Greek Fire

Greek Fire

By

James Boschert

The Fourth Book of Talon

Penmore Press
www.penmorepress.com

Greek Fire by James Boschert

Copyright © 2013 James Boschert

ISBN-13: 978-1-942756-02-6(Paperback)
ISBN   -978-1-942756-03-3   (e-book)

BISAC Subject Headings:
FIC014000FICTION / Historical
FIC032000FICTION / War & Military
FIC031020FICTION / Thrillers / Historical
Cover artist Oliver Frey: www.oliverfreyart.com
Editing: Chris Paige
Cover Illustration by Christine Horner

Address all correspondence to:
Michael James
Penmore Press LLC
920 N Javalina Pl
Tucson AZ 85748

Acknowledgements

Journal of Sport History, Vol. 8, No. 3 (Winter, 1981)

Sports of the Byzantine Empire

Barbara Schrodt*

Baba Tahir: "A Fool of God"

Rumi : Poetry

Wikipedia

Judith Herrin : Byzantium The surprising life of a Medieval Empire

Colin Wells: Sailing from Byzantium

Tess Malos: The Greek Cookbook

Anna Komnena: The Alexiad of Anna Komnena

Rainer Maria Rilke: Poems

John Julius Norwich: A Short History of Byzantium

The Rubiyat of Omar Khayyam

Rudyard Kipling

The research and help of Danielle Boschert

The advice and council of Chris Paige and Midori Snyder

Table of Contents

Map of Byzantine Empire 1165

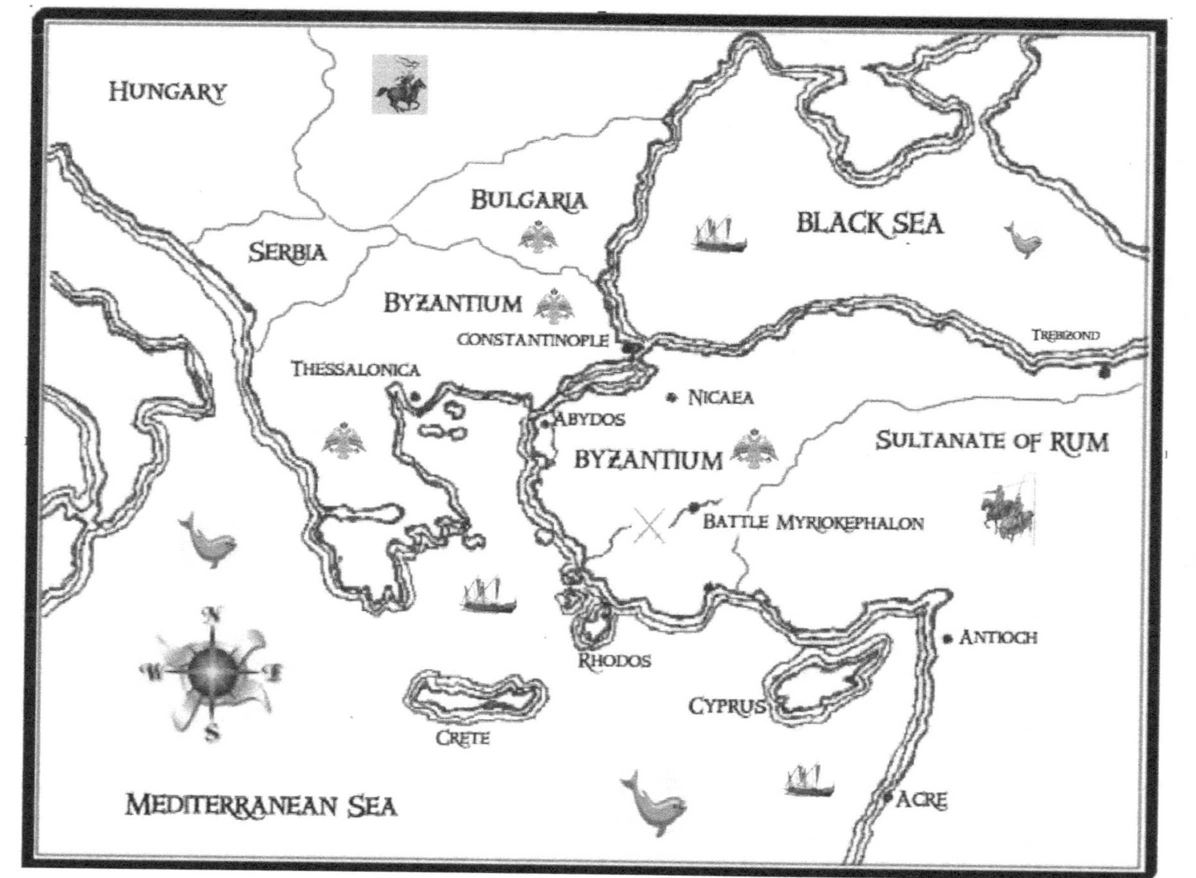

Map of Constantinople

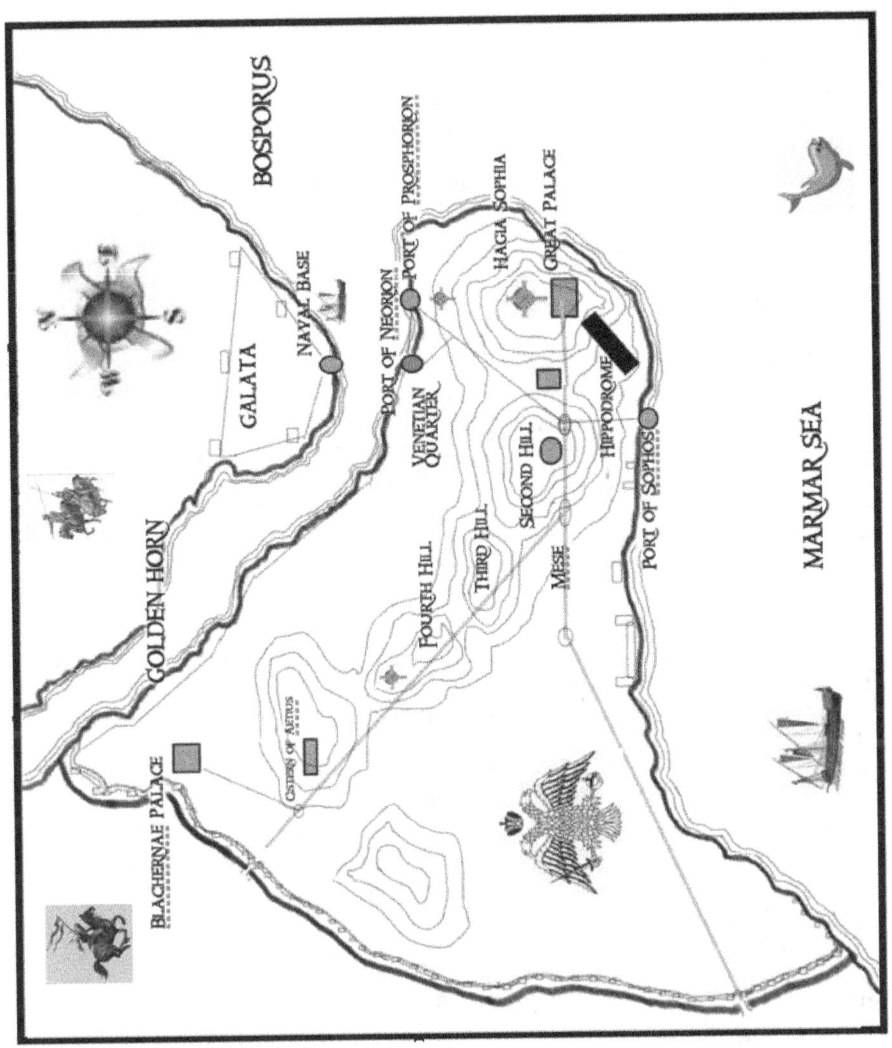

Names Byzantium

Royal Family Byzantine

Manuel I Komnenos:	Emperor of Byzantium
Isaac Komnenos.	Brother to Manuel I
Porphyrogennitos:	Those born to the purple.
Basileios	Eunuch representative of Andronikos
Komnenos	
John Axouch	Megas Domestikos (Right Hand Man)
Michael LourKouas	Patriarch of Constantinople
King Baldwin IV	King of Jerusalem
Alexios Bryennios	Negotiator for marriage. Prefect of
Constantinople	
John Komateros	Negotiator
Baldwin of Antioch	King of Antioch killed at Myriokephalon
Theodore Mavrozomes	General, friend of Senator Kalothesos
John Kantakouzenos	General, Killed in Myriokephalon
Andronikos Kontostephanos	Rear Guard General at Myriokephalon
Tarchaneiotes	Vice Admiral
Nestongos	Full Admiral of the fleet
Leontios	Officer in Abydos
Meletios the Phalangarches	Commander of Abydos
Captain Petrous	Ship's captain
Ioannes	Operator
Philippos	Officer in charge of the regiment

Templars

Sir Talon de Gilles	Knight Templar
Sir Guy de Veres	Knight Templar Senior
Claude	Sergeant to Sir Guy
Max Bauersdorf	Sergeant Templar
Henry	Captain of *Falcon*
Nigel	Companion
Guy	Companion
Brother Jonathan	Monk
Brother Martin	Monk
Dmitri Doukas	Ship's Guide
Ship	The Falcon

Palace officials

Eunuchs

The Chief of the officials	Parakoimomemos
Protospatharios	
Stephanos	Harbor Manager
Nikoporus	Principle to the Emperor (klarrissimos)
Chamberlain	
Andronikos	Praipositos or high ranks who control ceremonies
Gregoras	Parakoimomenos. (Sleeps across the door of the emperor)

Family Kalothesos.	**Family Name**
Damianus	Father
Joannina	Mother
Alexios	Son and Emissary
Eugenia	First daughter: Lady in Waiting
Theodora	Youngest daughter
Irene	Servant to Theodora
Makarios	Agent for the family
Giorgios	Assistant agent
Isaias	Agent in Rhodes
Joseph	Servant to Alexios
John	Servant to Damianus
Ariadne	Maid to Theodora
Nikoporus Tagaris	Friend of Alexios Mandatores
Antonina	Girl friend of Nikoporus
Theodoulos Melachrinos	Officer friend
Gregaros Aggalon	Squad officer
Isaias	Island agent
Varangian Guard	
Asmundr	Varangian chief
Eirikr	Second norse man
Gudridr	Third Varangian
Cuthberht	Saxon
Eadgar	Saxon
Genoese	
Caravello	Genoese captain
Christophas Levaggi	First Mate
Davide Chelone	Bosun
Family Spartenos	
Pantoleon Spartenos	Charioteer
Basileios	Eunuch in high places
John Spartenos	Senator
Constance	Wife of Spartenos
Markos	Eunuch for senator
Choumnos	Chief assassin
Psellos	Second assassin
Turks	
Kilij Arslan	Sultan of Turks
Yigit	Leader of Turks
Burak	Son of Yigit
Arabs	
Saieed Fakhouri	Arab Admiral invading fleet
Aarif Mejid	Arab ship officer
As-Salih Ismail al-Malik	Son of Nur Ed Din. Syria
Nur Ed Din	Former Sultan of Syria
Salah Ed Din	Sultan of Egypt

Book One
1176 AD

Then came to him the King Tafur, and with him fifty score
Of men-at-arms, not one of them but hunger gnawed him sore.
"Thou holy Hermit, counsel us, and help us at our need;
Help, for God's grace, these starving men with wherewithal to feed."

From "The Leaguer of Antioch"

Chapter 1
Acre and the Templars

The Officer of Stores and Requisitions leaned back against the hard wood of the chair and placed both hands flat on the papers piled upon the desk.

"It is apparent that you do not understand the Rules of the Order...sir," he said with a sardonic twist to his lips, addressing the men standing in front of him. His bearded face was dark with annoyance and not a little smug.

"What rules are we discussing here, Sir Julian?" Max Bauersdorf demanded. His scarred face was flushed with anger. He glanced at Talon de Gilles standing next to him, and then placed his knuckles on the table and leaned towards the officer.

"We captured the ship without any help from the Order and brought it here to Acre full of prisoners, whom we had released from captivity and a slow death at the oars! It therefore belongs to Sir Talon here, as he was the commander at the time. He brought us here alive and well, with a dromon that will make a great difference to the fleet, but it is his by right to do with as he pleases."

"You should remember your place, *Sergeant*." Sir Julian glared back up at Max, who slowly stood upright. Talon could see his companion resisting the ingrained urge to stand to attention.

Sir Julian continued; it seemed to Talon that officials of this kind always adopted a patronizing manner when they knew that they held the upper hand.

"The Rules state that everything that is captured by those of the Order belongs to the Order, and it is we who shall dispose of the ship, Sergeant," Sir Julian barked. "Neither you nor Sir Talon here can dispute this. If I were you I would yield the ship with good grace, and then we can all get on with more important business."

Talon gave Max a half smile, then turned his gaze upon Sir Julian. "If what you say is correct then you will have no objection to my discussing this issue with Sir Guy de Veres." He kept his tone pleasant.

Sir Julian stared at Talon. "You know Sir Guy de Veres?" His tone said he did not believe it. But he looked a little uncertain.

"We do, very well too," Talon lied.

Sir Julian shrugged, only half-believing him. "You are welcome to do so, Sir Talon. We all respect what you've done. Still, there are the Rules, and I cannot help you in this matter." He took up a quill and dipped it into an inkpot. "Now if you do not mind, I am a very busy man." He reached for a parchment.

Talon nodded, then took Max by the upper arm and turned his irate friend away.

"God be with you, Sir Julian," he said pleasantly in parting.

They strode out of the chamber. Max managed to slam the heavy wooden door with a loud crash as they walked out and strode down the narrow stone corridor.

"I despise those people, Talon," he growled. "By what right do they take the ship from us and toss Henry and the others out onto the quayside as though they were vagabonds who have no place? This isn't much of a welcome for men who have just escaped the Egyptian galleys!"

Talon chuckled. "Max, my dear friend. I detected a look of uncertainty in Sir Julian's eyes when I mentioned Sir Guy, so I wonder..." He too was feeling unsure of matters in this new environment in which they found themselves. Acre was proving to be less hospitable than either of them had imagined.

"He is a little, jumped-up official who is greedy for our spoils," Max complained. "Meanwhile, Sir Guy de Veres is not in the city at present and no one knows where he is, so we have an uncertain time ahead of us."

"But Max, I am not sure what we would do with a ship. Neither of us knows how to sail one. Henry now, he is a sailor and a navigator so he could do so, but what would we do with one if indeed we were allowed to keep it?"

Talon was referring to one of the men who had been rescued in Egypt and had navigated the captured dromon to Acre for them.

Max looked up at the sun. "I have to attend to some duties, Talon. I will see you later at the inn?"

Talon nodded, clasped hands with Max, then waved him off and made his way out of the Templar stronghold down to the harbor and along the wharf to the main gates. Once he was through the gates he was in the city itself, where all the stench, grime and noise of the town assailed his senses.

He had been appalled at the squalor of the city known as St Jean d'Acre. He wondered at the difference between this place and Cairo, which he had come to know reasonably well during his enforced stay there. No attempt had been made to plan Acre's streets, other than in the Jewish quarter, which was hemmed about by the many winding, narrow streets and poorly constructed houses and hovels built by the Christians. Filth lay in piles along the center of the main streets and in corners where it had been swept by the last rainfall; often there were carcasses of dogs and other small animals that had either died of disease or were there because someone had killed them. Either way huge rats feasted well on the corpses and other offal that lay about rotting and stinking in the hot sun. The streets were never cleaned other than when it rained hard enough to wash it all into the sea, or for religious holidays, and then it was only the main thoroughfares that were swept. As he walked along the street that led to the eastern sea wall, Talon pondered his situation.

Other than a brief flurry of excitement upon their arrival, Acre had been less than welcoming to him and his companions from Egypt. They were all now heading for poverty in a place that was already overflowing with beggars and the destitute, many of whom resorted to petty theft and purse cutting, or worse. He had to shoulder his way along the crowded streets where vendors shouted their meager wares of cloth, crude wooden carvings and relics, which they all claimed were the genuine article. There were many gullible pilgrims ready to believe them, for was this not a great city on the edge of the Holy Land?

Knights on their huge destriers rode tall above the moving crowds, their way cleared by their squires and servants who shouted at the slow movers as they pushed forward. Priests and monks there were aplenty, as the church had large numbers of both for the benefit of the multitude of sinners who inhabited the Holy Land. The former walked with a touch of superiority while the latter hoisted their habits and walked in pairs.

Soldiers of almost every description from crossbowmen to pikemen and common footmen were to be seen everywhere, many of them drunk and staggering. Fights broke out and spread like brushfires as others, equally drunk, joined in the general melee. The city guard was kept very busy and Talon imagined the jails were full by now. He traversed one small square where some freshly hung thieves were still twitching and the crowd not yet dispersed.

Talon barely paid these events any attention, other than to take another street to avoid them, as he had his own worries to deal with. Another thing he found disconcerting was that people in this city were pushy, loud and rude to everyone. It reminded him of Agues Mortes where he had first landed in Languedoc on his way to find his parents. He wondered, not for the first time, if he had not made a bad choice in coming to Acre when he could have remained a welcome guest in the calm beauty of the Fayoum of Egypt and lived like a lord. But the choices there had not been easy either. He could not have left his new companions and Max to whatever fate might befall them when he had the means to bring them to their chosen land.

The street where Talon had his lodgings was narrow and full of debris drying out in the hot afternoon sun. The stink of garbage and the wailing of hungry infants made Talon wrinkle his nose and wish for some wax for his ears as he climbed the rough cut wooden stairs to his single room. It would not be long now before he was thrown out of even this miserable lodging for lack of coin.

*****

Later, in a small, shabby tavern just off Armory Street, Talon was seated alone, morosely sipping a cheap wine and eating the meager fare that he could only just afford. His money was almost gone. He had given a large amount of the coin he had brought with him from Egypt to Henry and the crew of their galley to help them stay alive while in this expensive city. None of them knew what was to happen to them. The Captain of the City Guard, an officious and pompous official to Talon's mind, had forbidden any of them to leave, but there was almost no employment for them either, so they lived as they could. He ignored the noisy crowd of soldiers and sailors gathered at the other tables playing at dice or cards, betting their meager earnings away and getting drunk at the same time while trying to grope the few whores who were rash enough to wander among the tables looking for customers.

After attempting to persuade him that their wares were available for a small coin, the three whores who plied their trade in the inn withdrew, casting lingering looks at him. None of them could have been older than eighteen, but the careworn lines etched into their features and their crudely made-up faces gave the impression they were thirty or more. He barely noticed them, for his thoughts were elsewhere as he brooded on what the future might hold.

The rough cut leather curtain at the main entrance to the inn parted and Henry pushed his way in with Nigel just behind him. Both men had been with Talon when he had escaped from Egypt, having been galley slaves until Talon had them released to fight for his allies. They had sailed the ship he had stolen from Al Qahira to Acre and now, like him, they were down to their last coins and their clothes were in rags.

Henry peered into the gloom and then spied Talon in the corner. He nudged Nigel as they made for his table.

"Well met, Talon!" Henry boomed.

"God's blessings, Henry, Nigel. Where's Guy?"

"He'll be here soon," Henry said. He looked uncomfortable.

"He is entertaining a whore," Nigel said with a wry grimace.

"He can afford one?" Talon pretended shock.

"You know Guy. The city is full of all sorts of women, and many whose husbands have died in the wars or been taken prisoner. Some have become whores just to stay alive in this pestilential place. They need to earn a living too, I suppose, even if it is on their backs. But I can only guess what Guy pays them—he is as short of coin as we are," Nigel said.

The two men seated themselves and called for wine and bread. Both had lost weight since their arrival and Talon wondered just how much longer they would have to languish in this city before any of them knew their fate. It had been weeks now, and still no employment was offered. He felt reasonably certain he would be taken into the Templar Order, but he was no longer sure he wanted to become a full Templar knight. And what about his friends?

"Still no employment, Henry? What are you going to do these coming weeks? It will be winter soon." Talon asked.

Henry took a swig of the wine from his leather beaker and scowled. He wiped his mouth with the back of his sleeve. "Devil take this piss, I miss good mead," he grumbled. "There's no employment in this rat-infested city for any of us. The slaves, miserable unfortunates that they are, at least have that."

"What? You now want to become a slave again?" Nigel teased.

Henry rolled his eyes. "No, you clown, but a man withers when he is idle week after week with nothing to look forward to." He sounded cantankerous. The enforced idleness was getting to him.

"We might find ourselves in the army of the king before too long. I hear he is recruiting for another fight with the Syrians," Nigel said gloomily. He sucked on a chicken bone plucked from Talon's bowl of thin soup. His dirty, lank blond hair fell over his protuberant brows and deep-set, pale blue eyes, making him look unkempt and villainous. His large fleshy lips and straggly beard added to the effect, suggesting a man who might be a little mad and certainly dangerous.

Henry hunched his shoulders in a familiar manner. Talon knew his sailor friend was growing ever more frustrated with their situation.

"Soon we will not be able to sign onto a ship going back to our own land even as deck hands, we will be too weak for the labor. I am buggered if I want to stay here without any work to do during the winter. We would starve," he growled.

"Where is Max these days?" Nigel demanded.

"He is attending to his duties within the Templar stronghold. We will not be seeing much of him henceforth, and I too might have to go back to the Templars and complete my service."

"Much help that would be for us," Nigel said gloomily, rolling his eyes around the room.

At that moment Guy, their companion from the Egyptian galleys, pushed his way into the crowded room. He wove his way between the tables and clusters of patrons to tower over them.

"God's blessings, Talon," he said with a grin on his wide bearded face. When Guy grinned it showed his bad teeth, most of them slightly apart, although his good nature was always to the fore.

"Well, since you can afford a whore you can also buy us another drink of this swill they call wine in this flea-infested place," Nigel said with a grin of his own.

"Was she worth it?" Henry asked looking up with a leer.

"No, but you always have to find out or you'll never know, will yer?" Guy answered. He pulled a stool over from under an empty table before easing his large frame down.

"I swear you have an appetite for women that would astonish a sultan," Nigel said. He sounded envious.

"It is just an itch."

"I do not know how you do it, Guy. It is not as though you are a handsome bugger, is it? Wish I could catch women like you do," Nigel said wistfully.

"Not your fault, Nigel my old friend. You just frighten them off!"

Nigel shook his head and rolled his eyes at the other two from under his brows. "And this is good advice from a troll, mind you."

"We do not want to hear any more about it," Talon laughed.

They were finishing off the remainder of the wine and the scraps of food on the table when they became aware of trouble brewing at the other end of the room. There the whores, who were offering their services to whoever could part with a coin, were clustered. They were a poor lot. Talon could see the desperation in their eyes even as they tried to appear seductive to the rough soldiers and seamen who frequented the inn.

There was a shouted argument going on and then one man gave an angry yell. He must have been a foot soldier, for his greasy jerkin was covered with iron rings sewn onto the padded material. He seized the arm of a girl who had been standing nearby, making her cry out in pain as his hard fingers gripped her upper arm in an attempt to pull her away. The man rose to his feet and backhanded her, causing her to fall backwards. "I gave you coin!" he shouted. "Now it is time to pay up!"

The man gave a raucous laugh as he followed after her. Tossing her skirts up, and despite her scream of pain as he forced her thighs apart, he was about to take her then and there.

Before Talon or any of his companions could react there was a roar of outrage and Guy strode three long paces from their table, seizing the man by the back of his leather jerkin. He jerked him backwards and tossed him two tables away to crash in among some drunken sailors. The man, his features registering utter surprise, slid across the table, sending jugs and cups in all directions and spilling wine over the men where he fell. One of the sailors reacted by shoving him off the table before grasping a knife in his hand and lurching to his feet with a roar of his own.

Within a few seconds Guy was surrounded by drink-maddened men who were all shouting and yelling and trying to get him on the ground where they could pound him senseless, or stab him to death. Guy was a large man and shook them off like a bull would terriers, but it was clear that things were becoming perilous.

Nigel glanced at Talon and Henry, then shrugged. "Silly bastard always did have a soft spot for women! Come on," he said. "We can't let him get beaten up by these pigs."

Reluctantly Henry and Talon waded into the fray. Screams from the women and outraged yells from the proprietor did not help the situation, nor did the fact that a knife had appeared in the hands of another one of the seamen. Talon grabbed a three-legged stool and hammered it into the upper arm of the man who had drawn the blade. The seaman yelled, clutching his arm before retreating from the menacing look that Talon gave him. Talon smashed the stool on a table and then, armed with two of its solid legs in either hand, he struck left and right at any limb or head that presented itself.

Nigel and Henry, both yelling like madmen, were alongside as they fought their way through the mass of struggling bodies to get to Guy, who was tossing men in all directions. He shrugged off one attacker, then seized him by the throat and banged his head against that of another who he had managed to grip his jerkin. There was a dull, sickening thud as their heads came together and both men's eyes rolled upwards. Guy dropped them and turned to see who else wanted to fight.

Nigel had just finished clubbing a soldier to his knees with another stool, a wicked grin on his face while Henry had just pounded what remained of another man's teeth out of his head with a broken wooden leg. Both men seemed to be enjoying themselves.

Talon found himself confronting a large bearded soldier in ragged chain mail. Holding a very long knife, he had been making his way towards Guy with the aim of skewering him in the back. Talon shook his head at the man, who focused red glazed eyes upon him and snarled, baring his broken teeth and lunging at him with the knife. One stool leg snapped forward and smacked the man alongside his temple while the other one flashed down and with an audible crack struck the wrist that held the knife. The man did not even shout with the pain. He fell limply across a table face down. Whirling about Talon blocked a blow from a man with a short sword in his hand and poked the other leg into that man's eye. The seaman screamed and clutched his face, then staggered away moaning, blood pouring from between his fingers.

Then Talon heard shouts. From behind him the doors crashed open, the leather curtain was hauled off its rail and armed men crowded into the room. He had time to see Guy standing among a clutter of unconscious bodies and Nigel, a mad grin distorting his features, triumphantly beating another man senseless with a metal bowl before a shout, almost in his ear, caught his attention.

"In the name of the City Constable, you will stop! You are all under arrest!"

"Nigel! Stop it!" Henry bellowed as he dropped the stool he had been using. He put his hands out to his side, palms up, as the points of two sharp spears hovered within inches of his throat.

Talon dropped his two weapons and looked around him. Other than himself and his companions there weren't too many people standing other than the new arrivals. The women were clustered near the back door with the proprietor looking fearfully about. But the officer in charge of the soldiers was all business.

"You are going to jail for disturbing the peace. Hold them!" he commanded his soldiers, who hastened to obey.

*****

Three days later Max arrived at the door to the communal cell and beckoned to Talon. He got up from the putrid straw where he had been squatting with his companions.

"I thought we would never see Max again," Nigel commented as Talon rose.

Max was dressed in his Templar uniform of dark hose and overcoat. He was clearly uncomfortable within these surroundings. Talon assumed that he had been reissued clothing from the Templar stores. The jailor nodded and allowed Talon to go outside with Max.

"Hello Max. I'd hoped to see you before this. It has been three days."

"It took almost two to find out where you were taken, Talon. I've been a busy man. There is someone who wants to see you."

"Not that idiot Sir Julian? I do not think I could bear that," Talon groaned.

"No it is someone much more important so be on your best behavior."

"Who then? Do not torment me, Max."

"Sir Guy de Veres. You do remember him don't you? He wants to see you, Talon. Now!"

Talon was acutely conscious of his shabby dress and unwashed state as they came to the fortress within a fortress and were allowed entry to the inner keep of the Order.

Max led the way along narrow stone corridors past open doorways where the army of clerks and scribes worked feverishly to keep the financial empire of the Order functioning. After knocking on a stout wooden door they were admitted by a servant and walked in to find Sir Guy seated at a heavy plain wooden desk with papers piled high on either side. Behind him a fire was burning, as there was a chill in the air and the stone building denied the warmth of the sun in these chambers.

Sir Guy put down the large feather quill he was using and smiled at them, waving them into chairs.

"Ah, Sir Talon and Max, God's Greetings. Come in and be seated."

"God's blessings, Sir Guy," Max said. Talon nodded politely. Max decided to stand but Talon elected to sit on one of the curved leather chairs with no back placed on the other side of the desk.

Talon stared at the knight seated in front of him, who calmly regarded him in turn. It had been well over two years since they had last met. That time Talon had been in chains, having been captured by the Templars who, mistaking him for a Saracen, had imprisoned him prior to identification by his Uncle, Sir Phillip. The last time he had seen Sir Guy had been just as his ship left Acre for Languedoc.

The Templar wore full chain mail, as well as the white woolen cloak of the Order with the red cross stitched onto the left shoulder of the cloak and onto the left breast of the white surcoat. He wore no helmet, and his chain head protection was thrown back to form a heavy collar at the back of his neck. The stocky man was greying at the temples and beard, his face weathered and scarred, denoting many fights in his time.

Sir Guy assessed Talon with a keen eye. "I see you are no longer the boy I sent away in chains. Is it correct what I hear, that you are now a knight, Sir Talon?"

"Well met, Sir Guy. Yes I am. I am oath bound to Count Roger of Tranceval, and I think to the Templars too," Talon responded.

Sir Guy's eyes flicked to Max, who was by now rigidly at attention. "Be at ease, Sergeant. It has been a few years since I saw you last, Talon. Max here told me about your uncle Phillip."

"He died protecting my father's home...in a foul ambush," Talon added, his tone grim.

"May God be merciful and welcome his soul to Heaven. Phillip was a good and Godly man," Sir Guy intoned, crossing himself. "You must tell me about it some time in more detail. I both respected and liked Sir Philip. He was a good Templar."

There was a brief silence and then he said, "It seems we have much to discuss. I have only this week arrived in Acre and I consider it fortunate that I encountered Max, as I would have left this evening had I not heard the impassioned pleas of the Sergeant here on your behalf.

"You look almost as bad as you did that first time we met," he continued. There was the glimmer of a smile in his gray eyes as he regarded Talon in his filthy clothes. But then Sir Guy leaned back in his chair, steepled his fingers, and looked at Talon appraisingly. His expression grew stern. After a long moment he spoke.

"We seem to have met in a similar manner the last time we encountered each other, Talon. I arrive in the city to hear that you and your disreputable companions have all but destroyed an inn along with half of its guests. The Master of this citadel informed me that the City Marshall, who has seen much, could not recall destruction to this extent wrought upon the victims—and all of it done without swords! Everyone was up in arms. They want you and your companions either flogged or hung! What am I to do with you?" he enquired.

"I, er...I could not let one of my companions be knifed for no good reason, Sir Guy," Talon muttered.

Sir Guy raised his hand for silence. "I have been acquainted with the facts of the matter by Sergeant Bauersdorf here. However, it is not that which concerns me at this time."

Talon made to speak but the knight held up his hand.

"Allow me to finish, Talon." Talon did not miss the lack of a 'Sir' in the address. He nodded and shifted in his chair uneasily.

He remembered Sir Guy from those years before and had liked and respected him even in the short time he'd known him. Talon realized that he was in a difficult position at present and needed all the help he could get. It had been an unpleasant time in the jail alongside his friends. The flea-infested cells were poor accommodation even compared to that of his meager lodgings.

"It has come to my attention that you did a great service to the Order when you brought a ship full of Christians from out of Egypt with you. According to Sergeant Bauersdorf here, you have been poorly rewarded for your efforts."

Talon looked surprised but held his tongue.

"Let's go and take a look at this vessel of yours," Sir Guy said and got up.

They climbed the stone stairs that led up to the battlements and stopped on the ramparts overlooking the harbor. The stone was warm here, as the sun could reach it, in sharp contrast to the dark and cold stone chambers within the formidable Templar stronghold.

Talon took a deep breath of the fresh sea air and paused to enjoy the space. He was not entirely sure when he might again.

"Where is this ship?" Sir Guy enquired.

Talon pointed it out in the harbor below. "It is that one, Sir. The galley."

There was a lot of shipping in the pool but the dromon was easy to pick out from the heavy merchant and transport ships that lay at anchor all around. The galley was anchored among them, and although there was no activity on board and it appeared quite abandoned, this ship stood out from the rest as a predator and not a transport ship.

"That is a good looking vessel," Sir Guy commented staring at it with interest. "It is indeed a war ship and one of the best I have seen for some time, certainly within this harbor. She looks sleek and deadly, of the kind that is made in Byzantium. The Arabs copied them. Is she as fast as she looks?"

"Very fast, Sir," Max said, as he leaned back against the battlements. "We outran two of the Sultan's best to get here."

"I have heard rumors of that adventure and Max has been filling in the gaps. It is an impressive tale."

"They want to take it off Sir Talon here and add it to the Templar Order fleet!" Max burst out.

Talon placed a restraining hand on Max's arm. "He means the ship, Sir Guy. The Templar Order is claiming it."

,Sir Guy stood back from his observation of the busy harbor. "The Rules do apply here, Sergeant."

"It is wrong, Sir Guy," Max entreated. "The ship belongs to us, at least to Talon here, who guided us out of Egypt. All of us owe our lives to him, especially me. None of us would have made it here without his leadership."

Sir Guy looked past Max to Talon, who met his stare with a level gaze of his own. For a long moment Sir Guy stared at Talon as though assessing what he had just heard.

"Come to my chambers this evening. I am tired and would rest a while, but then we will eat and you can tell me what became of you these last few years; and we can also discuss this ship of yours. In the meantime you are free to move about the city and your friends will be released. Please do not get into any more trouble, as next time I might not be able to influence the Master of the Order here in Acre."

Talon left Max and Sir Guy on the battlements and hurried off to find his friends. He dared not hope too much that Sir Guy had something in mind for them, but for the first time since he had arrived in the city he felt a faint hope that perhaps something might just transpire to their benefit.

*****

That evening he presented himself at the Templar stronghold, cleaner and slightly better dressed than before. He still felt poorly garbed compared to even the simple attire of the people who inhabited the fortification. Max met him at the gates and escorted him up to Sir Guy's chambers. Sir Guy greeted him with a smile and bade him be seated.

"Sergeant Bauersdorf has had nothing but praise for you, Sir Talon. He has told me most of what he knows about your time in Languedoc and in Egypt. I am very impressed with his report and I know enough of him to know that he does not exaggerate."

Talon glanced at his friend with raised eyebrows. Max grinned at him and shrugged depreciatingly.

"The ship, do you have a crew to man it and sail it for me?" Sir Guy asked, addressing his question to both of them.

Talon sat up and stared. His heart began to thump.

Sir Guy smiled at his surprise. "I have a commission to perform for the Order. It is secret and will need speed and skill to complete. God willing I can find a ship and a reliable crew with which to accomplish it."

"I...I am listening, Sir," Talon said, trying to control his breathing.

"I want you both to swear you will disclose nothing of this to anyone, not even to the people you will have to recruit for the mission. Once we are at sea I can tell some of it."

"I so swear," Max said.

"As do I," Talon affirmed. "I swear." They looked at one another hardly daring to believe what they had just heard.

"Very well. I am ordered by the Grand Master to go as an emissary to Constantinople on behalf of the King of Jerusalem, to deliver secret papers to the hand of the emperor himself. I need a fast warship. It would be nice to arrive ahead of the letters written by the spies of the emperor and those of the Arabs for once."

He smiled at the two men who were gaping at the news, enjoying their surprise.

"I do believe that there is a fast warship in this harbor, and I am looking for resourceful men to assist me in my endeavor. Besides, it would seem that you, Sir Talon, have once again overstayed your welcome. At least you'll not be leaving in chains this time." He gave a chuckle.

Talon was the first to overcome his astonishment. "How long do we have to prepare, Sir?" he croaked.

"Three days."

"Where exactly is Constantinople, Sir Guy?" Talon asked.

Sir Guy reached for a rolled up papyrus. "This is a chart of the region," he said as he unrolled it and spread it out on the desk, placing the heavy ink jar on one side and his dagger along the other to hold it flat.

What Talon saw was a lot of straight and curved lines with writing and incomprehensible squiggles that meant nothing to him.

Sir Guy observed his bewilderment and then said with a smile, "Have you never seen a chart before, Talon?"

"No, Sir, I have not, but I would wager that Henry knows how to read this. What is it telling us?"

"If you can imagine that this is a picture of the land we live upon and it shows where there are other lands, then you'll be able to understand it better," Sir Guy said. "Here is where we are." He pointed with his forefinger at a squiggle on the chart. Talon read the name Acre in elaborate letters. "The coast we are on is that of the Kingdom of Jerusalem. This is land over here"—he swept his hand across the space behind the wavy lines—"while these lines mark the change from land to sea."

Sir Guy's finger moved up the chart to stop at an odd looking image. "This is an island called Cyprus and it belongs to the empire of Byzantium. We the Templars would buy some of it if we could. It is rich in crops and vines, and it also has salt marshes that are worth a great deal of money."

His finger moved further up the chart to cross another thick, uneven line. "This is the empire of Byzantium where we are going, and this," his finger moved quickly towards the left of the land, "further up is Constantinople, the center of the Empire." Talon gazed down where Sir Guy's finger rested.

"What are these?" He pointed to a jumble of irregular shapes gathered below the city of Constantinople.

"Those are the multitude of islands that exist in that region. They too, belong to the empire, for the most part anyway."

Talon had begun to understand the difference between land and sea, but there was a plethora of other detail he could not understand. Straight lines emerged from some complex looking device artistically rendered on the chart to fly off in all directions. There were pictures of gods blowing winds here and there, with men on horseback and castles on what he assumed to be dry land, while porpoises played around in places where he assumed it was the sea. He realized that they were about to embark upon a significant undertaking and that Henry and his men would be essential to the endeavor.

He also resolved to know and understand 'charts' in future so as to be able to use them to tell him where he was in the strange new world they were about to enter.

"Will Max be coming with us, Sir Guy?"

"I have decided to leave the ship and its needs to you, Sir Talon. Max will accompany us in the capacity of your Sergeant. I expect to sail on the third day; after dark, as this mission does not need the attentions of the dozens of Turkish, Venetian or Byzantine spies who doubtless reside within the city walls. Unfortunately I am known as an emissary by many, but this journey I would keep secret, at least until I am arrived in Constantinople and have delivered the letters, which will give me the advantage of time."

Talon looked at Sir Guy. The knight regarded him with a smile on his lips. "I believe you have a ship, Sir Talon. Can you man it and take me where I wish to go?"

Talon took a great breath. "I believe I can, Sir Guy. Er...will I be paid?"

Sir Guy pushed a small leather bag across the table that chinked with the sound of coins.

"This is an advance. Sir Julian himself provided it, somewhat unwillingly, but I managed to convince him eventually. There is enough to provision the vessel for a voyage and to refit where necessary. I think you should buy some clothes, as you are now a knight. Please do not disappoint me. I used up much of my credit with the Master of the Order by putting my trust in you and your companions."

Max laughed. "He is a knight, Sir Guy. I vouch for that, on my honor."

"Before you go you need to know that I will not be the only passenger. There will be myself, my Sergeant Claude, a monk, and an emissary of the empire with a couple of servants who wishes to return to his Emperor. He is familiar with the protocols we will be obliged to observe in Constantinople and can guide us well in that regard. Please ensure that the cabins at the back are made fit for the passengers."

*****

Later that evening they hurried off to find Henry and his companions, for their news could not wait until the morning.

They found the three men in another inn, morosely contemplating their future and spending their last coin on some wine. Talon and Max sauntered up to the trio and sat down trying to look casual.

"Ah, something's happened, or you would not look so smug, either of you," Henry said. His look was questioning.

"I forget, Henry, did you say you knew how to sail a ship?" Talon asked.

Henry gasped and sat back on his stool. "I do not believe it! You got the ship?" he asked, his expression incredulous.

"Not only that; we got the ship and some place to sail it to," Max said.

"Where?" All three of the men at the table asked at once.

"That will have to wait until we are out to sea."

"Mother of God," Nigel said in awe. "What are we going to be doing? Are we going to be pirates?" he demanded.

"We're not allowed to talk about it, and neither are you, but we all have much work to do," Max said, barely able to contain his own excitement.

"We should celebrate," Henry said.

"We have no money," Guy announced, a doleful expression on his face.

"If you had not spent your last coin on a whore we might have had," Nigel said, his tone caustic.

Talon dropped a small silver piece on the table. "I think we can celebrate tonight, my friends, but no brawls or we lose it all; and tomorrow we must go to work. Sir Guy has great expectations."

*****

The next three days were hectic. It took two full days to round up men from their former crew to man the ship, and more were needed. Most of them were too drunk or hung over to really understand what was happening. Henry and his companions rowed some of them out to their destination so inert that it was hard to decide whether they were alive or dead when they were heaved onto the decks of the vessel. But Guy and Nigel, along with their former crew-mates, took over, throwing sea water onto them to rouse them from their alcoholic stupors and prepare them for work.

Talon wondered how men could stay drunk for so long on so little coin.

Slowly the ship began to take on a life of its own. Supervised by Nigel and Guy, the men were put to work preparing the vessel from stem to stern for the voyage to come.

"I know someone we must have," Henry said to Talon on the second day as they stood on the deck of the gently rocking ship. Men were swarming all over the vessel overhauling the rigging and hauling barrels of water on board from a large lighter that was alongside.

"Who are you thinking of, Henry?'

"Remember not all of us were from the north, Talon? Some of the oarsmen were from the islands, the Greek islands. The best of them was Dmitri... Dmitri Doukas, remember him?"

"Yes, I think so. Short with red hair, built like a boar. Strong man as I recall."

"I need to find him if he is still here," Henry said.

"Why? Do you think we will need him?"

"Yes, because we are heading north regardless of exactly where, and he is the only one among us former rowers who might know what to expect."

Henry left that evening to hunt Dmitri down in the alehouses in the hope that the man hadn't slipped past the gate guards and gone off somewhere else, while Talon was left to marvel at how Henry might have divined their destination. He hoped no one else had done so.

Henry returned the next morning with Dmitri lying in the thwarts of the rowboat, senseless from drink but otherwise unharmed.

"He would like to go home," Henry said in a matter-of-fact manner. "He lived in Byzantium for many years before he took to the sea. We might need him if we are going near that country."

On the third night all was in readiness for departure. It was close to midnight but Sir Guy had not yet arrived. Talon stood on the now silent afterdeck with Henry and Max. No one said anything as they waited in expectant silence for Sir Guy to arrive.

Nigel was at the front of the boat waiting with some of the crew to haul in the anchor stone. Guy was amidships with other men prepared to hoist sail and start the rowers at Henry's command.

Talon listened to the creaking of the timbers as the ship rocked in the swell of the harbor. The occasional slap of water against the hull and the rattle of a loose rope against a spar or mast were the only sounds at this time of night. The men who would work the oars were in place and would be ready at a moment's notice to leave, even though most of them were asleep. The normal bustle of the harbor had subsided considerably at this late hour. The large Templar cargo ships were silent and the work on the wharf had stopped for the night.

"Even a slave has to have some sleep," Max had remarked as though divining his thoughts.

A light gust of wind blew from the hills to the east, rattling the lines and snapping the pennants flying from other ships' masts. Talon looked back at the looming fortifications that guarded the harbor.

"They come," Henry whispered, pointing towards the Templar quay where they could see dark figures illuminated by a couple of torches held high, moving along the pier. He told the dozing steersmen to wake up and be ready. Then sent one of the younger seamen scurrying down the ladder to alert Guy and Nigel.

Not long after, Talon peered into the darkness and could just make out what appeared to be a crowded boat moving between the other ships in their direction.

Soon it bumped and scraped alongside the hull amid whispered curses from the crew above to watch the sides of the ship. Within moments Sir Guy came over the side, then climbed the ladder to stand on the rear deck, where he clasped hands with Talon and Max.

"God's Blessings, Talon. Is all ready for our departure?"

"God's Blessings, Sir. We are well manned and provisioned for our journey as long as we can obtain fresh water from time to time," Talon replied, repeating what Henry had told him.

Another two men arrived on the mid decks and Talon could just make out that they were armed men, so he assumed they were the Sergeant and the emissary.

Then there was a yelp and a splash, followed by some grunts and suppressed snickers in the boat below. Finally another figure was assisted aboard. It was clear from his garb that he was a man of the church, and that his habit from the waist down was soaked. Now he stood on deck, wringing out the wet material. As he muttered to himself, another man in the same form of dress was helped aboard. The two were followed by others who appeared to be servants, for they supervised a large amount of baggage that was soon piled into a small pyramid of trunks and boxes in the waist of the ship. Guy solicitously stood by and made sure that several boxes arrived safely on the deck, then that they were removed to the rear cabin by seamen.

"I fear one of our Godly persons has had a little dip in our pristine harbor waters. I had only needed one of them, but the Bishop imposed another upon me," Sir Guy murmured to Talon as they watched from above.

The four new arrivals did not tarry. The monks and the man whom Talon assumed to be the emissary were led out of sight to the cabin below, while the fourth man made his way up the rear ladder and presented himself to Sir Guy. He was a large man with a huge beard and strong shoulders, standing even taller than Max in his chain mail armor. He placed a shield against the side wall of the ship with a muted clank and came to stand with Sir Guy.

"Ah, Claude. This is Sir Talon, and you know Sergeant Max." The men nodded to one another in the dark. "Talon, this is Claude, my sergeant. Claude, the man standing by the steersmen is Henry who captains this ship. Is that not right, Sir Talon?"

"Yes, Sir Guy, he is my captain. I will introduce you to my other two companions tomorrow. Do we sail now?"

"Yes, we sail...as unobtrusively as we can. We have with us a Byzantine emissary named Alexios Kalothesos, who will be our guide and assistant while we are in Constantinople. I will introduce you all tomorrow."

With Nigel supervising, their crew quietly hauled in the anchor stone of the galley. With orders given in whispers and relayed to the crew, the ship was rowed slowly towards the entrance of Acre harbor. Curious sentries on other ships called questions that went unanswered as the ship glided by. A soft call of farewell came from the Templar guards standing on the battlements overlooking the harbor entrance as they passed through, and then they began to feel the swell of the outer sea.

They slipped past the Island of Flies looming on their port side, its beacon flaring in the freshening wind, and then slowly the bright lights of the beacon and those on the harbor towers receded into the darkness. At a low command from Henry to Guy in the waist of the ship the sails were raised; they flapped briefly, bellied, and were hauled taut by the crew. Soon, with the aid of a steady offshore wind, the ship was driven westward. Henry ordered the oars to be shipped and the men below deck to stand down. The ship began to happily play the swell, all the creaks and humming of taut rigging began their familiar song as it headed into its element. The dark shadow of land disappeared and they were finally at sea.

The crew who were not on duty found their niches and went to sleep wrapped in their cloaks or blankets, as did the passengers, while the night watch moved about quietly lashing down equipment and stowage. Soon the humming of the rigging was matched by snores as tired men took their rest.

Baba Tahir

Chapter 2

A Journey by Sea

While the oarsmen and passengers slept, Henry set a course by the stars and murmured the commands to Guy who stayed on duty with him. The crew hauled the sails around to allow the wind to do the work, and the ship sped out to sea on a westerly course. For Talon it was yet another journey into the unknown; and worse, it was at sea. He recalled the ill-fated journey from Languedoc and the loss of his horse Jabbar, drowned in the shipwreck that had deposited Max and himself unwillingly in Egypt. He prayed that God would protect them from the elements and ensure they made a safe landfall.

He gazed up at the clear night and the canopy of stars and remembered another time, another night, when he and his old friend Jean the priest had stared up at the heavens and wondered at its majesty, before they set out on a journey into the depths of the valley of the 'Assassins.

His thoughts drifted off to Isfahan: a garden and a villa where he had known so much happiness, but also so much sorrow. He turned away with a murmured prayer. One day, he promised himself, he would set out to discover what he needed to know. Until then, his benefactor Sir Guy had entrusted him with a mission that needed to be completed in a new country with new customs and language. There was much to be learned.

Before dawn the wind freshened and the ship began to pitch and roll as she made her way through the heaving seas. Although it was not severe and the waves were not high, Talon had a queasy feeling in his stomach as he recalled the dreadful experience of his disastrous voyage from France. For an awful moment he wondered if God had ignored his prayer and was about to subject them to more misery. However the feeling passed after one day, and he was able to stand on the deck and keep his balance, enjoying the wind on his face and watching the bows nudge aside the small whitecaps, spray flying high to either side of the curved prow and wetting the men in the waist as the galley dipped and rose. Recovery was not so easy for the monks, who stayed in their cabin.

Sir Guy and the man who was the emissary came on deck the morning after their departure. As the emissary leaned over the side and stared forward, Sir Guy approached Talon.

"I am relieved to get away from their moaning and the stench of their illness. They are no sailors, those two," he remarked with a grimace.

"I have been meaning to ask you something," he continued.

"About what, Sir Guy?"

"The last time we met...it was not under the best of circumstances and you were constantly facing eastward. For one so young you were a tortured soul. You do not seem to be so much now. Has your time away taken some of the edge off that need to go back to the eastern parts that you seemed so sick for?"

Talon said nothing for a few long moments as he considered the question. Finally he turned to Sir Guy and said, "Sir, you are right, I have been away for well over two years now, almost three. I still have a quest to fulfill, but I have had no word of my friends. I had hoped for tidings to reach me, perhaps in Acre, but events have moved swiftly, and now I find myself heading off in another direction altogether, and I fear that I have become entangled in this life that you more or less chose for me. One day I shall have to go east, if for nothing else than to discover what happened to them and put my soul at rest, as it is still tortured and will never know peace until I do."

Sir Guy nodded. "You do not wear your thoughts on your sleeve, Talon, but I suspected as much. Perform this task for me and you will come to realize that that chapter of your life is over and that you can do great things in this world. The Templars have need of one such as you. I have waited for this time to come and I am sure that I am right."

"I shall serve you, Sir Guy with my, our ship, and to the best of my ability. But there will come a day when I ask for release, and then I beg you to grant it."

Sir Guy put his hand on Talon's shoulder and looked him in the eyes. Talon's pain must have been visible to him, for he said in a quiet tone, "The Templars have taken you in, Talon. You have to spend time with the Order as that is the expectation, and I too expect it. The Order gave you succor when you needed it on two occasions now. You could be languishing in a jail or worse but for the Order, so now there is a debt to be repaid." His tone was firm but not unkind. "In due course, and God willing that it be possible, I shall do all in my power to allow it...when the time comes, Talon. Not yet, however."

*****

A little later Sir Guy introduced his guest, Alexios Kalothesos, who nodded with a disinterested glance at Talon. He spent his time on deck with Sir Guy, talking quietly in a secluded corner. But after several days he approached Talon, who was alone on the top deck. Talon liked to be here with his thoughts, but he also learned much as he watched that grizzled navigator Henry guide the ship through the mysterious seas. Alexios presented a curt bow, then asked a question.

"Sir Guy said that you speak our language, Sir. Is that true?" he asked in Greek.

Talon reacted with surprise. "I did not understand all that you said, Sir, but some of it is familiar. I was taught some Greek when younger." His response had been halting and he stumbled over some words, but Alexios appeared to comprehend.

"Your Greek is of the street kind. But we can at least communicate. Sir Guy has asked me to teach you our ways because he says that you are a quick learner and would be willing to learn."

"Sir Guy is right, Sir. I do want to learn and I am very interested in the kingdom where we might be going."

Talon regarded Alexios with interest. He wore a tunic of heavy, richly embroidered material, the hem of which came to mid calf. The cuffs of the sleeves came down to below his elbows but he wore an under shirt of expensive looking material which enclosed his forearms. Talon assumed it to be silk or very fine woven cotton. His short boots were of the finest chamois leather, as was his belt that supported a short but business-like sword of a kind Talon was not familiar with. His short black hair was oiled and worn in tight ringlets. His beard and mustache were well trimmed. Talon's nose caught the scent of some perfume. The man also wore a long cloak and a tall, strange looking hat that seemed to serve little purpose for keeping the weather at bay but did give Alexios the appearance of being taller than he was. Talon stood a good inch higher, so he often found that he was addressing the hat rather than the man, and he found himself looking down upon him when they talked, which seemed to disconcert the Greek.

"It is an empire," Alexios corrected, looking past him to the horizon. "And I think it will be hard to teach a Frank our ways, as you are such barbarians. You are good fighters but have no manners and are not what one might call civilized. Acre is an appalling place with no baths or any substance, and the food is disgusting."

His dark eyes flicked to engage Talon's then drifted off to the horizon as though just looking at Talon was a chore. Talon observed the bejeweled rings on the Greek's fingers, which failed to hide the swordsman's callouses.

"I agree that Acre is not a grand city, as I too like a bath from time to time. And I am not so stupid that I cannot learn the basic manners to which you allude, Sir," he remarked politely, but with an edge to his voice.

Alexios brought his focus back to Talon and looked him up and down. His lean dark features expressed disapproval of Talon's rough attire, even though Talon was better dressed than his companions, who were at present wearing a compilation of patched rags.

"There might be time to teach you the better forms of phrase and how to address your betters. Sir Guy tells me that you are not like other Franks, that you speak Arabic," he said, raising one eyebrow.

"I speak the Arabic and some Latin, but I have not used that for a long time," Talon responded.

Alexios immediately switched to Arabic, speaking very rapidly. "Do you really comprehend the language or merely a few words?"

"Do you want me to tell you a dirty joke to prove I can speak it well?" Talon asked in the same language, wanting to provoke a response.

Alexios' lips twitched in the ghost of a smile. He then gave Talon a keener look as though reappraising him. "While I do speak your Frankish language I do not find it very refined, so I prefer to speak either Arabic or my own. We can leave Latin to those two seasick monks you have brought with you," he rejoined in Arabic.

"If you are willing to teach me more Greek I am willing to be your student," Talon said. "I would know more of your laws and medicine, for instance."

"Our Roman laws are far more advanced than your primitive Feudal laws, and better chosen than those of the Arabs, who have no universal laws for the people of all ranks, as we do. Nor do we confuse our governing and criminal laws with our religious laws."

"We Franks use Feudal and Church law separately," Talon said defensively, remembering his talks with Bartholomew in faraway Languedoc. He was becoming mildly irritated but he was determined to extract as much as he could from Alexios despite the man's supercilious behavior.

"Humph," Alexios almost snorted. "Both are very tribal and quite unsuitable for a great administration such as ours. We will discuss this when you know more Greek. We should begin as soon as possible. Do you know the game of Chess?"

"Yes, I know the game," Talon responded cautiously.

Alexios' eyes betrayed his interest. Then he recovered his aplomb and said with a tinge of skepticism in his voice. "Then we shall play as we speak. We shall see how good you become at either one." He sighed as though the whole thing was a massive imposition upon his precious time and he would rather be doing something else.

Talon held his peace.

*****

A week later they sighted a coastline and after a brief consultation with Sir Guy, Henry decided to land and take on fresh water and supplies. The edge of a storm had pushed them closer to the south coast of the empire of Byzantium and much further east than they had wanted. Sir Guy informed them that they were near a potentially hostile land, which meant they would have to sail due west, following the coast line until they sighted some place that lookcd like a safe haven.

Dmitri was now one of the appointed steersmen under Henry's supervision. Talon was glad that Henry had found him, as Dmitri provided an independent voice on the subject of the empire. The Greek was very grateful to both Talon and Henry for having first saved him from slavery and then from the wasteland of Acre's back streets. He sported a jagged badly repaired scar that ran from his forehead splitting his right eyebrow to finish at his cheekbone. It made him look most villainous, but he had a cheerful nature and liked to talk about his life in Byzantium. He stated that he knew the coast from Syria to Constantinople, so he had become their unofficial pilot. Now he pointed out the high cliff on the western side of the huge crescent bay rimmed with dazzling white sands.

"That looks familiar to me, Sir Talon. That castle is still in our hands. It is Roman."

Not for the last time Talon would hear that the people of Byzantium thought of themselves as Roman, although they spoke Greek.

They were moving into the bay with the aid of the rowers, and Dmitri stated with some conviction that he knew of this place, which was a Byzantine stronghold on the south coast of the empire.

Alexios confirmed what Dmitri had said. "It is called *Kalon Oros*, or 'Beautiful Mountain' in Greek," he explained to Talon as they drew near to the tiny fortified town. "Those mountains over to the north are called the Taurus Mountains, and that is where the Sultanate of Rum has begun to encroach upon our empire." He spoke with an edge to his voice.

"Is not 'Rum' the Arab word for the Romans?" Talon asked.

"Yes, it is, and alas, that region is no longer a part of the Byzantine Empire," Alexios told him. "However, it has yet to be decided whether the Turks remain or whether we can drive them back over the mountains into Persia."

They were standing on the side away from the two steersmen, who were taking their orders from Henry as he guided the ship carefully towards the landing beach, which was tucked into the curve of the large isthmus on the western side of the huge crescent bay. As usual, the three sailors worked together. Guy was in the bows watching for shoals and sand banks while Nigel was in the waist ready to haul the sails down at Henry's command.

Talon noticed a long, high wall near the beach, while on the top of the cliffs now towering hundreds of feet above the ship stood a small castle. They anchored, and while Sir Guy stayed on board, not wanting to bring attention to himself, Henry and Talon went ashore with Alexios to find where they might obtain fresh water and even some provisions, to be paid for with gold coin. Alexios was received with polite ceremony by a young officer and his guard who had noticed him as he came along the landing place; when he indicated that he could not stay but wanted to continue his journey, the officer ensured that they left with some fresh fish, caged chickens, some goats and even some green vegetables to sustain them on their way and reluctantly bade him farewell.

Talon was struck by the elaborate ceremony that seemed to be part of their meeting even in this remote corner of the empire. It reminded him of his time in Persia. He observed that the officer appeared to be very disappointed that they could not stay.

He remarked upon this to Alexios as they stood on the deck of the ship watching the beach recede.

"We are a nation of ceremonies, Sir Talon," Alexios responded. "At the palace, as you will find out, every minute of the day is organized by protocol, and by the eunuchs who are masters of the game. It can sometimes be very tiring. That man over there," he pointed with his chin at the officer still standing on the quayside, "might have done something that got him him here as punishment. There is nothing for him to do outside the dreary routine of his command, and he might be there for years before some administrator in Constantinople remembers to replace him."

Talon looked at him. Alexios had changed his demeanor towards him over the weeks they had been at sea, and although he was still very reserved and somewhat distant, he did not condescend to him in the irritating manner he had at the beginning of their relationship. In fact, Talon now enjoyed the games of chess they played—even winning the odd game or two, much to the Greek's annoyance.

Alexios, once he discovered that Talon had a talent for languages, spent a considerable amount of time with him providing very intense instruction on the elaborate Attic Greek.

*****

Setting sail again they headed towards the long point of the isthmus, the furthest end of which resembled a snake lying in the water with its head well out to sea. As they rounded the head of the snake, keeping a prudent distance from the rocks, Talon stared up at the walls of the castle high above them and wondered how long it had been there. Sir Guy crossed the deck and stood by him, also looking up at the walls and the small figures standing watching them from the battlements.

"What ghosts prowl its walls at night who have watched ships like this sailing by for how many hundreds of years," he murmured.

Talon looked at him. "Is this land really so old, Sir?" he asked.

"As time goes it probably is not, but this land has known great empires for a very long time. Today it is the empire of the Greeks, and although we do not share their philosophy of the Holy Trinity they are still people with whom we must deal. I would not doubt that the Persians, then the Romans, and before them the Greeks, and now again the Greeks have stood guard on those battlements and watched ships of our kind and others sail by for eons."

"How long has this empire been here, Sir Guy?"

"Nearly a thousand years. It was here when we in our own lands were still heathen."

"They are Christian though, are they not?"

"Yes, but therein lies the issue. Although we both face a greater peril from the Islamic world, the Roman church which we serve and the Patriarch of Constantinople cannot agree upon even the most common thread of Christian theology."

One of the monks had finally emerged from the cabin where they had spent the last week in suffering. He looked pale and thin from lack of food and sleep, but there was a deep-set fire in his slightly pale blue eyes that peered out at the world from under his heavy brows and thick, coarse cowl. He was fidgeting with his prayer rosary as he stood staring with absent gaze at the cliffs and the surf pounding the rocks at their feet. Clearly he had overheard the discussion, for he pointed to the land and said, "That land claims to be of the Christian faith, but they are heretics in all manner of ways and God will one day strike them for it."

Talon looked around to see if Alexios was anywhere near. He was down in the waist of the ship and would not have heard the remark.

"Perhaps we should try to learn from them nonetheless," Sir Guy said mildly.

"Have a care, Sir Guy. You are a soldier of Rome. The path that Rome has set is the one true way. Theirs is a way both strange and steeped in wickedness."

"Why are you going to Constantinople, monk?" Talon asked. His voice must have betrayed some of his irritation, for Sir Guy touched his arm.

"They come with me for a special reason," he murmured. "The gifts for the emperor are from the Church." Then he addressed himself to the monk.

"How is Brother Martin doing below, Brother Jonathan?" he asked pointedly.

"He will survive this Hellish journey with God's help, as shall I," Brother Jonathan snapped. After a glare in Talon's direction he turned away and made his way with care down the steps to the cabin below.

"How is it that you are saddled with a man like that at your elbow, Sir Guy?" Talon asked.

"God help me, Talon, I sometimes wonder myself at our brothers in the church. The Bishop chose that idiot at the last moment as another, far better qualified, was sick. Brother Martin, now, he is different, mild and interested in what we are about. I suspect that Jonathan is a spy for the Bishop and will hold suspect everything we do. I expect too that all that transpires on this journey will find its way back to the Pope eventually."

Sir Guy continued, "He speaks a little Greek but no Arabic, so we can converse in that tongue with Alexios while in front of him. You now know that Alexios speaks what is known as Attic Greek, which is spoken by the aristocracy amongst themselves. The Greek we speak is of the streets and is not 'refined' as he puts it, but at least he is willing to share this with us. You will find that snobbery is a characteristic of the aristocracy in Constantinople. But when you consider how rude we Franks are by comparison it is difficult to blame them for looking down their noses at us barbarians." His smile was thin.

"It seems a case of them needing us and we needing them," Talon remarked.

"Exactly my sentiments, Talon. But you would be surprised at how difficult it is to get agreement on anything that is necessary for our mutual safety from the Greeks...or from Rome."

Although puzzled by the lack of information, Talon did not press Sir Guy. He knew that in his own time the knight would tell him what he needed to know.

*****

Four days and nights later they saw the coast receding and Henry informed them that their course was now set due north. Still keeping the coastline in sight, they sailed with Henry, Nigel and Guy keeping a sharp eye on the sun by day and the stars at night to reckon their course. Talon was impressed with their seeming confidence even when there was no land in sight.

One morning Alexios came on deck and the customary lesson in Attic Greek began. The steersmen studiously faced forward while Talon and Sir Guy sat with Alexios under an awning.

Later Henry wandered over and asked if they wanted some food. Talon and Sir Guy agreed heartily. A sailor who worked for the ship's cook came up on deck and presented them with a small basket of biscuits and some chunks of relatively fresh meat floating in a delicious smelling gravy in a wide, shallow dish. A few of the chickens had been killed for the purposes of feeding the men the day before. Talon was becoming tired of stews and biscuits, but they had a few days to go before they landed for fresh provisions, so he took out his spoon and dagger, preparing to eat.

Alexios held up his hand and said, "Wait, Sir Talon, Sir Guy, I think we should do something different today." He waved for his servant, Joseph.

"Joseph, go and bring up the 'forks'," he ordered.

With a knowing glance, Joseph nodded and left. A few moments later he reappeared with three items that he handed to Alexios.

Alexios held one up for them to inspect. It was a slim item about one-and-a-half hand-widths long with two long prongs that had been carefully beaten out of steel and inserted into a slim wooden handle by a tong.

Sir Guy sat back with a tiny smile on his face. Talon glanced at him, then peered suspiciously at the device and said, "Can it not wait, Alexios? I am hungry."

"No, Talon, it cannot wait, and furthermore I shall command that unless you can master this device you cannot eat this meal today, as you may only eat with the fork," Sir Guy said with a laugh, but it was clear that he meant it.

Alexios gave one of his cool smiles and handed one of the implements to Talon, then passed one to Sir Guy, retaining the last for himself. He leaned over the morsels of chicken in the pot and speared a large one that Talon had already decided was his and took it to his own bowl. Talon watched as Alexios then held the meat in place with the strange device and dissected it with his knife. He followed that up by picking one of the smaller pieces up with the fork and placing it between his lips. He chewed with obvious satisfaction, all the while keeping his eyes on Talon who was in danger of gaping.

Sir Guy copied the action with more care, but it was clear that he was no stranger to the device.

"Now, Talon, it is your turn."

Talon gripped the fork in his right hand like a weapon and stared at the food. "Why do I have to do this, Sir?" he asked plaintively.

"Because no respectable person is allowed in the royal palace to dine who does not know how to use one of these," Alexios informed him.

"Am I expected to dine with people at the palace then? I thought that it would be you, Sir Guy," Talon asked.

Sir Guy ignored the question and speared another piece of meat. He ate with relish and motioned to the bowl.

Talon tried to spear a piece of the chicken with too much energy; it slipped away from his fork and he came up empty. He stabbed again and this time splashed the sauce out onto the decks. He heard a snicker from the steersmen. He shot a glare in their direction but those worthies were staring forward with intent, wooden expressions on their faces.

"You are not going to get far at the table if you continue like this, Sir Talon." Sir Guy sounded severe but there was a twinkle in his eyes; Alexios was looking smug. Patronizing swine, Talon thought to himself.

"Show me again," he said with a glare at his table companions.

Alexios took the fork in his fingers and gently pierced the very morsel that Talon had wanted and took it away to his bowl. There were now only two more pieces in the bowl and Sir Guy took one just to prove how adept he was at the art. Talon hated him.

His stomach was now rumbling. Talon emulated their moves, but this time he first trapped the piece against the side of the bowl and then speared the meat. He brought it triumphantly up in the air, but just before he brought it to his plate it slipped off the fork and fell into his lap. He stared at the meat resting on his tunic, mortified more by his companions who roared with laughter than the mess it made. He had not realized that Max and Claude as well as Henry had been watching fascinated while he struggled with the new device.

"Have you not got anything else to do but laze about?" he yelled at them, his face red with embarrassment.

This only provoked more roars of laughter. He scooped up the morsel of meat with his fingers and popped it into his mouth with a defiant glare at Sir Guy. His consolation prize for the meal was the soup remaining in the bowl, which he tried to soak up with the hard biscuit and sips from his spoon.

*****

Alexios gave him no respite, and each day at noon he was forced to use the fork. It was not long before he managed to handle it comfortably, if not with the skill of Alexios; at least he did not go hungry.

His companions, Henry, Max, and Claude, teased him by pretending to eat with forks and stabbing themselves in the face, as he had done once when not paying enough attention. The pain of that encounter and the embarrassment, aggravated by the lack of sympathy from everyone around, stayed with him long enough to make him not to want to repeat it. He noticed, however, that when Sir Guy challenged the others to use the fork they all found other things to do, which made Talon smirk in derision.

Max later told him that Brother Jonathan had witnessed the display and the training and had commented that it was a sin to eat food like that, as were not a man's fingers, provided by God himself, good enough for eating? Both Talon and Claude had shaken their heads at this.

"I am a man of God, indeed, we all here are servants of God, but this idiot irks me. It would be a good thing to throw him overboard one dark night," Claude had muttered, his tone ominous. Talon half believed him.

"What would we do about a confessor if you did that?" Max enquired with a grin.

"There is always that other young pup, Martin."

Talon decided that Claude was a good man to have around.

The other skill he worked hard to master was that of navigation. He was enthralled by the strange symbols on the large sheet of velum that Sir Guy had brought on board with him. One of the charts appeared to be a picture of all the countries on the eastern seaboard of the Middle Sea. He discovered that the cartographer had captured the essence of Egypt and the Nile, although it was clear that he had left much in the way of detail. The artist had marked in the Dead Sea and Jerusalem, followed by the Principality of Tripoli. For the first time Talon began to see the region from another perspective and his interest grew.

"It is as though we are seeing the world we live in as through a bird's eye, but higher, if that is possible. We would have to be close to the sun to see this much," he commented to Henry and Sir Guy while they were in the cabin staring down at the charts. Henry laughed, but he said, "Yes, in some ways that is so, but these charts only give us a rough idea of where we are. The other important indicators are the sun at any given time of the day and the year, and what the stars are telling us."

Henry would then take Talon on deck and ask him to remember the chart, while trying to figure out where they might be with respect to the land mass they had kept on their starboard side for many days now.

"Are we heading north? South? Which direction are we going?" he would ask Talon.

At first Talon could tell him with some conviction that they were going north but little beyond that.

At his request, Henry, Nigel, or Guy would call Talon to the deck at night to show him the stars and make him memorize the constellations, their positions in the sky, and how these positions seemed to change over the course of hours. Talon's respect grew for the three sailors as he began to understand more fully how important was their skill to find port in this wasteland of water. It was not long before he could estimate where they might be with respect to the chart, but then Henry told him something disturbing.

"These charts are just pictures of what men think the world looks like, Talon. They do not tell us the whole truth, as no one knows how to chart every single bay and cliff along the coast. That is an art we have not yet been able to master."

"So it is mostly guesswork and hope?"

"Men get to know a particular sea well, Talon. And God's help is important, but yes...there is a lot of praying." Henry grinned.

When mornings came Talon would often be yawning mightily as he struggled with the Greek, much to the annoyance of Alexios. But Talon understood that he was learning an art that was without price and such an opportunity would not easily present itself again, so he persisted. His companions were flattered by his interest and pleased with the progress he was making.

The day came when Dmitri pointed out that the land was converging directly to their north and they were heading into a narrow band of water. "The land we have been following on the east is about to meet that land over there," he said, waving his hand to the northwest. "We will sail into that gap there, and after about a day or two, depending upon the wind, we will be in the Marmara Sea. We are almost there!" He sounded excited to be returning home after several years at sea and in a galley.

Henry, with Dmitri and Alexios at his side, navigated the straits comfortably despite the dense shipping sailing to and fro they now encountered. At one point they saw a large fortified city on the east coast, which Talon mistakenly thought might be Constantinople.

Dmitri laughed. "No, Talon. That is the city of Abydos. You will not be able to mistake Constantinople when you see it. Nothing can match it!"

They sailed on along the slightly curved straits packed with sails. The dawn of the second day, a cool misty morning, found them emerging from the straits of the Hellespont. Talon stepped onto the deck and noticed that the land mass had begun to recede into the distance on either side of them. He glanced up at the sky and, despite the mist, could discern that their course was unchanged. They were still sailing due north.

There were still many other sails to be seen, but they kept their distance; one ship, however, changed direction and began to come their way. Henry ordered the crew to prepare for trouble. Talon came to stand with him on the upper deck to watch events alongside Alexios and Sir Guy, both fully armed, as were he and the two sergeants.

It soon became clear that the other ship was coming to investigate theirs. It was a warship, a long sleek three-masted galley, but Alexios reassured them.

"I think it might be one of the Byzantine naval ships that scouts these seas, and we would be well advised to stay on course and not run from it."

All the same, there was heightened tension as they watched the approach of the larger vessel. It was indeed a Byzantine warship: Alexios pointed to the pennant flying from its forward masthead, showing the image of a double-headed eagle. The ship appeared to be well manned by a large crew as it sailed directly towards them and then hove to within hailing distance.

Henry, at a signal from Alexios, had already furled his sails but had ordered the rowers to take their places as a precaution.

Talon observed the men standing on the deck of the strange ship with interest. The crew appeared to be composed of tough looking seamen all dressed in a similar manner. They were armed to the teeth with spears, sabers and even axes. The cluster of men on the rear deck next to the steersmen was composed of elegantly dressed warriors in fine gleaming armor, flowing robes and plumed helmets. The only person on his own ship dressed in anything like this manner was Alexios, who jumped onto the side of the ship and held onto a main stay as he shouted across the sea-swell between them.

Talon was chagrined to find that despite the long hours he had spent with Alexios learning that man's language he barely understood a word that was shouted between the two ships.

He beckoned to Dmitri and asked him what had transpired. Dmitri seemed embarrassed.

"I do not speak his Greek very well, Sir Talon, it is Attic. But I think he is telling them that he is on a mission to our Constantinople and that we are escorting him."

Indeed, after a lot of shouting to and fro the men on the other vessel seemed to want to come aboard.

Alexios turned to Sir Guy and said, "Their captain wants to verify that we're who we say we are, Sir Guy. Do you give permission?"

"Do I have a choice?"

"No, Sir, you do not."

Sir Guy glanced at Talon and the men around him, then gestured to Alexios to call over to the other ship. There was more shouting and then a boat was lowered from the other ship into which several crewmen jumped, followed at a more dignified pace by someone of rank.

"Do you see that tube pointing our way from the middle deck, Talon?" Sir Guy murmured, lifting his chin to point.

Talon followed his gaze and noticed a group of men clustered around some kind of apparatus placed on the deck. A large tube was being maneuvered so that it pointed directly towards them. It was made of some kind of metal and its muzzle was blackened.

"What is it, Sir Guy?" Max asked. He had joined them as they watched the small boat cross the short distance between them.

"It is known by many names, but I know it as *Greek Fire* and that is what delivers it. We have to be careful, for if they shoot its flames at us we have no defense at all. We would be burned to the water within minutes," Sir Guy said quietly.

Talon and Max stared at him, their faces registering shock. There was no time to discuss the strange weapon, however, for Alexios rejoined them. The small boat bumped alongside and an officer was assisted aboard, followed by some large, well-armed men who stood behind him protectively while he looked around the ship. His gaze was keen, that of someone who knew what he was looking at. He wasted no time but strode to the ladder that led to the deck above where Alexios and Sir Guy awaited him.

There were elaborate greetings between him and Alexios, who seemed to be speaking on behalf of the ship. Alexios motioned several times to Sir Guy, offering explanations for his presence. He even showed the man a paper that he had brought on deck for him to examine. The officer finally nodded and raised his hand in salute, then he prepared to disembark. Alexios accompanied him to the side of the ship and waved him off.

Henry did not give the command to drop sails until Alexios gave him permission. Meanwhile the other crew, demonstrating a smart example of seamanship, hoisted their own sails and moved off southward at a fast pace, tacking into a brisk wind. Talon was impressed by this display of naval efficiency.

"Overlooking Constantinople"

Chapter 3

Constantinople

They saw the city long before they arrived. It loomed out of the early dawn like some magical creation from a glowing legend.

Talon went forward with Max and Alexios to see better from the bows while Henry and Sir Guy stayed on the back deck. He could only stare. The massive fortifications encircling the city seemed to go on forever and to rise straight out of the sea. Behind the fortifications he could see a row of low, uneven hills upon which were dense clusters of buildings of every shape and size. There were enormous, square-looking constructions with many pillars, and lesser buildings planted all over the green hillsides. In the distance he could see the domes of numerous churches rising among the red tiled housing, denoting a pious population. What dominated the entire city, however, was an enormous complex of domes and towers that Alexios pointed to with pride.

"The Great Palace and the Hagia of St Sophia." There was reverence in his voice as he spoke.

"It was built for the Glory of God," Brother Martin said as he joined then. "It is magnificent! I must go there to pray at the earliest opportunity."

"I will come with you, Brother Martin," Talon said. He rather hoped that Jonathan would decide not to come but had faint hope of that.

These buildings were built on the highest point of the peninsular ridge to the right of the harbor, and the church was without doubt the most magnificent Talon had ever seen. Apart from its general size he could tell that the width of its dome was immense, and he wondered how men could build such a structure. Its dome dominated, yet clustered about the round central building were many others, each with a lesser dome. He gazed in awe at the most enormous and beautiful city in the world that sprawled over a long tongue of land jutting out into the Marmara Sea.

He pointed to a huge construction with many arches nearer to them. "What is that building over there, Alexios?"

"That is the Hippodrome, it is where we race chariots."

He began to point out many other places, from palaces to barracks, as they drew near to the walls of the city.

After three weeks of traveling all of them were ready to step onto dry land and stay for a while, but the men on the ship were silent as they contemplated this huge city that they were about to visit. The journey north had been interesting, Talon reflected. They had spent most nights anchored off the coast of the islands along the way. The sea was dotted with them in this area, and fortunately Dmitri knew many of them and had guided them unerringly northward through the archipelago. What harbors they had visited had been populated with Greeks who were part of the empire, so Alexios had been able to obtain fast service from the authorities when it came to resupply and fresh water. At the first sign of any bad weather, Henry had sought the shelter of an island inlet, anchoring and waiting out the rough seas that followed.

Alexios had begun to thaw towards Talon as they spent time together speaking the complicated Attic Greek, which, he had reminded Talon, would provide him with a passport to higher society when the time came; and besides, the court affairs were all conducted in Attic.

They had played chess often and Talon had begun to hone his skill. He enjoyed the game, which, Alexios told him, had come from Persia. He remembered his time with Reza, his friend, and the games they had played in Isfahan.

Talon had not had much to do with the two monks, who had shown up on the deck from time to time. Sir Guy wryly told him that he had to keep them engaged as they were part of his entourage, but even he had begun to tire of the incessant carping from Brother Jonathan. Brother Martin, once he had recovered from his initial bout of seasickness, had spent time on deck keeping Max and the others company. He was young and eager to please, but clearly scared of Brother Jonathan, who imposed his authority at every opportunity. He endured the treatment cheerfully enough, seeking the company of the sergeants when he could, his thin features ever ready to smile. Even Sir Guy seemed to like him, although the boy kept a respectful distance from the exalted man.

The sea they were now sailing across was full of shipping. Galleys, merchant ships large and small, and fishing vessels abounded, ploughing up and down the straits of the Bosporus. They passed five huge war galleys speeding south on some errand, their oars rising and falling in perfect unison as the rowers drove their ships forward. Talon asked if the rowers were slaves, at which Alexios gave him an odd look.

"They are soldiers, who row when they are needed and fight otherwise. Any other way would be wasteful."

Talon thought about this, remembering the slave-driven galleys of the Arabs.

There were the large sea dhows from the Arab world, perhaps even from Egypt, and Alexios pointed out the massive cargo ships from Genoa. They sailed by another batch of war galleys that were anchored, passing within hailing distance. The officers and men on board observed them without curiosity. They were just another vessel coming to the great city.

This cool morning the sea was choppy with white caps and a wind blowing from the southwest, so they were using only sail as they headed towards the southern border of the golden city. Sea gulls were in abundance, wheeling and diving into the choppy waters or shrieking at the ship and landing on the sides, their beady eyes searching for food, or swooping at discarded items they discovered in the crowded waters.

Alexios stood with Henry and pointed out landmarks ahead of them that would be useful. He told them that they would be docking at the Harbor of Julian, which was on the southern tip of the peninsula not far from the Hippodrome and the Great Palace itself.

Two hours later, when the sun was high in the sky, they drew close to the great walls of the city. Talon wondered if Alexios had made a mistake, for he did not at first see the great metal grill set into the wall between two towers towards which they were sailing. Then Alexios said to Henry, "Be careful here, Henry; we have to stop just before the walls and a pilot will come out and guide us in."

Henry bellowed orders and the crew ran to do his bidding. The sails were furled and the rowers were told to put their oars out. The ship slowed and they drifted in silence, the oarsmen at the ready. All of the passengers were on deck, including the two monks. Everyone stared in wonder at the walls and towers that now loomed above them. The entrance they were hoping to take was a gap in the walls with a square tower on either side.

"I hope the pilot is going to come out soon," Henry grumbled to Sir Guy. "I do not like drifting about so near to the shoreline with this wind behind me. It will be hard to get off the shore if it increases."

But they did not have long to wait. The huge grill set in the walls began to move to the side with an audible rumble, and then a boat shot out of the entrance, rowed by an energetic crew. The small craft came alongside and a man climbed nimbly up the side of the ship to pause on the deck and look around.

He was met by Alexios, who walked forward and saluted him. They had a conversation in rapid Greek and then the man walked aft to climb onto the after deck. Ignoring the people standing around, the man concentrated on giving Henry instructions, which Dmitri translated.

Henry gave the crew orders and the rowers began to work again. They backed the ship some hundred yards, then rowed the vessel between the two towers and into the still waters of the harbor. Talon watched with interest as the soldiers on the walls above them cranked some mechanism and the enormous grill slid across the entranceway behind them to crash to a stop against the other wall, locking them into the harbor.

They had arrived in a quiet place without much movement, which was a surprise to Talon who expected many more ships to be inside.

"This is only used for the visitors, naval vessels and emissaries like yourselves, who come to pay their respects to the emperor," Alexios informed him on being asked.

Their pilot guided the ship to a space alongside a high stone quay where Henry expertly set the ship into place. At a shouted command, the oars were shipped and ropes were tossed to men on the quay who pulled them in so that the side of the ship bumped hard against the thick knotted ropes hanging down from the stonework. Next, several people on shore tied the thrown ropes to big metal rings set into large stone pillars sunk into the stone pavement of the quay. The pilot, after a quick word with Alexios, received a coin then jumped ashore and disappeared into the crowd of people working on the quay.

"We have arrived," Alexios informed them. He was clearly pleased, and Talon sensed that he wanted to depart as soon as was polite.

"We must wait for the customs and harbor officials to come and verify we are who we claim to be, so you should not go ashore until they have completed their business. Here they come now." Alexios pointed to a group of people walking along the quay. They did not seem in any hurry, so it took some minutes before they were standing in front of the ship, which gave Talon and the rest of the passengers time to observe them.

The officials were dressed in expensive robes, which seemed somehow out of place in a rough place like a harbor. Their leader was tall and willowy, more richly dressed than all who accompanied him. His tunic was of the finest silk material and came down to his ankles, almost brushing his fine leather sandals. He wore an over-tunic that was more like a long coat and this was bound at the middle with a jeweled belt and a buckle of silver. On his head was a tall ornate cloth hat, which might have been the symbol of his rank. He wore no sword, but was accompanied by four well dressed men who looked like scribes and several armed men who resembled some of the soldiers they had encountered in the various harbors they had visited. But these men were far better dressed and armed.

Alexios murmured to Sir Guy, "This man is one of the *Logothetes tou Genicon* and answers only to the *Logothetes tōn sekretōn* of Constantinople, and *he* is directly responsible to the emperor for revenues, so this man is very powerful."

"What do those names mean?" Talon asked with emphasis.

"He is "One who counts" and is responsible for all taxes and revenue that come in through the ports. One should always be respectful to his kind," Alexios said in a low voice, as the official was only a short stone's throw away by now.

The official looked at a paper that was presented to him and glanced across the quay towards the men standing on the deck. "State your business!" he demanded in a high falsetto voice.

Alexios stepped forward to the ship's rail.

"This ship carries emissaries from the Kingdom of Jerusalem to see his Holiness the Emperor, bearing letters from King Baldwin of Jerusalem," he called back.

"Do you have proof which will allow you to remain in this harbor?"

"I have a letter prepared," Alexios said, and handed it down for one the minions to receive. The man hurried over to accept it and then presented it with a deep bow to the customs officer, who read the document and murmured something to a scribe standing nearby who quickly took some notes.

"Very well, you may stay, and there is no tax; although my officers will be coming to inspect the ship. If you are providing false information you will be imprisoned and the ship confiscated."

Alexios nodded. The official turned and, followed by his men, strode off in a stately fashion towards the land gate and buildings further down the quay.

"That man is a walking king's ransom!" exclaimed Guy looking after the departing group.

"What was that all about, Dmitri?" Henry asked

"He is the Customs officer for this port. He is the eunuch in charge of all customs duties that are collected here, which is not much, as this is for special visitors."

"What is a eunuch?" Guy asked naively.

"He is had his balls cut off." Max made a theatrical gesture by his groin.

"What?" this came from all three of the sailors.

"That is what they do in the Arab lands too," Talon said.

Guy put his hand over his genitals. "By God, I cannot imagine that!" he said. "He sounds like...a woman, well not quite, but something like one. How is it that he is in charge of everything when he is a whatdoyacallum?"

"Are they all like that?" Nigel asked as he came up to join them from the lower deck.

"Like what?" Talon asked.

"He looks odd. Long and thin."

"He is a eunuch, and here in Constantinople they are all like that," Sir Guy said. "To them we are known as 'The Bearded Ones.' They don't grow them."

"I could retire on the jewels he is wearing on his belt alone," Henry said enviously, scratching his beard.

"You'd give up your own jewels in order to obtain the riches he has on his belt?" Nigel asked wickedly.

"No you numbskull, but he has the riches by the look of it...it is something for what he is missing." Henry retorted.

This was greeted with snickers from his companions.

Talon had time to observe the soldiers who had accompanied the Logothetes. They wore a style of armor he had never seen before. He nudged Max. "Have you noticed their armor?" he asked.

"Yes, it is curious. They look like they're wearing long thin metal tubes down their arms. And I see slightly wider tubes sewn onto their thigh tunics. They might be good to stop a swipe with a sword, but how do they deflect a stabbing blow?" Max said, examining the men on the quay with a professional air.

"You or I could slip either a knife or a sword blade in between those rods or tubes unless they have something underneath that I do not see. Their shoulders look well protected, but not their necks. Their helmets seem to be made of bronze, which good steel would cut into if the hit were in the right place, and which a mace or an axe could destroy easily."

"Those large round shields they carry look like they are bronze plated, Talon. They make a nice polish, but I wonder how useful against a lance?"

"They wear nothing on their lower legs or their lower arms. Good targets in a close quarter fight, wouldn't you say?" Talon said.

"What are you two talking about?" Sir Guy joined them as they leaned on the ships rail.

"We were doing what we cannot help, Sir," Max said with a grin. "We're discussing the merits of their soldiers' armor and we find it wanting."

Sir Guy glanced casually over at the soldiers. "I would agree with you, Max. Our chain mail Hauberk is superior to that which the Byzantine foot soldiers wear. Their armor looks as though it hasn't changed since the time of the Romans, which was ages ago. Then again, those men might be in ceremonial dress. I am not sure. They do have armor on their elite cavalry that is every bit as good as chain, at least I hear it is."

Talon filed this information away for future reference. He was not about to underestimate these people. After all, they had built the most enormous and beautiful city he had ever seen, and the fortifications were formidable. They must be doing something right.

*****

They waited impatiently for another interminable two hours, but no one came to inspect the vessel. Possibly the customs official deemed Alexios to be a reliable speaker for the ship yet had omitted to inform them they were free to leave.

Alexios finally said it was time for him to go. "I will send a messenger to you before too long, Sir Guy. It will be my responsibility to make sure of the preliminary arrangements for your visit to His Holiness the Emperor. You will have to accompany me on several occasions to meet with the right people and to make sure there are no complications. Meanwhile there are inns on shore up on the side of that hill. You will have to arrange for permissions at the gates which are shut at night, as there is a curfew on all the harbors."

He gave a handclasp to Sir Guy and Talon, then climbed onto the quay with his servants and disappeared into the crowd.

"This is only one of how many ports for this city?" Henry asked, his tone incredulous.

"There are five ports, and one or two of them are larger than this one," Dmitri said.

"I have never seen a city like this before. It makes Acre look like a village," Max stated. "Perhaps Alexandria had something of the same, but this place is beyond my belief!"

"When you peasants have finished 'Ooing' and 'Ahing' at everything, I want to get off the ship and find a place to sleep that is not heaving and rolling," Sir Guy stated. He had been listening with some amusement to their comments.

"Dmitri, you will take me to find a place for us to stay. The passengers will be in one inn, that includes our Godly kinfolk, and then find a place for Henry, Nigel and Guy. Henry, the crew will have to stay on board."

Henry nodded. "Yes, Sir Guy, I agree we should not leave the ship alone. Nigel, you stay for the first day until we know where we are staying and what is going to happen."

"Be prepared for a stay of several weeks, maybe longer. Things do not move swiftly here," Sir Guy said, his tone dry.

"Come, Talon, we will go with Dmitri. Max, you and Claude will accompany us."

They collected their baggage, which was not much; the monks had even less; then they left the ship to push their way through the crowd of workers on the quay. They strode to the gates where they were asked their business, and finally after many explanations and much gesticulating on the part of Dmitri they were allowed through; but the guard officer, dressed in a fine tunic, gleaming breastplate and sandals, made them carry a paper that explained who they were.

"They seem to have rules for everything here," Talon remarked as they set off along a crowded street that led up the hill away from the harbor. "Where are you taking us, Dmitri?" he asked.

"We are going to see a friend of mine who once had a very good inn, Sir Talon. It has been many years since I was here so I do not know if he is still about, but if so it is not far," Dmitri told him.

Before making much headway, they heard the roar of a crowd and all of them halted.

"What was that?" Talon asked.

"They must be having a race at the Hippodrome. Do you see it? It is that large building over there." Dmitri pointed. "That is why there are so few people on the streets today."

Talon stared at him in amazement. The streets of this city teemed with people, beasts of burden and stray dogs. Then they all turned to look at the long, massive building from which was coming another roar.

"What kind of race?" Max asked.

"They race the chariots...do you not know of that?"

"This I must see some time," Talon said.

He glanced at the two monks. Jonathan looked disapproving but Martin looked interested.

Dmitri led the way along the busy street that went in a steep incline straight up the hill. Talon noted with amazement that the entire street was paved with stone. He could not remember where he had seen anything like this other than in Alexandria. Certainly not in Acre and never in Languedoc, although in Carcassonne there might have been some paved streets, he could not remember. It was not a particularly special road either from what he could tell. There were houses along both sides, many built of stone and mud walls with russet colored clay tiled roofs. It looked as though the side of the hill was scaled with red in places, the houses were so densely packed and the side streets very narrow.

Vendors were established all along the side of the road shouting their wares of food and drink and trinkets and cloth of amazing colors. The tantalizing smell of roasting chicken and fish mingled with the sharp aroma of spices wafted towards them from the open shops on either side of the street. Talon realized just how much he had missed a good meal. The shipboard food, despite frequent stops at the islands and the fish they had hauled out of the sea along the way, had gradually become less and less palatable.

Many people were moving about the market stalls. He noticed a few women who wore veils and scarves and bright colors but who were unaccompanied. Others had their servants with them, but no one showed concern over single women walking along a street rubbing shoulders with wizened old people and young men alike. He had noticed this in Acre too. Greek Christians did not seem to have the same inhibitions as the Arabs regarding their women folk moving around unescorted.

They pushed past groups of well-dressed men who were chattering and gesticulating animatedly and glanced at them as they passed but did not hinder their passage. Talon assumed they were merchants; the manner of their dress told him that some at least were not from these parts.

There were even soldiers lounging at the entrances of what Talon took to be taverns, some of them inebriated even at this early hour. He observed that the men were of many different nationalities and wore distinctive clothing that identified them as such, although he had no idea where most of them might be from.

There were numerous beggars, lying or hobbling about on crude crutches. Many were maimed, riddled with disease and sores that could see through their filth. Talon wondered if these unfortunates might be the detritus of past campaigns. Beggars called out to them as they passed, waving wooden bowls and shaking their fists or sticks at them if they did not provide any coin. Martin was visibly distressed and flinched when a particularly aggressive beggar hobbled over to him and began to shout in some strange language. Max and Claude move to intercept the man and pushed him carefully out of their way. Jonathan did not seem to notice the beggars, but his gaze roamed over the younger women, many of whom were engaged in one occupation or another.

The street they labored up was home to many industries and merchants. They passed a bakery that had a long queue of people outside. The tantalizing smell of fresh baked bread made Talon feel even hungrier than before. There were soldiers outside keeping the line under control.

"Why do they need soldiers outside a bakery when there are many other kinds of shop along this street?" he asked.

"Bread is for everyone who can produce a lead token to prove they are a citizen. We might be able to obtain tokens for the crew, as they will need food, and we are after all a delegation. I shall ask," Dmitri assured him.

Leather workers plied their craft close to smiths banging away at curved metal pieces of armor. There was even one who offered to sharpen a man's sword to the point he could shave with it. One such craftsman waved a thin blade in the air and demonstrated as he shaved a small strip of his forearm and then held onto his crotch and boasted that a man with a sharp sword never did without a lady. Because he spoke in street Greek only Dmitri fully understood him, and Talon barely. Dmitri asked the man if the inn was still in operation, to which the man replied yes. It was further up the hill; they still had some way to go.

Talon wondered, "Dmitri, if this is only one of the busy streets of this great city, where is the bazaar and what treasures does it hold?"

"Bazaar, Talon?" Dmitri looked confused. "Constantinople does not have one of those rabbit warrens. All our trading is done on streets like this one. There are many special streets, for instance on the other side of this hill there are the tannery streets that used to be run by those scummy Venetians. Thank the Lord I heard they are all in jail now. Then there are the Jewish streets where gold, silver and the like are worked. The streets of the silk merchants are farther the east of here. Caravans come to Constantinople from many countries. They camp outside the western walls."

Talon filed the information away, as he thought he might need to take advantage of the Jewish bankers some time. Dmitri finally stopped outside a stout wooden gateway that was the entrance to a large rambling house. There was a man well past his prime posing as a guard outside who demanded their business.

Talon was glad now that he had spent so much time with Alexios learning the language. This was street Greek, but he could just follow the conversation.

"We are visitors who will be needing rooms. Is this place still an inn?" Dmitri asked

"Go inside to see the innkeeper," the guard said, and opened one of the gates. "Only one allowed in until we know if you are going to be guests."

Dmitri was the obvious choice so he went inside while the others stood watching the pedestrian traffic go by.

It was hard not to notice a two storied house just a few hundred paces up the street. Men were coming and going, some clearly in their cups, while others lounged outside seated on crude benches. But what caught the attention were the women who stood on the balcony overlooking the street. They were for the most part young and dressed in light, revealing tunics. As they were some distance away what they were saying to one another was indistinct.

"What is that place over there?" the monk Jonathan asked, looking interested.

"I would guess it is a brothel," Claude said, watching with amusement as Jonathan crossed himself and looked outraged.

"I can sense that this is a place of great sin. I sense that God is not paying attention, may he forgive me for saying so," Jonathan whispered to Brother Martin. He wiped his dripping nose with his already filthy sleeve. He then fingered his beads as he peered about him with a disapproving look at the people on the street.

Talon rolled his eyes at Sir Guy but said nothing. Max grinned at Claude.

They heard a shout from the street outside the brothel and some drunken men began to roll about in the gutter punching one another. Others pulled them apart and the two men fell against the wall of the house. They soon settled down over some cups of wine their companions thrust into their hands.

"We must pray to God that he guide us, Brother," Martin said in a soothing tone when he noticed Jonathan flinch. "I am sure that there are holy places we can visit while here. I hear there are many relics of the saints in this city." The young monk did not seem to be in the least bit intimidated by his surroundings; instead he seemed excited and eager to see more of it.

Talon smiled to himself. "This must be one of the supply streets for the harbor," he remarked to Max.

"Everything is either going to the harbor or leaving it along this street. Look at those carts! They are huge!" He pointed to one that was laboring up the hill pulled by six oxen. The drover walked alongside the beasts cracking a long whip, shouting for passage and urging the straining animals to pull. As the monstrous wagon creaked by, its iron wheels grinding on the stone road, they could see large bales of cloth and many clay pots with wax sealed tops. The drover walked right by the two monks and gave them a cheerful salute, then spat in the roadway as he moved off.

It was not long before Dmitri appeared with a pleased look on his face. "I have found rooms for everyone, but the two Brothers will have to sleep in the same room," he announced cheerfully.

"That will be just fine for them. They can console one another in the dark about how sinful this place is," Claude muttered to Max.

Jonathan must have heard because he shot Claude a venomous look but said nothing.

"We must pay for the first few days in advance," Dmitri stated.

"Very well," Sir Guy replied. He had come prepared so he placed several silver coins in Dmitri's outstretched hand. Dimitri disappeared again, then after some minutes came back and waved them in.

They all trooped into a cool, long, low beamed room where it was cooler than outside. hey were greeted by a small rotund man with an ingratiating smile, who wiped his hands on a large stained apron and bowed. Dmitri identified him as the innkeeper. He beamed at them and spoke some words of welcome, which Dmitri translated.

"He says that he is very happy to have us as guests and that if you need food he can provide that in the garden out at the back."

Talon glanced down the corridor and could see a pleasant garden with a table and stools set for a meal. Servants were bustling about serving people. It was almost noon so the midday meal was in progress. A mouth-watering smell of roast chicken, herbs and garlic emanated from the kitchens somewhere down the corridor. He was hungry, but he decided that he wanted a bath more than a meal right now.

"He also said that there are public baths nearby which will cost a small coin for anyone who is interested. The maid servants can take care of laundry on the premises," Dmitri said.

Talon glanced at Max and Sir Guy. "I am very interested in having a bath before anything else, Dmitri," he said.

Sir Guy nodded agreement and so did Max. "Claude will come with us," Sir Guy said firmly.

Max grinned at Claude, who looked uncomfortable but did not refuse.

"The innkeeper will have servants show the others to their rooms if they do not wish to join us," Dmitri said.

The two monks were looking uncertain as to what was going on so Sir Guy explained for them. "We have rooms and the servant over there will take you to them. After this we are going for a bath. Do you want to come?"

Jonathan looked dismayed and crossed himself. "It is a sinful thing to do. I shall indeed not indulge in that Godless activity. Sir Guy, I must bring myself to say it, but should you be going to the bath?"

"There are people who say it is Godly to take a bath from time to time in order to wash away the dust of one's travel, Brother. While we have not walked the dusty road all this way from Acre I am still quite sure I need to clean myself, and the sooner the better. Brother Martin, will you be coming with us?"

Brother Martin looked uncertain but a nudge from Jonathan, who was glaring at him, made his mind up for him.

"I shall keep my Brother company and pray to our Lord to thank him for our safe arrival while we await your return; then perhaps we can eat?" There was entreaty in his voice, and he declined the offer with some reluctance.

They deposited their baggage and then Sir Guy, Talon, Max, and Claude left for the baths.

Dmitri hastened back to the ship to escort Henry and his companions to another inn nearby before joining them in the baths.

*****

Talon was smiling to himself as he surfaced in the lukewarm water of the large pool. The other four men were seated on the side of the pool relaxing and talking. There were few other clients about at this time of the day. He suspected the bathhouse would fill up in the evening. It was different from the bathhouses he had become used to in Egypt, but its function was the same and very welcome after the long voyage. Dips in the sea had been enjoyable but to be clean was even better.

He waded over to stand in the water facing his companions. They were all naked and he observed that between them they could boast many a battle scar. He noticed too that Claude had relaxed and showed signs of enjoying himself now that his earlier fears about bathing had proved groundless.

"What were they doing to you in that back alcove, Dmitri? You sounded as though they were torturing you," Max demanded.

Dmitri laughed.

"You should have the oil and massage treatment, my friends. They cover you in oil, the olive oil you understand, and then they massage you and then they scrape it all off with a blade. It is such a delight to be back!" He almost crowed.

"What part was it that made you squeal?" Max asked unkindly, "The scraping with a knife or the massage?"

Dmitri just grinned. "You just wait, Max, you'll try it one day. I promise that you will like it."

"I feel much better from just the bathing," Max said. Ever since his experiences in Egypt Max had tried to obtain a bath whenever he could, which in Acre had not been easy. Eventually he and Talon had become guests at the Jewish baths, where they had been accepted with wary hospitality.

"My regret is that we will have to put up with the stink of those monks during the meal," Sir Guy remarked. Talon stifled a laugh while the other three grinned openly. It was quite unlike Sir Guy to be so blunt.

"I am almost glad that they did not come, as I do not think there is enough water to wash off their accumulated muck," Talon said. The others laughed.

"Did you see the expression on Martin's face? He would have come if that miserable idiot Jonathan hadn't pulled him back. I do not mind Martin," Claude growled. He was not a man of many words but usually came to the point. He drew his hand down his full beard to clear it of excess water. Talon liked Claude for his blunt ways. He wondered what had brought him to the Order but it was not a question anyone asked of another. There were many in the Order who had a very dark past, so the unwritten rule was never to ask.

"Well, I am well bathed, but I have noticed that Dmitri seems to have enjoyed the massage so I shall be back for one myself," Talon stated. "In the meantime I am starving."

The others agreed.

Before they left, Dmitri pointed to an archway at the other end of the bathing area. "Do you know where that leads to, Talon?" he asked with mischief in his eyes.

"No," Talon said, peering into the somewhat gloomy recesses in the direction indicated.

"It is noon so they won't be up as yet, but that is where the women are to be found in the evenings."

"Then thank God for small mercies that we did not bring Brother Jonathan with us," Sir Guy muttered. "We would all be condemned without trial to Hell and damnation for merely being here."

Talon laughed, as did Max. Claude looked interested.

"What sort of women?" he enquired with a guilty glance at Sir Guy.

"Have you ever seen a beautiful Greek woman, or one from Bulgaria, or Macedonia, or even those blondes from the Slavic tribes?" Dmitri said with a leer, placing his fingers and a thumb to his lips and kissing them.

"It is time to go and have a meal," Sir Guy said firmly.

*****

Despite the dour attitude of Jonathan the meal was a success. They dined at the inn on the food that was brought to them, as there was no choice in the matter of fare, but Talon could not fault what was placed in front of them.

The harried, scrawny young waiter brought them a jug of wine and leather cups, then left to obtain food. He promised to find something for them from the kitchens despite their late arrival. Sir Guy made it plain he would reward the man well. True to his word he arrived back after twenty minutes, bearing two large loaves of bread with thick crusts accompanied by pots of plump olives and light olive oil in a wide bowl in which there was crushed garlic. There was a tan colored paste in another wooden bowl that Talon recognized as humus and a large pottery jar of soft white goat's cheese.

Talon and Max showed the two monks how to eat this and Martin took to the food immediately. The wine helped and his normally pale young face was soon a little flushed. Jonathan picked at the food as though it were a duty, but the others ate like starving men.

The humus and olives were speedily consumed and were followed by a dish that the waiter called *skioufikta*. The roasted lamb was delicious. It had been marinated in butter and aged cheese then roasted with herbs and thyme. With this the waiter produced another mouthwatering side dish called *dolmades* that consisted of grain and ground meat mixed with chopped vegetables and stuffed into vine leaves, which he explained had been cooked over a slow fire. He followed this with a dish of sour cream pies stuffed with chopped raisins and apples laden with honey. They had not eaten so well for weeks.

It was clear that the monks and Claude were altogether new to this kind of food. Claude belched happily as he leaned back on the bench while Martin suppressed one with embarrassment as he took another sip of the resinous wine.

Jonathan finally excused himself and dragged a reluctant Martin off with him. Dmitri gave an elaborate yawn and left as well, but the others stayed at the table. The garden area was empty of other people now, so they had it to themselves. The servant cleared the table and left them alone after Sir Guy had placed several copper coins on the table for him. The reckoning for the meal would come later. The skinny man bowed obsequiously and left them in peace.

"I suspect that even Jonathan would have to admit that this was a good meal," Talon remarked.

"I am sure he will go to the nearest church and pray for forgiveness for having enjoyed himself," Claude said. "I swear that if we eat like this every day I shall become as fat as a Bishop."

"Claude, it will be you who has to go and beg forgiveness if you say things like that; and worse, it will have to be to, Brother Jonathan to whom you go for your confession," Sir Guy admonished him in his dry manner.

Claude gave a theatrical shudder and rolled his eyes. The others laughed at his lugubrious expression.

Sir Guy looked around to verify they were alone, then leaned forward over the cleared table.

"Not all of you know the real reason we came to Constantinople," he said.

Talon and Max sat up. Talon stifled a yawn; he yearned for a nap, but it was clear that Sir Guy wanted to discuss things of importance.

"I am personally enjoined by the king to negotiate not one but two items with the emperor. Neither of them is going to be easy to accomplish, as His Majesty Manuel, although supportive of our presence in Palestine, is nonetheless at odds with the Normans—in one particular: Lord Roger of Sicily's son William—and we must not forget his difficult relationship with the Lombards and the Venetians."

What are these two items, Sir Guy?" Talon asked.

"The first is for the Templars as well as for the kings of France and Germany and the Holy Roman Empire; the second is closer to home for the King of Jerusalem. I am here to open negotiations for a right of passage past Constantinople for a third crusade."

Talon gasped. "I am not very familiar with the way things have gone between the Frankish Kingdom and the emperor, but did not the last crusade that passed through here end in disaster?"

Max nodded. "It did, Talon, and there were Templars even then trying to assist. The German effort failed, for their emperor fell seriously ill along the route. He was brought back to this city where he was attended to by no lesser man than His Holiness the Emperor Manuel himself. The German army evaporated while the French King Louis took a seaward route and arrived in Palestine, but then he led an assault on Damascus."

"That was a debacle and cost us the neutrality of the city. It also brought Nur Ed Din into the game, whom we might have been able to deny a place in history had we not been forced to attack Damascus by those idiot crusaders," Sir Guy said somewhat bitterly.

"Were you both there?" Talon asked.

"We were all there, your uncle included, Talon. God forgive me, but I do not have kind words for that king. He left us with such a mess to clean up that we are still paying for it today," Max said.

"Then why are we supporting another crusade which could end in a similar manner?" Talon asked bluntly.

"Because that is what we are about, Talon." There was a mild rebuke in Sir Guy's voice.

He continued. "The Templars cannot hold the entire Kingdom of Jerusalem and Tripoli and the northern provinces on our own. It is simple arithmetic. We need fresh soldiers and more people to come and live in Palestine. The losses exceed the births in all the areas; we need farmers, builders, tradesmen and men at arms to maintain our armies or we will be overrun eventually."

"I am sorry Sir Guy...I did not mean to be disrespectful," Talon said, his tone contrite.

"You ask questions, Talon, and that is a good thing. There is much talk of another crusade from France and the Holy Roman Empire of Germany, and we have been asked to see if the emperor will agree, in principle at least, to an army coming through."

"You see, Talon," Max said, "the last time an army of crusaders came through this area there was havoc wrought across the lands in between, and the Greeks probably remember this with anger and fear."

"He will not even countenance an audience with anyone from the western countries at this time, so we Templars, who have gained some respect because we defend the Holy Land, have been asked to open the negotiations and find out if it is at all possible," Sir Guy added.

"Why do they not all come to Palestine by sea?" Talon asked. It seemed an obvious solution to him. "Most of the Templar knights come in by sea, why not the crusading armies?"

"I am sure that many will travel by sea, but to do so means many, many ships and the western countries cannot provide such a fleet. Besides, there is always the likelihood of storms and such like. The Middle Sea is unpredictable. You and Max were shipwrecked, so you know of the hazards.

"The west does not have the same skills as, for example, the Genoese or the Venetians at building fast and seaworthy ships. The Templar fleet is too small for an endeavor of this magnitude, and while there are other shipbuilders, the Basque people for instance, and indeed the Kingdom of Aragon and the Catalans who can build good ships, they do not have the resources to build enough large troop-carrying vessels. The Venetians are the best ship builders in the world, but they hate the Byzantine emperor for imprisoning their merchant people, so it is very unlikely that they will help."

"It does pose the question, Sir Guy. Why does not the emperor finance and send an army to Palestine himself?"

Sir Guy chuckled. "There was a time when the Byzantine army was invincible, but in these latter generations that hasn't been the case. The Komnenos emperors have done well, Alexios I, John his son, and now Manuel, but they inherited an empire in disarray. It is all the emperor can do today to hold onto what belongs to him. It is being nibbled away by many enemies who clamor to come to this city and sack it. You probably know of whom I speak. There are the Arabs, and the Seljuks of Rum, and Roger of Sicily who gave us Franks a bad name by behaving like some pirate on the seas. His son wants this empire for himself. I do not think Manuel would dare to stay away from home long enough to allow that to happen."

"What is the other item you mentioned, Sir Guy?"

"Ah, that is on a more delicate note. Our king, Baldwin, is offering a treaty to the emperor based upon marriage of his son to a close relative of the emperor. The emperor is married to Marie of Antioch. They had a son in 1169 named Alexios, after his Grandfather. King Baldwin would like to propose a marriage of alliance between the young prince and one of Duke Raymond of Tripoli's daughters."

"How would that be a good alliance, Sir Guy?" Talon asked, although he thought he already knew.

"This would help to bind the principalities of the Holy Land to Byzantium and that would be a good alliance, as then Manuel could concentrate his efforts upon keeping William of Sicily and the Venetians at bay. So although they are only children it would be a profitable alliance for both the empire and our kingdom," explained Sir Guy.

"So this is why we are here without fanfare and trumpets," Talon said with a grin.

"I like to be able to negotiate in secret and have certain things agreed before any announcement. It is known that the emperor is somewhat capricious, so our negotiations are better kept secret until there is something hammered out in writing for the Bishops to announce."

"Then what are these two monks doing here, Sir?"

"It was decided that the gifts we would present to the emperor would be illuminated volumes from the church of the Holy Sepulcher. These two Brothers would do the presenting, as they are holy books. Jonathan is a spy for the Bishop who knows about the mission. He is supposed to speak Greek and was therefore to be of use to me. His companion Martin is more of a servant. This is why I wanted you to learn as much Greek as possible before we arrived. I do not entirely trust Jonathan."

"So...then we do not talk about this in front of the two monks," Talon stated.

Sir Guy nodded in silence. "Jonathan will be present for the negotiations in the first instance, as will you three, but you are all the escort I wanted and the Grand Master agreed."

"Why is Jonathan so distrustful of these people, Sir Guy? Martin does not seem to be so against them."

Sir Guy turned to Talon and said, "You have been in this part of the world since your birth. You should know that there are three rules that govern any relationship with your neighbors out here. Only three."

Talon sat up. "Three, Sir Guy?"

Sir Guy nodded. "They are pragmatism, coin and trust. Trust is the most fragile and most easily broken, but these Greeks understand all three just as well as the Persians, the Turks and the Arabs. We Franks, whom they call the Latins, do not."

He got up to leave. "Now I shall take a nap. We might have a busy day tomorrow. My old friends Alexios Bryennios, who is still the prefect of Constantinople, and his companion John Komateros will be wanting to meet with me, very soon I suspect."

"Who are they, Sir?"

"They are the men who came to Jerusalem to negotiate for the Queen Marie. We met then and I grew to like both," Sir Guy said over his shoulder.

Claude, who had remained silent for most of the discussion, got up and said, "I shall leave you two worthies to talk about these things. I too need some sleep after that meal. It is getting hot and I need to rest my old bones. God Protect."

"God protect," they answered in unison. Max threw a crust of bread after him. Claude grinned and waved as he left the garden.

Talon took a sip of water and regarded Max. "Did you know any of this before, Max?"

Max looked injured. "No, Talon I did not. Remember, I arrived with you from Egypt and it was not until Sir Guy called us in that I knew we were even coming here."

"Well, it seems that we must support Sir Guy in all ways, as it is doubtful that the bishop's spy, as he calls Brother Jonathan, will aid us in any way. The more I listen to Sir Guy the more I want to learn from him."

"I would even go so far as to say that it is the bishop that Sir Guy does not trust, Talon," Max said in a low tone after first glancing at the entrance to the garden. They were both facing the ingress, having seated themselves instinctively in the best place to observe quickly any untoward activity.

"Why is that?"

"The bishop like all of his kind is a political animal, and the Templars sometimes diverge from his goals. I remember it being like this when I was in Palestine before. Your uncle Phillip, may God be kind to his soul, used to tell me that Sir Guy was often frustrated by those of the Church who disliked the Templars."

"Could the bishop profit from the failure of this mission? Is that what you are telling me, Max?"

"I do not know in all honesty, Talon. But I think it would pay us to be on our guard."

What course of life should wretched mortals take?
In courts hard questions large contention make.
Care dwells in houses, labor in the field,
Tumultuous seas affrighting dangers yield.
In foreign lands thou never canst be blessed;
If rich, thou art in fear; if poor, distressed.

Posidippus

Chapter 4

Visitors

A good week after the Templars arrived, another group of people landed on the other side of the peninsula. To the north side of the city a ship eased into the harbor of Neorion. The master of the ship was Byzantine, but his passengers were from the Sultanate of Rum. The ship carried thirty of the Sultan's men and their horses. Yiğit, leader of the Turks, stood at the bows of the ship as it came into the harbor, contemplating the huge city that dominated the slopes above him. His son Burak walked along the narrow deck to stand beside his father.

"How is it that we do not have cities like this in our lands, father?" he asked.

His father turned to his son, irritated by the awe in his voice.

"Because we have no need of them. Is Konya now too small for you? There are too many people here and they are Christian and therefore unbelievers. You should remember why we have come."

His son looked at him and said, "To gain time for the Sultan?"

"Precisely, to gain time to strengthen our hold on the Rum in the south. That is why we are here."

"How will we accomplish that, father?"

"That you will know in good time. We are about to land, so go and see to the horses. I want them unloaded by this evening. We have yet to be met at the gates and I do not want to be late."

Their horses were unloaded by the Byzantine sailors, who used the booms attached to the masts to lift the horses over the side where they were lowered into the water and made to swim to the shore. Later, when all were safely disembarked, the master of the ship received pieces of gold from Yiğit, then took his boat away from the shoreline and anchored out in the small bay.

The Turks looked up at the massive fortifications and wondered at this empire that appeared to be so powerful. At the gate of Neorion two sentries watched the contingent of nearly twenty riders unloading from the ship.

"Go and fetch the Captain," one of them told the other. "We have visitors from the Turkish lands."

The captain hurried up onto the battlements and peered down at the Turks from the gate tower.

"We have been expecting them, but make them wait. Their escort has not yet come to meet them and I am damned if I will let that group of barbarians in until I know they are being taken in hand."

The Turks stopped their horses at the closed gates and stared up at the impassive soldiers on the walls, calling out that they needed entrance.

"We have come with letters from the Sultan of Rum, His Majesty Sultan Kilij Arslan. We come in peace and ask for entrance," Yiğit announced, and ordered his translator to inform the men on the walls. There was a shouted exchange and then their interpreter turned to him.

"The captain says you will wait until an escort can be provided. They are not here yet."

The Turks were not happy but Yiğit told them to be patient. "They cannot very well let us all in without an escort, as we might overpower them and take their precious city," he joked. There was laughter from his men.

They waited for four hours, during which time the Turks dismounted and made fires upon which they brewed tea. Finally a shout from above warned them that something was happening.

The gates creaked open and the Turks, who had hurriedly remounted, were faced with a unit of heavily armed cavalry who glowered at them. The stares were hostile so Yiğit warned his men to be careful and not to do anything stupid like pull out a sword or even a knife. A man in a fine uniform and gleaming plate armor rode forward with another next to him.

The contrast between the two groups of riders was stark. The Turkish men were mounted upon small horses, shaggy and unkempt. Their stirrups were short, which gave them better control in a fight, and they all carried bows in sheaths under their thighs or hanging off their belts, and quivers over their shoulders. Almost to a man the Turks had long black braided hair and sported long mustaches, but were rough shaven otherwise.

With the exception of Yiğit they were all clothed in rough woolen tunics, which came down to their knees over heavy cloth pantaloons. Despite the heat of summer many carried a rolled up pelt cloak or jacket tied to the cantles of their saddles. Each wore a fur hat of some type that was suited to the cold winters of the high plateaus around Konya and further east. Each man carried a small shield or buckler strapped to his left arm or hung off the pommel, and each carried a lance. One significant feature were the clumps of hair hanging off some of the lances and more grizzled warrior's belts. These were the scalps of their enemies.

Yiğit in contrast to his men wore a tunic of rough worked silk and a cloak that had been taken off a dead enemy some time back. His boots, as those of the others, were made of scuffed horsehide and were well worn. Over his knees were crude metal disks attached with straps. Their swords were of poor steel but it would have been a foolish man who had any doubt that they could use them well.

In contrast, the Byzantine cavalry were dressed in white cotton tunics with embroidered hems that came down to their thighs, under which they wore tight-fitting trousers made of heavy leather with metal plates sewn onto the upper thighs. Over their tunics they wore hauberks composed of many small metal plates sewn onto thick cotton material. Each plate gleamed and chinked as they rode. Their forearms were bare but they carried shields that were far larger than those of the Turks. They too carried long slim lances with shining points, and long, slightly curved swords that were deadly when used by a skilled horseman. Each man had a metal helmet of bronze that had been polished to a high shine, on top of which was set a crest that identified his unit. Their legs were protected by greaves on their shins. Their horses were a good hand higher than those of the Turks and groomed to a shine.

The officer approached and said something that Yiğit's man translated. "You are to come with us. Do you have papers proving you are delegates from the sultan?"

Yiğit, who pretended he could not speak Greek at all, waited until the words had been translated then reached into his tunic and brought out an elaborately sealed document that he passed along to the interpreter, who in turn handed it over to the officer, who in turn passed it to another man behind him.

"You will be taken to accommodations which will be provided. You are to stay there and not to leave without permission. Anyone who tries to leave will be arrested by our soldiers and put in jail. Do you understand?"

"Tell him we understand." Yiğit said, after his man had translated. Yiğit felt angry at the tone and contempt displayed by the officer but held his tongue.

The officer continued, echoed by the translator. "You will also disarm your men and leave the weapons outside the city walls. You have no need for them here."

Yiğit looked hard at the officer. He had not expected this. He was affronted but there was nothing he could do if he wanted to achieve his objective, so he gave a terse nod and told his men to comply.

They protested but followed his orders, and tossed their swords and spears into a pile with a clatter. Soon there was a heap of weapons on the ground outside of the wooden gate. The officer indicated the bows and quivers that were still hanging off the saddles of the Turks.

"They need to disarm. Everything."

"They are my bodyguard," Yiğit tried to explain.

"Then they will not enter this city. The choice is up to you."

The men obeyed the muttered command from Yiğit, scowling and casting ugly looks at the Byzantine soldiers, but they tossed their bows onto the pile.

Yiğit shouted to some of the men whom he had ordered to stay by the seashore to come and collect their weapons. Several hurried over to do his bidding.

"This area is known as the Venetian quarter," the officer told him through the interpreter. You will be taken care of here. The Venetians have no need for it at present." One of his men snickered.

"How long must I wait before I can speak to your king?" Yiğit asked.

"You will be told when you can have an audience with His Holiness the Emperor. In the meantime, do not leave this area or you will be hunted down and placed in prison."

Yiğit held his peace. He was here for a good reason and would not provoke the man who clearly viewed him and his entourage with disdain. He felt naked without his sword and other weapons, but his dagger was still hidden under his coat, as were those of his men.

They were taken through the gate and then turned to the west along a stone paved street. As they rode the cavalry surrounded them and kept close by, as though the Turks at any moment might make a break for it and disappear into the dark streets of the city. They rode in wary silence with the officer alongside Yiğit and the interpreter until they came to a wooden palisade, where they stopped.

"You will stay here," the officer said.

They were shown to their quarters and left to await the pleasure of the emperor.

*****

That same evening another ship slipped into the Prosphorion harbor, which was adjacent to the Neorion. This ship was a galley, similar to the dromons that were a large part of the Byzantine navy, but this one had been converted to a merchantman. The master was a Genoese, named Caravello Levaggi. He was a very experienced ship master who plied the eastern Mediterranean sea boards from Egypt to Genoa and even as far west as Andalusia.

This time he was here with a cargo of iron and salt. He hoped to meet with the agent and unload his cargo within a few days. It was late in the day so he anchored in the harbor near other ships. He would be called to the quayside in the morning and met by the *Logothetes tou Genicon,* who would ask him questions about his cargo and charge the reduced fee of seventeen solidi, a favor now given to the Genoese instead of the Venetians.

He was rowed ashore by his two most trusted men, Christophas and Davide. Davide, a big hulk of a man and Caravello's longtime bodyguard, accompanied him as he stepped ashore. They made their way through the gates and into the city with the confidence of long familiarity with the surroundings. They headed towards the center of what was known as the Genoese quarter. It was early evening and the Genoese were relaxing around their inns and eating places. They did not mix much with the Greeks of the city of Constantinople; indeed they were discouraged from doing so by the authorities. They had their area and were expected to remain there, especially after curfew.

Caravello knew this, as he had been to Constantinople many times before. However, he also knew how to move around the city without attracting attention despite the fact that he was a solid looking man and a Latin, as his people were called by the Greeks. His rolling gait gave him away as a sailor, but then the city was full of sailors. His dress was similar to that worn by the locals: a tunic of rough cotton cloth with an expensive hem. He wore a short sword on his belt, a felt cap on his head, and a greasy jerkin that had known better days.

He stayed in the Genoese quarter long enough to take the measure of the crowd and to share a simple meal with Davide. The people around him on the street and in the inns and alehouses seemed relaxed and a good deal less tense than the last time he had come to the city. It was while he was finishing his meal of roasted eels and city issue bread washed down with rough wine that he felt a touch on his arm. He turned sharply to find a man standing near by. The fellow was dressed in a long tunic with an over cloak, the pointed hood of which was pulled over his head so that his face was indistinguishable in the dark.

"We have been waiting for you," the man said quietly. "You were expected a week ago."

"I was delayed by storms off Crete. We had to take shelter for four days," Caravello responded.

"You are wanted at the villa. You must be there two nights from now," the man almost whispered. "Come when you are sent for."

Caravello nodded and turned away to take a swig of his wine. When he looked back the man had disappeared.

"Did you see that? Where did he go?" he asked Davide.

Davide shook his head. "I saw him come but I did not not see him leave. He was like a ghost."

"This city is full of ghosts and odd people. Never could trust a one of them. Look what they did to the Venetians," Caravello muttered uneasily.

*****

The messenger came again on the third evening, when Caravello and his two companions were seated on board his ship waiting for just this. As he boarded, his hood fell back, revealing angular, pock-marked features. He told Caravello he was expected at the villa that night. Having accomplished his mission, the man dropped back into the small skiff and was rowed back to shore, where he disappeared into the throng on the wharf.

Caravello considered his situation, for just walking through the city after sunset was in itself dangerous for a Latin. A citywide curfew had been imposed on all the Latin people, including the Genoese, because of their rowdy behavior in the past, to ensure that they did not get up to any mischief during the hours of darkness. They were obliged to stay in their quarter and not wander about. Caravello was well aware of the Greeks' dislike for the Latins, but he now had a pressing errand and it was long past due.

As the sun set in a blaze of glory behind the low hills of the city and darkness flowed over the seaways and plunged the hills above the harbor into darkness, Caravello ordered his men to row him ashore. Once there he told Christophas to wait for his return. Accompanied only by Davide, he walked unobtrusively through the gates of the harbor, turned south up the steep slopes of the hillside, then slipped out of the compound. They made their way up the North slope of the hill following the stone road that lead past the palace of Botaneiatis amid its extensive gardens.

Their destination was a villa that was situated on the Second Hill near the top, not very far from the Severin Wall, which was the second-most inner city wall. The city had outgrown several walls in its time. As the broken battlements loomed on his right Caravello turned left to take a path along the side of the hill. He was now well into the older part of the city, a far more dangerous place for him to be. If the night patrol found him here without a good reason, they would put him in jail and it would be weeks before he could get out. Indeed, at one time a patrol did tramp by, their hobnailed sandals scraping on the stone surface, while the two sailors hid in the deep shadows of a bridge archway. They waited several minutes before abandoning the cover of the darkness and continuing on their way.

Caravello, followed by Davide, walked with the confidence of having been here many times, so it was without hesitation that he stopped outside a small doorway set into a substantial wall. He tapped gently on the door and waited. A dog barked in the street further down, but other than the incessant chirp of crickets and the croaking of frogs the area was quiet. Further along he could hear the muted sound of a city that never seemed to sleep.

He tensed as they heard footsteps coming towards the door on the other side of the wall. There were several people coming towards them.

"Who is there?" a voice demanded.

"Visitors from Cyprus," Caravello whispered. It was a code that identified him.

A bolt scraped and the door creaked open on leather hinges. A tall, thin figure that Caravello knew to be one of the household eunuchs greeted him. Next to the eunuch was a servant bearing a torch, but there was also a hooded figure behind the slave who seemed poised for any trouble.

"Hello, Markos, you know me; and this is my bodyguard. Tell that assassin to keep his distance. I am here to see your master."

The thin man nodded and led the way in silence along the garden path towards the main building. The villa was as large as a small palace. A low second story marked it as the residence of someone of very substantial means.

They were shown the way through an entrance into a long passageway to the rear of the house that was quiet at this late hour. Only the night servants and the sentries would be about.

There was a glow of lamps burning in a room at the end of a long cool passage lined with stone columns and recesses that held busts and plants. The ceiling was so high he could not make out the details of the intricate workmanship in the dark. Their footsteps clicked on the polished marble tiles, which gleamed with the reflection of the torch carried by the silent servant who led the way. Caravello could see two armed soldiers with shields and spears on either side of the doorway they were approaching. He had a distinctly uncomfortable feeling about the hooded man who walked soundlessly behind him.

The servant stopped at the entrance to the room and, with a nod to the sentries, led the way in. Caravello signaled to Davide to remain at the entrance and then walked into the room.

"The Captain Levaggi, Sirs."

The murmur of conversation halted at their arrival. There were two others in the large spacious area in front of him. One of them stood up to greet him. The other continued to recline on a couch near to some low tables laden with the remains of a light dinner.

Markos bowed himself out of the room but the hooded man remained just inside the door. As he left Markos shut the main door so that the occupants would have complete privacy.

Senator Spartenos stood up and greeted Caravello with his arms wide, although he did not embrace him.

"Ah, Caravello, finally you have arrived! It has been a long time. I trust you had a good voyage?"

"Nothing but the usual hazards of wind and weather to contend with, Senator," Caravello said as he accepted a silver goblet of wine. He sipped it appreciatively as he was shown to a seat near to the other man in the room.

He was well used to the decor of wealthy houses in the great city of Constantinople and he had been here before, but this room was sumptuous and always impressed him. The polished tiles and pillars reflected the light from a dozen oil lamps burning with almost no smoke, which told of very clean and expensive oil. The floor to ceiling shutters were open to allow a light breeze from the sea to cool the room, making the diaphanous curtains billow. He glanced around in awe at the beautiful stone statuettes, gold and silver wares, and frescoes illustrated in gold leaf and colored tiles. Just the contents of this room would buy him another ship, he thought wistfully.

He forced himself to pay attention as the senator spoke.

"We can discuss your voyage, and perhaps then we can talk about the main purpose of your visit. I apologize for the time it took before I could call the meeting, but these things have to be done with care."

Caravello nodded. He had not minded waiting; he had made several decent deals while kicking his heels in the Genoese quarter. He would have a full cargo no matter how it went.

"This man takes an interest in what we are about tonight." The senator indicated the man who was now sitting up, watching Caravello with large grey eyes from under thin manicured eyebrows. Caravello noted that the senator had not given the man's name. He was dressed in a long colorful tunic that had intricate patterns and colors sewn into the fabric. It could only have been made of silk, Caravello decided. The man was obviously very rich but not particularly strong looking, although his eyes were sharp and regarded him with interest—but also distrust. Caravello wondered if he were a eunuch. Not a few had climbed the social ladders to arrive near the top in this empire.

"You were able to trade with the islands and bring in my cargo, I hear," the senator said. "I am pleased, as that will make us all better off."

"I sailed to Crete and managed to convince the authorities that I was a licensed trader for the Venetians. I only had to show them one of the forged documents. They fell for it easily." Caravello barked a laugh. "They are greedy people who want their cut of everything, and so long as they get it they do not really care where you come from. The silk sold so fast that I wish I had doubled the load or brought another ship with me. The icons do well too, though, alas, they are in short supply now, as you know. The cargo I brought back is of iron, salt, and dyes, and of course the coin we gained in the process."

There were dry smiles from the other two. "The important thing is that you managed to trade despite this suffocating ban imposed by the...administration. I shall send my man down to collect my coin tomorrow."

"Then he should bring someone to help him, Senator, with a guard." Caravello grinned, "As long as the Emperor keeps all the Venetians in jail I can make a big profit. In one fell swoop he took away all our competition. I will never understand why he did it, but I am not complaining." Caravello took another swig of wine.

"You still have to be very careful not to advertise for whom you are doing business in this city, or we will find ourselves explaining things in front of the *Logothetes tou Praitoriou.*

"Remind me who they are?" Caravello asked, puzzled.

"The authorities of the law. More powerful than the customs people you know. It is forbidden to trade at any Venetian controlled country at present, and as you were doing so on my behalf they would throw you in jail to join your friends."

"Ah...yes, you did say so before. But they are no friends of mine, I assure you." The captain sipped his wine and reached for a sweet cake.

"Not all the Venetians are in jail, but we will leave that for another time," the senator said with a glance at the other man. He went on. "You must listen very carefully now."

Caravello sat up.

"I need you to go to Cyprus and then come back via Rhodes, where I will have another task for you.

"I am at your service, Senator." Caravello smirked.

Spartenos gave him a long, hard look. "Very well. It is a simple task, but a very important one that I want you to carry out. You have done me many favors, and I trust you. But you must swear upon all that is holy that you will divulge nothing of this to anyone, anyone at all."

He stopped, staring hard at Caravello, almost as though he was reconsidering making his request.

"What is it you want done?" Caravello asked after a long pause.

The other man in the room said, "You have to tell him something, Senator. Warn him and then tell him."

"Understand, what I am about to tell you this evening is dangerous for all of us. if a single word gets out we will all be tortured to death. You included."

Caravello was not a coward but this jolted him. At the same time, he smelled profit. "Go on, you know I am to be trusted."

The senator nodded. "But...just in case you forget, even for a moment, remember this. In this room is a man who is a master assassin, and he will find you, no matter where you hide, and you will not be able to sleep because he will be there when you least expect it."

He pointed to the hooded man standing silently by the door. "Constantinople has many of these people and I own several of them. You won't forget, will you?" he asked gently as he stared into the captain's eyes.

Caravello took a swig of wine and nodded. "I truly swear by all the saints and the Holy Mother of God."

The senator reached forward and clapped him on the shoulder. "Good, then we understand one another. There is an Arab fleet in the vicinity of Rhodes, which you will guide to a certain destination. In Rhodes there are two Byzantine warships that are on duty. You are to follow them when they leave the island to patrol the seas nearby. They do this very regularly. When it is close to darkness you will signal the Arab fleet as to the whereabouts of the patrol ships. That is all you will have to do. Do you understand what I am telling you?"

"Yes, you want me to tell the fleet where the Byzantine ships are going to be on a certain night. Why, what are the Arabs up to? Do they intend to strike at the island?" Caravello asked.

"That is not your concern. Your task is very simple. No danger to you whatsoever. You will be given instructions as to how to contact the fleet later. Now you must go about your business as though nothing is happening.

Caravello's mouth was dry as he contemplated the request. "This is treason...although you say there isn't is much danger to me!" he whispered. He licked his lips and took another long swig of his wine. He would have preferred something even stronger at this moment. He knew he was on dangerous ground, but he also wanted something so badly that he risk a great deal to bargain for it.

"If I agree to...to this mad scheme, what is in it for me?" he demanded. "Gold will not suffice this time." he added.

"It is part of a far greater purpose than just wealth for you or me! It will free us of the yoke of the emperor and his capricious actions which are destroying our empire." The senator almost hissed that last part."

"It is not my empire...I merely trade with it." Caravello said as calmly as he could.

What do you want? Land? More ships?" Spartenos demanded.

"No Senator, I have those aplenty," he lied. "I want...I want one of those machines, one of those liquid fire machines," Caravello blurted out. He almost wanted to take his words back when he saw the icy expressions on the faces of the senator and his companion.

There was complete silence in the room for some long moments.

"Do you have any idea what you are asking for?" Senator Spartenos finally asked with a distinct edge to his tone.

Caravello gulped. "Yes...but you are asking me to put my head on the block for you. At least reward me properly. I shall not do it for less."

"I could make you rich with lands here in Byzantium." Spartenos offered.

"With the Greek Fire I can make myself rich...wherever I choose to be!" Caravello retorted.

The Senator nodded his comprehension, "Ah...I see." His gaze drifted to the figure by the door.

The tension in the room was palpable and Caravello glanced nervously towards the dark, hooded figure near the door, half expecting it to come for him he was so nervous. His armpits began to sweat.

Finally, after a long look at the other man seated nearby, who gave an almost imperceptible shrug, the Senator nodded, staring at Caravello, a speculative look in his eyes. "Very well...I will see if it can be arranged. But know this, once you have the fire apparatus on board you will be complicit in this scheme and there is no turning back."

"D'you think I am mad? By God and all the saints! You are granting me power on the seas that no one has outside the Byzantine navy. Of course I will not say anything. I swear it."

You had better be sure of yourself, Caravello, because I meant what I said earlier."

"I told you, I swore an oath, and I shall repeat it if you like," he muttered with another glance at the ominous figure by the door. He felt a little cold; the atmosphere in the room had changed.

A vision flashed before Caravello's mind. He was watching a ship burn to the water. It was his ship that had caused it and the burning vessel was Venetian and all her crew were dying, burning as though roasting in Hell. He detested those people.

Caravello licked his suddenly dry lips. "By God, I would have one of the most powerful ships in Christendom. Outside of the Byzantine navy, that is," he whispered, and took a long draught of his wine. His pulse was pounding.

"Then it will be arranged. Stay on your ship and wait. Before long you will receive a signal, which will tell you where your ship should be placed so that we can load it."

"I will need people to work the machine. No one outside the Greeks knows how to operate it."

"That will be taken care of when the time comes. I want you to remain in harbor for the moment, but move the ship to the Neorion harbor within a day or so. I will obtain the necessary papers to allow this."

"May I ask why I should move out of Prosphorion?" Caravello asked.

"Prosphorion has a wall right across the entire harbor with steel gates, whereas you would be anchored in the bay of Neorion and able to take on cargo and eave without notice when the time comes. Do not forget you have goods to deliver to Cyprus before you sail back to Rhodes. We will make good money out of it and it will be tax free, I promise you. Do not forget to come back, will you? You work for me." His smile was cold.

Caravello glanced at the assassin and shuddered.

They spent the next hour discussing locations and timing, as well as how messages would be relayed back and forth. The Senator never did get around to telling him about the others who were involved.

Dawn was only an hour away when Caravello left the villa. He slipped out of the same door he had entered, with Davide on his heels. The captain gave one backward glance to the entry as though he expected the man in the hood to be there, but there was no one. He turned his attention to making his way back to the Genoese quarter without being caught. It was long past the time when the patrols bothered to tramp around the streets of Constantinople, but they took great care in any case. Despite his elation he was cautious. It would not do to be careless in this city.

*****

After Caravello had gone, the two men continued to discuss their plans.

"Do you really think you can obtain the liquid fire and get it onto his ship?" the seated man asked. His tone was skeptical.

"Constantinople is at the center of the empire and as such anything, anything at all, can be purchased at the right price, my friend. You know that. Yes, I am sure we can find what we are looking for."

"Our patron is impatient to move as soon as possible, Senator."

"All in good time, my friend. Listen, Basileios, you must persuade him to be patient. There are many dangers and risks involved, and I for one do not wish to move without a sound base. The emperor might have many enemies, but he also has friends in the Army and the Navy, although I cannot understand why any of the generals would want to stay with him. A number of them are firmly on our side. They are sick of the incessant taxes and rapacious officials who are bleeding this empire and the nobility white, while the emperor spends lavishly on his feasts and visitors. Manuel is no Alexios, nor even in the same league as his father John Komnenos, whom I admired. He panders to the Latins one moment and then strikes at them the next. Who next, the nobility of the empire?"

"When are you going to meet with the Arabs? What our patron is offering them is horribly dangerous for us if it goes wrong, you do realize that do not you?" Basileios asked.

"I do know, but how else can we neutralize our own navy when the time comes? I cannot afford to allow anyone to stand in our way when everything hangs on securing the harbors and hence the city. We need to secure the naval base on Galata."

"Why can't we use some mercenaries to do the work instead of the Arabs? I worry that they will betray us at the last moment and take the fire anyway."

"Because mercenaries are unreliable people and you can never pay them enough gold to buy their loyalty. They will run at the first sign of resistance, whereas the Arabs will stay with the plan. Besides, they are the only ones that will make for a credible threat when the time comes. It has to be seen as a real threat whereas a few mercenaries in dhows will not. I have met with Al Fakhouri and we are in accord. He is a pirate by nature and not interested in doing more than I have asked. His main condition was that we provide him with fire devices. With the fire in his possession his power at sea will become virtually unassailable...for a while. Then we will take it all back from him. He will stay on the plan and our navy will be neutralized long enough for us to make our move within the city."

"I heard a rumor that the emperor might be preparing for a campaign on the eastern mainland against Arslan. Have you heard anything? That might be an opportunity to move then."

"I too have heard the rumor but I do not think he will make a move for some time as yet. We cannot make our own move until the autumn in any case," the Senator said.

He continued, "We have prepared treaties with Nur Ed Din's son As-Salih Ismail al-Malik, who will assist us against the Turks. They like the idea of sending Arslan packing. He has accumulated far too much power in Rum and now threatens Syria. Arslan is ambitious, but the Sultan of Egypt, a man they call Salah Ed Din, is also very ambitious and he does not want the Turks to own Syria, he would prefer to have it for himself. We will provide men and arms to assist him, and then he will help us to drive out Arslan and regain the center of our empire."

"And that, of course, is the goal. On that we agree fully. I am confident that the prince will bring back the glory of our empire. Manuel and his sycophants wallow in ceremony and beggar our empire." Basileios said.

"Do you know what the Templars are doing in this town?" Senator Spartenos asked. The question was asked abruptly and made Basileios blink.

Basileios' brow wrinkled in puzzlement. "I think it is about a marriage proposal. Why, do you know something more?"

"No but I suspect it *is* more than that. They arrived without any ceremony and suddenly they are here preparing to have an audience with the emperor. But...I know of someone who might be able to find out."

*****

Four nights later Caravello and his crew waited on their ship in the darkness. It was late and the harbor was quiet. Long after the city had gone to sleep there came a low call from the seaward side of the harbor of Neorion.

Davide opened a small lantern and displayed a light that would not be seen from shore. There was no moon but the men on deck could just make out the dark shapes of two boats heavily laden approaching their ship.

Before long, one of the boats bumped gently against the side of his ship and a familiar figure climbed aboard. Even in the darkness Caravello could make out the lithe form of the messenger Psellos. Their greeting was brief.

"I have some cargo for you and some people," Psellos rasped. "Keep an eye on the prisoners, get them below as quickly as possible."

Caravello nodded and nudged Christophas. "Get them on board and then we deal with the cargo," he ordered.

It all went quietly for a time as the six men huddled in the boat below were brought up onto the deck of the ship one at a time. They looked cowed and Caravello could smell their fear. The fifth prisoner, his hands roped in front of him, was assisted aboard by rough hands. He spoke to his companions, beginning to raise his voice, but as quick as a snake Christophas smashed his fist into the side of the man's head. There was an ugly crushing sound and the man fell as though pole-axed. He did not move again although Davide nudged him with his foot.

'You fool!" Psellos hissed. You have killed one of the operators, you dog's turd! Wait till the Se-" he checked himself abruptly, "...our master hears about this."

"Get the rest below and hurry up about it!" Caravello snarled at his men. "No more damage to them, just get them below and make sure they are secured properly."

"What do we do with this one?" Christophas asked, his tone contrite.

Caravello shook his head.Why he employed the thick-skulled man he did not know. He served well enough as a bodyguard but was useless otherwise.

"He looks like he is dead, there is blood on the deck. Make sure you don't make a noise when you toss him overboard." He had to control his anger and the urge to strike Christophas. Psellos looked as though he was about to do so.

But just at that moment the last of the prisoners to come aboard saw his companion lying on the deck. He took a pace back, shouted something, then made a break for the side. He jumped far enough out from the ship's side to miss the boat below and fell with a noisy splash into the water and disappeared below the surface.

For one stunned minute the men on deck stared at the place where he had been, then they rushed to the side to look for him. Psellos with an angry curse threw off his cloak and leapt out after the prisoner. He plunged into the water near to where the Greek had disappeared then struggled to the surface looking for his quarry.

The men on deck had seen the fugitive splashing about twenty yards away and with low calls indicated where the man was going. It was not hard for Psellos to find him in the dark. The man's hands were still bound and he was floundering desperately towards the distant shore and the dim lights of the city. He called out feebly but water choked his words off. He must have known that someone would come after him but did not know how quickly.

Psellos paddled hard to catch up with the fleeing man and seized him around the neck, choking off any cry, and then the knife was shoved in from behind. The body convulsed for a few long seconds, then went limp. Psellos let it drift down into the water below. There were many murders in this city for many different reasons, so one more stabbing would not elicit any real interest when the body resurfaced bloated and half eaten by the fish and crabs.

Psellos paddled his way back to the boats and was helped back onto the deck where he stood dripping water, catching his breath.

"That was well done, and quickly too!" Caravello remarked.

"Well now you have four to work with," Psellos muttered drily. "Make sure that you get what you want from them, as there will be no more. The master will not be pleased to hear of the losses and you can be sure there will be no replacements.

Caravello wanted to ask where the men had come from in the first place, but he knew that now was not a good time to ask.

Psellos took charge again and directed the other boat alongside. There was a distinct smell to this boat and the cargo that came aboard was heavy, carefully packed in sacking, and it gave off an unholy stink.

It was nearly dawn before the last of the cargo was loaded and the boats disappeared.

William Blake

Chapter 5

The Invitation

Talon made his way out of the harbor of St Julian onto the avenue of Ta Amantio as he followed Joseph, Alexios' servant, who had come to collect him and bring him to the villa of the family Kalothesos. He noticed the great walls of the Hippodrome off to the right as he climbed the hill towards the Mese, which was the longest and widest of the main roads running in roughly east-west through the city.

Joseph first lead him towards the Forum of Constantine, one of the great circles that coincided with the Mese; then they took a left turn along the huge avenue, and soon thereafter climbed the second hill to where Alexios's family lived. Alexios had told him that their villa overlooked the Golden Horn and the Latin quarters facing north.

When he had climbed the steep incline to the Forum of Constantine, Talon had paused and turned to look back. Despite all the pedestrian traffic and beasts of burden that used the street, he was able to make out the ships in clear detail that were anchored in the small port. He could even make out his ship tied up alongside the quay and the tiny figures working nearby, and the guards walking along the sea walls that effectively enclosed the entire harbor.

He gazed out at the Sea of Marmara where the waves were white capped and the sea dark blue in sharp contrast to the azure of the sky above. The sun was beginning to set on the horizon, sending up rays of golden light to paint the few clouds in the sky deep rose as though they were on fire. Talon noticed that for some reason the waters of the Marmara always tended to be agitated. Perhaps it was the winds that came off the northern mountains. He turned back again to follow Joseph who was patiently waiting for him to continue.

They had to pause while crossing, as there was a disturbance along the main thoroughfare. Talon heard cheers and shouts of excitement and from the east of the avenue came a chariot drawn by four horses. The pedestrians, carts and individual horsemen who were using the avenue moved over to the side and waited while a magnificent sight came into view. A line of four horses abreast drawing a chariot swept past them amid cheers and waved hats. Talon stood with the servant and watched it passing.

"What is it and where is it going?" He asked.

"The charioteer is going to the great palace to receive an honor from the emperor himself for his courage and skill at racing," Joseph told him.

Talon glanced up and down the Mese looking for more of the same, but the crowds had resumed their business and everything had gone back to normal. He realized that the Mese resembled a backbone of the city, with lesser streets and avenues flowing off its huge avenue like ribs on a fish. It followed the ridge of the hills known as the First, Second, and Third Hills; from the top of any one of these mounts the view south was spectacular. After they had climbed the Second Hill and had pushed their way through the forum area with its market stalls and crowds of pedestrians, men, women, and children of every rank and class, their route took them downhill and north towards the Tower of Eirene. Talon was impressed by the number of women he saw on the streets of this city, many accompanied by children but without appearing to need guards or escorts.

He glanced to his left and perceived another hill, upon which stood yet another magnificent structure, but this one looked somehow deserted in this evening light. He marveled at how the setting sun colored the stone of this strange palace pink and ochre. The men who built it were masters of stonework, he thought, as he observed its pillars and archways and even what appeared to be grottos built in among the conventional stonework.

As they descended the incline Talon could now observe the other side of the city that overlooked the waters of the Golden Horn, with the fortified town of Sycia on the other side; and he could just make out the tower of Galata at its northernmost area and a cluster of naval ships. He stared across the wide body of water known as the Bosporus to the distant mass of the mainland belonging to the eastern Byzantine Empire. Even at this late hour the sea was dotted with the sails of many crafts which plied up and down a strip of water that to Talon's astonished eyes made even the Nile around Cairo seem provincial.

Joseph, who was walking just ahead of him, indicated a building to the right, and now he could see the roof of a villa and extensive grounds. The road was very quiet and lined with old trees that reminded him of Isfahan. There were a few pedestrians about on this early evening. The trees here were large, mature cypresses and plane trees interspersed with the odd pine. The whole effect was cooling, especially at this time of year.

All the villas in this area had high walls surrounding them and Talon did not doubt that behind these were guards for every house. Constantinople might be the greatest metropolis in the world, but he was becoming aware from conversations with Alexios and Sir Guy that it was not always at peace with itself, and the wise owner of property protected his own.

Joseph came to a halt in front of some large wooden doors and shouted his name, then banged on the door. A dog barked a deep resonant bark, then they heard a movement behind the doors and a challenge. Joseph, with an apologetic look at Talon, shouted back that he was bringing a visitor to the family on invitation and wanted entrance immediately.

Bolts were drawn, the doors creaked open, and they were confronted by two guards. Talon noted that they were dressed in an assortment of crude protection made of leather and armor plate, and he was surprised that the family Kalothesos did not provide their guards with better gear. From Alexios' behavior on board, he had gathered that the aristocratic family was wealthy. The men looked tough, however, and regarded Talon with suspicion. One of them held on a chain choker a huge dog that had its mouth open, displaying large teeth. It regarded Talon balefully, as though he might be worth attacking. Talon watched the animal warily.

Joseph brushed past the guards without so much as a word of greeting and led the way along a tree-lined alley that took them to a wide yard surrounded by stables and other buildings. Situated above these buildings, dominating the view, was the main villa. The sharp smell of horses pervaded the yard and Talon glanced at the stables to see some purebred horses being fed and watered for the night. He experienced a sense of nostalgia and wondered if he would have the chance to ride out some time while here. He had grown a little tired of ships and the water. He felt a sudden pang of loss as he remembered his faithful horse Jabbar and how he had died in the shipwreck off the coast of Egypt.

Talon had to concede that it was a beautiful building. It reminded him of the abbey near Albi and was every bit as large, although this was for just one family. The walls of the buildings were all of stone and mortar, and in the case of the villa they were coated with white lime plaster to hide the stonework. This, combined with the heavy wood supporting beams that held up the tiled roof, made for a very pleasing effect. The row upon row of tiles made of red and ochre clay reminded him somehow of the scales of a great red fish, the perfect foil to rain and harsh sunlight. They suited this villa perfectly.

He was led through the wide loggia that ran almost all the way round the building into a cool antechamber. Here he was invited to be seated and his cloak was taken by another servant who disappeared. He held onto his sword when a servant came to take it from him. The servant shrugged and left.

Joseph had disappeared to find Alexios, and while he waited Talon looked around. There was a pleasant scent of beeswax and lavender combined with the smell of oil lamps emanating from the rooms of the house. In between the tall marble pillars the walls were decorated with murals of hunting scenes depicting what he took to be classic Greek forms of women and ancient warriors with huge shields and very long spears. Most of the men were naked, while the women wore diaphanous tunics that flowed around their bodies, revealing much. He found himself staring. One would never see this kind of thing in Acre, let alone in Cairo, he reflected. Two of the murals showed heroes who had died and were being carried on their shields by their women folk to their last resting places. He could hear water splashing from a fountain in an enclosed courtyard that he had glimpsed as he was ushered into the house, and sparrows chirped outside. The combined sound lent a cool and peaceful atmosphere to the surroundings.

It was very quiet after the endless noise and bustle of the harbor where he had spent the last week. He imagined there to be a bath and envied the owners of the villa this luxury. He and his companions, those who actually did bathe, went to the public bath near the inn where they were quartered. He thought about other countries he had visited and compared their lifestyle to the one he witnessed here. The Arabs perhaps came close, and the wealthy people in Isfahan too, but for the most part the wealth in those countries was concentrated in the hands of the upper aristocracy and royalty, whereas in this city it was not so well defined. The house that Alexios lived in was sumptuously appointed and from what Talon knew about him his father was merely a senator, which Talon supposed to be some kind of prince.

He was sitting on a stone bench when he heard the tap of a stick on the polished tiles coming from down the corridor in the direction of the fountain. An elderly man walked into view, accompanied by a eunuch. Talon was now able to recognize eunuchs by of their long limbs and tall frames, and while many Greeks shaved, their distinctively smooth cheeks were a characteristic of these people. This had been pointed out to him by Alexios when they had first arrived.

The old man stopped just inside the door and peered at him. Talon stood up and regarded the man in turn. The newcomer had a slight stoop and was dressed in a loose tunic that looked like linen and had many folds to it. It looked cool and appropriate for the warmth of late summer. He possessed a good amount of white hair and his full beard was graying. His features were lined but strong and his intelligent eyes peered out from under bushy eyebrows.

"What have we here, John?" the old man asked the servant accompanying him, squinting at Talon.

"My name is Talon, Sir. I am here to see Alexios," Talon stated.

At that moment Talon heard the slap of sandals on the tiles and Alexios hurried into the hallway.

"Talon, greetings. Please come this way." He led the way into a large comfortable room off from the anteroom and bade Talon be seated. Then he addressed the old man who had followed them. "Father, this is Talon, whom I was talking about earlier."

"Ah yes, the Frank. A Templar I believe. What is it exactly that you Templars do?" The old man's tone was not friendly.

"The Order of the Templars was formed to protect pilgrims on their journey from the coast to the city of Jerusalem because of the bandits along the way, Sir."

"I hear they are a grubby lot, never bathe. Do you bathe, boy?"

"Talon," interrupted Alexios, "this is my father, Damianus. He is a little off color today. Father, Talon is my guest and I would be grateful if you would be nice to him. This is his first time in Constantinople."

"You said he was a Frank. Of course it is the first time he has been to our city. They do not even have cities in the Latin countries, do they, boy?"

Talon was brought to mind of the statement his friend in Languedoc had told him about Paris and the muddy streets where wolves roamed in winter. He decided to hold his tongue.

"Father, please!"

Damianus stared at Talon with his keen eyes. "My family can trace its ancestry back to the time of Belisarius, young Frank, which for your information was almost six hundred years ago. What do you think of that? And you? Are you just another of those ignorant barbarians without any ancestry worth commenting upon who have come to stir up trouble for our emperor, as if he does not have enough problems to deal with already?"

"Well, Sir, I did not come here to stir up any trouble, and I might just have some ancestry. My family name is Gilles and the Duke Raymond of Edessa was a very distant relative."

"Ah, yes, of course! Isn't he the one that was beaten recently by the Turks and had his head pickled and sent to the Caliph of Baghdad?" the old man said with a smirk.

"Father! That is a grossly distasteful thing to say!" Alexios said. His face was flushed with anger.

"Talon, you must excuse my father. He is getting old and forgets that a visitor should be treated better." He cast a hard look at his father who got up and said, "My son, the Franks, of whom this is one, have been stabbing us in the back in the form of Robert Guiscard of Sicily for a decade now. Norman, Frank, what is the difference? What makes you think that this one is going to be any different from the rest of those pirates? Why in God's name did you bring him here? Lest you forget, this is my house...at least until I die."

Talon stood up, "I am sorry, Alexios. Sir, I should perhaps leave, as it is clear to me that you do not wish me to be here."

The old man glared at him from under his thick grey eyebrows. "I see you speak Greek? Well, that is a start, I suppose. None of the other Franks I have met seem to be able to master another language."

"Father, Talon speaks Persian, Arabic, and our own Greek." Alexios was fuming. "You should follow your own advice and give people the benefit of the doubt before you judge them."

"It seems that you have won my son over, Frank. It also seems that I do not have the right to choose who comes inside my doors any more. I shall leave you now. Goodbye."

He glared at his son and, leaning heavily on his stick, waved to one of the hovering eunuchs to help him out of the room.

After they had gone there was an awkward silence in the room. Talon was still standing. He felt sorry for Alexios, who was clearly upset and deeply embarrassed by the old man's behavior. His normal cool and aloof demeanor was replaced by one of acute embarrassment mingled with anger.

"I am very sorry for that display from my father, Talon." Alexios said. His jaw was clenched.

"I should probably leave, Alexios. I did not want to embarrass you and should not stay further. I also wanted to tell you that Sir Guy had other business and could not come in any case."

"Embarrass whom?" a voice said.

They both turned towards a woman who now stood at the entrance of the chamber.

"Ah, Mother. This is Sir Talon of the Knights Templar who is visiting us on a mission to the emperor. Father has just been inexcusably rude and insulted him beyond redemption. So I fear that he is about to leave."

The tall, slim, middle-aged woman seemed to glide into the room. She was elegantly dressed in a light green robe that was more of a sheath with rich embroidery on its hems which could only have been made of the finest woven cotton or silk, for it shimmered as she moved. Talon caught the scent of rose flowers as she approached.

Her slippers were of finely worked leather and she wore gold bracelets on her wrists that gave off a light jingle as she walked. Her jet-black hair, streaked with gray, was pinned high, enhancing her height. She was a classically beautiful woman, with a long, elegant neck and a slightly long face. Her full, sensuous mouth and large, dark, deep-set eyes and strong nose made for striking features. Her eyebrows were plucked to a thin line and her lips were painted with something that made them red. Talon had not met a woman so well groomed or so elegantly dressed since he had left his Aunt Fariba behind in far away Isfahan.

Intelligent eyes watched Talon as she walked towards them and presented her cheek to her son. He leaned down and kissed her with affection.

"So it was your father who embarrassed this knight, my son?" she asked, not taking her eyes off Talon as though sizing him up.

"He is old and becoming senile," Alexios said, clearly upset, "and Sir Talon is not as the other Franks that we have known. He has travelled to many countries, more than I have, and has much to tell us of those places. I thought he would like to visit us and you might like to hear about his travels."

"My dear, do not be so disrespectful of your father," she admonished him with a smile to take away the sting of the words. Then she turned to Talon and said, "Well, you cannot leave now, even if I also have to apologize for my husband's behavior." She tilted her head to one side and gave Talon a sweet smile. She was, he decided, a very beautiful woman who was many years younger than her husband.

She indicated the couch with an elegant hand and sat down herself. "Please, Sir Talon, how can we make it up to you?'

Talon grinned despite his annoyance. "Madame, the discomfort on Alexios's face was apology enough. I shall stay a little longer perhaps."

Alexios breathed a sigh of relief and grinned back. "Thank you, Talon. My father is getting old. He was once a general and fought for John Komnenos, the emperor's father, winning many honors and much wealth. He fought just about everyone at some time or another, and now all he has is his memories of those battles. It makes him...somewhat irascible and unsocial, and we have to put up with it. He is also an unspeakable snob about family, as you might have gathered."

He turned to his mother. "I have also forgotten my manners. Talon, my mother, Joannina."

Talon bowed from the waist. "I am honored, My Lady."

"He speaks passable Attic, how so?" she asked Alexios, looking surprised.

"We spent some long weeks on the ship getting that right, Mother," Alexios said with a wry smile.

She laughed. "Do not worry about my husband. We won't see him again today. Tell me what you are doing here in Constantinople, Sir Knight. What do you think of our fair city?"

"I am in awe of this great city, My Lady. Utterly in awe!" Talon told her sincerely. "It is magnificent! I have never been to a city so full of such impressive architecture, such beautiful churches and enormous palaces. I had not known that a mere street could be so wide and...so beautiful, paved from one end to the other with stone."

Joannina glowed at the praise almost as though she herself were being complimented. "Do you not then have palaces and cities of this stature in the Latin countries?" she asked.

"I must confess I have not traveled much in those countries, My Lady. Only for a brief time in Languedoc, which is the home of my parents, and although the city of Carcassonne is an impressive fortification it cannot compare to this city in size nor beauty."

"And where exactly is this Languedoc you are talking about?"

"It is near to Aquitaine, My Lady."

"Of course we all know where that is! It is the land of the beautiful Queen Eleanor, who came through this city many years ago. I was but a small girl then but I did get to see her."

She gave her son a quick glance. "Ah, now I understand. You are the strange Frank who has lived his entire life in the Arab countries and Persia. Alexios has been talking about you."

Talon glanced at Alexios then nodded. "Indeed, My Lady, I have lived in these countries. I grew up...as a boy in Palestine."

She appeared to make up her mind. "Will you not stay for the evening meal, Sir? I would hear more of your travels."

Talon glanced again at Alexios, who grinned. "You cannot refuse my mother, Talon."

Talon smiled at both of them. "Indeed, that *would* be bad manners. I would be honored to stay, My Lady."

"It is Joannina, and I shall call you Talon," she said with a laugh.

The meal was a success and his hosts made every effort to make him feel welcome. Being used to eastern foods the delicate, well prepared food did not come as any surprise to Talon, but it was of a far higher quality than even the good fare he and his companions had come to enjoy for over two weeks now.

The servants brought many servings, from most of which the family members took only a small portion before the dish was whisked away, presumably for the servants to finish off in the kitchens. Talon was seated at one end of a huge polished wooden table laid for five people, but there were only the three of them present. Servants hovered silently in the background or moved around the room, presenting food of differing kinds and flavors. Despite his experience with Eastern cuisine he was bemused by the variety of dishes placed before him. They were predominantly Greek, but there was much similarity to the food he had eaten in Persia and in Egypt. He was familiar with *dolma*; however, he was surprised at how many varieties of *dolma* could be presented: some were stuffed with chopped mushrooms in a sharp sauce, others with chopped chicken morsels over which pomegranate sauce had been poured, or mackerel paste mixed with hot spices that brought tears to his eyes.

They were served wine of a kind Talon had never tasted before; it left a pleasant taste in the his mouth and he resolved that he must learn some more about the way it was made. The deep red color and the taste on the back of the palate prepared him for the next course, which was a thick paste of sour goat's cheese with bread on a small glazed pottery plate that a servant slipped under his nose. Following the actions of his host and hostess he tore off a piece of crisp baked bread and scooped up some pate and then, following the example of his hosts, he dipped it into a saucer of olive oil and chewed. It was delicious, and he closed his eyes the better to savor the taste.

"You seem to like our food, Sir Talon," Joannina observed with a smile.

He nodded in silence and smiled. "Your food, My Lady, would melt the mouth of a statue of stone."

She smiled, then she pushed a dish of something towards him. "Try this, Sir Talon. I think you will enjoy it."

It was a dish of fish roe the color of light wine, and it tasted slightly salty but was of a creamy texture and quite delicious. It was followed by anchovies and chopped olives in garlic and rosemary. While he was munching on the bread he noticed a device next to his plate alongside a spoon. He picked it up and looked inquiringly at Alexios, who gave one of his tight smiles.

"It is the infamous fork, Talon," he murmured.

Talon held it in his right fist, the two prongs upright. Joannina was smiling mischievously but Alexios kept a straight face and said, "Now you can spear your meat with it and bring it to your mouth without getting your hands filthy. Try the *apaki*." He pointed with his own fork to the dish of meat slices covered in gravy that had been placed on the table nearby.

"What is that dish?" Talon asked, brandishing the fork and pretending he had never seen one before.

"It is lamb smoked over sage branches, then marinated in salt and vinegar, and then roasted over a charcoal fire" Joannina said. "I am sure you will like it. My cook is one of the best in this city." She spoke proudly but looked as though she was about to giggle.

Alexios gave Talon a stern look that said *enough of the play-acting* before demonstrating the practical use of the fork by spearing a chunk of the lamb and placing it on his own plate. He cut it with a knife and then picked up a morsel and brought it to his mouth. He chewed with evident enjoyment. Talon remembered and the hilarity that had followed the first lessons on the boat.

He examined the fork in his hand. Its handle was made of ivory and the two prongs might even have been made of silver. He held it properly in his fingers and very carefully speared a piece off the main plate, then moved the fork towards his plate, where he cut a piece off and took it to his mouth, being careful to watch the fork all the way until his eyes nearly crossed.

"You do that very well, Sir Talon. It is almost as though you have done this before. Have you never seen this device before, Talon?" Joannina asked with an amused but impressed look at him. She looked as though she were about to explode with laughter. Even Alexios looked amused.

"I have indeed, My Lady, er, Joannina. Your son was good enough to teach me while we travelled here. It seems like a good idea, but do you not spear your mouth from time to time?" he asked, remembering when he had done so.

"I have not so far," she said with dimple at the corner of her splendid lips. "Here in Constantinople in high society it is important to know how to use one. The use of fingers at table is frowned upon at the palace and now we all use forks. I am sure that it will be viewed with great distrust by your Frankish comrades if they should ever encounter one."

"They will probably think it is some kind of weapon for use at the table upon their neighbors," Talon said with a self-conscious laugh. "Where did it come from?"

"Why, the palace of course! They are always innovating, and as they spend a lot of time at the table I suppose this just came about. I am sure the Franks never use them, but do your Arabs and Persians?"

"I cannot say with certainty, but before your son showed me I had never seen one before," Talon said.

"Ah, my son clearly wanted to prepare you for the palace," she said.

The meal had progressed to the third course when they were joined by a girl of about fourteen who made a silent entry into the room dressed in a simple cotton tunic that came down to her ankles. She kissed her mother on the cheek and her brother, who greeted her with obvious affection, then she sat down with barely a glance at Talon. A servant quickly moved forward to provide her with a plate of small pastries. Talon had been told they were *sfakiani*; they reminded him of *baklava* but the bread was not the same as the thin flakey pastry of *baklava*. These were small pita bread pies with sour cheese and honey inside. She helped herself to several.

"You should apologize for being late, Theodora," Joannina admonished the girl, attempting to sound stern. "Where is your sister?"

"She is out with her friends, Mama, but has to be back to the palace by tomorrow morning," the girl said with her mouth full.

"Sir Talon, this is my little sister, Theodora. Theodora, this is Sir Talon, Knight of the Templars," Alexios stated.

Theodora bobbed her head and stared at Talon.

"Are you a Frank? You look like one."

"Theodora! Mind your manners. He has already been subjected to your father's idea of a welcome."

"I am sorry, Mama," she said, sounding not in the least bit contrite.

"I am a Frank," Talon told her. "But I live in Palestine."

"What do you do there? Are you a crusader? Do you fight a lot? Manuel says that the Franks fight all the time."

'Er...yes, I suppose we do," Talon said, taken aback by this small squall of questions. "But not all the time and there are many other things that we do as well."

"Such as?" Her eyes never left his face while she forked morsels of pork into her pretty mouth. Her use of the fork was adept and Talon admired the way she slipped the food into her mouth apparently without the slightest fear that she might stab herself on the lips or tongue. He on the other hand used his fork with care.

Theodora resembled her mother in some ways but appeared even more delicate of frame and her eyes were a lighter brown. Her hair, almost auburn, was swept back into an untidy ponytail that showed off the fine bones of her face, which was marred only slightly by a high ridge to her nose, more pronounced than that of her mother.

"Well we...build castles all over the place," Talon told her sounding serious to his own ears. She did not smile.

Alexios laughed. "Talon, my sister will prove even more difficult to talk to than Papa. She always has her nose in a book of some kind and understands the politics and history of the Romans even better than I."

"That is because you have not read the memoirs of Auntie Anna and thus do not have a good foundation, brother," Theodora said disdainfully, her mouth full.

"She is referring to my distant aunt, Anna Komnenos, who was an aunt of Manuel," Joannina said, as though she had heard this discussion before. "My dearest, please do not talk with your mouth full; and if I might say so, you need to leave the library on occasion and spend a little more time on your duties around this house. How are you going to manage when and if you ever get married?"

Theodora sniffed. "Mother, you are so old fashioned. Auntie Anna never had to do household work. She had servants and eunuchs to do her bidding, as will I, married or not."

"You will have to find the right person who can afford you, my dear. There are more poverty-stricken aristocratic youths in this city than anywhere else in the world, I am sure." Joannina turned to Talon. "Times are hard of late, Talon. Many of the great landowners are reduced to poverty because of the predations of the Seljuks. But you do not want to about hear that." She looked uncomfortable.

"Who is Manuel?' Talon asked to change the subject.

"Have you not met the emperor yet?" Joannina asked, her eyes swiveling towards Alexios in surprise. "I thought you said that he was here as an emissary, Alex?"

"Yes, he is an emissary, but no, Mother, he hasn't yet met Manuel. You know how long it takes for an emissary of any kind to obtain an audience with the emperor, even," he gave Talon an apologetic look, "one from the Knights Templar. It can take weeks sometimes. The Templars are here on business for the king. King Baldwin to you, little sister. Tuck that away in your head and see if you can remember his name."

Theodora was slouched in her chair over her plate, her spoon in the air, contemplating without enthusiasm some stewed apple that had been placed in front of her. There was a bored expression on her face.

"He is not an important king, is he? I mean, not like, say, Manuel? So why should I want to know all about him?" she said disparagingly.

Talon nearly choked on his wine as he suppressed a laugh. Alexios sent Talon an embarrassed grin and shrugged, his hands palm up. "Ignore her. I do not know where I found this family of mine," he said.

"I am sorry. I didn't know you were referring to the emperor. I did not know you knew him so well," Talon said with surprise in his voice.

"Of course we know him. We are related to the emperor through his aunt Anna, who was also a Komnenos," Theodora said with a sniff.

To change the subject again Talon asked, "There is a huge palace on the large hill to the east of this one. What is it called?"

"Do you mean the structure on the hill nearby?" Alexios asked. Theodora smirked.

"Yes, I think so. It looked deserted."

"That," Theodora said imperiously, "is the *Nymphaeum* of this fair city."

"And what does that name mean?" Talon asked reasonably.

Theodora gave her brother a wicked grin. "It is where the sacred Nymphs live."

Talon looked surprised. "Nymphs are...?"

"They are creatures of the ancient gods," Alexios said hurriedly with a glare at his sister.

"They are *na...ked* women who belong to the gods," Theodora said, drawing out the word and looking at Talon from under her brows.

Joannina, with a frown of disapproval at her daughter, said, "You were going to tell us a little of your experiences in the Arab and the Persian countries, Talon."

Talon shot her a thankful glance and began to tell them of Egypt and some of his experiences in that country, then he talked about Persia, leaving out the fact that he had been trained there as an assassin.

His audience was silent for the most part, only prompting him for more information from time to time. Even Theodora was drawn into the discussion and her attitude began to thaw. Her expression was rapt when he described the hospitals of the Arab world known as Bimaristans.

"We too have hospitals, Talon," Theodora spoke up. "They must be just as good as those of the Arabs, are they not, Mama?"

"I believe so, my child, but we do not interact with them as much as we used to, so we do not know." She turned to Talon. "It is a sad thing to say, but the perpetual wars in these parts make it difficult to learn from other people and their ways. There could be much learned from others, and perhaps we could teach them something too."

Talon looked at her with surprise. The Christians he had met up to this point, either in Palestine or even Languedoc, had been very ignorant of the sciences in the East and displayed no interest in learning from the peoples of these regions. He was being made to reevaluate his opinions of the people of Byzantium yet again.

"Theodora goes to the Palace of Magnaura, one of those halls within the Great Palace complex, which is also called the *Pandidakterion*, Talon," Alexios interjected. "I went there when I was studying Law and Philosophy."

"I am studying medicine!" Theodora said with pride.

"I applaud your interest, My Lady. I would very much like to visit this place some time," Talon said seriously.

"We will take you. I am sure that there will be time to show you all of the city and show off our churches and places of high learning," Joannina told him.

They were soon deep into a discussion of the various merits of some medical procedures for fevers and the herbs required for their treatment that Joannina knew very well. Theodora piped up and informed him somewhat pompously that in Constantinople the doctors even understood much about the eye. She winked her left eye for effect and said, "They know how to remove the milk from the inside of an eye so that a person can see again. Do your Arabs and Persians know about that?" She said it as though she doubted it very much. Talon himself was unsure, but he concluded they might because he had learned while in Egypt that the huge Bimaristan in Cairo had a section devoted to the eyes.

"I really cannot say, My Lady," he said politely. "But there have been some extremely well respected physicians in their world. Avicenna for instance, he was a genius and helped invent much that is used today. There are many others who devote their lives to medicine. My...uncle was a physician and I believe he was greatly respected while he lived. There is a very famous Persian physician, Seyed Esmail Jorjani, who has written a huge volume on medicine and it is used in the Bimaristans of Cairo. It is just as an important a work as those of Avicenna."

"We have studied some of Avicenna's work! Mama, he knows of these things! You may call me Theo," she said, her tone patronizing. "I will one day be a physician too."

Talon was astonished by this pronouncement.

"Did you ever get into one of those harems?" she asked, changing the subject so abruptly that Talon stared and then grinned.

"No, that would have been difficult, as they are well guarded."

"I think it is terrible that they lock women up like that," she said.

He smiled and replied, "You appear to be very well informed. How is it that you know so much?"

She looked at him scornfully. "You think because I am fourteen I should not know anything?" Theodora asked, contemptuously waving her spoon. The stewed fruit was untouched in front of her and a nervous servant was hovering about ready to rescue the food.

"Both boys and girls go to schools in all the towns across the empire," Alexios informed Talon.

Talon was impressed. "In the country of the Franks where I spent a little time, a girl of your age would not know anything of what we have talked about this evening. I for one have found our discussion of great interest," he said, addressing Theodora with elaborate respect.

He left that night thinking hard about the kind of people he had just met.

*****

Later that evening, Alexios, a his mother and sister were seated in the loggia overlooking the Venetian quarter. To the east of that darkened area was the Genoese quarter, full of lights and muted noise. Out at sea the occasional glimmer of a lantern could be seen belonging to a ship braving the darkness, but otherwise the evening was quiet and the distant sea as calm as a pond. Even the crickets were stilled, although now geckos ran along the walls in and out of the lamplight chasing moths, and the croaking of the frogs in the pond down in the gardens had begun to fill the night with song.

"What did you think of our Frank, Mother?" Alexios asked.

"He moves like a cat, a large dangerous cat. But I still like him, although there is something in those green eyes that frightens me."

"Yes, I saw something of Talon on the ship coming here from Acre. The Franks are a rough crowd, very rude, hard people. Sometimes they would practice with sticks to stay in form while on the journey. But none of them could even touch him when they played, he is so fast. He could beat them all including the largest of them, a man called Claude. I was going to try my luck, but Sir Guy, his senior, dissuaded me and said it would be a humiliation and he would not have that." Alexios's smile was rueful. "Sir Guy once mentioned that he did not know anyone as dangerous as that man, although on the surface he appears gentle. I think Sir Talon is more than he appears to be; but I have come to like him, and more than that, I think I trust him too."

"Why would you trust a Frank, brother?" Theodora asked skeptically.

"Because he is not like the others, not at all. What did you think of him, little sister?"

"I think that had you not shown him how to use a fork he would have used his fingers and thought that perfectly normal. But...I suppose...Oh, how would I know anyway?" she demanded and abruptly got up and stalked out. If her brother had been watching, as her mother was, he would have noticed a certain flush to the girl's cheeks.

"Is he really one of those Templars, Alexios? I have heard strange things about them."

"He tells me that he is only an associate, but Sir Guy gives him all the respect of a full knight."

"I think you should invite our Frank to stay, Alexios. He could learn good manners and seems willing. We can all go to the Hippodrome next week. I hear there is to be a grudge race. Your friend will be running for the Blues."

"I shall, Mother, but what about Father?"

"Oh, do not worry about that. I shall talk to him."

*****

Talon made his way back up the now silent street deep in thought. He followed the servant carrying the torch as they crossed the almost deserted Mese. Most of the shops that had been open during the day were closed and shuttered, but food stalls were still busy and the smoke from cooking fires drifted through the night air, and evening crowds moved about.

Talon observed that the south side of the city was far from asleep. It was almost as if another type of person was abroad at night: these people mingled with one another in the darkness amid loud conversations, laughter and curses. As Talon and the servant descended the hill towards the harbor, heading for the inn where he was staying, and he noticed that the crowd along the street became noisier and more raucous as they progressed. To his surprise there were women on the street who simply mingled in the crowd, sometimes they were alone, sometimes in pairs. He was tired and this evening had given him much to think of, so he ignored the drunks lurching about near the entrances of the many inns and ladies of the night with their whispered invitations.

Sophocles

Chapter 6

The Chariot Race

Two days later Talon was at breakfast t with Sir Guy, the two monks, and the sergeant when the landlord came hurrying over and told him someone was at the gate with a message.

Talon looked at Sir Guy in surprise but rose and went with the man to where he encountered Joseph.

"Good morning, Sir. I am bid to tell you that my master and his family will be going to the Hippodrome tomorrow. There will be chariot races and they would like to host you and your party there in the afternoon. The emperor has commanded their presence at the races and wishes that your delegation be present with them. Please meet them perhaps two hours after noon. The Master Alexios will meet you at the forum of Constantine. From there we will guide you to the Hippodrome. The emperor will be present, so you should dress appropriately," Joseph said diffidently.

Talon nodded assent and dismissed the man, then made his way back to the table. He sat down and addressed himself to the grilled sardines, which had been getting cold, before he told the others what had transpired. They contained their impatience with difficulty while he ate.

"We are invited to watch some chariot races tomorrow," he stated between mouthfuls.

Sir Guy looked interested. "I have heard that can be quite the spectacle in this city," he remarked. Then he followed up with the comment, "The story goes that the spectators are unruly and often riot over nothing more important than a winner or a loser." He looked sideways at Brother Jonathan, keeping a straight face as he did so.

"Then I shall devote my time to prayers," Jonathan stated with a pious look upwards and tore off a piece of the bread before dipping it in olive oil. He had grown very fond of the food in the inn, Talon noticed with wry amusement. Still, it allowed the rest of them to move around without his suffocating personage attaching itself to them all the time.

"I...I would like to see this spectacle," Brother Martin volunteered hesitantly.

Jonathan glared at him. "It is not for us to watch the unruly masses behaving like sinners and animals, Brother. You shall stay with me and we will read the psalms.

"I am sure that God would not approve of your going either, Sir Guy," he added pointedly. You should confess your sins for going when you come back."

"How can it be a sin to accept a command that you cannot deny?" Claude asked. His tone was a shade belligerent. There was clearly no love lost here.

"These entire people are sinners and will be punished one day, you mark my words. This is a Sodom and Gomorrah."

"I should have let him fall into the harbor the very first day we came to the ship," Claude muttered in an aside to Max, who grit his teeth as he tried to suppress a chuckle.

"I am sure that it would be foolish to refuse an invitation from people as influential as the family Kalothesos, especially at this sensitive stage of our negotiations, Brother Jonathan. Indeed, Talon said that the emperor has commanded our attendance, so I am sure that God will understand the reasons for our wishing to stay in their good graces," Sir Guy said in a placating manner. "Talon and I shall take the sergeants with us, for protection mind you, and you may pray for our safety. As I have never witnessed either a chariot race or a riot before, and there is the risk that we will see both, I shall need an escort. This is simply another facet of the people of Byzantium that we must endure. We must also dress our best, as we have been informed that the emperor himself will be there."

Jonathan glared at him.

Talon looked at Max and could see his friend's face was going red as he tried to contain his laughter. Claude put his hand across his mouth and scowled ferociously at the sparrows playing in the huge wisteria vine that cast a mantel of dark green leaves over the corner where they were seated.

*****

Talon and Sir Guy, dressed in their Templar uniforms and accompanied by Max and Claude, walked up the steep street to the Forum of Constantine where they were met by Alexios and his servant, Joseph. They wore cloaks this afternoon, as the sky was grey and there was the promise of rain. There was a cool, blustery wind blowing in from the north off the Bosporus. The vast forum was almost deserted at this time of day, as most of the loiterers had gone to the games. Talon noted that even the shop keepers were shutting up; was little business to be had when the chariot races were taking place. It was as if the huge Hippodrome had sucked the streets of the city clean of people.

Talon and Sir Guy walked around pieces of the statue of Constantine, which had formerly dominated the forum. Alexios joined them as they admired the fallen stonework. He wore a fine ankle length tunic with soft leather boots, his sword hung from a wide sash inlaid with gold and silver thread. His hair had been oiled and curled and his beard trimmed. He looked very much the aristocrat as he strode over to them and clasped hands with Sir Guy and Talon with a brief nod to the sergeants.

"How did it come to be in this condition?" Talon asked him, nodding to the huge pieces lying about.

"A great storm came through and it was blown over, about sixteen years ago. Now as you can see there is a cross for our Lord in its place."

They all stared up at the newly built cross. Talon thought that restoring the original would have been a better choice. He looked to the east and the west where the massive monumental gates marked the entrance of the forum through which the Mese passed.

"I have never seen a road like this...anywhere," he stated.

"This is the main great avenue of our city. To the east it is known as the Regia or Imperial Road, as the emperors of olden times used it for their victory parades. We will see the emperor come along here again before long," Alex said with pride in his voice. "His life is full of ceremony. I could not endure it."

"Does the Senator not accompany us?" Sir Guy inquired.

"My father was taken to the Hippodrome earlier, as the senators have to be seated before the emperor arrives," Alex explained, "and my mother and sister went ahead to avoid the crush of the crowds."

They walked east along the Regia which ran straight eastward, ending in the great square in front of the Hagia Sophia. Talon had by now walked it often and liked the wide spacious stone paved road with its plane trees and regular rows of columns on either side. Unlike the western side of the forum, where the merchants and shops were situated in between the columns, there were small palaces and villas along this section of the avenue, although they were well hidden behind dense rows of tall Cyprus trees and high walls.

They passed the Cistern of Philoxenos, which Alexios explained was a large reservoir, and the entrance to the church of St. Euphemia, and finally the small palaces of Antiochos and Lausos. Then they were in front of the massive construction of the Hippodrome, which dominated the south side of the avenue. Talon had been amazed at its size from a distance; now he had to crane his neck to see the edge of the rooftop. They joined the throng of people preparing to enter at front of the Hippodrome, but Joseph and the escorting guards pushed through the people standing about and lead them them through to another entrance. This, Alexios explained, led to the private balcony of the family.

Some turned and watched curiously as Sir Guy and his entourage went by. Realizing that they were Franks a few of them called out insults, but not too loudly as they noticed the escort of ten tough-looking guards who came with them. Others, noticing their badge of the Order, remained quiet. Several called a blessing, because even here in this great city so far from Palestine people knew of the Order of Templars. Talon smiled at an old woman nearby who blessed them.

"Bless you, soldiers of God," she called out.

The low murmur from the crowd both inside and waiting to enter the Hippodrome was unlike anything he had heard before. It was a living, seething thing and Talon was not sure that he felt comfortable with it all.

They were led through the milling groups of people to other guarded entrances that were placed along the north wall. Here an officer asked for identification, whereupon the eunuch presented a lead token. The officer then ordered the soldiers to open the doors. They walked along a dark tunnel approximately fifty feet long before coming to another opening that was barred. Soldiers stood guard at several doorways in the tunnel from which stone steps led upwards into the gloom.

Joseph indicated that they should follow him up one set of stairs. It was quiet in this vertical corridor other than the scraping of their boots on the stone steps until they neared the top of the echoing stairs, then the noise from the crowd inside the Hippodrome increased. Eventually the eunuch stopped and pulled aside a leather curtain, whereupon they found themselves on a balcony overlooking the arena. Talon was stunned at what he saw. All four Franks stared around them in awe at the sight laid out below them.

The Hippodrome was shaped in the form of an immense oval with tiers of seats that rose from the sand to a height of at least forty feet. The upper tiers were protected from the sun and rain by a tiled roof that went all the way around the top. The tiers were separated from the newly raked sand of the actual arena by what what seemed to be a narrow moat of water some six feet wide.

Down the center of the arena was a low, thick wall. It went for about two hundred and fifty feet and stood about five feet high. Perched all along its length were statues and obelisks of many different shapes and sizes. Some of them were immense.

Alexios noticed the direction of Talon's gaze and said, "That wall is the *Spina*, and as you can see it is decorated with many monuments placed there by past emperors. Look at the statue over there, it is one of Hercules; and over there is an obelisk from Egypt that was brought here when Egypt was part of our empire."

Talon could only stare. The statue of Hercules was enormous. Talon thought that if he stood next to the lower leg his head might just be as high as the knee. Further along was a massive representation of a woman holding a life sized horse and rider in her hand. He saw a bronze eagle with outstretched wings, which had holes in them to allow sunlight to pour through onto a sundial.

Nearer to hand was a magnificent lifelike bronze of four horses pulling a chariot that commanded the end of the *Spina*. He pointed it out to the others and asked Alexios, "Is that what we will be seeing today?"

"Exactly so. Although these competitors will not be made of bronze," Alexios smiled. "It is known as a *quadriga*. It is four horses, just like those you see, and has been part of Roman legend for generations. These represent the chariots of the ancient gods. Do you see those dolphins?" He pointed to the end of the *Spina* where Talon noticed a row of what looked like gleaming bronze fish with huge heads, each exactly the same size, their large open mouths gaping up at the sky, set along a bar suspended from a gilt frame.

"There is a rope attached to each one, and as the chariots complete one round a dolphin is pulled so that its mouth is facing the ground. That way the crowd knows how many rounds there are to go." Alexios stated.

Talon glanced to his left and noticed that above them and over to the east side of the Hippodrome, almost midway along the straight part of the arena, was another, much larger balcony. It was wide and deep and already there were many important people standing or seated in its large space, many dressed in the garb of Senators. Alexios informed him that it was the *kathisma* where the emperor would be seated.

"The races cannot start until the emperor arrives, and he is still to come," Alexios stated. "You might be able to see my father in that crowd over there." He pointed.

The fact that the Senator was one of the emperor's invited guests was not lost on Sir Guy de Veres.

"I am impressed at how well connected your family is with the emperor, Alexios," he remarked.

"Ours is an ancient family and my father is a senator, as was his father. I too will become one some day."

"How long is the arena? It looks enormous!" Talon asked.

"The circus, as we call it, is about twelve hundred feet long, and the arena itself is nearly one thousand feet," Alexios stated.

From their lofty position on the balcony Talon could see other balconies on either side and above, but none so high as that of the emperor, which had to be about forty feet or more off the sandy ground it overlooked. The stands were filling up rapidly with people and he noted that there were four main colors on display in the form of banners: Red and White and Green and Blue.

"What do these colors represent?" he asked, pointing to the banners.

"Ah! Those are the colors of the various factions within the city. They are ancient and used to be more important than they are today. The Greens and the Blues are still quite important, but not so the Red and White banners, although people still support them for sentimental reasons. I have no idea why though. The Greens and the Blues are paid by the government to attend various ceremonies and to attend the emperor whenever he moves about the city, as he has done today."

Talon noted that soldiers were posted at regular intervals along the aisles between the seating and wondered why out loud.

"They are there to keep order, Talon. People become excited during the races and sometimes misbehave." Alexios told him.

Alexios talked briefly with Joseph before he took a seat next to Talon. Sir Guy was already seated and gazing about him in wonder. He and Talon looked at one another.

"I wonder what Brother Jonathan would have made of this," Sir Guy murmured.

Talon grinned.

Max and Claude, as befitted their station, stood at the back of the balcony, although they could see well enough.

"I have never in my life seen anything like this before," Sir Guy admitted with some awe in his voice. "This...Hippodrome as you call it, Alexios, is larger than the Coliseum in Rome, I am sure of it. And that ancient building is a ruin now."

Talon looked around. The Hippodrome was built in a rough east-west direction with the flat section of the arena to the eastern end. The western end was curved to follow the shape of the internal sandy area. Anyone anywhere had a clear view of the rest of the arena except those at ground level, as the *Spina* obstructed the view of its other side. Their balcony was one of many on either of the straight sides.

"It feels like it is almost a living thing," Talon said, indicating the mass of people beginning to crowd the stands.

"It is like an animal. Wait a while and you'll see it come to life," Alexios said, his tone dry.

Joseph reappeared with wine and fruit for them to enjoy while they waited. But Talon could not stop looking around. This was not the first major construction he had visited during his brief time in the city, but it left him astonished and humbled at its sheer size and magnificence.

Every inch of the sides of the *Spina* was covered in either frescoes or cut stone imagery. People dressed much as the Greeks around him were depicted in battle as spearmen or cavalry. Most of the imagery was devoted to the glorification of the emperors of the past. Defeated enemies were kneeling and offering homage to the emperors of Constantinople, laying gifts of slaves and gold at their feet.

He could see clearly to the other side of the arena where slaves were making last minute preparations for the races. Some were still raking the area while others were collecting rubbish tossed onto the sand by the spectators. He noted pillars at all the four corners of the *Spina* and asked Alexios about them.

"Those are to tell the charioteers that there is a corner coming, and to protect the statues of the *Spina*. You will see that they come very close."

The crowds in the stands were beginning to settle down now. The smell of cooked meat wafted up from the stands below as vendors walked about hawking meats and fruits on trays, shouting their wares and doing a roaring trade.

"Here I see no women, Alexios. Where have the Lady Kalothesos and your sister gone?" Talon asked.

"It is tradition. My mother and sister are above the *kathisma* with the empress and ladies in waiting. Do you see the grilled windows up there?" He pointed above the emperor's balcony. "You cannot see them, but they can see very well from there without being noticed, and they remain protected from the vulgar masses. If the crowd becomes too noisy the ladies can easily retreat to the Great Palace without any danger from the rabble." Alexios sniffed.

Talon was always amused by Alexios when he started to be haughty and displayed some arrogance. It did not suit him at all.

They were interrupted by the blare of trumpets and the crowd slowly hushed. Then Talon realized that all eyes were on the Imperial Box.

Emperor Manuel I walked slowly up to the rail of the royal balcony; he raised his arms and made the sign of the cross. The crowd roared its approval. He was dressed in magnificent silken robes that glittered in the watery sunlight, the tall wide hat of office, and he wore a bejeweled sword on a belt studded with precious stones and gold that gleamed. He was escorted by several of his closest officers of the administration.

"He is signaling the start of the games," Alexios explained. There was a distant rumble of thunder. He glanced up at the sky overhead, which was still clear of rain clouds. "I hope it does not rain."

The emperor stood for several minutes at the front of the royal balcony and the crowd cheered and roared its greeting. He appeared to be enjoying the approbation of the crowd. Whenever they seemed to be flagging, one or other of the colored banners would be waved and the crowd would start cheering again. Talon thought they must be hoarse before the event had even begun.

Eventually the emperor dropped his arms and signaled to someone, then he took his seat in front of the large group of guests on the balcony so that his view would be uninterrupted. To Talon's astonishment a strange sound began to emanate from the top of the walls behind their balcony. He realized that it was music, but of a kind he had never heard before. It sounded as though a number of huge pipes were being played. Some of the notes were so deep that no person could have made them on any instrument he knew. Others were so high that again he could not even imagine how they came about.

He looked his puzzlement to Alexios who laughed. "Have you never heard an 'organ' playing before, Talon?" He pointed towards the far end of the stadium. "There are two in the Hippodrome and they work with the help of water. Do not ask me to explain; only an engineer might. They are wonderful, are they not?"

"I have not heard anything of the kind. It is indeed a strange and wonderful sound," Sir Guy said.

Talon nodded agreement. The sound filled the air all about them, and because the walls of the Hippodrome were high the notes were captured and resonated around the stands, creating an incredible sound that stilled all voices for several minutes. The music continued even when, upon an unseen signal, gates were opened below their balcony and the first of the charioteers drove his quartet of horses into the arena.

He was greeted with a roar from the crowd and much waving of colored banners. Talon looking down upon the chariot could see that the horses were of the finest and were pulling as a team in one line, shoulder to shoulder. The man who held them looked strong and lithe; he held them well in place with a firm hand, the muscles on his back rippling through the thin material of his tunic as he controlled them. He talked to them all the while, not permitting them too much freedom, just enough to allow them to strut and look magnificent as they pulled the light vehicle behind them. The chariot had been pared back to the most basic of frames, open at the back to make it lighter; even so, it was elaborately decorated with the color of its patrons, the Blues. The driver wore a long tunic of light blue material, with a thin gold belt at the waist and fine leather sandals on his feet, but little else. His short black hair was oiled and curled.

He allowed his team to cavort and prance their way to the front of the emperor's balcony, and then with a shout he hauled them to a stop. He bowed to the emperor from his chariot and called up praises; after an acknowledgement from the emperor he drove his team round to stand at a place indicated by some slaves, who held the horses to keep them in position and to quiet them. The arrival of three other teams of horses was repeated in a similar manner.

As each driver saluted the emperor his color in the stands roared their support and waved their banners and flags in the air.

By the time the last man, representing the White team, had driven his horses out and performed his salutes, Talon could feel an almost palpable tension in the entire arena. Even Alexios was leaning forward in anticipation of the starting trumpets, his eyes intent upon the Blue driver. He had declared for the Blue team, explaining that his father and his father's father had supported them for generations. "It is tradition, but today the driver is a friend of mine," he explained with a shrug.

The strange music had stopped and there was a dense silence in the arena. The highly restless teams of horses were being held in place by both their drivers and nervous slaves who were hanging onto their bits; horses were plunging and fighting for their heads, tossing flecks of foam from their mouths into the air. At one time the Red team appeared to be almost out of control: the horses were so excited they made sharp, nasal whinnies; one tried to rear and was coaxed down by the tense driver and a slave hanging onto its bit.

The waiting stretched out interminably, but although the crowd was silent their palpable impatience and excitement reached the spectators in the balconies, adding to their own anticipation as they waited.

Then the moment arrived. The emperor gave a small hand signal and a trumpet blared. The drivers all at the exact same moment slapped their horses' rumps with the reins, shouted and cracked their whips. The horses plunged forward with a jerk that would have thrown anyone less experienced off the back of the chariots, and in a spray of sand they were off. The crowd as one gave a great roar of excitement. Spectators howled and shouted and prayed for their team to win, waving the tokens of their bets as the four teams of racing horses bowled down the first straight run of the course in a spray of sand, straining horses and the blur of galloping legs. The lightweight chariots were hauled along at a great speed, the thud of many hooves on the sand all but obliterating the whir of their lightweight wheels and the slap of the traces. The slaves who had been holding the horses scuttled off for the doorways; their lives depended upon getting out of the way before the teams came back around.

"They must circle the arena seven times!" Alexios shouted over the din. "You can see the dolphins at the eastern end of the *Spina* being hauled down as they go by to indicate a lap."

Talon barely heard him; he was so intent upon the horses and their chariots racing away from them in a pack. It was very hard to see who was in the lead as they hurtled along the sandy track, and for a while he could not tell which color was which as they rounded the end of the *spina*. The crowd howled as the chariots raced by each section, the noise grew louder coming straight towards them. As the chariots swept by the screaming spectators stood up in a strange kind of human wave that surged alongside them. The screams of encouragement from the crowd drowned out the sounds of the chariots and their pounding horses as they raced by.

He could just make out the tense faces of the charioteers as they leaned over the edge of their light chariot frames, eyes intent upon the way forward. They shouted at their horses, alternatively encouraging and cursing. It was as though the horses understood what was needed, for the drivers did not use the whips at this time; it was clear the animals were giving their all. They were bunched and Talon wondered how they could control the four animals and the bouncing fragile vehicle and at the same time not run into one another and become destroyed in the process.

Their skill was extraordinary and he marveled that the innermost chariot could negotiate the turns without striking the pillars or running into another chariot. The teams raced around the corners in a flurry of sand and then were off again down the straightway.

"How do they do it?" he yelled at Alexios, who was on the edge of his seat shouting at the teams as they went by. Gone was the stiff and haughty man Talon had first met in Acre.

He turned an excited look upon Talon. "They train from boyhood! They know what they are about, but just wait, it has only just begun. Curses on the Green team, they are in the lead! Get going, Pantoleon! You call yourself a charioteer?" he shouted at the Blue driver. "What are you doing?"

Talon grinned at Sir Guy, who was clearly amused at this unusual display of emotion.

Indeed the green flags were being raised in the areas where the Green supporters were standing, and shouts and insults were being flung at the other supporters, followed by laughter and obscene gestures from all quarters. Talon was struck by how uninhibited the people of Constantinople behaved when in the stadium. The reserve he had seen from many a Greek he had encountered outside was certainly not on display here.

He watched with keen interest as the teams swept around the nearest post during the fourth round, admiring the skill of the charioteers as they controlled the four racing animals. They were bunched again, although the Green driver had gained some distance on the others and went around the pillar without difficulty, teasing the reins and shouting encouragement to his animals. A second later they raced off along the straight line of the arena in a spray of sand and dust. Just behind him, however, the three following teams were competing to take the lead position. The inside man, the White driver, appeared to be dangerously close to the side of the *Spina*, the wheels of his chariot spinning within inches of the stone wall. Talon held his breath as the chariot raced towards the pillar the Green had negotiated only a second ago. He noticed the Blue chariot pulling across the path of the White at the last moment while the Red chariot was closing on the right side of the Blue.

Suddenly there was nowhere for the White driver to go. He turned a panicked face to the Blue driver and screamed at him to give him room, but that driver had his own problems. He was sandwiched between the Red and the White teams and could only scream back and haul on the reins. Then the White driver made a bad decision; he seized his whip and lashed at his horses, trying desperately to gain vital yards that would allow him to get round the pillar before the other two. It was too late, and before the horrified eyes of the entire crowd the White team galloped straight into the pillar. One horse ran directly into the post, which shook but stood. The shocked horse crashed to the ground, twitching. In doing so it brought the entire team down in a tangle of bodies and equipment.

Panic stricken horses tried to evade the wall and pillar but were caught up in the traces and the haft of the chariot, and try as they might they could not free themselves. The driver of the White chariot was thrown sideways to strike the wall hard and appeared to be knocked out by the blow, as he tumbled to the ground in a limp heap. One of the horses struggled off to the right and almost managed to break free, but the other two chariots swept up and the head of the struggling horse was struck by the shoulder of one of the oncoming horses of the Blue chariot. The animal was thrown back into the mass of kicking and screaming animals to lie inert and bleeding. The horses of the Blue chariot staggered for a few paces but then resumed their headlong pace.

The Blue and the Red chariots had slowed, but neither stopped. They swept around the mass of struggling animals and the wreckage of the chariot almost in parallel and raced off in a cloud of dust and sand.

F For a brief moment there was a shocked silence from the crowd, but then there were shouts of alarm and then anger. Fists were waved and shouts of abuse came from the White enclosures as they realized that their chariot was out of the race, their man was injured and quite possibly dead from the accident, and their bets were now lost. Their anger was directed at the Blue driver and now rubbish was being thrown.

"They believe the Blue driver caused the accident and are very angry. And it is just like Pantoleon to do such a thing," Alexios said with some apprehension as the shouting and traded insults grew noisier.

"Why did the White driver not pull up when he saw there was no room?" Talon asked.

"I suppose he thought he could squeeze by," Sir Guy said.

"It was a mistake he might not live to regret," Alexios said in a grim tone, as they watched the slaves race out onto the sand to try and sort out the mess at the corner.

"Will they not stop the race?" Sir Guy asked, his voice incredulous.

"It depends upon the emperor. But Manuel is unlikely to interfere, I would say." Alexios glanced over to the royal balcony. Several people were remonstrating with the emperor, but he dismissed them with a wave of his hand and they were forced to sit down and watch the events unfolding below.

The slaves managed to retrieve the body of the White driver and get him out of the way before the teams came racing back towards the tangle of horses and the overturned chariot. They hugged the wall of the *Spina* as the drivers hurtled past. As soon as they had gone by the slaves went to work to cut the horses free and run the surviving ones out of the arena. The two dead ones were dragged off after another round by the charioteers.

The drivers, who knew what they were doing, were careful to slow and negotiate this corner with care before racing off again. The cheering grew louder and more intense as the Blue driver was catching up with the Green chariot. Their horses were covered in sweat and struggling to maintain their former pace. It was now that the whips came out and the drivers lashed their teams forward with yells and strikes. The finish of the race was now between the Blue and the Green team. The Red driver despite all his efforts could not drive his team to match those of the others, perhaps because their horses were without doubt the best bred and the most expensive. He came a far third now, although he continued to drive the laboring animals on with shouts and curses.

It became evident that experience might be the telling point in this race, and Talon could see by the way the Blue driver guided his animals that he had an edge, although it was not by much. He was able to get the best out of his horses without belaboring them with the whip, unlike the Green driver, who was now looking over his shoulder at the four horses galloping almost alongside his chariot. He drew back his whip and lashed it forward to strike the lead animal on a back already streaked with welts.

The Blue driver calmly called a word to his straining animals and his chariot surged forward. They were now only two hundred yards from the finish marker, half way along one of the straight sides of the arena and almost in front of the emperor's balcony. Talon watched approvingly as the Blue driver drew alongside the other chariot, his horses, while covered in sweat and streaked with foam from their bits, still seemed to have reserves left; but the Green team was laboring, their legs and sides soaked with sweat and their sides heaving with the effort.

The Blue's rival looked across the short gap between the racing chariots and spinning wheels and shouted something to him. Although he could not hear over the noise of the screaming crowd Talon was sure it was an insult, as the Blue driver glared back but did not lose his temper. Instead he took out his whip and cracked it over the ears of his team. The horses plunged forward, seeming to leave the Green team standing. The Blue chariot streaked past the finish line to the cheers and yells of the now standing crowd in the Blue sections who waved their banners and howled their approval. Alexios jumped to his feet and yelled too. Talon laughed and so did Sir Guy.

The Green team raced over the finish line a good five yards behind. The charioteer hauled his horses to a stop about fifty paces further down the course, once again shouting something to the Blue driver. In response the Blue driver turned his team around and walked back to face his Green opponent. As he drew near he raised his whip, snapping it with force straight at the Green driver. The tip of the long plaited leather cord struck his target on the chest. The blow threw him off his chariot with a startled yelp of pain. The Blue driver then stepped down from his chariot and walked over to the stunned man, who was lying on the ground clutching his chest. The Blue driver then kicked him hard in the ribs. But this time, the other man bounded to his feet and the two set to wrestling with each other. They were quite oblivious of the Red chariot, whose driver was now desperately hauling his team to a stop for fear of running them over.

The crowd erupted to its feet; those on the other side of the *Spina* were confused and shouted questions to those who could see properly. There were boos, jeers and shouts of excitement as viewers took in what was going on. The banners began to wave and men of different persuasions began to wave fists at one another across the dividing lines between the color sections. Rubbish and old food were thrown as people screamed insults at one another. A man wearing a blue tunic jumped into the moat and swam across it to join in the fight, bellowing insults as he did so. He was quickly followed by other spectators from the Blues and Greens. In a few short minutes there was a mass of struggling men punching and kicking at one another and rolling on the sand. Talon and his companions the other Franks stifled their laughter as members of the crowd belonging to all colors lifted their tunics to bare their behinds or their genitals before daring their opponents to come and fight, none of whom seemed loath to do so.

Soldiers and slaves appeared on the sand like magic and restrained the two drivers who, already exhausted from their race, were now staggering about trying vainly to hit one another and not succeeding. Then the soldiers chased off the spectators who had joined in the scrap with the sharp ends of their spears.

Talon glanced at Alexios who said calmly, "There's going to be a riot now unless the soldiers can quiet things down."

Heavily armed soldiers were beginning to hasten down the aisles between the tiers of seats with their shields and spears at the ready. An officer who seemed to know what he was about shouted to several of them to get into the struggling mass of men who were punching and yelling at one another. Others of the crowd were cheering the fighters on and many were laughing, clearly enjoying the spectacle.

"It is not very serious," Alexios remarked.

"What will happen to the Blue driver?"

"He will be acclaimed the victor and that will be the end of it."

"Does this kind of thing happen often?" Sir Guy asked.

"Not that often, but when it does it can become a full blown riot, and then the soldiers come and break heads or even kill a few of the crowd to restore order."

Talon and Sir Guy looked at one another.

Indeed the soldiers did restore order very quickly. Several of the more rowdy spectators in the crowd were hustled off by soldiers and then slaves ran back onto the sand and guided the now calmer drivers to a place in front of the emperor's balcony.

Manuel was standing waiting for them. He had obviously enjoyed the affray as he laughed at the charioteers, wagging his finger at the Blue driver, then he told them to make up and be friends again.

"It was a good race and the winner deserves the prize!" he shouted down at them. He raised the laurel leaf crown on high, and at this point the crowd began to chant.

"We ask for equal share of your victory that comes from God,
An equal share of your victory, Master,
The faith of Kings prevails!"

Manuel waved his hand to the spectators and then handed the wreath to a slave who carried it down to the Blue charioteer. The servant vanished from sight but almost as quickly reappeared on the sand. He walked up to the Blue driver and placed the wreath of dark green, tapering leaves upon his head. The crowd roared its approval while the charioteers saluted the emperor and then in procession performed a victory lap. The organs played a sonorous melody to which the spectators sang along with some raucous songs.

They were to witness several races that day, most of which ended in a clear winner and few accidents.

On one occasion a team was so badly bumped that the chariot tipped over on its side, spilling the driver unceremoniously into the moat with a big splash amid laughter and jeers of the crowd. He crawled out of the water looking bedraggled and filthy while his horses were hurried out of the arena. Many spectators were by now intoxicated with wine, which seemed to be flowing freely. This induced arguments and then fights erupted in which empty wine skins were used as weapons to slap opponents about, and once more the soldiers came and restored order. Then there was a flash of lightning followed by the crash of thunder, and the rain began to fall.

The emperor seemed to think it was a good time to leave and stood up. The music played and the crowd cheered as he left the balcony. The races were over.

*****

Later, back in the inn, while they were sitting under the loggia watching the water dripping from the tiles, Sir Guy remarked, "I am glad we went to see the races as it gives us a better idea as to who these people are."

"They don't seem to mind a scrap," Claude said with a laugh. "I have never seen men showing off their bare arses like that just before they go and have a fight. I was terrified." He rolled his eyes theatrically.

Talon choked on his wine.

"No one can tell me that the Greeks aren't an excitable people after this," Max laughed as he thumped Talon's back.

"It is very different from their behavior when they're not in the Hippodrome," Talon spluttered and caught his breath.

"Yes, they seem very reserved when you meet them. But just look at Alexios! He went mad when his friend won and then got into that fight," Max replied. He laughed again, shaking his head.

"I think that the less we say about the whole affair to our beloved Brothers the better," Sir Guy said as he watched Martin approach.

Talon had no doubts as to whom they would all confess when the time came.

Chapter 7

The Emperor and Liturgy

The following day Sir Guy was informed that they were all commanded to attend the emperor's parade, which would then be followed by a possible audience. They feverishly trimmed beards, brushed clothes and cloaks and polished boots that had not been attended to properly for some time. Sir Guy even managed to force Bother Jonathan and Martin to have their habits washed, which Talon and Max deemed to be a singular achievement.

"Today you will witness pomp and ceremony such as you've never seen before," he told them all at breakfast.

The great parade from the Palace of Blachernae to the Great Palace on the eastern side of the city was almost a mile long, so that by the time the emperor arrived at the Forum of Theodoseus and was well on his way to the Great Palace, the end of the train had only just begun to move from the Blachernae itself at the other end of the city.

Talon had never before witnessed the rituals of the Byzantine Empire and its Church, and although he had been a spectator at more than one parade in his life he'd never been present at one of this magnitude. Sir Guy had told him that the ceremonies were ancient, indeed, there was a preoccupation with the preservation of these ancient rites, and what he witnessed on this day would remain with him for the rest of his life.

Soldiers lined the Mese from one end to the other. Many of them looked very like Norse men to Talon. In the van of the parade were the emperor's heralds and eunuchs who were of the household staff—some holding high office if their costumes were any indication of their status. These rites and the costumes worn by the high officials of the church and the court denoted a culture that was more ancient than anything he had ever witnessed before.

The standards and great crosses, carried by slaves, officers of the court, and exalted eunuchs alike, were made of crimson satin, heavily fringed and attached to gilded poles that rose high into the air. The bearers and musicians wore identical uniforms: bright white tunics of fine white silk cloth with intricately sewn gold and colored thread depicting saints and holy men, crosses and other saintly imagery.

The horses they rode had bright plumes of feathers on their heads, and their manes, bound with ribbons and tassels, combed as fine as silk, moved and flowed with every step the animals took. Each harness was inlaid with gold filigree and semi precious beads, while the saddles were studded with silver. They stepped high with their heads arched so that their chins almost touched their glossy throats, and the foam on their mouths from the bits only added to the sense that this was a living parade despite the expressionless faces of their riders. The riders wore crowns and diadems looped, strung and fringed with fine gold chains, and their freshly oiled hair shone bright in the sunlight, from pure blond gold to deepest black. The over robes the riders wore were tight fitting and encrusted with precious stones, gorgets and bands of gems that had been worked generations before. So heavily stitched and embroidered were the costumes that they could have been armor.

Every rider's back was as straight as a spear and their faces painted such that aside from their eyes and their hair color the masks of paint were all alike: impersonal white coverings, elongated holes for the eyes to see through, the mouth a cupid bow of red paint. Even the ears and necks of the masked riders were painted white. The leading riders of the train reached the Forum of Constantinople, its great ring of flag stones densely packed with people of all races and classes, from aristocratic families waiting to join the procession to the ordinary people of the city there to gawp and cheer. Because of the circle the line closed up upon itself and the emperor and his private train closed with them. Talon felt overwhelmed by the pomp and the many people clad in such finery.

The personal guard of the emperor was a mixture of fierce looking Norsemen. They were large, blond, and most wore big mustaches and short beards, although a few were beardless. The uniforms over their chain mail were of the finest cloth with richly embroidered hems. Each carried a distinctive one-bladed axe along and bore a kite-like shield on a wide strap across his back. Most of them wore round helmets of plain, polished iron. In some cases the entire face was protected with chain, exposing only the eyes, giving them a dangerous aspect.

Alongside the Norsemen were soldiers of another kind. They were layered in gold and their tunics were of golden hues, rich with embroidery. They carried large shields of burnished bronze that gleamed in the sunlight and their long spears were painted gold. Their helmets were of bronze with gold filigree embossed into the metal, while their upper bodies were clad in molded polished bronze breast plates and shoulder plates that Talon sensed were from another era.

Trumpeters led the procession and their instruments blared at regular intervals, while among them heralds called out praise for the emperor at almost every step of the way. Standard bearers both mounted and on foot carried banners of every color and design it was possible to imagine, but predominant was the double-headed eagle, the crest of the empire. Their ornate felt and silk banners of red, white, blue and green waved in the light breeze as the solemn procession moved slowly by.

As the emperor approached the great ring of the Constantine Forum, young boys and girls walking ahead began to throw late blooming flowers mixed with small clusters of leaves in his path, chanting in high melodious song. The emperor was flanked by men who looked like priests of some kind, whom Talon assumed to be confessors and priests of high office. His horse, clad with a jewel-encrusted harness, was of the whitest pelt and its groomed mane and tail flowed like silk as it moved. Its head was bowed in a collected form that forced it to lift its feet high as it was led slowly forward by two young boys dressed in white tunics holding onto its bridle.

The emperor seated deep in the saddle, held in the crook of his right arm the Imperial Crosier; over his left he carried a long swathe of silk which trailed below his buskin-clad foot, which rested in a silver stirrup.

His tight fitting tunic, stiffened with stays, was of embroidered silk of many colors and patterns. His head was held high above a high stiff collar sewn with gold threads and with twin eagles of the empire on either side of the collar. Emperor Manuel's swarthy visage was calm and his black eyes stared straight ahead, looking neither to right nor left as though he was spiritually removed from the clangor of the parade. His hair and beard were curled and oiled under the wide gold crown from which strings of pearls hung glistening like rain over his broad shoulders which were clad with a golden mantle. The cheering of the crowd, the blaring of the trumpets and the shouts of the heralds were deafening as the procession passed by. Talon glanced about at the cheerful people milling around him. Most appeared to genuinely like the emperor; clearly they liked the parade, which provided a break from their normally humdrum lives.

Immediately behind the emperor and his escorts came the Empress Maria and her glittering escort of notables and ladies in waiting, all mounted upon the finest ponies and horses Talon had ever seen gathered in one place. Her tunic was as richly ornamented as that of the emperor. She wore a cloak of the finest silk with gold and silver thread woven in a wide band around its hem and collar. Her mount, as pure white as her husband's horse, was led by young eunuchs. Talon noted with some surprise that she was a tall woman with hair the color of honey coiffed in long tresses that were held by a jewel-encrusted diadem over which was a diaphanous veil that did little to hide her beauty. The hand that held the reins was as white as a lily, every finger almost hidden with rich and costly rings. The crowd cheered her too and some threw flowers onto her path to join the already trampled clusters of leaves and flowers lying on the road. A light scent of rosewater and lavender lingered with her passing.

Behind her the train of men and women and youths, of officials, nobles, senators and churchmen stretched far off down the tree-lined avenue. Talon could see the riders' plumes dancing to the rhythm of their horses movements while the tramp of the iron shod sandals of the soldiers vied with the shouts of the heralds and the cheers of the crowd.

Alexios explained who the various kinds of soldiers were as they rode by. The Norsemen were indeed Scandinavian and Saxons from the English isles; they were known as Varangians, he told Talon.

"Their company was formed by the grandfather of the emperor Manuel, Alexios I, after whom I was named. They are the personal guard of the emperor."

Alexios pointed to the emperor's immediate escort, each of whom carried a long bladed spear, gilded with gold. Alexios explained that these men were the traditional executioners; their office dated back to the earliest Roman times when the Caesars and emperors of Rome had employed them.

A troop of heavily armed cavalry followed the detachment of Varangians. Their horses and armor gleamed from all the polishing that had been lavished upon them. These horses were of a slightly heavier breed than Talon had encountered in Persia but still lighter than the Destriers he had become familiar with in Languedoc.

"They look like they could be effective," Talon murmured to Sir Guy, who was watching with equal interest as the impassive cohorts rode by, leaving behind a smell of waxed leather and horse sweat.

"I belong to that Tagamet," Alexios said with pride in his voice. "They are called the *Athanatoi*, the deathless ones," Alexios smiled. "I would be riding with them but I am charged with being your host today. Most of the men in this Tagamet belong to the aristocracy, either here in Constantinople or from great families in Thessaly and Thrace and other provinces. Our family came from Anatolia but today most of our possessions lie to the north. We are also known as the *Oikioi*, which means 'Those of the Household.'"

The men of the heavy cavalry were dressed in what appeared to be a type of old fashioned armor, but Alexios assured Talon that the fishlike plates were very solid and could withstand a spear thrust without giving in. Talon observed their expensive gleaming armor, their conical plumed helmets and their kite-like shields. Some of the helmets the men wore were beautifully made of steel with gold and silver inlaid work depicting saints and elaborate images of the Christ. These men carried laminated bows similar to the one he possessed but slightly smaller. They also carried large maces at their belts and long spears with pennants.

He wondered how it would be to face this kind of unit in the field. As he had never been in a full-scale battle before he could only imagine what the effect of such a force would be like. He recalled the Templars and their disciplined charge. These cavalry units looked just as effective.

Behind the heavily armed cavalry came units of heavy infantry, whom Alexios called the *Peltasts*. They tramped by on hobnailed sandals, clothed in heavily padded over-tunics with heavy steel and bronze plates and laminated arm armor. Their spears were about three yards long.

Talon observed with interest as detachment after detachment of armed men rode or tramped by. He noted the light cavalry and related to them, as these men appeared to be fast moving units who rode small but well-bred looking ponies that could be useful against their opposite numbers in any Arab army.

He shook his head. The parade was something quite new to him and he could find no comparison. Despite its splendor, it had been as though hundreds, even thousands of gilded and finely dressed and armored wax dolls had been carried by on horses.

Talon, Sir Guy and Alexios, who had been standing among the dense crowd at the Forum, joined the procession as it moved the last few hundred yards to arrive at the entrance to the Great Palace at the south-east tip of the peninsula. As they approached the huge square in front of the Great Palace, which was packed with soldiers and cavalry of various rank, Talon noted a group of strangely dressed men who were accompanied by an officer of the Imperial guard.

"Who are those people, Alexios?" Talon asked, pointing.

"I am sure that is a Turkish delegation, come from the Sultan of Rum to negotiate with the emperor." Alexios sounded dismissive.

The men they were discussing wore bright single color tunics over trews and knee-high leather boots, jackets of unrefined stitching, and a wide array of felt hats of differing colors. Their clothes denoted tribal origins and were very plain in comparison to those worn by other notables who were present. The men, although dressed differently from the Greeks all around them, were as dark-skinned; but they were easily distinguishable by their long braided hair and huge mustaches. Their fierce dark eyes were watchful as they moved with the rest of the crowd now heading for the maidan in front of the Grand Palace. Talon regarded them without too much curiosity, but he recalled what Sir Guy had said about the Sultanate of Rum pushing into the former empire.

The Turks, Sir Guy had told him, were the main reason that the first and second crusades had happened at all, and the next crusade would without doubt have to cross dominions now held by Seljuk Turks which were no longer those of the former Byzantine Empire.

He also noticed a group of finely dressed men of a lighter complexion who were accompanied by a group of Greek officials dressed in what he now knew to be togas. Alexios, who knew much about the complex array of official titles, told Talon that the escorting Greek notables were *Protospatharioi*, the same senatorial rank as his father. The delegation being escorted was an important one from Persia. They too were known enemies of the Sultan of Rum.

By the time they were moving through the maidan themselves Talon's head was swimming with the information Alexios supplied on the multitude of different nations who were there to witness the parade and, as in their case, seek an audience with the emperor himself. He had seen an Arab delegation and wondered if it had come from the Sultan Salah Ed Din, or Damascus, or perhaps even further afield. There were many groups of emissaries who had clearly come from Europe by their constrained woolen dress that was positively provincial compared to that of the Greeks.

Then there were others who came from Russia and the far north. All had come to see the emperor and seek favors or alliances for trade or military purposes. Alexios was scornful of many that he pointed out and dismissive of some, saying that they were just traders and wasting their time, as the emperor was far too busy to see them all. Most delegations came many times to this square and waited for hours before being rewarded with an audience.

"If we are approached by the *parakoimomemos* we will know that this day you will be received by the emperor." Alexios sounded nervous.

"I shall never get used to all these complicated names. Which one is he?" Talon muttered.

"He is the leader of the Senate and as such will guide you through the interview with the emperor. Since a treaty is in question he will conduct all subsequent discussions and report to the emperor on our progress," Alexios said with a trace of impatience.

"I would like you to become familiar with much of this nation, Talon," Sir Guy admonished Talon out of the corner of his mouth. He got no further, as Alexios was hurrying them along to make sure they had the best view of what was to come.

Talon had no time to dwell upon Sir Guy's admonishment, instead he turned his attention to the huge building they were about to enter. They had to push and squeeze past many people who wanted to watch the spectacle within and who gave way only reluctantly. The large wide square in front of the church of Saint Sophia only just accommodated the procession and the visitors.

He gazed up at the huge construction in front of them. The wide archways supported by slim carved marble pillars were topped with many small domes that guided the eye towards the center tiers, where there were more towers and even more domes on either side of a much larger one; but above that again was the enormous, great dome of the Hagia. The whole building, while massive, gave the impression from the ground where he stood of being rather squat; but he noticed that the further away one stood the taller the whole seemed to be. He had never seen a place of God that was so huge. None of the mosques that he had encountered in Cairo or Alexandria came even close. The builders in those places were only just experimenting with brick and learning its potential, while here the architects seemed to have mastered the basics of brick building and leapt further ahead with stone and marble to create something extraordinary.

As the emperor arrived at the steps that led to the main entrance of the Hagia Sophia on the north side of the square, the Patriarch and his entourage emerged from the entrance of the great church to greet him. This was a no less a magnificently dressed group of people. The white bearded priests, most of them old, some seemingly ancient, wore high black headdresses and jewel encrusted vestments that sparkled in the sunlight. They and their eunuch servants carried large, beautifully wrought crosses of ivory and gold, while the icons set in gold inlaid boxes they held on high were of priceless gold-inlaid carved wood with painted, gold leafed figures of the virgin and child.

The emperor dismounted and, assisted by plumed and bejeweled eunuchs, slowly approached the Patriarch, Michael III of Anchialus. All knelt as the Patriarch and the emperor met and exchanged the kiss of the faith on both cheeks.

Sir Guy seized Jonathan by the scruff of his neck and forced him to his knees. Martin rapidly followed suit. Talon had anticipated the moment and with Max and Claude crashed to his knees along with ten thousand citizens of Constantinople in a mute sound of shuffles followed by a suspended silence of respect.

The two most powerful men in the empire of Byzantium walked sedately side by side into the vast interior of the Hagia Sophia followed by the most noble and important officers of the realm. Those who were envoys hopeful of an audience this day were allowed in behind them, and this included the Knights Templar and their two monks.

"We will stay on the edge of the crowd and wait for a signal," Alexios whispered to Sir Guy as they followed the perfumed royalty and their nobility up the wide stairs. "The Liturgy will be said by the Patriarch and then the main service will commence," he added.

There was a long silence inside the vast chamber, broken only by the occasional cough or snuffle, but even that died down as the crowd within waited in hushed anticipation for the service to begin. Talon stared about. This place of worship was brightly lit by hundreds, perhaps thousands, of candles, some as thick as a man's upper arm. The walls were covered from top to bottom with fine, intricately worked gold and silver inlaid frescoes of saints and emperors that gleamed with an ethereal glow in the candlelight. Huge brass chandeliers hung overhead alongside bronze pots that smoked with incense, supported by chains that disappeared into the gloom of the dome. Intricately carved stonework was suspended from pillars and arches overhead while in places along the curved wall were long, thin windows, through which streamed beams of sunlight. Talon and his companions could only stare in wonder and awe at the magnificence that surrounded them.

In the echoing vault of the great church the voice of the Patriarch was lifted in prayer that broke the silence.

"In peace let us pray to the Lord."

"*Lord have mercy,*" the crowd chanted.

"For the peace of God and the salvation of our souls, let us pray to the Lord."

"*Lord have mercy.*"

"For the peace of the world, for the stability of the holy churches of God, and the fear of God, let us pray to the Lord."

"*Lord have mercy.*"

Talon became aware that the strong smell of incense from the pots hanging overhead was beginning to permeate the air within.

The passion and the echoes of the divine liturgy of the Greek Church climbed to the great heights of the vast dome of Sophia and echoed off the pillars and curved walls. It was a haunting refrain that had been repeated down the long ages since the time of Constantine, and all who heard it were imbued with a sense of holiness.

The liturgy and the canon with its refrains was replaced by the high tenors of song. Talon heard the strange music of what he now knew to be the organs that, although hidden, resonated through his very soul. There was now a solo voice chanting.

"*Who is great like our God? You are the God who performs miracles.*"

This was followed by the chant from the mass of people clustered in the naves and under the great arches of the church. "*Lord have mercy.*"

Then the high voices of the boys in the choir soared as one crystal clear note above the crowd to penetrate deep into the shadows and crevices of the massive ancient church, which rebounded with echoes so that the notes seemed to come from everywhere at once. All present were now absolutely still, even those who had been here a hundred times, as the *castrati* went through their song of praise to God.

Talon felt the hair on his forearms tingle as he listened. He craned his neck to stare into the high shadows of the dome, past the light from hundreds of lamps, candles and smoking incense pots, and wondered to himself at the power of song and praise. He became aware that these ceremonies he was experiencing had been repeated for centuries in this church that was the shrine of heaven on earth, while the emperor, the consecrated leader and lord of his people here in Constantinople, was to these people the ambassador of God on earth.

Despite himself he was awed by the majesty of the ceremony and the rite as it unfolded before him.

The Patriarch went through the *First Antiphon* and the second then the third, followed by the Psalms and the *Apolytikon*. Talon's mind became almost numb from the repetition.

Then the choir began to sing the *Akathesos Kotakion* and the boys' crystal clear voices again soared into the heavens above. Talon stood stock still and absorbed the music both from the choir and the organs through his very being. It was clear that the entire assembly was rooted to the intricately tiled mosaic of the floor as they listened to the heavenly music, which eventually died away, leaving a strange empty silence behind. Talon's breast ached and he could almost imagine men weeping at the loss of that sound. Then after a long silence when the very last of the echoes had died away, the Patriarch's low voice could be heard again.

"Lord, You have given us grace to offer these common prayers with one heart. You have promised to grant the requests of those gathered in Your name. Fulfill now the petitions of Your servants for our benefit, giving us the knowledge of Your truth in this world, and granting us eternal life in the world to come."

They stood for seeming hours as the service continued towards its conclusion and the *Eucharistic* rites drew to a close, leaving Talon exhausted. He glanced at his companions and found Sir Guy staring up into the deep recesses of the dome while Max and Claude heads were bowed over their clasped hands.

Martin was on his knees, a look of wonder on his young face, his hands clasped together under his chin. Brother Jonathan was on his knees too, but on his face was a scowl of disapproval. Talon wondered why.

Later came the blessing and then the dismissal, followed by the scrape of shoes and boots on the smooth marble and the rustle of expensive silks and stiff clothing as people roused themselves. Nobles, Senators and officials prepared to leave the church, and some would even leave with the emperor.

The Patriarch and the Emperor left first, led by a boy who waved the chained incense bowl to left and right, letting the light smoke drift to either side. The two leaders were followed by the empress and her ladies, who were accompanied by the royal children dressed in their finery, looking straight ahead as they departed for the Grand Palace on the opposite side of the square, where they would remain for the rest of the day. The crowd in the naves and under the arches of the Hagia gradually dispersed, most leaving the square, but the emissaries coagulated into their national groups in front of the massive gates of the Grand Palace to wait the pleasure of the emperor. The troops who were to go back to their barracks formed up and were marched out of the square, the rhythmic crash of their hob-nailed sandals receding into the distance, leaving a curious quiet in the maidan. But then the buzz of conversation in many tongues commenced.

Rainer Rilke

Chapter 8
The Audience

The two Knights Templar stood out in their chain mail with the crosses embroidered on the left breast of their surcoats. They wore their distinctive white cloaks with each side thrown back over their shoulders, and as they did not carry their helmets their heads were bare, their chain hoods down. Their sergeants were dressed in darker clothing, almost black, denoting their rank, and they too wore chain. The two monks were clad in their threadbare habits with the hoods thrown back, which showed that they were tonsured men of God. Talon wrinkled his nose at the smell emanating from Jonathan. Martin had somehow managed to become reasonably clean, but Jonathan's nose still dripped and the sleeve of his habit was again becoming stiff with dry mucus from the wiping. He and Martin carried the presents from King Baldwin for the emperor wrapped in better cloth than they wore: two gold inset books of the saints that had been painstakingly put together by the monks of the Church of the Holy Sepulcher in Jerusalem. Sir Guy had said to Talon somewhat ruefully, "They are poor gifts for one such as the Emperor of Byzantium, he who must have had riches beyond measure presented to him from kings of Persia and Europe before. But...the Kingdom of Jerusalem has the one thing no one else does: the center of the Christian Faith. Hence the books."

It was many minutes of waiting in the sunlight before Alexios touched Sir Guy on the arm and nodded in the direction of a small group of Greek officials making their way toward them through the crowd of would-be supplicants.

"See the large hat?" he murmured. "That would be the *protospatharios*. He is a very high-ranking officer in the Sword bearers, the Emperor's Body Guard. I think we will be commanded to follow him."

They were all suddenly alert and self-conscious. The official, accompanied by several other men including four golden guards, walked up to Alexios and, with a polite nod to Sir Guy, asked a question.

"Are the Templars ready to be taken before the emperor?"

"Yes, my Lord, they are ready," Alexios responded.

"Then you are to follow me." Without another glance at them he turned on his heel and led the way through the murmuring crowd of many nations.

Talon glanced at his companions and was glad to see that they seemed as awed with expectation as he was. The two Brothers were speechless, which was gratifying in the case of Brother Jonathan. Martin, he noted, was looking around with eyes bright with interest. The boy seemed to prefer to stay close to Talon as though their similar ages might be reassuring.

The extravagance of the interior of the palace halls was spectacular. They were led towards another tall building across a courtyard populated with statues and fountains. Gold inlaid bronze statues of children and dolphins gamboled in the water of the fountains, while the carved stone of the many pillars was remarkable. The amount of gold mosaic and precious metal inlay made one blink when struck by sunlight. The multitude of different palace troops and the army of exotically dressed servants and eunuchs hurrying to and fro were overwhelming to the small group of Templars who followed their guide to a tall edifice that Alexios called the Court of Daphne. They were informed at this point that their swords were to be handed over to the guards and they could collect them on their way out.

The interior of the building was ablaze with light from the hundreds of candles in every hall that reflected off the gold and silver hangings. They passed several other parties of emissaries, and again Talon caught a glimpse of the Turkish delegation. This time they passed close enough for the men in each group to size one another up. The man who appeared to lead the Turkish group was tall and well built. A long scar across the top of his forehead ended over his right eyebrow. It gave him a stern, concentrated look that Talon felt bore into him even after they had passed. They exchanged cool stares but otherwise did not pause as their respective guides hurried them along. Perhaps the Turks had already been before the emperor, for they were being ushered in another direction.

To Talon's surprise he heard Farsi being spoken as they walked past a large group of elaborately dressed Persians huddled in a corner near a sleek marble pillar. They paused to stare after the Templars as they went by, so Talon did not hear anything more than the brief word. But he did notice a smaller group of men who stayed apart and turned away as they passed. Their mode of dress looked familiar, but he could not in that moment remember where he had encountered it before; besides, he needed to focus, as they were now being ushered into an inner sanctum. This would be where Sir Guy had to make his case for the Templars.

Two Officers of the Imperial Guard stood in front of the double bronze doors to the throne room. These men were armored in molded cuirasses and carried the lozenge-like shields of bronze. Their helmets were gleaming bronze with elaborate inlaid silver depictions of the saints. Alexios muttered to Talon that although they looked like doorkeepers, they were in fact important officials of the court and should be treated with great respect whenever encountered on the streets.

They were announced to the company at large by the *protospatharios* who had led them this far. Their names and titles were called out and called out again at the other end of the room while they waited. Talon could see down a long passage between a rainbow of colorful costumes on both men and women to the throne of the Emperor, and to his left another where sat the Empress of Byzantium.

The chamber was lined from the door to the thrones at the far end with people. Down the center of the path straight to the thrones lay a thick woven carpet of Persian origins along which the small group now walked very slowly behind the *protospatharios*.

Talon observed the vaulted roof supported by slim marble pillars, on either side of which were arched windows of colored glass that tinted the sunlight pouring through. Where the floor of polished marble met the walls, the frescoes began. They depicted former emperors and empresses surrounded by angels and their followers. The tiny tiles fitted so well that they gave the impression of being facets that gleamed in the lamplight, the gold and silver colors lighting up the walls. Many of the frescos depicted emperors and their wives accompanied by their children and wise men of the church. Patriarchs with long flowing beards stood or knelt alongside the emperors, their eyes raised to heaven, their hands clasped in prayer, their heads surrounded by golden halos.

He saw someone step onto the dais before the throne of the emperor, kneel, and present him with a large parchment that was the one Sir Guy had taken to the first meeting with his counterparts several weeks ago.

Both thrones were of ivory and gold, with rich felt cloth emblazoned with the eagles woven into the corners. The two figures seated were motionless, as though they were large gilded marionettes. Talon did not detect much life in them until they drew near. Then it became clear that the man on the throne was of a strong athletic build, and despite the finery Talon sensed a person of strong will and intelligence. He sensed too that their party was being scrutinized as it approached.

He cast a quick look at the empress and was struck again by her golden beauty. Her hair was spun gold and her calm features were white as snow. At her side and behind the throne was a small cluster of her ladies-in-waiting. They resembled angels gathered about their Madonna. All were of singular beauty and their rich dresses and glittering diadems gave them an ethereal glow. Again he felt that they were being watched with interest, this time by the ladies-in-waiting as they approached.

The Emperor lifted his hand and the official stood up and stepped to the side, but he beckoned to their guide that they should come forward. Talon was pleased with himself for remembering that this man was the *parakoimomemos;* the High Chamberlain, who was a eunuch; dressed in his finery one would have been forgiven for mistaking him for royalty itself.

Talon also remembered that Sir Guy had been told that both he and his entourage were expected to fall to their knees before the throne and shuffle forward in that mode before kissing the ground in front of the emperor. Sir Guy had discussed this with his group and said, "I might be a supplicant, but no Templar kisses the feet of anyone; so you will follow my moves exactly and do nothing else. I am the only person allowed to speak, and this will be done through an interpreter. You, Talon and Brother Jonathan, will listen carefully and relate all you have heard to me later after the audience."

Their guide, the *protospatharios,* began to walk forward in a slow, deliberate gait towards the thrones. Talon became aware that among this glittering throng, especially gathered near to the throne, were many very powerful men who might well influence the final decision of the emperor at some stage. He did not envy

Sir Guy his task after what he had heard about the previous crusade. At about ten paces before the throne their guide went down upon his knees and shuffled forward to stop directly before the throne of the emperor. At this point he kissed the foot of the emperor and then sat back on his heels, his head bowed.

Sir Guy, instead of going to his knees, bowed very low. The other men followed suit, and then Sir Guy walked forward, Talon one pace behind and the two sergeants one pace behind him, with the monks one pace behind them again. Sir Guy walked the remaining distance then went down on one knee before the emperor and again bowed his head.

The maneuver had brought a hiss of surprise and disapproval from the attendants and nobles clustered about the area near the front of the throne, but Sir Guy ignored them. He lifted up the document that carried the seal of King Baldwin with both hands for the *parakoimomemos* to take. The man presented it to the emperor, who touched it with the fingers of his right hand, and the document disappeared into the hands of the dignitaries clustered behind the throne.

Sir Guy indicated to the two monks that he wanted the presents brought forward, and these were passed to him still wrapped in silk cloth. He held both out towards the emperor with his arms straight and his head bowed. Talon marveled at his strength, for the books were huge and doubtless heavy. A eunuch took the presents and held them before the Emperor and Empress with the coverings taken off for a few long moments. No one opened the books.

There were formal murmurs of appreciation and the presents were whisked out of sight.

Sir Guy and his men stayed in front of the emperor in the kneeling position, heads bowed, awaiting his pleasure.

Manuel I spoke. Talon found with surprise that he could follow most of the words, but he did not show it and kept his head bowed. The strong voice stopped and the man who interpreted, the *hypobolius,* commenced to translate the emperor's words into flawless French. Talon could find no fault with the words and concentrated on what was being said.

"We are pleased to see the notable Order of the Templars in our court once again."

Sir Guy responded, "It is a great honor for me to be present before your most Exulted Majesty and to represent my Order and King Baldwin before you today, Sire."

"We have read your petition from the King of Jerusalem, Sir Guy, and we will ponder its implications."

"On behalf of the King of Jerusalem, Sire, I am to pass to you his sincere greetings and love. We are in your debt and will await your pleasure in this matter."

Another voice spoke. "Will your Majesty allow me to talk to the Templars to hear the news from Jerusalem?"

It was spoken in French and came from the empress by his side; the emperor responded in the same language.

"I understand your wish, my Queen. We will have time for that after we have made our decision on the first subject, but your opinion will be required for the other matter."

"Thank you, my Lord."

The emperor lifted his hand and the interpreter said, "His Majesty has finished the audience. You are to await his pleasure."

Sir Guy responded, "Your Majesty, I thank you for this great honor. May we stay in the city and await your summons?"

The emperor spoke in rapid Attic Greek.

"They are to stay in the palace, as I wish to speak to them in my private chambers after I have completed my audiences here. See to it, Senator. Within two hours at the most."

The *protospatharios* bowed his head to the floor and slid backwards to stand beside Sir Guy.

"The audience is over, Sir Guy. We will leave now."

Sir Guy stood up and waited until his small retinue had done the same. He then bowed very low and backed away from the thrones. When they were about ten paces back he bowed again, then turned and led the way past the curious throng of courtiers and notables who had been watching them. The murmuring receded as they exited.

As they came out of the main entrance they collected their swords and then waited until the Senator had joined them.

"Do we leave now?" Sir Guy asked the *protospatharios*.

Talon held his tongue.

"No Sir Guy, he wishes to see you within two hours at his private chambers to which I shall now take you. We will await him there."

"Will the Empress be there too?"

"I cannot say, Sir Guy."

Both the *protospatharios* and the *hypobolius* stayed with them as they made their way down long passageways lined with marble columns and very lifelike statues of warriors and athletes to an anteroom where they were invited to be seated.

Servants brought honeyed cakes and clear water for them while they waited.

Sir Guy did not invite conversation at this point, having warned his men previously that everyone in the palace was a spy and anything they said would be reported back to the emperor. He did not want any loose tongues to jeopardize his mission.

In fact they waited three hours before the same official, the *parakoimomemos*, came to collect them and guide them along some more corridors to another bronze door. Again they were relieved of their weapons and allowed to enter another sumptuous room. This time, however, there were only a few attendants upon the emperor. Talon noticed that the empress was absent.

Emperor Manuel the First was standing this time, as though he had tired of being seated. There was a small throne under a canopy at the far end of the room. He waited through the repeated introductions and the kneeling of the knights then addressed Sir Guy, "Please rise, Sir Guy. Your men may stand."

Manuel addressed Sir Guy in Greek, although it was now clear he could speak good French. Talon supposed it was for the benefit of his senior advisors, as not all of them spoke that language. The *hypobolius* translated, and the emperor spoke again.

"We have some serious concerns about the proposal for another crusade coming through our lands, Sir Guy. What guarantees do the kings of the west make that there will not be a repeat of the pillaging and rapine that accompanied the last crusade?"

"My Lord, Your Majesty. That is the reason I am here in my capacity of Knight Templar. It is the wish of the Grand Master of my Order that we the Templars meet the crusading armies at your borders and ensure from there onwards that there is no untoward behavior."

The emperor stroked his beard thoughtfully. "We understand that the Templars are a well disciplined body of men and we respect that. They demonstrated their discipline the last time but... not even they could enforce the law and police the Germans and the Franks when they arrived at the gates of Our city. Had I not reinforced my own walls it is quite possible that their barbaric hoards would have assaulted my city and pillaged it for themselves!"

"I was there, your Majesty. I was deeply shamed by what happened, but my Grand Master and indeed the king have both pledged that they will insist that the kings or leaders of any further crusades abide by strict rules of the march. Oaths will be taken to that effect. The Templars are pledged to stay with them all the way from your western borders to the time when they reach our lands in the south."

One of the officials leaned close to Manuel and whispered something to him. The emperor nodded as though in agreement

"Sir Guy, my advisor the *Korapalates*, my Master of the Household, has mentioned something of importance. How will the armies feed themselves on the march?"

Sir Guy glanced at the official as though assessing his opposition. The official was older than most in the room, his grey-flecked beard and lined face denoted a man of great experience. He returned Sir Guy's enquiring look with a trace of defiance.

The advisor addressed Sir Guy directly after a nod of permission from the emperor.

"Sir Guy, one of the singular problems for an army on the march has to do with its provisions. Some march with the aim of feeding off the country as they go. This is what happened the last time and it led to terrible hardships for those in its path. The two armies were as locusts. The Germans in particular took most of what they wanted without payment of any sort, and when they were resisted they simply plundered. When the Franks came behind them it was worse, as there was nothing left to provide them with. We cannot allow that to happen the next time...if there is a next time." He glanced at the Emperor as he said this. "How do you propose to avoid this situation?"

"Your Majesty, my Lords." Sir Guy addressed the entire company. "I have been given dispensation to negotiate the beginning of this agreement, but only in principle. I anticipate that there must be more negotiations, of course. However, I am authorized to inform you that The Templar Order has pledged that it will finance much of the provisioning for the armies in question. This can be either payment to you or to them for their needs."

There was silence while those present digested this piece of information. Then the same official said, "Can the Templars indeed afford to pay so much?" His tone was surprised and even skeptical.

Sir Guy gave a wry smile. "We were originally asked to finance the building of a fleet, my Lord. That we could not do without grave loss to our treasury, but we could certainly help a king feed an army."

"You need those armies in Palestine, Sir Guy. I understand," the Emperor interjected. "Perhaps we can think about this some more."

He went and sat down on the throne, and then he leaned on his elbow as he spoke.

"You must understand that my father and I have had work to do just to regain losses sustained on all our borders. We are threatened by enemies from the east as well as to the west so it would be very hard for me to provide an army to assist the kings. However, if the Templars are ready to place a reasonable amount of money on the table in the form of compensation, I will do what I can to assist. There is much to negotiate, and Our mind is not made up as yet. The people of my country have very long memories."

Sir Guy bowed low. "Your Majesty, my Lords, I am honored that you have even given me the opportunity to put my case to you, and I thank you on behalf of the Grand Master and King Baldwin of Jerusalem."

The Emperor clapped his hands and servants came hurrying in with trays of sweetmeats and wine.

"Then let us celebrate our continued relationship with the Order of the Templars despite any disagreements in the past," he said.

The people in the room visibly relaxed and Talon and Sir Guy were offered wine.

"Who is this young knight who accompanies you, Sir Guy?" Manuel asked in French.

"Your Majesty, may I present Sir Talon de Gilles, a trusted colleague and...a friend." Sir Guy smiled at Talon as he said this.

Talon bowed very low. "Your Majesty. I am deeply honored to be here in your presence," he spoke in French, which was rapidly translated.

Manuel nodded his head.

"I see we have Alexios Kalothesos with us today as well. How is your father?" he inquired.

Alexios flushed and bowed. "My father is well, your Majesty. He hopes to be in attendance at the next chariot races if it pleases you."

"Well, let us hope that Pantoleon does not start another riot this time," Manuel said. His comment drew a titter from the attendants. "We will be watching the games of *tzykanion* within the next few weeks here at the palace. We will be pleased for you to attend, Sir Guy."

"I shall be honored. Sire. Sir Talon has played Arab Polo. I am informed that he is very good at it. May I bring him too?"

This last comment was greeted with a low murmur of surprise from those present.

Manuel raised his eyebrows and looked at Talon as though reappraising him. "The game of *tzykanion* is not the same as that of the Arabs, Sir Talon, but as you will see it is somewhat similar. I am sure you'll enjoy watching it. I did not know you Franks played Polo with the Arabs, Sir Guy. That is interesting. I thought you were at war."

Sir Guy had the wits to remain silent, but he bowed his head just a little in acknowledgement of the barb.

"The sport that was given us from the Frankish lands was that of jousting," Manuel continued. "I myself have taken part in this and enjoy it, although my officials disapprove, but I have not met a Frank who could play the 'Game of Kings' before." He seemed to be amused as though he did not quite believe Sir Guy, but he was in an expansive mood. "Bring all your people, Sir Guy. We would like to entertain you while you are here."

He looked as though he was about to dismiss them when the chamberlain moved forward and whispered to him.

"Ah, yes, I had almost forgotten. We wish to invite you and Sir Talon here to a banquet this evening in honor of the Empress. We can discuss the other matter at a later date, Sir Guy."

Sir Guy bowed low. "I thank you, your Majesty. I will be honored to attend."

They bowed themselves out of the chamber.

*****

That evening Sir Guy and Talon, accompanied by their two sergeants, presented themselves at the main entrance to the Great Palace. By now Talon knew that this place name embraced at least five palaces he had heard mentioned. An officer who stood with the sentries inspecting papers at the doorway scrutinized the letter provided by the chamberlain. He waved them through without taking their weapons this time and motioned for a eunuch to lead them to the palace where the banquet was to be held.

Led by the eunuch, who was dressed in expensive colorful clothes that made the Templars look plain by comparison, they made their way along corridors and across wide, echoing hallways to their destination. The bustle of the day had been replaced by activity in places other than the huge administrative complex.

It was not long before they heard the murmur of many voices as they approached the entrance to another enormous room. It was as richly furnished as the audience chamber but somewhat smaller, and contained several large tables placed right in the center of the room. There were two chairs for the royals placed upon a low platform that overlooked the tables used by the guests. The thrones were placed to face the room but behind a low table.

From the glazed marble floor to the distant roof, the walls were decorated with frescoes depicting the royal families of previous generations and charioteer races. Ubiquitous among all the artwork were the saints and the members of the Patriarchy, all of whom were decorated with golden haloes. The chamber was ablaze with hundreds of oil lamps.

The eunuch led them along the central corridor covered by priceless hand woven carpets towards the banquet table where other guests were already seated. The two sergeants were officially on duty, so they joined the guards standing along the wall to the chamber. The Templars were to be treated as special guests, seated near to the high table of the Emperor and his Empress.

Sir Guy was on a nodding acquaintance with several of the guests and he greeted in a friendly manner Alexios Bryennios, the Prefect of the City, and John Komateros. These were the men with whom Sir Guy had been working over the details of the marriage alliance. They nodded and smiled at Sir Guy as he and Talon sat down. Talon realized that the negotiations must have gone reasonably well if they were to have a dinner with the royal family.

They heard the sound of trumpets and a eunuch announced the arrival of the Emperor and his Empress. All stood while Manuel with his Empress Maria made their entrance. There was no special fanfare; they walked in and greeted the guests, then when they had been seated, Manuel waved his hand and the guests took their seats. The moment the Emperor sat down to dine they heard the sound of flutes and pipes in the background. The gargantuan feast got underway in a most orderly manner.

*****

Talon and Sir Guy made their way back to the inn in a state of bemused astonishment at the huge variety of food that had appeared and disappeared in front of them. They had learned belatedly that one only took a small portion each time a dish appeared under one's nose, as to eat the whole plate required speed and left one with little room for the next, which arrived the moment the Emperor decided that he was ready for another.

"I swear that the only dish I really remember from the feast is that fish," Talon said and burped as though to emphasize his statement.

"You mean the fish stew, the one called *Kakavia*?" Sir Guy asked as he stopped to take in the view, for the moon was high and the sight north of the city at this time of night was worth the pause.

"I had thought we would be discussing the marriage at the feast."

"No, we were simply placed high at the table as a mark of regard. It can do us no harm," Sir Guy said.

Talon remembered how remote from the guests the royal couple had been. The food that came their way was sealed before it left the kitchens and only unsealed by a eunuch just before it was very carefully placed in front of them. They would take a nibble and then wave the food away. It was almost comical, because the guests could barely get hold of a morsel before it too would be whisked away and another equally delicious, mouthwatering serving was placed in its stead. Thus there had been little conversation at the great feast. The guests had been concentrating on eating what they could get their forks to in a timely manner.

Chapter 9

Stone Work

Sir Guy, being of a pious disposition, never tired of visiting churches and the massive monuments, be they Christian structures or the ancient temples of past gods or the memorials that were to be found in almost every corner of the city, and Talon was eagerly shared that interest.

He pointed to the complex of domes and pillars of the Grand Palace in the distance and asked Sir Guy, "Is that where the Emperor lives?"

Sir Guy shook his head. "No, not any longer. They used to, but now the Emperor and his Empress live at the other end of the city. It is possible that the Blachernae Palace is a much quieter area of the city. The Great Palace is now where the government of the empire is conducted."

Talon had to digest that, then he asked, "Does he rule by decree like the King or a Sultan?"

"There was a time when the Emperor used to have to go to the senate for consultation before he undertook a great task like war. Today it is different. He rules and they agree." He gave his slow smile.

Talon laughed. "Then it *is* by decree."

"It is complicated but very efficient, because there is much that he does not have to concern himself with and that is taken care of by officials at the Great Palace. I could swear that every administrator there who deals with money or taxes or organization, such as for armies and the provisions for the navy, is a eunuch," Sir Guy said with a dry laugh. "The Emperor simply makes a statement and they implement it, but that gives them great power too."

*****

Sir Guy had to go off to the Great Palace to negotiate with the Greeks for the conditions of the dowry. Talon begged off from that arduous task and contented himself with walking among the crowded avenues. He would take Martin with him on occasion, as it was clear from the young monk's demeanor that he enjoyed every minute of these expeditions.

Once their curiosity took them down an unusual street. Hitherto Talon had seen all the usual trappings of an industrious city: the leather makers at their tanneries and the stink of urine that went with them, the shops of pottery workers and of carpenters, where they saw the most incredible carvings he had ever seen and which made Martin almost drool as his hands caressed the smooth curved shapes of animals and designs.

This street, however, was one of the quietest they had ventured into; everywhere they looked they could see great blocks of marble, limestone and alabaster lying in open yards alongside the street. Most of the waiting blocks had grass growing all around them, indicating that they had been there a long time. There was even a large wagon parked against a wall with a huge block of white stone tied to it but no activity nearby. As they walked down the street, passing open doorways, hearing the sound of crying babies, and observing little urchins watching them from the steps, they heard voices and the tap-tapping of metal tools on stone. Approaching a large archway that led into an enclosed yard, they saw that it was full of men sitting, squatting and standing on top of ladders tapping away at stone statues and forms of every size and shape.

A man in a short tunic and a leather apron around his waist into which he had placed his tools in fitted pockets noticed them and beckoned them in. Martin shot a look at Talon, who nodded, and they stepped into the yard. The man smiled and asked them a question, but neither understood. He repeated the question more slowly this time, and this time they both understood. Martin pointed to Talon.

"He is a Templar, we are from Palestine," he said in Greek, smiling at the man.

"Ah! You are here to visit our fair city." He nodded and clapped his hands together, creating a small cloud of dust, then he offered his hand for them to clasp. His palm was as hard and dry as a piece of weathered wood. He was covered in dust from the top of his gray head of hair to his sandals, but his smile was welcoming.

"You like the stone work?" he asked with a gap-toothed smile, waving his arms at the activity all around. Talon glanced about and noted that many of the workers were mere boys. They were covered from head to foot with stone dust making them look oddly white.

Martin nodded happily. "I admire stone work. We use limestone in my home country." The man seemed pleased and then proceeded to show them about the yard. Talon noted that Martin seemed enthralled by the intricate work they were witnessing and unable to keep his fingers off the smooth finished work.

Finally the man, whose name they had discovered was Sabas, brought them in front of a complex piece of stonework and stopped.

"This is for the palace, and we are behind with the work but it is almost finished, as you can see."

They could see, and Talon was amused to note that Martin, while he blushed like a girl, was unable to take his eyes off the finely finished and smoothed piece in front of them.

It was a half-sized stone statuette of a slim nymph standing near to a pond leaning over with one delicate hand poised to touch a huge carp that had its head out of the water and its mouth open. Her body was draped with a tunic which was clearly was not meant to hide her form. Talon was astonished to note how well the stonemason had captured the expression of deep tenderness on her features that were framed by hair that had begun to escape from its combs. Her feet were encased in sandals, which were perfectly cut, while her shape was that of a lissome young woman.

Martin was blushing furiously and glanced guiltily at Talon, who was watching him and returned the look with an amused smile. Talon was surprised when Martin reached out and touched the stone, almost caressing it. "It is so beautiful. How it is done to this detail I cannot tell." He turned to Sabas. "Who made this?" he asked, his voice full of awe.

"I and my apprentice." Sabas shrugged as though it were nothing.

"You are a master!" Martin exclaimed and clearly meant it.

Sabas smiled in a depreciating manner and offered them wine, but Talon wanted to rejoin his companions at the inn, as he thought Sir Guy might have returned from his meetings. They bade the stonemason goodbye and made their way back up the street.

While they were walking back Martin was silent until finally Talon asked him, "Did you not like the stone work, Martin?"

The boy turned to look straight at Talon. His hazel eyes were bright with excitement and the look he gave Talon was almost challenging.

"These creations they have made can only be there because God gave them the inspiration. I love the stonework, I...I almost became a stone worker, but my father, who was a mason, said that the Church was a better place to live and learn. But sometimes I miss the feel of stone and what it feels to make it mine." His tone became wistful.

Talon was taken aback by the emotion in the monk's voice and stopped in the middle of the street.

"You did not feel they were blasphemy, Martin?"

Martin shook his head vehemently. "Of course not, Sir Talon. The churches and buildings in this city are akin to a gateway to heaven." He stopped, his eyes widened as though thought he feared he might have said too much, but Talon took his arm and said, "No, Martin. I agree with you, and wholeheartedly. There is so much beauty here. I cannot get enough of this great city, but...I am surprised that you, a man of the church...of Rome, should say this when your companion, Jonathan seems to find nothing to please him in this city."

The monk shook his head. "He is really a good man, Sir Talon, but...he follows the doctrine very closely, and there is disagreement between the churches. He does not care to see beyond that. It does not mean that one should decry their art and creations. We see nothing of this in Acre. I wonder why?"

*****

After the first invitation to the villa of the family Kalothesos, Talon found that he was a regular guest. Joannina appeared to like him and invited him to walk with her in the gardens, where she plied him with questions about life in Palestine. He realized after a while that the Greeks yearned for access to the Holy Land but were restrained by the feeling that it was a crude and barbarous place now that the Franks had invested in it with their own people.

Even her daughter Theodora had thawed enough towards him to offer to take him to the schools she went to, buried in among the buildings of the Great Palace. His fascination with the city evidently appealed to her, and thus it was that she became something of a guide. She took great pride in showing him the churches that seemed to be everywhere. Often he heard bells chiming a light sound that rang with a high note. It was quite different from the quiet of the mosques he was familiar with, and the other thing he noticed was the lack of people calling men to prayers. He had become so used to *Adhan,* the call to prayer, sung out by the *muezzin* in the mosques of Cairo five times a day that he actually noted its absence.

He observed too that the churches did not have the cool squares and archways that characterized the mosques, where the imams and students could sit in the shade of the trees and discuss the laws and codes of Islam in the calm atmosphere of the enclosed courtyards. However, they more than made up for this lack of comfort with their exquisite frescoes and the stunning images of saints and Emperors depicted in pious stances with more gold leaf than he had ever seen before. He understood that these were a very pious people despite their wide assortment of dress and their freedom of expression.

*****

Alexios was determined to help Talon improve his Attic Greek and kept him working on the language by challenging him to chess, which they played in the mornings under the shade of the olive trees that dotted the gardens of the villa. Theodora once came by and challenged him to a game. He found it unnerving as she took him to pieces very quickly, much to his chagrin and the vast amusement of Alexios, who later admitted that she could beat him too, more often than not.

While walking with them in the garden one day Talon felt they had become friendly enough to ask, as he turned to Alexios and Joannina, "Tell me, why does the Senator dislike the Franks so?"

Joannina spoke up. "His opinion of them is not high. The Franks appear to be ignorant of most things other than fighting and have little wish to learn from anyone. They and the Germans came through here twenty years ago on their way to the Holy Land and left a swathe of destruction. We could not believe how barbaric their ways were! They quarreled with everyone, and each other, and the whole city was in fear lest they plunder Constantinople instead of going on their way."

"You will have noticed, Talon, that we Romans have certain... refinements that do not sit well with Franks," Alexios said. "No one doubts that they can fight well, but that seems to be all they can do. Even their fighting prowess was not enough for them last time, because they were defeated by the Turks. The Germans had to scuttle home, and the story is that the French King blundered about all over the countryside before he finally made it to Jerusalem. That crusade was a debacle!"

"Hmm, what you are saying is that the Latin people, we Franks, do not believe in 'Diplomacy' as you call it?"

"Exactly, Talon! When faced with a superior force, diplomacy and negotiation are often the answer, although Manuel might disagree with me on that point from time to time. He has used the bludgeon more often than diplomacy lately."

"What do you mean?"

"You might not have noticed, but the area designated as the Venetian quarter is empty. The emperor Manuel arrested every one of the Venetians a few years ago on suspicion of treachery and threw them all into prison. Our jails are full of those people; only a very few got away."

"Why would he do this?" Talon asked, puzzled. "I thought you told me that he liked the Latin ways as they call them here."

"He is a man of contradictions. But the Venetians were very much disliked. They had special trading privileges that no one else had, not even the Genoese. They paid only seventeen instead of the usual thirty solidi for each ship that sails into Constantinople. As a result the Venetians became richer than anyone else very quickly. Furthermore, the Venetians were arrogant; they rioted and clashed with the other Latins, the Genoese and Pizans, then with the Greeks of Byzantium. It vexed the citizens no end, I can tell you. Eventually they put pressure upon the Emperor to do something to curb their excesses."

As they were walking up to the loggia, they were joined by Theodora, who linked her arm with that of her brother. She had just overheard the last remark.

"They were pigs!" she stated as though that explained it all. Talon had to control his laughter at her decisiveness.

"Theodora! Mind your tongue, young lady!" her mother said sharply. Theodora scowled, quite unrepentant, then directed a cheeky quirk of her mouth at her brother who pretended to be looking elsewhere.

"Were the Venetians very important to the empire to have gained so much in the way of privilege before they fell into disfavor?" Talon asked when he had recovered his composure.

"They were and perhaps are still very important to the empire, as they have the ability to muster large navies. But they are always looking out for the Venetians and they caused many problems. They, and most of the other Latins, are disliked by the local merchants in the city. None of us like them very much."

"We are not merchants, my dear," Joannina admonished her son.

"Aristocrats do not deal with those mucky people," Theodora stated; it was clear she was pretending to sound pompous.

Alexios looked exasperated. "True, Mother, but we, like many people, invested in trade with the Venetians through agents, and some lost all they had when those people were arrested. Merchants we might not be, but Papa still invested heavily with them, as you know. We stand to lose even more if they stay in prison much longer. Makarios is desperate; he does not know how to dispose of what we have in our warehouses."

Joannina looked pensive and looked over to Talon. "You must understand, Talon, that our family used to own large estates in those areas now under the control of the Turks which they call Rum. We were fortunate in that we were able to bring a lot of that wealth out with us. But here one must place one's money somewhere, so we employ agents. We could still lose much because there have to be ships to take our goods to other countries to sell. The Venetians used to do this for us."

"In what sort of things do your agents invest, My Lady?"

"I have no idea whatsoever. Alexios can tell you, I am sure," she responded with a vague wave of her delicate, ringed fingers.

"I can tell you," Theodora said with a smug look on her face. "The agents collect the silk and the olive oil that comes from our estates in the west and buy the spices that come in huge caravans of camels from far away to the east. Isn't that right, brother?"

"I told you she was bright." Alexios looked at his sister with pride. "Yes, and more, but without ships we cannot send it to destinations in the Middle Sea and sell it."

"I know of these caravans," Talon said. "I remember seeing them while I was in Isfahan. I had no idea that they came this far west."

"You know of these things!" Theodora was clearly warming to him.

"Yes, My Lady. Isfahan is a lovely city on the edge of a great desert called *Dashte Kavir,* which means the desert of salt."

"How is it that you were there?" Joannina asked.

"I was taken there by a man to whom I owe much," Talon said, evading the question. "He was a doctor, and he passed along what skills I could understand in medicine." He briefly allowed his mind a glimpse of his 'uncle' Far'jan and 'aunt' Fraiba.

"What about the Genoese and the Pizans?" Talon asked after a pause, to take keep the conversation where he wanted it to remain.

"I would trust a Genoese even less than a Venetian!" Alexios said bitterly. "They are now the cock of the coop and are crowing loudly about it. They don't have reliable agents and you never know if you will be paid back on your investment or cheated. As for the Pizans, they are upstarts and barely know how to sail a ship according to Makarios. How could I entrust a cargo to them?"

Talon thought about all the slaves and staff needed to run this villa and wondered how they managed when the trade was so poor; slowly the germ of an idea began to take hold in his mind.

The sun had set and he could see the servants lighting candles and oil lamps. To Talon there seemed to be more candles in the dining room of this house than he had seen in all the churches of Acre combined. Here was wealth despite their protestations to the contrary.

"We have guests for this evening. Talon, would you not stay and share our meal?" Joannina asked.

Before he could protest Theodora unexpectedly joined her mother's plea.

"You will stay, will you not, Sir Talon?" she asked with a coy look and with emphasis on the 'Sir.'

He glanced at her brother, who grinned. "I shall join with my mother and my sister and ask you to stay, Talon. We enjoy your company."

"That is settled then," Joannina stated with satisfaction. "Senator Spartenos and his wife will be here but Pantoleon will not, as I hear he is practicing for a chariot race, though how he does that in the dark I do not know. Theo, your sister will be here, so you can ask her to help you with your hair. It looks as though... well, never mind; please just try to look as though you have tried."

She departed, holding her daughter's arm tucked into hers, while the two men sat on the loggia and watched the evening draw in. Talon enjoyed the the view as he could see right across the Golden Horn to the hazy landmass on the other side. He glanced down the garden and observed the bee hives placed in a corner near to the fruit trees. It was a far cry from Acre, he thought to himself.

"Don't pay any attention to my sister, Talon." Alexios said, surprising him out of his reverie. "She has inherited all of my father's ill graces, but one has to make allowances. She is very bright."

"She is remarkable, Alex, quite remarkable," Talon said with a grin.

"Is this the same Pantoleon of the chariot races?" he asked.

"Yes, he is the son of the senator who is coming to dinner. I know very well that he is not practicing this evening; he is probably in one of those high-end whore houses and I am sure that his father knows this, but, well, Pantoleon is a little spoiled. It is a rare thing for Senator Spartenos to want to come and visit, as he and papa are usually at one another's throats in the Senate. I don't entirely trust him. My guess is that he has heard of you Templars and wants to find out more about why you are here. I shall be circumspect, I promise."

A servant appeared and announced that the guests had arrived. Alexios got up and went inside, telling Talon to remain where he was and that he would come and collect him after he had performed his duties.

*****

The guests arrived in litters, with torch bearing runners alongside and to the fore to guide the bearers to the front steps. Talon kept out of the way while the guests were greeted by the Senator and his wife, with Alexios standing by. But then Alexios came to fetch him and took him to the ante room where several newcomers were standing. One of them was a man almost as old as Damianus but less stooped and in possession of a muscular frame despite his advanced age, his greying hair cut in the tight curled manner the Greeks favored. His features were strong and showed a determined jaw but with a sensuous mouth, while his deep-set brown eyes seemed just a little close together on either side of a fleshy nose. He wore a full-length white tunic, with silver and gold thread woven into the fabric on the sleeves and hem, over which he wore a traditional toga denoting high rank. His whole bearing denoted a man accustomed to power and unafraid to use it.

The other man was clearly a member of the Greek clergy. He wore dark vestments, embroidered with small crosses, that came down to his feet; the cloth looked expensive, as did the white silk shawl and the huge silver cross formed in the Byzantine design set with rubies and precious stones on a long chain around his neck. His long greying beard resembled those of several Templars Talon had encountered. The features behind the beard were kindly, although the deep-set dark eyes were enquiring and sharp. The rounded, silk-embroidered hat with no brim that he wore on his head gave the impression of height.

Both the churchman and the senators were in the middle of a discussion when Alexios brought Talon forward. *"Preoteasa* Anthony, Senator Spartenos, may I present Sir Talon, who is one of the Knights Templar we have as our guests in the city."

The Senator greeted Talon with a nod and a cool look. "We know of the Templars, Sir Talon. What is it that brings you to our fair city?"

"It is a mission from King Baldwin that my superior Sir Guy is better suited to tell you, Sir. I am here merely as his escort."

The *Preoteasa* addressed Talon next. "We have heard much that is good of the Templars, Sir Talon. We respect your Order, although it is lamentable that our Byzantine church and that of Rome seem to be at odds all the time."

"You will have to forgive me Sir," Talon responded. "I am a mere soldier of the Order and unacquainted with the complexities of the dispute, if that is what it is. Surely we are all meant to face the same way if we are to defeat the Seljuk and retain the Holy Land." He knew he was falling back upon an easy way out and wished Sir Guy were here to further the discussion, as the Priest seemed eager to talk a without rancor.

Anthony smiled." It is most probable that there is more for us to agree upon rather than disagreeing, Sir—"

The conversation was interrupted by Senator Damianus, who seemed irritated to see Talon and did not waste any time in calling his guests away to discuss some item or other. He left with a glare at his son as he took the senator's arm and steered him and Father Anthony off towards a corner. Alexios seemed to give a mental shrug and walked Talon over to where Joannina was standing with another woman. She appeared to be older than Joannina, somewhat frail, with very delicate bones. Her small oval face was covered with some white powder and her eyes made up with something dark, while her lips were painted redder than they needed to be. But her smile was friendly enough and her greeting warm.

"We hear of the Templars, Sir Talon. They are a bastion of defense against the Saracen and guardians of our sacred places. I pray every day that God will smite the enemy and bless his soldiers in their mission."

Talon bowed politely. He was uncertain as to what to add to this pious statement, but Joannina came to the rescue by looking up and saying, "Now that is an improvement."

Talon turned to see what she meant.

Theodora made a grand entrance, with her sister just behind her. She had clearly made a considerable effort to bring her unruly hair under control and wore a little make-up that had been administered by someone with understanding of its effect. She was dressed in a fashionable ankle-length tunic of many colors that shimmered, held with a slim belt around her waist and some gold on her arms. She looked self-conscious and awkward and held her arms straight down at her sides.

But behind her walked an apparition and Talon stared.

"Be careful, there are flies around and you will gulp one down if you do not shut your mouth, Talon," Alexios whispered gleefully. "But I think my little sister is seeking to impress as well. I have not seen her looking self-conscious in my lifetime. You must have had an effect upon her. Beware!" He chuckled. "Now I shall introduce you to my elder sister."

The lovely young woman glided up to them with her eyes respectfully lowered to greet her mother and brother with a kiss on either cheek that barely touched.

She was even more beautiful than her mother, Talon decided. Her lustrous dark hair was carefully coiffed and curled to show off a perfect oval face while the make-up, which most women in the city seemed to over use, was carefully applied and served to enhanced her large dark eyes and her wide sensuous mouth. She had the family nose, but not as pronounced as that of her younger sister, while her cheekbones were just a little more prominent making for regular and very attractive features.

She turned to observe Talon and her brother said, "Eugenia, this is Sir Talon, about whom we have talked before. Eugenia is a Lady in Waiting at the palace. She is not here as often as we would like, as her duties take her away too often."

She gave a dimpled smile and a curtsy, offering Talon a cool wrist to lean over. He was learning and did not touch the alabaster skin with his lips. He was reminded of the stone nymph leaning over the pond.

"I am honored to meet with you, Sir. I have heard very much of you and look forward to hearing more of your country," she said. Her voice was well modulated and although it was an automatic reply her eyes stared into his for a moment longer than perhaps intended.

The senators must have finished their discussion, as they began to walk towards the small group. Joannina took this to be a signal for them to all move towards the dining area where the servants had laid out a feast on the large table.

As they were seated Senator Spartenos eyed Talon sharply from his position almost opposite, next to Alexios. The men were seated at one end of the table while the women at the other. Talon was conscious of Theodora watching him and on one occasion caught her look and smiled at her. She dropped her eyes immediately and concentrated on picking at her food. Gone was the slightly brash, confident girl with whom he was acquainted, replaced by a bashful young lady with nothing to say.

Her sister was seated next to her and she too, while listening politely to the conversation between her mother and the visiting lady, seemed to be preoccupied with something else. Talon noticed her glance more than once at Senator Spartenos, who was involved in an intense conversation with Damianus and his son and Father Anthony.

Talon realized that they were discussing a hunting expedition. Alexios looked over at him.

"Can you understand what we are talking about, Talon?" he asked.

"Is it a lion hunt, Alex?"

"Yes, and one that went badly wrong for someone," he returned, and then concentrated upon what Senator Spartenos was saying.

"They went high into the hills to the east of the city where there are still a few of them to be found and it is not too far to ride."

"Who was on the expedition?" Alexios asked.

"Prince Isaac and his retainers and one of the Bulgarian princes. You remember the young one who always wanted to play *tzykanion* but his father would not let him?"

"Why not?" Alexios asked.

"Because he said it was too dangerous! Ha! Now he is dead, or nearly so, as the lion jumped directly onto him and his horse and took them both down." The senator evidently enjoyed the story because he went on to tell them in gory detail what had transpired.

Talon ceased to hear him at this point, remembering his own experiences with a lion, and he had not had the benefit of a score of other men with spears to help him. He felt sorry for the Bulgarian who might well die from his wounds.

Finally the senator tired of the story, but not, it seemed, of being the center of the discussion. He turned his attention to Talon.

"A Knight Templar in Constantinople? I do wonder what might have brought you here, Sir?" He asked again, staring hard at Talon.

Talon glanced at Alexios. "We came to see the wonders of the city, Sir. My Master has some business with the Great Palace, but I am in ignorance of his purpose."

"Perhaps it is to do with another crusade?" Spartenos asked with a knowing look at Damianus.

"You seem to know exactly what is going on at any time in the city, even the empire," Damianus said. Talon thought he detected a note of irony in his voice.

"You know as well as I that it pays to be aware of what is going on."

The senator looked over to the women and seemed to share a moment with Eugenia, but she did not seem to like the look; she turned away with a frozen expression on her face. Talon wondered what understanding might be there. He assumed they must meet often enough at the palace, but it was clear to him that Eugenia did not like the senator.

The senator persisted in his questions until Alexios came to the rescue and brought the conversation around to the topic of chariot racing. It was not long before the senator was bragging about his son's accomplishments in the arena. It was clear to Talon, however, that this man was determined to find out more about the Templars' activities. He decided that he was going to be very circumspect with his answers in future.

Chapter 10

A Game of Tzykanion

A few days later Talon received an invitation from Alexios to join him at the villa belonging to Senator Spartenos; furthermore, Alexios sent Joseph as a guide. By now the knight knew enough of the intricacy of the streets to find his way, but it was customary for a well-to-do person to be accompanied by a servant. He was dressed in clothes newly bought from the market the day before. He had shed the light flowing cotton robes he had worn in Palestine and now looked more like a Byzantine than an Eastern Frank, and this suited him well enough. He felt that the more he could blend in with his surroundings the better. The Greeks were not coy about pointing at the Templars and making comments about them, not all of them complementary.

Although the majority of the population of the city was Greek and many of them as dark as any Arab, the city could boast almost every shade of mankind, from the pale blond ghosts of the northern steppes to the black people of the African lands below Egypt, so he did not stand out as he would have if he had kept to the dress of his Templar uniform.

They arrived at the entrance to the villa to be greeted by the noisy barking of a watch-dog on the other side of the tall gates. The grill snapped open and a guard peered out at them through the hole in the door and demanded their business. After Joseph had provided the reason for their presence the smaller postern door opened and they were allowed to enter. A large dog strained at its chain leash, held hard by another guard a few steps back.

Talon felt the malevolent glare of the animal was intended for him; he kept his hand near to his knife just in case. The guard bade him good evening and waved them on.

Joseph led the way toward the house and barns that comprised the villa. This was yet another house set among trees and gardens, bearing a similar look to that of the Kalothesos family residence only a few hundreds of yards away. At the door a smartly dressed eunuch greeted him politely and asked their business. Joseph mentioned Alexios and then, while Joseph stayed outside, Talon was led into some rooms from which could be heard loud conversation and reedy music. There were a lot of people present. They stopped at the entrance and the eunuch indicated that Talon should wait. He then disappeared for a few moments only to reappear with Alexios, who greeted Talon with some enthusiasm.

"There you are! I was about to send another servant to collect you, Talon," he exclaimed as they clasped hands. His breath smelled of wine and he seemed in a lighthearted mood. "I want you to meet some friends of mine. We are having a small party to celebrate the promotion of one of my friends and his recent win at the games. Come in. Come in."

He led the way into a room crowded with young Greeks. There were perhaps thirty people gathered there, standing or seated in small groups. The servants were moving among them with long slim porcelain jars containing what Talon supposed was wine and hydromel, a form of fermented honey, or carrying trays of sweetmeats. The atmosphere seemed to be congenial and everyone to be in a merry mood as there was a lot of laughter, and he noticed with some surprise that there were several young women among the guests. The light, reedy music played by three musicians could barely be heard over the general babble of conversation and bursts of good humored banter. It reminded him of Carcassonne where he had enjoyed the company of the nobles and Lord Roger of Tranceval under similar circumstances. There too, ladies had been present at gatherings where wine was drunk and amusement provided by jesters and musicians.

A silver beaker full of bright red wine was thrust into his hand, and Alexios led him towards a group clustered about a man of similar age.

"Panto!" Alexios called out as the group opened to receive them.

The young man stopped what he was about to say and turned with a slight frown on his handsome face to see what Alexios wanted.

"Everyone, I want to introduce a friend of mine, Sir Talon de Gilles, who is visiting our fair city," Alexios said for all to hear. He turned to Talon.

"Talon, this is Pantoleon Spartenos, a friend of mine, who is with us today in his new capacity of *primikeroi*. He is now a senior officer in our regiment. We are celebrating his promotion."

Talon nodded to the young man. Without doubt the man was very handsome, and it was also clear that he knew it. His fine light color and regular features were offset by broad shoulders and strong arms, indicating a man who was very fit; he nodded back and gave Talon a cool look.

"Talon is a Knight Templar," Alexios explained to the group around. There were surprised murmurs, and Talon received some curious looks.

"I am honored to be here in Constantinople," Talon said to the assembly at large. He spoke carefully in the Attic Greek he had learned from Alexios, and this was greeted with a few pleased murmurs of surprise. Then he remembered the charioteer who had ridden for the Blues. Here he was in the flesh. Talon was impressed; the man not only knew how to master the complicated method of guiding a chariot to victory but was a senior officer as well.

"We must welcome you, as your people are defending the holy places," Pantoleon said, but his tone was cool and almost dismissive.

Talon was not sure he liked the tone of voice from the somewhat too sensuous lips or their slight curl of disdain as Pantoleon regarded him. A young woman was leaning on Pantoleon's arm looking up at him adoringly. She giggled and looked boldly at Talon with large dark eyes.

The chatter began again and the group turned its attention back to Pantoleon, who held forth on one of his encounters with another charioteer. Talon drew back to look around. Alexios had left the group, perhaps assuming that Talon could look after himself. But he felt a little lost and wondered what he was supposed to do. Thoughts of escaping and going back to the inn crossed his mind. He was sure that Max and Claude were having a far better time with Henry and his men.

He searched nervously for Alexios, but his friend was talking animatedly to some other people. Talon moved towards the open balcony, but as he did so he was intercepted by a man of about his age,who waved his cup at him and spoke.

"You must be this Sir Talon the Frank that Alexios keeps talking about. How do you like Constantinople?"

Talon decided that although the man was perhaps a little drunk the words had not been rudely spoken, so he responded.

"I am he, and I am very impressed with this magnificent city. Who might you be?"

"My name is Nikoporus and I am drunk."

Talon laughed. The young man grinned back at him and said, "I see you have just met...our new Senior Officer, who is holding court over there." His tone was dry as he waved his goblet in the direction of the laughing people Talon had just left. Talon looked at him. Nikoporus was as tall as he, slim and fit, but without the muscle of Pantoleon. His narrow face and slightly long jaw were offset by a long nose, flanked by intelligent gray eyes that looked back at Talon with some amusement.

"I take it you are not a part of his entourage?" Talon asked, his tone equally dry.

Nikoporus peered at him and then chuckled. "Is it that obvious?"

"Hmm, yes, I am afraid it is."

"Well...I have to wonder how it is that some people get promotions and others do not," Nikoporus said.

"Take Alexios over there....he is far too nice to complain, but he is a much better officer; and what is more...he shows up to do the necessary work with his men."

Talon glanced over at Alexios. He wondered why Alexios had come to the party, if this was the case.

"I have only once been to something like this, and that only in Languedoc where my family live. You call it a gathering, and everyone is drinking wine, including the women..."

"Gatherings of this kind are not that common, and women rarely come to them. Panto told us at the training barracks that his parents were away for a few days on the estates to the north and the house would be empty. I do not think his mother would approve, and as for the crusty old senator, he would probably burst a blood vessel if he knew."

Talon grinned at the thought of the Senator Spartenos exploding. His thoughts went to Alexios' father, another crusty old senator with whom he had had an unpleasant encounter. Perhaps being unpleasant and crusty was a qualification for the role.

"What training do you do at the barracks?"

"They are cavalry officers and therefore they train with their men in maneuvers and such like on the large parade grounds."

"You do not train with them?"

"Sometimes, but I am in the Navy. I am a *Mandatores*."

"What does that mean? I am very new to all these names you Greeks have for yourselves. They are complicated and confusing."

"Ha Ha! Yes, perhaps, but *we* know what we are talking about. My rank is *Mandatores*, which means that I am an equerry, I carry orders from the Admirals, the *Topoteretai* who are the fleet commanders, to the captains and others who command squadrons." Nikoporus looked at him. "You look tough enough. Are you a cavalry soldier too?"

"I am a Knight Templar. Does that count?"

"Ah, yes, of course, Alexios mentioned that. He also said that you were well versed in the languages of the Arab and the Persian."

"What is this? Do we have a linguist among us?" A light voice interrupted them.

Both men turned to see a small but very pretty young woman standing facing them with a smile on her oval face.

"Well, are you not going to introduce me, Niko?" she asked with a dimple, her bright hazel eyes looking straight at Talon as she spoke.

"Yes of course! Sir Talon, I would like to introduce Antonina, who is a very good friend of Alex's family and of mine." He reached a long arm over her shoulders for a brief hug. She clearly enjoyed the intimacy of the gesture.

"What were you two talking about when I arrived?" she asked, offering her hand, wrist up, to Talon who bowed over it.

"I was saying spiteful things about Panto, as usual. I do not agree with this promotion, as you also know. It should have gone to Alex," Nikoporus said with a grimace.

Antonina laughed, showing good white teeth, her eyes merry.

"Niko, we all know that you do not like him much, but you have to admit he is very handsome and his father is very rich. Not only that, he is a first rate chariot driver and has won vast amounts of gold in the Hippodrome and fortunes for those who bet on him. It does make a difference in these things."

Nikoporus took a swig of his wine. He smiled ruefully. "Yes, this is all true, but I am sorry for Alex. He wants his father to be proud of him and I think he deserved it more; but then I am just a sailor, so what do I know?" He turned back to Talon.

"We were talking about the army and horsemanship and languages. How is it that you speak Greek? Do you know, Antonina, I have just realized that this Frank is speaking to us in

Greek! You speak it passably too, if I may say so, although your accent is a give away. ” He laughed and clapped Talon on the shoulder.

“Niko, you are so silly! Now I know that you are drunk and your slaves should take you home,” Antonina said, laughing with him. “You must excuse Niko, Sir Talon,” she said, smiling at him. “He can be such a fool at times, but he is adorable and we all love him. How is it that you have learned Arabic, and what was that other language? Have you lived long in Palestine?”

“I was born there,” Talon said to her with a smile. He liked her open, relaxed behavior and was beginning to feel more comfortable. “He was just telling me all the complicated names of your navy. I have to admire our ships; they look businesslike and are very fast.”

“There is a rumor that you came in a galley, Talon. Alexios said there is a lot of mystery about that ship but he had conflicting reports about it. He also said that you had something to do with the whole story.”

“It is not a long story, Nikoporus.”

“Call me Niko.”

“Very well...Niko. We stole it from the Egyptians and made our escape to Acre with it. Almost the whole crew came with me and my sergeant Max when we escaped.”

Nikoporus gaped and almost spilled the contents of his beaker.

“You *stole* the ship from the Egyptians?” He and Antonina gasped almost at the same time.

“Now this I have to hear about. This beats anything Panto can brag about!” Nikoporus said as he took a gulp of his wine. “Start at the very beginning and do not leave anything out! Alex, come over here!” he called. “Your friend Talon is about to declare the mystery of his ship!” Alex waved but he was engaged and obviously did not hear; he stayed where he was.

Talon gave them a very brief account of the shipwreck and their subsequent adventures, concluding with the escape through Dalmatia and the chase out to sea where Henry had finally lost their pursuers.

Nikoporus said, “You certainly had an interesting time of it. For such a good tale I want to take you to visit one of our warships sometime. Would you like that?”

“Yes, I would like that very much Niko. Thank you.” He meant what he said. There was a mystery of sorts on the Byzantine ships that he wanted to clear up for himself too.

Nikoporus gave Antonina another hug and then said, "My beaker is empty and I need some more. Where is that servant?"

He wandered off to find more wine, leaving them alone.

"I have never been further afield than Thessalonica, and that was just so that my father could check on his estates. We stayed for three months and then came back. I cannot remember being so bored!" she laughed as she sipped the glass of wine she held in delicate, bejeweled fingers. Talon observed that what jewelry she did wear was expensive but sparse. Her thick lustrous hair and her slim neck were very attractive.

She noticed his glance and smiled then said, "How does our food compare to that of the Franks in Palestine?"

He laughed. "It does not compare at all. It is superior in every way!"

They were deep into a discussion of the food he had encountered thus far in Constantinople and delicacies that she described, making his mouth water, when Alexios sauntered over with another man trailing along. This was a youth who was only in his teens and looked awkward dressed in his finery. He gave the impression of being a gawky boy and bore a slightly glum expression on his angular features. His beak-like nose stood out from between large, innocent brown eyes.

"Theo, I want you to meet Sir Talon, Templar Knight. Talon, Theo is on our Tzykanian team. His father owns more horses than a cavalry division," Alexios said by way of introduction. "I noticed that Niko was talking to Talon, but I seem to have just missed him," Alexios said, as he took Antonina's hand and kissed the back of it, exaggerating the gesture. She pretended to simper, dipping one leg as she did so. Talon could not help smiling at the playacting.

"Your loss, Alex. Hello, Theo. Talon was telling us how he came by his ship. Niko said that there was a bit of a mystery about it; well, now we know and you do not!"

"What is this?" Alexios asked. "Talon, did you tell them something I do not know? That ship of yours, yes, there is a mystery there."

"Well, he told us that he stole it from the Egyptians and escaped with the entire crew to Acre," Antonina stated with almost possessive pride.

Alexios stared at Talon. "I did hear rumors on the ship while we were sailing here but no details. Everyone on that ship is very closed mouthed. Now you have to tell it all again, not just for my benefit but for my other friends too. Where is Niko?"

"He said he was going for more wine but I think he has had enough and is probably gone to find his servants in order for them to carry him home," Antonia said.

"Oh no, he hasn't!" Nikoporus said, leaning over her with a leer. "I want to hear more about this Frank of ours. He said he was a Knight Templar but did not explain whether this meant he was a good horseman or not," he said with a grin at Talon.

"Niko! Where did you come from?" Antonina squeaked in surprise. "Niko is fishing, Talon. Beware!" She said this with a laugh and shot an affectionate glance at Nikoporus.

"The Templars charge into the enemy as a unit and destroy them. Is that not true?" Alexios asked.

"It is true the Templars charge as one. It seems to be very effective, especially against lighter cavalry and of course infantry," Talon said.

"I am talking about real horsemanship, something you Franks do not do," Nikoporus said with a sly glance at Alexios.

Alexios sighed. "He is talking about *tzykanion*, Talon. Perhaps you have never seen it played."

"But what is it? Is it played with horses?" Talon asked.

"It is played on horses on a large field," Alexios began.

"The riders use a stick to drive a ball through a pair of poles and that counts as a score," Nikoporus interrupted, lifting his arm and swiping at the air with it, spilling some wine in the process.

"Niko, settle down!" Antonina exclaimed with a giggle, moving out of the way.

"But that is Chogan!" Talon said, his interest rising.

"Chogan as the Persians play it?" Alexios asked.

"Yes, that is what I mean, with a mallet and a ball. Several players and you score goals."

"We use a stick here too, but it has a small net at the end and you can flick the ball through the air or carry it, but not for long, as the other players will smack you hard for doing so. They sound similar but not quite the same. So do you play Chogan, Talon? Is that what Sir Guy called Arab Polo?" Alexios asked.

"I have played...yes." Talon did not want to give too much out as there might be a reaction, but he wanted to see this game.

"Well, Niko plays like a demon and Theo here plays really well, as do I of course." Alexios pretended to preen. "And then there is the champion of champions, Pantoleon over there, who has his own team."

"I would very much like to see this game," Talon said.

"You could play too if you like. We are always looking for more players." Niko grinned. It sounded like a challenge.

Before Talon could say anything another voice interjected.

"Is this right what I hear? The Frank says he knows how to play *tzykanion*?" It was Pantoleon who said this, and his look at Talon wasn't particularly friendly. The same girl he had been with before was hanging off his arm and still smiling vacuously. She was clearly too drunk to know much about what was happening.

"I know it as Chogan, but from what I hear there are differences," Talon replied, his tone mild.

"I wonder. You Franks point spears at one another and then ride in a straight line. It is not what we call horsemanship," Pantoleon retorted.

Nikoporus gave a wicked grin. "Better not let Manuel hear you say that, Panto. He thinks jousting is the best thing since...well, there is only one way to find out. You have your team and our Alex's team is short a player. Perhaps Sir Talon,"—he emphasized the Sir—"would like to play with us in a friendly game?"

Alexios gripped Talon's arm. "This is a dangerous game, Talon. You do not have to play."

"I am willing to participate in a game, Niko," Talon said in an even tone. He knew that Pantoleon was out to humiliate him and was not sure why, but he was not about to back down. "Unfortunately I do not possess a horse at the moment. So unless someone is very generous I shall have to run about on my own two legs."

Antonina laughed merrily and Alexios joined her. "I shall provide you with mounts, Talon. Niko can provide a couple as well so that you do not ride mine into the sand."

Pantoleon looked smug. "It is settled then. Why do not we play in two days' time at the barracks where there is a small field?"

Alexios looked a little worried. "That is the parade ground, Pantoleon. If someone falls there will be a serious injury—why not the fields to the west of the city just next to the walls?"

Pantoleon ignored him and stared at Talon with a challenge in his dark eyes. "Well, you have the horses now; are you still willing to show us how well the Franks can ride?"

"I shall be there," Talon said, his tone neutral.

Pantoleon sauntered off, taking his girl with him.

"Now what was all that about?" Nikoporus asked, looking puzzled.

"It is your fault, Niko. If you had not opened your big mouth Panto would not have heard and Sir Talon here would not be forced to play that silly game." Antonina looked annoyed.

Nikoporus looked hurt. "Panto will do what he wants regardless of what I say. Why he is picking on Sir Talon I do not know."

"Probably because he does not know the difference between a Norman and a Knight Templar. And he has a good team. He is probably just showing off as usual, and at the expense of someone else," Alexios stared after Pantoleon with a look of distaste on his face.

"I am under the impression that Franks are not much liked in this city," Talon remarked.

"No, they are not, but it is unpleasant of him to have challenged us to a game and to have used you to do so," Nikoporus said. He appeared to be sobering up. Talon decided that he liked him.

"You see, Talon, it is not really you he wants to humiliate, it is Alex and me."

"I do not understand," Talon said.

"We trounced him about six months ago and now he sees an opportunity for revenge," Alexios said.

"Well, that is very likely if you have me on the team. I am used to Chogan, not this tzyka...this complicatedly named game you play here."

"You need to understand, Talon. I am not sure how you Franks do things, but horsemanship is a very important skill here. Pantoleon is not only a superb rider and player, he is also a champion charioteer. He is a member of the Blue team and has won many laurels."

"I recall seeing him the last time in the Hippodrome."

"The game is called *tzykanion*. Let's discuss the differences between the game you know and the game you do not know," Nikoporus said.

*****

Two days later Talon, accompanied by Sir Guy, Max, and Claude, appeared at the gates of the barracks.

The guards appeared to have been alerted to their arrival, as the officer motioned them in politely and then guided them to the parade ground, which was bare except for two thick poles at either end, spread about twenty feet apart.

The horse lines were packed with animals and men attending to them. Talon noticed that Alexios and Nikoporus were waiting for them. Both men were dressed in tunics and hose with short boots, as was Talon, who intended to be unencumbered when he played.

They had spent the last two days practicing and Talon had by now managed to convince both men that he knew how to ride. Now they were nervous that there would be an accident; in his role as emissary for the Templars that could make for a scandal none of them wanted to be responsible for. Pantoleon, however, showed no concern about that and was at the other end of the field with his six men, cantering in lazy circles as he swung his stick.

Talon had discovered that the stick used in the Byzantine game was made of cane, just as the mallet he was used to; but at the end of this stick was a small leather net that could just accommodate a wooden ball about the size of a man's fist, which was made of willow root.

In many respects the games were similar in that once a player possessed the ball he tried to hurl it at the goals on the opposing side, on a field that was about two hundred paces long. The other players would try to stop him...and that was where the game became rough. However, there could be no striking of the ball, as it was not a mallet but a net.

Sir Guy was annoyed when Talon had told him of the challenge and had almost forbidden him to participate, but realizing that this would put Talon in an embarrassing position he had relented and then decided to come along.

"To see fair play," as he put it, and also to remind the other players that Talon was a guest of the Emperor and, as such, should not be harmed. He wore the Templar uniform to make his point.

Once mounted Talon cantered his small but fast and responsive pony out onto the field, leaving Sir Guy, Max and Claude standing near the horse lines with Alexios, who was also preparing to mount.

Talon felt a rider come alongside him and found that Pantoleon was riding a beautiful pony nearby. He stopped and greeted him.

"God's Greetings. You have a good-looking animal there, Pantoleon. How are you today?"

Pantoleon surprised him by greeting him in a pleasant manner. "Greetings yourself, Frank. Thank you, she is one of my best and knows this game as well as I. Perhaps we will have a good game today." He smiled, showing white teeth, then rode off.

Talon looked after him and thought about that.

The game began with a throw in from the sides by a soldier, and then the players went at it trying to hoist the ball out of the sand into their nets and carry it a small distance before hurling it in the general direction of the opposition goals. The game thundered back and forth along the length of the field with the riders pushing and barging into one another as they tried to take the ball from each other. Good-natured curses and insults flew as the teams faced off against each other.

He made good progress but the other team began to put the pressure on, and by the end of the game his team mates were bruised and definitely beaten.

He rode off the field on yet another horse he did not know alongside his new friends, who were not particularly despondent about the defeat.

"You did well there, Talon. I think that with some practice you could become a very useful player," Nikoporus remarked. Both he and his pony were sweating from their exertions in the hot morning sun.

"Yes, you did. I was watching and I liked the way you avoided Pantoleon when he came after you. I think he was frustrated at how well you could evade him and still carry the ball. I had the feeling he was trying to make you fall," Alexios said he rode alongside, his pony's flanks still heaving from the game.

"Wouldn't surprise me at all. He is an arrogant bastard. You did well to not get injured, Talon."

"I am bruised all over from the whacking his team delivered to me," Talon said in a rueful tone.

"Oh, do not worry about that. You got off lightly. At least they did not poke you in the eyes. Go to the baths and get a good massage and you will be fine," Nikoporus said with a laugh.

"I think that we are probably done with *tzykanion* for the time being. Honor seems to be satisfied for the moment," Alexios remarked to Nikoporus as they dismounted.

"I agree," Nikoporus said with a glance over his shoulder at the other team. "Talon, as I said, I want to show you around one of our warships one of these days. How about it?"

"I would like that very much, Niko," Talon said, and went to look for his Templar companions.

Sir Guy pretended to be upset. "Max told me that you were a good Chogan player, Talon. So this game is all about being chased all over the field by others with sticks and they try to beat you?"

Talon glanced at Max, who was grinning, and wagged a finger at his friend.

"No, Sir, but in Chogan at least one can hit the ball and control the play that way. This game is about taking the ball to its destination or close to it and then trying to score. As you can see, the other side beat us handily, but I think I could get used to this game too."

"You managed to stay out of most of the trouble at least," Sir Guy rumbled, but Talon could see that he was not displeased at the way he had acquitted himself.

"I am very bruised and will need to rest and recuperate, Sir," Talon said with a grin. "But I do have an invitation to go and visit one of their warships. Would you like to come too, Sir Guy?"

Sir Guy stopped in his tracks and stared at Talon. "So this is what you are up to?" he asked slowly.

"Only partially, Sir. I like to play Chogan, I mean *tzykanion* too."

"Yes...I would like that very much," Sir Guy said. "But do not put your friends in a position where they have to explain my presence on one of their war ships. Perhaps upon reflection you should go alone, at least the first time, and not in Templar uniform."

*****

In the Blachernae Palace that evening the Emperor listened to the reports coming in from his officers. Several of them were eunuchs whose sole purpose in life was to keep in touch with everything that went on within the city walls. There were others who were messengers from the outlying provinces who had come in with intelligence on the condition of the empire. A few of his most senior officers were nearby to offer comments and further information about reports delivered from afar.

It was a custom Alexios I, Manuel's grandfather, had set for each week, and his grandson followed suit, having found it wise to do so. The first reports were to do with the Bulgarian border and the murmurings of unrest in the region of the city of Dorostal, in the northeast of the empire.

Today, however, Manuel was more interested in what what the Venetians might be plotting. "Have we heard anything that might indicate they're planning something perfidious with their fleets?" he asked the eunuch who was charged with watching the Venetians.

"No, Your Majesty, but it is clear that they would like to join forces with the Normans and make a bid for Chios and Lesbos."

"Can we stop them if they make a determined attack?"

The chief of staff eunuch looked uncomfortable. "I am not sure, Your Highness. We do not possess a sizable fleet anymore and to divide it...might be unwise."

"What are you telling me?" Manuel demanded with some impatience.

"Sire, we do not have enough ships in the south to protect our colonies and at the same time keep the seaways clear of pirates and other predators."

"Then send ships from the Grand Fleet! They sit there doing nothing most of the time."

The eunuch looked very uncomfortable at this point. "I shall pass along your wishes, Your Majesty, but you yourself did say the fleet must remain intact and near to the city while we prepare for our campaign."

"Why do we not have a fleet in the south? Why can't we just build more ships to do this?" he demanded with much annoyance.

"Sire, there is not enough in the treasury to both build ships and pay for the upcoming campaign," said the unhappy official.

Not for the first time Manuel, Emperor of Byzantium, felt himself in a corner as he contemplated his empire's demands. It did not put him in a good humor.

The affairs of state required the Emperor's attention for another two hours, after which he stood and dismissed most of the officials with a wave of his hand. He took some wine and then motioned an officer of the light cavalry who had been waiting patiently near the entrance to the room to come forward.

"Tell me of the game that was played at the barracks today. I heard that the Templar, Sir Guy, came to watch the other knight play against our chariot champion."

He listened with interest to the officer's account of the game and how the players had performed. This report was merely one of the many that were presented to the emperor during the course of a day. His spies and agents were always on the lookout for anything out of the ordinary going on in this volatile city. The intelligence was useful for deflecting trouble before it could mature into a riot. The game of tzykanion was one of those games that Manuel was passionate about; he enjoyed playing immensely, as did his brother Isaac and others of his family.

"How did the game go? Did Pantoleon win?" Manuel asked.

"It went well, Your Majesty. He won easily."

"How did the Frank play?"

"He is unfamiliar with this particular game but there is no doubt he can ride with the best of them in a game of this type, Your Majesty. They say that he played Chogan with the Arabs, Sire."

"Sir Guy de Veres said the same thing when we gave audience, did he not, Your Majesty?" the *parakoimomemos* murmured from nearby.

"Yes, I believe he did," Manual said. "This Frank is different from the usual barbarians we meet, it would seem. I hear that Pantoleon challenged him to play our game. Perhaps he feels threatened by the Frank? Now that is amusing."

He came to a decision. "Who are the players in the game I am to watch in two days?"

They gave him the names of the teams.

The Emperor began to make changes to the listings with a smile on his face. "This should prove interesting. See to it," he said. "Tell Isaac he now has a different team to play against."

*****

Talon received the news that he was to play at the Grand Palace with dismay. He was told by no less a person than Alexios, who hurried down to the inn where Talon was staying and woke him up to tell him.

"I cannot play in the tournament!" Talon exclaimed. "I do not have the experience, and besides, there must be many others who can really play well."

"Well, the Emperor can be rather whimsical about these things," Alexios said, his tone anxious. "He is a great sportsman himself and this game is very close to his heart. It is *the* game in Constantinople for the nobility, and close behind the chariot racing in popularity. Do not forget that Pantoleon is one of his favorite players too."

"But Pantoleon is a very experienced player!" Talon protested. "Why in God's good name did he choose me to play as well?"

"It is worse than that. Isaac, the Emperor's older brother, wants to play. The Emperor agreed."

Talon gaped at him, his eyes wide. "Dear God protect us; so we are going up against the royal family now!" he groaned.

"He not only chose you but me and Niko, as well as a couple of other players who are in the top rank, so you will have our company at least," Alexios said, his tone excited and apprehensive at the same time.

Talon did not find it comforting in the least.

"Talon, be aware that this is a great honor for the Emperor to have chosen us for a game in his presence. We will be playing on the *tzykanisterion*, the grounds within the Grand Palace. They are not as hard as the ones in the barracks but it will be a rough game, as Isaac, his brother, is one of the best players in the city."

"Thank you for telling me that good news," Talon muttered.

"And what about ponies? I do not have any of my own, and certainly nowhere to put them."

"That is the least of your worries, Talon. We have been given horses from the royal stables. You will have your pick, and I would suggest that you pick at least eight. You might need them all."

"What did we do to earn this...honor?"

"What the Emperor wants is what he gets," Alexios said. Talon could see that he was worried but also very excited.

*****

Talon had a sense of déjà-vu as he sat on one of the ponies he had chosen and lined up with the other players at the throw in.

All around them were terraces covered with cropped grass that led up the slope to the palaces lined along the summit, much as there had been in the Hippodrome, but these were packed with noblemen and their wives, while the far end was crowded with servants, idle soldiers and eunuchs. The grounds extended from the base of the Great Palace complex almost to the edge of the seashore, bounded by the great city walls that enclosed not only the palaces but the city itself. On this day the walls were lined with spectators eager for a grandstand view of the game. The silken banners of the emperor, embroidered with the twin-headed eagle, fluttered proudly from every tower along the walls.

The nobility were dressed in all their finery of rich colorful fabrics, diadems and huge hats. Bejeweled officials from the administration complexes vied with the ladies for colorful tunics and over dresses. This occasion was nothing like the vulgar spectacle of the chariot races, but as Alexios had said, "It is a game for kings and their nobles."

A light wind was blowing off the Marmara Sea bringing with it a sharp taste of salt, which Talon hoped would cool the players. It was now late August and the full heat of summer was waning. Talon was glad, as the city streets became smelly and suffocating when it was very hot, although there was usually a bit of a breeze to cool a heated forehead.

He glanced at his team members and was reassured that Alexios and Niko were well mounted and relatively calm. He recalled the instructions of Niko when he had come to talk about the game.

"Talon, this match is about keeping certain other players out of the game. We, Alexios and I, have decided that you might not be good enough to score as yet, but there is one thing you can do for our team that will be priceless."

Talon had felt a brief twinge of indignation but then scolded himself for being selfish and paid attention. Alexios and Niko then said he was to mark Isaac out of the game, if he could.

"You stick to his stirrup like sheep's shit to a cloak, Talon. If you can stay with him at all times and never let him pick the ball up we might have a chance. Will you do this?" Niko asked him. His expression was very earnest.

Talon nodded assent.

"Do not be disappointed, Talon. We have seen how you can ride, it is not a question of that. It is tactics, and Niko understands the game very well," Alexios said in a consoling tone.

"Who will stay with Pantoleon?" Talon asked the obvious question.

"We have young Theo for that!" Alexios said with a grin. "He is very young and looks as frail as a stick, but he is as tough as leather and, like you, he is a very good rider, besides not being at all afraid of Panto. We want to neutralize the opposition before the game even starts. The strategy for a game like this is decided even before it is played," he added with a grin, pretending to sound pompous.

Talon looked across the short divide to the tall, strong looking man in his late forties whom he now knew to be Isaac Komnenos, the Emperor's brother. The man was dressed in a close fitting tunic and tight knee-high boots. His short curly black hair was streaked with grey. There was nothing weak looking about this man. He sat into his sleek pony as though they were one, and his unwavering gaze never left the stands from where the soldier would be throwing in the ball. Talon took a deep breath and tightened his fingers on his stick. He was sure that the task ahead of him was not going to be easy.

The two teams lined up alongside each other, each player almost knee to knee with his opposite number, facing the royal tent and a man standing on a platform holding a ball in his hand.

Talon eased his pony a little closer to the right side of Isaac and prepared to play. Ponies were tense and already snarling at one another, as horses do when excited and crowded against one another. One tried to kick and got a good thrashing for his temerity from his rider. Riders talked to their mounts, calming them, or exchanged insults at close quarters. Pantoleon was one of those who liked to taunt the opposition. He was just ahead of Talon and Talon could hear almost every word he said to the passive Theodoulos, who ignored the taunts. By contrast the Emperor's brother was silent and focused, barely even glancing at Talon.

A trumpet sounded, sharp and clear, and the soldier on the terrace overlooking the huge field threw the ball into play. It came directly over the heads of the front players who stood in their saddles and tried to catch it with their sticks as it flew by, but it landed right in front of Isaac. He immediately spurred his animal to pick up the ball and take it away. Talon decided that this was the moment to rap his stick sharply on its end with his own just before Isaac captured the ball, causing him to miss. Isaac's forward momentum was too great to stop and try to regain possession of the ball, and besides Talon had rammed his pony into the rear end of Isaac's, jolting him out of the immediate play. Isaac grunted and whirled in the saddle to see who had done this and his eyes landed on Talon. His surprised glare became threatening.

But there was no time to pause, as others had gathered up the ball and one man had broken free. It was Pantoleon, who had had better luck against Theodoulos, evading him easily and scooping up the ball.

Now he raced off with Theodoulos frantically chasing after him in a vain attempt to stop him. It was fortunate that another of their team had anticipated this and slammed his pony almost at right angles into that of Pantoleon. Both ponies staggered and nearly went down, and but for some good horsemanship might have, but once again the ball was free. Alexios galloped up, leaning well forward, his stick scraping the ground as he tried to scoop up the ball before another from Isaac's team smacked his stick out of the way. Both riders rode hard into one another, elbowing and trying to stop and turn all at the same time. Talon swiveled his head to find Isaac and nearly lost him. That man was not dwelling on the last issue but was concentrating on taking the ball off Niko, who had succeeded in picking it up. Isaac slammed his pony into the side of Niko's, causing the pony to stagger sideways, while Isaac smacked Niko hard with the haft of his stick on the upper arm. It was a very sharp blow and was meant to disable the rider and force him to let the ball go.

It had the desired effect; Niko gave a howl of pain, his arm fell to his side, and the ball was again free. Isaac swept his net towards the ball, which was now bouncing on the slightly uneven ground ahead of the riders.

Talon was almost alongside; Isaac ignored him as they galloped flat out down the field. Men were shouting from behind, although Talon couldn't make out what they were saying. He did remember what Niko had said though, and once again he rapped Isaac, but this time he struck him on the back of his hand. Isaac snarled with the unexpected pain and again lost the ball.

They galloped on, both looking back over their shoulders as they tried to bring their racing ponies around. There was a lot of dust in the air by now thrown up by the galloping animals, so Talon had a difficult time seeing just where the ball was when suddenly out from the melee came Alexios with the ball tucked into the small net of his stick.

"Go up, go up!" he shouted as he spotted Talon ahead of him. Talon needed no persuasion. He brought his pony back under control, spun it on its haunches and drove it forward to stay well ahead. He was about twenty yards ahead of Alexios when the ball whirred by his head and bounced on the ground in front of him. He heard a shout from behind from Alexios but could not make out the words from the noise of the pounding hooves and his own concentrated attempts to follow the line of the ball. It was not hard for him to scoop it up and then carry it forward. He saw the goal posts coming up and decided to have a try at them.

It meant that he had to swing the stick behind him to get momentum, but just as he did he felt a hard rap on his stick and lost the ball. Others had anticipated him.

Niko, however, had been watching and he swooped in and caught the ball at an impossible angle and was off before anyone could catch him. This time the ball was swung back and hurled at the goal posts. It soared high over the goals to a delighted roar from the crowd. The spectators on the stands and the walls were waving their hands in the air and shouting encouragement.

Alexios rode alongside Talon as they cantered back to the middle for the throw in. "Well done, Talon. You blocked Isaac twice. He is not used to that, so keep it up. Niko and I will try to get some more goals."

"I doubt they are going to let us get away with this for very long," Talon nodded at the scowling opposition who were already lined up.

"No, but we will give them a bloody nose in the meantime," Alexios grinned at him.

Talon joined the line, but just as he did so Isaac leaned forward and glared at him. "You, Frank. Do not try that again, or else!" he snarled.

The ball interrupted any other comment, but this time it landed well forward of them. They jostled for position as the ball was pushed one way or the other but eventually someone got a net over it and hauled it up out of sight, followed by a lot of shouting as one of Isaac's team raced away with it. He did not get far before one of Alexios' team caught up with him, but before he was almost knocked off his mount he managed to hurl the ball high into the air towards their goal

Pantoleon, with Theodoulos in hot pursuit, galloped hard up to the bouncing ball and swept it up into his net and headed for the opposition's goal. This time he screamed at one of his own team who was galloping flat out toward the goal posts. In one swift motion Pantoleon hurled the ball with great force at his teammate, who caught it in midair and tossed it almost nonchalantly underhand into the space between the goals. The move was greeted with roars of approval from the spectators, as it had been a well executed piece of horsemanship and team play.

Once again they headed back into the middle. "Stay with Isaac, Talon. Theo should not have let that happen," Niko said, as he cantered by with an annoyed expression on his dusty face. He began to speak rapidly and urgently to his young chagrined teammate.

Now Talon had to watch every move made by Isaac, who was aware of what was going on and played Talon, sometimes beginning to race away, dodging and stopping and then galloping hard for opportunities that presented themselves. Talon had to ride hard and well to stay with him but still managed again and again to thwart his efforts at gaining control of the ball. Talon knew full well that should Isaac gain the ball a goal was almost certain.

Theodoulos, having been chastised severely by Niko, paid more attention to Pantoleon, and even as he was sticking to Isaac, Talon could see that it was having some effect. Pantoleon was impatient and it began to tell. After interrupting yet another maneuver Theodoulos was forced to back off in a hurry as

Pantoleon finally lost his temper. He rode directly at Theodoulos, slamming into his pony and thrashing at him with his stick, which Theodoulos blocked with his own. Pantoleon was clearly enraged and wanted nothing more than to hurt the boy.

But Niko and Alexios had been waiting for this. They stopped playing and charged into the fray. Alexios put his pony between Pantoleon and Theodoulos shouting, "Stop that, Panto! You cannot attack a player who does not have the ball!"

"Tell the skinny little bastard to stay away from me then!" Pantoleon raged.

"What? You can't manage to evade him? Are you so poor a player that even a boy can upset you?" Niko teased, goading Pantoleon even more. His face was mottled with anger and he was clearly on the edge of doing something dangerous.

Talon thought he might even attack Niko, which of course was exactly what Niko wanted, as it would show Pantoleon up as a bad player and might even get him thrown off the field. Isaac rode up then accompanied by his shadow, Talon, and coldly told them all to shut up and play the game. He glowered at Alexios and Niko.

"I know what you are up to. The gloves are off now and you will be thrashed. You can look forward to that."

He took his team back to the center of the field, calling over to the Emperor's box for a rest period.

As their team rode slowly back to their horse lines, Niko was chuckling.

"Well done Theo, well done! He is as mad as a hornet now, and when Pantoleon is this upset he can't concentrate on the game at all! You too, Talon! I am quite amazed at how well you stuck to Isaac. You really took me seriously, eh? Like sheep shit to a cloak, ha ha! Be careful, Theo, but don't stop what you are doing."

Theodoulos laughed with delight. He was definitely not afraid of Pantoleon. "But I am not a boy, Niko!" he replied, sounding indignant.

Nikoporus leaned over and put his arm around Theodoulos's thin shoulders. "I know that, Theo, but I wanted to provoke him." He laughed. "You are doing a man's job here!"

"I think you might be getting under Isaac's skin, Talon." Alexios laughed. "Watch him, though. The Emperor's brother isn't a very nice man to cross. Watch your back. We will too."

They remonstrated with the others of their team but it seemed to Talon that these two players were quite content to have things going this way. They had unsettled the opposition and that counted for a lot when facing such a good team.

They spent a little time with the new ponies. All of them were new to Talon, so he made haste to get onto his new pony's back and run it in tight circles, testing its responsiveness. He could not complain. The royal stables had not stinted him for good animals. This one was supple and quick to respond to the back and leg. Talon sat deeper in the light saddle and wondered how the rest of the game would go.

Once the game resumed it became evident that Isaac had decided to change tactics. From being a somewhat condescending opposition, confident they could win no matter what, the other team took the offensive. They went after Alexios and Niko and two others of their team, often without provocation, as in a melee it was hard to see who was striking at what. There were many angry yells from Talon's teammates as a stick or an elbow found its mark.

In one breath-stopping incident Nikos' mount, having been struck from behind, stumbled forward and then at a flat out gallop nosed into the ground. Nikoporus as quick as a cat allowed himself to be tossed forward out of the saddle and then rolled once and bounded to his feet, stepping lightly out of the way of the thrashing hooves. The pony, however, was not about to get up so quickly. Slaves ran onto the field to assist the trembling and now limping animal off the field while Nikoporus leapt onto the new animal they had rushed out for him to use and resumed play, almost as though the incident had never happened. The crowd clapped enthusiastically at this display of horsemanship, to which he gave a cocky wave of his stick.

Isaac's team scored two goals in rapid succession despite Niko and his team's valiant efforts to stop them. On one occasion Isaac, despite Talon's best efforts, managed to obtain and then pass the goal, making a shot to one of his players who threw it into the goals. On another occasion, because of a simple mistake by Niko, one of the other team broke away and carried the ball all the way to drop it contemptuously just over the line. The crowd, unaware of the tension that was building, roared its approval.

As they walked their sweating and tired ponies back to the line at one of the intervals Talon was again joined by his friends. Both were the worse for wear: Alexios sported a swelling on his right cheek and his forearm was scraped raw. Niko had a black eye and there was a large bruise on his upper arm where Isaac had struck him yet again. He rubbed his ribs and flinched as he did so. Talon had not escaped the general mauling. His leg felt like it had been twisted half off at the hip and his shoulder ached.

They were all beginning to feel the strain of the game. The constant turning and scrapping for the ball, the hard riding, which hurt both horse and rider because it was so violent, were beginning to take their toll. Everyone was panting and the ponies' sides were heaving with the effort.

"Not too long to go now," Niko panted.

"You two hang on, you are doing your jobs well," Alexios gasped in between sucks of water from a leather skin he was holding.

Talon poured water over his head to try and cool off. He, like the others, was panting and sweating copiously in the heat. The light breeze from the Marmara Sea was not making the slightest difference to those on the field.

"If we can score just one more goal I will consider our honor satisfied," Niko said, wiping the sweat off his face and casting a fierce look down field to where the other horse lines were located.

"What do you mean, Niko? Bulls balls if I am going to just let those eunuchs win!" Theodoulos piped up. His voice cracked and the others laughed.

"Better be not to let Isaac hear you say that!" Alexios laughed.

It took some of the tension out and relaxed everyone. Immediately the mood changed from pessimistic to optimistic. Talon liked the change.

The game resumed and once again it became a bitter fight for the ball and the elusive goals. Alexios managed to take a long pass from Niko off a capture from Pantoleon and scored a goal. The team was elated. As they cantered back to the center they heard the approving shouts from the crowd who had thought they were defeated and the game virtually over.

The game became even more ferocious after that. Isaac had still not scored and it was clear to Talon and the rest of his team that he was seething with anger at being blocked by Talon from doing so. Talon never gave him an opportunity. He stuck very close to him as they rode along the field. Isaac even resorted to insults and jabs with his elbow to try to shed this shadow. All it did was to make Talon more determined to stop him at every turn.

The activity on the field was not lost on the Emperor and his entourage who all knew the game well and could appreciate what was going on. Surrounded by his generals and secretaries he commented at one time, "It seems that my brother is not having the game all his own way for a change."

"Indeed, Your Highness, it would seem that the Frank is staying with him," his Chamberlain commented tactfully.

"I would say Isaac is going to get very angry if he does not score a goal in the entire game," Manuel laughed. Everyone nearby who had heard the remark laughed too.

"See that?" Manuel pointed as Isaac rode into Talon hard. "He is getting very angry. I hope that Frank is good enough to avoid him when he finally loses it."

*****

Out on the field tempers were coming to a boil. Isaac was becoming dangerous. He flailed at Talon on one occasion when Talon leaned over and just tipped his stick so that once again Isaac missed a pickup.

"You Frankish barbarian!" he shouted, and if Talon had not skittered out of the way on his pony the end of Isaac's stick would have slashed his face. Talon said nothing, he just watched and waited until another opportunity arrived to thwart yet again Isaac's attempts to obtain the ball. As his opponent became ever more enraged so Talon became more collected. He finally had the measure of this man.

It was late in the game now and Alexios had scored once more with a terrific pass from one of his players that allowed him to gallop almost unimpeded to the opposition goal and return the insult by dropping the ball just inside the goal posts. He even nudged the ball a little with his stick to emphasize the point.

All the players and ponies on both sides were near exhaustion. Faces were streaked with sweat and dust, features were tight with fatigue, their clothing was wet through, and in many cases there was blood. Their ponies, although replaced frequently, were rapidly tiring and the players were becoming sluggish. A small opportunity arrived for Talon.

He snatched the ball out from among the legs of yet another melee and was almost unobserved as he did so because of the dust surrounding everyone. The thrilling thought flickered through his mind that he might not have been detected when a roar almost in his ear cleared that up. Isaac had seen what he had done, but by this time Talon and his pony were fleeing like the wind toward the other side's goal. Isaac was not that far behind, however, and behind him were the other players. The audience, sensing that the foreigner might be about to score, began to shout encouragement.

As Talon approached the goal lines Isaac rode up behind him and struck him a blow on the back. It was a blatant foul and made Talon arch his back with the pain, but no one was going to do anything about it and Talon knew it. He gripped his stick all the harder and drove his spurs into his pony to gain that last few yards before he could toss the ball over the line. They rode over the line together, Isaac on Talon's left side hammering at him ferociously while Talon leaned away from the blows. Then, standing in his right stirrup and anchoring himself to the pommel by just his left heel, he leaned all the way out and tossed the ball through the goal posts as he passed by.

He did not even have time to see if the ball actually went through the goal as he resettled into his saddle and Isaac brought his pony up on it haunches and swung its shoulder into Talon's side. Instinctively Talon swung his arm up to defend himself and the back of his hand connected with Isaac's snarling face, which was very close. Talon felt the impact of his backhand but did not realize what he had hit, only that he was suddenly alone. The pain in his back made him stop his pony and bend over the pommel before sliding off its back to land on bent knees leaning against its heaving sides as he tried to bring the pain in the small of his back under control.

He was quite unaware of the people running past him until he heard Niko approach and say, "Dear God, what happened?"

"He hit me in the back. Lord it hurts!" Talon groaned.

"Not you, Talon. Do you not know what happened?" Niko exclaimed.

"No, what? Did I score?" Talon gasped.

"Yes, you idiot. But...look what happened...look over there." Niko pointed.

Talon glanced at him, noticed the alarmed expression on his face, and turned to look back the way he had come at the field. A small crowd of people were milling about around someone who was lying on the ground.

"You knocked the Emperor's brother off his horse, Talon," Niko said. His tone was grim. "I think the game is over now."

"Dear God, what have I done?" Talon groaned and leaned his head against the sweaty neck of his pony, which had its head down and its sides heaving. He wondered if he would survive this wretched game at all.

Alexios rode up and hurriedly dismounted, throwing the reins and his stick to one of the grooms who ran up to collect the pony.

"Well, it looks like we are finished here," he said, his voice toneless. "Isaac seems like he is in pain. The Emperor might have something to say about this."

Talon looked at his two battered teammates. If they felt anything like he did then they were in pain too. They were all bruised and battered. He welcomed the finish, although he did wonder what might happen to him now that he had apparently committed a dreadful sin. Alexios wiped the sweat off his face and neck with a cloth provided by one of the grooms. He shook his head with a worried look.

"I am sure the Emperor saw how Isaac struck Talon the way he did," Niko said nervously as he took a deep breath and handed off his pony to another groom.

"We will have to see. Look, they are taking Isaac away on a bed! He must be hurt. I think it is his arm. Oh my God! The physicians are putting his arm in a sling! He must have broken it when he fell."

Indeed the physicians were attempting to ease Isaac's arm into some kind of sling, but the loud roars of pain and cursing were hampering their efforts to make their patient comfortable. A man came running up to Alexios and spoke to him in rapid Greek.

Alexios turned to his companions and said, "We are bid to make our way to the center of the field for a ruling from the Emperor." He sounded very apprehensive.

They mounted up and with the rest of the team made their way slowly to the center of the field and the pavilions where the Emperor and his nobles awaited them.

When they were alongside the remainder of the opposition team they lined up in silence and waited. Manuel took his time, keeping them waiting while he conversed with members of his entourage. Finally he stood up from his comfortable chair and walked to the edge of the terrace where he now stood looking down on the nervous teams. His feet were about level with their heads.

"It was a good game to watch and well played; all of you played well and did honor to this stadium. As to a winner? I shall award the game to the team of my brother as the final goal is disallowed due to a foul. There will be a banquet tonight to celebrate the game and to reward the winning team. You are dismissed."

The ritual cheer praising the Emperor was shouted by all, then the teams turned away to go back to their lines.

Talon turned his pony away along with the others. Niko was muttering under his breath and Alexios bore an expression of disbelief.

"How could he do that to us?" Theodoulos gave an angry yelp. "I saw what happened, Talon scored a clean goal. Prince Isaac was the one who played foul."

"Shut up, Theo," Alexios said grimly.

"I can bet that Panto is feeling pretty smug right now, the bastard," one of the other players said between his teeth.

Most of them thought that Talon had done nothing wrong, and without talking they formed a protective group around him as they came to the horse lines. Then everyone disbursed, but not before they had all promised to meet up and drink some wine to celebrate the game.

"We did well out there today," said one of the players whom Talon did not know. "They were the better team going onto the field without a doubt, but we hammered them."

"Your tactics worked really well, Niko. You'll make a good general one day."

"Do you mind?" Niko said, pretending indignation. "It is an Admiral I shall be, one day for sure, not a mere General. That will be for lesser beings like you."

The banter continued. All of the players were full of praise for Talon and Theodoulos for taking Pantoleon and Isaac out of the game.

"It was great play, Talon, but I do not remember telling you to break Isaac's arm in the process," Niko said putting his arm over Talon's shoulder. It drew much laughter; Isaac it would seem was not a popular man.

Talon said goodbye to his newfound friends and began to leave, only to find Sir Guy, Max and Claude waiting for him on the edge of the horse lines.

"We have come to ensure that you get home in one piece, Sir Talon," Sir Guy said with one of those small smiles of his.

"And I appreciate that," replied Talon, "but could we please stop at the bath house on the way?"

Chapter 11

Negotiations

The day after the game on the *Tzykanisterion* the Emperor held an audience with the Turkish delegation.

Unlike the audience with the Templars there were many irksome formalities inflicted upon the Turks who had been waiting around in the Venetian quarter for almost a month by now. True, the officer placed in charge of them had been rigidly correct in his behavior toward them, but he had not kept them informed as to what was going on in the palace, so they had no idea when they would be called upon to attend the Emperor.

Eventually, after complaining vociferously to the officer, Yiğit had won a concession. They were allowed to walk under escort along the walls to the Gate of the Neorion to greet their companions who had been left on the beach to fend for themselves. They were not in a very good way, having been denied entrance to the city even to buy food. They had resorted to fishing and paying such vendors as there were on the shoreline exorbitant prices for other necessities. There was much discontent and indignation at such treatment of emissaries.

Yiğit had been furious and had demanded that his men be allowed to join him in the confines of the Venetian quarter, and also demanded that as an emissary he be allowed the freedom to walk at liberty around the area. It took much argument and pressure from him to gain these meager concessions from the officer, who finally received permission for Yiğit to walk about freely, though his men were to remain within the confines of the quarter. Yiğit realized that he was not going to gain much more from the Byzantines so he accepted the situation with as good grace as he could.

Now he was to be presented to the great emperor of the Greeks to make the case his sultan had commanded him. He knew it was a difficult mission and was not sure how much he could accomplish given the animosity that existed between the two nations. He had done all he could to clean up his disheveled best coat and breeches. He had his son polish his boots till there was a nice sheen on them and he had his mustache trimmed. He knew in his heart that his dress was shabby by comparison to the opulence of the court, however, and dreaded having to make an appearance before all those elegant Greek courtiers. How he longed for the wide open spaces and the fresh air of the grasslands around Konya. This place was stifling, and the constant hum of activity even at night was beginning to make him feel tired and irritable.

Their escort took them up the hill to the monstrous buildings at the eastern end of the city, past curious people who pointed at them and sometimes laughed at their strange clothing. Although he could barely understand them, it was enough that he gathered their meaning. He gritted his teeth but pretended to pay no attention as he strode proudly forward.

Yiğit had brought his son Burak with him and two of the more presentable warriors who carried presents for the Emperor. They were ushered into the huge entrance hall by strange blond warriors with ice-blue eyes. In this effete company they seemed to be the only people who would be able to put up a fight. He stared with contempt at the gilded manikins masquerading as warriors standing at some of the doorways through which they were admitted. Bracing himself for the ordeal to come, the Turk greeted the perfumed eunuch who came to meet them politely enough. They used an interpreter.

It was with some dismay that he beheld the brightly lit and glittering audience room ahead of him. It was filled with nobles and officials, many of whom were definitely not Greek as, for instance, the group of Arab ambassadors standing near the doorway. The Arab dignitaries were dressed in outfits of the finest silk and cotton, any one of which would have purchased Yiğit half a dozen herds of sheep. He told his son to wait for him at the doorway. Then he squared his shoulders and walked proudly alone behind the eunuch towards the figure seated on the throne at the other end of the room. His two men heaved the caskets of treasure along several paces behind him.

He went through the humiliation of the crawl to the throne, but then his pride took over and he rose to his feet. There were gasps of disapproval from all around but he ignored them. He threw back his cloak and took a stance proudly in front of the Emperor and waited. He was a representative of the sultan, was he not?

The Emperor spoke some words in Greek which were translated in a high falsetto by a eunuch standing near the throne.

"We greet you as an ambassador of the Sultan Kilij Arslan."

Yiğit gave a deep bow. "I am honored to be in the presence of Your Majesty. I come in peace with gifts to your Eminence from my Sultan."

He had the boxes of treasures opened in front of the Emperor, who barely glanced at them, although the Sultan had gone to great lengths to send beautiful objects of gold and silver to please him. It did not matter very much that some of the items had been recently plundered from the southern reaches of the Seljuk holdings. The Emperor nodded acceptance, the treasure was whisked away out of sight, and the real business began.

Yiğit had already glimpsed a familiar face among the crowd so he knew that the emirs of Danishmend were here to make sure that the Emperor maintained his support for them in exile. Perhaps even Shahishah, that snake from Danishmend, was lurking in the background trying not to be seen but doubtless taking a keen interest in the outcome of this particular audience. It gave him a malicious sense of amusement that they might even have recognized a few of the baubles he had presented to this Greek emperor.

The Emperor was speaking again. "We would know for what reason you are here today. We have sent messengers to the sultan but have thus far received no answers that please us. Do you bring letters from him?"

Yiğit nodded, bowed again and drew out of his jacket several rolls of parchment that he had been keeping safe all this time.

"I bring messages of good will from my Sultan, Your Majesty. He asks only for peace and reconciliation between our peoples."

While the words were being translated he handed the rolls to a eunuch who held them in front of the Emperor, who touched them with bejeweled fingers before they were carried away.

"We will read them. Peace between our nations seems to Us to be a good thing, but your Sultan has broken treaties of long standing. Not only that, he has refused thus far to hand over much of the lands he took from the Danishmends who are our vassals. We do not consider this to be an act of friendship, nor of peace."

"Sire, my only mission is to beg for peace between us," Yiğit said calmly. "My Sultan does not want war and will do much to avoid one. What message may I take back with me to assure him that this will be the case? I am sure there is a misunderstanding with regard to the territories you have mentioned."

"There is no misunderstanding. You will return to your sultan and inform him that our patience is at an end. He has six months to comply with the terms of our treaty, after that it is ended."

Before Yiğit could elaborate or even try to explain the Turkish side of the argument the interview was at an end.

Yiğit was forced to bow deeply and walk backwards to the door feeling humiliated and frustrated. He had not expected such an abrupt termination. As he walked backwards he heard quite clearly words muttered in Turkish from one of the emirs who watched him with undisguised hate. "Tell your Kilij Arslan that the Emperor is going to crush him and take back that which he has stolen. The next time you appear here it will just be your head on a plate, and hopefully his too," the man hissed.

As the Turks exited the palace at the main gate and waited for their escort, Yiğit pondered his situation. He was seething with rage at the treatment meted out to him. What difference was there between his delegation and that of, say, those perfidious, flowery Arabs whom no one trusted anyway? The Sultan had ordered him to negotiate for time; the intent was to avoid a war on his western front while he was engaged in consolidating his gains in the south. The Byzantine army was capable and disciplined and could indeed crush any army of the Turks in the open field.

Yiğit felt apprehensive. The Sultan did not take kindly to failure even if he did like and respect his emissary. But to Yiğit's chagrin there had been little he could do. It was very clear to him that these sophisticated, pretty colored peacocks did not see the necessity of dealing with the Sultan, let alone a mere emissary. Yiğit was sure that the six month warning was hollow and that it would be much sooner than that when an army came to challenge the Sultan.

Yiğit stared across the busy square to the immense building of the Sophia and wondered at the skills of these arrogant people. Despite his anger, shame and the overriding hate he now felt, he grudgingly admitted to himself that they certainly knew how to build great palaces.

A man walked by and stared curiously at the Turkish delegation. He was dress like most Greeks on the street, but his cloak, which was of white wool, carried a red cross sewn onto it. To Yiğit it was just another of those Christian emblems that these people wore. What caught the Turk's attention was the intensity of the look from the other man, who was accompanied by a pretty young girl with a slightly large nose who carried with her several of those books he had heard about.

They paused and the two men stared at each other for a few long moments, taking each other's measure. Then the escort arrived and Yiğit turned away, but not before he had noted the strong features of the man and the scar running down his jaw. The eyes that had made contact were direct and hard. It only lasted a moment or two; then the girl pulled on the man's sleeve and they walked off to join the throng on the Mese. But it left Yiğit wondering about the encounter.

*****

Talon walked along the Mese with Theodora in a thoughtful frame of mind. He had just spent the day with her at the Magnaura, where he had listened to a lecture on mathematics followed by another on some obscure philosophical point that completely eluded him. However, when Theodora took him to see the medical facility he was impressed. It compared very favorably with the Bimaristans in Isfahan and Cairo. He wondered, not for the first time, at the utter disinterest of the infamous leeches of the western nations in the medical knowledge available here and in the Arab world. It was not as though they did not have the opportunity to learn from either the Byzantines or the Arabs, as both were in close proximity to the Kingdom of Jerusalem and both had a profound knowledge of medicine.

There had even been a discussion about dissection and examination of cadavers, which he knew even the Arabs and Persians could not do, at least not legally. He was very impressed with the fact that the physicians in this city knew all about Avicenna and notable figures like Ibn Hubal, who wrote impressive books on the subject of medicine, in fact a copy of the Arabic work had been on display at one of the libraries among the multitude of Greek books on the same subjects.

It was while they were crossing the large square in front of the Palace entrance that he had seen the Turkish delegation exiting the gates and had paused to look at these wild looking men who seemed completely out of place among the more refined population of Greeks. He paused to stare at them, taking in the clothing and their features. The Turks had not been very popular in Persia the last time he had been there.

The man who appeared to be their leader must have felt that he was being observed, for he turned to stare back. Talon could see he was angry about something, as the glare from his light brown eyes was fierce and hostile. Talon noted a scar that travelled down his brow and continued down his upper cheekbone. Then he felt a tug on his sleeve and walked on with Theodora, who was chattering about the lecture, oblivious of the exchange between the two men.

Theodora interrupted his thoughts. "Talon! I've been talking for some minutes now and you have not said a thing. What happened back there? Did you see something?"

"I was looking at those Turks just outside the palace. That man looked very angry for some reason. How is it that you have Turks in the city? I thought they were the enemy of Byzantium."

Theodora frowned, as was her manner when irritated by something that she considered elementary. "Talon, it has been the policy of our emperors to allow emissaries of all people to come to this city. Some come to make trade while others come to plead a cause of some sort, and others to negotiate with our empire. Is that so difficult to understand? These men probably had an audience with the Emperor, that is my guess."

Talon smiled, nodded and asked, "Do you believe in fate, Theo?"

"I believe in God and his saints and if he ordains a thing then that is to be my fate. Why do you ask such a question, Talon?"

"Because I've just had a sense that that man and I are fated to meet again," he said.

She stared at him and glanced back at the Turkish delegation. "Are you superstitious then, Talon? I would not have thought so."

"I am a soldier; we are all superstitious, Theo."

*****

Two days after the game of *tzykanion*, word came from Alexios to the Templars that they were to attend the Emperor the following day. This time, they were to go to the Palace of Blachernae, which was at the western end of the city on the shores of the Golden Horn. Only the knights were to be present at the meeting, by command of the Emperor. The distance they had to travel would require horses, which Alexios said he would provide if they would meet him at the Forum of Constantine.

Sir Guy had spent some time with his counterparts Alexios Bryennios and John Komateros and told Talon that the negotiations for the hand of the princess were making progress, but the final word had to come from the Emperor and nothing was going to hurry the Greeks along.

"I suspect that they've learned much from the Persians about negotiating, or perhaps it is the other way around," he remarked with a shrug. "They study every advantage and then move a piece on the board...slowly. I shall no doubt have to take inadequate answers back to our king."

"But they have not said 'no' to either of the requests, Sir?"

"True, and I should consider that progress I suppose," Sir Guy answered; he sounded somewhat resigned.

"I think it is telling that the Emperor does not want our monks present, Sir Guy."

"Indeed it is, Talon. It would be naïve of me to suppose his spies do not know why they are here. Besides, Jonathan probably disgusted them by wiping his snotty nose on his sleeve at the last audience, and Martin tripped over the hem of his habit on the way out!"

Talon stifled a snort of laughter. Sir Guy clearly found the monk Jonathan irritating in the extreme.

They walked all the way up the hill to the Forum of Constantine where Alexios greeted them. He was mounted and had a small escort of his own cavalry with him. He smiled a crooked smile as Talon walked up to him and they clasped hands."So how are you today Talon?" Alexios asked with a grin. Alexios' eye was puffed up black and blue and he moved stiffly.

Talon grinned and winced. He felt battered and would have preferred not to be visiting the Emperor in his present condition. There was a huge welt on his back and he was still bruised all over from the battle two days previously. He had planned on visiting the baths and trying out the recommended services of a masseuse that day. For Dmitri had insisted with a leer that these were among the best in the city.

Sir Guy, on the other hand, looked rested and ready to continue the discussions. They moved off, cantering along the crowded avenue and shops that lined the entire length of the vast street right up to the Forum of Theodosius. From there the road angled southward to the Forum of the Ox, but they turned right on the northerly route of the Mese, finally arriving at the great entrance to the Cistern of Aetus.

"This is only one of the great water reservoirs within the city walls. They have allowed us to survive very long sieges," Alexios informed them as they trotted their horses past the huge pillars at the entrance to the cistern. Then he led the way down the paved road northwest by an array of churches with the familiar domed roofs, topped with crosses, beyond which were the roofs of the several palaces of Blachernae. The two riders in front called out to the pedestrians to clear a passage and any of them who were too slow were shoved out of the way.

Alexios pointed to a building and said, "This is the palace of the *Porphyrogennitos.*"

What significance is that?" Talon asked.

"It is where the Imperial children are born. The babes are said to be born "to the purple" for only they may wear clothing that is dyed with the royal purple. All our emperors and ladies of the Imperial house are born there and much value is placed upon that. Foreign princes want to marry princesses born to the purple as it brings them much prestige."

They were by now entering an area of vast gardens and wooded avenues which surrounded the palace of Blachernae. The panorama of the busy waters of the Golden Horn was spectacular. They did not have much time to dwell on the view, however, as they had arrived at the main courtyard of the palace. Here they were met by a small group of men dressed in rich costumes topped with huge, unwieldy looking hats of different shapes, from incongruously tall to extremely wide. Talon noted the familiar crest of the double-headed eagle with the small crown between the heads and the crossed keys carved into a large stone plaque over the gateway.

He wondered why this place was so remote from the Great Palace, but as everyone was preoccupied with preparing for the audience he did not ask, but followed Sir Guy and the reception committee through the great gates into the hall where they were told to wait and hand over their weapons to the attending Varangian officer.

As they stood on the polished marble flagstones staring at the statues and the gold and silver leaf frescoes and murals on every inch of the walls, Talon remarked to himself that this palace was much quieter than the bustling Great Palace they had previously visited.

There was a hushed atmosphere in this building where people went about their business quietly, with only murmured conversations in corners. The army of eunuchs was much reduced. He noted, however, that in all the strategic places, such as entrances to private chambers, the huge Norse warriors stood as impassive but imposing sentries.

In some distant chamber of the palace a voice was raised in song and they all listened as the crystal clear tones soared and dropped and climbed yet again before eventually fading away into silence. He realized that it could only belong to one of the *castrati*, boys who had been castrated to ensure that their voices remained pure. Yet another item to ponder in this multi-faceted civilization.

They waited for about an hour, during which Alexios and Talon told Sir Guy of their part in the game and the infighting that had gone on. Sir Guy was amused that Prince Isaac had been thwarted so badly by Talon but did not comment. There was still the aftermath of that game to deal with. The Emperor might not have been very pleased.

After what felt like an interminable wait a bejeweled eunuch silently entered the room and glided along the polished floor toward them. Talon wished he could afford a fraction of the expensive, shimmering silk clothing the man wore, and he smiled to himself as he looked at the belt. Henry could buy his own ship with he jewels laid into the silver and gold filigree on that item—or retire.

The eunuch bowed and asked them to follow him. They complied in silence and walked along corridors that were as elaborately decorated as the anteroom. Talon by now had become somewhat inured to the rich display of wealth, the statues of marble inlaid with gold, and frescoes of silver and jewels, but he still found himself gawking like some country bumpkin at some new creation that they passed.

Then they arrived at the main entrance to the Emperor's chambers. The two Varangian guards came to attention and another, an officer, opened the door quietly.

The *Parakoimomemos*, the Chief Minister, was there to greet them at the door; they were told that they need not go through the normal procedures of crawling, but they were expected to advance to the throne and bow very deeply, then wait until spoken to.

They were announced by the accompanying eunuch, who moved ahead of them down the rich carpeted floor to face the throne where the Emperor and Empress sat. This was quite different from the crowded hall where they had first met the

Emperor. Here were just a few advisors and the Emperor himself, seated on a throne that, while not as magnificent as the one in the main reception chamber of the Great Palace, was nonetheless worth a king's ransom. The arms and back were intricately carved ivory set into dark wood that had been polished to a fine sheen. The empress, clad in shimmering golden splendor, sat by his side on an equally priceless throne.

Both Sir Guy and Talon stopped ten paces before the throne and both went down on one knee, heads bowed. They waited.

Manuel spoke, but this time in French. "Welcome, Sir Guy of the Templars. I welcome too Sir Talon, who has, so it seems, made a name for himself on the field of *tzykanion*." His tone was dry.

Both Templars looked up and saw the Emperor smiling. Talon almost sighed out loud with relief. He had fully expected to be chastised and that would not have boded well for their mission.

"Sire, I beg the forgiveness of Your Highness. We deeply regret the accident to your kinsman by my unworthy knight. If there is anything we the Templars can do by way of atonement I beg you to name it." Sir Guy sounded contrite and very sincere. He had warned Talon that if a punishment were to be meted out then Talon would have to face it, unless it was too severe in which case he, Sir Guy, would ensure that he got out of the city safely.

However the Emperor raised his hand and said, "One of my relatives, Basil the First, was a great player and was rarely defeated on the field. Alexander died of exhaustion from the game. We Komnenos are not afraid to go onto the field of battle, whether it be *tzykanion* or even your sport of jousting, and least of all against our enemies. My older brother knew the risks and feared not to take them."

"I pray that your brother has a speedy recovery, Your Highness."

The Emperor shrugged. " He will recover. Your man played well for someone who was newly come to the game and we commend him. As for punishment, there will be none. However, we request that when you leave our shores to take your answers back to your king that Sir Talon remain here with us and learn more of our ways. I hear that he has proven to be a keen student of our language and culture, so we would see more of him."

Talon sent an astonished look at Sir Guy and gave the briefest nod. Sir Guy looked back up to the Emperor from his still kneeling position and said, "We are deeply flattered that Your Highness has taken such an interest in our knight. We would be honored for him to remain here in your magnificent city and learn from your people."

"Then it is settled," Manuel said, and indicated that they could stand. As they stood the Emperor continued, "As to the question of a crusade being permitted to come through our lands, there will be conditions that must be agreed to or there can be no crusade."

Sir Guy nodded and replied, "My Liege, I am aware of the concern of the people and Yourself regarding the behavior of the armies we expect to muster and march across your territories. What may we do to relieve this concern?"

Manuel steepled his fingers and looked at him. "There shall be a payment made before the armies come even close to our borders, Sir Guy. I expect the Templars to fund this side of the agreement. The payment will be held in safe keeping as a means to ensure that any damages incurred will be recompensed. We cannot live on promises from princes or kings from those countries when we know full well they do not possess the coin to pay any reparations. You will be permitted to work out the details with my officers after this meeting.

"We, for our own part undertake several commitments.We will allow the armies to come through, provided they pay their way and do not cause harm. Their unruly behavior and acts of vandalism have not been forgotten by our people. It will not be tolerated again. We will commit to assisting them to cross over the Bosporus, but they cannot stay outside our gates for any length of time." His voice was firm.

"As a further sign of our commitment we intend to mount a campaign against the Turks in the very near future. They have broken treaties of long standing with us and the Sultan Arslan is trying to extend his territories at our expense. We will drive him back to the Toros mountains, which will leave the path clear for the Latin armies to follow unimpeded right down to Syria, where you will be able to retake the lands lost in Antioch."

There was a long silence while Sir Guy digested this information. Then he replied, "Your Majesty, I am sure my leaders will be pleased to hear of your agreement in principle to the request I came here to present to you. I will make it my business to return to the king of Jerusalem at the earliest opportunity and make known to him the terms, and then we will be in communication with the Pope, as it is he who will then inform the kings of the west of those conditions."

Manuel nodded. "There will be documents prepared with the conditions so written. See to it," he ordered his chamberlain, who bowed acknowledgement.

"On the more delicate subject proposed by your king we will continue the negotiations, and you, Sir Guy, have our permission to do so with our officers Alexios Bryennios and John Komateros with whom you may meet at the Great Palace in the next few days. You may take back with you the understanding that we are interested and wish to continue the discussion."

Sir Guy bowed low and said, "Your Majesty, I am deeply honored to hear your words and I shall make haste to carry them back to my king, who I am sure will be delighted to hear this wonderful news. I wish to assure you of the respect and honor we, the Order of Templars, hold for your person. May God protect you."

Manuel nodded and motioned that the interview was over. Both knights bowed themselves to the door, which opened to allow them to exit.

*****

Several hours later Sir Guy and Talon were seated at the inn with their sergeants and Henry, eating a hearty meal of roasted pork and duck garnished with herbs and covered in a rich gravy of oil and meat juices. The bread on the table was crusty and warm from the kiln.

Jonathan and Martin sat with them, but Jonathan was sulking. He was clearly upset at not having been a party to the audience. Martin kept silent while Sir Guy passed along information that he knew would go straight to the Bishop once Jonathan arrived back in Acre, so he chose his words carefully.

At the end of the report Jonathan accepted the situation calmly enough. "We should leave at the earliest opportunity," he said as he wiped his dripping nose for the tenth time on his filthy sleeve. "The sooner we leave this den of iniquity the better I shall feel. Why is Sir Talon to stay?" he asked. His voice was querulous.

"The Emperor has commanded it," Sir Guy said curtly. "Had I refused it could have jeopardized all I have worked for these past weeks. Sir Talon shall stay and be our eyes and ears until I come back or send for him." He put a hand on Talon's forearm.

"I am sorry, Talon. I did not intend that you should stay beyond our agreed time. I know you would have preferred to come away with us, but we cannot gainsay the Emperor. He is known for his whimsical behavior."

"If this is punishment then I am relieved, Sir Guy. Will Max be able to stay with me?" Talon was actually not disappointed. He found the city fascinating, the culture extraordinary, and he wanted to learn more. Now was his chance to do so. He had difficulty hiding his excitement.

"Of course! Max, you must stay to protect Sir Talon," Sir Guy said, a deadpan expression on his face.

Max grinned at Talon. "Yes, Sir Guy, that I will try to do. God willing."

"Then it is settled. Henry, prepare the ship to sail within two days—with your permission, Talon." He gave a small nod in acknowledgment of his ownership. "I want to reach Acre before the winter storms make it difficult." A tiny smile twitched his lips as he observed Jonathan cross himself fervently.

Talon, watching the thin-faced monk, was glad at least that he would soon be gone. He had tired of the man's incessant carping about the Greeks and their foreign ways.

Talon waited for the monks to retire before he asked a question that had been uppermost on his mind.

"Does the Emperor really intend to attack the Turkish people of Rum, Sir?" he asked Sir Guy.

"It is entirely possible, Talon, but not, I think, because of his commitment to another crusade. Maybe it is to impress us. Since Nur Ed Din died the Turkish Sultan Arslan has consolidated his power and he has gained even more lands for himself in the south of his empire, not a little of which used to belong to the Emperor. Your Salah Ed Din has not yet shown much interest in Syria, but I am sure that will change. Manuel has spent too much time taking care of his enemies in the west and has failed to curb Turkish expansion. He wants to take back what was lost even before his father came to power. He has dreams of regaining much of the old empire. If he can succeed, then he will have achieved much; not least to demonstrate that he is a committed ally. The motive really does not matter. I hope he succeeds."

He stopped and squinted as he continued, "I found it intriguing that Manuel's advisors have informed him that we have treasure enough to pay for the protection. Their spies are everywhere! That was clever; if we pay in advance for the launching of a third crusade it means we, the Templars, are committed to ensuring its success."

Talon thought about this and wondered what it was like on the main land they could just see across the Bosporus. This must be to where the Emperor would lead his army should there be a war.

*****

In the palace of Blachernae the Emperor was in conference with his chief advisors. The business at hand was the invasion of the Sultanate of Rum. Their objective was to strike a two-pronged blow at the sultanate and bring it into submission.

He addressed one of his most senior generals. "I want to destroy Iconium, as it is the heart of his kingdom; so we must assemble a very large force with siege engines. It must be so large that they will not even dare to engage us. We will advance upon Iconium with a great army, while you, Androikos Vatatzes, will advance upon Amasia with another legion and destroy it."

"We should use the towns of Doralaeum and Sublaem as supply bases and bring the armies through them before we move into their territory, Your Highness," one of his other generals suggested.

"How long will it take to move supplies in readiness for the main assault?" Manuel asked.

"Merely a matter of weeks, your Majesty. We should notify the officials at the Grand Palace as soon as possible and they'll begin to move everything into place," he replied.

Not for the first time Manuel was pleased with the vast bureaucracy that he had inherited from his predecessors.

Avrahim Ibn Ezra

Chapter 12

The Passes of Phrygia

Within a week of Sir Guy's departure Talon received an urgent message from Alexios while he and Max were eating breakfast. A breathless servant came running down to the inn to deliver it: they were to come back with him immediately.

They donned their cloaks and hastened up the hill to cross the already busy Forum and then struck up the narrow street that led to the top of the Second Hill. Soon the din of the Mese receded as they climbed. From there they hurried over the crest and down between the plane trees and the large stone-built walls of villas on either side to arrive at the gates of the villa Kalothesos.

Alexios was waiting for them on the long northern loggia, striding to and fro. He looked agitated. His normally calm features were furrowed in thought. He turned as they were escorted forward by a eunuch and smiled with relief.

"There you are Talon, Max." He gave a perfunctory bow.

"God's blessings, Alex," Talon said politely. "You called for us. It sounded urgent."

Max said nothing but bowed to Alexios.

"Um, yes it is urgent." Alexios sounded distracted. "But I forget myself. Joseph, please bring wine and refreshments. Please be seated." He waved at the basket-like chairs grouped around a low table. Talon nodded and sat. He liked the view from here of the Golden Horn and the Bosporus off to the east, both waters busy with sails moving across the bright sunlit waters.

"Yesterday the command went out that all officers and soldiers were to report to the barracks and prepare to march within a week. There's to be a new campaign!"

Talon and Max sat up, fully alert now.

"Where are you going, Alex?"

"If you look over there," he pointed to the north at Neorion and Prosphorion harbors, "you will see many more ships than there were before."

Talon and Max stood up to stare down the hill at the locations of the two harbors. Now that it had been pointed out Talon could see that they were crammed with vessels of every type and description.

"I see they are full of ships," Are those to take your army to the mainland?"

"I see that the navy is also clustered out in the straits," Max said. "I do not think I have ever seen so many ships in one place before!" he exclaimed.

"It was all done within a night and a day. But the preparations have been going on for much longer." Alexios sounded proud of his country's ability to organize even as he looked worried.

"It is very impressive, Alex. How long do you think you'll be gone? This is a campaign against the Turks, is it not?"

"I do not doubt it, although I am not party to the details. The sultan has broken too many agreements and the Emperor has decided to teach him a lesson. But there is something else...and it concerns you," he said.

Talon looked at Max. "What is it, Alex?"

"You are commanded to accompany the army and you are expected to stay with the Emperor's entourage while he is engaged upon this enterprise." Alexios sounded unhappy.

"This is a command?" Talon asked, wondering if he had heard correctly.

"It is a command, Talon. To refuse would...well, it would be unwise."

"We are Templar men, Alexios," Max growled. "Our liege is the King of Jerusalem."

Talon thought about it for a moment. "In fact our liege is the Pope, not even Baldwin can gainsay his command. Yet I see what you mean, Alexios. Should we refuse we would be thrown out of the city *persona non grata*, and the mission of Sir Guy would be jeopardized, most likely refused. Is the Emperor so...what I mean is, I am just a lowly knight. What significance does it show for me to be a part of this?"

Alexios frowned. He knew exactly what Talon had refrained from saying, that the Emperor was willful and impulsive. He nodded reluctantly.

"I suspect that it has much to do with the game we played. I do not know if this is a form of punishment but I should take it as a compliment instead and submit gracefully to the command. You can join me at the barracks within the week. I will send a messenger for you."

After they had left and were on their way back to their accommodation Talon glanced at Max and asked, "What are you thinking, Max?"

"I am thinking that it is not our war and that we should not go, but the alternative is not a pleasant one. Besides, Sir Guy left you here for precisely this reason, to learn more of them, which includes how they make war. We have no choice but to go. I hope the Emperor has not underestimated the Turks."

Talon remembered the fierce Turk he had seen in front of the Hagia Sophia and felt sure that these people should not be underestimated. He hoped the Greeks had not.

*****

The day was the seventeenth of September in the year of Our Lord AD 1176. Talon and Max rode at the tail end of the Emperor's personal guards. Talon looked over his shoulder at the seemingly endless column of men that stretched back over the rolling plains to the low foothills they had marched across that morning. This army, he had learned, was known as the *tagmata* and it was enormous. The long lines of infantry and cavalry wound back many miles behind the division led by the Emperor, and there were even more divisions of infantry in front of them. The multitude of banners, crosses and standards of the empire and its regiments carried by men on foot as well as on horseback fluttered in the light breeze creating a bright and colorful parade for all to witness. The emblems and flags proudly told the world that the largest army Byzantium had amassed in decades was on the march and woe betide the enemy who dared to meet it in the field.

Having never before been in the company of military force of any size, Talon was struck by the ever-present noise and smells that went with thousands of men on the march. He heard the creak of leather and chink of metal armor, as well as the soft clop of thousands of hooves and the thump of sandals on the dusty surface of the track, and the murmur of voices all about as the army wound its way across the plain, engulfing his ears with a diversity of sounds. He likened it to the buzz of millions of active bees. It rose and fell as groups of men began to talk or swear while others, having been talking for some time, subsided into silence. The murmur grew to near silence as the dust and lack of water dried out men's throats, and then surged up again as men found something to discuss or complain about. He sneezed; his nostrils were full of the dust raised by their passage and he adjusted his shemagh over his nose and mouth. His horse snorted, as it too seemed to be having trouble breathing through the dust.

The other impression Talon had was the incredible variety of dress, armor and uniforms of the many units that composed the branches of the *tagmata*. Alexios had pointed out the differing cavalry units and named some of them. "You see those mounted men with bows and lances, Talon? They're the *prokoursatores*, our light cavalry. The Heavy cavalry, over there, with long lances and very good armor like mine are, the *kataphraktoi*, our shock troops. They can destroy the enemy when they charge into them as a wedge. The Emperor keeps them close to his person as many of them are from wealthy families."

It was clear the infantry came from numerous origins. He recognized the Varangians from the parades and the imperial *Oikos* surrounding the Emperor and his staff, but there were also units from Thrace, Bulgaria, Antioch and places he had never heard of before.

He noticed that the men in front were beginning to bunch up. The van of the army had stopped at the massive entrance to a gorge cut through the heavily wooded mountains through which ran the river Meander. Here it was a fast flowing stream. Men were breaking ranks and filling their water skins.

He was uneasy. For the last few days the army had made its way over a series of low hills then across the plains of Philomelion, subsisting off its transported rations and foraging for what they could off the land. However the Turks had burned most of the crops and high grass as they withdrew, leaving wide swathes of blackened countryside. The air stank of burned grass and trees, and there were still columns of black smoke in places where the Turks had burned entire villages in a scorched earth attempt to slow the Byzantine army.

Most of the wells that they had come to had been poisoned. The choices left to the commanders were few. Eventually after much debate and acrimonious discussion between Emperor Manuel I and his generals he had ordered the army to leave the plains and seek water from the river, which they were now following. Looking off to the north Talon could see squadrons of the Turkish archers watching them from a distance, obviously preparing to move in closer and inflict what casualties they could on the column led by the *protostrator*, General Theodore Mavrozomes, the second in command to the Emperor. He was accompanied by his best soldiers, a mixture of his personal guard the imperial *Oikos*, many of whom were young aristocrats with little experience in war, and the Varangians, who were Nordic and English mercenaries with much experience.

Someone with a sharp eye yelled and pointed at the Turks, who had begun to move forward on their ponies and then came in a rush, their yells and battle cries loud in the dusty air. Talon took out his bow from its place under his left thigh and knocked an arrow. Taking aim he waited until the Turks were within a hundred paces and then loosed his arrow. His bow was stronger than most and his aim good; the arrow plunged into the front ranks of the Turks, striking a rider high on his left chest. The man toppled off his horse, to be run over by his companions who had not anticipated an arrow to find its mark a this distance.

A shower of arrows loosed by the Byzantine light cavalry greeted the rest of the Turks, who responded with their own arrows, and men began to fall on both sides. The Turks wheeled their horses and rode away but continued to shoot over the backs of their horses even as they raced away, inflicting more casualties among the ranks of the Byzantium soldiers. Their small, shaggy ponies were ideal for this kind of skirmish, responding to the leg aids of their riders who used both hands to fire their bows while holding their reins in their teeth. The Turkish skirmishers regrouped, wheeled their ponies around, and repeated the maneuver.

An arrow whispered past Talon to strike another man behind him. The man shouted with pain as the arrow embedded itself in his thigh. Not for the first time Talon noticed that the strange looking tube armor worn by the lighter cavalry did not do well against a direct thrust or arrows. The man gripped his saddle front with his right hand, trying to prevent himself from falling off as he clutched at the wound, the arrow protruding. He grimaced and his eyes squeezed shut with the pain. His companions sidled their horses up to him and helped him to dismount. A eunuch rushed up and extracted the arrow, which judging by the yelling was very painful. They then bound the wound and assisted the pale man to remount and continue.

Some cavalrymen who carried long maces along with their lances, exasperated by this harassment, shouted abuse and brandished their maces at the enemy threatening to dismember them. They wanted to chase after the retreating Turks but their officers savagely shouted them back into line and the march continued. Talon looked about. The Emperor was just forward, accompanied by his two generals and well protected by the palace guards and their cavalry. There were many Varangians in this group, as they were the highly respected palace guards, but there were also Latin knights who came from many of the countries of Europe and he had been able to converse with several whose families had been in Byzantium for over a generation serving the emperors as heavy cavalry.

They carried the kite-shaped shields that Talon was familiar with, although he did not carry one as he found it interfered with his bow, so he carried a small metal shield on his forearm. Max, on the other hand, bore the shield of the Templars with the distinctive cross decorating the front slung over his back, as did many of the other knights. The two of them had initially received many curious looks from the other Frank and German horsemen when they joined the Emperor's entourage, but these veterans soon began to talk to the newcomers, asking them what they were doing in the country and why they were with the army. Max told a few of them as a joke that Talon had knocked the emperor's brother off his horse and was now paying the price for such impertinence. Talon wondered if that wasn't partly true.

Now he observed the generals staring forward and discussing the steep gorge opening in front of the army. Their conversation was animated and Talon even fancied that General Mavrozomes and General Kantakouzenos might be trying to dissuade the Emperor from entering the narrow defile, at least not before it had been thoroughly scouted. But he could see that there were some younger officers who were eager to enter the gorge and proceed; he thought he saw Pantoleon Spartenos in among them.

Then the men in the very front of the army halted and messengers were seen galloping back toward the Emperor. Talon and Max glanced at one another, then edged their horses forward to try to hear what was being said. The messengers came from Baldwin of Antioch, who was in the van of the army with his divisions. There was a Turkish delegation waiting to speak with the Emperor at the entrance of the gorge. The messengers were sent rushing back to bring the Turks to the Emperor, where they dismounted and prostrated themselves in front of him. Manuel remained seated on his horse with his officers and guards placed in a semicircle behind him.

Talon noted that the leader was a tall, strong looking man with a scar down his forehead who looked familiar. He and Max were too far from the group to hear what was being said but there was much gesticulation from the Turks, who waved back at the pass. The translators were kept busy, but before long the Turks bowed very low and remounted to then be escorted back to their own men. Within minutes the entire delegation had vanished into the maw of the towering pass.

Word came back that the Turks had come to sue for peace and that they had tried to persuade the Emperor to abandon his enterprise and negotiate a new treaty. Men chuckled at the news and made jokes at the expense of the rough clad people who had the temerity to try to stop such an army. Talon wondered if scouts had checked the route and seen any evidence of the Turkish army along the way. He feared that their scouts had not been deployed forward far enough to make a difference and his stomach tightened. The gorge would be a very bad place to be ambushed. He said so to Max.

Max said quietly, "See if the Emperor can be persuaded to send in some scouts. Not to do so would be folly."

Talon nodded agreement and turned to Alexios.

"That is a perfect place for an ambush, Alexios. Are they not going to order a scouting party to go in and check that the Turks are not there already?"

"I agree with Talon, Alexios. We shouldn't just go into such a place without making sure first that we do not have a welcoming committee," Max said.

"I shall go and ask the generals what they're going to do," Alexios said nervously. He clearly did not relish riding up to the exalted group and telling them how they should be conducting their war. Nevertheless he rode forward, pushing through the men and junior officers until he could ride alongside one of the generals. The columns were bunching up on each other's heels as their commanders, realizing that they were to enter the gorge, were uncertain how to proceed. After some respectful talking and bowing to the emperor, Alexios beckoned to Talon, who with Max moved forward to stop in front of the emperor, who glared at him.

"You, Sir Talon, with all your vast military experience, you think there might be a problem with going through the gorge?" His tone implied that Talon had been highly presumptuous to suggest such a thing.

"It is certainly a risk, Sire," Talon responded carefully. "We should at least make sure the Turks do not hold it."

Both General Mavrozomes and Kantakouzenos looked angry, but he was comforted by the approving looks they gave him. Clearly their anger was not directed at him. Mavrozomes slapped his thigh as though exasperated with the conversation he had had with the younger soldiers but held his peace. But now one of the more impetuous officers pushed forward. Talon turned his head to see Pantoleon, who was sitting his horse glaring contemptuously at him.

"We should push on, Sire. The Turk is on our wings, not in front. This Frank does not know the Turk as we do, and besides, look at the size of our army! Who can stop such an assembly?"

"Yes, we have seen what the Turks can do on the plains, which isn't much, so we should push forward, your Holiness," another piped up.

Pantoleon smirked and addressed the assembly at large. "Are we going to sit here like women and wait, as this...Templar would wish? Are we not warriors? The Turks are just a tribal rabble compared to our might."

Talon placed both hands on his pommel and rested his weight on them for a moment easing his seat in the saddle. He did not bother to answer but faced the Emperor in silence. He could feel Alexios seething by his side.

It was general Kantakouzenos who responded and his tone was angry. "Your Majesty. It would be good policy and prudent to allow a scouting party to go and check the passes. We do not know what awaits us in there and we have much to lose if we walk into a trap."

The Emperor grinned and said, "My generals, I do not think we will have any trouble. We still have a long way to go. But as you are so sure of yourself, Sir Talon," he laughed and gestured to the gorge, "very well; Alexios Kalothesos, take Sir Talon here with you and you shall lead the scouts into the gorge. We shall wait until you have returned. Take some of my personal guards. Be quick about it, as it is getting late and I wish to be out the other side by nightfall."

One of the polished and well-dressed cavalryman who was in attendance whispered behind his hand to his companion in like dress; both were staring at Talon and Alexios. The man laughed, his face contemptuous. They clearly did not think there was anything to be concerned about. Talon stared back at the two young men. They were about his own age but clearly felt superior to a scruffy Frank. They looked away.

The Emperor turned to his officers. "Generals, we can wait here as there is water aplenty for the men. They can rest by the river and perhaps we can take some respite from those accursed Turkish skirmishers over there."

Talon was joined by twenty of the cavalrymen from the personal guard, the *kataphracktoi*, under a young officer who clearly knew Alexios. They exchanged a curt greeting and then, with a curious glance at Talon, the officer put spurs to his horse and led the way into the steep the gorge.

It was somewhat cooler once they passed between the huge ramparts of the entrance, a great relief from the heat of the plains they had just left. The river, which Talon had learned was called the Meander, was shallow and became a tight torrent in places with rapids. Talon noted that the hills on either side were steep, high and craggy with bluffs and overhangs that towered over the track along which they were riding. The slopes were too steep to allow a horse to climb and in many places there were dense clusters of stunted trees interspersed with heaps of rocks and large boulders. Alexios rode in front, talking to the young officer. They were not paying much attention to their surroundings, but Talon's eyes were everywhere and he knew Max, a veteran of skirmishes in Palestine, was watching for any movement in the hills.

"This is perfect lion country," Max murmured as he rode alongside. He scratched at his chin—always a sign he was uncomfortable. His fingers made a rasping sound in his beard.

"I agree, but the Turks could well be here and we would not see them if they did not want us to. I think it is perfect Turk country too, Max," Talon muttered in return. He could feel the sweat cooling down his back under his heavy mail shirt now that they were out of the sun.

As they rode along a trail that followed the banks of the fast flowing Meander River, occasionally splashing through the water as the trail dipped, he nervously scanned the high slopes above them. In places the gorge was so narrow that only a single cart would be able to pass along the embankment and even then risked losing a wheel. The passage was well used but all along the route there were clusters of boulders and his instincts told him that these would make perfect ambush sites for archers, while high above them he could see even more piles of rocks strewn among clumps of long grass along the hillsides.

Despite the incessant rasping of crickets there was an ominous feel to the gorge as they climbed the steepening track, and even the two officers in front finally stopped talking. The only other sound became that of the horses' hooves on the uneven surface and the creak of leather and the rattle of accoutrements attached to their saddles. A man coughed and the sound was amplified by the walls of the gorge. Talon had a queasy feeling that he was a mouse about to walk into a death trap. Max whispered to him, "I feel uncomfortable Talon. There's something going on here that I do not like."

Talon nodded but said nothing. They had to have definitive proof before they could go back and declare it unsafe, but despite all his searching he could not see any sign of movement or people in the rocks above nor ahead of them. They gorge began to widen and they could finally see the opening in the hills that denoted the beginning of the high plains. Talon noted that the grass was dry; it would make a merry fire should someone put a flame to it, he reflected. Now the late summer sun blazed down upon the sweating men and horses. They had been climbing steadily for about an hour but although the mountains were still towering all about them the canyon gave way to foothills and pastures. The officer decided they had gone far enough.

He turned his horse and headed back the way they had come, and as he passed Talon and Max he gave a condescending smile and said, "You see, Frank, the Emperor was right: we have nothing to fear from this gorge. We should go back and inform His Majesty as quickly as we can. There is nothing here to be afraid of." His tone was neutral but Talon sensed what he was implying. The officer muttered something to Alexios, who looked annoyed, and one of the men nearby snickered.

The officer went on without another glance and even cantered his horse back along the way they had come. All the men wheeled their horses and followed him but for Talon, Max, and Alexios, who watched them go.

"We might as well join them, Talon," Alexios said in a resigned tone. "Your idea was correct, it was wise to scout ahead, and we have done so. But now the army must come through." He moved past them and trotted his horse after the others.

Talon nodded and again said nothing but glanced at Max, who shrugged.

"You were right to insist, Talon. Like you, I sense trouble and am almost sure this is a trap, but try as I might I cannot see anything to alarm me. They probably think we are cowards."

"There is nothing to be gained by staying here, Max," Talon said. He was chagrined and felt humiliated by the attitude of the officer, but there was nothing he could do about it.

They cantered down the slope and reentered the gorge itself. They had about four miles to go back to join the army, and as the Emperor had pointed out, the army had to march through here before nightfall.

They caught up with the men jogging back down the trail, but both Talon and Max were still very alert and scrutinized every slope and crag above them. They had nearly a mile to go when they heard it: the sound of a rock falling down the north slope. It was not a large rock and could easily have been dislodged by time and weather, but as his eyes darted up to the source of the sound he saw what he had feared. There were men up there who had been too slow to move out of sight.

"Alexios! Look! Do you see that? There are men up there!" he called ahead.

"I heard the rock, Talon, but I did not see any men...I do not see them."

"There! There are more on the other side! Look!" Max called.

Now several of the other men had also seen movement on the slopes. They pointed and called to the young officer, who had stopped his horse and was staring intently up the mountain. He too had seen movement. He appeared to be undecided as to what to do. Alexios rode up to him and exchanged urgent words. He nodded and they both pointed up the mountain. The Turks were moving into position for an ambush. There was suddenly a lot of activity on the slopes above them where formerly there had been none.

"We have to alert the army. This is a trap!" Alexios called back to Talon. There was nothing else to do. Putting spurs to their animals they galloped as a group down the trail heading for the distant opening at the west end where the army was stopped. Talon prayed that the Turks had not closed the trap behind them as they passed earlier.

But as they rounded one of the sharp bends in the trail and were onto the last half mile they were greeted by a sight that stopped them in their tracks. To their dismay the army was on the march.

*****

High above the small contingent of Byzantine cavalry a tight group of Turks crouched among the boulders. Yiğit was among them.

He had been one of the delegation that had spoken to the Emperor of the vast horde approaching the gorge, and once again he was smarting from the sting of the arrogant rebuff and the contemptuous laughter that had followed them as they left. However he had prepared his men well over the past few days when it became certain that the Byzantine army would come this way. He had hid his men in every possible crevice on both sides of the pass, having them prepare clusters of rocks and boulders in strategic places where they could do the most harm. He peered down at the scouts below now as they galloped off. He swore under his breath and vowed to take the head of the fool who had shown himself before the signal. His men looked at him apprehensively. What would the Byzantine army do now, they wondered out loud. He shook his head but said nothing, praying that they would still come.

The Turks did not have long to wait. One of the men further down the steep slopes and in a good position to see the entrance stood up and waved back at them. Incredible though it seemed, the enemy was marching into the trap. Yiğit could barely believe his luck. Now he would have his revenge for all those humiliating days spent in that vast city being treated like an ignorant peasant by those pretty peacocks with their condescending attitude to his people. He clapped one of his men on the shoulder. His grin was ferocious.

*****

The trail was full of infantry marching in good order toward them. Alexios hauled his horse to a stop and yelled at the men in front to halt, calling out that the Turks had the heights above them. He pointed back up the trail and waved his arms, pointing up the slopes.

An officer rode over to him and there was a heated exchange. Alexios and the young scout officer were pointing back up the trail and were arguing insistently. The officer, who seemed to be senior, stared up the trail, but as Talon approached he heard the man say, "The Emperor grew tired of waiting and ordered the army forward. I cannot halt my men now. We will see what happens. It might just be some villagers who plan mischief. We can march past them without casualties."

Alexios was clearly frustrated and now alarmed. He turned to Talon and asked, "Did you hear that, Talon?"

"Yes I did. The only thing we can do is to try to warn His Majesty and the generals. If it is in earnest the infantry will be halted and the army can withdraw before too much damage has been done. God help us all if he insists on proceeding."

But it was not so easy to move past the tramping infantry; they packed the trail from side to side leaving almost no room for horses going in the opposite direction to push past. In the end Talon led the way by taking to the river, his horse splashing through the shallows. The others followed.

Still more bad news greeted them just after the first division of the vanguard had marched past. It appeared that the rest of the army was following close on their heels. The leader of this division was none other than Baldwin of Antioch and most of his soldiers were either men from Antioch or Frankish and German mercenaries. They wore familiar chain armor and rode big horses. Many of the Franks carried lances, axes and huge swords. Baldwin was impatient. He glowered when Alexios again explained what they had seen and insisted upon continuing up the road hard on the heels of the vanguard.

They came upon the center of the army just about to enter the gorge and Talon saw the clique of senior officers in the middle of the moving mass of men and baggage carts and huge siege engines all heading slowly for the entrance of the gorge. The Emperor paused long enough to listen to the respectful report offered by Alexios and the officer, casting a glance at Talon as they were speaking, but he shook his head in an irritated manner and dismissed them with a gesture.

Alexios withdrew after a deep bow from the waist and joined Talon as they in turn joined the moving throng that was marching into the gorge.

"What did you tell him?" Talon asked.

Alexios looked stunned but answered, "I told him what we had seen and that we should be cautious."

"What did he say to you?" Max asked.

"He told me that his army was the largest this country had seen for many years and that a few Turks perched on a hilltop were not worth waiting for. 'We will brush them aside if they cause any trouble. The infantry can clear the hills of them as they go. That is what they are there for,' he said. That swine Panto' almost accused me of cowardice. I could have struck him dead for that." Alexios was fuming.

Talon gave a resigned nod and said, "We are committed then. There is a trap about to be sprung and we are the mice walking into it."

Alexios shrugged. "We have no choice now but to see what fate has in store for us. We have done our duty." His tone was dismal.

Max drew close to Talon. "This is not even our fight, Talon. Why did the Emperor order you to come? I wish that you had been able to refuse."

"It might have cost my life and possibly yours had I refused, Max. Besides, we were instructed by Sir Guy to keep an eye on things. But next time I shall be careful whom I knock off his horse when in a game. Stay close and let's see if we can protect Alexios but...I have a terrible feeling that there are many more Turks up there than we saw."

"So do I! God protect us, because these fools do not have any sense at all," Max said under his breath. His grizzled features were grim as he loosened his sword in its scabbard and hitched his shield around to cover his front. Talon hauled his bow out of its sheath under his left thigh and took out an arrow. He shifted his light shield on his forearm to a more comfortable position. He felt a familiar tension in his stomach.

They joined the mass of cavalry and baggage wagons that labored up the winding track. Instead of the former silence it was now all noise as the drovers shouted and whips cracked and the oxen heaved at their huge loads, the iron shod wheels grinding deep grooves into the dry path, churning the already arid track to a fine dust that rose in choking clouds to torment the men and horses following behind. Once again they entered the cool mouth of the canyon, its menacing crags towering over the winding mass of men, horses and slowly moving wagons. They were followed by the rearguard under an experienced general named Kontostephanos whom Talon had met and liked while on the march. His men were well disciplined and fully capable of holding off the irritating Turkish cavalry who followed the army from behind. They moved painfully slowly up the trail for another mile.

Talon tried to think what he would do if there were an ambush. He pondered gloomily what might happen once the bulk of the army was well into the pass. Would the Turks seal both ends and then slowly cut them to pieces? He began to wonder if it had been his imagination and if indeed the people they had seen on the slopes had actually been the Turkish army or just villagers seeking safety and watching them from on high.

He could hear nothing but the clamor of a large army of men and animals on the move, and the dust that now obscured most of the route ahead did not help his confidence. The bellowing of the oxen pulling the carts and the crack of the drover's whips prevented him from hearing anything that might be of use, but his eyes never left the steep hillsides and the clumps of trees high above them. Nearby several soldiers were trying to hold in check some fighting mastiffs who strained at their leashes, pulling their masters along. Occasionally these would join in the general din by barking and growling. They were huge dogs and he did not like the thought of one of them coming after him. Their tawny coats were streaked with the saliva coming from their open jaws.

"They look as though they could kill in an instant," he remarked to Max.

He noticed Max watching the dogs too. As if understanding what was going on in his head Max gave a tense grin through gritted teeth and said, "If the arrows begins to fly then stay close, Talon. Those dogs will be useless in a battle other than as a distraction."

Talon nodded as he cast a glance at Alexios, who was slumped on his horse as though he was contemplating his future with no optimism at all. He should not be blamed for trying to do his duty, Talon thought. But he was already beginning to understand that the emperor, while a brave man, was also impetuous and frowned upon caution as a weakness.

"I put him in a bad position where his courage was called into question and now he could be disgraced," he said to Max.

"No, you did not, Talon. He was trying to do his duty but no one was paying any attention."

Talon nudged Alexios and indicated his shield. "Be ready, Alex. We cannot help what has been done but we must prepare for what is to come."

Alexios nodded and hitched his shield round and looked to his armor and his weapons. He began to pay attention to what was going on around him again. Talon felt relieved.

Meanwhile the Emperor and his staff continued about a hundred yards ahead of them, talking and laughing amongst themselves, giving all the appearance of being quite content with the progress of the army.

If things went badly he was going to make sure that the three of them worked together, Talon decided. He was thus preoccupied when he became aware of a lot of activity about half a mile ahead of them just before the road turned around a bend that hid the rest of the army. The long column of men up front had halted and he heard the distant sound of trumpets baring the alarm.

208

Chapter 13

The Battle of Myriokephalon

Talon stared ahead and saw something that made his blood run cold. High above the men in front there was now activity on the slopes. To his horror he saw a group of Turks heaving at a huge boulder until it finally came loose and began to trundle down the slopes gathering speed as it went. More followed until there was an avalanche of rocks and boulders thundering down the hillside straight at the men on the road. The luckless horsemen and infantry could see what was hurtling downwards but despite their frantic efforts to get off the road the boulders and rocks crashed into their massed ranks and wrought awful destruction. Horses and men were either crushed immediately under the weight of the avalanche or thrown in all directions, many falling into the river down the steep banks to lie broken and maimed in the fast flowing waters.

The yells and screams came clearly to the ears of those behind witnessing the moment with horror. At first the sight left men numb and unable to move with shock. Then they began to shout and point. But it soon became apparent that this was just the beginning. There was a startled cry from nearby as a man pointed up at the hills directly across the river above them.

"They are here too! Dear God, we are lost!"

There was a rumble from above and every eye turned in that direction. To his horror Talon saw a mass of boulders roaring down slopes of the gorge directly at them.

There was only one place where they might be safe. Across the stream was a high bank, which might just protect anyone sheltering under its lee from the avalanche hurling down the slopes. If they could make it, then the rocks would pass over head.

"Come on Max, Alexios!" Talon shouted as he spun his horse to the right and spurred it down the short bank straight into the river, heading for the other bank. The river was not deep here, so his horse had no difficulty crossing it. Alex and Max realized in the instant what he was about and were right behind him. They slammed their horses into the cover of the other bank, hauling them to a stop. Just as they did so, a rain of rocks and larger boulders careered overhead with a roar, bouncing, whirling just over their heads to smash into the wagons and men still clustered on the trail beyond.

Talon watched appalled as, once again, the missiles wreaked havoc. The avalanche destroyed a whole wagon train of oxen, crushing them where they stood, their flesh and bones mingling with that of the men and their mounts. The air became full of shrieks and cries of maimed men and horses but no help could be provided. Everyone was desperate to escape the carnage. It became a scene of utter panic as men and loose horses milled about among the crushed remains of their former comrades.

Miraculously the Emperor and his generals were unhurt, as they had been just far enough forward to avoid being crushed. But then it became complete chaos on the trail. Men on their horses fought to stay mounted as their screaming horses either tried to bolt or climb straight up into the air. Everyone cast fearful looks up the hillside while footmen and drovers who had survived the first avalanche ran about calling on God to help them. Some were hiding under the wagons from smaller stones still hailing down upon them, while others fled into the river bed.

Some had the sense to join Talon and his companions but they were horribly exposed to anything that came from the other side, and indeed Talon could see men on the hill across from them launching more rocks. One of the dogs, which appeared to have escaped its master, huddled with them as though hoping that these humans might know where safety lay.

Max noticed the danger on the opposite slope above as well. "We must leave, now!" he yelled and put spurs to his horse. They splashed downhill along the riverbed and away from the mob of men and animals and rode through a thin stand of trees that gave them a small amount of shelter. Looking back Talon saw the rocks they had just escaped sweep more men and horses in a tangled mass of wrecked bodies into the river. Most lay where they had been tossed; few moved among the pile of mangled flesh blood and bone.

Talon's mouth was dry and his stomach tightened into a knot; he felt sick. The Turks had planned this carefully and he had no doubt that the pass was now sealed because he heard a roar from downstream. Looking in the direction of the sound he could see a lot of commotion in the rear. Kontostephanos was busy with his own problems. Talon looked for the Emperor and was stunned to see that he and his officers were still on the trail almost where they had been at the commencement of the engagement. He wondered at their inactivity. Why were they not hastening to the front to lead the army out of this terrible predicament? It was as though they were paralyzed.

Then the arrows came whispering down upon the survivors and suddenly there were Turkish archers darting all over the hillsides. They had appeared as if from nowhere. Talon lifted his bow aiming at a small group of men splashing along the river toward them. They were clearly Turks from the distinctive tall colorful felt hats they wore despite the heat, and they wore a mixture of plated and leather protection. Some even had undressed skins covering their upper bodies by way of armor. They shouted battle cries and waved their swords and spears menacingly.

"They have placed ambushes all along the gorge!" Talon called to his companions. "Stay close."

He loosed three arrows with deadly effect, but then the enemy was too close for more and he was forced to draw his sword. With Max and Alexios close behind he spurred his horse into the remainder of the Turks. It was a small well armed party, but they were no match for mounted men. And now the war dog had joined in and was worrying a man into the river, tearing at his throat and growling ferociously. The engagement was brief and savage; after four more Turks were taken down, the rest lost heart and ran back up the steep slopes to get out of the way. Talon was shocked to notice that the river was beginning to run red with the blood of man and beast. Max whistled to the dog to come back and he was surprised that it did.

"By God, did you see that?" he exclaimed astonished. "It killed one of them!"

"I saw it!" Alexios shouted, even though he was close by. He was exhilarated from the fight.

He then shouted that he was returning for the Emperor and wheeled his horse to spur it up the bank. With a glance at each other and a shrug Max and Talon did the same. Once they had regained the road, stepping over bodies and other shattered obstacles, they hurried along the short distance to where they had last seen the staff officers. In passing Talon thought he saw the broken body of one of the young men who had sneered at Alexios earlier. The young man's frozen features bore a look of stark terror.

The dog for its own reasons decided to accompany them and kept pace as they approached the Emperor's men. The situation had changed. The rain of rocks had stopped, but now there were Turks all over the slopes raining arrows down upon the dense mass of men and animals still struggling to escape along the trail. The Emperor's guard had moved up the trail another hundred yards and was clustered about a small knoll near the road.

The Emperor's men were holding off an attack by a ferocious band of Turks who were screaming and brandishing spears and swords as they charged with reckless courage at the personal guards surrounding the monarch. The Varangian Guard greeted them with fierce battle cries of their own, meeting the attackers with equal ferocity. The fight raged back and forth as the Anglo and Norsemen men hacked at the Turks with bloodied axes and the Turks fought back with bloodied spears and curved swords of their own. Soon the ground was slippery and the screams of the wounded drowned out all other sounds. Some Latin knights joined in from the sidelines with maces and axes to assist the Varangians in the center.

It was an uneven match and the Turks were soon driven off to seek easier pickings than these berserk blond men with huge axes. But arrows still flew and men still fell, including the Varangians, who were not archers. Talon and Alexios, with Max right behind them, galloped up to the group and Talon began to return the Turkish fire with his own arrows. The mercenaries shouted their appreciation of his shooting in their own incomprehensible language, waving their weapons and yelling encouragement to him every time a Turk went down.

However it was clear to all they were in desperate trouble.

The Turks had sprung their trap well.

There was a brief respite in their particular area around the knoll, although the battle raged furiously elsewhere. Alexios called over to Talon to join him. He had dismounted and was kneeling next to a body that lay at the feet of a small cluster of men.

Dismounting Talon tossed his reins to Max, who was already on foot making friends with the dog. Talon hurried over to join the men around the body.

Lying on the ground lay General John Kantakouzenos covered in blood. He was dead, having taken many wounds. "He was caught by a band of Turks and slain. He fought and died as a soldier should," someone muttered as Talon approached

He glanced up past the group and saw General Mavrozomes, himself appearing to be lightly wounded, talking intensely to the Emperor. The Emperor was sitting on a rock with his head in his hands.

"What is he planning to do?" Talon asked pointing with his chin at the seated man, Alexios stood up in his saddle to look.

"He is doing nothing, Talon. It...it is like he is frozen." Alexios sounded disgusted.

"What in God's name? We have to fight our way out or we are surely dead men!" Talon exclaimed.

Evidently this was what Mavrozomes was saying too, as he added with a shout, "Your Majesty, we cannot stay here! We can marshal our troops and fight our way to the end of the pass. We must! Your Majesty!" he bellowed, ignoring the startled looks from the men all around him. "We must leave. Now!"

Manuel roused himself long enough to take his hands away from his face and to look up at his general.

"What do you suggest, my general?" he whispered. His helmet was gone and his long black hair, streaked with gray, was plastered to his dark features, which wore a look of defeat.

"Stay with your bodyguard!" Mavrozomes said as he waved his arm around him at the wolfish crowd of bloodied Varangian soldiers. "I shall collect others to form a wedge, then we shall fight our way forward. I had word from Kontostephanos that the way back is blocked completely. He is trying to join us as I speak. We do not have such a clear picture of what is happening to the front, but I think the van and Baldwin's men might have managed to get through." The general turned to his men. "Stay together, do not get cut off, because we cannot stop for either the wounded or anyone who is left behind."

His words were greeted with a growl of acceptance from the Varangians. The eunuchs said nothing. Manuel shuddered and tried to stand. Alexios stepped in quickly and helped him. The Emperor stood, dazed and bewildered by the awful turn of events, and then became aware that all around him were battle torn men, most bloody from their own wounds or others' blood, who surrounded him in a protective circle. Everyone was staring at him.

With a loud sigh he appeared to pull himself together and stood erect to gaze up the road. Fighting was raging all along the track as Turkish soldiers hurled themselves with mad bravery onto the massed ranks of the Byzantine army, who still put up a stiff resistance if not a cohesive one. There appeared to be heavy casualties on both sides as the Turks, determined to finish off the Byzantine army, attacked recklessly and the Byzantine troops fought for their very survival.

The Emperor nodded and to a collective sigh of relief from all around motioned for his horse to be brought to him. It took a few minutes to gather enough men and add them to the ranks of the Varangians, before they pushed off the low knoll and back into the cluttered trail. It was slow going, as they had to negotiate the wreckage of baggage wagons and enormous siege engines that were now abandoned and get past the carnage all around them. The mangled bodies of oxen, which had died in the traces from the arrows and flying boulders, were mixed with those of horses and men. The ground was slippery with blood from animals and men alike and the stink of blood and disemboweled men and animals made many retch. Their newfound friend the dog sniffed at a mangled mess and whined over what had once been another dog still tied to its dead master, but when Max whistled it lifted its head and looked as though it understood. It followed him closely as they moved off. Talon glanced down at the splintered wreckage of one wagon and noticed sheaves of arrows tied in bundles.

"You!" he called to one of the eunuchs. "Do you see those arrows? Take as many of them as you and your companions can carry! We will need them."

The eunuch nodded agreement and, reaching into the jumble of equipment, took hold of one sheaf and tossed it to Talon, who caught it in midair, nodding his thanks. The other archers saw what he was doing and called for more.

The Turks were everywhere, so the Varangians, who knew how to make a formidable shield wall, led the way with a hard wedge of men with axes and spears to the front. They shouted as they stamped each foot forward and stabbed and hacked to some kind of awful rhythm, cutting a swathe of death that moved forward without being overwhelmed by the smaller groups of Turks. The light infantry, eunuchs and other servants walked right behind the front ranks and finished off any of the wounded enemy with long knives or even thrust past the Varangians at the enemy with long spears.

Talon, Max, and Alexios, with several other men who had obtained bows and scavenged arrows, rode behind on horseback, which gave them the height to see over the heads of the front ranks and to support them with arrows. The Emperor, his guards, and his general with some of his own men closely followed. A rag-tag of soldiers, once they saw that this group was making progress, attached themselves to the back of the column where they were shoved into the ranks by the more experienced soldiers to help to fend off attacks from the flanks and the rear. Alexios was one of the most energetic of the officers. He would stop by an exhausted man who was seated on the side of the track and seize him by the shoulders, shout words of encouragement, then haul him to his feet and push him into the ranks of fighters. Men were gasping and stumbling with exhaustion and thirst brought on by the heat of the sun burning down upon them. Talon wiped his eyes free of sweat with a rag he had around his neck and concentrated his gaze forward.

They finally made it past the last of the great baggage wagons only to find a large group of Turkish cavalry and footmen blocking their way forward. This group had slipped into a gap between the two divisions and, having seen the emperor's entourage, or what was left of it, were now preparing to attack.

Without being asked Talon and the other bowmen loosed arrow after arrow at the Turks and had the satisfaction of seeing men go down. Undaunted, the Turks responded with their own arrows and inflicted yet more casualties upon the group. Men went down with strangled cries as arrows found their mark.

"Keep your shields up! Stay in a crouch and move forward!" Alexios shouted, his voice hoarse. Another man bellowed orders to the Varangians. He was an officer of the elite infantry, but Talon could not see his face as it was covered by the helmet that protected his head, leaving only his deep blue eyes uncovered.

Talon felt exposed sitting high on the back of a horse, certain that he was a target for more than one of the enemy archers. At that moment an arrow pierced the chain mail of his upper left arm. The mail stopped the arrow from going deep but it made him gasp and it knocked him sideways in the saddle. He looked down and saw the arrow sticking out of his arm. Gritting his teeth he pulled it out and cast it aside. He retaliated by taking down three of the enemy in quick succession before his arm became too numb to use for a while. Slight as the wound was it still made Talon feel momentarily weak, so he stopped and attempted to bind it.

Max sidled his horse alongside. "Here, Talon," he said, and bound the arm quickly with a rag.

"Thank you, Max," Talon said through parched lips. Max grinned and slapped Talon on the back.

The Turks decided this was the time to attack again and hurled themselves at the Varangian wedge. The impact shook the shield wall as savage men bellowed their war cries and hacked and stabbed at one another, grunting with the effort of pushing back and holding their places in the line. The crash of shield on shield, the rasping of sword blades rang out, and the screams of wounded men deafened Talon's ears. The Byzantine group was the more determined, and, to Talon's relief, the shield wall held and prevented the Turks from breaking through.

Try as they might the Turkish footmen could not prize the overlapped shields apart. Max, unable to restrain himself, handed his bow to another man then joined the ranks of the Varangians in the melee on the line, and Talon could see him in the thick of the fighting. His sword moved like a piston, stabbing back and forth while he batted aside the blows from the enemy with his long shield. But he too took a wound, in the mid thigh, made him stagger before he decapitated the man who had struck him.

It was Talon's turn to bind his friend's wound while Max leaned panting against his horse. The wound, while not deep, was clearly painful. Eunuchs nearby were administering to others in the same manner and one passed a bandage to Talon. The dog sidled up to Max and lifted its head, locking eyes with Max, clearly concerned. Man and beast appeared to have bonded.

"Do not worry, Dog. I am fine and so will you be," Max said as he patted it on the head. The animal whined.

"You should stand back, Max. They are doing fine just now," Talon told him.

Max nodded, but then gave Talon a slap on his arm—forgetting that it was his wounded one—and plunged back into the fray. He was joined by the dog, which growled in one continuous note, its huge jaws snapping ferociously at any exposed flesh that presented itself.

Talon felt the friendly slap hurt as he mounted. Max's exuberance! He smiled ruefully as he rubbed his wounded arm.

Slowly a mound of bodies from both sides began to grow in front of them. A few Turks with reckless courage ran at the shield wall in a tight formation and managed to create an opening with their stabbing spears and maces taken from the Byzantine dead. While the gap was quickly closed and the brave men slaughtered, one managed to get past. Incredibly he evaded the surprised men behind the wall and drove straight at the Emperor, who was easy to identify because of his white horse. The Turk dodged past a stabbing spear and leapt at Manuel. His astonishing move brought the horse down and the Emperor with it. The Turk was first to recover. He lifted his sword to finish the still dazed monarch, but then Talon hurled himself off his own animal to hammer his small shield edge onto the neck of the warrior, who rolled off the Emperor and died in silence of multiple stab wounds inflicted by the Byzantine men around.

Talon and Manuel stared at one another, panting. Their eyes met and the Emperor blinked the sweat out of his eyes. The shocked officers scrambled to pick Manuel up and assist him back onto his horse, while Talon grabbed the reins of his horse from a eunuch and remounted. Manuel himself looked too dazed and disoriented to know what had just happened but General Mavrozomes called over to Talon.

"You saved his life with your quick action, Knight. It will not be forgotten."

"If we live though this I shall be grateful to God for just having preserved my own life," Talon said to Max.

Several other Turks attempted the same feat of wild courage but the Byzantines were now ready for them and spit them on spears as they charged; in one case the eunuchs stabbed the man to death with their long knives once he got through. The reckless attacks of this nature soon stopped.

Despite the pain in his arm Talon joined the other archers and shot arrow after arrow into the packed ranks of the Turks from his vantage point on his horse, and before long this intense barrage of arrows from him and the other archers had its effect. The Turkish warriors could not reach the Byzantine archers to destroy them because of the immovable ranks of the Varangians, who were disciplined and ferocious fighters. Eventually with sharp cries of defiance the Turks pulled back, waving their fists and weapons, unbeaten but frustrated.

Talon heard the sound before it happened. There was a low roar from behind followed by a gust of hot wind that startled him. He spun in the saddle, half expecting another barrage of rocks to come flying at them only to see a wall of dust being blown up the valley.

Within seconds a strong wind that suddenly roared up the valley, bringing with it a dense cloud of dust, swept over the combatants, blinding everyone with swirling particles that stung and burned their exposed skin. Within the howling storm that encompassed everyone in the valley the men around the Emperor groped for one another and Talon heard the general shouting. "Hold onto one another but keep moving, we must keep moving! Blow the trumpet to tell our people where we are."

A trumpet sounded but it was soon cut off as the trumpeter choked on the dust.

Men from all about began to call out and even the Varangians joined in, shouting for one another in their own language. Talon looked around for Max and found him winding a cloth around his lower face. Max lifted his hand and then rode in closer to Talon. The dog came with him, cowering near the horse's legs.

Talon whirled as he felt a heavy hand on his shoulder. But it was only the general.

"God has sent us help! We must keep moving! How far to go now?" Mavrozomes shook Talon by the shoulder questioning him. "You came up here before; how much further?" he demanded over roar of the sand storm.

"Perhaps several hundred paces and we leave the gorge, general," Talon responded. He coughed from the dust as it went into his throat. Pulling out a rag he wound it around his lower face. It was incredible that a dust storm of this kind should spring up so quickly from literally nowhere. They must use it to their advantage, he thought.

They pushed on through the blinding dust , tripping and falling over bodies that were in places stacked four high. Turks and Byzantine soldiers lay sprawled all about in the rictus of death. Disoriented and as lost in the sandstorm as the Byzantines, small groups of Turkish soldiers would blunder into them. There would be a brief fight and more men would fall, and then the Turks would disappear into the swirling dust. Men of their own army were found sitting on the ground having given up. They were kicked to their feet by the unsympathetic Varangians and officers and beaten back into service, swelling the ranks.

The ordeal felt as though it lasted an eternity as men and horses staggered forward. The men on horseback, their faces covered with cloths, squinted desperately to see far enough forward to tell if there was yet another ambush to overcome. No one had any water so they were parched with thirst, but none dared to leave the ranks of the main body to seek it even as close as it was known to be.

After an hour or more the keening, buffeting wind abated and they began to see that they were exiting the gorge, and before long, men noticed that a large fort on the flat area on some high ground. Talon knew it had not been there when he came up before. The wind all but died out and the soldiers began to exclaim with joy at their deliverance. In front of them was the van of the army and the troops from Antioch behind a crude makeshift defensive barrier thrown together from rocks and trees.

Men began to take heart, wanting to run to the enticing safety of the defenses, but General Mavrozomes held them together with his fierce will and marched them as a unit until they were finally within the walls of the barrier constructed by the divisions from Antioch.

The men with the Emperor staggered into the temporary safety of the fort and collapsed with exhaustion and relief. Some men even fell to their knees and raised their clasped hands to the heavens calling their thanks to God for their deliverance.

There was even enough water for all, brought from the river by a few courageous souls determined to obtain water despite Turkish harassment.

Ragged groups of men trickled in for the rest of the day. Most were disoriented and many were wounded; all were fearful and dispirited. There was little to be done for the wounded other than bind their wounds and give them some water. The eunuchs took on the task of creating a makeshift hospital where wounded men were sent. The rest of the men stayed near the barriers of rocks and trees, prepared to defend them at a moment's notice.

The Turks were not inclined to give up the fight. Their mounted cavalry made determined incursions, seeking weak spots and opportunities, the warriors riding their ponies in hard and loosing flights of arrows over the defenses. Many of these arrows found their mark and made life very uncomfortable for those inside. Talon and Max found themselves alone with Alexios. They were all three exhausted and lay on the ground with the reins of their horses held firmly in one hand, oblivious of the occasional arrow that thudded into the ground nearby.

"Well, now we know for sure that the Turks were in the gorge, by God," Max panted. Talon croaked a laugh.

"Yes, I wonder what the Emperor is thinking about that now."

"It is very serious," Alexios said gloomily. "We have lost all our baggage and our siege weapons. We cannot go forward to Iconium without those and we cannot go back because it is clear the Turks hold the passes."

"Do you think the Emperor will be able to negotiate a withdrawal?" Max asked, sitting up on one elbow.

"We might have to, but it will be on their terms. They have won this battle as far as I can see."

At that moment there was a great cheer from the men standing by the defenses facing the gorge. Talon and his companions got painfully to their feet and went to see what was going on.

The sight they was worth cheering about. General Kontostephanos was marching his men out of the passes and it appeared that they were relatively unscathed. The men of the main army greeted them with enthusiasm as they marched into the encampment.

"I am going to see what has been happening with the Emperor," Alexios announced. He walked slowly towards a group of senior officers gathered around Manuel.

Talon and Max watched him go and then sat back down on the stony ground to discuss their situation.

"It looks as though we have ourselves in a pretty pickle this time, Talon," Max remarked, chewing on a length of dried grass.

"Yes, we are trapped, unable to go forward and unable to go back. And it looks as though the other army did not fare so well either, if the head the Turks displayed earlier today really was that of Andronikos."

"You mean the general leading the other army?" Max asked, for he was not as aware of events as Talon, who could understand the Greek being spoken all around them.

"Yes, that's him. His army was supposed to go to Amasia and cut the Turks off."

"Looks like they didn't make it then. God be merciful on their souls, for the Turks will not have been," Max said.

"Any army as powerful as this and as well organized cannot function as it was designed to in an ambush like that. The Turks knew what they were doing. They have all but destroyed us. Ugh, what a stink!" Talon exclaimed.

He had just caught a whiff of excrement left by men with dysentery. If seemed that many of the soldiers were afflicted.

"The men have had the flux since we were on the plains," Max said. "I am even feeling the effects of something. The food is terrible."

Talon wrinkled his nose. "We have not been here even a few hours and those men are shitting all over the place. It is a perfect breeding ground for disease!"

"Do you have anything in your saddle bags?" Max asked.

"I thought you said that you were feeling sick."

"Only at the other end. The front end," Max said pointing to his mouth, "tells me that my stomach thinks my throat has been cut."

Talon laughed. Max never seemed despondent when things were going badly.

"Little enough, but we might manage for a day or so."

"God help us but that will not be long enough, I fear. We need to find some water for ourselves and our horses." Max indicated their two mounts, which were standing with their heads down, clearly exhausted, their flanks heaving. "They are in a sorry state."

Talon beat his fist on the ground. "Why did he not listen, and why did he not bring the Turks to battle on the plain of Philomelion when he could have?"

"The plain of what?"

The plains we were on before we entered that God forsaken pass. This army could have minced the Turks out in the open. They knew it and so did general Kontostephanos; he argued for us to stay out of this place."

"Well, now we are here." Max stated. "It is almost as though the dust arrived at divine command! Never seen anything like that before." Max said.

Talon nodded agreement. The dust storm had been an extraordinary occurrence and had arrived just in time.

There were thousands of perspiring and exhausted men and animals within the confines of the crude defenses and the noise was deafening, made worse by the cries and groans of the wounded.

"I wonder what we can expect from the Turks?" Max muttered looking towards the plains.

"Not much," Talon answered. "Their leader Arslan is probably crowing with delight right now. We gave him the victory with our own stupidity. God willing we will get killed and not end up as slaves of those hairy men on ponies. I have to give it to them though, they know how to ride and shoot. It reminds me of the time I was in Persia."

There were anxious shouts from the barricades and a shower of arrows flew overhead, so they scrambled to their feet and hurried to the defenses. Another attack was upon them and the Turks seemed determined to make life as miserable as possible for the Byzantine army.

After the attack had been beaten off with spears and arrows, Talon and Max found themselves seated next to some of the men from the Varangian guard. Some of them spoke bad Greek, so they could communicate.

"You two are pretty good with the sword and the bow," one of them commented. "I am Cuthberht and I come from the Norselands," he explained.

"You are not so bad yourselves! What is it that brings you to this country so far from home?" Talon asked.

"Gold and curiosity. The gold I do not have anymore and the curiosity might get me killed this time." Cuthberht laughed and spoke to his companions.

They were a tough looking crowd with their thick blond beards, heavy tunics, and chain mail that made no concession to the heat. Their long blond or red hair fell in braids down their backs from under their helmets. Many bore wounds, but their blue eyes were sharp and undaunted by their circumstances. These men did not give up easily, Talon thought, looking at them. Their axes were encrusted with blood from the fighting. They chuckled at whatever it was that Cuthberht told them.

"They seem to be mighty handy with those axes of theirs, I noticed," Max remarked.

Talon translated for Cuthberht, who guffawed. "Yes, these axes are for chopping people up, not for wood!" he said with his thick accent. He took off his helmet and rubbed his forehead where the rim had worn a red welt. His red bearded face was flushed with the heat and he was sweating copiously. Indeed, the slim but wide blades of the axes made for intimidating weapons.

"Where are you from? Are you Franks?" one of the other men asked.

"We have come from the Holy Land," Talon told him.

They were interested. "You Christians have conquered that land?"

"That was nearly a generation ago," Talon informed him. He was rubbing a nub of grease into his bowstring as he spoke. His arms ached from the shooting and his wound, he felt bone weary.

"You know how to use that, Frank," the same man said. "You were killing them at a greater range than they could from their horses. I saw you kill one at more than a hundred paces. That was a feat."

"Has anyone got any food to share?" A Varangian called out. We should share our food."

Men immediately checked their satchels and pockets, while Talon and Max retrieved some bread and cheese from their saddlebags. Someone made a small fire and shared out the rations to the men clustering about.

"By the Gods but I miss a good Herring Matjes!" one named Erikr said, his tone wistful.

"What is that?" Max asked.

"It is pickled herring fish that is salted. Tastes fine with ale or mead," Erikr said.

"I prefer Surströmming," another Varangian who introduced himself as Eadgar told them, smacking his lips through his ginger beard.

Cuthberht chuckled. "Now that will put hair on your chest!"

Eirikr noticed the puzzled looks on Talon and Max's faces.

"It tastes like rotten fish marinated in cat's piss," he laughed. He pretended to gag.

"Thus speaks a man without any couth who cannot tell good food from bad," Eadgar retorted.

Talon and Max sat back and enjoyed the argument that ensued. For a few brief moments they all forgot their predicament and were able to laugh at these good-natured but formidable warriors from the countries far to the north. They spent the next few hours around the small fire chewing on the meager rations they shared with one another.

The talk went back and forth as night fell and the men tried to make sense of their situation. Despite their apprehension there was a sense of comradeship engendered by their dire situation and the fact that they all knew they had fought well together and survived thus far. Men tried to joke and pretend that it was not as bad as it sounded. But everyone knew that this day had been a disaster and that the army was trapped and could well be destroyed by the next day.

Much later Alexios joined them and told them an extraordinary thing.

"The Emperor and his generals do not know what to do over there," he exclaimed angrily after he had settled in between Talon and Max, who made room for him around the fire.

"What happened?" Talon asked him as he passed a piece of stale bread to him.

"Well I am probably finished in this world anyway, but they were talking about leaving the army and trying to get away as a small group." Alexios' tone was despondent. He chewed without appetite on the scrap of bread.

"They were what?" There was an indignant chorus of voices from those men who understood him.

Alexios swallowed and took a sip of water before saying anything. "I told them that they could not desert the army, it would be shameful, and if they did then they were more likely to be taken prisoner before the rest of us anyway. We know full well that we cannot surrender to the Turks. It is slavery or worse for anyone who does."

"You might have misheard?" Cuthberht enquired.

"No...I did not."

"I bet they did not like being told that," Eadgar said, almost under his breath. "Treacherous whoresons, and to think that we're expected to defend them with our lives. God protect us all from leaders like that."

"I imagine that Kontostephanos did not disapprove of your words," Talon said by way of encouragement.

Alexios did not respond, and Talon guessed that his friend had been shocked at his own presumption. One did not address the emperor in that way. Talon looked around him in the gloom of the early night and wondered who would still be with them in the morning. The men nearby wore the exhausted and haunted look of people who do not have any hope that they will survive.

There was another shout of alarm and they all scrambled to man the crude defenses.

Chapter 14

An Army at Bay

The army of the Byzantines battled for its life through much of the night that followed, standing at the crude defenses which had been feverishly thrown together from branches and rocks by the Antioch infantry the previous afternoon.

The struggle was often hand to hand as the Turks attempted time and again to break in and finish what they had almost won the day before. In the flickering light of the makeshift torches and the fires that had been started by the eunuchs and other retainers, the men of Byzantium fought with desperation against a howling mass of Turks. The press of men surged back and forth around the defenses as they stabbed and hacked at one another, or fell in an embrace of death, some even biting at their foes as they died.

Talon and his companions held a place alongside the contingent of Varangians who were not directly responsible for the defense of the emperor. Men from the Edessa infantry joined them, fierce fighters who wielded long spears and could hold off the raging opposition while Talon and others like him picked off their leaders with arrows fired almost at point blank range.

From time to time the Turks would succeed in pulling a man out of the packed ranks of the Byzantines with long hooks, and then would butcher him screaming in front of all. At one time Cuthberht was almost seized: his sleeve was hooked and the Turks began to drag him out. But Max had seen what was happening, and with a shout he leapt forward and slashed the shaft of the hook in two. Both he and Cuthberht were hauled back into their own ranks by many willing hands.

"I owe you!" Cuthberht shouted, wiping his face. He then hacked fiercely at one of the enemy who was within range of his huge axe, almost cutting him in two.

In the process of blocking a cut from a Turk Max's blade shattered. He was left for a moment holding the remains of his sword and was very vulnerable. But Cuthbert was watching out for him, and as Talon shot an arrow at the Turk, he seized the sword off one of the dead Varangians at their feet and tossed it to Max. Max caught it in midair and went back to the fight, his new blade flashing in the torchlight.

The carnage along all parts of the wall was terrible and bodies were piled high. Finally even the Turks had had enough and left the wall to fade into the night, leaving the defenders panting and licking their wounds.

The exhausted defenders watched numerous fires spring up all over the valley as the Turks settled down for the night. The moans and screams of the wounded were a dreadful sound that Talon wished he could block out from his ears. Eventually some of the *Tagmata*, the light infantry, stole out into the dark and finished off the wounded Turks nearby who were calling out in their own language for water from anyone. There was no mercy. A scream would suddenly stop or a voice would be pleading in the darkness only to be followed by abrupt silence.

When the scouts could find them in the dark, they hauled their own wounded back into the confines of the stinking camp and attended to them as best they could. Water was short, so a few brave souls with some reluctant guards ventured to the river and came hurrying back with enough for the Emperor and his entourage. Although it was late at night the canopy of stars overhead gave off enough light to see the boundaries of the camp and the huddles of men who were resting while they waited for the next attack. Talon saw men slip out and guessed that they too were going for water. No one was challenged, so it seemed as though the Turks were as exhausted as the Byzantine army.

He thought of them all as Byzantine but the truth was that few of the men in this army were in fact Greek. Many of the units were mercenaries who had come to the empire to earn good money, as had the Varangians and the men from Antioch, who had lost their king Baldwin just the day before in the gorge. There were units of Bulgars, Franks and Germans on large horses, and many other native auxiliaries whose homes used to be in this general region before the Turks displaced them.

Talon, Alexios, and Max, with his new-found friend Dog now constantly at his side, took turns to sleep but it was nearly impossible with the din and the stink. Despite this Talon managed to get in a little rest and woke to see the beginning of dawn in the eastern sky. Alexios was still sleeping, but Max was standing with the dog at his side looking to the east where the Turkish encampment lay.

Talon clambered to his feet feeling stiff and sore. He came and ruffled the head of the dog, then stood next to Max, who was standing with his feet apart leaning on his new sword. Talon looked at the shining blade. It was of brighter steel than normal swords and it bore an inscription. Max noticed his stare and lifted the blade for him to look at it.

"It is of harder steel than my former sword. I have heard of these, they are a legend among the Northern warriors. They call such swords by this name, *'Ulfberht'*—look! See the letters? They are stamped into the steel! There is even a small cross with the letters at the beginning and between the H and the T. Cuthbert gave me a fine sword indeed. From all that I hear this metal is as good as any Damascus steel."

"Then that is a fitting blade for a Templar, Max. You have earned it," Talon said.

They did not say anything more to one another. There was no need. Talon rubbed his eyes, which were gritty with lack of sleep, and felt his beard, which was matted with filth. His arm burned and his shoulders ached painfully from all the work with his bow. He looked at Max and the other men nearby, mostly them Norsemen or English. They all looked haggard with exhaustion. None of them had bathed for days and their eyes were sunken in gaunt faces that were muddy or smeared with blood. Their armor or chain mail was dented and rent, while their tunics were torn and stained with their own blood and surely that of others. This was an army in no condition to take the fight to the enemy. He wondered what was going to become of them.

The sky changed from a pale grey streaked with pearl to a light shade of blue; eventually the sun climbed over the edge of the mountains and another hot day had begun. The army woke and manned the walls, 'standing to their places' in case the Turks decided that they would have another attempt at them. Nothing happened, however, although they could clearly see groups of horses tethered in the distance. The Turks, it seemed, were content to let the Byzantine army wait until they were ready.

Far off in the distance Talon and Max heard the sound of the call to prayers and noticed an increase in activity at the enemy camp.

Alexios woke and came to join the other two and announced that he was hungry. None of them had anything to share so he wandered off to see if he could scrounge something from the emperor's attendants. He came back with a few crusts of bread and some salted fish, which he shared.

"This is all they would give me," he grunted as he gnawed at the fish, which was dried and tough.

"I don't care, this fish is fine for breakfast, but you'll have to do better than this for lunch, Alexios," Max said. He gave a morsel to the dog, which gulped it down gratefully and looked at him with a beseeching look for more. He patted it on the head.

"There is nothing else for any of us, Dog," he said.

Alexios grunted and managed a weak grin. Talon watching him thought of how he had changed since the first time they had met. The arrogance was gone and he had lines of exhaustion on either side of his mouth but he was holding up. The rest of the army was eating what they had left but the future now looked bleak. They had no supplies and were effectively cut off from any retreat.

Alexios waved off the circling flies that had appeared just after dawn and now swarmed around the army.

"Damned flies!" he complained.

Talon was not surprised. Excrement, urine, and blood were everywhere. The place stank worse than a dung heap. To this noisome stink was now added the fetid odor of the corpses piled high all around the perimeter.

"I am sorry for the wounded. The flies will make life hell for them now," Max remarked.

Talon had a thought. "Has anyone seen Pantoleon?" he asked.

Alexios shook his head. "Not since the rocks began to fall. I... we have been too busy."

Talon knew what he meant. They had all been too busy trying to stay alive to worry about others outside their immediate circle. There was a brief silence.

"Perhaps he is with the Emperor even now," Max suggested.

"I did not like him much, but he was a fighter. He should have been with us at the walls. I do not remember seeing him with the generals either," Alexios said softly.

Max voiced his thoughts. "We cannot go anywhere and the Turks are staying put. I wonder if there is a plan to break out and rush back down the gorge."

"From what I have noticed, those nearest the Emperor have not got a plan," Alexios said. He sounded resigned and bitter.

"Then we must look to ourselves, for when the Turks come today it will be to finish us off or to ask us to surrender."

"What do you intend to do, Talon?" Max asked, as he picked some dried fish out from between his teeth with a dirty fingernail.

"I do not intend to be taken prisoner, Max. If the Emperor wants to surrender that is his business, but I intend to find a way out and you are coming with me."

"God's will, that I shall," Max agreed.

Alexios looked at them both. "I would like to come too, if...you will accept me."

"Good," Max said. "Three is better than two, and perhaps we can persuade some of the Norsemen to come as well, they will make good company. And I am taking the dog with us."

"Good idea, Max. Then we should check our horses carefully and make ready for anything."

They did not have much to do. Their mounts were standing among a forlorn group of horses held by some younger men who had been ordered to keep them from bolting. The animals needed water but apart from many scratches and a few nicks from a sword or spear they appeared to be in reasonable shape. They left the horses and went back to the walls to stare at the Turkish encampment.

Finally the Turks began to assemble out on the plain and the call to man the defenses was shouted to the tired men of the Byzantine army. The Turks wanted to engage at a distance at first, loosing many arrows into the crowded ranks of the defenders and riding off when there were too many arrows coming back at them. Talon worked with others to make them keep their distance.

Eventually, however, the Turks became bolder and began to rush the defenses as though looking for weak points. They howled battle cries as they jumped off their horses and rushed recklessly at the rocks and branches confronting them. They were met with yells and shouts from the Varangians and men from Antioch who stabbed and hacked at the enemy as they tried to break through.

Once again the fighting became a savage close quarter affair on a wide front with Max and Talon fighting in the company of the Varangians accompanied by Alexios and some spearmen.

Suddenly they heard a lot of shouting in the distance and the Turks in front of them began to fade away. Talon turned to see a group of Byzantine cavalry charge out through a gap opened in the wall to attack the Turks, who retreated hurriedly as the heavier horses came sweeping out. But the Byzantine cavalry were not archers, and they soon began to find that they were exposed to the accurate fire of arrows from the retreating Turks who shouted at the cavalry as though daring them to follow. Talon recognized the leader of the Byzantine cavalry and wondered if he would be stupid enough to do so, but John Angelos was not a fool. He chased the Turks long enough to make his point then ordered his men back behind the relative cover of the defenses.

The harassment began again, but this time the Turks were content to rain arrows upon the Byzantine army, inflicting many injuries, but few were fatal. Once again the cavalry sortied out to chase them away; they were armed with bows, but once again they had to retreat before they were sucked into the ambush the Turks had prepared. It was Constantine Makrodoukas who led them, and the frustrated general had to acknowledge that his cavalry could not engage the Turks and their mounted bowmen. Talon and Max watched the whole thing from inside, then in mute accord, they went back with the dog in tow to look at their horses and make sure they were ready to leave at a moment's notice.

"Those Turks are incredible riders! I have seen you do the same, Talon. So is this where you learned that skill of yours with a bow on horseback?"

"I learned Persia, and you'll note that the Byzantine cavalry cannot fight them on equal terms."

"Indeed I do. How is it that they have not learned this skill better?"

"That I do not know, but they have had long enough fighting these people to learn how to adapt and use it. They do not seem to have learned much at all. Some of them can use a bow on the horse, but few as well as the Turks."

"There seem to be fewer Turks about today, Talon. I could have sworn they were everywhere yesterday."

"They are probably looting our baggage trains and do not have much time for us right now. We can't go anywhere."

As they were talking the men on the walls facing the main Turkish encampment began to shout and point. Thinking they were under attack again the two of them looked at one another and then rushed to join the mob of men heading for the fortifications. As they jostled for position in their usual place alongside the cheerful Varangians who were chattering in their own guttural language, they were greeted by the sight of a small group of Turks riding to their camp, bearing white flags. Everyone stared at the oncoming men and wondered what they might be about.

The Turks stopped a discreet arrow length away. One of them who spoke Greek called out that they wanted to speak to the Emperor. Alexios was on the wall, and as the officer nearest to the visitors, told one of his soldiers to run and alert the Emperor and his generals. As the man sped off the soldiers stared at one another across the divide. The Turks appeared calm and content to wait, sitting quietly on their ponies who fidgeted and whisked flies away with their tails. The silence hung heavily on both sides as they waited.

Then General Kontostephanos hurried up to Alexios; there was a brief discussion, which Talon could not hear, but Alexios pointed at the Turks.

The general peered over the battlements at the delegation and raised his hand acknowledging their presence. Then Alexios called a man over and explained something to him. The man nodded, stood on the rocks, and shouted in Turkish to the waiting men.

Three men broke away from the group and walked their horses slowly towards the defenders. One of them was carrying the white banner, another was leading a splendid horse by an ornate silver inlaid bridle, while the third carried a long slim item wrapped in a silk cloth. They dismounted at the wall and a space was made which just allowed them to lead the horse though. The Turkish soldiers outside the compound held their own mounts. The envoys were then taken up to the general, who curtly acknowledged them and then walked with them and the magnificent horse towards the place where the Emperor and his remaining entourage waited. Kontostephanos waved to Alexios to come and join him. Alexios needed no persuasion.

"If I know my horses, that is a Nisaean, bred from the Turcomans in Persia," Talon said to Max.

"Beautiful animal," Max commented with approval as they watched the dark chestnut with the glossy hide and flowing mane and tail walk by.

The Byzantine army waited impatiently for the seemingly endless discussion to come to an end. The conference was held in the open as there were no tents, but the Varangian guard surrounded the Emperor, his officers, and the Turkish delegation so no one could see or hear what was going on.

"I have an uneasy feeling that our lives are being bartered away along with most of the rest of the army," Talon said to Max.

"I agree, Talon. He is a weak man, that emperor. He just wants to save his own skin. I do not trust him anymore, not that I did much to begin with." Max sighed and rubbed his stomach. "I am not sure if it is hunger or my bad guts," he complained.

"Even if we can escape this place it is a very long ride home, Max. Also, you have seen how good the Turks are. We will have to go like the wind."

"A good two days hard riding on the road, and that depends upon our horses. Now what?" Max pointed with his chin at the Emperor's guard, who were opening their ranks. General Kontostephanos and some guards escorted the Turkish delegation back to the makeshift walls. The Turks rejoined their companions on the plain who had waited patiently for them, and without a backward look the group of horsemen rode away.

"Here comes Alexios," Talon nudged Max. "Well...have we surrendered and are we off to slavery? What happened?" he asked Alexios as he came up to them.

"You will not believe me when I tell you!"

"Tell us, man!" Talon and Max demanded. A chorus of other voices joined theirs as other men who had seen him rushed up wanting to know what had transpired.

"The Sultan of the Turks, Kilij Arsan, sent an envoy, Gabras, that large man over there," he pointed, "and that horse he brought with him and a sword were articles of good faith. The Sultan is allowing our army to leave the field of battle and go home!"

For a long moment everyone just stared at him. Then there was pandemonium. Men hugged each other and shouted with joy and surprise. They were incredulous. Cheers had erupted elsewhere as the news reached men on the other side of the camp.

"How can this be?" Talon asked Alexios when they had finished embracing him.

"I do not know, but I swear by God that it is true. Even the Emperor cannot believe it and probably thinks it is divine intervention. I certainly do," Alexios answered, his eyes shining.

Max gave him a thump on the back that made him stagger. "I agree, God's will, and we are going back to the city," he said happily.

"The Sultan wants peace. He is allowing the entire army to leave. There are conditions, however."

"What are they?" Max asked, suspicion in his tone.

"The Emperor has to destroy two of his forts. One is called Dorylaeum; it is on the border we passed on the way here."

"Is that all?" Talon asked. He was still incredulous. This appeared to be far too good to be true.

"If I understood the translator correctly that is about all there is to it. Please do not ask me why it has come about like this; I am simply glad that we are going home." He indicated the feverish preparations being made by the rest of the army to leave. "We are going now, and none too soon for me. God be praised."

It took but a couple of hours for the Byzantine army to form up and prepare to leave the noisome place. As they marched out they left behind many graves and all the filth and detritus of an army defeated.

Talon, Max and Alexios were invited by the captain of the Varangians, Asmundr, to stay close to them and the Emperor, who did not appear to be altogether aware of his surroundings. The first divisions left the temporary sanctuary of the fortifications to head south down the gorge. These men, the van of the surviving army, were led by General Kontostephanos.

In the center came the Emperor surrounded by his personal guards and a dense contingent of cavalry, while behind them came the soldiers of the Antioch who that had first made it through the gorge and put up the defenses.

They moved with great caution, as no one quite trusted the enemy despite the truce. The first troops who entered the canyon were greeted with a horrific sight. Their shouts of anger and dismay echoed back to the middle of the army where the Emperor and his men were placed.

"What are they seeing?" Manuel called to his men.

A runner came panting back to them. "A message from the general, Your Highness."

"What is it? What is it?" The Emperor shouted.

"They have scalped everyone...and..."

"And what?" bellowed General Mavrozomes

"They...they have castrated everyone...everyone!" the runner gasped, then began to weep and wring his hands.

The silence that greeted his words was eerie. Nothing whatsoever was said by anyone. The soldiers cast sidelong looks at the accompanying eunuchs, who looked elsewhere. Everyone was appalled by the news, but they had yet to see for themselves what the Turks had done as they marched back along the trail of destruction which littered the gorge.

Not content with looting the remnants of the army baggage train and destroying the siege engines, most of which were still smoldering, the Turks had decided to confuse everyone by making sure that no one knew who and how many of their own had died in the battle for the gorge. It was an utterly ruthless thing to do but it was calculated and hugely demoralizing to the army that had to witness the result as it made its way back along the gorge.

The horror of the sprawled, mostly naked bodies that were piled high along the road through the gorge shocked everyone. Exposed skulls gleamed red in the sunlight, although most were swarming with flies. As if that were not bad enough, the crotches of most of the corpses were blackened ruins of what had once been their genitals.

Even the most hardened warriors were appalled. With every step they were forced to not only relive the battle of the previous day, but to witness the butchery of what the looters had left behind. Many men wept as they marched past the remains of their comrades; worse yet, it was almost impossible to identify individual comrades from the enemy. There was complete silence from the army other than the shuffle of sandals and the sobs of men who were undone by what they encountered.

"I sometimes wonder at the suffering we men inflict upon one another and who rules it," Talon murmured to Max.

"No one rules over suffering, other than the Devil, who reaped a good crop today, Talon," Max said as he stared out over the carnage.

Alexios and his friends made an attempt to locate the body of Pantoleon when they arrived near the area where he might have been killed. The dog whined as it nosed around at the remains of one of its kin in the same area. There was no sign at all of Pantoleon's body as they searched through the corpses of animals and men that were already bloating and beginning to stink after a day in the heat of the sun. It was a despondent group that proceeded to the entrance of the gorge.

The men of the forward divisions emerged from the claustrophobic confines of the pass after two hours of fast marching to find that the enemy was waiting for them. There were howls of anger as the Byzantine army stared at the enemy and contemplated the march to come across the plains and into the distant hills with the Turks still harrying them.

"So much for the promises of the Sultan! May he perish in Hell eternal!" someone shouted near the Emperor, who looked up from his blank contemplation of the ground. He had not been paying much attention up to this point, but now he lifted his head and asked what was going on.

"We are confronted by Turks. They have broken the agreement already," General Makrodoukas growled angrily.

"They are Turcoman tribes, my Lord," Talon offered.

"So what is the difference? They are still Turks, are they not?" The general said, his tone acid.

"Yes, my Lord, they are. But it is probable that the Sultan does not have as much control over them as he does the Seljuk."

"It does not make any difference now. We will have to fight them no matter what," the Emperor said.

They all looked at him. He appeared to be bracing up, which was a good sign. This was not the defeated man who had sat on a knoll in the gorge but the Manuel whom Talon had come to like in Constantinople.

"If we hold the divisions together and do not allow our troops to become separated we should be all right, Your Highness," Makrodoukas said. "However, we cannot wait for those who are wounded and cannot either ride or walk. There aren't enough of us to carry them and fight."

The entire army clustered along the banks of the river Meander and took what water they could for themselves and their horses before the orders went out that all the columns should form up into solid blocks of infantry with cavalry support on either side of them to chase the Turks off should they grow too determined.

It soon became clear that the Turcoman riders were looking for easy pickings from an army they considered defeated. They would charge at the Byzantines with shouts and yells and loose off arrows, then gallop away as soon as the cavalry showed signs of giving chase.

For all the attempts to close ranks and march forward, the foot soldiers were in poor condition; they lacked enough of both water and food for the journey back to the Byzantine frontier, which was a good two days' march away.

"I hope that someone on the other side of the border is waiting with fresh water and food, otherwise we are going to lose a lot of men," Max remarked to Talon as they rode alongside the marching Varangians.

"We are losing men already, Max. Look at how many wounded are being left behind."

Alexios looked back to where Talon was pointing. There were men lying where they had fallen to arrows that were fired into their massed ranks by the agile Turks. These men would be finished off and their corpses plundered before they were cold. Their piteous cries reverberated among the numb men who marched on with faces set like stone trying to ignore them. Every one of them knew that within an hour it could be himself lying there begging for help. In one or two cases a comrade would break ranks and bring some water to the wounded man.

In one horrific case the man reached up and gripped his comrade by the tunic in a desperate hold and begged to be killed before the Turks got to him. His companion wept as he stabbed the wounded man to death and then ran back to the rest of the men wiping his dagger on his tunic.

"I am witnessing the defeat of one of the largest armies ever to have been sent against the Turks," Alexios said, his tone despairing. "I think this side of the empire is gone forever."

He turned to his companions and said, "If I am wounded to the point where I cannot ride my horse then I wish you to take my life." His face was tight as he spoke, but it was clear to Talon and Max that he meant it.

They did not say anything, averting their eyes and riding on, while watching for more visitations from the enemy riders.

*****

The Turcoman tribes people were not to be denied their chance to harry the army, and the attacks continued all that terrible day as the Byzantine army staggered towards its own borders.

At one time Talon noticed a large Turk pointing out the Emperor and his contingents and wondered what he was telling his men. Just to make life difficult for him Talon loosed an arrow directly at the man, but his horse shifted and the arrow embedded itself in another rider just behind his target. There were howls of anger but a man was down and the Byzantine men nearby who had witnessed the action called their appreciation to him. The distance was well over one hundred yards.

"You are quite the bowman!" someone called. Talon looked around. He noticed the Emperor staring at him.

"Where did you learn to shoot so well? On a horse at that!" Manuel called over to him.

Men around them began to take notice.

"I learned from our enemies, your Majesty," Talon pointed to the retreating Turks.

"It is a useful skill. Why do we not have more men like that?" Manuel demanded, but the question was a rhetorical one and his attention drifted off.

Then Talon noticed that a very large group of Turks was assembling off to their right. "They are going to charge! Be prepared!" he called.

"Max, Alexios, stay together. They're going to make a bid for the Emperor. He would be the best of prizes for them."

Alexios nodded. "I agree. We should stay behind the pike men and the Varangians. Use that bow to good effect, Talon."

The more experienced officers on the flanks had seen what was about to happen and halted their men then faced them out. This was no skirmishing group come to loose arrows. These men were going to try and break the wall and get to the Emperor.

With blood curdling screams and yells the Turcoman cavalry smashed into the Thracian spearmen and all too quickly broke through to engage the Varangians in a vicious close quarter fight to the death. It became a mad melee of horses and men fighting hand-to-hand, howling at one another. Men fell and were trampled to death if they still lived as they fell. The screams of wounded men and horses filled the air. Talon could hardly see in front of him from all the dust, but he loosed arrow after arrow into the ranks of the attacking horsemen, knowing that approaching mounted men were the enemy.

But then the wall of Varangians caved and a determined group of riders pressed through, hacking down at the Norsemen on either side who could not retaliate with anything but their axes. Their spearmen defense having broken, it was up to them to fight the harder.

Several staggered backwards, brandishing their axes and shouting abuse at the Turks who could not see their objective clearly for the dust and the crush of men, but this appeared to make them all the more determined to break through. Talon drew his sword and urged his horse into the fray. Max was at his side screaming something as he dismembered a man in his path. Talon drove his sword forward and felt it jar on a man's body armor before it drove on into his chest. The man's mouth opened in a wordless scream and he fell out of sight.

Talon spurred his horse into another man and found that he was facing the large man he had fired his arrow at earlier. Talon stared into the fierce brown eyes of the rider, seeing the distinctive, somehow familiar scar that ran down his right temple to stop at his eyebrow. The man bared his teeth and swung a curved sword at his neck. Talon easily parried the blow and returned it with one of his own, stabbing up in a feint to the man's eyes. Up came the shield and his sword flicked down to drive at the man's midriff. But the horseman was suddenly falling out of the way. One of the Norsemen had hacked the front legs off the luckless horse so that it fell in a welter of blood, screaming its agony.

The Turk tumbled to the ground, but as quick as a cat he was on his feet, and another man who had seen the event kicked his horse alongside. Seizing a stirrup the man held on as his comrade rode away from the fighting, out and away from the mass of struggling men. As though this was a signal the rest of the Turks abandoned their efforts to reach the Emperor and hurriedly left the field. Talon watched as they streamed away out onto the plain, leaving the Byzantine army to nurse its wounds.

Talon stared after the retreating Turks. Now he remembered the man. It was the same one he had met in front of Hagia Sophia. And he was also the emissary who had all but begged the Emperor to stop at the now infamous gorge. Talon felt a cold chill of superstition.

He shook his head and made the sign of a cross over his chest then looked about him. His first thought was to find Max. He saw him dismounted, kneeling next to another man lying prone. Talon knew with a sinking feeling that it was Alexios before he reached them. He glanced around him to make sure that the Emperor was well protected and then dismounted.

Alexios was lying with his upper body cradled in Max's arms. Alex's teeth were bared in agony. His thigh jerked and bled while blood flowed between his fingers as he clutched at his midriff. Max had a nasty looking gash on the side of his head. Talon wondered how his helmet had been dislodged. There was a lot of blood pouring down his face as he held Alexios, who was staring down at the large gash in his side. He also had a wound just under the front of his left knee, which Talon knew must be agonizing.

Talon did not ask any questions. Quickly, he ripped a strip off his own sleeve and bound it around Max's head to stop the immediate bleeding, and then tore away the the armor and opened Alexios' tunic to lay bare the area of the wound. He peered hard at the inside of the wound to see how deep it was. He was worried that he could see the blue of his friend's intestines just under the surface, but that might have been his imagination. It would need stitching, but of course there were no tools for this to be found anywhere now.

"It is bad but not mortal," he told them. All the same, it needed serious medical attention and he could not provide it here. "I must bind you up quickly and prevent more loss of blood."

He tore some cloth from the cloak of a dead man nearby and, making a thick wad, pressed it against the wide open wound, then wrapped strips of cloth around Alexios' torso, binding it firmly in place. Even so blood seeped through the bandages, which worried him. He then did the same for the knee wound. The pain was so great that Alex passed out for a couple of minutes, which allowed Talon to complete the task unhindered. That wound alone meant that Alexios would be unable to walk away from this place.

"How does it feel?" he asked when Alexios came to his senses and ground his teeth from the pain.

"It hurts like Hell," he gasped. "God help me, but I should never have lifted my shield at that moment." His face was gray and he licked his dry lips. "Is there any water? I am parched." He stared up at them with unfocussed eyes. "Are they going to leave me here?" he asked, trying hard not to show fear in his voice.

"No," Max said. He touched his head where the bandage covered the gash.

"Will you be all right, Max?" Talon asked with concern.

"It will take more than this to put an end to me. God save us but that was close." Max gave a lopsided grin.

Talon smiled back, but it was a worried look he gave his friend. He wondered if God had even been present to witness this last fight.

Talon looked about him at the mess left from the skirmish. The Turks had done much damage. Men lay about either dead or wounded, while those still unhurt began to form up again in preparation to continue the march. There was a water skin lying not very far away. He retrieved it before anyone else could as it was a precious commodity now and allowed Alexios a sip of water. Max pointed to Alexios' horse. "Do you think you can ride?" he asked.

"God help me, but I must," Alexios winced with pain.

"Yes, you must," Talon agreed.

They lifted him up and half-carried him over to the horse. With difficulty they managed to get him astride his animal where he sat hunched over the pommel trying to stifle a sob of agony. Max and Talon looked at one another. Max absently stroked the head of the dog that had never left his side.

"This does not look good, Talon. Look, the Emperor is moving off already, leaving the wounded behind," Max said this under his breath as he watched the army begin to move away

"I do not know what choice he has, Max."

"He will leave these men behind to die and we cannot take them with us either, but that one we should take with us." He pointed to one of the Varangians who was limping along trying to keep up with the others. He had a wound in his calf that had a crude bandage wrapped around it. Eadgar was trying to help him along.

"It is Cuthberht! Quick, Talon, get hold of that horse over there!" Max said with an urgent note in his voice. "No one seems to have noticed it."

Talon scrambled off to catch the horse, which did not try to escape. He knew very well that Cuthberht would never be able to make it to their destination without one.

Max meanwhile called over to the Norseman. "Get on the horse, Cuthberht. It is your only chance."

Cuthberht looked back at them. Despite the bandage he was bleeding copiously from his wound. There was a desperate look in his eyes that changed to one of pure relief when he saw Talon holding the reins out to him. He slapped Eadgar on hte shoulder, said something to him then urged him to go on with the others. He limped back and took the reins and said, "God bless you, Frank. I am in your debt."

"Can you ride?"

"Does it matter? I will ride no matter what," he replied. "What? Should I wait for the Turks to come and geld me?"

"Let me look at that wound," Talon said.

Cuthberht held onto the reins of the horse and sat down hard. Talon realized what an effort it had been for him to walk with the wound. It was a nasty and deep cut, but he was able to stop the bleeding with a tight bandage and patted the man on the knee.

"You can get up now, Cuthberht, it will take more than this to finish you." He helped the man onto his horse.

"I shall stay with you, Frank. I owe you that."

"I am, Talon. You do not have to," Talon said.

"I shall, Talon. The Gods have given me a second chance. I thought I was finished just then."

"Then stay with us, as I think we are about to be left behind," Talon remarked with a lift of his chin toward the emperor's entourage. "You will be good company."

"Stay together and we will be fine. Keep that axe of yours with you, Cuthberht. You might still need it," Max said. Talon had a very uneasy feeling that they might not survive, but it made sense for them to stay together.

There were many wounded but all who could not walk or ride either on their own or with the help of a comrade were to be abandoned. Some made a pitiful effort to stagger to their feet despite their gaping, crippling wounds.

"In God's name, do not leave us to those barbarians!" they cried, but the remainder of the men who could continue to march had the wide-eyed stare of men who have seen too much horror and are simply trying to get out of hell. Talon and his companions were being slowly left behind, which could be disastrous, for the Turks would surely come back to loot the dead and finish off anyone they found alive.

"We must keep up at least until dark," Talon said to his companions. Alexios looked dazed, Max was squinting, but Cuthberht was alert and his bright blue eyes watching both the front and the back of them.

They rode flanking Alexios, at times holding him upright as they walked their horses. He was in great pain but Talon felt that as long as they could find clean water and food soon he might be able to keep his friend alive. They were falling further and further behind the emperor's entourage, but there was nothing they could do about that. Alexios could barely stay on his horse. Talon was worried, and he wondered, not for the first time, why he was here at all. It was not his or Max's fight. But then again perhaps it was, as the Turks were moving in large numbers all over the former Christian world. All the same, he knew full well that he would have remained in Constantinople if the Emperor had not ordered him to come.

"Do you think he will make it?" Max asked Talon of Alexios as they watched the sun setting.

Talon pointed. "We are close to some low wooded hills that the army has to negotiate, after that we should be near the border and with God's help I can look after Alexios until then. Cuthberht will be all right as long as he has his wound stitched up and cleaned. Alex's wound did not go deep enough to open his guts, but it came close. He needs to be stitched up or it will fester and then..."

Talon did not have to elaborate to Max, who knew full well what that meant.

Cuthberht remained with them and they were grateful. His wound was painful and he knew it would have meant death had he not had a horse to ride. He spoke very bad Greek so Talon had to strain to understand him. All the same he provided company, which was sorely needed, and there was something reassuring about his large muscular frame and the huge axe dark with dried blood that he gripped in his right hand as he rode on the left side of Alexios.

They arrived at the base of the wooded hills as the setting sun shone red in a flame of glory low in the western sky. The Emperor was for moving on, and his generals did not gainsay him. The army would march along the well-defined track that would take them through a low pass in the hills and then bring them to the plain beyond and the first fortified towns that belonged to the empire. It was a matter of five or six hours continuous marching. The Turks had drifted away as evening settled in so the army had for some hours been unmolested.

As they climbed the slopes of the first hills Talon looked back and saw the detritus the mass of men had left in their wake. Wounded and dead men and horses lay strewn along the side of the road among the baggage and equipment the men could or would no longer carry.

It would be rich pickings for the Turks in the morning, and more terrified men would stumble crying with frustration and fear along the road as they realized that they would not be able to march any further for loss of blood or the agony of their wounds, to await the cruel vengeance of the Turks. He turned his attention back to Alexios who was in a bad way; his normally dark features were ashen. The pain of the wounds and loss of blood were taking their toll.

Max glanced forward toward the Emperor and his entourage who were now some distance ahead of them. No one from that group so much as looked back to see how they were faring. They were now almost at the end of the marching rear guard who paid them scant attention as they staggered up the hill.

"We should stop and allow Alex to rest, Talon." Max said. His face was grim and his jaw set. He knew full well what this could mean.

"If we stop then let us ride well off the trail and work our way into the hills. We know where the road is so we can regain it later."

Max nodded. He looked as exhausted as Talon felt, but neither wanted to leave Alexios to the tender mercies of the Turks. They would have to stop.

"A couple of hours...it is all we can afford," Max stated. "I have the headache of all headaches," he complained. Talon said nothing. He hoped that the gash on Max's head was all it was and not something more serious. He asked Cuthberht how he was feeling, and the Varangian said he would be fine.

"I am concerned about your comrade. He looks in a bad way," he said, nodding at Alexios.

"He is, but with us three beside him there is a chance we can make it through."

"Your dog likes that one there," Cuthberht indicated the dog that remained close to Max.

"Max seems to have a way with it. It might be useful if we get in a scrap. It knows how to fight."

"I have seen that," Cuthberht said with a grin. His big round face was almost hidden by his bushy red beard but the exposed skin on his forehead was scabbed with sunburn and his bright blue eyes looked tired. He had massive shoulders and his large frame was too large for the small horse he was riding. Talon thought that he looked like a troll perched on the horse, which he made look small, but Talon was glad of his company.

They rode their horses off the darkening road, eliciting some disinterested looks from the dust-covered men marching past, but no one tried to stop them. Once they were well out of sight of the road Talon dismounted and walked back along their trail. He made sure there were no obvious signs of their having left the track and then went back to remount. Holding onto Alexios' horse, Talon led the way up the slope among the thick trunks of stunted trees, their horses slipping and struggling for a foothold until they came out onto the crest of a low hill. From here, still under the cover of the trees, he could see the dust rising along the road from the army marching, but just as easily he could see some way back along the way they had come. He looked at the men filing slowly

past and wondered whether they would see the Golden City ever
again.

The World is a raging Sea
Whose depth and width are vast,
And Time is a rickety bridge extending across it.

Yedaya Hapenini

Chapter 15

The Return

Talon was concerned about Max but his friend, although groggy from the blow to his head, still seemed to be able to function and was taking care of Cuthberht. Having settled the Norseman against a tree Max joined Talon as they considered Alexios.

"We can settle here for a while; let's get him down."

They eased Alexios off the horse and laid him against the bole of a gnarled old tree near to Cuthberht. The dog plopped itself down alongside the roots of another tree, his tongue hanging out panting and watching them. Alexios groaned with pain but otherwise said nothing. His eyes were closed and his face pallid. It was as though he had lost interest in his surroundings. Talon looked down at him.

"I am going to go down the other side of this hill and see if I can get some water. There might be a stream somewhere nearby," he told the other two men. They were too exhausted to do more than nod acknowledgment.

Taking his bow and the now empty water skin, he left Max and Cuthberht to watch over Alexios and the horses and moved silently down the other slope of the hill to where he thought he might have heard the distant sound of water. The dog scrambled to its feet and accompanied him, keeping close, its head up and lifting its feet as though sensing that it should not make any noise. Talon was not disappointed; there was a trickle of water flowing along the almost dried up bed of a stream. Despite his eagerness for the water he approached with great care, taking the dog by the collar to restrain it. It was very possible that the Turks were somewhere near and the last thing he needed was to stumble upon any of them.

The cicadas were rasping loudly in the evening twilight, making it hard to distinguish other small but important sounds as he approached the water, but he heard nothing that sounded like men and their animals. He watched the dog carefully as he went but it displayed no interest in anything that might spell danger, so he cautiously moved to a dense thicket that was very near the water and began to fill the skin. He leaned over and took a long drink of water to slake his own thirst.

A small lizard leapt up, surprising him briefly as it skipped over the dried grass to stop and stare back at him, then it did three small press ups and ran off under a nearby stone. The dog leaned over the low bank and was about to jump in after the lizard when Talon placed a restraining hand on its shoulder and pushed it down. It obeyed him with a reproachful look, then lapped the nearby water, looking up at him with questioning eyes. Suddenly, its attention flicked downstream and it gave a low growl.

Talon instantly followed its gaze and was shocked to see that downstream, only about one hundred and fifty paces away, there were indeed some dismounted Turkish warriors who were letting their horses drink. He berated himself for having missed them the first time he had checked.

Clearly they did not think there was any danger, as they were squatting comfortably alongside their horses talking. Talon froze for a few long moments and then very slowly slid back into the bushes behind him, whispering softly to the dog to follow. It stood up and moved after him as he walked carefully away from the water. He had a full skin so there was no reason to tarry other than to see which direction they would take. Eventually the Turks mounted up and headed back downstream away from his position. He took out an arrow and knocked it just in case, but then made his way silently back up the hill. There was no sign of pursuit and the rasp of the cicadas continued undisturbed.

He arrived back in the resting place to find Max and Cuthberht both looking worried.

"You were gone so long I was concerned," Max said, as the dog went up to him and offered to lick his face. He fondled its ears then pushed it away.

"There were Turks or Turcoman warriors watering their horses. I had to be sure which way they would go when done. I would not be surprised if these woods are crawling with them."

Max's eyes widened. Cuthberht went straight to his horse and took down his axe. His wide red face displayed apprehension.

"I do not think they heard or saw me," Talon said as he handed the water skin to Max, who took a long pull and then passed it to Cuthberht. Max allowed Talon to undo the bandage on his head and clean the matted hair and wipe most of the blood off his face before replacing the bandage. The wound was long but not deep. It would heal if it was kept clean, Talon reasoned. He squatted next to Alexios and nudged him awake.

Cuthberht assumed the role of guard and gave a low call to the dog to come with him to stand on the edge of the small clearing, watching and listening.

"Do not say anything, Alexios, as there are enemy all about," Max whispered while Talon was attending to him.

Alexios stared up at him and nodded. "Where are we?" he whispered.

"Well off the road, resting, but we cannot stay long. I want to dress your wounds and then we must move on or we will be trapped behind the Turks who are following the army. By dawn we must be over the border or we are in serious trouble," Talon whispered back.

"Why do not you leave me and save yourselves?" Alexios muttered. He ground his teeth as a wave of pain washed over him and his knee gave a spasmodic jerk. He gave out a low moan.

"We do not leave our friends behind," Max told him.

"God bless you for this...if we survive I will not forget," Alexios whispered.

Talon unwound the bandages and inspected the wounds. The knee wound worried him most because it was deep. From what he could tell a spear had penetrated just below the kneecap and done considerable damage to the tendons and the cartilage. All he could do was to bind it tight with more rags torn from his own cloak and do the same with the blood-drenched bandage wrapped around Alexios' stomach. At least the bleeding had been reduced to a mere seepage.

"We can stay for another hour and then we must leave. There will be a thin moon tonight, which will help us, but we will be in constant risk of discovery. You must do your best to stay awake and to make no noise."

Cuthberht remained where he was while Talon and Max settled down near Alexios, who was dozing in a pain-filled state. Occasionally he would give out a low groan but otherwise he tried bravely to keep quiet.

The moon was climbing into the sky and the crickets were sounding off in the woods and frogs had taken up the song contest from the stream in the valley when Talon indicated to the others that it was time to leave. Max helped Cuthberht onto his animal then he and Talon assisted Alexios onto his horse, tied him to his saddle, then lead the way with their own animals down the hill towards the road. The dog stayed close to Max, silent and attentive for untoward noises as they moved through the trees. They moved very cautiously, although Talon was reasonably sure that the Turks would not be traveling on the road during the night. The Turks had every reason to believe that it was all theirs and they had time to do what they liked during the day. Nevertheless he worried that there might be a loose band of pilferers out looking for advance pickings.

A hot breath of wind came up the hill behind them. There was a flicker of light that briefly illuminated the distant mountains to their rear and they heard the ominous sound of thunder in the distance. Watching the lightning flicker over the area of the fateful gorge Talon thought of the dead abandoned to the elements; it seemed as though some strange gods might be hovering over the battleground investigating the battlefield and arguing over their portions.

As though reading his somber thoughts Cuthberht said in a low voice, "The gods and ghouls are feeding well tonight, I think."

The air around them changed perceptibly from the dry heat to which they had become accustomed to a heavy pall, making them sweat under their thick hauberks and chain armor.

"This might be a good thing," Talon whispered to Max, indicating the storm.

"If God decides to send it our way," Max whispered back and Cuthberht growled assent. Rain could help them travel undetected.

They arrived on the road to find it quiet and apparently deserted. They stopped and listened very carefully for any sounds of horses in either direction before walking the horses slowly up the hill. They still passed pieces of equipment and discarded baggage but not in any great quantities. The army had dumped most of its unwanted equipment down on the parched plains. Cuthberht went and retrieved a discarded bow. He hefted it. "I cannot understand why anyone would leave this behind." Then he picked up a full quiver and climbed painfully back onto his horse.

He grinned at Talon and Max. "I too can use a bow. Not as well as you, Frank, but well enough."

They gained the crest of the low pass and began the descent toward the plains beyond and the border without incident. The night was quiet now; even the cicadas had stopped, so they could listen to the more subtle night sounds. Behind them to the south the storm they had seen on the horizon had moved closer and the lightning began to be followed more closely by the rumble of thunder, but the sky was still clear above them.

The moon climbed higher, a thin crescent which bathed the countryside in a faint silvery glow that reflected off the white rocks, but scudding clouds were beginning to move across the sky. The only sound was the muted thump and click of their horses' hooves on the stony road. At one point they were startled by a dark bundle on the side of the road that moved and a voice croaked in Greek.

"Mercy, God have mercy on my soul. Water! Water!"

Talon hurriedly dismounted and took the water skin over to give some relief to the wounded man.

"God bless you, whoever you are for your kindness," the man babbled; then he stiffened and fell back. Talon noted a fresh wound in the soldier's side. This meant that the Turks must have followed the army right up the road while they were resting. He immediately became even more alert. he ran back to remount his own horse and whispered to his companions, "The Turks have been on the road. This man was wounded only a matter of hours ago. I am surprised that they did not kill him."

They moved on, trying to put distance between themselves and the dead man, but now there was the added tension of knowing that they had to get past the Turks, some of whom were sure to be ahead of them now.

Two hours later the moon and the stars were gone, replaced by racing clouds as the storm swept over the top of the hills. It became very dark and the spatter of rain heralded a huge flash of lightning that lit up the surrounding hills and woods, followed by a crash of thunder. The jagged edge of the fork was so close everyone flinched and the horses began to fidget fearfully. Talon nudged his mount closer to that of Alexios. He did not want a runaway at this point.

The crash of thunder was almost overhead but still there was no more than a spatter of rain. Then with a suddenness that surprised Talon they heard a roar behind them and a wall of rain swept over them. In seconds they were drenched to the bone. Horse and man were engulfed in water and a buffeting wind that tore at their clothing and made it hard to breathe. It lasted for only a few minutes and then was gone, leaving them dazed and soaked. But soon after it began to rain in a steady downpour that chilled them right through.

"We must keep going!" Max shouted. "There is no shelter except in that big wood ahead. Do you remember it?" The bandage around his head had slipped half off giving him a rakish look; his hair was plastered to his face.

Talon did not respond other than to urge his mount to move on as fast as it could. He checked the bindings that held Alexios, who was conscious but leaning over the pommel of his saddle in too much pain to care what was happening.

They had gone another mile when the dog that was trotting alongside Max's horse stopped and stared forward into the dark. Max nudged Talon and leaned close.

"Something has alarmed him."

Talon glanced at the dog's indistinct form and then peered ahead. To his dismay he saw a flicker of light. Someone despite the rain was keeping a fire alight, which meant more than one and quite possibly many of the enemy right in their path. He decided to move in closer. The rain had subsided by now and there was a light mist coming out of the cleft of hills about them. He dismounted and threw the reins to Max and then, holding his bow with an arrow knocked, he crept forward along the trail. As he suspected there was a party of men ahead, their dark forms clustered about a fire which they had lit about forty paces off to the right of the road under the cover of some stunted trees. Their horses were a dark mass of animals behind them up the slope. There did not appear to be any sentries that Talon could see. He wondered about the horses. A stealthy, closer examination revealed that they were tied to the low branches of nearby trees and a man who should have been looking out for them was huddling against the roots of a tree that afforded some shelter.

Talon hastened back to Max and the others and explained to them what he had seen. "The only way we can do this is if I can chase the horses off and you can ride by. I do not know how else we can slip past them. If they have horses they will catch us for sure."

Max gave a tired mutter in the darkness and said, "How will you manage to catch up with us?"

"Take my horse and get past the camp, but go quietly and do not rush. With some luck they will be chasing after their horses in the forest, and I hope to be able to meet up with you several hundred paces from here. Stop and wait for me, but if you hear horses on the road you must flee."

He did not wait for Max to answer. There was no other way for them. None of the others were capable of a fight and certainly not in the dark. He slipped out of sight to make his way with great care back to the horses of the enemy. They stood in a forlorn group with their heads down close together, trying to keep warm as the rain continued to fall and drip off the trees onto their soaked backs.

He counted twelve horses and then made his way silently down the slope to observe the group huddled around the glowing embers. From time to time a man would get up and throw another wet piece of wood onto the fire, making it smoke and hiss with steam before catching, then the flames would briefly light up the dark mustached faces of the Turks under their hoods. No one spoke and most of them seemed to be asleep where they sat cross-legged on the ground, huddled under their cloaks and oblivious of their surroundings. One of the men threw another log on the fire that briefly flared, illuminating his face. Talon was startled as it looked familiar, then he realized that this was the warrior who had almost managed to get to the Emperor during the savage skirmish earlier that day! Again a superstitious chill went through him. They seemed destined to meet again and again.

He moved back from the region of the campfire, heading silently for the sleeping form of the sentry. The man barely struggled as his lifeblood flowed away. Talon eased him back against the tree and then proceeded to untie the horses. They appeared to wake up as he worked at the ropes, but he whispered encouragement and they settled down into an apathetic quiet and allowed him to begin to lead them away through the trees. He wondered when someone would notice the absence of the horses, but it was not until they were a good thirty paces away and well out of sight of the fire that he heard a yell and he knew that the sentry had been discovered.

There was no time to waste. He gave a great shout and laid about him with the flat of his sword on the rumps of the horses, yelling and striking them in the dark. The now terrified animals bolted in all directions but to his satisfaction not towards the road. They crashed into the forest thickets and could be heard galloping off among the trees. He now heard the men yelling in anger and fear as they discovered their dead companion and then heard the neighs of the fleeing horses.

It was time to leave the area and rejoin his companions. Talon fled up the slope for a few hundred paces until the sounds of the agitated Turks receded and then struck off to find the roadway, hoping he had not over-shot his companions As it happened he crossed the road further along and had to make his way back to meet them. The dog greeted him with a whine, and then Max muttered an exclamation of surprise as Talon appeared right under his nose before taking the reins of his horse from him. The other two men were almost unaware of what had just happened.

"If we move off at a reasonable pace they'll not hear us and we can make some distance before they realize what has happened," Talon said.

A flash of lightning illuminated the now deserted track well ahead of them, followed by a more distant crack of thunder. The wind blew their way and after a few moments and it began to rain again in earnest, which while adding to their discomfort at least allowed them to force the horses into a trot and gain some distance from the enemy who were still trying to retrieve their terrified animals.

*****

Morning found them at the base of the range of hills. The sky was grey with low scudding clouds and it was still raining, but not as hard as before. They moved slowly along the trail through an obscuring mist that hung over the woods along the road, which had been transformed into a track of oozing mud. Their horses splashed through the ruts and pot holes full of water.

Talon was very concerned about Alexios, who muttered feverishly to himself. Cuthberht rode ahead of them acting as a scout, while both Talon and Max spent a lot of time watching their back trail for any sign that would herald the appearance of riders. Indeed, just as the sun began to rise into the sky they saw what appeared to be movement down the long straight road behind them.

Talon gave a low shout to Cuthberht, warning him to get off the road, then drove his horse into the bushes with the other two. They just had time to get into the trees and hide before a group of Turks splashed by, heading along the path in the direction of the fleeing army. They watched the riders go by and once again Talon noted the leader. It was the same man with the scar who had been back at the fire. They would not be treated well if they were caught, but the Turks were too intent upon the way ahead to notice there had been others on the road recently. The warriors galloped by in a spray of water that hung in the misty air after they had passed.

*****

Yiğit rode like a man possessed. He had discovered his man dead at the base of the tree shortly after he had decided to check on him. In the darkness it had been hard to tell at first and he had kicked the inert body, thinking his man was asleep, and was about to administer rough punishment when the body fell over exposing a slit throat dark with blood all over the front. After staring at the body of his sentry for a brief shocked moment Yiğit had drawn his sword and roared out the alarm. Then he noticed the horses were gone.

Almost as he did so there was a bloodcurdling scream from the woods above. Then he heard the whinny of one of the horses and the galloping of the mounts as they panicked and fled into the denser trees away from him.

His men came running up from the fire, their blades out, to stop and stare at the bundle on the ground at his feet and then to peer into the trees above listening to their horses galloping away.

"Go after them!" Yiğit shouted. "Find the horses!" He had wondered briefly if it might have been some men from a rival clan who had committed the killing, but now he was sure it was a band of Greeks. He would hunt them down instead of heading back to the Sultan's army. With any luck he might be able to intercept them before they made the shelter of the fortress a few hours away to the west.

His men sheathed their swords and ran off into the darkness and the rain. It took hours for them to find even half the horses but as soon as he had eight of the twelve Yiğit decided that he had enough to take up the chase for whoever had visited them in the night.

Driving their horses brutally, they rode like madmen along the road on the chance that whoever did the killing would be fleeing towards the army of the Byzantines. They rode into the dawn and the mists that partially obscured the woods on either side of the muddy track they were following—and completely missed the men hidden among the trees.

*****

"I fear we're in trouble," Talon muttered to Max. "Are they not the same men we passed earlier last night?"

"God alone knows. I wonder if the army has made it to safety or there is more fighting to come," Max said.

Talon edged his mount next to Alexios. "Alexios, wake up. We are not far from the border."

"What? Where are we?" Alexios called out as he woke up.

Talon put a hand on his shoulder to calm him. "We think we are not far from the border but we are not sure. Do you know this place?"

Alexios looked about him, his eyes bleary and unfocussed. He shook his head. "This is the large wood about five or so miles from the border town of Dorylaeum," he said. "I think it is anyway." He began to shiver and to mutter prayers to himself.

Talon and Max looked at one another. Five miles was good news, but anywhere along that road the Turks could be scavenging and they could ride right into them.

Talon shrugged. "We have no choice, Max. We must go on as fast as we can. My guess is that the Turks are almost done with the army and are going home too."

"I hope you are right, Talon," Max rasped. "But if so, those men were going in the wrong direction."

Cuthberht reemerged from his hiding place and waved silently to them, then rode cautiously forward. Talon was very glad of his presence. They might well need his help in the coming hours. Their horses were streaked with sweat and in a poor way. Talon glanced down at himself and realized that he looked as bad as his companions. He felt cold, hungry and nervous, for they now had a gauntlet to run and Alexios appeared to be in no condition to ride on his own.

They tried to trot the horses to make up lost time but the movement was so painful to Alexios that he began to pass out. They were forced to slow down and resume their walk. The small group emerged from the woods after three long hours, glad of the sight ahead.

Ahead of them was the fortified town of Dorylaeum with its high walls. Talon could see that most of the army had already entered into the town, with the rear guard just about to do so. They had made very good time despite their enforced delay.

Talon glanced around him. The terrain was open grassland at this point with the town placed on a high mound right in the middle of the plain. There were several groups of riders, clearly not of the Byzantine army, off to the right and left that were moving away from the town. He watched the nearest of these groups with a wary eye to see what they were going to do, and to his dismay they began to turn in their direction with the aim of using the road. He urged his horse along the trail.

"They do not know who we are just yet but sooner or later we are going to have to make a run for it, Max. Is Alex tied firmly in place?"

They continued at their former pace, and it was clear that the Turks had become curious and were coming to investigate.

"It is time to run. God save us, but we have to go now!" Talon croaked; his mouth was dry. He did not think much of their chances.

"Yes," Max replied. "I see what you mean. We must get ahead of them before they reach the road. Cuthberht, come with me and help with Alex." His tone was sharp and tense.

With Cuthberht and Max on either side of Alexios the horses were readied for a gallop.

"Gallop hard, Max. No matter the pain to him. Are you ready?" Talon shouted. He prayed that his bowstring was not too wet.

Both men put spurs to their horses, Max dragging on the reins of Alexios' mount. "Come on, boy!" Max shouted to the dog, which needed little persuasion to follow hard on their heels. Talon slapped the animal Alexios rode hard on its rump with the flat of his sword; it snorted, bucked, and then began to gallop hard along with the other two men. Alexios swayed loosely in his saddle and Cuthberht clung to his for dear life, looking very unstable on his own animal. At any other time it would have been comical to see, but Talon was not watching; he was drawing his bow. It was going to be a race to the death.

They galloped along the muddy trail as fast as their tired horses could manage down the gentle slopes towards the town which was still a good two miles off. Their animal's hooves threw up a spray of mud. Much of it splattered Talon, as he was the one in the rear. Then Talon saw the Turks were coming after them at a hard gallop. They had realized that these were stragglers and were determined to catch them. Soon he could hear their yells as they urged their horses on.

He pulled out an arrow and checked the distance. It was narrowing slowly as the fresher horses of the Turks gained ground.

"Go on, Max, run! I shall do what I can to delay them!" he called.

The men in front needed no urging and pounded their horses' sides with their heels, hunched over their mounts' necks while pulling hard on the horse in the middle. Alexios had regained his senses; he too was pounding on his horse with his right heel and beating on it with a strap of the reins. The animal needed little persuasion with Talon bringing up the rear and screaming after them. They fled for the safety of the town but the Turks, by their yells of excitement, were sure of their prey and gaining by the second.

Talon turned to face back along the road, his bow taut, an arrow knocked. He loosed an arrow that flew high into the air and then vanished as it descended. There was no reaction from the Turks so he quickly set another and took very careful aim, judging the distance and the speed of their advance. This time the arrow flew true and a man toppled off his horse with a cry.

Talon loosed another arrow and a rider clutched at his shoulder. This time the Turks slowed down in evident surprise as they were still well out of range for their own bows. But they only hesitated a moment before coming on again. However, this tiny respite had gained many yards for Alexios and his two escorts and now they were within a few hundred yards of the town walls, and people on the battlements were beginning to take notice of what was happening on the plain. Talon threw a glance forward and saw the gates begin to open and men running along the battlements above.

He took another arrow out of the quiver and was startled to find that there were only three left. They all had to count or he was finished. The seven Turks remaining began to let loose their own arrows, having once again shortened the distance. Arrows began to whisper past and clatter onto the road nearby. He fired another two and had the satisfaction of seeing one more man go down. But the Turks were undeterred and howled their rage while thrashing their horses even harder in an attempt to close with him.

There was a sudden whoosh in the air above him and the next thing he knew the ground in front of the Turks erupted in a spray of mud and flying stones. His horse bolted then and he had to turn and pay attention to where he was going. Fortunately he was very close to the town gates, which were flung wide and crowded with men shouting at him and waving their arms.

As he neared the gates he heard a crash from above and saw a black object flying away from the walls and drop down upon the Turks, who had hauled their horses to a shocked halt. The great stone struck just in front of them and ploughed into their ranks. The two men in front could not get out of the way. Their mounts were thrown aside like toys and the men were borne to the ground in a shower of flying stones and mud.

Talon pulled up his horse and stopped just before the gates to watch the retreating horsemen. He was panting with the effort and the adrenaline rush but his horse was almost ready to fall over. Its head was down and he felt it shaking.

The stone had destroyed the group of horsemen. There was no one left on their horses but one animal did struggle to its feet and stand with its head hanging down next to a body.

Talon gazed at the destruction wrought by the huge stone which now lay a hundred feet from its landing place. He then noted that one of the bodies moved. He walked his horse closer with his bow taut and arrow ready.

Lying on his back with a couple of his men lying next to him in a tangle of torn limbs and broken bodies lay the Turk with the scar. As Talon approached the man tried to sit up but then winced and fell back with a groan. Talon cautiously dismounted and approached. He verified his earlier assumption that it was indeed the same man he had now encountered several times. He was covered in a light splattering of mud but it was surely he.

"You are wounded, but can you ride?" he asked the man in Greek.

"I am wounded," Yiğit answered after staring at Talon in surprise. "Have you come to kill me?" he asked, his teeth bared in a grimace.

"There is a horse nearby. I can help you get onto it and then you must ride away as they will be coming to kill you," Talon responded.

"I have seen you more than once before," Yiğit said and then groaned. His left arm was loose. He tried to stand up. "That infernal machine broke more than my arm."

"If you do not try to kill me I will help you onto the horse."

"I will not try to kill you," Yiğit answered through clenched teeth. "Ah, but that machine can hurl stones a huge distance."

"We do not have much time. Here let me help you," Talon said.

He assisted Yiğit onto the horse, which he had captured without difficulty, and then while the man leaned over the pommel holding his arm Talon hastily mounted his own animal and faced him. He glanced over to the town where people were clustered on the battlements watching. The gates were open but he saw no signs of any mounted men coming out.

"You must leave now." He jerked his head back along the way they had come.

"Why do you do this?" Yiğit demanded.

"There has been enough killing for one day," Talon replied.

Yiğit nodded. "Perhaps you are right. I lost some good men here...all because of a stone! One of them could have been my own son. I sent him back to the main camp yesterday. Fate!" he shook his head. "What is your name, Greek?"

"I am a Frank and my name is Talon."

"I am Yiğit, may Allah judge you kindly for what you have done. I shall not forget." He hauled the horse around and set off at a canter leaning forward over the pommel. Talon sat and watched him for a few moments and then turned his horse and walked slowly towards the open gates of the fort.

He dismounted and led the horse the rest of the way past the gates and the yelling crowd, his own legs wobbly with fatigue and the aftermath of the chase. Men were cheering all around and slapping him on the back, laughing and shouting. He saw Max ahead of him surrounded by men and realized that they were the Varangians who were shouting and laughing. Some of them came running to greet him.

Asmundr seized him in a huge bear hug. "We thought you were all dead! I even told Thor and the other Gods what I thought about that! You brought Cuthberht back with you too! By God, that was well done!" he roared and clapped a dazed Talon on the back hard enough to make him stagger.

"It was a close thing indeed, my friend," Talon gasped. "Is there any water to be had? I am so thirsty!"

A water jug was pressed into his hands and his horse led away while he drank from the vessel and poured the rest over his head. He gasped at the coolness as it sloshed down his neck and front. He noticed that his hands were shaking.

"Some of us watched the chase from the battlements," Asmundr exclaimed. "My, but you are a horseman and an archer. I've never seen the like before!"

At that Talon remembered some Welsh archers he had known once who could have argued with the statement.

But what was that about putting one of them on a horse and sending him away?" someone asked him.

"He was someone I've met before. Remember the envoy at the entrance to the passes? It was he!"

The men around him exclaimed but they said no more about his strange action.

Max and Cuthberht pushed through the crowd and they embraced.

"You were not with us when we went through those gates, Talon. But here you are and God be praised for it. I am right glad to see you safe."

"The Greeks threw some very big stones at the enemy, Max. I am sure those saved my life. I am right glad of it too. How is Alexios?"

"They have rushed him off to the physicians. The Emperor ordered it personally."

Talon looked surprised. "The Emperor? Well, I am glad. God willing Alexios will be in good hands now."

The jubilant Varangians who wanted to know all about their ordeal dragged them off to a wine house. It was several jugs of wine and much translating and joking before they were allowed to find some rest. Cuthberht elected to remain with his comrades, but before they left he embraced Talon and Max.

"A man does not forget. You are our friends and we will remember you," he said as he crushed Talon to his chest. "Be sure to come and see us when you get back to the city."

They fell asleep on rough beds despite the fact that it was midmorning. Talon did not even remember his head hitting the mattress.

*****

Someone shaking him by the shoulder waked him. The eunuch who had woken him jumped back with a startled cry; Talon's dagger was at this throat.

"What is it?" Talon croaked. His mouth was dry and pasty and his head ached.

"His...His Lordship the General Makrodoukas wants to see you, Sir," the servant quavered in his high-pitched voice.

"I am coming," Talon said shortly, and got up to follow the man out of the primitive accommodation he found himself sleeping in.

He was surprised to see that it was late evening and the sun had just set; the sky to the west was streaked with red. The servant showed him the way to the fortified building that housed the senior officers of the army. The building was bustling with servants running here and there, and Talon's nose detected the mouth-watering smell of cooking meat as the evening meal was prepared for the Emperor and his generals. Talon was shown to a room with marble and wide, red colored clay tiles on the floor. It was cool in here after the stuffy air of the street and the room he had just vacated. General Makrodoukas was seated there when he arrived, but now the general rose and walked toward him. He looked worn and tired and still wore some of his armor.

"Ah, Sir Talon, welcome," he said, and to Talon's surprise the general embraced him.

"Good evening, General, you sent for me?" He returned the embrace but then stood back.

"I did. I wanted to thank you, Sir Talon."

"What have I done, Sir?'

"You saved the life of the Emperor and I will not forget that, nor will he, as I shall remind him, but that is for later. No, I want to thank you for bringing Alexios Kalothesos safely to us."

"I, we could not just leave him; he is a friend, Sir."

"He is more than that to me. He is the son of Damianus the senator, who is very dear to me. I served under him when he was a general so his boy is important to me. The Emperor is out of sorts with Alexios because of his outspoken behavior in the gorge, so I shall do the thanking for him tonight."

"Ah...it was God's will that we came out of it at all," Talon said.

"Alexios will be well looked after here in the hospital, but there is still a long journey to go to get back to the city. I cannot stay, for the Emperor wishes to leave as soon as the army can stand on its feet. Will you escort Alexios back to his home for me?"

"Of course, Sir. I shall be glad to do so."

"There is more I would ask of you, Sir Talon."

"What can I do to be of service to you, Sir?"

"I would like you to stay for a meal with me and tell me more about the Templars. You are an outsider who fought well both during and after the battle. You are young, it is true, but I suspect that you are also observant and I would like to spend some time with you."

The general smiled and said disarmingly, "The whole thing was a disaster from beginning to end. The incident of the passes was terrible. We, the generals, had asked the Emperor to listen but sadly he did not, listening instead to some impetuous younger officers. We subsequently all lost friends in the gorge because of it. I lost my friends Baldwin and Kantakouzenos. But there were far too many others."

Talon was very tired and wanted to go to back to bed more than anything, but he began to like the general for his candor. He had, up to this point, found the senior officers of the Byzantine army aloof and haughty, but here was a man asking him for his opinions. Despite himself he was flattered.

"I saw how you dealt with the Turks on many occasions with that large bow of yours, Sir Talon. Tell me though, it is not a standard weapon for a Knight Templar, is it?"

"No, my Lord, it is not, but Sir Guy allows me to bring it along with me and right glad I have been of it from time to time."

"You made very good use of it during the battle from what I could see, and even today...they are still talking about the chase," the general said with a dry smile.

"Why does the Byzantine army not have more men with bows who are also cavalry, Sir?" Talon asked. "It is clear, at least to me, that the Turks are a fearless enemy who understand the use of the horse and the bow in a manner that your army does not seem to. I noticed that they prefer to hit and run rather than make a direct assault, but when they have to they do so without regard to their own safety."

They talked late into the night. As they were eating the delicious plain fare of olives and bread with oil and cucumbers in yoghurt and the lamb meat balls in gravy the general had ordered for the meal, Talon found that he was talking to a man who listened attentively and asked many questions.

The town bell was chiming midnight when he arrived back at the room he had left earlier that day. Once again he fell into a deep sleep, barely aware of the snores coming from Max's bed.

*****

Two days later the army left the town of Dorylaeum and marched off toward Constantinople. General Makrodoukas had several other meetings with Talon and during one of these he informed Talon that the Emperor had decided against demolishing the town as agreed with Arslan. The opinion was that the Sultan of Rum had broken his word when he allowed the Turcoman warriors to attack his army. Instead, the Emperor would demolish only the one fort. That was Sublaem, which was further south.

Talon heard that the general did not think they should demolish either of the forts and was worried that the affair was not over with the Sultan. But there was nothing he, nor the other generals, could do to persuade the Emperor otherwise, so it remained at that.

Talon watched the army marching off with a little more of its old cockiness from the battlements with Max at his side. He and Max would be remaining in the fort until Alexios was in better condition to travel. They would leave in about a week to accompany many of the wounded who had also been left behind.

"The Norsemen told me that they expected to see us back in the big city after we have delivered Alexios to his family," Max said. "I was told we should visit them at their barracks near to the palace of Blachernae after we return."

Talon nodded. He liked those rough men from the north. They watched the remainder of the army disappear from view and then headed for the hospital to see Alexios.

He greeted them with enthusiasm, his eyes lighting up at the sight of them. His color was back and he had been bathed.

"I owe you both my life. God's will, but I thank you for your courage and for keeping me safe," he called out to them as they walked into the large spacious room where he lay alongside some other survivors.

"We only did what you would have done, Alex," Max said.

"What do the physicians say?" Talon asked.

"They have stitched up my belly and they say that it will be fine as long as I do not do anything stupid like play *tzykanion* or go into battle," Alexios said with a feeble attempt at humor.

"The knee...what about the knee?" Talon asked with concern.

"Ah, now that is another matter." Alexios looked unhappy.

"What did they say, my friend?" Talon asked.

"They said that I might never be able to walk properly again." Alexios had tears in his eyes when he said this.

Max put a hand on his shoulder. "You will still ride, Alexios. You will get better and you will still be a good rider. That is the most important thing."

Alexios managed a weak smile. "I know you are right, Max, and I thank God for you both or I would not even be here but...well, I am not used to being in this condition."

"Hum. Even if you cannot run as you used to, Alexios, you will ride again, and I will teach you how to use the bow from the saddle so no one will even know the difference, my friend. You might even become a half way decent *tzykanion* player." Talon grinned at Alexios, who pretended to look offended. "Future battles with the Turks will be fought on horseback, of that I am sure," he added.

*****

It was a week before the physicians gave them permission to move on. Even then they were forced to use a cart. It was a very painful journey for Alexios as his knee could not withstand the jolting of the wagon for long periods and they had had to make frequent rest stops along the way. They had once tried to put him on a horse but he had almost passed out after only a short while, so he was placed back in the wagon along with some other wounded and the procession continued slowly along the now dry road that led to Constantinople.

After having traversed a range of hills they paused to look down into a wide basin of green cultivated land at the magnificent city of Nicaea. Once again Talon marveled at the industrious labor that created its massive walls which enclosed a bustling city on the shores of a huge lake called Ascanius. All roads seemed to join up at this city. He was startled to see a long caravan of camels ambling slowly towards the south gate where they were about to arrive themselves. It seemed very peaceful here in this fertile valley, a long way from the battlefield they had recently left behind.

A stopover at the city was deemed necessary as Alexios had become feverish. Talon made a point of cleaning and re-bandaging his wounds as well as his own and Max's at every opportunity, explaining that the infections of wounds came with dirt and filthy dressings.

Nonetheless the redness and puffiness of Alexios' knee wound worried him enough that while they were staying in Nicaea he sought out a physician who came with him back to the inn and examined the wound. He clucked his tongue, then pasted a sharp smelling poultice on the wound to draw the poison and redressed the knee. He complemented Talon on his care and encouraged him to continue in that vein until they arrived back in Constantinople. There he should seek out expert medical care, for the wound was complicated and would need a skilled doctor to ensure a good recovery.

Another painful week later, having paused at Helenopolis, Nicomedia and Calcedon along the way, they were in sight of the distant city of Constantinople across the sea and then they looked for a boat to take them across the Bosporus.

*****

They entered the great city at the Gate of St John of Cornibus located on the northern side of Constantinople. It was almost midday after three weeks on the road from Dorylaeum. They had taken a ferryboat from Gelation on the other side of the Golden Horn using some of the last coins that they possessed to pay for the crossing. As they sailed over the gap between the lands, Talon had seen the Byzantine navy at anchor and wondered if Nikoporus was somewhere there on a ship.

Max insisted on going straight to the Church of St Demetrius, which was a stone's throw from the gate, and giving thanks for their deliverance. As they knelt and prayed in a corner of the tall stone building they were watched with curiosity by some of the locals, and a priest even came over and stood near them. He looked askance, but Alexios, who was pale with exhaustion, still managed to explain briefly what they were there for and where they had come from. The bearded priest promised to say prayers for them as they left.

They were unsettled to see smoke rising from various places along the hillsides. The streets were almost deserted, which was unusual and those people who were there hurried past without looking at them or pausing.

Talon stopped one man who wanted to push past and asked him, "What is happening in the city?"

The man looked up at him. "You have been away? The army came back two weeks ago and the citizens have rioted. They are very angry at the Emperor." Talon would have asked him more, but he looked over his shoulder and started, then hastened away.

Down the road came a detachment of soldiers. Talon recognized them as Varangians. The officer in charge was none other than Eadgar.

He stopped the men and greeted Talon and Max as old friends.

"Well met, Sir Talon, Max! Where have you been?"

"We were delayed because of our friend Alexios here." Eadgar into the cart at the prone figure of Alexios lying asleep.

He nodded."You should hurry to your destination, Talon. There have been riots and burnings. It is not safe to be out on the streets. I will give you two men as an escort."

Talon thanked him and they proceeded at a faster pace towards the villa. Talon hoped that it was untouched and was relieved to see the walls intact and the gates shut. He thanked the two Varangians and sent them on their way.

Their arrival at the senator's house created pandemonium. Talon had to pound several times to get the attention of the guards, but the gates were eventually opened. The large dog named Belisarius barked loudly and tried eagerly to leap up at the cart as he sensed that Alexios was there, but the guard who was holding his leash tugged him away. He then contented himself with a raucous exchange of barks and growls with the dog accompanying the three men. Max called his dog to his side and they moved past the sentries. Despite the pandemonium Alexios was lying almost asleep in the cart barely aware of his surroundings.

Servants came running towards them with much shouting and cries of welcome to cluster about the wagon as the donkey dragged it creaking down the last few dozen yards along the tree-lined avenue toward the main house. Then there was a brief silence and all eyes turned to the steps of the building where Joannina stood with her daughters watching their arrival. She had her hand to her throat and looked very pale. Then very slowly, as though holding herself in check, she walked to the cart and stood looking down on her son. Alexios opened his eyes and squinted up at his mother.

"Hello, Mother. Am I home now?" he croaked.

Joannina looked at all three of them and said in a strained voice, "Welcome home. Yes, my son, they have brought you home." She was on the edge of weeping but Talon could see that she held herself together with an enormous effort of will. He admired her control as she began to issue orders to the waiting servants. Not so her daughters, who wept without restraint when they saw the pitiable condition of their brother.

As the servants carried Alexios with great care up the steps to the house they were followed by his sisters. Talon could not tell if they wept for joy or for pity.

Joannina looked up at Talon and Max. She was clearly shocked at their condition but said calmly enough, "The army arrived two weeks ago and there have been riots. People have been killed in the streets. We did hear from General Makrodoukas that Alexios had been wounded and that you would be bringing him home. For that I thank you from my heart and thank God for keeping you all safe along the way."

"God saw fit to keep us safe, madame," Talon said.

"You must stay here where we can look after you. I see you are both wounded and I wish to offer the best our house can provide. I shall send for the physicians immediately and they can attend to you as well."

"I thank you for your hospitality, madame." Talon said. "We will be honored to do so."

"It is we who are honored, Sir Talon. You have brought my son home to me whom I thought dead, as so many his friends are. My servants will attend to your every need." She could no longer keep her tears from flowing but turned away then and walked up the steps, her back as straight as a rod.

Later that day after they had bathed, been given clean tunics and had their injuries attended to by the physician, they rested in the shade of the loggia and discussed their situation.

"I wonder if the ship has come back from Acre," Max said.

"I too. How long have we been away?"

"Almost two months, but it feels longer. By God but I do not want to go through that kind of thing too often," Max said fervently. "I wonder why the riots."

"The citizens lost many of their own in that ill-conceived campaign, Max. I think they are angry and wanted the Emperor to know it. But I do not think that they could do more than that. The Emperor will have turned the same army loose upon the rioters and will surely punish them."

"You are right Talon. This is not a happy city at present." Max agreed

"We can rest a little while and then we should go and see if the ship has arrived. If it is back we should probably leave and return to Acre ourselves, Max. I do not know how much longer Sir Guy will permit me, or you for that matter, to loaf around in Byzantium."

"Is that what we have been doing, Talon?" Max asked with a wry grin.

Book Two

*Bring me my cup when the shadows lengthen
and the sun kisses the darkness's hand,
and its face goes pale like a man who's ill—
or lover stricken by passion.
The wine will drive out the legions of grief—
although it is weak, and has no weapons.*

Moshe Ib Ezra

Chapter 16

The Senator

Talon walked across the logia of the Kalothesos villa and down the stone steps that led to the rows of vines at the bottom of the slope. He had been summoned by the senator and was accompanied by John, the eunuch who looked after the senator's personal needs.

"He will be in among the vines, Sir Talon," John said respectfully. "He likes to come here and think."

"Does he make wine from them, John?" Talon asked, indicating the vineyard below.

"Oh yes, Sir. It actually makes for a pleasant wine, although a bit resinous, and he worries about it." They both smiled.

John halted and stood aside while Talon continued towards the old man, who was standing alongside a thick hedge of vines peering at the ripe fruit and talking to a servant who stood nearby.

Talon made his way softly between the rows until he was within speaking distance and then stood waiting for the senator to notice him. A bee hummed close to his head but did not tarry. Talon looked down at the end of the garden to the hives tucked up against the north wall.

"You need to weed these rows better, man. Remember the soil also needs to feel the sun between the rows," Senator Damianus Kalothesos was saying.

His tone was gruff but not irritable. Talon had the impression that the old man was content to be here among the bushes. Damianus noticed the direction of the servant's gaze, then turned slowly to face Talon.

Talon said, "God's Blessings, Sir."

"So, now you know where I retreat to when I have had enough of my family and need to think," he stated.

Talon nodded. "A garden or a vineyard, they both provide solace, Sir."

"Hmm, how do you know? You are barely as old as my son and he knows nothing of these things."

"I have in my memory a garden, Sir. It is where I used to go when I was out of sorts. But that was long ago."

"I like that, out of sorts. Eh? But you are right, young man. Sometimes one needs to go some place where nature rules and retreat into the mind and take a breather. Why do you think I chose the vines over the garden over there?" he asked abruptly and waved his hand at the rows of vegetables and herbs located on the other side of the orchards.

"Perhaps because here there is less work?" Talon said.

"Ha Ha! That is cheek." The old man cackled and struck a clump of earth with the end of his cane. "I am a senator, you know. I deserve more respect." But it was clear he was amused. "In fact there is just as much in either, but the rewards of a good wine outweigh those of root plants—although my wife might not agree."

"I apologize, Sir. I do not really know."

"I am an old soldier, retired and barely able to carry out my duties as a senator. In the old days of Rome they used to retire those legionnaires who had survived to the ripe old age of forty. They would give them a patch of land where they would traditionally grow crops for sale in the city. But most grew a few vines; soldiers like their drink. It was a man called Marius, a consul of Rome, who started that idea. The vine is a symbol that you have survived. It certainly is to me anyway. I draw comfort from the fact that I too survived to grow grapes and make a little wine. That way I can drink to those who did not and pour a libation to give their ghosts some peace. It will certainly be better than that awful swill they used to give us in the service."

Talon grinned, "I understand, Sir. It is a nice thing to be able to do."

"Well it isn't what I asked you to come and talk about, Frank. Go on up to the house and send John down to me. Go onto the loggia and wait for me there," he ordered. He turned his back on Talon and began to talk to the waiting gardener. "You must make sure the stray tendrils are clipped, Christophas. They will take from the fruit if you do not trim them well." He spoke as though Talon were not there anymore. Talon turned and made his way back up the steps to the loggia and in passing he indicated to John that the senator was waiting for him.

While he was waiting, Talon watched the ships moving about the Neorion and Prosphorion harbors. There was a large dromon with a Genoese flag anchored in the Neorion harbor but he paid it no attention. Instead, he took a deep breath and relaxed while he waited for the senator and enjoyed the peace and serenity of the view of the sea beyond with its myriad of sails. He wondered at the changed behavior of the senator. Their first meeting had not been a good one.

He heard rather than saw the arrival of another person. The click of a cane on the cool tiles indicated that it was the senator. Talon still did not take his eyes off the waters as the old man approached and sat down in a leather chair nearby.

The senator made himself comfortable while John fussed about him, wrapping, a blanket around the old man's legs.

"Stop fussing man...and leave us," Damianus said irritably.

The senator looked at Talon with rheumy eyes and waved him down.

"Sit, Frank, we need to talk."

Talon seated himself and looked attentively at the senator who seemed to be collecting his thoughts.

"I have misjudged you, Frank. You saved my boy's life. General Mavrozomes sent me a letter telling me all about it. He said that you and your sergeant risked your own lives to bring my boy home."

"It was God's will that he survived, Sir. We could not leave him. Not while there was a chance."

"Pshaw! God might have helped, but he helps those who look after their own. The army would have abandoned him, but you did not. We are in your debt...much as I hate to say it, Frank."

It irritated Talon to hear these words and the tone in which they were spoken, but he remembered what Joannina had told him. He decided to drag the subject into the open. "What do you hate so much about the Franks, Sir?"

There was a long pause and the old man stared back at Talon with faded brown eyes. He gave a bark of laughter.

"Forgive me...Frank. Just what is your name anyway?'

"It is Talon."

"That is a strong name, a good name. They tell me that you were born in Palestine?"

"I was, Sir."

"Yes, well then...Talon, the Franks—really it is the Normans, but we call all of you Franks. We are like the Arabs, we do not care to make a distinction. We can talk about that later. Now I want to know what really happened out there. That halfwit Manuel is claiming a victory, although from the reports I received it was more of a rout!"

Talon contained his shock at the irreverence for the Emperor and said. "May I speak openly, Sir?"

The old man laughed again. "You are in my home and now an honored guest. Yes, you may speak freely."

"It was a defeat and a bad one, Sir..."

The old man's jaw clenched and his lips became a thin line. "Continue."

Talon proceeded to recount the entire campaign from his own perspective. It quickly became clear to him that the old man knew what he was about when it came to military matters. He asked penetrating questions and shook his head at some of the events that Talon described.

When he came to the part where Manuel overruled his senior officers and listened to the hotheads like Pantoleon he hammered his cane onto the tiles, his anger visible. John appeared like magic enquiring as to the senator's wishes but the old man waved him away with a blue-veined, bony hand and said, "Go away John, I did not call."

John vanished and the senator turned back to Talon. "Those fools! Those fools! They learn nothing from our enemies and even less from history! The Turks are excellent light cavalry and will not stand and fight, for they are not stupid. They are men of the plains, brave to the point of insanity, but they know they do not have the power to go into a head on clash with our army on a plain. So they ambush us and to make matters worse we oblige them and walk right into a trap. God protect us from our inexperienced, arrogant young men and an impetuous emperor, they will destroy us without the help of outsiders."

Talon's respect for the senator went up several notches. "I agree with your analysis of the enemy, Sir. They are deadly in a skirmish and know full well they cannot take on the might of the Byzantine army on an open field, but they certainly knew how to sting over and over again. Then there was nowhere to go in that gorge and they carved us up."

The senator banged his stick on the floor again and John reappeared.

"Ah, John. Bring us wine, my wine, and some light refreshments, and be quick about it!" John disappeared.

"Was this your first battle?"

"Yes...I have been in fights before, but this was chaos on a huge scale and it was sometimes unnerving."

"Scared were you?"

Talon looked at the old man. "Terrified, Sir."

The senator nodded with approval. "You are honest. Yes, it is like that. My son said that he could not have hoped for two better men than you and your sergeant alongside him, and Theodore told me that you were an astute young man. He was right. Where did you learn to think?"

He smiled to take the sting out of his words. His beak of a nose and his chin appeared to join when he did so but it was a genuine smile.

"Tell me, Talon, was my son one of the hotheads I heard about?"

Talon looked him in the eye. "Your son pleaded with the Emperor to have a scouting party sent up the gorge, and when finally the Emperor permitted it I went with him. When we realized that the Turks were laying an ambush we rushed back to try and prevent the Emperor from sending the troops in, but they were already on their way, and despite your son's pleading the army went into the gorge anyway."

"My son told me very little of this. I do not understand why he feels that he is in some kind of disgrace. He won't tell me, but I know there is something gnawing at him and I want to hear from you what you think it might be."

Talon hesitated. "Sir, I am not familiar with the politics of the empire and how officers can discuss things with the Emperor but..."

"But what? My son is an officer in the elite cavalry, the *Oikos*, and as such had access to the Emperor, did he not?"

"That is what I think is the problem, Sir. He did speak directly to the Emperor, that night when we were trapped at the top of the gorge. He mentioned to us something about having told the Emperor that it was unthinkable to abandon the army and escape with his officers under the cover of dark that night. He told me they were talking about it and that it made him very angry."

"He told the Emperor that?" The old man's eyes were wide open, his expression incredulous. He sat forward in his chair gripping his cane. The blanket slipped off his knees but he ignored it.

"I believe he did, Sir."

The old man looked stunned. "Well I never...my son had the courage to tell the Emperor he was a coward and a fool?"

"I don't think he quite said that, Sir."

The senator almost glared at him. "By God, he as good as did so. Now I begin to understand," he said slowly. "Yes, that would not put him very high in Manuel's good graces, but I am proud of him. By God I am proud of him!" he almost shouted.

John reappeared with a servant hastening behind him. The two men silently laid out the food on a small table placed between their chairs. John placed wine goblets in front of them, poured wine, then topped the senator's cup up with a little water. He readjusted the blanket over the fidgeting senator's legs.

"He will find it hard to get promoted now, but we shall see," the senator said as John and the servant departed.

"No one can dispute the bravery of your son, Sir. He outshone many other officers in that he would not give up and fought without regard for his own safety."

"Have some wine," the senator said, looking pleased. "This is my wine and these cakes are bad for me but John brings them to me anyway. You might like them."

Talon took a glass and sipped the dark wine. It was a little resinous, but pleasantly bold on the palate, and he did like the pastries; they were the typical *baklava* honey cakes that he was familiar with.

"I thank you for this information, Talon," the senator said. There were tears in his eyes. He paused for a long moment staring at him.

"I should apologize for my behavior the first time you came here. It was, in the light of events, unforgivable."

"There is nothing to forgive, Sir." Talon's tone was stiff.

The senator looked at him hard and snorted with disbelief. "You asked me earlier why I disliked the Franks so?"

Talon nodded. "What have they done that makes them so offensive to you?"

"I should explain that we, the people of Byzantium, are part of an empire that began before the Franks, the Normans, the

Visigoths and the rest of those barbaric tribes in the west were ever heard of. Our civilization goes back to the beginnings of time, well before *Christos* even. We used to be the greatest empire the world has ever known. That is changing though and as much from rot within. But there is still much to this empire that is worth holding on to." For a moment his gaze looked far beyond the harbor below.

"I was a very young soldier under Alexios the First, Manuel's grandfather, then I soldiered for his father John Komnenos. I served in almost every part of the empire. I became a general and as a result I was witness to much that went on in the palaces and armies of our own country. I commanded men against the Bulgars and the Turks—and the Normans too."

He took a sip of watered wine and squinted into the distance as though reflecting upon something.

"You must understand, Talon, that the empire of Byzantium is a great light in a sea of darkness. Constantinople is the greatest city in the world today and is the foremost shining example of civilization. It does not matter where you go in the world; anywhere from Baghdad to the cities of Persia or even those of Andalusia, which I hear are remarkable places, there is nowhere that has more to offer than this city in this empire. That is why we are surrounded by enemies: nations, tribes and others of a more barbaric sort who envy us and are jealous of our achievements. They want to take what we have and destroy and pillage what has taken centuries to build."

He stopped and stared out at the sea for a long pensive moment before continuing.

"The Normans and Franks were a part of that envious crowd in the form of one Roger of Sicily, who is dead now, thank God. May his soul burn forever! But he had a son who is just as unpleasant, William, a grasping pirate! There are other adventurers who have all but taken over Italy and want to take us down too. Those Lombards will bear watching, and the Venetians, who are a murky crowd of pirates.

"The Arabs have tried and failed. They came to our very walls and died of starvation in front of us, eating their camels as they left. The Bulgars and the Pechenegs, God rot them all, have come and gone, as have many others of a like mind. Even today it is not over. They all want this city. They are like moths attracted to the flame but they do not understand it. They only envy us and just want to loot our city and take what plunder they can back to their own hovels." He sounded bitter.

In the silence that followed Talon gazed out at the east seaway that was bathed in the last of the evening sunshine. The harbors were now almost in darkness and lamps were beginning to glow in the streets and houses below them. He was beginning to understand the perspective of this man who had ridden out many storms in his time and had little patience for those who could not or refused to understand his people. He turned his attention back to the senator.

"What angered everyone here were the Franks who came through these parts on their way to Palestine. They came with the Germans about twenty years ago with that pathetic king of theirs, Louis, and his stunning wife...can't remember her name now."

"Eleanor?"

"Yes, that might be her. They looted their way across the countries they passed through, paid for almost nothing, and left a trail of destruction behind them, killing every Jew they could hunt down along the way. Then when they arrived here they had the gall to tell us that they were here to save us from the infidel! The pious hypocrites!"

The senator gave another of his barking laughs. "We who have been fighting the Persians and the Arabs for three hundred years before those barbaric nations even knew the Arabs existed, let alone the Persians or the Turk! You are a Knight Templar, I hear, so I suppose you know the difference between an Arab, a Turk and a Persian by now?"

Talon grinned. "Yes Sir I do...now."

The old man smiled dryly. "Then you will know that one deals with one's enemies each to his own traits and characteristics. The Turks are tribal and pastoral. They want land for their sheep and goats and do not give a fig for our kind of civilization—and that makes them dangerous as they are great fighters.The Arabs know full well what we have as do the Persians, who have been our enemy of ages. The empire of Byzantium, whatever its faults, is a bastion of Christendom and the only barrier against implacable enemies and yet the Latin people despise us.

"We have dealt with each of our enemies separately, with negotiation and diplomacy, because, my young friend, when you have more enemies than friends you cannot fight them all. Instead, you play them off against each other. Our empire has had to deal with our enemies with guile and cunning. This has meant sending delegations to their camps and cities and bringing their emissaries here to Constantinople to make deals that allow us breathing space. There is little enough to begin with."

"Is that why I have seen so many delegations here in the city and at the palace, Sir?"

"Yes. You cannot just go out and hope to crush all your enemies all at the same time. You need to know where their pieces are on the chessboard and play the game, concealing your true intentions but finding out theirs before they can use them. The Franks and their German cohorts naively consider this treachery. God preserve us from 'friends' like that!"

At this moment there was a light step at the entrance and Joannina walked out onto the loggia.

"Ah, there you are, my dear. I have been looking all over for you. You should know better than to be out here at this time of the evening. The insects will be biting and then you will have the fever to contend with. I am here to take you inside." She smiled at Talon. "Talon, excuse my husband please, he likes to talk about the grand scheme of things. Would you join us for dinner?"

Talon rose from his chair. "I would enjoy that very much, my Lady Joannina." He turned to the senator. "I thank you for taking the time to explain some things to me, Sir."

Joannina helped the senator struggle to his feet.

"You listen well, Talon. I am an old man who talks far too much," he said as he hobbled off with his wife.

Talon bowed and went off to find Joseph.

Later, dressed in a comfortable knee length tunic, he made his way to the lamp-lit dining room where he found the others already seated. The senator was absent, as was Alexios, who was still convalescing, so Talon was presented with three women who regarded him with interest by the light of many lamps. Even Theodora appeared pleased to see him and greeted him with a smile.

"We were just talking about you, Sir Talon. I hope your ears were burning?" she said with a malicious grin.

He smiled back and then fingered his ears. "I had wondered why they were so hot. Greetings, Lady Joannina and Lady Theodora. God's blessings, Lady Eugenia."

Joannina gave an enigmatic smile. "The empress has granted her some time with us so that she could see her brother."

Talon bowed and looked at the young woman as he took his seat. Her beautiful dark eyes were accentuated by kohl, making her already large eyes seem larger, but they also were a shade calculating as she watched him take his place at the table.

"The senator will not be joining us this evening, but he wanted me to assure you that he enjoyed the afternoon in your company and wishes you to know that he looks forward to doing it again."

Talon nodded. "He honors me. How, may I ask, is Alexios? I have not seen him since the physician told me he could have no visitors for a while."

"He is...on the mend." She put her hand to her breast.

He felt eyes upon him and looked up from his plate. Eugenia regarded him with eyes that were speculative. She looked very beautiful.

Talon smiled tentatively at her inspection and received one in return, but it was cool. He then concentrated on the excellent grilled fish that was being placed in front of him. There was a short silence as they enjoyed the food. Talon was hungry but he paid attention to his use of the fork, surreptitiously watching the women as they used the instrument with absent-minded skill.

Theodora ate with the speed of a teenager who wants to get it over with but is too hungry to not be present. This did not stop her from interrogating him.

"Alex has not told us much about the great battle and the journey home, Talon. I expect you to tell us all about it."

"Theodora! Please mind your manners."

"I only want to know how they managed to escape being taken prisoner, Mama," she protested.

"I shall tell you as much as I can," Talon said with a grin at Joannina.

She gave him a warm smile and sipped her wine but she gave her daughter a look that said, *Do not overstep any bounds.*

Talon told the story without adornment and finished with their arrival in Constantinople. In the silence that ensued he could feel their eyes on him but it was Eugenia who spoke.

"Did you not think you might die out there, Sir Talon, and not come back at all?"

"It did cross my mind, my Lady."

Theodora gave an exaggerated sigh and said, "Of course he could have died! But he did not, and furthermore he brought back our brother safe and, well...not so sound."

Her sister gave an irritated shrug. "I just asked. We can all give thanks to God that they did survive."

"I want to know what the Turk warriors look like, Talon. Are they like the ones we met in front of the Grand Palace? And why did not the Emperor listen to his scouts? It was stupid!" Theodora said. Her tone so resembled that of her father that Talon had to suppress a laugh. Before he could answer her sister replied.

"Theodora, my dear sister. You had better watch that flappy tongue of yours or someone might cut it out." Eugenia's tone was acid.

"But it is true, isn't it, Talon? It is all over the city. Why else would the citizens be rioting and screaming abuse at the emperor?"

"Whether it is or not you should learn to keep that kind of thing to yourself, little sister. It is not wise to spread rumors," Eugenia said.

Theodora glared at her sister but subsided and pretended to pay attention to her bowl of fruit.

Joannina interjected smoothly. "It is clear to all of us that it was a desperate time and we do give thanks to God for the preservation of our beloved Alexios. Nikoporus has sent a message to say he is coming to visit soon. I trust you will stay the night, Talon? We would be honored," she continued.

*****

Before retiring for the night to the guest quarters, Talon decided that he wanted to take a relaxing bath. It was late and the bathroom was deserted and quiet, although there were a few oil lamps still burning that shed a faint light on the dark water of the pool. He would have liked to have a massage for his new wounds ached, but the water was sufficient for the moment. He spent some minutes soaking, then swam before pulling himself out onto the side. He glanced at the scar forming on his arm and rubbed it, feeling that the wound was tightening. He remembered with appreciation the physician who had stitched it up. The man had clearly known his trade as now the wound only gave him an occasional twinge.

He sat on the side of the small pool, enjoying the quiet of the darkened room and the muted sound of running water from the garden fountain. The oil lamps cast long shadows that flickered among the pillars and alcoves. The villa was asleep at this late hour. His thoughts were interrupted by a small sound off to the side in the darkness.

Instantly he was on his feet seeking a weapon. The only thing of any use was a long brass candlestick on the stone table in an alcove behind him. He scurried silently into the alcove and retrieved the thin length of brass and then stood, dripping water on the marble floor, listening hard.

The small sound came again. This time he identified it as a footstep on the marble. He peered out from the alcove across the dimly lit pool into the gloom at the far end but saw nothing. He drew back into the concealment of the alcove and waited. Nearer to hand came the same small noise and he raised the stick, ready to strike.

A voice said, "You can come out now. Ah, our hero is on the prowl, and quite bare too! Is this how you greet a woman?"

Talon snapped his head at the sound of the voice. Eugenia was lying on one of the lounge chairs watching him with an expression of amusement on her fine features. Talon moved toward her but then became aware that he was quite naked and began frantically to look for some form of cover. He put the candlestick down on the side table and reached for one of the many folded cloths. It was very quiet. This late at night that would not be unusual, but he was sure there had to be a servant around to attend to the needs of Eugenia.

As though anticipating his thoughts she gave a low laugh and said, "You need have no fear, Sir Talon. I am quite alone, and the servants have been sent to bed. I might ask why you are here at such a late hour, but I imagine it was because you thought you would be alone too?"

"How did you know I was here?" he asked. He felt self-conscious and foolish. He had been so absorbed in his thoughts that an assassin with real intent could have finished him.

"I didn't. I first went to your room and discovered you were not there, but your sword was and I assumed this would be the first place to come."

He looked down at her and realized that she was very scantily clad herself. Her slim form was covered only by a diaphanous veil that did little to hide her long slim legs or her breasts. She lay in such a manner as to show off her best without being too obvious, but it was clear that this was her intent. Her robe hung over the back of the divan.

He found he was staring. In the dim light of the lamps she was very beautiful, her fine oval face surrounded by a halo of dark hair that was now unbound; the jewels that had adorned her neck and arms were gone, adding to the impression of nakedness that he found very seductive.

"I am beginning to see that you are pleased to see me," she said with a smile, and then she licked her lips like a cat and beckoned him closer. "My, but you have some serious looking scars. How did you get them?"

"I should leave, My Lady. I...I should not be here," Talon croaked.

"Do not leave now, Sir. That would not be...knightly, and besides I do not want you to go," she whispered. "I have wanted you since the first day I saw you, and from what I have heard about you and now see, I still want you. I, too, have come dressed for the occasion."

Talon knew it was dangerous and foolish to allow this to go any further, but here was a lovely woman inviting him to bed her and he found it very hard to find an excuse to leave. He wondered what the punishment might be for bedding the daughter of a senator in his own house. They liked to blind people in this city, he knew. But his own desire was getting the better of him. Despite his misgivings he moved over her and leaned down to kiss her.

She met his kiss with her own soft lips and then pulled his head hard down onto her mouth, her teeth clicking onto his. Their tongues met and fought and it was as though he had opened a dam. For a long moment they kissed, tasting one another. They separated and he felt his heart pounding and his breathing short. Her breath also came in sharp gasps as she looked up at him with eyes that were almost predatory. Without a word she reached up and seized his arms and pulled him down. There was no room alongside so he landed more or less on top of her. But then after only a brief pause while he inhaled her perfume she forced his head down and pushed her breasts up to be kissed. He kissed the one while fondling the other and heard her gasp then moan with pleasure.

His lips made their way down over her full breasts down the silky smooth surface of her stomach to her belly and lingered there before moving on. He looked up and saw that she had her eyes shut and her head back, her lips parted. Her body gave a spasm and she gave a low cry. Her hand reached down and caressed his manhood, pulling him up so their lips met again and and she thrust her hips up at his.

Their motion was slow at first but as he moved inside her he could sense that there was an urgency that she did not want to control. Then she raked his back with her nails and cried out into his shoulder.

She shuddered as she climaxed, wrapping her legs about him as though to pull him into her as far as she could. He moved harder and felt himself about to climax and she came again, but this time she bit him on the shoulder then threw her head back and her mouth opened in a silent scream as her body arched back under him. The sharp pain of the bite brought him to his own peak which felt as if it would last forever.

They lay together gasping for breath for long moments before Talon slid off her wet body to land on his knees on the hard marble floor. His hand was still lying on the slippery skin of her belly, while she lay back against the rise of the divan with her eyes shut her breasts rising and falling as she recovered her breath. Her left hand strayed to her belly and rested for a brief moment on his hand then slid off while her right hand played with his head and hair. He lowered his head to enjoy the fingers caressing him.

"So there are things the Franks can do well. By the Saints but that was what I needed more than you could know."

He sat back on his heels and looked up at her. The flush of their exertions was still on her face and the scent of lovemaking hung in the air.

"What do you mean?"

"You know that I am a Lady in Waiting for the queen?, Well, our duties are many, but for the most part they are very routine and very, very, boring. We dress up and look pretty and then make the empress look pretty and then we all stand around the throne and watch the officials and merchants and princes and foreigners fawning and crawling up to the throne as they beg for favors and try to influence the Emperor or the Empress. There is no excitement in our lives and no men...the eunuchs sometimes serve, but unless you threaten to cut their tongues out they will talk. They can be worse than the other women about that. I have one friend... but."

She stopped abruptly and left it in the air. Then she surprised him by asking. "Why are you here, Talon? You are a Templar and they do not visit this city very often, but you Templars have been to see the Emperor at least twice."

"We are here to..." he stopped.

"To do what?" she probed.

He sensed that she was perhaps too keen to know and felt a tiny alarm inside. He lifted his head and stared at her then said lightly. "Why, does it matter why we are here? The Templars are independent of the King of Jerusalem and wanted to establish a cordial relationship with the Emperor." He knew he sounded evasive but Sir Guy had sworn him to secrecy. Eugenia regarded him with eyes that told him she was skeptical of his answer.

"There is a lot of gossip in the palace as to why you came. Was it about another crusade?"

This was too close to the mark and he wondered again why her interest.

Instead of answering he changed the subject and asked her,"You do not have an arrangement for marriage to look forward to?"

She shook of her head emphatically. It made the thick mantle of her hair move across her face and she gave low laugh, almost as though she understood why he had shifted the ground. But then she said, "It is true that we Ladies in Waiting are prime marriageable material, especially those born to the *porphyrogennitos*. I have no doubt that the empress is contemplating potential alliances among the smelly foreigners who try to paw at us while we dine at the feasts."

"What is that title you just mentioned?"

"The *porphyrogennitos*."

"Ah yes I remember, Alexios showed it to me," he said.

"Then you'll understand that we lesser Ladies in Waiting do not have the best choices awarded to us."

"What do your parents have to say about this arrangement?"

She snorted. "Nothing! They have done their duty by me, their daughter, after all. It is probably the best they could do under the circumstances."

"You sound bitter." Talon could not help wondering if she bedded others like himself. It was clear that she was no stranger to the game of loving.

"It might be because I am. I desire more than an arranged marriage to a barbarian. Even Ladies in Waiting can go higher. It depends upon whom they know. There is one who...well, that is for another time. I must go now, Talon. You too must go to your bed, as the servants and eunuchs will have much to say if they find us together here." She laughed again.

In one lithe movement she slid her long legs off the divan, reached for her robe and stood. Talon stood with her and she moved into his arms. "Hmm, you seem ready for more!" she teased and slid her hand along the scar on his jaw, but then she gave him a brief kiss and disappeared into the darkness, leaving behind the scent of her rose petal perfume.

Talon wrapped his towel around his waist and stood for a long moment looking after her, reliving the moments of their lovemaking. Then he shook his head in bewilderment. Later as he headed back to his room it was easy to avoid being seen by two of the slaves who were mopping the floors.

He woke later than usual and hastened to dress. He was still bemused by the events of the night before but decided that he must act as normally as possible and make his excuses to get back to the inn and rejoin Max. He went out into the loggia where he met Joannina, who greeted him with a smile.

"Good morning, Talon. God's blessings on you. I trust you slept well?"

He nearly jumped. Did she know anything? He felt that he had guilt painted all over his face as he scrutinized her face for any sign of mockery, but the only emotion he detected was that of concern.

"God's Blessings, my Lady. I, er...yes, Joannina I did sleep well," he finally responded.

"I am about to go and see Alexios. Will you come with me, Talon?"

"Yes, I will," he said, feeling relieved, and he got up to follow her down a long cool corridor to the room where Alexios was convalescing.

Alexios was propped up on the wide bed with pillows all around. He kissed his mother with affection and glanced up to see Talon coming into the room. He looked pale and tired.

"Talon! There you are. I was beginning to wonder if you had left the house for that inn of yours!"

"God's Blessings, Alex. I was invited to stay by your mother and...the senator."

Alexios blinked. "Father invited you to stay?"

"Your father has decided that Talon, although a Frank, is not as bad as those he remembers and has invited him to stay as long as he wants to," Joannina said with an amused look at Talon that lingered.

"How are you doing?" Talon asked.

Alexios shifted in the bed. "I still cannot use the leg but the other wound seems to be improving. God willing, I will be out of this bed and back on duty before too long." He winced in pain from the movement and leaned back, clearly tired from even this exertion.

"I shall leave you, my son," Joannina stated. "Talon will stay for a little while, but you must not be too long, Talon, as the physician insisted that he rest."

Talon grinned. "I shall not stay too long, Joannina, I promise."

She swept out touching his forearm as she left. Talon looked after her as she moved away, leaving a subtle scent of some warm exotic wood.

He turned back to find Alexios regarding him. "Mother is one of those ladies who enslaves all who meet her," he said in a jovial tone.

Talon relaxed. "She is an unusual woman and yours is an unusual family, Alex. Tell me, how is that knee doing?"

For answer Alexios threw aside the bedclothes and exposed his lower leg, bandaged from the shin to mid-thigh.

"The physician said that had the wound not been dressed regularly on the way I would have certainly lost the leg and perhaps even died. I have you to thank for that Talon."

Talon peered at the leg then bent over the knee to sniff the area as he had learned to do in Egypt. It smelled clean and he could not see as much of the puffy redness that had so worried him while they were traveling.

"I believe that it is mending nicely," he said. "I am glad the physician was pleased."

"We are all grateful to you and Max, Talon. Where is he today?"

"He is at the inn."

"Why does not he stay here? He knows he would be very welcome."

"Max feels uncomfortable in this kind of place, Alex. Besides, he is with our new dog—remember Dog? He has not even given it a name yet as he does not know what to do with it and the inn keeper is not happy that it is there. It frightens everyone!"

"He could leave it here as guard dog," Alexios suggested.

"That sounds like a good idea; I will talk to him about it," Talon agreed. "But also we await the ship and he wants to be on hand when it comes in. It is due in any one of these days."

Alexios looked pensive.

"What is the matter, Alexios?" Talon asked. He had by now come to recognize when his friend was worried about something.

Alexios looked up at him, struggling to find the right words. He finally said, "You have always been honest with me, Talon. Will... will I ever be able to walk again?"

"It is very much in God's hands and that capable physician, but I see no reason why not," Talon stated with a conviction he did not entirely feel. "You will hobble about for a while and then hopefully the knee will heal and you can do all the things that you used to," he lied.

To change the subject and to break the silence that ensued he said, "I want to talk to you about something very different."

Alex tried to sit up more and winced. Talon hastened to help him by placing the cushions to prop him up more comfortably.

"What do you want to talk about?" Alexios asked.

"Some time ago we talked about the problems associated with shipping goods to their destinations. You said the Venetians are all in prison and the Genoese were untrustworthy."

"Yes, that is right. Our ever capricious emperor decided he had had enough of the Venetians, but it was not simply that. They have played us off against the Normans, getting rich in the process. As for the Genoese, they are just like all Latins. You give them some concessions and the next thing you know they are strutting about the city as though they own it."

Talon nodded. "But your family's involvement in the production of silk and the trading of spices is still very important, is it not?"

"Of course! We are now more than ever dependent upon being able to sell our silk, spices and oil."

"But you do not have ships, or rather, people with ships who you can trust to dispatch your goods to where you want to send them?"

Alexios stared at him. "Do you mean what I think you mean?" he asked slowly.

"Well...I am neither sailor nor navigator but...I do have a first rate navigator and just as importantly a ship. Yes, that is what I mean," Talon said with some hesitation in his voice. He did not know how his friend might react, given the aristocratic aloofness toward merchants.

Alexios reacted in quite another way. "Are you sure, Talon? Dear God! I mean...yes, this is worth thinking about. If you are serious then we should discuss this." He sounded excited.

Talon breathed a small breath of relief. "I am serious, Alex. I own a ship that from time to time must do the work of the Templars, but in between times it should work for me and Max and my friends: Henry, Nigel, Guy and the rest of them. I need to pay the crew or I can't sail the ship. A ship should not be idle, should it?"

"No indeed," Alexios breathed. His eyes glowed. "We shall have to tell Father...eventually, but perhaps not at first. We should see what we can do to prove it would work for us."

"We will need to find out where there is a demand and what we can exchange for your goods. Not everyone has gold to buy with, but I think there are many places where we can trade for valuable cargoes and bring them back here," Talon said.

"I must get the charts out and have a look. But Makarios, our agent, will most certainly know. I shall send for him," Alexios stated. For the first time in weeks he sounded excited.

"Would you be on the ship, Talon?"

"Of course I would. I would not want to have my ship sailing about the sea with a precious cargo on it without being there to protect it," Talon said with a bravado he did not feel. He cringed at the thought of being in another of those ferocious storms hat seemed to rise up out of nowhere.

Alex nodded almost absently, but it was clear he was thinking hard.

"There will have to be an agreement between us. This is what the Merchants do. We must calculate prices and what we want in exchange."

"What do you want in exchange for your cargo, to be brought back to Constantinople?" Talon asked. "It is here, is it not, that the gold will be?"

"Indeed it is, Talon. This city needs salt and wheat, a lot of it for the citizens, and we must not forget the army will want to salt their meat and fish. Then there is copper and iron, hides, and grain too if that is possible. The bakeries used to depend upon Egypt for their grain but cannot anymore."

"Sir Guy mentioned that there is salt on the island of Cyprus. I know there is salt in Egypt as well. That is a start."

Joannina arrived later with the physician. Both were agitated to find Talon still there with Alexios. Papers and drawings done with charcoal sticks were strewn about the bed and both men were so deep into their discussion they were barely aware of the visitors.

"Alexios!" Joannina exclaimed. "Talon! You promised not to stay and tire him!"

The physician, a thin man in a long robe with a leather bag hanging off a long strap from his shoulder, clucked in alarm and hastened over, almost pushing Talon out of the way to lean over Alexios and feel his brow.

"Hmm, he is a little flushed, my Lady. Sir, you should be resting," he admonished Alexios. The physician took his wrist and felt his pulse then he looked alarmed. "Your pulse is high, Sir! I must insist that you stop what you are doing and rest!"

The less than contrite Alexios glanced up at Talon and grinned. "Till next time, Talon...Thank you. God Bless."

"God Bless, Alexios." Talon turned and gave Joannina a disarming grin; she gave him a reproachful look as she guided him out of the room.

"What have you two been talking about, Talon? But I must say Alexios seems to have woken up! He is looking better than I have seen him for the last two days despite what the physician says!"

"We were discussing ships and places where they can go for trade."

She looked surprised, then laughed and waved a dismissive hand. "Alexios has always had this interest in ships and merchants. It does not please his father, but if it keeps his mind from going stale while he is recovering that is a good thing." She spoke with a degree of uncertainty in her voice. "His father, of course, will want him to rejoin his regiment as soon as he recovers and can walk and ride again." This time she sounded more convinced.

My Heart is in the East-
And I am on the edge of the West.
How can I possibly taste what I eat?
How could it please me?
How can I keep my promise
Or ever keep my vow?

Yehuda Halevi

Chapter 17

Thanks Giving

Not long after their arrival back in the city Max announced that he wanted to fulfill his vow to give thanks for their delivery and safe return at the church of Saint Demetrios.

He and Talon were once again at the inn where Talon retained rooms for the sake of privacy and because it was close to the harbor. When the ship returned one of them wanted to be there to greet it upon arrival. Talon had come from the villa to the inn to have breakfast with Max and to enjoy his company before they planned for the day ahead.

The dog had been left with the stable hands at the villa Kalothesos where the grooms promised to look after him. He had whined as Max walked away with Talon, but with a few words of encouragement from the groom holding his lead he had settled down to watch their departure quietly enough.

Talon was tired. "The church is all the way over on the other side of the city, Max. Why could you not go to one near the Mese, Saint Mary of Diakonissa for instance, or the Forty Martyrs? That is even closer!"

But Max was in no mood for compromise. "Talon, I made a solemn promise and I have not kept it for one reason or the other for two weeks now. I will have to go to confession and declare myself unfit to be a Templar if I do not go and pray there." His bearded chin jutted out in a determined manner.

"Jonathan is gone to Acre, Max, who are you going to confess to here in Constantinople?"

"These priests are not heretics, although Jonathan thought so. I think I can confess to one of them," Max sounded defensive.

Talon looked at his friend with some amusement. "You are right, Max. I am guilty of being lazy and you are the honorable one. Come, let us finish breakfast and then go. It is a nice day and we will enjoy the walk."

Max smiled. "You have been somewhat preoccupied of late, Talon. Not like your usual self."

Talon grinned back. "I am just getting lazy; that journey back was tiring." He did not add that his thoughts were drifting eastward and he had been wondering when he might return in that direction.

Max nodded. "At one point I thought that we were finished. God protected us though, and here we are. Must give thanks, it is important to me, Talon."

They walked out of the inn and turned up the street. The city was humming with activity, both along the busy avenues and down along the several harbors. The nearby brothel was quiet, as it had stayed open until the early hours of the morning. The usual beggars were on the streets, their rags fluttering in the light breeze coming in off the sea. Filthy urchins were aggressively begging and running errands, while tradesmen and their workers were out and about, either putting up scaffolding or working in open shops along the way.

The two men arrived at the Forum of Constantine and walked down the straight paved road that followed the curved line of the wall of Byzantium, which was falling into decay now that the city was encompassed by huge walls a mile and a half to the west. They had a grand view of the Golden Horn and the Bosporus sea, which was full of the sails of all manner of water craft. Their arrival at the church coincided with a small ceremony being enacted just outside the building. There was a marriage in progress.

"We have come at a bad time for a moment of quiet prayer," Max muttered.

"We can always attend and then pray. Look, they're about to enter the church. Let's follow and stand at the back where we can observe the ceremony."

They were standing at the back of the crowded church watching and listening as the priest went through the process of the marriage ceremony when Talon felt a light tug on his sleeve. He turned to see Max staring at someone just ahead of them.

"Talon, I recognize that man," he whispered out of the side of his mouth, indicating with his chin some people ahead of them.

Talon peered into the half light. "Which man are you talking about, Max?" he whispered back.

"The one who is standing sideways to us, talking to that big fellow."

Talon stared at the two men. There was something familiar about the person Max had indicated.

"We must leave...now," Max whispered. There was an urgent tone to his voice.

"What about our reason for coming?" Talon protested as they passed through the church's doorway into the sunlight. Max took Talon's arm and moved them firmly out of the way of the steps so that anyone who came after would not immediately see them.

"Who is it that you saw in there, Max?" Talon demanded.

"I am sure that he is the one we met in Alexandria."

"Who did we meet in Alexandria?" Talon asked, confused.

"Talon, did you not recognize him? That was the captain of the ship we nearly managed to take to Cyprus before we were captured!" Max actually took Talon by the shoulders and shook him he was so agitated.

"Max, calm yourself." Talon gently disengaged himself. "Are you very sure?"

"Wait until they come out and then see if you agree with me. By God if it is him I will take his life today!" Max was clearly upset. "He betrayed us and abandoned us to our fate and let Montague die right in front of his ship!"

"Wait! Wait, Max! I will stand here with you and we shall see who this is."

The light cheerful music of flutes and a tar being played for the wedding came to a stop, and after a quiet period during which the priest blessed the couple, the families and other attendants began to leave the church. Somewhere within the church a bell began to chime. Both men stared hard at everyone who left the building. The wedding crowd paid no attention to them as they ran down the steps of the church laughing and joking. The musicians struck up their instruments and played a merry tune as the bride and groom walked down the steps to the cheers of their families and friends, her hand on his arm, a flush of happiness on her face.

Talon concentrated on locating the two men Max had pointed out. His memory went back to that terrible day almost three years ago when they had been captured in Alexandria. He recalled the fight, the heroic death of their companion Montague, and their subsequent interment in the city prison. He remembered the captain of the ship who had taken their silver in the foul wine shop, and the last view of the man as he had shrugged and watched them being hauled off by soldiers.

"He is coming now, look!" Max whispered.

The man was just walking down the steps of the church toward the street. He was well dressed in the Latin style, which made him either Pizan or Genoese. He wore a finely stitched doublet with wide sleeves over a clean white linen shirt. He was talking to a heavyset man who was balding on top and had long strands of lank hair hanging over the greasy collar of a once white shirt.

Talon thought he recognized the well dressed man, but he was fleshier than he had been the last time Talon had seen him; clearly life had not been unkind to this man. There was a paunch beginning to form over his wide leather belt. His hose and pantaloons were of fine felt and his knee length boots were of the best leather. He carried a good sword at his belt and a long knife in an expensive leather sheath near to the money pouch on his right side. His huge blue felt hat had a feather stuck through it, giving him a rakish look. His trimmed beard and hair tied back in a tidy queue indicated that this man had some money to spend upon himself.

Talon sharpened his stare and concentrated. Max was right; there was a resemblance and it was not just a vague one. It was confirmed for Talon when the man gave a casual glance at the two Templars. Talon recognized the features instantly, but it was equally clear the recognition was not reciprocated. The man turned his head away without seeming to recognize either of them.

"By the Saints, Max, I believe you are right," Talon breathed.

"He looked straight at us!"

"While we might recognize him it is doubtful he could do the same for us, Max. Remember we were three vagabonds looking for passage. Not two Templars."

"What should we do, Talon?" Max asked. "I want him to pay for what he made happen to poor Montague."

"It was really that other man, whom I killed, who betrayed us. All the same, I am curious as to what he is doing here. We can follow him and see where he goes. Come on, Max."

As unobtrusively as they could, the two of them set out. Talon quietly voiced a concern.

"I am uncomfortable doing this in our Templar uniforms, Max. We stand out in this Greek city as outsiders. It will be hard to miss us should he look behind him more than once."

As it happened they did not have far to go. The two men in front of them, still talking together, strode through the now unguarded gate of the old wall of Byzantium and walked into an area that was noticeably Latin in character. The streets were narrow and dirty, the tops of the houses almost touched at the top floors, and there were many wine houses and eating-houses along the street.

The two men ducked into one of the taverns and disappeared. Talon took Max's arm and said, "We cannot follow them into that tavern. He might recognize us if we did and I do not want that."

"So you agree with me it is he?" Max asked as a final confirmation.

"Oh yes, it is him all right."

"I want to avenge Montague. God save me, but I want his skin," Max ground out the words. "Had it not been for this man Montague would be alive today."

Talon looked at his friend with compassion. "Do you know, Max, I want to find out what he is doing here in Constantinople. The Venetians are all in prison and the Genoese are high on the hog's back right now. It would be nice to know more. Come, we should leave before people get too curious. We are already attracting attention."

"I have an idea, Talon." Max said. "You are the more conspicuous with your Templar white. Go and find some other clothes while I wait and watch. Look, I shall turn my cloak over so that the cross is on the inside. We do not want to lose this man now that we have found him."

Talon agreed. Max in his dark clothes of a Templar sergeant was much less conspicuous in the crowded streets, and they most certainly did not want to lose the Genoese captain at this time. He hurried off to the inn.

A good hour later Talon arrived back at the tavern where he had left Max, but his companion was nowhere to be seen. The street was less crowded now as it was almost noon and most people had retired to enjoy a meal or take a rest. The habit of going home for a few hours in the middle of the day was popular in this city. He cast about for any sign of Max but there was none. All he could do was to investigate the tavern in the hope that the Genoese might still be there, but again he found no sign. He reasoned that Max must have followed the men when they left the tavern and wondered in which direction he might have gone.

He need not have worried. Max strode up to him from the area of the harbor walls.

"I hoped that you would be here, Talon."

"Where has he gone, Max?"

"He is indeed a sailor and he is at this time on his ship!" Max sounded triumphant. "I knew the rogue was our man. I could swear that God's hand is in this. Why, I just wanted to pray and give thanks and He led us to this rascal. There might be justice after all for Montague."

Talon grinned. "Show me where his ship is berthed."

It took only a few minutes for Max to retrace his steps and lead Talon to the banks of the natural inlet called Neorion Harbor.

"There, that is his ship. He climbed aboard with that other fellow." Max pointed to a long, slim, two masted galley anchored in the middle of the harbor. The ship was distinguishable by the fact that it was not one of the many rounder merchant ships clustered all about the waters.

"If I needed confirmation, this is it, Max. Remember our captain had a galley, not a merchant ship." Talon clapped Max on his shoulder.

"Well, what do we do now? I am hungry but I do not want to lose sight of him."

"You go and get out of those clothes, eat some food and bring something back for me. It is my turn to watch. I want to make sure that the gates are not shut during the night, as that could become difficult."

Max agreed and left. Talon settled down to watch the harbor and to see what their quarry might do next.

*****

The message arrived while Caravello and his two companions were aboard his ship waiting for just this. They had attended a wedding that a distant acquaintance had invited them to earlier that day. The note was delivered by the same wiry man with angular pockmarked features. Having accomplished his mission the messenger returned swiftly to shore and disappeared into the still busy throng on the wharf. Caravello unrolled the letter and read the words.

You will come to the usual place after sunset it said, nothing more.

Caravello was exasperated by this, as just walking about the city after sunset was in and of itself dangerous for a Latin, even more so now in the wake of the riots. However, this was a pressing errand and it was long past due.

Caravello told Davide to row him ashore. Once there, he told Christophas to wait for him and then, accompanied by Davide, he walked unobtrusively through the gates of the harbor. As the sun set and darkness flowed over the seaways and covered the hills, he turned north to climb the steep slopes of the hill.

Sometime later he tapped gently on the door of the same villa he had visited earlier and waited. A dog barked in the street further down, but other than the incessant chirping of crickets and the croaking of frogs the street was quiet. He had no sense that he had been followed.

*****

Keeping to the shadows Talon had experienced little difficulty following them through the gates that isolated the harbor from the city. He noted that there was no moon that night and they were heading up the hill past the gates of the palace of Botaneiatis. The two men were walking in the general direction of the villa Kalothesos. Intrigued, Talon maintained a discrete distance and kept his quarry in sight.

The Genoese seemed to know exactly where they were going, glancing back once or twice as they walked along the narrower streets. There was one occasion when a patrol tramped by but Talon disappeared into the shadows; then he waited for the Genoese to continue, as they too had hidden from the patrol. They stopped outside a small doorway set into a stone wall that enclosed one of the great houses, distinguished by a second story that marked its owner as one possessing considerable wealth.

A dog growled, then the door opened and the Genoese men disappeared, leaving Talon to wait outside. Talon decided that having come this far he might as well find out what else he could. The wall did not look like an obstacle he needed to worry about; although tall it was easy for him to scale. He lay along the top of the wall and listened. The presence of the dog worried him. He would have a hard time with one of those huge mastiffs if one were on the property and sniffed him out.

Listening and watching as still as the stone wall itself he soon gained a good idea as to the layout of the extensive gardens of the property. At one point he realized that this was the villa he had visited for the party. It belonged to Pantoleon's father, the senator Spartenos; he was sure of it. He remembered thinking that the buildings were more impressive than those of the family Kalothesos. The area he was able to observe from his perch was the back end of the compound and was full of shrubs and olive trees as well as some vines in a corner. He also noticed that there were guards patrolling the grounds, one of which had a dog on a lead. Lying absolutely still along the top of the wall Talon could see that the man with the dog was going to come right under his position. Deciding that detection was not going to help his cause, he slipped back down the outside of the wall and waited, leaning against the stonework and listening.

There was a murmur of voices as the guards walked by on the other side. To Talon's relief neither they nor the dog seemed aware that there was an intruder nearby. As the low voices moved off Talon once again scaled the wall. He wanted very much to get inside the villa and find out what it was that had brought the Genoese captain to this place.

*****

Caravello and Davide were led to the rear of the house by the same servant Markos, again accompanied by the torch-bearer and the hooded man.

They stopped at the entrance to the room. After a nod to the sentries Markos lead the way in. Davide stayed behind under the watchful eyes of the guards.

"The Captain Caravello, Sirs."

The murmur of conversation halted. There were the same two men in the spacious area in front of him as before. Senator Spartenos stood up to greet him. The other continued to recline on a couch near to some low tables laden with a light dinner. Markos bowed himself out of the room, but again the hooded man remained just inside the door.

"Ah, Caravello, I trust you had a good voyage?"

"Nothing but the usual hazards of wind and weather to contend with, senator," Caravello replied as he accepted a silver goblet of wine. He sipped it appreciatively.

The senator spent a good hour going over what he wanted Caravello to accomplish. It was very late when he finally dismissed the Genoese.

*****

Talon slipped over the wall and dropped into the shrubs at its base without a sound. He crouched in the dark, listening intently. Now he not only had people to deal with but also a large watchdog, perhaps even more than one, and he had no illusions as to what they could do to a man should they attack him.

Silent as a ghost he made his way towards the dense black outline of the buildings. He was thankful that there was no moon. His night vision was allowing him to see into some of the deeper shadows and watch for any movement that would betray the presence of someone in hiding or simply on guard. Wondering where the dog might be he moved with great caution across the grounds, keeping to the darker shadows wherever he could. He had encountered no one by the time he finally made it to the base of the brick steps leading up to the loggia, which wrapped around this side of the main house. There did not seem to be any lights on, which made him wonder where his two Genoese might have gone. He decided to move around the building and find out if there was any way to gain entry.

He had managed to slip around the north corner when he noticed a dim light coming from a large window above him; he could hear the low murmur of voices coming from the opening. He moved very cautiously into the shrubs at the base of the terrace, trying to get closer to either see or hear what was happening in the room above, but the space ahead of him was bare with nowhere to hide. He was sure now that he was close to finding out what the Genoese was doing here. He noticed that just above him was the window to another room. If he could get into that room he might be able to hear more and perhaps even see who was present in the other room.

Talon climbed the rough stone terrace, which was only about three paces high; then he could just haul himself into the darkness of the room. As he slid over the windowsill he thought he heard the word Rhodes, and several men walked past. Realizing that the Genoese were leaving, he almost followed them. At the last minute he decided to investigate the house instead and proceeded to climb into the room, but as he did so he caught the hem his tunic on a splinter of wood. Despite his care there was a tiny sound of ripping cloth.

*****

After Caravello had gone, the senator and his visitor continued to discuss their plans.

"Our patron is impatient to move as soon as it is possible, senator. Have that Genoese back from Rhodes as soon as possible. I hope that the fleet is right behind him and closes off the Hellespont. If we can achieve our objective, winter will curtail shipping enterprises until the spring."

"All in good time, my friend. You must persuade him to be patient. The pieces on the chessboard all have to be in their rightful places before we can call checkmate. The Emperor still has powerful friends in the Army and the Navy—although after this last debacle I cannot understand why any of the generals would want to stay with him. Andronikos Kontostephanos and Andronikos Angelos are now firmly on our side, and Issac is disgusted with the huge loss we incurred at Myriokephalon. He blames Manuel for the entire fiasco."

"And what of the Arabs?"

"The Genoese will act as the signal and then they will come. Their mission is to draw the navy away from the city down into the Hellespont, nothing more. They will be well rewarded. Some liquid fire apparatus will keep them happy. This will keep the navy out of it and then when they come back they will find another emperor in the palace."

*****

Talon had no sooner entered the room than he became aware that something was very wrong. A cool draft indicated that a door had been opened. He could see very little in the darkness but realized with cold certainty that someone was in the room with him and quite possibly about to attack him. A chill made its way down his neck and back. He had not expected to be caught in this manner. His adrenaline was already high but it seemed to jump a notch. He slipped his knife into his left hand and drew his sword very slowly. In the dense silence of the room he could hear the slip of its passage from its sheath as he drew it out. He held it ready as he stepped very slowly and with great care towards a darker corner where he planned to stop and take stock of his situation.

He had no time. There was a tiny noise to his right and he felt a presence very close by. He whirled, his weapons up on the defensive. His blade was struck hard by another one; so hard and unexpected was the blow that it hurt his wrist, the shock running right up his arm to his shoulder. The blades made a harsh rasping sound and a tiny stream of small sparks flew out from the rasping blades. In that moment it was enough to briefly illuminate a hooded figure holding his sword in both hands. The force of the strike drove Talon back a pace, his wrist rigid with tension as he held off the other's blade. He struck almost blindly at where he had last sensed his opponent but his blade merely cut the air. He ducked instinctively and was glad that he had. He could feel the wind of a blade pass overhead. He again stabbed out in a wild hope that he would make contact with something other than the air of this ghost's passage. He was rewarded by a short gasp and knew that he had indeed struck something, but he did not want to tarry. Whoever it was in the room with him was very good and extremely dangerous. Detection was not what Talon had wanted so now he needed to escape.

He made for the window but found it blocked by a darker patch of shadow that suddenly appeared right in his path. The next thing he felt was a stinging cut along his side. He wondered fleetingly if it was going to be fatal but it was only a shallow slice and he charged straight at the other. Ducking once more as he approached, Talon struck low at the legs of his opponent and was again rewarded by contact and a hiss of pain. He knew that he had not made a killing blow, but it was enough to allow him to slip inside the guard of his opponent and strike him hard in the face with the pommel of his sword. There was a grunt and the figure stumbled backwards to fall onto the floor. A blade clattered onto the tile floor.

It was time to leave. Talon jumped through the open window and landed silently on the verandah, then ran back the way he had come wondering if he should not have killed the man, but it was more important to get out of the place than to leave bodies lying about in his wake.

Talon fled across the silent and dark loggia, making his way through the shadows, expecting at any time for the alarm to sound and the whole place to wake up. Soon he gained the base of the wall, which he shimmied up and slipped over to land in a crouch on the other side. He heard a shout back at the far end of the garden, men calling and the barking of several dogs; the alarm was well and truly sounded.

*****

Back in the villa there was pandemonium. Having heard the commotion in the other room the senator shouted for more lights and for the guards to open the doors.

"Where is Choumnos?" he shouted.

Servants appeared, frightened and bleary-eyed. "Find me Choumnos at once!" he bellowed.

The guards stood aside to allow the formerly hooded man to enter the room. He was limping badly; there was blood all over his thigh and it dripped onto the floor. He looked as though someone had smashed his lips and nose with something hard.

The senator gasped. "What in God's good name happened to you?" he asked finally after taking in the damage to his retainer.

"We had a visitor, Sir."

"It would seem so," the senator said with a dry tone. "Have the guards secured the grounds? Where are the dogs? Why have they not taken care of this intruder?"

"We...we have all the guards out on the grounds with the dogs, senator," one of the eunuchs stammered.

"Well, what are you waiting for? Find whoever it was!"

"You, Choumnos, tell me exactly what happened." The senator's voice was now very calm.

Choumnos, who would have preferred to have his wounds dressed, staggered.

"Sit down man, sit down. You there, get some dressing and see to his cut; I do not want to see his blood all over my furniture!" the senator barked at the frightened servant standing by the door. The man fled.

Choumnos thankfully almost fell onto one of the couches where he dripped more blood onto the leather surface. The senator regarded the man and the mess he was making on the divan with distaste.

"I thought I heard a sound, just a feeling, but it turns out I was right. I had left little traps lying about for the unwary and any unwanted visitors, you can never be too careful. I heard the sound of someone entering the room next door through the window and I suspected he was trying to find out what was going on in here, Sir." The man winced at the pain in his leg and then composed himself with an effort. "I went there to find out and he attacked me."

"I can see that," the senator said. "Do you think he heard anything?"

He was not in the least bit interested in whether Choumnos was going to live but whether the intruder had heard anything significant.

"I...do not think so, Senator. I got into the room very quickly and had the impression that whoever it was had only just arrived. It was very quick...he is as fast as a snake and very good; I did not get a look at his face." Choumnos looked as though he was professionally impressed, but then he brought his attention back to the senator. "But I winged him, I am sure of it."

"Then perhaps there will be a trail to follow," the senator said.

"There might be, but we will have to move fast as he has probably escaped over the wall by now."

"You sound pretty sure of that," Basileios said, speaking for the first time.

"He was good, Sir."

"Hmm, not so good that you did not detect his presence."

At that moment one of the guards rushed in and bowed to the men in the room.

"What is it? Have you found the intruder?" the senator demanded.

"No, Sir, but the dogs are agitated at one place near the wall. There is some blood there."

"Where is Psellos?" the senator addressed Choumnos.

"I am here, Sir," replied a man dressed very much like Choumnos, in a long plain tunic with his hood thrown back. His hand was on his sword as he bowed to the two men. He was the man who had been the messenger for Caravello.

"You two, find this man. I do not care who he is or where he is from. Enlist the aid of your murky friends in the city if need be. There will be gold in payment. He is probably one of the Chamberlain's spies, but you will find him and kill him. I want his head—as soon as possible. Go!"

By this time the servant had returned with bandages and lint for Choumnos. He approached the couch but the senator waved him off.

"Get out of here, all of you. Fix him up somewhere else; I do not want him bleeding all over my furniture. Find that intruder," he snarled as he turned away.

He waited until they had all gone then turned to his guest. "As you can see, there are spies everywhere, and I am sure this is the work of the Emperor's Chamberlain. You had best leave for the time being, but do not leave the city. You will of course inform Prince Andronikos?"

"That should not be a problem."

"He has already jeopardized his position with his philandering," the Senator said, the irritation heavy in his voice. "That girl from the family Kalothesos is a liability; he should never have involved himself with her at this crucial stage, it is insane. She is a Lady in Waiting to the Empress, for God's sake. What if she talks? It is dangerous enough that the prince is in the city. If the Emperor's spies find out, he will be blinded and the rest of us will be headless, and that only after we have suffered at the hands of the Emperors imaginative torturers."

"I agree. If that was a spy for the Emperor it might already be too late. I trust you to find him before he can pass along anything he might have learned, Senator." There was no mistaking the threat in Basileios' tone. It was odd to hear that level of menace in the eunuch's high voice. "Also, I must be kept informed of what the Arab fleet is doing. We have mercenaries waiting on the mainland to come over as soon as the Byzantine fleet has left to deal with the threat at Abydos."

"Very well. I do not think it will take long for us to find this man; he is wounded. Nevertheless we should probably not meet until things have cooled down. The plan is in motion as soon as the Genoese sails. After that the bones are thrown."

The senator called for one of his servants, and when the man arrived he told him to find Eugenia Kalothesos and bring her to him.

Chapter 18
Family Affairs

Talon stopped to draw breath several hundred paces from the villa and considered his options. He could hear the pandemonium at the estate he had just left, although it is clamor was now diminished by distance and the houses and trees in between.

Here in the darkness of a side street the night was very quiet, even the insects and frogs seemed to have gone to bed in the predawn hours. He was very sure that the dogs would be sent after him despite the fact that the city patrols were in the area. He had to keep moving. Max would by now be very worried and wondering what had happened. He put his hand to his side and felt the sting of the cut and the wetness of blood.

It did not have the numbing pain of a deep wound. He knew he had to bind it up thoroughly so that there would be no blood dripping on the ground. It was likely he had left some on the wall he had climbed. Ripping the hem of his tunic in a wide bandage he wrapped it around his waist and made sure that the bleeding was contained. Some blood had trickled down his leg so he had to wipe what he could feel, hoping he did not leave traces on the road. Then he heard loud barking and it sounded as though it was getting closer. It was time to move.

He decided that he had to get off the streets as fast as he could and hope that Max would trust to his instincts and find him in the morning. Max could figure out how to avoid the patrols and get back to the inn. He might spend a sleepless night, but he would most probably come to the villa to investigate in the morning. Talon set off at a lope towards the villa Kalothesos.

It was not hard to find his way. He decided to run up one or two of the adjoining streets in an attempt to confuse the dogs, but steadily made his way back to the villa of the Kalothesos. The sound of the dogs receded, for which he was thankful, and he was soon at the wall that surrounded the villa. Again he climbed into someone else's property without permission; he was quite sure that if the dogs did trace him to the gates the sentries would give him away, either intentionally or unintentionally. They did not strike him as being particularly bright and he did not want to take that chance. There was a brief shock for him at the top of the wall: a cat was sitting on the wall watching him. It hissed and arched its back while he jerked backwards and almost fell, but then it vanished into the garden below and he released his breath in a long quiet whoosh.

The shrubs of the garden were good cover for him and the guards here at the villa Kalothesos were a good deal less alert than they were at the other place, in fact he could have sworn they were asleep; it was easy for him to climb into the house through a half open window and slip down a corridor to his own room.

He walked silently into his room but with sudden alarm he realized that once again he was not alone. All his internal alarms went off and his dagger was out in a split second as he crouched just inside the door, scanning the room desperately trying to see where this new danger came from. He waited. Something stirred on the bed, and in two paces Talon pounced and had his dagger at the figure's throat before it could more than sit up.

There was a terrified squeak, the figure froze, then fell back onto the cushions with a faint gurgle. Talon followed it down and hissed, "Do not move." The figure shook its head in mute obedience and he eased the knife off the its throat.

"Don't hurt me!" a voice gasped in a terrified whisper.

"What are you doing here?" he whispered back, thinking it might be Eugenia.

"I...I was waiting for you to come. Where have you been? It is almost dawn." Something about the voice made him stop and peer hard at the figure on the bed. The voice was a woman's but not the one he had expected; the perfume, light as it was, did not fit.

"Who is it? Stay there!" he ordered in a harsh whisper.

He hastened over to the small table in the corner and struck a flint onto the wick of one of the lamps. It took slowly but soon there was a bright glow in the room that cast many shadows and he could see who it was. Instinctively he kept his wounded side turned away from view.

Theodora was sitting up in the bed holding the sheets up to her chin. Her hair was in disarray and she looked frightened and vulnerable. Her face was very pale and she was beginning to shake with reaction to his behavior.

With an astonished grunt at the sight of her Talon held the lamp on high and walked toward her. Her wide eyes regarded him fearfully.

"What in the Saints' good names are you doing here?" He realized his tone was none too friendly.

His heart rate was slowing as he recovered from his own surprise, but now he needed some answers.

Theodora looked sheepish. "You frightened me!" she accused him.

"What are you doing in my bedroom, Theodora?" he insisted, more gently this time.

"I...I wanted to be with you," she stammered, but then she looked back at him with defiance. "I love you, Talon. I am not a child." Her tone was defensive.

The sheet shifted and he realized that her clothing was on the floor and she was naked in the bed.

"Yes you are, Theodora, you are only fourteen and you should not even be in this room. What if anyone heard you or saw you coming in here?"

"Fourteen is old enough for love. My sister knew a man when she was sixteen." Theodora was fast getting over her fright and was prepared to argue the point.

Talon was pulled up short by the memory of his encounter with her sister. He shook his head. "Sixteen is not fourteen."

"Queens get married to kings when they are twelve, Talon," she reminded him, her tone acid.

He almost laughed.

"That is not the point, Theodora. You should not be in this room. You must go. Immediately."

She stared back at him, defiance in her eyes coupled with hurt, but then they widened and she gasped.

"Talon, you are hurt! What happened to you?"

He sat down on the edge of the bed suddenly tired. "It is nothing that I cannot deal with. You must go, please go."

"No! Not until I have seen to your wound," she exclaimed. She let the sheets drop and clambered out of the bed quite naked and reached for her tunic. Talon turned away quickly to allow her some privacy.

She slipped her tunic over her head and was just pulling it down over her knees when he turned back. She bent over to him and stared at his side, which was red and wet.

"You must let me help you with this, Talon. I can help," she almost pleaded, her hand reaching out tentatively to touch his side.

Talon was tired and wanted to be left alone, but he relented as she began to take off the rag he had wrapped around his waist.

"There is clean water by the window. There should be a towel there too," he muttered.

Theodora was of a sudden all business.

She brought the basin full of water to the bedside and helped him to take off his tunic, leaving his torso bare. Her eyes wandered over his body and widened as they took in the old scars and the new wound. He liked the fact that she did not seem unduly bothered by the sight of blood.

"It is not serious, it just needs to be cleaned and bound. But you must hurry," he said. A cock had crowed out by the barns heralding the dawn and he heard stirrings in the yard. The household would be rising to start the day any minute now.

She nodded and quickly wet one end of the towel, then wiped the sides of the long thin cut that ran from his last rib on the right side a hand span down to his belly. He winced but held his tongue as she concentrated on the wound. Soon she had it cleaned and ready for a bandage.

"How did this happen, Talon? You should have stitches for that," she added as she carefully wrung out the rinsed cloth and began to dry the area around the wound. He glanced down at the thin cut. "I was walking back to the villa when I was set upon by street robbers. One of them did this before I could get away."

"At this time of night? It is almost dawn, Talon." She sounded skeptical.

He did not say anything. Instead he helped her tear up another towel with his dagger and wrap it around his lower chest. Theodora was kneeling on the floor wiping up some spilt water when he got up.

"Do you know anything about Greek Fire?" he asked casually.

"All I know is that it is a secret weapon that our navy uses in battle. It burns ships," she said with a puzzled look on her face. Talon's face was inscrutable.

"You must leave now, Theodora. If anyone finds you here then we will both be punished, and you probably worse than I."

Without a word she stood and slipped her hand up along his chest, then seeing his unrelenting frown she nodded and hung her head. "I just wanted..." She did not finish.

He took her chin in his hand and lifted her head so that she had to look into his eyes.

You are a lovely girl...I mean woman, Theodora, but this is not the time, nor the place," he said, trying to comfort her, as there were now tears in her eyes and one rolled down her cheek. He wiped it with a gentle thumb then took her head and shook it gently.

"I shall see you tomorrow, Talon? You will not...go away?" As she asked her eyelids fluttered. He had difficulty keeping himself from grinning. Instead he tried to look even more severe.

"I shall be here tomorrow. God bless now, you must go."

She stood on tiptoe and kissed him on the lips. "Good night and God Bless, Talon," she whispered, some of her old irreverence coming back.

He smiled and watched as she glided through the door her hips swaying more than they needed to. "Dear God," he thought to himself, "this whole family is nothing but trouble!"

*****

He catnapped for a couple of hours, then woke up with the sun shining into the room. His thoughts about the events in the villa gave him no peace; besides, he needed to see Max as soon as possible. He got out of bed feeling stiff and sore, washed, and then checked the wound. It had not bled very much but he replaced the dressing with another and bundled the bloody cloths up into another towel. Dressed in a clean tunic he walked along the corridor to the dining room. To his relief no one was there except a servant who provided him with some bread, honey yoghurt, and a pear which had come from the orchard. He ate hungrily, washing it down with clear water. He wondered how he could look the Lady Joannina in the eye after what had transpired the previous night. Breakfast over he was on the verge of going down to the inn when Max was announced by the servant, who showed him in then left.

"Where on this God given earth did you disappear to, Talon? I waited..." Max said, his tone just a little loud.

Talon put his finger to his lips signaling silence and then took a chunk of bread and cheese and placed them on a platter. He picked it up, handed a jug of wine to Max, then walked out of the room into the gardens. Glancing about he did not see anyone, not even the senator, who was normally an early riser and could sometimes be found puttering about in the vineyard. Max followed quietly, visibly trying to contain his impatience. Talon found a stone bench under some olive trees far enough from the house to provide some privacy and sat down, motioning Max to do the same. He indicated the bread and cheese.

"I had no choice, Max," he said quietly. "We have stumbled upon something and I nearly did not make it back at all. God protected me last night, of that I am sure."

"What is this all about, Talon?" Max took a bite of bread and popped a piece of cheese into his mouth. "I came back to the harbor and saw that all was quiet, but not a sign of you. I waited; it must have been three hours at least; it was very late when I finally decided that you were not coming back. I decided that you would be either at the inn or here, and so, I am here. What happened?"

Talon told him in short sentences what had transpired the night before. He showed Max his bandaged ribs and the little bundle of rags; if Max not been convinced before, they served to convince him now.

Max exhaled a long breath. "So you got into the house but someone was there waiting. I know you, Talon. You can walk into a bedroom past the guards without them ever knowing, but this time someone—perhaps someone as good as you—nearly took you down! Did you at least hear anything from the other room before you had to leave?"

"I thought I heard the word Rhodes, and I am sure I heard the words Greek Fire, but more than that I cannot be sure. Max, there is something going on but I do not know what. That villa belongs to a very wealthy man, Senator Spartenos. I went there when Pantoleon was alive and met Niko there. The senator can afford to hire skilled killers to guard it. What is our Genoese captain doing visiting a place like that, and in the dead of night, I wonder?"

"Well, you survived, and as this is not our business we should go about our own now and forget it happened," Max stated.

"What about your intent to bring Caravello to justice for what he did to us in Alexandria, Max?"

"If it means that you are going to be cut up, then perhaps we should reconsider. We are out of our depth here in this city, Talon. Perhaps there are things we should stay away from especially—a wealthy senator. They wield power here," Max said.

Talon was not satisfied but he held his tongue. His friend was tired and out of sorts. He needed to think about what had happened, and then there was the vexing problem of Theodora. He leaned back against the stone, his thoughts going back to their encounter. This slip of a girl was intelligent, perplexing, and it seemed, determined to become a woman. He would have to be very careful it did not happen while he was there. Suddenly the inn seemed inviting. Max interrupted his quiet reflections.

"Isn't the ship due back, Talon?"

"It is, and I have something else to tell you, Max."

Talon then went on to recount his meeting with Alexios, their animated discussion the day before, and their plans.

"First, though, we should pay our respects to Alexios, who is wondering why you have not been to see him much lately."

Max nodded agreement and slapped Talon on the back. "I would like that," he said.

They went inside, but just as they did so they saw Joannina with another guest. It was Nikoporus.

Talon and Max bowed to Joannina, who smiled. "Good morning, gentlemen. As you can see we have a visitor who wants to see Alexios."

"God's blessings on you, Niko," Talon said, as Niko embraced him in a fierce bear hug which made him wince from the pain it caused his wound.

"God's blessings on you both, Talon, Max," he said with tears in his eyes. He embraced an awkward Max and then stood back and looked at them.

"I heard many, many rumors about the campaign, and most of them were of the worst kind," he said. "My lady Joannina told me part of the story about how you brought Alex out. I thank you from the bottom of my heart for doing that." He spoke with a catch in his voice.

Max answered gruffly. "Many did not come back from the slaughter, Niko. We were the lucky ones, and it was our duty to bring him back safely if we could."

"I know that is true, Max, but you did it when many would have thought only of their own skins."

"Come," Joannina said softly. "I shall take you to see my son. But this time, Talon, you must promise me on your honor that you will not tire him."

"My Lady, it was all his fault he wanted to talk about..." Talon gave her a guilty grin.

"I know, but you will have to take charge or I shall come and chase you out myself. Now go in there and cheer him up," she said, but it was with a smile.

*****

Alexios was delighted to see them. He had been looking out of the open window at the garden when they walked in. Talon caught the pensive expression on his face but that cleared at the sight of them, replaced with surprise and pleasure. "Niko! About time. God's blessing!"

Nikoporus laughed and shrugged. "The Admirals keep me busy; besides which, although the army returned with a great deal of noise, your arrival was much quieter."

Nikoporus and Alexios embraced while Talon and Max stood back and watched. It was clear that these two fast friends were very glad to see one another. Nikoporus was getting emotional again so Talon asked one of the servants hovering about if he would bring some wine.

The wine came and they drew up stools in a cluster about the bed of the invalid.

"I thought that *tzykanion* was supposed to give you the skills that prevent you from getting knocked about in a battle, Alex. What happened?" Nikoporus said in a feeble attempt at humor.

Alexios grinned sheepishly. "The knee injury came from nowhere. I was busy trying to protect my middle when I was struck in two places almost at the same time. That, my friend, not even you, dexterous as you might be on a horse, could have avoided."

"The important thing is that you came back," Nikoporus said, his tone somber. "Tell me about it. All I have had up to now has been second-hand stories."

They told him the whole story: their attempts to stop the army from going in, the advance through the gorge fighting for every inch of ground, and then the hideous night in the makeshift fort. Alexios told most of the story but asked Talon and Max to fill in where he was vague, which was for most of the final effort to reach

Dorylaeum. Nikoporus was uncharacteristically silent through this part of the story. When they had finished he shook his head. "Abandoning so many men the way it was done...that cannot have helped morale, and I hear that it has done the emperor's reputation no good either."

"What do you mean, Niko?" Alexios asked.

"The army arrived back in a sorry state, thoroughly demoralized, and then the rumblings of anger began. I heard that voices were raised in the senate but no one has openly criticized the emperor, none would dare. But there is much discontent in the army and the city at our losses, and more than that, our humiliation at the hands of the Turks."

"I do not know what else he could have done, given the circumstances, Niko," Talon remarked.

"The army could not stay and fight. The Turks were stinging our flanks but they were too clever to stand and fight it out," Max added. "To stay would have meant the destruction of what remained of the army."

The conversation continued for over an hour, at which time Talon was looking over his shoulder apprehensively for Joannina to arrive and chase them away. He stood, indicating that it was time to leave.

Nikoporus embraced Alexios and they left the room, saying they would be back within a couple of days. On the way out Nikoporus said, "He looks exhausted, Talon. What do you think about that leg of his?"

"God help him, Niko, but he isn't going to walk far on that leg again. The wound is very bad."

Nikoporus stared at him in disbelief. "Are you sure? That is terrible. Does he know?"

"I think so, but he will not admit to it. Soon we need to get him up to exercise the leg, but the physician will have to allow it when the time is right."

"Will he be able to ride again?"

"I think so, but I doubt if he will be able to play *tzykanion* again."

Nikoporus looked sad and shook his head. "He loved that game," he said. Then he changed the subject.

"I have to go back to the harbor, the same one that your ship came into originally, Kontoskalion. My ship is there now and I wondered if you would like to come with me and have a look? You and Max?"

Talon and Max needed no persuasion. Waving to the distant Joannina, who was stepping into the gardens, they exited the main house and hurried down the path to the gates. Talon could not wait to leave. He wanted to get rid of his little bundle of rags before someone noticed.

Within a short while they were down the hill and near the harbor of Kontoskalion. Nikoporus was recognized and they were quickly waved through the gates by the sentries and a youthful officer who saluted him. Alongside the quay was a large, sleek looking battle dromon. The walkways were crowded, but overseers kicked and pushed slaves out of their way as they strode along the stone quay. Nikoporus stopped at the gangway and waved his hand at the ship.

"What do you think of it?" he asked. His tone was proud, even proprietary.

Talon looked over the warship with its many colorful pennants snapping in the breeze; one of the pennants bore an image of the two-headed eagle, the symbol of the empire of Byzantium.

"Is it your ship?" Talon asked. He liked what he saw.

"Yes...well, no, not quite, but I am the most senior officer on it so I am acting captain at present," Nikoporus said.

Talon's eye followed the graceful lines of the vessel tugging gently at its moorings. It was larger than his own ship and looked very businesslike with its long and menacing ram that was half under the waterline. Rising sharply from the ram in a sweeping curve that defined the bows of the ship was the figurehead, shaped in the form of a mythical creature of the sea, its jaws open wide and its claws rising out of the wooden frame that supported it. There were two tiers of rowing ports that extended from the rear decks to the base of the forecastle—something his own ship lacked —and he noticed that among the usual clutter of a ship there was something else on the deck. He could not make it out very clearly, but thought it might be one of the fearsome weapons he had heard about.

There were two masts, one just forward of the center of the boat and one aft where a lateen sail could be rigged to assist with steering, thus making the ship very maneuverable in all kinds of weather. That was about as much as Talon could understand about a ship.

"Come on," Nikoporus said and walked up the gangplank. Their arrival had been noticed. Men ran to the forecastle and covered the strange looking device with a thick cloth of some sort, and in the waist there was further activity. Nikoporus was greeted by an officer who saluted him respectfully as they boarded.

Talon looked at their companion with new eyes. He had thought that, although a nice fellow and a very good *tzykanion* player, young Niko was nothing more. The fact that he was in charge of this deadly looking weapon of war impressed Talon, and evidently Max as well, who gave Talon a surprised look with one raised eyebrow. They followed Niko willingly enough onto the deck where introductions were made and translated for the benefit of Max.

Nikoporus motioned the officer, a young man about the same age as he, to lead the way onto the upper aft deck. Talon would have preferred to have a look at the forecastle where that the strange looking device was now completely covered, but then he realized that there were some of the same items squatting in the waist of the ship on either side of the deck pointing out through openings in the sides.

They were taken up to the aft deck where they could see the length of the ship. Talon glanced about with interest before casually asking about the odd looking things on the main deck. He pointed innocently at them.

"Ah, those." Nikoporus cast a meaningful look at his colleague. "These are our fire weapons. They are known as 'Sea fire' throwers."

Talon remembered the comments of Sir Guy. He had called it 'Greek Fire.'

"What do they do?" he asked, as though he had never heard of it before. He thought he knew but he wanted to hear what Niko would say.

"We can maneuver near to an enemy boat and throw the liquid from these tubes onto their boat and set it afire," the officer said. His tone was guarded.

Talon translated for Max, who crossed himself. "It sounds like an infernal device," he said.

When Talon explained what Max had said to the two Greeks they both laughed grimly.

"It is indeed an infernal device, but God has given us the knowledge to make it and use it, and we have been able to do so effectively against the Arabs. Twice we have defeated them at sea because of this weapon and saved our city," Nikoporus said.

"How does it work?" Talon asked. He was very curious, but the officer shook his head and Nikoporus said quietly, "It is a closely guarded secret, one that only those who operate the device know.

It is all very confidential, Talon, and even if I did know—which I do not—I could not tell you on pain of death. I can tell you this, however. If we throw the substance at another ship even the sea will boil and that ship will burn to the water no matter what the crew tries to do to stop it."

Talon was awed. This was truly a terrible weapon, and his mind went back to the evening before when he thought he had heard the name. All he could see was a long tube sticking out from under a thick oilcloth covering, nothing more. He did notice that the end of the tube was smudged black.

"Have you ever seen it happen?" Talon asked Nikoporus.

"We both have," Nikoporus said with another look at his colleague. "We were on patrol at the entrance to the Hellespont one day when a pirate attacked a merchant ship. He saw us coming and tried to run for it, but we came up behind him and fired the liquid at his ship. It burned down so rapidly that few of the crew survived. I shall never forget how quickly the ship went up in smoke and flame." He shook his head. "The pirate ship had no chance at all. Nor did the people in the water."

"So there are many people who would like to have this device, your enemies perhaps?"

Nikoporus shot him a sharp look. "Many have tried, but no, none have managed to steal it from us as yet. God forbid that they do." Now it was his turn to cross himself. "Why do you ask?"

"I think that must be obvious," Talon returned. "This is a deadly weapon for the sea. Those who possess it are almost invincible, am I not right? Your enemies must desire it greatly, both for offense and defense."

Nikoporus nodded. "You are right, of course."

A huge roar from the crowd in the Hippodrome on the hillside above interrupted further conversation. The chariot races were taking place once more.

"They will miss Pantoleon," Nikoporus said.

The visit did not last very long, there was only so much they could be shown, but Talon left impressed with the condition of the ship and the apparent discipline of the crew. Leaving Nikoporus on board, Talon and Max headed for the inn to have lunch and talk about what they had seen on the boat.

*****

By morning Senator Spartenos was seething with rage. There was no sign of the intruder. His men had scoured the streets of the hillside and found no trace of him. There was only one thin clue and the dogs had provided that. They had guided the hunters to a wall that surrounded the estate of the senator Kalothesos. The dogs had become quite excited, milling about the base of the wall, whining and looking up at the top, but the men could not go into the property. Besides, they had woken up the guards within, who enquired rudely as to what they thought they were doing making so much noise outside a senator's house.

Psellos had shouted, "We are following a fugitive from justice who we think might have gone over the wall. Have you seen anything?"

The guards inside had looked at one another and promptly denied that any such thing had happened. "We have been patrolling all night and would have seen someone come over the wall, you can be sure of it. This is the estate of Senator Kalothesos and he will not take kindly to you making all that noise. Shove off!" they had shouted back.

Psellos had grimaced with disbelief and called his men away. "They were probably asleep or playing around with one of the servant girls," he muttered. Soon after, they had trooped back to the compound of senator Spartenos.

Reporting to the senator, Psellos mentioned that he thought the guards might be lying.

John Spartenos looked thoughtful. "I will pay the house a visit and see if there is anything I can find out for myself. In the meantime, think of how the man could have even known to come here. Was that oaf Caravello followed here perhaps? Find out."

Psellos nodded and his deep set eyes flamed briefly. Despite the lack of sleep he was enjoying the attention. Choumnos being out of action, even if not for long, left him in charge of the hunt and he liked that.

"I shall go down to the harbor immediately, Sir," he said.

Spartenos turned away and called for his litter. He preferred riding in the palanquin to walking, and besides, it made for a grander entrance.

It was not long before his servants and bearers were standing outside the house of his colleague Senator Kalothesos. Servants from the household were bustling about, agitated that a man of his consequence should have arrived unannounced. He waited patiently for his men to put his litter down and then walked up the entrance stairs to be greeted by an obsequious servant who showed him into the anteroom.

He was standing admiring the frescoes on the wall when there was a light step behind him. Turning he smiled at Joannina who was coming toward him. He allowed himself to indulge in the appreciation of this beautiful woman. Despite her mature years she could still stir a man, he reflected as he watched her. Perhaps she felt his intense gaze as she approached because she lowered her eyes modestly. However she greeted him warmly and held out her hands to his, which he held for just a few moments longer than than he needed to. She released his hands and said, "It is good to see you, Senator. We share your grief for your wonderful son."

He lowered his head for a moment then lifted his eyes, bright with unshed tears to gaze into hers. "My son Pantoleon would have made a great general one day. To lose him in the prime of his life is a devastating blow to myself and Constance. My wife is inconsolable. All because the Emperor could not make the right decisions that day!"

Joannina had tears in her eyes. "May God receive his soul and grant it peace in Heaven. They all say that he was going to be a great man, just like his father. We too mourn his loss."

"Please call me John. Our families are friends, and there should be no formality here, do you not think? May I call you Joannina, my Lady?" he asked, his tone deferential as he wiped an imaginary tear away with the hem of his toga.

"To what do we owe the honor of this visit...John? It has been a little while since I saw you last," Joannina asked him, indicating that he should be seated. She glanced at one of the hovering servants, who disappeared to obtain some refreshments.

"You will stay for a while, will you not, and honor our house with your presence?"

"It is I who would be honored. I apologize for the early hour," he returned, his smile avuncular.

At this moment there was the sound of footsteps outside and Theodora walked into the room. She stopped in surprise as the sight of the visitor and then made a clumsy curtsy.

"I am sorry, Mama, I did not know we had company," she said.

Joannina smiled affectionately. "John, do you remember my youngest daughter, Theodora?"

Spartenos looked at the young girl with the slightly beaked nose without much interest. "Of course I do, but it was some time ago. How you have grown. Why you are almost a woman now, and a very pretty one too!" he said with an attempt at a friendly smile that showed off the gap in his front teeth. He did not notice the flicker of annoyance that crossed the girl's face and the slight pout of her mouth at the patronizing tone, as he had turned his attention back to Joannina.

"Were you looking for something, my dear?" Joannina asked her daughter.

"I was looking for Talon, er...to ask him about some medicine we talked about," Theodora improvised.

"Talon is our new guest," Joannina explained to Spartenos. "Do you recall the Templar delegation from Acre, Senator? Well, we have one of them staying with us at present. He it is who brought..." She stopped herself abruptly, her hand going to her mouth. "I am so sorry, John. I simply forgot. Please forgive me."

He shook his head. "Like many others, I am sure, I have wondered what the Templars were doing here in our city. If I am not mistaken that is the young man who knocked Prince Isaac off his horse in the now famous—or perhaps infamous—game a month or so ago?" He forced a laugh.

Joannina gave him a grateful look. "The same. A very well behaved young man, not at all like the Franks we are all so used to." She looked at her daughter. "He knows a lot about medicine and my daughter is very interested in things of this nature. Well, Theodora, now you are here you can stay and help me entertain the senator. Ah, here is the wine. Thank you, Antonia," she said, as the servant girl placed the cool wine jug with real glass goblets on the table in front of them. Small honeyed cakes and biscuits were placed nearby.

"I believe Talon has left with Max and Nikoporus to visit a ship or something," she added as an afterthought.

Theodora looked disappointed but said nothing. She sat demurely on the couch opposite the senator, clearly trying to contain her impatience. If Joannina noticed she said nothing.

"May I ask how my dear friend Damianus is these days? I saw him last at the chariot races." Spartenos did not really care about his colleague. They had sparred often enough on opposite sides of the forum for him to dislike the crusty old general.

Joannina gave a tiny shrug. "He is well, but like you, I dare say, on a cold night his old wounds bother him. But God is kind and he is happy with his vineyard. Do you wish to see him?" she asked. "He might be in the garden, but I can send someone for him." She looked up from pouring some wine and then handing a glass half full of the deep amber liquid to their guest.

"No, no, I do not wish to disturb. In fact I just came because..." his hesitation was not all a pretense. He wondered just how much he would be giving away by making his enquiry.

"Is it because of Pantoleon?" Joannina asked.

He took a sip of wine but left the cakes. "No, Joannina, thank you for your concern, but it is about another matter altogether."

Both the girl and Joannina looked polite and attentive. Theodora evidently could not resist taking a small cake. Her mother gave her a disapproving look.

"Please go on, John."

"Last night there was a great disturbance in the grounds of my property. Some thieves we think, who perhaps thought they could sneak in and steal something. Who knows. Our guards intercepted them, but unfortunately they got away, although my men tell me that one of them was hurt."

Joannina gasped. "No one was hurt on your staff, I pray!" she exclaimed with genuine concern in her voice.

He smiled and shook his head. "As a matter of fact someone on my staff was injured, but not seriously. However, we set the dogs out and they tracked one of them to your compound wall."

It was clear immediately that he had taken Joannina utterly by surprise, but his sharp eyes detected something very strange about the girl at this point. She suddenly looked very agitated, her hands shook and she seemed to be trying to control them by placing them in her lap, one on top of the other, and gripping them hard; he cake was almost crushed in her fingers. It was for a very brief moment and then she appeared to pull herself together, took a deep breath and then a small bite out of the cake. She noticed his sharp gaze and attempted a weak smile.

"I wondered if your guards had reported any event of this kind last night?" he asked gently, looking hard at her.

Joannina interjected. "I have had no such report, John, but I shall definitely ask the guards for information, you may be sure of that. I did not know that anything of the sort had happened until you just mentioned it. How peculiar!"

The senator turned to look directly at the girl. "Did you see or hear anything, my dear?" he enquired in a soft tone.

Theodora had regained her composure by now and looked him in the eye. "No, senator. I sleep like a stone so I would not have heard a thing. I am sorry."

He looked intently at her for a moment longer. "Very well then. I apologize for asking, but it is a serious matter which I need to get to the bottom of." He smiled again as though dismissing the whole thing and sipped his wine. It was a good wine, he noticed, and said so in order to change the tone of the visit.

Although he was now impatient to leave he tarried a while longer, making small talk and sharing with them some court gossip. A scandal had been unearthed that involved a visiting princess from one of the Latin nations and a eunuch. The eunuch would probably go to the scaffold or simply be strangled, and the princess sent home in disgrace. Both women pretended to be interested in the gossip although he could see that neither was very amused. Eventually he made his excuses and Joannina accompanied him to the steps of the loggia to see him off.

*****

The senator was deep in thought when he arrived back at his own compound. He called for Choumnos and when the man arrived he made him stand, even though he was limping from the wound he had garnered the night before. It would serve him right, the senator thought, he should have been more careful. He was paid gold for being one of the best and he had allowed this to happen.

"Well, they could tell me nothing...of course, but I am almost sure that the girl knew something."

"How is that, Sir?" Choumnos asked.

"Her reaction to my question. I think there is something going on there. We will wait for your friend to bring us further news before we do anything else. I am going to bed for a few hours. When they get back have me woken up and report what they have found. Keep looking. Where is the girl Eugenia? I need to talk to her."

*****

When the senator had left Theodora turned to her mother and said, "That man frightens me, Mama. His joke about the princess was horrid." She mimed being sick.

Joannina frowned, then took her daughter gently by the arm and steered her back into the house. "My dearest, you will really have to control your feelings when there are guests about, even when they make tasteless remarks. The senator is a very powerful man and we should be polite to him whenever he makes one of his visits."

"I know Papa does not trust him one little bit, and I do not trust him either. I know that he has some strange men in his compound who Joseph says are evil and dangerous."

"That is as may be, darling, but he is our neighbor and Joseph should not be spreading rumors."

Theodora went to her room and lay on the bed curled up into a ball. Her mind was working furiously. Could it have been Talon who had been the intruder? He had come into his room like a ghost at night, she had not heard anything until he was on top of her holding a knife at her throat. And even worse, he had been wounded by someone. Joseph had looked fearful when he talked about the men at the villa Spartenos. It all fit with what the senator was saying, but she could not understand how. Talon was a Templar warrior, not someone who crept about at night like one of those terrifying assassins who infested the streets of the city. She had heard some blood curdling stories about men who were assassins. Most were former soldiers or mercenaries who killed for pay. Life was cheap in the city what with all the wars and corruption. She shook her head. This could not be Talon! But then something her brother had said about Talon came back to her and she shivered.

Theodora had woken that morning feeling anxious and depressed. She knew for a certainty that Talon would not tell her mother about the incident, but she was still mortified and wondered if he would shun her—and that would be more than she could bear. Tears came and stung her cheeks but with a flash of anger at her weakness she wiped them away and determined to find him and tell him of the visit by the senator.

Calling for her maidservant she donned a pretty tunic that came down to her ankles and put on some fine sandals, flung a cloak over her shoulders and pulled the hood over her head before leaving the compound with her maid in attendance. She thought that the most likely place Talon would be was the harbor, so she walked up the street and over the top of Second Hill across the Mese, which was busy with people, and then walked down the street that led to the harbor. Just as she was half way down the street she spied Talon and sergeant Max walking up the hill toward her. With a glad cry and a wave she began to run towards the two men. Talon glanced up when he heard her call and stopped in his tracks. Max looked at him and then followed his gaze.

Theodora came up to them breathless and threw her arms around Talon's neck, her relief was so great to have found him this easily. The light hood she had put on to hide her face fell back. He held her gently with a bemused expression on his face. A couple of whistles came from the men in the crowded street but she ignored them.

"Oh Talon, I am so glad that I found you! There is danger and I must speak to you."

Talon took her arms from around his neck and pushed her back gently, holding her with both hands. "What in God's good name are you talking about, Theodora? Danger? What danger?"

"Hello Max," She gave him a tense smile but then said in a whisper, "Not here, Talon. I must speak to you and Max. There is real danger, please!" she pleaded.

Talon glanced at Max, who shrugged. "Gods blessing, my Lady. We are near to the inn; we could go there and have something to eat while you tell us of the er...danger?"

"Yes, that would be perfect. But we must hurry."

Max led the way with a strange look at Talon, while Theodora stayed close and the maidservant walked behind them. They entered the inn and were greeted by the innkeeper who gave a small leer as he noticed them with two females in attendance.

Max gave him a look and said, "Find us a table that is private, and on your life do not say anything or you'll regret it." The man nodded, chastened. Hastily he took them out to the almost empty gardens, seating them under the wisteria well away from eavesdroppers.

The two men helped Theodora and her maid to sit, and at a sign from Max the innkeeper vanished, having promised to bring olives and bread, cheese and wine within a few minutes.

Talon gave the maidservant an enquiring look and Theodora caught herself. "Yes, she can stay. Ariadne, you will swear that whatever you hear today will go no further. Do you understand?"

The maid blinked and then said, "Yes, my lady, I understand. I swear by the Holy Mother of God I will not tell anyone about this visit."

After making her maid swear by a dozen saints Theodora relaxed a little, and then Talon prompted her. "What is all this about, my Lady? You seem very agitated and we need an explanation."

Theodora drew herself up and took a deep breath. "Very well, Talon. You were not at the house this morning when we had a visitor."

Both men looked interested.

"It was from one of our neighbors, one Senator Spartenos who lives not far from our house on the same hill." She looked hard at Talon to make the point.

His green eyes stared back at her, waiting.

Theodora was losing patience.

"Do not you want to know what he said?" she demanded.

"I think you are going to tell us." Talon gave a tiny smile.

"Yes well..." she became flustered by this intent audience.

Just then the innkeeper came bustling back with his hands full of food and drink that he placed on the table amid the silence that attended his arrival. After asking if there was anything else, he departed.

"You were telling us of the visit by the senator." Talon kept his tone bland.

"He told my mother and me, I was right there when he told us, that last night there were intruders in his compound and that there was a fight. Someone on his staff was injured but the intruders escaped. However..."

She let this drag out, wanting to see a reaction. "One of the intruders was wounded. He left blood around for the dogs to find and then led them to our walls! Imagine that?" she exclaimed, watching his face all the time.

Talon stared back. His face gave nothing away other than polite interest.

"Did they ever catch the intruders?" he asked.

"Um, no, but the senator wanted to know if our guards had seen anyone. We do not know if they did or not, as Mama did not get a report this morning about that. She is finding out. Do you think they saw anything?"

Talon held up his hand. "Let me tell Max what you have told me," he said.

He translated for his friend, who looked noncommittal and glanced at her from time to time without comment. Max spoke a few words of Greek now, but not enough for a lengthy conversation, so it was up to Talon to translate.

Theodora watched the two men carefully. They were without doubt a hard looking pair of men and their faces gave little away, so she had no idea what they were thinking, which frustrated her.

"What are you going to do, Talon?" she asked, interrupting their conversation in her impatience.

He looked at her and then shot a glance at the maid. "Thank you, Theodora, for the information. It is very interesting, and I can understand how you would be upset that intruders struck so close to your own villa. But right now after we have eaten we will escort you home," Talon said firmly.

Despite her agitation she realized that they would not talk freely in front of the maid, so it had to rest there.

"Will we be able to talk more about this later, Talon?" she asked.

"Yes, of course, and there is no danger so please do not be so worried. It is really nothing and we should forget the whole thing," he said.

Theodora glared at him. He winked. She gaped. Then he said, "We should eat. The food here is not as good as at your house but it is passable, and I am hungry."

*****

Psellos had himself rowed out to the Genoese galley. He was met at the side of the ship by Christophas, who grunted a greeting and without further ceremony took him below deck to see Caravello. The captain had just finished a late breakfast and was preparing to go ashore.

"Oh, it is you," he said when he recognized Psellos. "What are you doing here?"

"Did you know that last night someone followed you to our compound?"

Caravello blinked and then sat back in his chair. He motioned Psellos to be seated and then said, "What do you mean? You must be mistaken. No one came with me except Davide. We did not see anyone following us."

"These people, or this person, did not want to be seen and wasn't, up until Choumnos discovered an intruder in the house. He winged the intruder, but the fellow was fast and wounded Choumnos before he left."

"Choumnos? That is something to hear. I thought he was one of the best."

"He was. Perhaps he is losing his edge," Psellos said with a curl to his thin lips. "So you do not remember seeing anything yesterday that might have stuck in your mind?"

Caravello stared at Psellos. The man's lean, pockmarked face with his high cheekbones and deep-set eyes resembled a fleshed out skull. His mouth was a slash under his sharp nose. His lithe frame bore no discernible fat and his slim but strong hands were calloused with the use of the sword and knife. Caravello did not want to get on the wrong side of this man. He shouted for Davide. There was a clatter of boots on the steps and he poked his head into the cabin. "Yes, captain?"

"Did you notice anything out of the ordinary yesterday? Think, man, anything at all?"

David grimaced and screwed up his doughy face, which almost hid his small eyes while he pondered.

"We went to a weddin' yesterday, remember? That was good, but you wouldn't let us go to the feast afterwards, although those two Templar fellas probably did."

"What two Templars?" Psellos' tone was sharp.

"There are some Templars in the city. They came into the Genoese quarter, they were right behind us, do not you recall? I did not see them after we went to have a bite in the tavern."

Caravello looked thoughtful. "Yes, now I remember them, the Templars, but I do not see what they have to do with what we did later."

Psellos agreed. He got up. "Well, I am wasting my time here. I will see you before you go to Rhodes."

Psellos spent another hour walking about the harbor asking casual questions about strangers who might have been hanging about the wharves the day before. He was just about to leave in frustration when a beggar with only one eye clad in tattered rags sidled up and asked for a coin. He should have used his good eye to judge who he was asking. Psellos shoved him away, his pockmarked face distorted into a snarl.

"They tell me that you have been asking questions about strangers," the beggar whined as he staggered back.

"What of it?" Psellos demanded.

"I might be able to help you." The man gave a gap-toothed grin. His breath stank.

Psellos stared at him hard then tossed him a small coin. "This had better be good. You'll go swimming if it isn't."

"Two men were here yesterday. One dressed in dark clothes with a cross on his tunic, an older man. Another younger man was with him, but he left."

"You need to do better than that. What did they look like? Their faces, man?"

"I didn't get a good look at the older man, but I did the other younger man. He spent a lot of time watching the ships. He sat over there." The beggar pointed to the place where Talon had spent the afternoon.

"His face, man! Did you get a look at his face?" Psellos spat out the words. He kept his face impassive but inside he felt that he might just have stumbled upon a clue.

The beggar cringed. "He was young, looked strong. Had a scar down the left side of his face here." He drew his fingers down his own face to illustrate his point. "His eyes..." the beggar hesitated.

Psellos seized him by his throat. "What about his eyes?"

The filthy creature whimpered. "They looked...dangerous."

It took a little time but Psellos managed to get a fairly accurate description of Talon out of the beggar before he sent the man sprawling in the dirt. "Here, drink yourself to death," he said and tossed another small coin at the wretch.

He arrived back at the villa later that afternoon and asked to see the senator immediately.

Senator Spartenos arrived looking disheveled. "This had better be worth it," he grumbled as he took a sip of water. He did not offer any to Psellos, who stood before him.

After Psellos had delivered his report the senator sat down, his face thoughtful.

"So, the idiot Genoese did not notice they were being followed and perhaps led one of those men all the way here from the harbor. I wonder who they were?"

"Caravello's man said that there were Templars at the wedding who were on the same path they took to go back to the Genoese quarter, but that might just be coincident," Psellos offered.

The senator looked at him. "Templars? Yes...there are Templars in the city at present. But what they might have to do with this makes little sense to me. I can't see those people creeping about in the dark." He shook his head. "Well, I cannot understand that at present, but there is something else too. Our neighbors know more than they are telling...of that I am sure."

Psellos looked surprised.

"I want you to keep an eye on the younger daughter. Her name is Theodora. I think she knows about our intruder. When I asked about it this morning she looked as guilty as though I had found out about a lover!"

"What do you want me to do, Sir?"

"I want you to watch her movements. Post someone near the gates to that house and report any movements of people to and fro. I want to know more about where she goes and whom she talks to, but do not interfere with her. Just watch and report. Do I make myself clear?"

Psellos nodded and then said, "What about Choumnos? Shall I bring him in on this?'

"He is still licking his wounds. Leave him to it. He might be more careful after this. I need you and your friends to get to work immediately."

Psellos concealed his smile of satisfaction. He was going to be the headman for the senator if things worked out for him. Choumnos had failed a test and faced demotion, which could mean his promotion if he played it the right way. Psellos bowed low to the senator and stalked out, lithe as a panther.

The senator watched his departure. Psellos was a nasty piece of work but seemed loyal and might prove an asset. He shook his head in irritation at Choumnos' condition. Just when he needed him the worthless man got himself cut. He knew Choumnos' reputation and skill with most weapons. The man had an impressive list of kills behind him. The senator wondered who could have winged a man like that.

Thibault of Champagne, King of Navarre

Chapter 19

Preparations

Two days after the incident in the villa Talon and Max were walking down the street near to their inn when Talon, ever on the lookout, spied a ship approaching the southern walls heading directly for the harbor of Sophia.

"Max! They have arrived! It is the ship! It is our ship!"

"God be praised, they have made it back!" Max said with a whoop.

They rushed down to the harbor and after explaining who they were they were allowed by the sentries to go through the gates that led onto the wharf.

They stood on the quayside and watched as their ship came alongside. Henry and the others waved and shouted greetings to them as they approached. Talon looked at the ship with a critical eye. There was no visible damage to the vessel, such as he had seen on some others that had limped into the various harbors around the city. The ropes were cast to men on the quayside and tied off against large stone bollards, then the ship was at rest.

The customs officials led by the *Logothetes tōn sekretōn* came marching along the quayside and sternly demanded to know of the cargo. Henry replied, once Talon had called out the translated questions with the help of Dmitri, that there was none. They were in Constantinople to collect their emissary. He pointed at Talon.

After a doubtful look at Talon the official reluctantly agreed to allow the ship to dock, but only on a temporary basis. It might have to be moved to the other side of the peninsula at a later date, and sooner rather than later. Talon agreed and bowed the official away before grabbing Max by the sleeve and heading for the gangway.

Henry, Nigel and Guy met them at the side, and after they had all embraced and exchanged greetings Talon asked Henry how the voyage had been.

"Thanks be to God, it was uneventful. One storm, but we slipped by it and had no damage. It was a smooth trip and God protected us all the way. I have papers for you in the cabin from Sir Guy, Talon."

"How is Sir Guy?" Talon asked.

"He and Claude send their greetings. They were on their way to Jerusalem as we pulled out of Acre harbor."

"I want to talk to all three of you as soon as you get off the ship. Bring your baggage to the inn where Max and I are staying."

"Good, it is close to the baths—and the whorehouse is even closer!" Guy joked.

"I do not think that he has talked of anything else since we left this city," Nigel grumbled, rolling his eyes.

*****

Later they were all gathered around their favorite table under the wisteria that provided a welcome shade from the warm autumnal sun. Their friends had heard about the ill-fated campaign and were questioning them about it when Talon decided that the time was ripe to discuss his plan. He had no intention of telling them about the encounter at the villa. That was something he would have to deal with on his own.

He thumped his metal goblet on the table to attract the attention of the others. Henry nudged Nigel to get him to pay attention.

When he was sure that they were all listening Talon began.

"As you know, the ship has been given into my possession thanks to the good graces of Sir Guy. I know Sir Guy de Veres well enough by now to hazard it was not from the goodness of his heart alone but for practical reasons too. He wants a ship with a crew he can trust which can take him discreetly from place to place."

There were murmurs of agreement and the wine was passed.

Talon continued. "However, there is one great flaw in that plan."

"How so?" Guy asked.

"Shut up and he will tell you, Guy." Nigel said, jabbing his friend in the ribs.

"The ship will be idle for many months in between escort duty, and we will not be able to live off that," Talon said.

Nigel slumped in his seat while Guy gave a lugubrious sigh and scratched himself under his arms.

Henry sat back, his eyes narrowed as he stared at Talon and Max. He appeared to be waiting for more.

"But...do you have any ideas, Talon?"

"You three remember Alexios, do not you?"

"Of course! The pompous emissary, right? But you said that he was badly wounded. What does he have to do with our ship?"

"A great deal." Talon watched his friends. He had their full attention now.

"Why are all of you scratching...all the time?" he asked, his patience evaporating. All three had been scratching themselves since their arrival.

"Fleas!" Nigel said, sounding annoyed.

"How did you come to get them?" Max asked as he hastily shuffled down the bench away from Guy.

"I think it was that monk, Jonathan. He never washed. Devil take him!" Henry grumbled.

"I think it was those chickens we brought on board in Acre. Dmitri warned me that they were crawling with something, probably lice."

"Henry, I shall not travel on that ship if it is full of vermin," Talon stated. "Max and I have only just cleaned ourselves up from the campaign. I will not go through it all again on my own ship! All of you are to go and get deloused at the baths and do it today. Then you are to clean up the men, Henry...and the ship." His tone was ominous.

"It shall be done, and I will smoke the ship out, Sir Talon." Henry sounded contrite.

"Do not keep us in suspense Talon. You were about to tell us something important. We are sailors and need to be kept working," Guy rumbled.

"That is especially so in your case!" Nigel said.

Talon resumed his earlier conversation. "I know you remember Alexios as aloof and arrogant, but he has changed... considerably."

Max nodded in agreement. "He has indeed. I actually like him now."

The others stared at him skeptically, remembering the priggish, haughty individual of their voyage.

"Alexios wants our ship sail for him and carry cargo."

Henry gasped. He had been holding his breath but now he let out a great shout.

"Dear God, but this is incredible news, Talon! God be praised!" He crossed himself and beamed, then scratched his belly.

Nigel and Guy were slapping each other's backs and yelling with glee.

"What kind of cargo?" Henry asked when they had all settled down and had drunk some more wine.

"He has an agent who will help to load the ship in the Prosphorion harbor, which is on the other side of the city. We are to take silk bales, spices and oil to Rhodes and then on to Cyprus. And we are to bring salt and copper back with us, along with some grain if we can get it in Cyprus."

There was a silence while the crew thought about this.

"You do know where Rhodes and Cyprus are, do not you, Henry?" Max asked with real concern in his voice. He was even more ignorant of the sea than Talon.

"Well, if he does not there are charts and things, so we are bound to bump into it along the way," Nigel said with a wicked grin at his nautical companions, who were both grinning, which changed to laughter as they watched Max's alarmed expression.

Henry gave a booming laugh. "Fear not, Max, we three do know where the islands are and how to get there."

Max relaxed and shook his head. "I should have known you three pirates would. What about those sea dragons and serpents that inhabit the water around the islands?"

"We shall pray to God that he protect us from such creatures and brings us home safe," Nigel intoned solemnly with a glint in his eyes.

Despite his determination not to worry Talon gave an inward sigh of relief. Ever since he had discussed the possibility with Alexios he had worried that his nautical friends might not have a clue where these places were and they would become lost in that vast empty sea. He chastised himself for doubting them, breathed a silent thanks to God and continued.

"Alexios is concerned that without the Venetians his produce will rot in warehouses and the family fortune will disappear. He is putting enormous faith in our ability to carry out this mission for him, my friends. I have nothing personal against the Venetians but...well, this seems to be an opportunity."

"Then we must see to it that we do not disappoint him," Henry said as he gulped the last of his wine and held his cup upside down, shaking it as though there should have been more.

"I hope the Venetians continue to rot in their prisons while we fill the gap. When do we start, Talon? I have your letters with me here, so once that business is taken care of we can sail within the week." He looked at the other two.

"Which means that you two will have to get a bath, get deloused and get a woman very quickly, because, my friends, there is work to do!" he bellowed out his delight. The others happily banged their mugs on the table in agreement, causing the innkeeper to hasten outside and ask if there was anything more they needed.

"Bring some more wine!" Max ordered.

"What is the news from Acre?" Talon asked.

"The news is that the king, may God protect him and grant him a long life, is not in good health. There will most likely be no issue, hence there is no heir. The Hospitaliers are building castles in the south and the Templars are losing popularity in the coastal cities. There is much talk of another invasion of Egypt, but I think that is only hearsay," Guy told them.

They talked late into the evening at which time the lamps were lit and the inn began to fill up with customers looking for a good meal. The sailors excused themselves to go and get baths. Guy, who had fidgeted most of the evening, almost ran out of the garden.

He was followed by a sardonic comment from Nigel. "He will fuck his hard earned coin away no matter what, that man."

"At least that will bring him home to us like a homing pigeon every time. He is a good sailor," Henry growled. "But for the girl's sake, I hope he bathes first!"

*****

That evening Talon read the missives that had come in Henry's care.

The first one he read was from Sir Guy.

God's blessings be upon you, Talon. We have arrived with Henry's good navigation and God's help at Acre in good time and I was able to bid a fond farewell to the Bothers.

Talon grinned to himself.

There is much going on in the Kingdom of Jerusalem, some of it is of concern. King Baldwin's condition of leprosy is worsening. However, he has sent important letters to the Emperor. You are to deliver them as soon as possible.

Talon glanced at the bulky package that was wrapped in oilcloth and realized that it was sealed with the Royal seal of the King of Jerusalem. He read on.

I have encountered the now famous, or perhaps infamous, Raynald de Châtillon who, having been released from prison with the Arabs, is now bent upon pursuing his ambitions here in the kingdom, to the advantage of no one but himself. Therein lies a problem for us in the future, I fear. His time in prison does not seem to have dampened his arrogance or his enthusiasm for trouble making. I recall that the Emperor detests him after the Cyprus debacle, so I am trying to make sure that whatever mischief he gets up to does not impact Byzantium.

There are rumbles of trouble on the borders of Egypt. My agents—remember our friends the Bedouin in the Negev who do not love the Sultan of Egypt—tell me that Sal Ed Din's brother has finally conquered all of Yemen and had a hero's welcome back in Cairo. There is the possibility that he and Salah Ed Din might come north to Aleppo before too long.

I should say rather that there is much happening among our neighbors. Since the death of Nur Ed Din the Sultanate of Syria is in turmoil. I understand that Kilij Arslan is busy in the north. I hope that you will be able to provide word on his activities, as reliable information is sparse here.

It is ever this way, as you might be aware. The Sultan dies and his many progeny backed by others with ambition and greed support the one or the other and try to destroy each other. In this case the person most likely to succeed is the son As-Salih Ismail al-Malik, but he is far too young to be able to rule, so there will doubtless be a bloodbath in Syria. Should he come to power I would consider that a temporary victory, as your friend Salah Ed Din will now be free to exercise his newfound influence upon these regions to the north of our kingdom. This does not bode well for the dukedom of Antioch, nor even in the long run that of Tripoli. However, I do not consider this to be immediate.

The Arabs still have their eyes upon the jewel of the entire region, and that is Constantinople. They have been defeated twice at sea but despite their own internal conflicts they would like to take the city one way or the other and, here is the irony, to prevent the Turks from doing the same. There is a rumor that a fleet of corsairs is lurking in among the islands not too far from Rhodes. There have been reports that there is an alliance of sorts between the Arabs and the Turks, but I find that somewhat unlikely. There is little for either party to want to agree upon. All fear the Turks, as they are great fighters and have defeated the small Arab armies sent to fight them of late. Arslan is an ambitious man and his Seljuks fierce fighters.

Talon gave a wry smile at this comment. Sir Guy could not been aware of the battle of Myriokephalon when he wrote, although Talon was in little doubt that he would know of it by now. Such a defeat would not fail to be passed along to the Christians in the Kingdom as rapidly as the wind, further adding to their sense of isolation. Not for the first time he wondered at the knight's keen knowledge of the players in the region. He continued to read.

I shall ask you to keep your eyes and ears open to the situation regarding our mission. I left with the understanding that we could in principle continue to work for passage across the Greek lands, but I am also painfully aware of how quickly things can change. If the Normans of Sicily continue to press for war it will not be to our advantage. I need to know as soon as you can tell me if there is any danger from the west or even the north to the empire, as all this will affect the attitude of the emperor.

Another concern is the consequences of the Battle at Legnano, in which you will recall the Lombardi alliance defeated the emperor Frederick Barbarossa. I am interested as to Manuel's intentions there, as despite an alliance with him against Frederick they could now lay claim to most of the region of Italy that formerly belonged to Byzantium. Please inform me at the earliest opportunity as to whether his advisers are taking this into account.

Sir Guy finished with comments on the terms of the agreement that he had written for the emperor's advisers. He expected a response as soon as Talon was able to send one.

Talon read the instructions carefully, as they referred to the offer of marriage to the emperor's son. The dowry was beginning to look impressive. The Greeks were apparently hard negotiators. Sir Guy was keen to know if there was anything to learn about the suggested crusade through the emperor's lands. As Talon was a de facto ambassador from Jerusalem he realized that he had more duties to attend to than he had bargained for.

He had had the faint hope that there might have been a response to his letter to his parents. Then he reminded himself that even if the letter had arrived by now a reply would not arrive before the spring of the following year. The season for sailing was fast closing this October.

*****

The next day Talon hastened to the villa to talk to Alexios, who had sent a messenger to attend him. He knew that Alexios would be well aware that the ship had come in by now; Joseph would have informed him almost the moment the ship had been sighted. Talon arrived at the villa in time to have moment with Joannina, who greeted him warmly and kissed him on the cheek.

"God's blessings. Good morning, Joannina. It is a beautiful day, but a little cold," Talon said, looking at the finely embroidered woolen tunic that reached her feet and the fur stole that was draped over her shoulders. Indeed, the cool wind from the north had swept any lingering clouds from the sky, leaving it azure blue. He noticed a small fire in the entrance hall and realized that winter was just around the corner.

"God's blessings to you too, Talon. Alexios is almost back to his old self and I am right glad of it. Do be careful not to tire him out too much, won't you?" She gave his arm a squeeze and a smile.

He hastened along the corridors to Alexios' room and knocked.

"Come in." Alexios' voice sounded stronger. Talon breathed a sigh of relief. His friend was on the road to recovery.

"God's Blessings, Alex."

"Ah Talon! God's Blessings to you!"

Talon sniffed. "That smells like cloves," he said.

"The physician has been using some kind of smelly paste that deadens the feeling around my knee," Alexios said. "He does not want me to stay on the sap of the poppy."

"He is right, Alex. You can become addicted to the poppy. So how is the pain these days?"

"It is a heavy ache and sometimes it itches badly."

"I think you are healing by the sound of it. Praise God!"

"It is about time. I am sick of lying about in this room," Alexios responded.

Another man was in the room respectfully standing near to Alexios. At the side of the bed in a loose pile were many papers, some of which had even slipped to the floor. It was clear that they had been going over them together as Alexios was sitting on the edge of the bed with a blanket over his knees and a quill in his hand.

"Talon, you have not met before. This is Makarios, my family's agent for our estates and our warehouses. Makarios, meet Sir Talon. You two are going to be working together."

Makarios was a small man in a plain tunic with a belt but no sword. He was balding on top but wore the greying hair that was left in a queue tied at the back of his head, unlike many Greeks who favored short curls. He sported a large bulbous nose with pits in it and sprouted hair from his ears. His light colored eyes were sharp but the glance he gave Talon was polite, and it was clear from his tone that Alexios respected him.

"You arrived in good time, Talon. We were just discussing the cargo and how we would get it aboard. How did the crew take the news?" Alexios asked.

"Need you ask,? They are delighted and eager to serve you well," Talon replied. He noted the reserved look that Makarios gave him and was briefly irritated, but then he realized that a great deal of trust was being placed in him going into this venture, and should it fail not only would he be responsible but the Kalothesos family would be ruined. He became very attentive.

They discussed the type of cargo and its destinations. Makarios told Talon that one of his men who knew the agents on both islands would be sailing with them to make sure that they did not have trouble with customs and that the agents stayed honest. Time passed very quickly to the point where Talon noted that Alexios was getting tired. Talon recognized the now familiar white lines at the corner of his mouth and sunken eyes.

"We must close this meeting and allow Alexios to rest," he said firmly after an hour of discussion.

Makarios glanced at Alexios, noted his condition and nodded. They helped him back onto the bed and made sure he was resting comfortably before leaving. His eyes were shut before they left the room.

"Makarios , I think it is important for you to meet my captain. When could you be free to do so?" Talon said to the agent as they walked down the corridor.

"The best thing for all of us is to get your ship around to the port of Prospharion where I can come aboard and meet him. When can this be done?" His tone was curt but not rude.

Talon assumed he was a busy man who valued his time. He had been impressed with the knowledge he displayed regarding the kind of cargo and the places where they could discharge it. His knowledge of the islands in the Greek seas south of Constantinople was very detailed.

"I shall ask permission to do so at once."

"And I shall see what I can do to get the cargo to you as quickly as possible. The season for sailing is almost gone so we have little time and must use it well," Makarios said. They parted at the entrance to the villa. Talon watched the man leaving with the rolls of papers under both arms, his short sharp stride carrying him speedily toward the gates.

Talon turned back to pay his respects to Joannina and possibly also the senator.

Joseph guided him to the back of the house and pointed out Joannina standing among the shrubs with her servants in attendance.

She saw him and waved, said something to her serving girl and then floated up to him.

"You have not exhausted my son, Talon?" she said her tone severe.

"I fear that I have, Joannina, but we left in time, I think. He is resting now." Not for the first time Talon caught himself admiring her fine features.

"What do you think of his condition?" she asked in a direct manner, which was unlike her.

"I think that it will not be long now before he is demanding to get around."

She laughed and he smiled back. Her eyes were merry and she linked her arm in his and said, "You will stay and eat? It is almost noon and I would have you tell us of your ship and how your men fared."

"Willingly, my Lady."

They made their way to the dining room and were just about to be seated when Theodora arrived. Her look was shy as she greeted him, and Talon wondered if her observant mother might notice.

"I hear that your ship has arrived, Sir Talon," she said with emphasis on the title.

He smiled at her and replied, "That is right, my Lady Theodora. It arrived today and before very long we will be sailing again."

She looked at him with large eyes. "You mean...you are leaving us...again?"

"What is this about leaving us?" Joannina asked, also concerned. "We had all thought that you might stay the winter. It is dreary enough, but better than Acre surely?"

Talon laughed. "My Ladies, I am about to embark upon a voyage into the unknown. Places with names like Cyprus and Rhodes," he intoned, pretending to look afraid.

"You are going to Cyprus and Rhodes? Those are not unknown, Sir Talon?" Theodora snorted. "At least not to us. Perhaps the Franks have never heard of them but they have been part of our empire for a very long time." Her tone was scathing.

"I so wish I could go to these places one day," she added with a wistful glance at her mother.

Talon grinned. "To me they are strange places, my Lady. I have never been to them and I pray that my captain knows what he is about when we set off."

"Does Father know of these plans? We have to tell Papa about what you are doing, Talon," Theodora said.

"What do we have to tell Papa?" said the senator.

They all looked up in surprise. The senator was standing at the doorway with the eunuch John supporting him. He waved his stick in the air and repeated, "What is this that I need to know?"

Joannina looked startled and Theodora glanced at Talon. "I shall tell him, Mama," she said after a hesitant pause.

"Papa, come in and join us please," she said and hurried over to him and kissed him on the cheek. "We can talk when you are seated. Look, Mama has ordered the cook to make your favorite almond cakes for us."

Theodora and John assisted the old man to sit next to Joannina at the head of the table and made him comfortable. A plate of pork pate with thin slices of bread along with a glass of watered wine was placed in front of him. The plate of cakes was moved near by.

He peered at Talon and said, "I remember...Talon isn't it? How have you been, my boy?"

Talon smiled and said, "Very well, Sir. I hope you are well too?"

"Passing well, passing well. What is going on? You tell me. The girls will muddle it all up and then I will get confused."

Theodora snorted and began to protest but her mother gave her a look and said, "I agree, my dear. Talon should explain."

"With an apologetic look at the women Talon cleared his throat then spoke.

"Sir, your son and I have decided that as I have access to a ship and he...you, have goods in warehouses to sell, it would be a good thing if we combined our efforts and worked together."

Damianus gave him a sharp look and Talon realized that old he might be but his faculties were still very much intact.

"My son has not shared this with me," he said; his tone was sharp.

"It is a passing thing, my dear. He will recover and go back to the army. You will see," Joannina said, her tone placating.

"We are a great family and not merchants!" Damianus said, his voice louder and color rising to his neck.

"Yes, we are aristocrats, Papa, but we have no fortune. The Venetians are in prison and Talon is offering his ship," Theodora said, trying to sound confident, but she shot a wide-eyed look at Talon.

"You have a ship? I did not know this!" Damianus was genuinely surprised.

"He told us how he won it, Papa. You would be proud of him," Theodora said with a sly look at Talon from under her thick eyebrows.

"You must tell me sometime, but now tell me all about this plan you and my wayward son have hatched. I am not sure that I approve, and indeed I might not permit it."

"Sir, there was no intention of going behind you. I have a ship that is unemployed and I am able to use it as I will, while you have goods that are going bad in warehouses, so it made sense to discuss it with Alex, I mean Alexios," Talon said. His tone was polite but he was becoming nervous. The senator could nix the whole arrangement if he disapproved.

Talon set out to convince the senator. He was so preoccupied with his explanations that he barely tasted the food placed in front of him. The others listened, and Theodora burst in with ideas of her own, which made Talon wince as he had no idea whether Damianus had decided in advance to shut the whole enterprise down or not.

They were on the last course of berries and cut grapes, which Theodora was spooning down in a hurry while Joannina only picked at her food, by the time he had finished. They all watched Damianus in the tense silence that ensued as he finally put down his own silver spoon and wiped his lips with a napkin.

"Do you think he is ever going to soldier again with that wound?" he demanded.

Joannina put her fingers to her lips, her eyes wide. Talon looked across the polished surface of the table at the stiffly erect man in front of him and knew he should not lie.

"No, Sir, I do not think so. He will ride again...one day, but he will not play *tzykanion* any more."

"The old man nodded, his lined face was sad. "I wondered, but you would know, I suppose. So what is to become of him?" he asked the table at large.

There was a disturbance at the entrance that made them all look up. Alexios was standing at the doorway supported by Joseph and another servant. He looked weak and drained but there was a determined set to his mouth and he motioned the two men to help him to the table.

"Joseph told me that you were grilling Talon about our plan, Papa. I decided that I needed to be here to explain."

Joannina had risen and rushed to help him, exclaiming, "Alex, my darling, you really shouldn't be wandering around the house like this! What will the physician say?"

"Mama, I am tired of lying around in bed, and besides it is time to talk frankly about the future of this family," Alexios said with some asperity.

He was helped to sit next to Talon so that the two of them could look up the table at the two women and Damianus. Alexios was breathing heavily by this time and he took a sip of water.

Damianus regarded his son with sharp eyes that could not altogether hide the sympathy he felt. All the same it did not look like he was going to make it easy for him.

"You have been making plans behind my back and I disapprove of that. What have you to say about it? You are supposed to follow me into the senate at some time."

"Papa, you have always insisted that we are not merchants and should not be involved in trade. But we're becoming impoverished for several reasons, not least because the emperor jailed all those Venetians."

"Pshaw! They're arrogant Latins and needed to be taught a lesson. And do not underestimate the influence of being a senator," Damianus said.

"That may be, Papa, but while the Venetians are being taught this obscure lesson, Makarios is sitting on many bales of silk that are rotting in our warehouses and we have lost much in the way of the spices. Those are hard to replace and costly. We do not have the resources to weather this 'lesson' much longer."

"Manuel will release them soon, I am sure of it. And we are members of the nobility; my ancestors put us there and I have maintained us in this position with my military service and now as a senator. You, on the other hand, have offended the emperor and your career is in jeopardy. How do you propose then to maintain our position in society?"

"Papa, how can you say that!" Theodora burst out. "Alex fought bravely and nearly died. That is unfair! We have an opportunity to regain our fortune using Talon's ship and our goods. It makes all the sense in the world!"

"Be quiet! Let him speak for himself," Damianus said, his tone harsh.

She subsided with a scowl and sent a look of appeal to her mother who opened her eyes wide and gave a tiny shrug in helpless sympathy.

Alexios had tried to rise, anger written all over his face. "I did not come here to quibble with you over our position in society, Sir. If that is all you care about then there is nothing else to be said." He sat back as though he did not care any more and glared at his father.

"There is much to be said! But you must stop going behind my back and have the courage to speak to me honestly and to my face!" the old man almost shouted. "Talon over there tells me that you showed much courage in the face of death and battle, yet you fear to talk to me about trade?"

Alexios glanced at Talon then stared across the table at his father, his mouth a tight line. The room was deathly silent for a long moment. Finally he took a deep breath and spoke.

"You are right, Father. I was wrong not to talk to you first. It is just that...you have always denigrated the merchants and made it clear that we should not dabble with them, so I saw no reason for you to change your position in that regard."

"I have changed toward this young Frank, have I not? Perhaps I can be persuaded to discuss the enterprise you two have hatched." Damianus glowered at his son, but there was a look in his eyes that no one missed.

Theodora was the first to react. She almost threw herself on her father and kissed him. "Papa, you are such a curmudgeon! Listen to them! I know you will love what they have to tell you. I know it!"

Damianus patted her on he arm. "Is there no respect left in this house? Stop smothering me, child, and sit down." His voice was gruff. "They have work to do this afternoon. I shall listen and give my verdict." His tone had lost its bite, however. "How does this child of mine understand all this stuff about trade?" he asked the world at large.

"She is a wizard with numbers, Papa," Alexios said.

Talon let out his breath. He knew in his bones that the old man was going to agree to the plan, but they were going to have to put a good argument before him. Joannina gave an exaggerated sigh of relief and said firmly, "The physician is coming this afternoon. You men had better get on with it. I do not want my son fainting from exhaustion, my dear," she addressed her husband.

Talon and Alexios spent the next hour with the senator explaining what they wanted to do. Theodora sat next to him now, Joannina having left to talk to the servants.

Finally the senator motioned for water and sipped it, his face pensive. "I am interested in the long term aspects of this plan, Talon. Tell me, will Sir Guy permit you to work with us for a year or two? Do you know if he will?"

"The ship is officially mine to use as I will, Sir. He made that plain, so I think that the answer is yes."

"That is good to know, as there is no telling what is going to happen between the Venetians and our emperor. I would prefer to know that we have a reliable means to ship our goods. You will have to have written permits from the Grand Palace if you do continue with this enterprise. Those are hard to obtain," he added.

All three of them stared at the old man. "So you agree...to the plan, Father?" Alex was hesitant.

"You are correct that our merchandise is languishing in the warehouses, and under the circumstances I would prefer to trust it to Talon and his merry crew than those Genoese, Pizans and the rest of those Latin pirates. You must not let us down, Talon," he admonished. "As for you, Alexios, you will begin work with my help to become a senator. Do not underestimate the usefulness of influence."

Alex turned to Talon and tried to embrace him. Talon laughed his relief. Then he murmured, "I do not think you will make a very good senator."

"Why do you say that?" Alexios sounded indignant.

"You will have to work harder at being a crusty old fellow. That seems to be a necessary qualification."

Alexios hid his face in his hands and shook with laughter.

Theodora embraced her father again, eliciting a gruff complaint, then she rushed over to embrace her brother and finally Talon. He sensed that there was more to the embrace than there should have been, but he held her tight nonetheless.

Damianus called for some of his own wine and they knew he had given them his blessing.

It was a tired Talon who was escorted late that evening back to the inn by the servant Joseph. Joannina had protested but he felt that he should get out of the villa and away from the risks of any more encounters in the night, so he had pleaded the necessity of planning with the crew.

On the way, he said, "Joseph, it was a good thing to get this done. I applaud you fetching Alex to the meeting."

"I merely mentioned that the subject had come up, Sir. Alexios insisted on getting out of bed and coming in person to talk to his father. He knew that it might be difficult."

"But he came with your help. It was just the right moment and I am very glad of it. Thank you Joseph." Talon then bade Joseph goodnight.

*****

The next day at breakfast Talon discussed the plans with the others and they in turn explained the advantages and the limitations of carrying cargo in a galley rather than a normal merchant ship.

"We will be able to move faster and that is a huge advantage if there is trouble. We can deliver a perishable cargo in good time and, I hope, beat the winter storms, which will be coming soon," Nigel said.

"The disadvantage is that we will not be able to take as much as those fat tubs the Genoese float around in," Guy pointed out. "Besides, I do not mind spending a winter here." He gave his usual feral grin.

"I do not doubt it!" Nigel said, his lank blond hair falling over sinister blue eyes. "But you will need money to spend, and there is none to be found by us in this city. We will soon have to change lodgings so that you can take care of all the women in a different brothel."

Nigel thumped his shamefaced friend on the back while the others laughed.

"It would seem to me that this is a trial run to begin with, so we need to prove ourselves," Max said.

"What is to be our share of the profits?" Henry asked.

"We get forty percent," Talon said.

"That is not bad. Not bad at all. So this is some kind of partnership? Does that also mean we do not get lumbered with the shipping tax? Who pays that?"

"How much is it?" Talon asked, his tone apprehensive. He had not even considered taxes.

"It is thirty solidi to everyone except the Genoese and the Venetians," Henry said. "We nearly had to pay it on our return but Dmitri persuaded the guard ship that we were picking up an ambassador. Their officer was not nice about it."

"That seems to be a lot of coin," Max said.

"It is," Dmitri spoke up. He had joined them from the ship. "That is why those cursed Venetians got rich so quickly; they only paid seventeen!"

"Speaking of coin," Talon said, "I should pay the crew, should I not?"

"Hmm, that would be a good idea, Talon, as they are owed. But better not do so until we're back at sea or you will have no crew for this next enterprise. They will disappear into every wine house or whorehouse there is like rats and we won't be able to find them again for a week," Henry said with a glare of warning at his companions. Nigel and Guy, who had brightened up at the thought of coin in their pockets, subsided with resigned sighs.

"Where are the crewmen at this time?" Max asked.

"I confined them to the ship and told the soldiers that they couldn't leave the harbor."

"Perhaps we could send down a cask of wine and some decent food to keep them sweet?" Guy wheedled.

Talon agreed and Henry nodded. "I shall see to it, Talon," he said.

Talon excused himself to write some letters. He had some documents to deliver to the palace but needed to be called first. He could not just appear at the doors. Alexios had promised to send a messenger to the chamberlain to let him know that Talon was seeking an audience.

*****

Sooner than any of them expected the command came for Talon to present himself at the palace of Blachernae in the east. The messenger came from Alexios, informing Talon that he would find an escort waiting for him at the gates of the harbor in the afternoon. He dressed carefully in a newly purchased tunic, which he had bought at one of the many small tailor shops along the Mese. He told the others where he was going and was escorted across the busy quay by Max and Nigel who told him to be careful and to come back in one piece.

True to Alexios' word there was a small escort of mounted men waiting for him at the gates of the port, and soon they were one their way to the palace. Talon was nervous. He was in awe of the wealth and power of the empire in evidence all around him. Not only that, there was the lingering memory of the disastrous campaign, and he wondered how the emperor would behave when he saw him again.

There was the familiar group of people to greet him, followed by the wait in the anteroom which was so quiet it allowed him to collect his thoughts and relax somewhat. He wondered for the hundredth time what the emperor might say. He had the letters sent by Sir Guy in his sleeve, but these could have been delivered without the complexity of another audience. He wondered why he was really here.

The wait this time was not as long as before. The same eunuch glided into the room and beckoned him to follow down the highly polished marble floors, past the intricate mosaics on the walls, and finally to the doorway of the audience room. He was cautioned as before to observe the protocols. He was to use the interpreter at all times and never to speak directly to the emperor unless that august figure did so first.

The doors were opened and he walked slowly behind the eunuch along the carpeted floor up to the single figure seated on the throne. Talon was struck by the contrast between the emperor in his palaces and his far less formal behavior in the field. He had little time to dwell on this, however, as he was now in front of Manuel. He went down on one knee, his head bowed, as the eunuch introduced him as though he were a complete stranger. It felt odd. Talon knew half the men in the room, as most were army officers that had fought in the gorge at Myriokephalon. He wondered why they were all here for this occasion.

"We are pleased to see you again, Sir Talon, Knight of the Templars," Manuel said. There was a pause while the translator repeated his words.

Talon glanced up and bobbed his head. "The honor is all mine, Your Majesty. I bring letters from Sir Guy and His Majesty Baldwin, King of Jerusalem. I am to offer their greetings and sincerest good wishes for the health of Your Majesties."

He offered the letters, holding them out in both hands. The eunuch took them and held them before the emperor. Manuel touched them and the letters were removed. Then Talon waited.

"We will read them with pleasure and you may expect a reply in due course," Manuel informed him by way of the translator.

Talon bobbed his head again. He thought this might be the end of the audience, but then Manuel spoke to him in French.

"My generals inform me that you saved our life on one occasion while we were...in the gorge."

Talon said nothing.

"I hear too that you brought one of our well beloved officers, Alexios Kalothesos, home with you even though he was grievously wounded. We would reward you for this exemplary behavior."

There was a brief silence at which point Talon realized that he was expected to speak. He looked up at the emperor and said, "Your Highness, I but did my duty. I would willingly place my life at your disposal again. I wish that I could have helped more of the men but there was no choice...for any of us, and Alexios has become a close friend."

He stopped and waited head bowed, but his mind was working furiously.

"We would ask again, what can we do to reward you for such sacrifice." Something about Manuel's tone indicated that he was uncomfortable with the interview.

Talon looked up into the dark eyes of the man on the jewel-encrusted throne. He made up his mind.

"My Lord, I own a ship and would ask for trading rights with your people."

There was an audible murmur of surprise from the military men gathered nearby, some of whom spoke French. This was clearly unexpected. He noted the surprise in the eyes of the emperor as he stared back at him

"You are a Templar knight, are you not? Why then do you wish to resort to trade?" Manuel asked.

"My Lord, with a ship I carry out my duties for the Order of Templars, but I must also find a way to pay for the crew. I note that there is a shortage of vessels for transport at present and would offer my services in this regard."

He was not expecting the response he got. Manuel sat back in his throne. His swarthy features creased with amusement and he laughed.

"My people have told me that you are an astute man, Sir Talon, but this is a surprise indeed! How do you propose to do this?"

"With your permission, my Lord, this is all I ask as a reward and I will not abuse this privilege, my Liege. I shall respect all the laws of this land, as God is my witness."

Manuel was still smiling. "This is unusual in the extreme. Does Sir Guy know of your ambitions?"

"No, my Lord, but of course I intend to inform him if...if you do grant me permission to trade with your people."

Manuel stared at him for a long moment and then said, "We shall think on this, Sir Talon. It is a very unusual request." He waved his hand in dismissal.

The interview was over. Talon stood and bowed very deeply before the throne then bowed himself out of the room. He wondered if he had overstepped himself. One never really knew with Manuel, as he had already discovered, and he almost despaired. He might have lost the one opportunity to achieve something for not only himself but for the family Kalothesos as well. If permission were refused he could not act for the family no matter how much he wanted to. That route would be barred forever.

But there was another surprise for him. In the extravagantly decorated anteroom the eunuch told him to wait, then disappeared. He sat on a stone bench with the impassive golden guards for company, wondering what was going to happen for almost two long hours during which he agonized over the whole scheme of things.

Eventually the eunuch glided back into the room accompanied by General Theodore Mavrozomes. Talon stood up immediately when he saw him and bowed respectfully.

"Ah, Sir Talon!" The general said with a broad smile. "It is good to see you again. I hear that young Alexios is doing well, thanks to you. You seem to be full of surprises. The emperor was still laughing after you had left. We were all surprised by the request."

Talon felt himself reddening. "How so, Sir?"

"He expected you to ask for an estate or many pounds of gold... as anyone else would have done. But no, you asked for a piece of paper!"

"It is an important piece of paper, Sir," Talon said. He was tense; the wait had not been easy.

"Indeed it is. Yes, indeed it is! I am here with Ionnikios to present it to you with the emperor's best wishes. I told you that I would make sure that your action was not forgotten."

Talon gaped at him. "I...I do not know what to say, Sir. How can I thank you enough? I wish I could thank His Majesty. I am deeply honored," he babbled, relief washing over him.

"Myriokephalon is still a somewhat sensitive subject and the less said about that particular campaign the better, but I think it is enough for His Majesty that you will use this opportunity well, Sir Talon. It was not hard to persuade him."

The general handed Talon a tightly folded and sealed velum package while the eunuch smiled and gave him another rolled paper also bearing a large seal with ribbons. "Sir Talon. You will want to keep these in a safe place. Please read them carefully when you get back to your ship. You do read Greek, do you not?"

Talon took the roll from him and slipped them both into his sleeve. He gave a small bow to the eunuch as protocol demanded and then gave a deep bow to the general. He was about to leave when the general motioned the eunuch to move out of earshot.

The General came close to Talon and said in a low voice. "I hope to see more of you in the future, Sir Talon. I am sure that there are enterprises we can discuss with Senator Damianus. I also think the emperor admires your action..." He laughed and clapped Talon on the shoulder. "He said as much, but not in so many words."

Talon left the palace in a state of high excitement. The first place he wanted to go was the villa to talk to Alexios and if possible the senator. He went at a fast trot all the way and arrived in time to find the family about to sit down to a meal. Joannina kissed him on the cheek and took his hand. Even the senator was at the dining table, as was Alexios and both daughters. Everyone greeted him as a member of the family and he was given a seat next to the senator, who beamed at him. Talon noted that Eugenia's warm smile was just a little proprietary.

"So you come from the palace, eh, Sir Talon?" Damianus asked.

"I do, Sir, and I have good news!"

He showed the two documents to Alexios, who almost snatched them out of his hand. He broke the seal and unfolded the velum package first and examined it.

His eyes widened and he exclaimed. "The emperor has granted Sir Talon trading rights anywhere in the empire! We will be allowed to move ahead with our enterprise. Thank God for all his mercies!" He looked up, his face pale with emotion.

Theodora gave an excited cry and jumped off her seat to rush over to read the paper that Alexios held in his hands. He passed it to her, and she scanned the papers quickly, then gave a whoop of excitement.

"Mama, Papa it is true. Sir Talon has the right to trade with the empire. Anywhere at all!"

Everyone was suddenly talking excitedly. It was clear the senator was very happy as he called for his wine to be brought to the table. They all drank to Talon.

"You do not know what an honor this is, Talon. Father does not bring his good wine to the table very often," Eugenia told him, her soft voice a little sardonic.

"You need to know what an honor the emperor has bestowed upon you, Talon. This velum is exceedingly valuable," Alexios informed him. "It can take many months and much in the way of bribes to obtain one of these."

They were interrupted by an excited shriek from Theodora. She was holding the roll in both hands and staring at it with shock written all over her face. Joannina jumped up and rushed to her daughter, putting her arms around the girl.

"What is it, my dearest? What is the matter?" she demanded as she held Theodora. Then, "You really should not open other people's letters, my dear!" she admonished as she realized with horror what her impetuous daughter had done.

Eugenia also rose but with less haste and moved around the table to stand next to her sister, peering over her shoulder to see what she was so excited about. Not for the first time Talon was struck at how similar she was to her lovely mother, but there was something harder about her features.

She too gasped as she read the paper and her eyes widened. She turned to her mother and pointed at the writing and the stamp. "It has the signature of the Emperor himself!" she all but whispered as she stared at Talon. "What did you do?"

Theodora lifted her face to the men and said in a voice full of awe. "This is incredible. You must read this, Father!"

"Read it child, you have it in your hand," the senator said, but a look of apprehension flitted across his face. Talon felt his heart sink. Had the capricious emperor laid down some impossible condition, he wondered?

Everyone was quiet, so quiet that they could all hear Theodora gulp, then she said, "It says that Their Imperial Majesties grant exclusively to Sir Talon, Knight Templar, the right to pay a Tax of ten solidi for every ship belonging to him that enters the ports of Constantinople..." She did not finish as it was now the turn of Alexios to shout.

He turned to Talon and cried, "Do you know what this means?"

"Er, yes, that I have to pay a tax for my ship every time I..."

"No!" he bellowed, his eyes blazing. "I mean, yes, but do not you see? We not only have the Emperor's formal permission to trade but you will have the best..." Alexios began, trying to stand. He fell back with a wince and his stick clattered to the floor. One of the servants hastened to pick it up and place it nearby but Alexios ignored him. Talon had never seen his friend so exuberant.

"Alex is quite right!" Damianus interrupted. He beamed at Talon. "It is much less than the rate the Genoese and the Venetians had to pay. They have to pay seventeen! Do you not see, boy, that the emperor has granted you a very special privilege?"

Talon could only stare at them all in a state of bemused surprise. "I...I did not know," he stammered.

Theodora swiped at her hair, which was now in disarray, falling all about her shoulders and across her face. She was enormously excited and tearful. She hugged her mother, pecked her sister on her alabaster cheek and then rushed around the table to embrace her brother, who kissed her back with enthusiastic affection. She restrained herself with difficulty as she strode up to Talon and almost diffidently handed him the paper and then impulsively kissed him on the corner of his mouth.

"I am sorry! I should not have opened it without your permission, Talon. You really must have done something very special to impress the emperor, so congratulations," she said, her tone was demure, but her eyes glowed with pride.

Theodora put her arms around her father's neck and embraced him, still looking up at Talon. Damianus patted her on the arm and kissed her cheek.

"You should be proud of yourself, Sir Talon. Few are granted favors of this kind. Be sure to keep that paper safe, as you will have to show it to the customs people before they will believe you." He laughed. "John, bring more of my wine! We have to celebrate this momentous occasion with our boy Talon here and salute the enterprise we are about to embark upon. Alexios, my son, may you and Talon here have a very profitable enterprise. We need some good luck."

Let us cast off the haze
Of the mists from our band,
Till with far-seeing gaze
We may look on the land.

Aristophanes

Chapter 20

Rhodes

Talon swiftly made his way to the wharf. He was greeted by a very curious group of friends at the ship's side, and once aboard he told them what had transpired not only at the palace but also the information held in the letters, which he produced with a flourish to the awed murmurings of his companions. Nigel and Dmitri did a small jig around the deck while Guy's smile of happiness would have frightened a lion.

"This could make us all rich!" Henry exclaimed, rubbing his beard furiously, which he did when excited.

"I thank God that we have now the passport to continue with the venture," Talon informed them, "but we still have some proving to do, and it is time to do so without delay."

Max laughed. "I do not know how you do it, Talon. But I applaud you."

"You must name the ship, Talon," Nigel said.

"A ship must have a name, its true," Guy agreed.

They all looked at him while he thought about that.

"We shall call her the *Falcon*, because of the carving on the front. It is like a bird of prey," he stated at last.

They all agreed to the name and had a noisy celebration at the inn that night. Nigel got so drunk that he wanted to sing and clambered onto the table where he swayed about blearily and forgot the words. He slipped off the table and fell into Max's lap and then remembered the words and tried to get back onto the table. Max restrained him amid much laughter at his lugubrious grimaces and shouts.

Some men at a table further across the room shouted at him to shut up and got up to follow up on their words. Talon got to his feet expecting trouble that he really did not want, but then Guy lumbered to his feet and smiled at them and gave them the come on with his fingers, then he called over, "Come over here and I will tear your heads off one by one then spit down your throats!"

Nigel cackled from under the table and Guy grinned. Talon could not decide which was the most menacing, but it gave pause to the Greeks.

They glowered at him for a long tense moment, during which Henry and Max also got to their feet, but then the Greeks all sat down again.

"I want to go and fuck something," Nigel slurred. "Guy, you got ta... take me to your fav'rit whore, le's go!" He climbed to his feet and with Guy holding him upright they staggered out of the door.

"Those two are true barbarians. Henry, you should go with them to make sure they get back to the ship in time. Do not forget the curfew."

"Do not worry, Talon. I am going with them anyway. You know us sailors, we have to take care of business before we sail, never know when if ever we will again. Are you coming?"

"Not tonight, my friend. Max, do you want to go with them?" Talon asked his friend.

"Go off to a whorehouse with those trolls? Not me," Max said with a grin at Henry. Then he and Talon headed back to the ship. Talon hoped that there would be no more trouble.

*****

The next morning they all had hangovers, but there was work to do. Henry might have had a woolly head but he drove the crew hard as the dawn lit the sky. Talon remembered Sir Guy's comment on the Templar interest in Cyprus and the possibility of some corsairs in the region of Rhodes. That troubled him, as he did not want to sail into the middle of an Arab fleet looking for victims. He had mentioned this to Henry the night before but the seaman had shrugged. "If we have the weather on our side and a good wind we can show them a clean pair of heels, Talon. I would not worry too much."

Talon had another worry to deal with. He had gone alone down to the harbor of Neorion to find that the Genoese ship had gone.

He stood for a long time on the beach looking out to sea thinking about the evening of his almost disastrous visit to the Spartenos villa. The event was still very fresh in his mind but there was little he could do about it now, there was too much else going on. Yet he had an uneasy feeling that it was not over.

This was confirmed when a one-eyed beggar sidled up to him with his dirty hand sticking out of the rags he wore. "Spare a coin, Sir. I am an old soldier with nothing now. God will bless you for your kindness," the man whined.

Talon looked at him and nodded, the battle of Myriokephalon still fresh in his mind. He reached into his purse and handed the man a copper. The money disappeared but beggar did not leave immediately.

"What is it?" Talon asked him.

"You was here the other day with a friend, weren't you," the bundle of rags stated.

"What of it?"

"If I was you I would watch my back. There are bad men, and they know about you."

"Who are you talking about?"

"The man who was here asking about you."

"How did he know to ask you?"

The beggar looked guilty and shuffled his rag bound feet in the sand.

"Ah, a few coppers would have done it, right?" Talon asked, not unkindly.

The man nodded. "A man's got to live somehow. I was once in the Emperor's army but then I took a spear to the thigh and a slash that took out my eye. At least I made it back, but to what? They do not care, they use you and and then throw you out onto the dungheap of this city to rot." He sounded apologetic and resentful at the same time.

Talon nodded. He could see these detritus of former battles all about in this city. "Well, what did you tell him?"

"I didn't have any choice," the man whined. "He scared me, wanted to know what you were doing here. But you have given me coin, so now I wanted to warn you. Watch your back."

Before Talon could demand more of an explanation the man had shambled off back to a corner of the walls where there were others in like condition squatting around a fire.

He did not think it worthwhile to follow so he made his way back to the inn deep in thought. He touched his side where it still ached.

*****

He was still deep in thought when Max entered his room and informed him that a message had arrived from the port authorities telling them to move the ship to the harbor of Prosphorion. He came down the stairs to find his companions preparing to leave.

He decided to embark with them, as he feared another difficult encounter with either Eugenia or Theodora. They left for the harbor of Prosphorion within the hour. With Henry at the steersmen's side they set off to round the curve of the peninsula heading for their new destination.

The view from the ship was magnificent. They sailed by the church of Saint Serglas, its domed roof peeking over the tops of several trees, the copper dome glowing in the sunlight. Next they could see the roofs of the palace of Bucoleon. Talon was able to point out the terraces of the Tzykanisterion where he had played.

"I wanted to come and watch that game," Henry said with regret in his voice.

"It was exclusively for the nobility, Henry, not the common riffraff or pirates like you," Max said with an exaggerated sniff.

"How then did you get in, Max, may I ask?" Nigel asked, his voice dripping sarcasm.

"Someone has to keep an eye on that lad, look at him. He'd be helpless without me," Max said. Guffaws of derision greeted this remark, but then Henry had to devote his time to navigating the shoreline.

Max and Talon stayed out of his way and stared at the magnificent sight of the many palaces and administrative buildings of the Grand Palace, which dominated the southeastern side of the peninsula, situated along the shallow slopes for all to see, and the buildings glowed in the autumn sunlight. The monastery of Hodegetia stood out, set amongst the green of many trees. Standing head and shoulders above it all was the massive body of the Hagia Sophia. Theodora had told him the name meant 'Church of the Holy Wisdom of God.' Talon never ceased to admire that huge structure, wondering as always how men could have been inspired to create such a place.

They rounded the northernmost peninsular tip and gazed up at the Column of the Goths that sat on the very top of the hill, its twisted marble shaft resembling a massive unicorn horn with a four spiked cap, which Talon had been told was known as a Corinthian cap. Then they had to arrest their course, along with many other boats. The massive machinery had to grind into gear, which allowed the great chain across the Golden Horn to drop sufficiently to allow ships to pass. While they waited Talon could observe the ships of war anchored in small groups all along the line of the chain. Several were anchored on the side nearest to the city, but he saw many more on the other side of the Golden Horn: formidable galleys of two and three masts; they looked menacing— even more so now that he knew what weapons they carried.

Their ship was boarded by a pilot who wanted to see their permit, after which they were guided through the fortified walls of the harbor Prosphorion into its still waters where, with shouted orders and much scurrying about by the crew, they hauled in the sails and dropped anchor with a splash.

This was an entirely different harbor. The wide bellied, two masted Genoese cargo ships which towered over their sleek galley were tethered in groups or lying alongside the wharves which seethed with activity as gangs of slaves loaded and unloaded their cargoes. Racks of salted Tuna fillets lined the harbor walls. The season was over for fishing, but the smoking and salting were underway and now the fish was being taken west to the Latin countries which vied for the meat.

Ferrymen plied their trade and boats were rowed from ship to ship offering fresh vegetables and just about anything else the crews might want.

Now that the ship was idle the men leaned over the sides and called out to the boats to come closer and show off their wares. The fastest of the boats contained women. There seemed to be a universal language where boats that traded in whores were concerned and the dickering was lively. Henry threw cold water on that, eliciting groans from all around when he informed the crew that no women were allowed on board. There had been none of this kind of activity in the other secluded harbor.

They had little time to relax. Now that he had a ship available, Makarios was in a hurry to see to it that they were loaded and sent on their way. He was rowed out to the ship that very day with papers that he wanted to discuss with Talon. They went down to the cluttered cabin accompanied by a younger man introduced as Giorgios. His hazel eyes were intelligent and he understood book keeping very well. Makarios told Talon that he would be sailing with him to the islands, as he knew the agents there personally and would be able to smooth over the official hurdles they were bound to encounter. Talon realized that Giorgios was a eunuch even before the man began speaking in a high falsetto voice.

Makarios left the ship several hours later, leaving behind a cheerful Giorgios chatting to Dmitri on deck while a bemused Talon scratched his head as he pored over what Makarios called a manifest of the goods they were to carry. His unfamiliarity with Greek letters and numbers did not help. He called Giorgios to come into the cabin where he asked him to help with the numbers.

A day later they were ordered to bring the ship alongside the quay where wagons were waiting. There was a vast amount of cargo to be squeezed into the ship and Talon wondered where it would all be placed.

"If we cannot get it all into the holds we will put the overflow in the main cabin and we can all sleep on the deck on the soft bales. How else are any of us going to sleep on silk again?" Nigel said with a grin.

The work started as soon as they were alongside the quay. The gang waiting for them was whipped into action and shortly after a stream of slaves were coming and going as the bales were hauled on board. Henry, Guy and Nigel, who knew something of loads and displacement, supervised the work with the help of Giorgio and Dmitri, who translated for the overseers. Talon and Max stood on the upper rear deck and watched the proceedings with interest.

"I confess that I am very glad of those men. I feel helpless when confronted with all the details," Talon told Max, indicating his busy companions supervising the loading.

"We are to become traders, Talon. This is not the way of the Templars, but I find it exciting all the same. May God bless this venture."

"I agree. We should go to the church of Saint Menas before we leave to ask for God's blessings." Talon felt apprehensive. It was a huge responsibility to carry this cargo and sell it for the family. They were coming into the autumn and the weather south of the Hellespont could be unpredictable according to Henry and Dmitri.

The slaves worked all that day and long into the night carrying bales of silk, barrels of olives and oil, and tightly woven sacks containing spices onto the deck of the galley. The pungent smell from these sacks dominated even the smell of olive oil. Talon observed the activity from the upper deck and thought back to his time in Egypt. There many of his own people were slaves, being beaten just as here, and dying or falling from exhaustion. The world was indifferent to a slave and his feelings no matter from where he came, as was being demonstrated on this wharf.

Eventually the last of the empty wagons rumbled off, drawn by its sleepy oxen. The exhausted slaves were marched off in their chains and the noise and bustle on the ship fell silent as the crew, also exhausted from their exertions, fell asleep almost where they stood.

Talon and Max spent some time on the top deck watching the harbor as the moon rose. A galley some ways off was slowly leaving port. Talon wondered who might be sailing off in the dead of night but was too tired to think about it. They found a place in the crowded main cabin where Henry and his companions were already snoring and they too fell instantly asleep.

*****

Late the next morning a message from Alexios arrived, asking him to come to the villa. Talon walked up the long straight street that paralleled the Wall of Byzantium, which he now knew to be the earliest constructed wall of the city. Citizens who wanted it for other purposes now that it served none at all had stripped its crumbling stone away in many places. He was met by Eugenia, who had been waiting to intercept him at the door to the main hall.

The greeting was a little forced, although the kiss she gave him on the cheek was warm and friendly enough. Talon was curious as to why she was there.

"God's Blessings, Talon. It is good to see you again," she said as her lips brushed his. She was still holding his hand in hers.

"God's Blessing to you too, Eugenia." He released his hand and looked at her. The memory of their previous encounter threatened to surface, but now was not the time to dwell upon it.

"I am delighted to see you, Eugenia, but what are you doing here?"

"This is my home, Talon, despite the fact that I am so often at the palace. I understand you will be traveling very soon now that you have all the right papers?" she queried.

"Of course it is your home. I meant, however, that I am surprised it is you who meets me. And yes, we are almost ready to leave," he answered.

"I hear it is to be Rhodes and even Cyprus."

"It is, my dear sister, although I have my doubts that Talon knows where they really are...even now." The voice belonged to Theodora, who walked up to him in a proprietary manner and kissed him on the cheek with her arms around his neck.

Embarrassed he loosened her arms and held her at arm's length. "How are you, Theodora?" he asked with a glance at her sister. Eugenia had a half smile on her face that was both patronizing and annoyed at the same time, while Theodora was simply looking possessive.

Eugenia ignored her sister and said, "You have come to see Alex, I am sure, Talon. Come, I will take you to him."

She slipped her arm into his and, with a bright smile at her scowling sister, walked him out of the room. As they walked toward the sunlit loggia she said in a low voice, "Talon, shall I see you before you leave?"

He nodded without saying anything as he could hear light footsteps behind them. He glanced back expecting to see Theodora following, but instead it was Eugenia's servant maid.

"Then I shall wait near the hall. Look for me before you go," she almost whispered.

Eugenia led him to where Alex was seated, surrounded by papers. His leg, heavily bandaged was propped up on a small table. Eugenia smiled at her brother and kissed him on the forehead.

"Look who I have brought with me, my brother. Talon and you have much to talk about so I shall leave you two," she said. Her eyes held Talon's for a brief electric moment before she turned and walked away.

"Ah, there you are, Talon. Good to see you." Alex looked rested and comfortable. He had recently been shaved and looked brighter than Talon had seen him in some time.

"Will you not stay? I know you worked with your companions half the night. Makarios said that you did not waste a minute of daylight."

They talked till the servants came out with lamps, but by then Alexios was tired. Talon escorted him back to his room and then returned to the loggia.

He ate with the family that night and stayed reluctantly, as he had no good explanation for leaving and thought it might even offend. He retired with everyone else and lay on the bed in the guest room wide awake, thinking about the impending journey, but also about what the beggar had said. Who was looking for him? It had to be the people from the villa, and it was very clear that the beggar had been afraid. He was still pondering this around midnight when he heard a faint noise. He had been expecting a visit. Eugenia had been very insistent when she encountered him in the corridor as he was leaving Alexios' room.

Ever cautious he slid out of bed and drew his sword, then waited as the door opened and a figure slipped into the room. He hoped it was Eugenia; then she whispered his name so he was sure. He replaced his sword and murmured a greeting.

She wasted no time but took his hand and led him straight to the bed where she proceeded to make love with a passion that left them both gasping. She threw her head back with a long hiss of breath and clawed his back with her nails as she climaxed, causing him to wince with the pain because her nails raked the slash in his side.

Lying back on the bed Talon caught his breath and wondered about the woman at his side. He gingerly touched the wound that had only just begun to heal and to his dismay found that it was bleeding again. He muttered something about needing to wipe his face and hastened to the bowl where he took a towel and dabbed at the wound. She lay quietly in the dark waiting for him to come back.

"I have missed you, Talon," she said as he came back to bed, and she slipped into his arms. "Where did you get that cut? She ran her fingers down the scabbed tissue from the recent wound. Talon hid his surprise that she had noticed and said casually, "It is one of the wounds I garnered during the campaign."

"My poor warrior," she said as she stroked him. "But that was some months ago now, did you not visit a physician to have it seen to?"

"It was really just a scratch, but it is taking longer than usual to heal," he said, hoping she would talk about something else.

They were silent for a while but then she asked a question that startled him. "My mother told me of an incident that happened with one of our neighbors the other day. Did you hear about it?"

Talon shook his head in the dark. "What incident, when?" A tiny alarm bell sounded in his head.

"You were here that night, I think. Someone tried to break into our neighbor's villa, probably to steal something. Not even our houses are safe anymore. Did you hear nothing of it?" Her tone implied that he should have been aware.

"No, indeed I did not," Talon lied.

"That is surprising, as my mother could hardly have kept that gossip from you, I am sure. Did my chatterbox of a little sister not say anything?"

"Tell me more about this...attempt to break into your neighbor's house," he said, leaning on his elbow.

"Well, I am more often at the palace, as you know, but when I came back the other day Mother mentioned it. She said the senator had come to visit and had told her all about the event. She had asked the guards about it but they said that nothing happened."

"Well, what did happen? Was it here or there?" Talon feigned confusion. "I thought that you said the break in occurred in the other villa." Why, he wondered, was she so interested in that event?

"Oh, that is because the robbers, or at least one of them, came over our wall and Senator Spartenos came to report it to us. Can you imagine that? Are you sure you did not hear about it? He said that his men and dogs followed the man to this house. I can't see that our guards would not have seen an intruder unless they were asleep at the time."

Talon shrugged in the dark. "Perhaps they were. Did they ever catch the thieves?"

"No, but there was a disturbance, which is why I am surprised that you did not hear it. You heard nothing?" she insisted.

"I must have been sleeping like a log, for I heard nothing at all," he murmured as he leaned over her and kissed her. This time he spent time with her, finally letting her fall into an exhausted sleep.

He slept very little that night, but as the cock began to crow in the stables he roused her and sent her sleepily on her way. He was left pondering her interest in an incident that her mother had barely mentioned but which Theodora knew all about.

*****

Eugenia woke late that morning and stretched like a cat and smiled as she recalled the night before. She looked at her hand that was still stained with blood from when she had touched his side. She was thoughtful for a while, but then realized that it was time to go back to the palace, but first she had a small detour to make.

Eugenia's litter was admitted to the house of Senator Spartenos and she alighted at the wide steps leading up to the main entrance hall. This was a far grander house than that of her family and she glanced enviously about her as she walked slowly up the steps. She was greeted by one of the guardsmen, who leered at her. She lifted her chin disdainfully and pretended to ignore the man. Right behind him was a well-dressed eunuch who bowed her in.

She was shown into the main living room where the senator was standing waiting for her.

"God's Blessings to you, my Lady. I was informed that you had come to visit me, my dear. It is a long way to come from the palace. Did you spend the night with your parents?"

"Gods Blessings, Senator," Eugenia said respectfully. She did not like the senator but she dared not offend him in any way.

"What may I do for you?" he asked with a silky edge to his voice.

"You asked me to report upon anything I heard that might be unusual regarding the incident the other day, Senator" she said.

"Please call me John. We know one another well enough for that, do we not?' he said, stepping closer to her.

Eugenia stepped back a pace and hurried on. "The Knight Templar who stays with us. You wanted to know more of him?"

"Yes, indeed." The senator stopped and cocked his head. "Well, what have you to say?"

"He says he knows nothing of the incident, and yet he was in our villa that night. Even my brother heard something, but the Templar says he heard nothing."

"Hmm, a little strange, but not unbelievable."

"Yes, but...he has a new wound. It was not there the last time I saw him."

The senator gave her a sharp look. "How did...? Ah...how fresh would you say this wound was?"

"He claimed it was from the campaign, but that was months ago now. I did not believe him and he tried to talk about something else. I think he knows more than he is saying."

The senator noted her hesitant tone and said, "Do not tell me that your Frank is beginning to get under your skin my dear?" His sneer was barely concealed.

She blushed with anger but said nothing other than to glare at him and bite her tongue. He stared hard at her. "I do not care if you rut with the Frank, Eugenia, but do not forget that it is I who tells you what to do. Your relationship with the prince is not known to anyone except me and you would do well not to try anything rash. Remember the consequences of that. A whore, even an aristocratic one, has a limited future." He came even closer and took her lower face in his hard fingers. "I might even feel like a payment or two myself."

She twisted her face away from his hard grip and put a hand up to feel the marks he had left behind.

"But you did well coming to me about this. There is certainly something going on here, which I intend to discover. You may go now. Be sure to say nothing to anyone about this visit," he said, briskly dismissing her.

Eugenia left hastily, tears welling in her eyes, feeling humiliated. There was nothing she could do, as the senator had pointed out, but she hated him for it.

*****

At dawn on the next day the crew roused themselves and began to make preparations to cast off. Talon woke to the sound of bare feet stamping about on the deck above and orders shouted by Henry and his two lieutenants, Guy and Nigel. He decided he was not going to get any more sleep so he threw off his coverings and got up from the pallet. He left Max still huddled under a blanket in the other bed and made his way up on deck. Henry greeted him from the steering oar where he was supervising the ship's guidance. Guy was down in the now cluttered waist of the ship with the rowers and the crew who were about to raise the sail while Nigel was in the bows seeing to the casting off of the ropes that had held them to the wharf for three very busy days.

As they drew away Makarios and his scribes arrived and stood watching from the quayside. Talon was surprised and delighted to see a litter being carried along the waterfront. As soon as it was placed on the ground by the sweating slaves Alexios was helped out of the litter to stand upright with the aid of a stick. Theodora jumped out and began to shout and wave her arms wildly. She danced up and down and then turned to her brother and hugged him. Then she stood with her brother's arm about her shoulders waving goodbye. Talon waved back with a strange feeling inside him as he watched his friends and heard the faint words, "God speed and safe journey."

While the ship turned in the wide waters of Prosphorion harbor he pointed up at to the masthead. A banner that Theodora and her mother had presented to Talon was snapping in the breeze. The lion's paw on a gold background and the ship of gold upon azure with a diagonal line dividing them was proudly flying from the highest point on the vessel for all to see. Talon had decided he liked the banner, but he would have them make a small but significant change to it when he came back. There was something missing.

Henry shouted to Guy to raise the second sail and begin the rowing, and they sped through the open gate and out into the swell of the Golden Horn. They still had the Marmara Sea and the

Hellespont to negotiate but they were finally on their way. Talon stared back at his friends, waving from time to time until they were lost in the mist rising off the waters.

*****

It took a week of sailing for them to make the journey to the island of Rhodes. Once clear of the Hellespont, Henry had sailed within sight of the coastline during the day, anchoring at night in some sheltered bay. He did not want to be far out to sea at this time of year, for storms were gathering in the west. Out in open water they might get caught unawares, unable to find suitable shelter in time as the storms were sudden and harsh at this time of year. Apart from one long rainy day, which they spent in the confines of a secure cove, the weather was dry with a good wind to keep them moving south. As Henry pointed out to Talon as he chaffed at the time it was taking, a Genoese tub would have taken a month to get this far. Their ship was ideal for an enterprise of this nature. Its speed was a huge advantage, even if they could not take on an equivalent cargo.

On the eighth day and they set off once more with the sun's rays glittering off the calm waters of the sea. Seagulls and other sea birds that Talon could not name dipped and rose as they fished, and there were only a few clouds in the sky to keep Henry's attention. It was only a matter of hours before the long line of an island was sighted by the lookouts posted at the top of the masts and Henry conferred with his crew. He included Giorgios in the discussion. They were certain it was the island of Rhodes and Giorgios indicated to Henry that he should take a more easterly course that would bring them to the town of Rodos, which rested on the easternmost point of the island.

"I have not been here for the last two years now, but I am sure that our agent Isaias will still be in Rodos," he told Talon, who was standing next to him watching the crew at work. In truth Talon could not have told where they were and asked Henry to show him on the charts. Henry pointed to the bottom of the big lump of land which he said represented Byzantium and showed him where the island of Rhodes was with respect to others with Greek names.

"Giorgios says that this island was taken by the Turks and then retaken by the Byzantines," Talon told Henry.

"True enough, Talon. We have seen no Saracen ships in our travels recently. I think the Byzantine navy rules these seas at present." Henry sounded comfortable.

He guided them along the rugged coastline of the island, passing many fishing vessels out plying their trade. A pod of what seemed to be large fish with grey colored skin that resembled the strange looking creatures on the chart gamboled alongside the ship for a few fascinating minutes and then disappeared into the azure depths of the sea. They had seen these before on their way north, but Talon was still fascinated by these large dark forms that drove through the water effortlessly watching him with their knowledgeable eyes. Guy wanted to spear one for fresh meat, but the creatures had vanished as though they heard him before he could fetch weapons. There were other fish that appeared to fly for brief moments, and then they too disappeared.

As far as Talon was concerned they had lived quite well and had no need to kill for any reason. They had brought chickens and pigs aboard for fresh meat and at night the men had fished, sometimes bringing aboard huge sleek fish with silver skins and pointed noses and crescent moon shaped tails. Dmitri called them Thunnos and said these were the same fish that they had seen on the wharves of Prosphorion Harbor being salted and smoked. The meat had been delicious when cooked over a fire on the beach.

They rounded a sharp cape and headed down the coast seeking the harbor of Rodos. They had to row now as the ship was driving into the wind. Henry had Nigel bring the sails down and set the crew to work, pulling hard at the oars. It was backbreaking labor but eventually they began to see the signs of a city. Perched on a hill overlooking a natural harbor was what looked like a temple, and near to that a fortification. Below these constructions were a cluster of buildings nestling against the hillside protected from the weather by the natural loop of the bay and fortifications that protected the entrance.

Henry with Giorgios and Dmitri at his side guided the ship to a place in the middle of the bay where they dropped anchor with a loud splash. The gulls screamed and dived into the glass-clear waters, while the sounds of activity on the quayside came clearly to their ears. Nevertheless, there was a hush within the confines of the low stony hills that surrounded them. The town was not large but the harbor was busy.

Talon noted that there were two large dromons in the harbor that seemed to be Byzantine ships of war. The familiar banner fluttered idly on both masts.

"Those are Greek ships," Giorgios confirmed as he came up and observed the direction of Talon's gaze. "They are probably here to protect this harbor from the Turkish and Arab pirates.

They come and go, but today they seem to be taking a rest from their onerous duties." His tone was sarcastic. Talon grinned.

"What is going on over there?" Talon pointed at the beach where there was a lot of activity. He could see the frames of what appeared to be the beginnings of large boats.

"These people make ships. This ship could even have been made here. There is another town on the other end of the island that is larger and makes even more. The Venetians and the Genoese come here for their vessels, as do the Greeks."

"Will our cargo have what they are looking for? Will they buy from us?" Talon asked. His responsibilities weighed heavily upon him, making him apprehensive now that they were finally here.

"Look about you, Sir Talon. Do these hills look as though they produce silk? Do they look rich with olive trees? Yes, there are some olives here, but more importantly we have spices and they have none. Let us hope that they have much gold and are willing to part with it!" He chuckled and rubbed his hands together with anticipation.

"First we must deal with the officials, don't forget," Dmitri said as he joined them, his tone dry. "They will want their cut."

"What have they done to earn it?" Talon asked.

"Nothing! But we will not sell a bale of anything if we do not oil their slippery hands. Look, here comes a customs official now. By God, but they do not waste any time, do they! Like flies."

There was indeed a boat pulling out toward them. The by now familiar form of a eunuch dressed in rich clothing was seated at the back being pulled by four lusty rowers; he was accompanied by a scribe and two soldiers.

"We must be very polite to him as he represents the empire, and above all make sure that he does not realize the full extent of our cargo," Giorgios said. "With your permission, Sir Talon, I shall meet him and we can go to your cabin to discuss things?" he asked diffidently.

Talon nodded and told Henry to stand the crew down until they might be needed. The official was helped aboard by Dmitri and Nigel, who despite being on his best behavior still looked villainous with his lank blond hair and deep set, slightly mad looking eyes. Once aboard, the official's sharp, experienced gaze swept the ship taking in every detail.

Giorgios greeted the official in Greek in such an oily manner that Talon shot him a surprised look. This was not the easy going, quiet and assured man with whom he had just spent a week. But he did not interfere as Giorgios unctuously bowed the man and his scribe along the deck and into the cabin. His voice was even higher pitched than usual, and he affected a manner that was distinctly feminine.

The cabin was just a space with pallets in corners and a low table that squatted in the middle. They squeezed into the cramped space, which even Talon could tell was beginning to smell of too much occupancy. The official wrinkled his nose but did not comment when Giorgios brushed by him—far too closely, but he did not seem to mind. He demanded to see their manifest, which Giorgios produced with a flourish and an elaborate bow. It was a large document that Makarios had shown Talon before rolling it up and handing it to Giorgios while they had been in Constantinople.

"This is the document that you show the officials," he had said with his usual deadpan voice. "You do not show them the real manifest. Giorgios will show you how it is done."

The lead stamps and the colored wax with signet stamps and beautiful calligraphy would have impressed any normal person, but this official seemed unimpressed. He ordered the scribe to take notes and then demanded to hear about the cargo from them, the agents they would be dealing with, and how long they intended to remain in harbor.

It lasted about an hour, during which Dmitri brought some wine. Talon was sure the plump official was going to spit it out it was so bad, but he swallowed it with a pained expression on his pursed wet mouth. His scribe did not take more than a sip before putting the stained leather cup back down with a grimace and did not touch it again.

A fee was suggested as a tax, which was met with horrified exclamations from both Giorgios and Dmitri, who waved their hands in the air in despairing motions, then translated for Talon as though he could not understand a word of Greek, and Talon added his own lamentations of poverty and pleas for reduction, but not in Greek. Giorgios began to wail in a high-pitched tone and begged the official to reconsider. He batted his eyes at the man and almost pursed a kiss as he pleaded for leniency.

Talon was about to explode with laughter at the performance, but he knew this was no laughing matter. A wrong step and they would do no trade here. He brought himself under control and forced his expression to look aggrieved along with the other two. They bargained for another half an hour, during which the price went down from exorbitant to just about reasonable amid much sighing and wringing of hands. It soon became clear to Talon that there were two masters of negotiation in the cabin, and Giorgios was probably the better man. His respect for him went up a couple of notches. As soon as the gold had been passed over in a small leather sack the official and his scribe placed a seal on the document and add another small lead stamp to the already weighty paper. The officials then quickly departed the noxious smelling cabin with its bad wine and dangerous looking crew, their duty done.

They were bundled down into the waiting boat along with their gleaming soldiers and Giorgios called out oily compliments as they rowed away. When they were well out of earshot Giorgios turned to Talon and said, "We seem to be free to trade, even if we have been shorn of some hair." His voice had gone back to normal and his expression was all business. Talon almost gaped at him.

Dmitri was not so restrained. He grabbed at Nigel and in front of the entire crew did a small jig, dragging the perplexed man about with him and laughing with excitement.

"You know of course what did it?" he told the others.

"Tell me when you two have finished," Talon said in a dry tone. Nigel extricated himself with a look of disgust. "Dmitri, let go of me, you horrible creature!" he exclaimed.

"Why, the shitty wine of course! And that stinky cabin of yours, Sir Talon. We did very well in there—as I am sure you could tell." Dmitri held his sides and roared with laughter.

"Other than paying a bribe which was barely reasonable I am not entirely sure what you mean."

"We paid much less than we would have if we had been one of those large fat merchantmen, Sir Talon," Dmitri said as he caught his breath. "Giorgios pared him back to the bone. I am willing to bet that he still does not know how it was done and will be scratching his head for the rest of the time we are here."

"Well done, Giorgios. I will tell Makarios of this when we get back," Talon said.

"God willing." Giorgios crossed himself and then suggested that they go ashore and find where the agent might be.

They were rowed over to the wharf and found themselves once again on dry land. It swayed a bit for Talon as he regained his land legs. Giorgios and Max appeared to be in the same condition; but Giorgios quickly set off, with a glance at Talon and Max to see that they were keeping up.

The buildings around the harbor were of much the same style as in Constantinople but not as grand, being more functional and less elegant. The lime painted walls and the tiles still made for a colorful backdrop to the calm blue waters of the harbor. Giorgios led the way past clusters of work gangs and slaves, past the shops and beggars, to climb a street that led up the low hill upon which stood the temple. He told Talon that it was known as an acropolis and was an ancient temple dedicated to the sun god Helios from the times before Christianity came to these parts.

They walked up the short steep street toward the house of the agent Isaias. Small boys ran about playing a raucous game of tag and old men sat on stools outside their houses sunning themselves and gossiping. They grew silent as the newcomers walked by and started up again as they moved on—the new subject certainly being the visitors.

Giorgios brought them to a low archway and banged on the wooden door. They waited in the silence that ensued. Eventually they heard a step and a woman's shrill voice asked who it was.

"It is I, Giorgios. I wish to speak to Isaias. Is he here?"

There was a muttered exclamation, the sound of retreating footsteps, and again silence. Then they heard someone heavy approaching.

"Is that really you, Giorgios?" called a man's voice.

"It is, and I have business to discuss. Open the door, man! We're tired and want some wine to ease our thirst."

The door was unlatched and a very portly man with tight, curly grey hair peered out at them. He blinked in the harsh sunlight but then he spied Giorgios and opened his arms to embrace him.

"Where have you been, my friend? I had given you up for lost," he said in a throaty rumble. "We have heard such tales from the city! Come in! Come in!" He beckoned to the others. "Anna!" he bellowed, "Bring wine and food. We have important visitors!" His jowls wobbled when he talked, his chin almost disappearing into the fat of his neck. His little button eyes, however, were alert as he examined Giorgios' companions.

Giorgios introduced Talon and Max, making it clear that Talon was in charge and that there was business to conduct.

"You are still our agent, are you not?" he queried Isaias, who now sat in front of them at the table in the garden. The stool he sat on was far too small for a man of his size.

"Of course, of course, and let me tell you there is much to discuss." Isaias' small eyes gleamed.

They sipped a very acceptable red wine and nibbled at olives in oil with some dried salted fish and large chunks of fresh bread. There was goat's cheese and some hard sausage slices to go with it.

"You have come at a very good time," Isaias told them. "Since the Venetians were taken out there has only been the occasional Genoese ship. Trade has almost dried up!" he lamented.

"When was the last time one of them came by?" Giorgios asked.

"Only a week ago, but he only came by to resupply and then left. It was a galley, not a cargo ship."

Talon and Max looked at one another, but Giorgios was suddenly very interested in finding out what was needed.

"Ours is also a galley, so we do not have a very large cargo, but we have spices and silk, oil and olives in our cargo. Will they sell?"

Isaias hesitated as though calculating. "Yes, they will sell. There is no doubt about that. All are needed here on the island."

"What is your fee?" Giorgios asked.

Within a moment the two men were haggling over the fee. Talon glanced at Max. He shrugged and smiled. It appeared that these two men enjoyed the art of negotiations, but by now Talon was reasonably sure just who would come away with the better deal, so he sat back and began to enjoy the food.

*****

Isaias had asked for fifteen percent, which made Giorgios throw up his hands and roll his eyes. "That is daylight robbery and you know it, Isaias. Where do you think I was born?" he exclaimed. "We had to pay the fee to the custom's official which nearly beggared us, and now you want to take what little profit is left for yourself?" He turned to Talon.

"When can we sail, Sir? The price here is too high."

Playing the game with him Talon made to rise.

"Wait...wait. I have to see the cargo first in any case. So why do not we do that, and then we can come to an agreement?" Isaias reached over the table and punched Giorgios on the arm gently. "You were always so impatient, my friend," he admonished with an ingratiating laugh. He gulped his wine and told his buxom wife Anna that they were leaving. He was clearly anxious to see the ship and its cargo.

They hurriedly finished their drinks and followed him out of the garden and down the street to the harbor. Isaias waddled along the quayside and shouted for a boat into which they all piled. The boat had a distinct tilt to the side where Isaias was seated.

They all clambered aboard ship, helping a wheezing Isaias onto the deck where he had to stand for a few moments to catch his breath. Almost as though they had never stopped, he and Giorgios fell into a deep discussion as they walked about, pointing to various bales that were on deck, and then they disappeared below to do the same thing. Isaias needed help down the narrow gangway to the lower deck.

Talon and Max retreated to the upper deck where they found Nigel and Guy squatting on the floor eating. "We will need to resupply before we take to the sea again, Talon," Nigel said.

"If we can unload some of our cargo we will do that, Nigel. The crew can go ashore when we get permission to dock at the quayside."

"Is he interested in our stuff?" Guy nodded in the direction of the two Greeks who had just emerged from the lower deck. Talon's ears pricked up as he caught the gist of their conversation. They were back to discussing the fee.

"My master over there will not pay more than eight percent of the profits, and we all know that you will make separate deals with your customers, so there is a handy margin in that for you. We still have to pay thirty solidi at the port of Constantinople whether the ship is empty or not." Giorgios knew perfectly well that the tax would be ten solidi, but Isaias did not.

They now stood too close to one another for Talon to hear properly, but they appeared to come to an agreement of sorts.

They did not say anything more as Giorgios came up the steps with Isaias in tow and stood in front of Talon. Giorgios looked serious and Talon's heart sank. He glanced at Isaias, but that man's fleshy face was inscrutable.

"What is it, Giorgios? You do not look happy."

"We have a problem, Sir Talon."

"Well what is it, man? Speak up."

"Isaias wants the whole cargo, Sir." They gawped at him.

"So, what is the problem with that?" Talon managed to croak.

"I told him that we had to go on to Cyprus with some of it to trade."

Talon wondered if this was another ploy on Giorgios' part. He glanced over at Isaias, who was now rubbing his hands together as though washing them. He appeared to be agitated.

"Its like this, Sir," Isaias interjected. I have empty warehouses and customers begging for these goods. They are in short supply and I could sell everything you have."

"We have been asked to bring salt back with us to Constantinople," Talon said. "It is in short supply at present and worth much. I suppose we could go without the grain, but we need to take salt back with us."

Isaias looked thoughtful. "Salt is important here too, but there is some of it in storage. It came from Alexandria, good salt, better than you will find in Cyprus. I could obtain gold for half your cargo and the rest in salt?"

For the briefest moment Talon wondered if the salt had come from the Al Fayoum in Egypt, then he took Giorgios by the arm and walked him to the far end of the deck.

"Is it as he says, Giorgios? Can he pay us in salt and gold?" he asked in a low voice.

Giorgios almost beamed. "Oh yes, Sir. Isaias is a reasonably honest trader, well, as traders go, which is why we use him, and he is certain he can sell our cargo very quickly. I am sure he is salivating at the prospect of making a killing. There are no other ships in harbor with our kind of cargo. He can get a good price for the silk and the oil, which will offset the salt, Sir Talon. However, we need your decision. It is your ship."

Talon went to discuss this development with his companions. Henry, Nigel and Guy joined him and Max at the far end of the after deck.

"It makes good sense to me, Talon," Henry said, rubbing his beard. "From here it could take us a week or more to get to Cyprus, and here we are with our entire cargo being purchased. Why would we not?"

"A week if we do not run into bad weather, you mean," Nigel added.

"You get good salt and we go home that much earlier," Guy said.

"Well, of course you would like to go back to that den of iniquity—isn't that what the monk called it?" Nigel jeered his friend. "We all know your reasons."

"Stop your bickering, you two. Why tempt fate, Talon? The season for sailing is fast closing and as long as you feel we have not been cheated, we should do this," Henry insisted.

"I do not think Giorgios would lead me astray on this.. Very well, we shall trade." Despite his hesitation he agreed with his friends. The season for storms was fast approaching.

He walked down to join the two Greeks, who were talking to Dmitri in the waist of the ship.

"It is decided. We stay here until the cargo is off the ship and we are paid. See to it Giorgios. Just make sure that we get paid. I will not be leaving without coin owed and the salt." He gave Isaias a hard look.

Isaias looked apprehensive. "I assure you, Sir, that I shall move with all haste and you will be pleased," he said as he clambered down into the boat below.

*****

He was true to his word. Somehow he managed to put it about that there was a cargo of silk and spices to be bought, and bids were coming in from as far away as the other end of the island.

Giorgios had warned Talon that salt was a difficult cargo to ship. It did not respond well to damp conditions, therefore they could not store it on the open deck and even the rowing deck presented a problem.

Guy came up with a partial solution. "Get some carpenters to make panels and we can surround the salt blocks with the wooden walls, which will keep most of the water away from them," he suggested.

The sound of hammering and sawing went on for a couple of days as this task was completed. Meanwhile the crew went ashore and spent a lot of time in the couple of small taverns to be found along the beach. Henry reported some short-lived brawls as drunken sailors got into their cups, but Guy always managed to restore order before any soldiers arrived, by cracking heads and laying out anyone who felt like quarreling with his authority. Talon and Max remained on the ship. They both felt that they needed to be on board in case anything went wrong.

They managed to offload the entire cargo within three days, and then the wagons carrying the salt began to arrive. Talon walked with Max onto the quay to have a look at their next cargo. The salt had come in ingots about two hands spans in diameter and two arm lengths long and they were partially wrapped in sack cloth. Talon had a curious sense of another time when he touched the smooth surface of one of the ingots. There was no need to remind Max of that dreadful evening when they had been betrayed and Montague had bravely fought to the death on another quay in another city. They looked at one another.

"I hope his soul is at peace," Max murmured.

They walked off together to the more respectable tavern to have a cup of wine with their friends.

Bitter breast-cares have I abided,
Known on my keel many a care's hold,
And dire sea-surge, and there I oft spent
Narrow nightwatch nigh the ship's head
While she tossed close to cliffs.

Ezra Pound

Chapter 21

A Fleet at Night

On the morning of the fifth day the ship was still tied alongside the stone quayside when Guy called down, "Another ship has arrived!"

Talon joined the others on the upper deck and watched as a dromon, its sails furled, slipped into the crystal clear waters of the harbor, its oars rising and dipping in unison as the rowers pulled. It looked vaguely familiar. Suddenly Max took his arm in a fierce grip.

"I am sure I know that ship. Is it not the one we were interested in, Talon?"

"I think you are right, Max. Well, well, our friend the Genoese is back with us. I wonder where he has been?"

"And what in the Saint's good name is he doing here?"

"If he has come to trade I am right glad that we were here first," Talon commented.

The ship glided between the naval vessels and the harbor sea wall. Activity on the dromon was minimal but Talon and Max still watched it, looking for a sign of the captain.

"There he is on the after deck. See him?" Max growled.

Talon glanced at his friend. He was like a hound with the scent of his prey in his nose.

"Max, we did not come here to fight with a Genoese pirate. We are about to load our cargo and leave with what we came for."

"I know, Talon, but I know too that I shall not sleep well until I have confronted that man."

"This I am aware of, Max. Let us see."

In fact the Genoese ship did not stay long at all. The men on the *Falcon* noticed activity on the naval vessels early the next morning and then the two naval ships departed, closely followed by the Genoese dromon.

*****

Their own departure took place a day later. They were passing a nondescript island to their east in the afternoon when the lookout called down to them. "There is something in the water ahead! Looks like pieces of wood," he called from on high.

"Where?" Henry shouted up to him.

"Off our port bow, by several points. There is something else there too, perhaps a man?"

This generated much excitement. Nigel ran to the front of the ship with some men prepared to throw ropes. Talon and Max stood near to Henry, peering into the distance, trying to make out the small spot in the sea to which the masthead was pointing.

"There! I see something. Do you see it, Talon?"

"I see it, Max. It looks like some wood beams or spars, and look, there does seem to be someone hanging onto the beams. What could have happened here? There is no evidence of a storm."

Henry ordered the men to the oars and the sails half furled so that he could come down upon the wreckage with care.

"I do not want to spear our hull upon some spar floating loose in the sea," he told Talon.

As the rowers pulled the ship closer Nigel shouted to them to back, as the ship was almost upon the floating debris. Then he exclaimed with surprise.

"Sir Talon, there are two men! They are hurt and will not be able to come aboard on their own!" Nigel shouted from the bows.

Henry directed Guy to lower the boat over the side and bring the survivors back.

They hauled the dripping men out of the water and assisted them onto the deck. Both of them fell onto the planks and stayed there, too exhausted to speak. Talon descended to the waist of the ship and stared down at them. Guy was kneeling, the head of one of the survivors in his lap. Both men were burned black across their faces, heads and shoulders. The flesh was peeling from the one who was barely conscious, while the other was waving his hands about in feeble gestures.

"How could they survive this?" someone muttered. "They're burnt like charcoal!"

"Look at the wood floating in the water, it is burnt all over! God preserve us, what has happened here?" someone else asked in a hushed tone.

"Here, take this," Nigel thrust a leather cup full of clean water into Guy's hand. "He will be thirsty."

Indeed the man gulped the water down and gasped for more, and then he tried to sit up.

"Where am I?" he asked in Greek.

"You are aboard a Frank ship and safe now," Dmitri said, kneeling beside him. "What happened to you? Who are you?"

"God be praised, and may He bless you all for your kindness. My name is Romanos. I am an officer from a Byzantine dromon. Our two ships were attacked at night, and all who lived were captured and locked up below. But then we broke out and fought back. We almost recovered the ship, until something happened to the fire apparatus."

"Bring the man below at once," Talon ordered. He motioned for Giorgios and Dmitri to come with him and Max. "Guy, Nigel, go and tell Henry there is danger about. Everyone be alert, especially the lookouts. I shall tell you all when we know more, but for now look to the ship."

The two men nodded and immediately jogged off to alert Henry and prepare the ship for any eventuality. Very soon Talon felt the ship heel slightly as the sails caught the wind and they moved forward, heading north again.

The two survivors were carried very carefully into the cabin then laid gently on the floor and covered. But their wounds and burns were clearly agonizing. One man's flesh was so badly burned it fell off in swathes. He screamed and writhed, then fell back moaning, throwing his head from side to side. What remained of his eyelids were gummed shut.

"This one will not live for very long, Talon," Max said in a low voice.

"Neither will the other with burns like that, Max, unless we can help him to a doctor. But we must know more, even if there is little enough we can do. Dmitri, Giorgios, I charge you to find out all you can before they die. We must comfort them as much as we are able, but I am sure their information is important."

He left Dmitri and Giorgios to patiently ease the story out of the one man who could still talk coherently.

*****

They returned to the deck looking shaken, and Giorgios went immediately to Talon and told him what they had learned.

The commander of the two dromons had lead the ships on a slow patrol, as there were rumors of pirates, and the two ships had anchored for the night in the harbor of the nearby island.

Before they had left Rodos a Genoese merchant had asked if he could come with them, as he was fearful of sailing on his own. He departed with them when they left Rodos and kept them company for most of the day. According to Romanos, he stayed well over to the east, which he thought was somewhat strange, because that was where the enemy pirates would come from, if they were there at all. It would have been more like a cringing merchantman to be on their seaward side where they could best protect him.

"Did he see the man who came aboard from the Genoese ship?" Talon demanded.

"He told us that he was portly, with a beard and swagger. Typical Latin, just like a Venetian.He came with a very large man as bodyguard," Dimitri said, then Giorgios continued.

"He told us they were Arab ships, and there were many of them —a fleet! Quietly they came in the dark: they sent assassins to board the ships and it was all over before they could do anything."

Privately Talon wondered at the lax sentry-keeping that could have allowed this to happen.

Giorgios clutched Talon by the shoulders. "They have captured the Liquid Fire," he said, anguish in his voice.

"How would they know how to use it?" Talon asked.

"Romanos told us that the Arabs began to cut throats until some men stepped forward. These were beaten to show how to make the equipment work, then they tested it."

"So what happened to his ship? Why would the Arabs sink it?" Nigel asked.

"They didn't. The crew of his ship tried to take it back and nearly succeeded, but then there was an accident with the apparatus on board. It caught fire and then exploded. While the survivors were trying to put the flames out the Arabs jumped overboard and swam to another ship that took them aboard, leaving these people to die."

"Come, we will have another look at these men to see what we can do to ease their pain," Talon said.

They trooped below.

Talon looked down at the groaning men and thought for a moment. "Ask him if he knew which direction the ships might be sailing?"

Dmitri asked the man called Romanos, who shook his head. "I do not know, but here is something strange. There was only one of the fire launchers in the waist of our ship when we came back on deck, I remember that. I do not know where the others went. They might have taken them off during the night, I do not know. There was a lot of noise and movement before we left the bay and many of the crews were taken away."

The other man woke up at this point and shouted something.

"What was that?" Max asked. He looked at the grim expressions around him.

"He said something about treachery. He said...he said they knew where to find them. He is blaming the Genoese." Talon said slowly.

Giorgios shook his head, as though to say this might just be the man's raving.

Talon glanced at Max. "I wonder..."

"We have lost two ships to the Arabs and both had four of our fire devices on them. That means eight of them were stolen! No, only seven, as one went to the bottom with his ship, but this is a catastrophe!" Giorgios wrung his hands in agitation.

"They could wreak havoc with seven different ships each carrying one of the Greek Fire devices. If those naval people had been paying more attention to their business they might not have had this disaster," Talon told Max in French.

"Well it is done now, God help us. What do you want to do, Talon?"

"I want to take our gold and our salt and flee for the Hellespont and get to Constantinople. I fear the worst, but we are not about to pursue an Arab fleet. However we owe it to the Byzantines to inform them that there is indeed a fleet of corsairs abroad and that they now possess the Greek Fire. That should get someone's attention. I pray to God that we can sail undisturbed the rest of the way without running into them."

He turned to Giorgios and resumed in Greek, "Make them as comfortable as you can, Giorgios." He put his hand on the weeping man's thin shoulder. "Stay with him for a while, Dmitri, but come on deck soon, as I want to talk to the crew." Dmitri nodded acknowledgement.

Talon and Max went back on deck and told their companions what they had heard. All three were grim-faced and agreed with

Talon that they should put on full sail. Henry set a course due north. He reckoned that if they did not tarry in island harbors he could get them to the entrance of the Hellespont within a matter of days rather than a week.

They sailed north all that day, and because it was a clear night with bright stars and a moon to illuminate the sea, Henry continued to sail through the night.

During the night the more badly burnt of the two men died. The other man held on, but Talon told Max that he did not give much for his chances. His limited knowledge of wounds and a few diseases had not prepared him for this kind of horror.

It was on the fourth day just before sunset that the *Falcon* sailed past the dark line of a large island on their port bow, which Dmitri called Lemnos. Henry, before handing off the ship to Nigel and going below to get some rest, ordered a change of course slightly towards the northeast. Several hours later one of the lookouts called down softly that he saw many lights ahead. Nigel immediately had the sails furled and sent one of the crew to wake Talon, Max and Henry.

As he came onto the deck, rubbing the sleep from his eyes and followed by Max, Talon realized that there was something wrong. Everyone was very quiet and the tension was palpable. The sails were furled and the ship was wallowing in the water. He made his way onto the top deck where he found Nigel, Guy and Henry having a muttered conversation.

"Why are we stopped, Nigel?" he asked.

"There are lights ahead, Talon," Nigel said in a low voice. "We are not due to sight land for another day at least. I thought to call all of you, as this is very strange." He sounded nervous.

"What do the lookouts say?" Talon asked.

"The lookout thinks it might be a lot of ships clustered together. Many ships, Sir Talon."

"Are you sure?" Talon asked. He felt the apprehension in the air. "Are you thinking that perhaps it might be the Arabs?"

"Yes we do, Talon," Guy said from nearby, "unless the Greeks have sent out a fleet to chase their ships away. But we do not know as yet, if they're coming our way or not."

"We should try to go around them, Talon," Nigel said.

"Have you not seen how many lights there are over there?" Guy said. "Come daylight they will move faster and then we will be seen hanging about on their wing. We cannot out-sail them by going all the way around and then get ahead of them during the night. God help us," he finished.

"How many do you three estimate?" Talon asked.

"Near to fifty I would say," Nigel said.

"I think there are more. I guess at sixty to seventy ships with all those lights. It would take us a day just to sail to the side of that fleet," Guy said.

"I agree with Guy, there are more than fifty ships out there. We need to know who it is and which direction they're sailing," Henry said.

Talon did not like the idea of running into the middle of the corsair fleet, if that was what it was. But it sounded as though it might not even be possible to get around that many ships.

"They are not sailing fast at all despite a good wind. I think they are keeping station for the night, and my guess is that they are going the same way as we," Guy offered.

"They have lamps lit on every mast. That is what we see, but I can also now see lights nearer to the water, which means we're gaining upon them," Henry said.

He was right. Peering forward Talon could now see lights bobbing about near to the surface of the sea. They were quite close. He instinctively checked to see that they had no lights showing. Nigel must have had them put out the moment he saw the other ships.

After a low called discussion with the lookout, Henry established that the ships ahead of them must be sailing northward. And that was indeed the same direction as the *Falcon*.

"If we try to sail through them we will surely be challenged and that will be the end. I for one do not speak Arabic well enough to talk my way past them," Guy said.

"But Talon does, and I do too. Although Talon speaks like an Egyptian," Max said.

That gave Talon an idea. "Max is right, my friends. If this is an Arab fleet bent upon mischief then we have to at least do our best to provide warning. What is the closest port to the entrance of the Hellespont, Henry?"

Dmitri, who had joined them on deck, answered that question immediately. "The city of Abydos is the nearest port to the neck of the Hellespont and to the Greek fleet, if it is on station, Sir Talon. Abydos is on the east side of the divide and very well fortified."

Talon nodded his thanks. "Thanks, Dmitri, that helps. Let us hope it is a Greek fleet, but I fear not. Perhaps we can bluff our way through. We will surely be challenged, but I do speak Egyptian Arabic, and in the dark we may seem to be just another ship of the fleet. It is when we are pulling ahead of the others that we will have the most trouble. This is a fast ship…" He left the rest unsaid and waited for Henry to speak. Henry nodded in the dark but he sounded uncertain.

"It will be a race for our lives if we do make it to the other side of that fleet. It is now only a few hours before first light. There is also the real risk of collision in the dark, and if that happens we will be finished. If we are going to do this thing we must decide now, Sir Talon." His formal address made it clear that Talon had to make the decision for them all. The others all murmured their agreement. There was a silence while he pondered what had to be done. He did not see much of an alternative.

"We could always turn tail and run from sight over the horizon in the opposite direction. We would be safe, but I do not like that idea, as this group of ships might well be trying to surprise the city of Abydos."

"We also know that they now possess the potent weapon of fire, so they can burn any shipping that is not fast enough to escape or seek shelter behind walls," Max pointed out.

"We cannot let that happen." Henry sounded adamant, and Nigel and Guy muttered agreement.

Talon shifted his weight on his feet. He was full of unease but everyone was looking at him; they were trusting to his judgment alone. For the first time he felt the full weight of command and the responsibility for the lives of his companions and the crew on his shoulders. It was not a comforting feeling. He took a deep breath.

"God help us my friends, but I see little choice. We are not cowards and we owe much to our Greek friends. We cannot run away, so we will go forward. Our fate now lies in the hands of God."

There was a collective sigh of acceptance and all of them crossed themselves at this, but to a man they nodded assent. Nigel stated what was on all their minds. "We will do as you say, Sir Talon. I think we are all mad, but I pray that God will be with us. You have led us out of danger before."

Talon warmed to him for saying it. They embraced each other hard with the sober thought of the danger and risk they were about to face; none of them knew if they would survive this ordeal.

"Henry to stay at the helm and guide us; Nigel, you come with me to the bows with runners; and Guy, you stay in the waist with the rowers and the sail crew. Max, you remain with Henry. I will be the only one to respond to any challenge, but Max, if I send a message, you talk in Arabic in a low voice as though issuing commands. Pass the word that no one is to speak at all other than

Max and myself, other than in whispers. All of you are to be armed in case of discovery."

"We should put our lights on. They will become suspicious if we have none at all. See to it, Guy," Henry said.

As he went down the steps to collect his bow, Talon thanked Henry silently for attending to this detail. Henry also ordered Guy to take the sails in so that they were moving at a speed that would bring them up to the other ships just fast enough to overtake them, but not going at so great a speed as to incur suspicion or risk collision. Nigel and Guy got into a discussion as to how orders would be passed to the rowers without giving away the fact that they were Franks.

By now the shipping ahead had become well defined silhouettes against the starlit sky. The word was passed to the crew, who cast incredulous looks at their officers but did not argue. The rowers were sent running to their seats and the men manning the sails stood by for orders. Men who would take the first line in a fight prepared themselves for battle and the crossbow men looked to their weapons. Everyone was taut with the knowledge of danger to come.

Talon retrieved his bow and a quiver full of arrows from the cabin and joined Nigel to make their way forward to the forecastle. As they walked by they saw men with bows, pikes and crossbows crouching against the high walls of the ship's sides where Guy had placed them in case they were needed. Nigel was worried the ships ahead might be lashed together, as was sometimes the case with fleets trying to stay close. The first ships loomed up as the distance between them closed. In the darkness Talon could see they were galleys that looked just like the ones he had seen with the Byzantine navy, and for a split second he hoped that they were Greek, but this was quickly dashed as someone noticed them approaching and called out a challenge.

There was no mistaking the language. At least it was now clear that this was a corsair fleet bent upon mischief.

"Ship that is approaching. Where are you from and what are you doing?"

Talon cupped his hands on either side of his mouth. "*Salaam Aliekom!* We are from Dalmatia and seek the commander. We carry urgent dispatches from the Sultan. Where is the Admiral's ship?"

He was guessing that the inherent obedience to command would inhibit an officer on the ship ahead from taking the initiative and making sure they were who they said they were. He prayed too that the men on the ships would not know where the Sultan might be and challenge his story. There was a long silence during which he could feel himself sweating. The *Falcon* drove ever closer to the other craft.

"*Aliekom Salaam.* What ship are you?"

"We are the *Falcon of the South*. Our mission is urgent." Again there was a silence as though the men on the ship might be discussing their appearance. He felt the tension building up all round him as the men of his crew, not comprehending the words, prepared for the worst.

"You need to move north and then some east, as his Excellency Al Fakhouri's command ship is in that direction. Move carefully! There are many of us and we are close together."

"Allah protect you and bless you. We go forward. Allah be Praised," Talon called back.

At a nod from Talon, Nigel sent the silent *Falcon* past the first two ships. The only sound from his own ship was the slap of the sea on its bows and the hiss of water flowing along its sides, the occasional splash of an oar and the creak of ship's timbers, but all around there was the sound of men at work and the clatter of gear being moved about the other ships' decks. They could hear men calling out as they went about their duties in the night.

"It is as though we have stumbled across a city on the sea. It is a living thing," Nigel whispered.

Talon could even make out the silhouettes of curious men wearing turbans leaning over their sides to peer at them as they went past. The oars were taken in on the vessels but the stench that came out of them told its own story of the slaves chained to the benches.

Nigel breathed a great sigh as they went past; Talon was sure that the stink of the ship brought back terrible memories, even though he said nothing. Then he sent a messenger running silently to tell Henry to alter course slightly to avoid a dense cluster of shipping that was looming out of the dark. Henry guided them toward a gap between two large galleys.

Once again they were challenged. This time Talon used the name provided by the men on the first two ships and again there was a long silence as they digested the information. He could even hear a shout as someone called for a senior officer to come and take charge. They were so close he could hear a conversation taking place on the after deck of the ship on their right, although he could only make out the occasional word.

But then, after what felt like an interminable period during which Talon, now very tense, was sure that enemy archers were being assembled behind their sides waiting for them to come well within range, someone on that ship called over to them in an authoritative voice to pass. Once again they slipped between two large galleys, Talon calling up his thanks and many blessings. He sent a message back to Max to start muttering so that the strained silence on their own ship was broken by what might sound as confident conversation on their afterdeck in Arabic, for all the world as if the steersmen were talking to one another. Nigel again heaved a sigh of relief as he realized that they had passed another hurdle.

They were challenged twice more by sleepy ships' crews and each time Talon used a little more of the information gleaned from a previous encounter to substantiate his story. Each time there was a tense moment as crew members pondered the answers and then finally decided to let them pass. As one ship disappeared into the gloom behind them another vessel would loom to their front. One officer in charge of the watch called over to them as they slid by, "You are too far to the west and need to move more easterly. Have you not been told this before?" His voice was querulous, probably because he had been roused out of his warm bed, but he did not follow it up.

"Yes, you are right of course" Talon called back. "But we need to maneuver and there are many ships. We do not want a collision. We will try for a more open space ahead of us. Allah's blessing upon you for helping us reach our objective."

All this time they had been working the oars when they needed them, but for the most part the sails had taken them through in a rough line from behind the fleet almost to the front. There only remained two ships between them and the open water beyond the fleet. It was a seductive thought that they should make a run for it between the last two ships ahead of them, but caution restrained him. Anything could go wrong at this point and all they needed was a little distance and then Henry could show a clean pair of heels. He steadied his breathing and waited for the next challenge.

As they approached, men on the ship to their left had been alerted to their arrival by the calls between them and the other ships, for they were clustered on the afterdeck waiting for them. But these men carried torches, which lit up the sea all around the back of the ship. Talon realized with a sinking feeling that they were about to sail right into this bright patch of water where the people on the other deck would have a good look at them.

"We need to stay clear of those torches and the light. They will see quickly enough who we are if we do not avoid them," Nigel urged. His two remaining runners were fidgeting with concern.

Again the questioning call and again Talon called back. Then he remembered something he should have thought of earlier. He wore no turban and neither did anyone else on the ship; it would be noticed.

"*Salaam Aliekom*. We carry dispatches for His Excellency Al Fakhouri. Allow us to pass as we come from Cairo on an urgent mission."

He could see turbaned men holding torches high and peering across at them over the dark water that glinted in the torchlight, rising and falling in the swell. He had an uneasy feeling that they were suspicious and not about to let them pass without some serious questioning first.

"Pull in your sail and explain where you are from. You are way off course for the command ship. You must have been told this before."

"We have been told, but there are so many ships gathered so closely together I have decided to go to the front and then change course when we are clear of other shipping, *Insha Allah* it will be safer to do so."

There was more shouting and calling and yet more men gathered on the already full afterdeck of the ship with which they were now almost parallel. Curious people were watching from the waist of the ship.

"What is the name of your ship?" The query was abrupt.

"*Falcon of the South*," Talon called up.

"I know of no ship with that name, but you may pass. Take care not to get in our way."

Talon breathed a sigh of relief and was about to turn to Nigel to pass along the information when there came a great scream from the back of their ship. All eyes swiveled to the entrance of the cabin where the sailor Romanos, who had survived the burning was standing. He was screaming and pointing at the ship across the dark waters and shouting.

"It is them! They are the killers who burned us. God curse them all!" He was quite naked; the ghastly burns across his face and chest were captured in the flickering light thrown out by the torches. Talon froze; the man was screaming in Greek for all to hear.

Talon swung his gaze back to the other ship. There was consternation as they began to realize what was happening on the ship passing them by. Several pointed, beckoning their comrades to come and look, and then men began shouting and running about. The alarm was sounded.

Henry with great presence of mind began to shout orders to Guy to get the sails fully down, and Guy in turn screamed at the rowers to get busy. As their oars were already out there was no delay and the water churned as they dipped and pulled with all their might.

The ship lurched and surged forward as the wind caught the sails and they began to gain speed as they passed by the last two ships. The crew of the ship on their port side had realized that all was not well and they too had sounded the alarm. Torches began to appear on their deck as men ran to illuminate the water in between the vessels. As Talon raced back to the after deck he noticed Max and Giorgios had seized the burnt sailor and dragged him back inside the cabin, but the damage had been done. They were in a race for their lives.

Talon cleared the steps to the after deck in three strides and turned to watch as Henry, calm as ever, guided the ship clear of the Arab vessels toward the open sea. They all ducked as arrows whispered overheard and slammed into the wood of the sides and the floor of the deck. Talon drew his own bow and sped an arrow into the cluster of men in the waist of the ship on their starboard side. A man fell with a scream and the rest scattered for cover.

But other men with bows on the Arab ships were in formation and the hail of arrows increased. Several of their sailors were hit and fell crying, to be dragged into the cover of the ship's side, the rest of the exposed crew fled for cover. Their own archers began to fire back with good effect. Both crossbows and long bows twanged, and the arrows and bolts began to take men down who made good targets in the light of the torches. Someone must have realized this as the torches were rapidly extinguished. One man had the idea of throwing his torch across the water at the *Falcon*. It fell with a hiss into the water not far from the side, and then others began to do the same.

Talon drew and fired at one man who was about to try. The arrow struck him in the chest and he fell over backwards, dropping his torch on his own deck. There was a brief panic as the crew frantically put out the beginning of a fire, and then the *Falcon* was moving out of range. Talon drew and fired his arrows until his quiver was empty, inflicting damage where he could. He wondered if fire might be used against them and prayed that it did not occur to the enemy to start shooting fire arrows.

Then Talon noticed something that made his blood run cold. Men on the starboard Arab ship were running towards a contraption in the waist of their ship and feverishly preparing something. Protruding out from the side was one of the dreadful tubes of the Byzantine weapon. He gripped Nigel by the shoulder and pointed.

Nigel stared and then breathed. "Dear God! They have the Greek Fire! We must flee!" he yelled. Henry shouted down to Guy and the rowers to pull for their lives and the crew to tighten sail.

The *Falcon* leaped forward and began to draw past, but the frantic activity on the Arab ship intensified. Whips were cracking and Talon could see men pumping something up and down, and then others heaved the apparatus so that the tube was pointing directly at their ship. Although they were a good twenty yards from the other ship and gradually increasing the distance Talon feared the worst.

The next thing he saw was a jet of flame spout from the nozzle of the tube and fly across the water at about deck height towards their ship. He was mesmerized by the spectacle of the liquid flame curling in a deadly arc towards them. All the ships nearby and the faces of the men clustered on their decks were lit up in an eerie glow.

Somehow, perhaps because of the haste in preparation by the Arab crew, the flame fell just short of their ship and dropped into the sea, but a few gobs of flame landed on the deck where they sizzled fiercely, burning into the wood. Talon looked at the water between the ships. A line of flame burned on the sea, hissing and bubbling before finally disappearing below the surface and going out in a cloud of steam.

In desperation one of the sailors on the *Falcon* threw a canvas bucket of sea water over the stinking puddles of flame, but they only flared higher, hissing like a hundred malevolent snakes. The flames reached for the bottom of the sails. Men screamed with fear and cowered away from the intense heat. To Talon it was as though the Devil had thrown his evil fire at them and his stomach lurched. They had no defense against this terrifying weapon. Then Nigel with great presence of mind seized some heavy sailcloth and threw it over the largest puddle of fire and jumped on the cloth, stamping and yelling a stream of curses. He then screamed at the petrified crew to do the same with the other blobs of fire that were igniting the deck.

They leapt to do his bidding and smothered the other flames in the same manner, realizing that they were doomed if they failed.

Then Max yelled from the afterdeck and pointed. Another terrible jet of flame was being pumped out of the tube. They all watched in frozen horror as the flaming jet arced out towards them, reaching for their ship like some live tentacle of fire. But this time it fell well short and they drew away ever faster, the light wind in their raised sails taking the *Falcon* out of harm's way. Still Guy roared at the rowers to pull for their lives, and the sweating, gasping men heard him and pulled. Their oars churned up the water and the ship fled out into the open sea.

*****

After what felt an eternity during which all on the top deck held their breath, they were well free of the two ships and out into what appeared to be clear water. Their sails were taut and the oars were driving up and down as the rowers worked furiously to gain as much distance as they could from what was now a thoroughly agitated enemy.

"We have a hornets' nest back there and they are going to come after us, Henry. You should get us as far away as you can," Talon called.

Talon knew full well that pursuit was inevitable. He could not make out individual ships anymore but assumed it would be at least the two they had just left behind that would follow, with perhaps more behind them. He saw a red burning flame arch high into the sky. It seemed to pause at its highest point and then plunge back into darkness, swallowed by the sea. Talon could not tell if it had been a signal or a missile meant for them, but it was followed by several others. And yet nothing reached their ship, and their lead steadily increased as wind and the rowers bore them swiftly on.

There was elation on the *Falcon*. Henry grinned at Talon and Max. "I did not think we would make it. God help me," he gasped, " but I thought we were finished when the fire came. Praise be to God and that crazy bugger Nigel!" The relief in his voice was pronounced.

Talon found Nigel in the waist standing over several hands' width of charred deck with some of the crew nearby. He looked up as Talon arrived.

"This is the Devil's fire, Talon. Look, it is still hot! Bring water —we can use it now." He ordered the men nearby. They hastened to obey. He showed Talon the burned rag of the sailcloth. "We were lucky," he said.

"How did you know what to do, Nigel?" Talon asked.

"I did not know, Talon. I just remembered that water thrown on burning fat is a bad thing so I just tried the sailcloth. Thank God it worked, but I did not know for sure that it would. If they had struck us with the whole jet of flame we would not be here now, of that I am sure."

Talon wanted to embrace Nigel his relief was so great, but instead he clapped him on the shoulder. "You saved the ship Nigel. We owe our lives to your quick thinking and I shall not forget it."

*****

Henry directed the ship into the night using the fading stars as his guide. He told Talon that he was fairly confident that he could outpace the enemy given their lead.

"But we have surely stirred them up." Nigel said, as he stood with the others looking back over the ship's wake.

"I did not believe we could get through that mass of shipping, but God protected us," Max said with relief. "Nigel my friend, you showed great courage back there."

"I thank God for it," Nigel said, embarrassed by the thanks from his friends, "But I thank Talon too. He talked us through the fleet!"

"You must have done a convincing job back there, or we would all be in chains right now," Henry said as he slapped Talon on the shoulder.

"They will come after us with their fastest boats, my friends. Henry, you will have to keep us moving as fast as you can all night and tomorrow too until we arrive at Abydos."

"Guy will pace the rowers, but we might all have to take a turn at an oar. I shall keep us on this course until we see land. It will be a race, that is for sure," Henry told him.

"I will willingly go to an oar when you ask me," Max said.

"I too," Talon agreed. "But first I need to see how our passenger is doing."

He found the man lying on a pallet in the cabin. The smell was noxious, for the corpse of the other man was still there wrapped in a canvas. There had been no time to deal with the body before now, but Talon realized that they would have to bury the man at sea as soon as it was dawn. The sailor was weeping and moaning with the pain of his wounds while Giorgios tried to comfort him.

"He did not realize what he was doing back there, Sir Talon," Giorgios said, looking up when Talon entered.

"We were at the end of our luck in any case, Giorgios. Tell him to live and we will get him to a physician as soon as we arrive in Abydos. I do not know what to give him to ease his pain. We do not even have the gum of a poppy to aid him, nor the mandrake. Keep giving him water when he needs it."

"Will we be safe, Sir Talon?" Giorgios looked frightened. Talon looked at him. Despite being a good and confident trader Giorgios was not a warrior and did not know how to deal with the dangers they were facing.

"With God's help we will make it to Abydos, but they will chase us, Giorgios. Still, Henry is an excellent pilot and we have a good crew. I am sure we will be fine," he assured the agent. "Pray hard," he added.

Talon took his cloak off a hook then went on deck to see how they were progressing. It was quiet except for the rush of water at the bows, a slight keening of the wind in the rigging, the creaks of the ship, and muttered conversations on the afterdeck. Henry had stood down most of the men and allowed the rowers to rest.

"The wind is well behind us and we're making good speed, Talon," Henry explained. "I want to rest them till we really need them, which will be in the morning, I am sure of it."

"It seems a pity that we cannot change course to deceive our enemy, but there is only one place to go," Talon said.

"We're fleeing into what seems to me a trap, Talon. We might be lucky and come across a Greek warship, but there is land to east and west, and we are surely the mouse now."

Talon thought that if they did run into some Greek warships, the fleet behind them would make short work of them. With their numbers and the new weapon they possessed they could sweep aside a patrol. The first light of dawn was in the east. Talon glanced back to the south but could see no sign of pursuit.

"We need to get some sleep while we can, Talon, you as well. Guy will stand helm while we sleep," Henry told him.

Talon nodded and wrapped his cloak about him, then went to lean against the side of the ship. In spite of the danger he was asleep within moments.

*****

He awoke abruptly several hours later, feeling stiff and cold. The day was well advanced and the wind had intensified. He shivered. Even though he lacked nautical prowess, he sensed that the wind might have changed direction and the sea was rougher than before. He clambered to his feet and walked unsteadily across the deck to stand next to Guy, who was still on duty.

Guy nodded and gave him a grin. Talon was reminded of a predator about to sink its teeth into its victim.

"Good morning, Talon. Look over there." Guy pointed back along their wake. Talon turned and a ship about a mile away. Without doubt it was an Arab warship and it was in hot pursuit.

"Now look over there." Guy pointed off to the west. Talon followed his pointing finger and saw a thick black line rising out of the horizon. Ahead of them the sea had changed color to a darker green while the waves, although still relatively small, now possessed white crests.

"Notice the wind has changed?" Guy asked. "We are in for a tempest, and if my judgment is correct it will be a bad one."

Talon's thoughts went immediately to the salt that was stored in the makeshift cabins. "How will we protect the cargo, Guy?"

"There will be no rowing in this if the storm hits. The sea is already getting too rough. This is going to be about seamanship. So we seal up the openings below and do our best to protect the salt. It would be a pity to lose that after all the hard work." He grinned again.

Talon looked to where their destination lay.

"Will we make it to land before the storm strikes, Guy?" Talon was apprehensive. His last experience with a storm had not ended well.

"It will be a race. And then there are those behind us." He jerked his thumb at the pursuing ship.

"I see only one of them."

"Thank God for it. I would have thought they would send a pack of after us. Perhaps they just want to stop us and take us back. But I for one will not be going back to that life." Guy scowled, and then he raised his voice. "Pay attention there, John!" he admonished the steersman. "Do not let the ship yaw or I will have your hide! I want to see those sails so tight that you can play a drum on them." He ignored Talon as he shouted down into the waist to the men there and ordered them to trim the sails. There was a rush of men to comply. Everyone knew their fate should they lose this race.

Talon left him to it and went below, to find something to eat and to see to the salt.

Roll on, thou deep and dark blue ocean-roll!
Ten thousand fleets sweep over thee in vain;
Man marks the earth with ruin-his control
Stops with the shore;-upon the watery plain
The wrecks are all thy deed, nor doth remain
A shadow of man's ravage, save his own,
When for a moment, like a drop of rain,
He sinks into thy depths with bubbling groan,
Without a grave, unknell'd, uncoffin'd, and unknown.

Lord Byron

Chapter 22

The Storm

Later in the morning, Talon and Guy were joined on the afterdeck by Max and Nigel,, and then Henry came up on deck rubbing his eyes.

"I cannot sleep with all that moaning going on below," He complained, referring to the burned Greek sailor.

This reminded Talon that they needed to dispose of the dead man. They brought his body up on deck, tied it into a canvas wrap, placed some stones in the sack, and then dropped the body overboard with a splash and an intoned prayer. It was a hurried and depressing event that only added to the feeling that they were hunted and that there was no time for niceties.

They ate a cold breakfast of mutton and goat's cheese, which did little to warm anyone. Henry, Guy and Nigel spent some time in a huddle talking about the oncoming storm. Henry took over from Guy, called the relief steersmen to attend him on the afterdeck, and sent Guy below to snatch some sleep. Everyone kept a sharp lookout and the men shivering on the top of the two masts were ordered to watch ahead and behind for any sign of danger. The after lookout confirmed that there was only the one ship, but that she had gained on them since the dawn. Indeed the ship was now clearly visible, although too far away to see any activity on the decks. Talon and Max stood staring back at it.

"We can only pray to God that it is not carrying any of those infernal fire machines," Max muttered as he huddled into his cloak. He looked a little pale.

"My guess is that they will not, that they cannot afford to spend that effort on one ship. They only have a few machines now that they lost the one we were told about. They will keep what is left close and use it for a surprise attack when they reach their intended objective," Talon said. He looked toward the west and noticed the ominous black line was much closer now. The *Falcon* was beginning to pitch and roll with water sluicing over the front despite their high prow. Henry trimmed the sails to adjust for the change in wind direction, but the ship was heeling over at an angle as she sped forward.

"I fear for our cargo, Max."

"My word, Talon!" Max said with a wan grin. "You have become a merchantman, I swear!"

"I am just worried about our responsibility to the house of Kalothesos, Max," Talon said a little too sharply. Then he grinned as he realized how pompous that sounded.

"I am sorry, Max. Perhaps you are right, but I have enjoyed the enterprise and would be sorry to lose what we have gained on their behalf. I fear that I shall never be a good sailor, however," he said, grabbing for a rail as the *Falcon* lurched into a wave.

Max gave a feeble laugh. "Nor I, Talon, and you are right. It would be a pity to lose our cargo now when we are so close to home. Pray God that the storm prevents the Arab from harming us, but that it does not harm us in the process."

They watched the menacing clouds scudding across a lowering sky. Talon could see isolated squalls of rain moving eastward and knew that they would be sailing in among them. He was fearful of their effect upon this small ship of theirs, but Henry was calm enough.

They had just sighted the low rise of land ahead and the lookouts had pointed out the gap that indicated the Hellespont when the first squall struck. Henry had been watching for it and altered course by a few degrees then held the ship steady while the rain slashed down at them, almost instantly soaking everyone on deck. Guy, their cargo in mind, had ensured that the hatches were locked down, leaving only one access for the crew to use as they came and went below decks. Nigel had gone below and had made sure that the oar holes were sealed with whatever they could find to plug them.

The storm swept in at great speed and a gust of wind laid them over at such an angle that Talon had to hang onto the railing to avoid sliding down into the steersmen. He glanced at Max and read the same fear in his eyes. Were they to be shipwrecked again?

"I hate the sea!" Max shouted over the wind.

Talon agreed with him and wished that he would never have to go to sea again, but knew he had little choice in the matter.

Talon stared back into the haze of rain at the dim shape of the Arab ship and wondered how that crew was faring. It had gained on them as they headed for the Hellespont. The Arab ship was now only about five hundred paces away, rising and falling in the troughs of the waves, its bow throwing up huge plumes of spray as it chased after them. He noticed it had more sail than the *Falcon* could muster. Everyone had made preparations for a fight: Talon had ordered the archers, both longbow and crossbowmen, to stand ready. The ship's officers, Nigel and Guy, were driving the crew to lash down everything they could, while Henry's main preoccupation was to get the very best out of the *Falcon* and gain the safety of Abydos before they were engaged.

Giorgios had informed Talon that the port was well guarded and the navy had warships stationed there, but he did not know how many.

"If we can get there in time we can take shelter under the walls inside the harbor, Sir Talon," he said hopefully. "Our pursuers will not dare to come into the harbor or they will be destroyed by fire from the walls."

Talon took some comfort from that, but he was uneasy at how quickly the other ship had caught up with them under the impetus of heavy sail and the rowing of its slaves. Henry and Nigel had been adamant about not using oars in these seas.

"We will take on more water than we can manage to bail out and tire the men, which will do us no good when we really need them, Talon. And they will not have much effect on our progress. Better to make the best use of our sails and hope to God that we can gain entry in time, or that the storm prevents them from catching up with us," Nigel had informed him.

Talon's attention was forced back to the *Falcon* as another gust of wind struck their port almost at right angles to the ship. Once again the ship heeled over and the starboard sides were forced almost underwater. The men crouching in the scuppers crossed themselves and sent anxious looks at the after deck. The ship righted itself slowly and shook off the water that was pouring out through the scuppers, taking with it some loose gear that had been improperly lashed down. Ropes and blocks crashed into the side of the ship. Guy shouted at his men to recapture the gear and lash it down tighter, and so they plunged on.

Now the troughs between the waves were deeper and the *Falcon* climbed up large waves to pivot dizzyingly before plunging down the other side and bury the breast of its high prow with the open beaked *Falcon*'s head into the next wall of water.

Then the ship would repeat the motion as the bows rose again till the cluttered foredeck was all that Talon could see ahead of him as it climbed higher and higher up the wave and obscured his view of the land ahead. He began to feel horribly queasy and lurched to the side downwind to empty his stomach overboard into the green, froth-mottled waters below. He found he had good company. Max was being very sick at the same time. His normally weathered face appeared chalk white. He gave Talon a sickly grimace then bent over the rail again, retching. Talon looked back at Henry, who waved at him and grinned. Talon scowled back, envying him for seeming so at home on a pitching, rolling ship like this.

Talon wondered how they were going to fight the Arabs while in this condition. Drawing and aiming a bow in this storm was almost pointless. Then a flash of lightning lit up the sky, followed by a deafening crack of thunder, and the rainfall intensified. Dashing the rain from his eyes and hunching into his sodden cloak, Talon looked behind Henry to see that the enemy ship had gained even more upon them and was now only a few hundred paces away. He could just make out turbaned figures on the front staring impassively ahead. They were good sailors, and they were keen to come alongside for a fight.

"They are not shy about putting on their sail! They are reckless about it!" Henry shouted. "That is why they have caught up with us."

"Can we not do more?" Talon called back, wiping his mouth and sidling past Max who was still leaning over the rail, but he already knew the answer.

"No! If this gets any worse we will have to take in our sails no matter what or we will lose a mast."

As Henry said this, Nigel yelled down to some of the men crouching in the waist. "He is coming alongside the port side—be ready!"

"This man is coming after us at all costs. He is mad!" Max shouted to Talon over the howling wind.

Men scuttled over to the side where they expected the Arabs to launch their attack. Those who possessed cloaks tried to protect their bowstrings from the rain but it was in vain. Everyone watched as the other ship surged towards them. Quite suddenly it was almost parallel with the *Falcon* and arrows began to fly. They were wildly inaccurate but they forced people to get their heads down. Both ships were plunging and rolling in the agitated seas with the wind howling in the rigging and tearing at clothing and the stinging rain slashing down in torrents. Lightning flashed again, making the men on the afterdeck flinch. It was followed immediately by a crash of thunder that split the air above them with a loud cracking and tearing sound, making everyone cower with fear.

The sporadic exchange of arrows continued but it was very ineffective. While Max stood beside Henry and his steersmen with his large shield ready to protect them from enemy arrows, Talon, still fighting his nausea, stood braced against the rail on the afterdeck and shot his arrows at the steersmen on the opposite deck, now a scant fifty paces away. Although his arrows could easily bridge that distance they went wide because of the pitching and rolling of the *Falcon*. He did not see any of the other archers' arrows find their marks, and the Arab bows were not as powerful, so many of their arrows merely struck the side of the *Falcon* or went into the sea.

Men began to adjust their aim and more arrows fell on the decks. The *Falcon*'s archers' bolts were telling despite the crazy rolling and pitching of both ships. At times the ships rose in unison, at others one would be plunging into a wave while the other was rising from a trough.

It was during one of those times when both ships were heaving together with sea water pouring off their decks that Talon finally managed to strike a target he had been trying many times to hit: a man with a large turban who was standing with the group of men gathered near the steering oar. It looked like a mortal blow and appeared to generate much consternation among that crew, as men ran from all over the after deck to cluster around his fallen body.

Then a bolt fired from the waist of the *Falcon* struck one of the two steersmen in the side. He was thrown back into the cluster of men standing and crouching about the other fallen man, which created even more confusion. Henry had been watching and he called over to Talon.

"Good work! But look over there! We are only half a mile from the water breaker of the city. God help us now!"

Talon spun around to squint into the driving rain. Again fear gripped his stomach, and the Arabs were forgotten as he stared at what lay ahead. They were so close! In his preoccupation with the other ship he had not been paying any attention to their progress. How they had come to be this close to the port he had no idea, but there it was and it gave him no comfort to contemplate the sight.

They were pointing directly toward a line of rocks upon which rows of waves were crashing, sending spray high into the air. Talon shot a fearful look at Henry, but the seaman was concentrating all his attention on piloting the ship, leaving the battle to him.

ThenTalon heard faint screams of alarm from the other ship. Without enough men to control it the steering oar had shifted with an adverse affect. The ship yawed and twisted, turning in an angle that sent its bows almost at right angles to the wind. Talon watched as men rushed to the vacant steering oar to try and correct the situation but they were moments too late. To make matters worse a flurry of arrows struck yet another man who fell back clutching his chest. Ignoring the menace of arrows the Arabs at the steering oar fought desperately to bring their ship around. The courageous men had nearly regained control when a another squall hissed in and struck both ships.

Talon hung onto the railing, horrified to see one of their own crossbowmen fall from the lookout's position at the top of the mast. He watched as the body passed by with a scream to plunge into the foaming sea between both ships. He disappeared without a trace.

Then they all heard a great crack which made everyone return their gaze back to the Arab ship. The center mast was leaning over. The sail was bellied but no longer held by its lashings and now it flew free like a monstrous banner. The other sail suddenly had to take the strain of the whole ship and before the Franks' astonished eyes it ripped and tore into rags, some of which flapped away into the wind like strange birds of the sea fleeing the howling wind. The Arab boat was transformed in one moment from a predatory instrument of war to a wallowing wooden raft that was about to be destroyed upon the rocks ahead.

The *Falcon* had been on a more easterly course so all the wind achieved was to drive the ship harder toward the same rocks. Guy instantly saw what to do and bellowed at the crew to reef both sails so that they were able to slow their headlong pace and approach the entrance at a more controlled speed. Henry waved his approval of the command from the after deck.

The Arab ship was doomed. The crew was frantically hacking at the tangle of rigging with axes and swords in a desperate attempt to save what was left of their ship and their lives. All the while they were still harassed by bolts and arrows from the *Falcon*. These were beginning to have a deadly effect. Men were falling even as they strove to save their own ship.

Talon gazed at the once fine cruiser that was about to be destroyed.

He leaned close to Henry. "Could we not save them?" he shouted

Henry gaped at him. "Those bastards are the Saracen, Talon! Why would you want to save them?" His words were being blown away in the wind. Talon leaned even closer. "They're finished, there is no need for them to be crushed to death on the rocks. Could we not try to tow them?"

Henry gave him a look that said he was completely mad but he shouted for Guy and Nigel to come to the afterdeck. They staggered along the heaving deck and stopped in front of Henry.

"Talon wants to try and save the Saracens..." Henry bellowed.

They too gawped at him.

"We would have the ship for ourselves," Talon shouted.

"If we do this crazy thing we need to do it now. We are but a few hundred paces from the entrance and any mistake will kill us all," Nigel bellowed.

"The wind is right behind us," Guy shouted over the keening wind, "and that ship will fall behind unless we throw a rope and bind them to us."

As if to emphasize Guy's words the wind and the rain eased but maintained a westerly direction. They were closer than ever to the other ship, which was now devoid of its mass of rigging and one mast, leaving a stump about the height of a man, and it was wallowing lower in the sea. Clearly the ship had taken on a lot of water. There were faint wails coming from the lower deck as the slaves realized they were near to death from drowning. There were many bodies lying on the deck, and the afterdeck was almost clear of men other than the cringing steersmen who could not leave their position despite the murderous stream of arrows from the Franks' ship.

Then Talon saw what he hoped to see. A soaked and bedraggled man staggered onto the crowded afterdeck of the Arab ship and two of them held high a patch of sail that blew out white for all to see. The captain of the ship was surrendering. Standing next to them was another man in good cut cloth, his armor gleamed and his turban even at this distant showed it was of some expensive material. Although he too must have been soaked to the skin from the pelting rain it was as though he disdained the weather. His young swarthy face stared back at Talon, defiance written all over it even as he accepted that he had lost the race and now faced death on his stricken ship.

"Henry, we shall take them into the port. Do what you can to save that ship!" he ordered. "Guy, have the men stop their shooting. They have surrendered."

His companions, albeit reluctantly, went to work; and as their ship moved past the Arab vessel thin ropes with rocks tied to them were thrown to the few members of the Arab crew who were left on deck, who eagerly caught them and hauled them in as fast as they could. The waves were still as high as ever and it looked like an impossible task to Talon, but once his companions were agreed they leapt into action. Orders were shouted and men came running up the ladder to the afterdeck hauling the end of a large cable of about a hand's spread in thickness behind them. This was tied to a weighted rope that was thrown across to the other ship, then the cable was hauled across the choppy waters, and another two cables followed.

The Arabs hastened to bind these to the foremast so that the towing could begin. It appeared to take forever to complete this task, and all the while everyone was watching with fearful eyes the gap in the rocks come closer and the monstrous columns of spray tossed into the air on either side. It was going to take all of Henry's seamanship to pull this off.

Talon muttered a prayer and wondered if he had not condemned them all to a watery death. He could tell that all the crew of the *Falcon* were aware of the fearsome end they were facing if there was a mistake, and he waited with bated breath for the first terrifying and final rending crash of the ship upon the rocks. He glanced at Henry and then down at Guy, prepared to relay commands to the rowers who were waiting tense and frightened in the dark for orders to pull when needed.

They felt a significant tug throughout the ship, and the cable that ran across the afterdeck became suddenly taut and hummed like a harp string as it took up the strain of the dead weight of the vessel behind them. Then the other cables did the same. Talon jumped aside and watched the cables, apprehensive that they might snap at any moment, but they held. The *Falcon* seemed to stop in its path for an instant and everyone held their breath. Then they began to sense movement in both ships. Guy brought the main sail down enough for it to catch the wind, which seized it and snapped it full. Then everyone held their breath again as the frightened steersmen, with Henry calling out orders, guided the ship to point at the middle of the sea break.

Men were praying out loud at this point, but most like Talon were frozen where they stood. The ships rushed into the foaming, spume-filled gap in the rocks. Henry's shouted commands were relayed to Guy, who bellowed down to Nigel. Oars moved up and down on one side or the other. Terrified sailors hauled the sail in, as the *Falcon*, with the vessel wallowing along directly behind, moved inexorably into the gap between the fearsome black rocks that stuck out of the sea like dragon's teeth waiting to devour them They were committed now, and all prayed fervently for God's help.

Talon and Max stood helpless and terrified on the afterdeck well out of Henry's way and away from the three cables that ran as straight as iron rods along the deck and out to the other ship. The roar of the seas crashing on the rocks on either side thundered in their ears and the spray flew like a mist all around them. The ship was drawn into the rush of water directly in the middle of the maelstrom swirling about the entrance, then they were swept through, as though sailing down fast-flowing river rapids. The oars were raised and men shouted in relief. Talon shot a glance back at the other vessel and gasped as it lurched through the opening. He saw that the captain had managed to bring his own oars to bear and thus ensured that his ship stayed precisely behind them and was therefore safe from the rocks. Both ships lurched into the choppy but much calmer waters of the outer harbor of the city of Abydos.

Men all around them were screaming with relief, crossing themselves and calling Hail Marys, raising their hands to the darkened, gray heavens above with unrestrained joy. Talon danced over the cables and pounded Henry on the back. Henry had tears in his eyes as he too crossed himself.

"I did not think we would make it through, but we did! I shall burn candles to all the saints by the bushel when we get back to the city!" he shouted as he and Max pounded one another and the equally relieved steersmen on their backs.

They were not done, however; there was still the task of finding good anchorage, and then they would have to deal with the Arab ship now in their possession. Talon wanted more than anything to board the other vessel and make sure of that.

Henry asked one more thing from the rowers, and that was to take them to the inner harbor. It was laborious work, as the dead weight of the other vessel held them back and Henry was loath to put too much sail on the booms as the wind was as fierce as ever. Yet the rain was easing, and they could now clearly see the curious people on the walls above them. After almost half an hour of hard work they were finally abreast of the fortifications, and Giorgios was calling up to the officers. The officers sent messengers running off, and the signal came to allow them into the calm of the inner harbor.

"You can anchor in that space near to the wall and that jetty," an armored figure shouted down to them.

The inner harbor was full of shipping, most of them refugees from the storm. Large cargo ships bumped alongside galleys from Pisa and Genoa. And there were indeed three warships in the harbor, including a *Chelandios* dromon, a much larger ship than the *Falcon* that could transport horses, as well as two small fast *Galleas* dromons the same size as the *Falcon*, battened down and riding up against their moorings.

Talon breathed a sigh of relief when he saw those ships. He wanted to talk to their commanders as soon as possible. But first they had to ensure that the Arab vessel could be salvaged. He waited impatiently as Henry, with Guy and Nigel assisting him, took The *Falcon* to the designated location and dropped anchor.

Tired though he was, Talon and Max, with Giorgios, some archers, and some well armed sailors, dropped into the lowered boat and were rowed across the short gap to the side of the Arab galley. Despite the strong wind, the stink of the ship made them wrinkle their noses in disgust. Two of the men had been galley slaves and muttered angrily.

"Do nothing without my orders," Talon said sharply.

Max reinforced the command. "Stay near and say nothing. This is Talon's work, men."

They clambered onto the deck of the ship, to be met by the young man who had stared across at Talon earlier in the afternoon.

On closer inspection he looked exhausted, with large hollows under his eyes and a pinched look around his mouth, and there was blood on the sleeve of his fine but soaked tunic. He stepped toward Talon with his sword still in its scabbard and presented it hilt first.

"I am Aarif Mejid, the second officer of this ship. I surrender the ship into your charge."

He was attempting to speak Greek, so Talon immediately said, "*Salaam Aliekom*. Peace be with you, Aarif Mejid. We can speak Arabic, as I am familiar with it."

The young man's dark features expressed surprise as he regarded Talon from dark deep-set eyes.

"*Aliekom Salaam*, Sir. You speak our language just like an Egyptian! My compliments. Alas, my captain is dead from his wounds and cannot pay his respects to you. I am the sole officer left, so it is my unpleasant duty to surrender the ship to you. May I enquire as to your name?" he said as Talon took the sword from him.

Talon wondered if it had been the captain he had killed with his arrow earlier but deemed it senseless to go into that now.

"I am Sir Talon de Gilles, Knight of the Templars. This is my Sergeant, Max Bauersdorf." He indicated Max nearby, dressed in his soaked Templar uniform. "I regret the death of your captain, Aarif. I shall try to help you with the authorities that will be here quite soon. Your crew I cannot do much for, but perhaps we can arrange a ransom for you?"

Aarif looked relieved. "You are Templars? I thought you were Greeks." He shrugged. "God's will. My life is in your hands, Sir Talon."

"I need your word that you will not try to escape while we are here on this ship."

It was very clear that should he try, Aarif would not get very far. He glanced around, then shrugged. "I give my word. Will you see to my wounded?"

"I shall talk to the authorities and ask for a physician to visit them."

Talon asked Max to take Aarif down to the cabin, place a guard at the door, and to stay with him until the business of dealing with the remaining crew and wounded men was completed. He took Max aside just before they left.

"See what you can glean from him, Max, why they were where they were and their ultimate destination. We might have to move quickly and I need to know."

Max nodded without saying anything and escorted their prisoner below.

Talon remained on deck with Giorgios, waiting for the local authorities to arrive. He glanced down at the sword, then eased it half way out of its jewel encrusted, gold inlaid scabbard. It was a magnificent blade, slightly curved along its slim length, made of very fine Damascus steel. He decided to keep it. Aarif Mejid did not sound as though he was from Egypt, so perhaps he was from Syria. One way or the other, there might be a good ransom to be had.

*****

It was only a matter of time before a boatload of Greek soldiers with an officer in charge bumped alongside the captured ship and clambered aboard. The young Greek officer, splendidly dressed in an expensive tunic and decorated breast plate, with a jewel encrusted belt and scabbard, glanced around the wreckage and then at the small cluster of Arabs standing disconsolately next to the stump of the main mast, surrounded by Franks holding pikes.

He introduced himself as Leontios, and a *Komes*.

Giorgios explained in a low tone for Talon's benefit, "This means he is in charge of about three hundred men…"

Leontios sounded not a little pompous and stared about him in a proprietary fashion, almost ignoring the people standing before him.

Talon asked in Greek, his tone curt. "My name is Sir Talon de Gilles, Knight of the Templars. Do you know an officer named Nikoporus?"

"Indeed I do. We have played *tzykanion* together before, until I was sent to this shit hole. Where are you from and how do you know him?" The young man was curious now.

Talon laughed and said, "I too have played *tzykanion* with him, and on his side, fortunately for me. But we have important news that concerns not only this ship but also a great danger approaching this city."

The whole attitude of Leontios changed in an instant. He gave a short but polite bow to Talon and exclaimed, "Niko is a great player! If you played on his side then you must also be a good player. He is somewhat particular in that regard! I apologize, Sir Talon. I had not realized you knew him. Now what is this about danger to this city?"

In a few short sentences Talon explained the circumstances of their arrival and described the fleet lurking out in the delta of the

Hellespont. He made it clear he did not know its whereabouts due to the storm but suspected that it was not far behind. Giorgios confirmed Talon's story to make sure there was no misunderstanding.

Immediately Leontios was all business, his eyes wide with concern. "This is very serious, and I must inform my commander. We watched what was going on out there at sea. In spite of the rain we could see much from the towers, and it looked insane; I dare say you will fill in the details. I would like to deal with them now," he indicated the prisoners, "and then you should accompany me to the garrison commander. He will want to know this information as soon as possible. I shall also send messengers to the ships' captains and ask them to be present."

He indicated the prisoners again. "Is this all that is left of the crew?"

"No, there are the galley slaves, but I want to talk to them first and see who are from my people. I will keep them."

Leontios looked uncertain for a moment, but the other news was so serious that he did not press the point and claim them as prisoners too. Talon breathed an inward sigh of relief. He would need a crew.

"Do what you have to do, Sir Talon, but as soon as you are done please report to the tower over there, he pointed, "and you will be escorted to the palace of the garrison commander, Meletios, our *Phalangarches* in charge of the city. I shall leave an escort for you at the tower."

Giorgios informed Talon that a *Phalangarches* was in charge of about three thousand troops. This gave Talon some pause, as the flotilla approaching them surely carried far more men than that.

Leontios saluted then took his leave, and soon the heavily guarded prisoners were being ferried off in boats. Their wails of fear and grief were muted by the wind, which picked up again, and once more the rain began to pour down. Talon and Giorgios pulled their cloaks about them in a vain attempt to keep dry.

Talon, accompanied by Giorgios, walked down into the gloom of the middle deck. The stench of the galley almost made him gag, reminding him of the time he had found Henry and his companions. He also heard the ominous slap of water and realized that the boat was at a danger point. Unless they could bale it out in time it would sink, taking all in it. He was greeted by shouts and wails from the men chained to the benches in front of him. They shook their chains and screamed for release. As there was no light he could only just see the ragged scarecrows seated immediately in front of him. The filth that floated on the greasy, foul smelling water was almost enough to make him hesitate but he knew he had to reassure them.

He called out in French, "Is there anyone here who is a Frank, Norman?"

Immediately there were hoarse yells and calls from the darkness. He listened carefully and decided that the vast majority on this boat were most likely prisoners from ships making their way to and from the Holy Land, hence there would be sailors and pilgrims mixed together, along with some criminals sentenced to the benches from the Arab world.

Regardless of their circumstances they were all desperate and shouted at him, pleading for release. Even now they had no idea what had transpired above them during the battle and the surrender of the ship, but the water sloshing about their ankles and rising was enough to generate great fear.

Talon looked at them. He decided he needed help. "Wait and be patient. We are here to help you. Do not panic; my men are coming to help you." He turned to Giorgios, who looked sick.

"Giorgios, get Guy and Nigel over here at once. Tell them to bring armed men but also hammers to strike the chains. We will be releasing some of these poor souls at the very least." Giorgios nodded and rushed up the stairs ahead of him.

*****

While Nigel, Guy, and their men set about checking the oarsmen to see who was from what country, how they were faring, and to strike their chains, Talon went below to the cabin. He nodded to the guards outside the door and told them to stay there. They grinned in acknowledgement and saluted him.

He found Max and Aarif seated on some cushions, talking. They looked as though they were comfortable with one another, but Max gave Talon a look that said *not much progress yet.*

Talon wanted something to warm him. He felt cold and wet, but there were no spirits here. Apparently alcohol was strictly forbidden on this ship. None of them had slept much in the last twenty-four hours and he was dead tired. He stared at the young man in front of him; his fine sharp features were swarthy; his dark eyes stared back at him with intelligence and interest, while a tinge of defiance remained. Talon noted that his turban was of fine silk and decorated in the front with a silver badge of some design unknown to him. He was an aristocrat, that was for sure, Talon reasoned, and not one to like a stone dungeon, which was where he might now end up.

"Allah protect you, Sir. Although our fate is unknown, you did risk your lives for us, and I shall not forget that act of courage," Aarif said as he touched his forehead and then his heart.

Talon nodded and replied, "We could not leave you to die on the rocks. God protected us all, and besides, we are not so cruel. What of your captain? Is his body still aboard?"

"I thank you for asking, Sir. He is wrapped in his cloak and placed in the main cabin. Our custom is that a man...but I am sure you know this."

"I know and will ensure that he is buried as soon as possible. You will write a letter that will be delivered to his family when we are able to do so."

Aarif was clearly touched and said, "Allah bless you for your kindness, Sir Talon. This too will be remembered."

"I do not understand why there was only one ship," Talon said. "I would have expected more to chase us."

"We thought you were only a merchantman. The officer on the ship sailing next to us told my captain to go ahead and capture you. So we came."

"Is your family rich enough to ransom you?" Talon asked. The question was so abrupt that Aarif blinked with surprise.

"Of course, as long as a message can be delivered which is written by me, they will ransom me."

"I need some answers first, Aarif," Talon said.

"I will answer what I am able to. *In Sha' Allah.*"

"What you tell me affects whether I turn you over to the authorities here, who will quite possibly torture you for any information, and then throw you into a dungeon along with your crew, where you will rot for years. On the other hand, I can arrange for a message to go to...?"

"Damascus," Aarif said. There was a tiny look of fear in his eyes. Talon knew that the man had thought it inevitable and only a matter of months before a ransom could be arranged. He had clearly not expected the alternative.

"Do you understand what I am saying, my friend?" Talon asked softly. "It is your choice. Others would torture you for the information that I need. I shall not be so crude, but you will never see your home again if you do not tell me why the flotilla was where it was and where it is going."

Aarif looked from one to the other. Max assumed a cold, indifferent expression and Talon just gazed back, his face bland, as though he wanted to help. It might have been that expression that unnerved Aarif, but Talon could see him fighting hard to be resolute. Talon was desperate for the information. Even as they were speaking, elements of the flotilla might be gathering close to Abydos and blocking the port, or even traveling further north to inflict mischief on shipping in the Marmara Sea.

"Are they coming here to besiege this city?" he asked, pretending not to watch Aarif too carefully.

He caught something in Aarif's eyes just before he nodded vigorously and said. "Yes, it is tAbydos we were coming to besiege."

"Why?"

"Why, in God's name? It is an entrance port to the straights that lead to Constantinople, that is why."

Talon sensed that something was not quite right. He spoke in rapid French to Max without looking at him, hoping that Aarif would not know the language.

"Do you believe him?"

Max was staring at Aarif. "No, I do not. There is something going on here but I cannot put my finger on it."

"I agree. Stay with him and keep the guards near at hand. Did you check him for his knife?"

Max nodded.

Talon rose to his feet. "I shall give you one hour to think upon this, Aarif. If I am not satisfied, then you go and join your crew, and I am afraid that you will stay there forever—or end up on a galley, perhaps?"

He left the cabin and made his way to the larger main cabin where he found a body wrapped in a fine cloth lying on a very beautiful carpet. He left the body undisturbed and gazed around the ornate cabin fittings, the pile of exquisite carpets and the cushions, along with the books and the chests lying about in casual disarray. The silent cabin was fitted for comfort and style, clearly the home at sea of a very wealthy man. Talon opened one of the chests and found papers and letters. He decided to look them over, hoping the ship did not sink before he could.

Something draped with silk cloths caught his eye in one corner. It was a small locked chest. He tried to lift it and found it very heavy. He took a beautifully etched dagger that was lying on the floor near a belt, a pair of gauntlets, and a helmet, and with a couple of hard blows broke the padlock and shifted the bolts sideways to open it. He was not surprised to find it full of gold coins. Talon was too tired to feel pleased, but he understood very clearly the significance of this find. If all went well he might have another ship, and there was gold aplenty in the chest to allow for repairs and much, much more. But there was also much business to attend to before he could feel safe.

Talon placed the small chest inside the larger one underneath the books and letters and then stepped out of the cabin. He jammed the same sharp dagger into the space between the door and the lintel, thus effectively preventing access without his knowledge. He made his way onto the deck and encountered Nigel on deck.

"Nigel, the captain of this ship is lying in the main cabin. I need you to send two guards. They are not to enter the cabin under any circumstances and they are to allow no one in, unless I have given permission."

Nigel nodded and shouted for two men to do as Talon commanded. Talon thanked him and went onto the afterdeck to observe the release of many of the oarsmen. They came staggering up into the light rain, blinking at the light and croaking their joy at their release. These men were led over to a corner of the deck and given some scraps of cloth to cover their nakedness and told to wait for the rest to join them.

Talon turned away from the dreadful sight of these filthy creatures that were once hale men. He had seen enough of this in Egypt. He turned and faced the sea and thought about what had to be done next.

An hour later he entered the cabin where Max and Aarif were talking. They stopped as he came into the cabin and sat down on the carpet across from them. Max was yawning but was still alert and watchful. Aarif was still sitting where Talon had left him, and there was a resigned look to his face now.

"Are you going to tell me more than you have?" Talon asked.

Aarif looked back at him and said, "Allah protect me but I have told you all that I know." He gave a shrug his shoulders slumped. He stared defiantly back at Talon, who looked into his eyes for a long moment.

Talon got up and went to the doorway and called for Nigel or Guy. When Guy arrived Talon said, "Take this man under tight escort to our own ship and have him placed under guard in the storeroom. I want him chained to the wall by the wrists until I have decided what to do with him."

Guy nodded and beckoned to Aarif. "Come along, you," he said in French, but it was clear what he meant. Aarif got to his feet.

"What is going to happen to me?" he asked uncertainly.

"You will have a little time to compose two letters, one on behalf of your former captain and the other informing your relatives that you are a prisoner and need to be ransomed," Talon told him as he walked out. The expression of relief and triumph he noted on Aarif's face was all he needed.

Turning to Max, Talon told him about the dagger in the door jam and the chest, and asked him to take the chest over to the *Falcon* and secure it in his cabin. Max departed and Talon considered his next task.

He rubbed his face. He was tired, but he had to go and see the *Phalangarches* and tell him and the ships' captains the information he had. He was rowed to the quayside where he was met by an officer and several men who greeted him politely and then escorted him to the gates of the fortress that overlooked the entire harbor and the sea. Talon realized that the people on the walls must have witnessed the whole pursuit, surrender and passage at the entrance.

It was a relief that there was no sign of any fleet out there as yet. He hurried after the officer along stone corridors and guarded hallways, eventually to be shown into a large room with a huge fire burning at the other end. Grouped around the fire were several men, all of them older than Talon by many years; one even had a grey beard. They were dressed in military uniforms and looked considerably better groomed than Talon felt. Standing several paces away was the young officer Leontios.

All of them watched Talon with interest as he walked the twenty paces it took to join them. Leontios made the introductions. He spoke in Greek, satisfied that Talon was competent in the language.

The officer with the grey beard turned out to be the *Phalangarches*; three of the others were captains of the ships riding at anchor, and another was introduced as a quartermaster. There were soldiers at the doors; Talon assumed they were there to ensure no interruptions.

"You had quite an interesting time out there in the approaches, Sir Talon." the commander Meletios remarked. His shrewd gray eyes regarded Talon with interest. "Leontios has told us briefly what happened. We would hear your story from your own lips, and do not spare the details." He offered Talon some warmed wine that the knight gratefully sipped.

Talon told them all that he knew, only leaving out the last hours spent on the Arab ship. They listened intently, especially when he explained the theft of the fire machines and the evidence that the Arab fleet possessed them. There were angry murmurs and much shaking of heads from the captains as Talon described coming upon the remains of the destroyed naval ship, but the men allowed Talon to continue.

When he had finished, Talon stood waiting. The officers began to talk in animated tones among themselves, at times too rapidly for him to understand.

Finally the commander turned to Talon. "How many ships do you estimate there were in that fleet?"

"My men and I think that there were in excess of sixty ships, Sir. But as it was dark we could only guess. There were many, many lights on the water. They were not worried about being seen from behind."

There was a buzz of low talk as the officers considered this statement. The *Phalangarches* nodded.

"Where do you think the enemy fleet was sailing?"

"I can only tell you what I've concluded from talking with the prisoner, Sir. He said that the fleet was coming to Abydos. However..."

"However, Sir Talon?"

"Sir, I do not believe him."

"Now you must explain yourself, Sir Talon." The *Phalangarches'* tone was sharp. "Why would they not come here and try to take the port? It would be a significant prize for them."

"Sir, I cannot explain it with solid evidence and, of course, I am sure that they will leave some ships to keep this port bottled up so that no one can go north to warn the fleets in the Marmara or the city of Constantinople; but every instinct tells me that they are going for a larger prize. It is not a small fleet of corsairs, it is a large fleet of more than sixty dromon warships and larger ones that take horses, and now they have at least four ships that carry the fire machines, if they share out the ones they captured. My guess is that the fleet will be sailing directly for Constantinople."

There was real consternation at this. The officers began to talk again, casting many looks in his direction. They appeared to be arguing about whether they believed Talon. After much shaking of heads the commander turned to him again and said courteously.

"We do not doubt your courage, Sir Talon, we witnessed it here today. Only a very brave man would have done what you did, or a very mad one." He smiled to take the sting out of the words. "But there does not appear to be much to the argument that they are going all the way into the Marmara Sea. I and my officers are not convinced of that. However...I shall send a warship, under the command of Captain Petrous here, to the fleet at Constantinople. We are sure to need them in any case if we are besieged. You may remain here with us, as I am sure you need to make repairs to your ship. You will be a welcome guest at my house. We have not had the pleasure of a Templar Knight's company before."

Talon nodded his understanding, but he knew what he needed to do. "Sir, if I and my ship might accompany your naval vessel I would be very grateful. I have pressing business to attend to and it cannot wait."

Meletios looked sharply at him, hesitated for a moment, then said, "Very well, but you realize that you will have to leave very soon. Once the enemy arrive we will have a chain across the inner harbor and no one will be able leave; the enemy will, I am sure, see to that."

"I realize that, Sir. I have to ask if we can leave the injured Greek sailor in your charge, for I do not think he will live much longer if he does not have the attentions of a good physician very soon. Likewise some of my men need tending, and also the Arab prisoners, unless the Greeks do not care and just throw them into the dungeons to rot."

"They will be seen by a physician," the officer said stiffly.

"The Arab ship I captured on the high seas, Sir. I believe it is now my ship, but it'll not be able to sail. May I leave it under your protection while I am gone?"

"Of course! Leontios will see to that. Leontios tells me that you know Nikoporus Tagaris?"

"Thank you, Sir. Yes, I had the privilege of playing *tzykanion* with him in front of the Emperor."

"Now I remember! The news of that game had come even to us here in Abydos. I heard that...wait, was it *you* who knocked the prince off his horse?" Talon looked hard at the commander, but the man only chuckled. "I would have liked very much to have seen that game," he remarked. "Well, you seem to be living up to a reputation for courage and fire, Sir Talon. We are honored to have made your acquaintance. I suggest that you hasten to your ship and prepare to leave. Negotiating that outer wall will be dangerous, as the light is going and the sea is still rough."

Talon clasped hands with all the men, and then walked out of the room with Leontios almost running after him. On the way they discussed the wounded men and where they would be taken. Talon was concerned about the other ship but Leontios said, "You have made quite an impression, Sir. Meletios will honor his word. I shall give instructions to the harbormaster to allow your men access and help with repairs."

Talon made his way over to the *Falcon* and called Henry and Max to join him, then sent a messenger over to the captured Arab ship to ask Guy and Nigel to come over as soon as they could.

Talon wanted to talk privately to Henry and Max. When the two men were seated on stools in the main cabin he broached the subject on his mind.

"I am sure that it has not escaped either of you that now we possess two ships instead of one?"

They nodded and grinned wolfishly. "We will need to fix it first, but given time I think we can," Henry said, rubbing his hands together.

"That is right, Henry. You are captain of this ship and we have a task still to perform but...Guy or Nigel, who should I put in charge of the other ship with a view to his being captain eventually?"

Henry stared at him and Max glanced at Talon. "You are not thinking of trying to sail it away, are you Talon?" Max began. Talon held up his hand. "No, Max, not yet anyway. Henry, which one can I leave with the ship here to make repairs and eventually sail it home?"

Henry scratched his beard vigorously. "My choice, but only just, is to have Nigel stay with the ship, Sir Talon," he said slowly. "Guy will not like it but...well, that is my first choice. Guy is a very good navigator and mariner too, so there is not much to chose between them."

"I am glad that you told me that, Henry." He did not continue, for just then they were interrupted by the sound of a boat coming alongside, and then the tramp of two pairs of boots on the companionway, followed by a rap on the door.

Nigel and Guy came in and noticed the serious faces. They took stools and sat down at the low table and Nigel said, "Is there something wrong, Sir Talon?" He always used the formal term when he was worried.

"Yes, we have been trying to decide which one of you pirates we should leave behind to the mercies of the Greeks in this town," Talon said.

Both men looked disheveled and filthy. Nigel pushed back his long lank hair, while Guy's sharp teeth made a short appearance as he grimaced.

"I have decided that it will be you, Nigel, who remains here. You will prepare the other ship for sea and you will have the help of the harbor master and that officer to do so."

Nigel stared at him with his watery blue eyes. "Er, I do not speak Greek, Talon, or have you forgotten that?"

"No, but Max now speaks enough to get by, and he will remain in overall charge to have a Templar presence. You will assume the position of captain of the ship."

Talon sat back and watched as his companions digested this information. Max was as surprised as Nigel.

Nigel was overcome. He reached across the table to clasp the hands of all there with tears in his eyes. Guy came around the table and they embraced as good friends. "I always knew you would make a good pirate someday," Guy said with real affection in his voice.

Talon spoke again. "Max, I want you to remain here in Abydos to act as my representative, but also to protect Nigel from the dangers of the officials. I shall leave Dmitri with you, as I know Nigel thinks the world of him." They all laughed at that. "He is a good man and you will be able to rely upon him, I am sure." Nigel nodded vigorously in agreement.

"I am truly honored, Talon. You will not be disappointed; we will make that ship seaworthy again. But...what about the Arab fleet?" There was concern in Nigel's voice.

They all looked at Talon and waited while he collected his thoughts. Finally he said, "Henry and I must leave within the hour. They did not really believe me when I told them of my concerns, so I need to deliver the message to Nikoporus myself and see if he will. I will also require help with another matter, which may or may not be connected, so I will take Guy and Giorgios with me. Be aware, however, that even if the Arab fleet does go up the Hellespont they will blockade this harbor and there will be real danger. Max, you are charged with ensuring that the men are protected as well as possible. God protect all of you."

After a brief silence the others immediately began to discuss what might be needed to get the *Falcon* ready. Eventually Talon chased the three sailors out of the room, leaving him alone with Max.

He went to the chest and took out the smaller box from inside. Opening it he exposed the contents to Max, who gasped.

"I found this in the cabin of the other ship, Max. You will need some coin." He laid out two small piles of gold on the table, which gleamed in the semi-light of the cabin. "The smaller pile is for the *Phalangarches* Meletios who commands the city. You must seek an audience with him as soon as you can and deliver this to him with my compliments. You know why I do this?"

"It will smooth our way for sure, Talon."

"I think so too. The other pile is to pay for repairs. I do not want them confiscating the ship under any pretense, so you should pay for everything as it needed. Now, make sure we have reliable men from the oars of that Arab ship. Ones you and Nigel can trust. He spent long enough in that kind of hellhole to know how to sort out the good from the bad. Help him make good decisions, Max. I plan to come back for you as soon as I can."

They embraced. "God go with you, Talon. Be safe, but get that bastard Genoese. I think he is behind this treachery."

"I am sure you are right, Max, but I also believe that a certain senator is as well. How deep that goes I have no idea. The first thing we must do, however, is to alert the fleet."

*****

Henry and Talon saw Max and Nigel over the side, and almost immediately Guy had the anchor hauled in. The Greek dromon they were to follow to Constantinople was already making its way across the inner harbor. The rain had stopped but the wind was still strong, although it had veered back to a more southerly direction. Talon wondered how Henry was going to get them back out through the sea breaker. He stared back at the cleaning activity on the captured ship and hoped that all would be well, but there was nothing to be done other than hope that Max and Nigel would come through.

He stood on the afterdeck as Henry maneuvered the *Falcon* out of the clustered shipping and into the area before the main entrance to the inner harbor. Following the Greek galley they rowed out between the tall towers, where many curious people

411

stood staring down.A ragged cheer rose from the walls as the crowd watched them leave. The captain of the naval ship knew what he was about, for he set sail as soon as he cleared the entrance and guided his ship unerringly toward the gap in the barrier, where waves were breaking over the rocks on either side of the opening.

Henry was calm enough, although Talon's stomach lurched as their smaller ship heeled when the wind caught the sails and they picked up speed to chase after the other vessel. Talon breathed a sigh of relief when he saw that the galley passed through the gap without much difficulty, and then they were passing through themselves. Guy shouted for the oarsmen to cease work and pull in the oars.

Once again the menacing roar of the waves crashing to either side of them deafened Talon's ears, and the water receding from the black and deadly teeth of the rocks was terrifying; but Henry, with the aid of the two steersmen, guided them through without incident.

Talon released his death-like grip on the rail and took a deep breath of relief. He looked back at the devil's cauldron of foam and spume and thanked God for the second time that day for his deliverance.

It was early evening and the wind was almost behind them. The grey cloud cover obscured the little light that was left of the short day. Instinctively Talon glanced up at the mast to see if there was any sign from the lookout of any ships other than their own, but the man only had his gaze directed to the south, searching. Talon turned his face northward toward a darkening horizon and a choppy sea and hoped that they could make good time before the flotilla arrived. He muttered a short prayer for his companions, who were in all probability now trapped in Abydos.

Guy and Henry shouted commands and the crew hauled on the sheets to lay on full sail in order to follow the Greek dromon, which was now on a northerly course, tossing the waters aside as it raced for Constantinople. The *Falcon* surged forward and spray flew high in the air at its bows as it slipped its constraints and sped after the other ship.

Treacherous time has put me in prison
where I've chirped away like a bird in a snare.
How pure and fine my inspiration
is and was and will be there.

Todros Abulafia

Chapter 23
Doubtful Haven

Senator Spartenos stood at the large open window of his reception room and gazed out through the rain at the Grand Fleet on the other side of the Golden Horn. It was late evening and lamps were being lit everywhere in the city and in the harbor below. He could see very few ships at sea and those were hastening to the safety of port. Just behind him were Captain Caravello, Choumnos, and the eunuch, Basileios. The squalls soaked the dry hills of Constantinople, obscuring the view of the town of Galata on the northern side of the Golden Horn as the rain intensified. Gusts of wind rattled the shutters of the house and the splatter of rain muted the words of their conversation. Winter was just around the corner and the autumn storms were taking their toll on shipping and roof tiles on the south side of the peninsula. Here on the relatively protected North side the wind was not as strong, but it was still chilly and wet; the room was being warmed by a brazier standing in one corner.

Caravello had arrived wet but smiling; his ship had sailed into the port of Prosphorion, from where he had made his way almost immediately to the villa. He had just completed his report on the capture of the naval vessels near Rhodes and the forthcoming attack on Abydos by the Arab fleet.

Spartenos was pleased. "It seems that you arrived just in time to beat the storm. Where do you think the fleet is now, and how many ships are there with it?" he asked.

"I estimated perhaps sixty ships, but it was hard to tell, and they did not encourage me to come too close. The two Byzantine navy vessels were locked into a harbor when I left. I sailed off immediately they had trapped the two ships, senator. My job was done as far as I was concerned. The apparatus you loaded onto my ship is still under wraps on deck, but I have the crew for it ready to work it. They are in chains below deck until I leave."

"Have you not learned how to use it yet?"

Caravello shifted his feet and his wide bearded face looked uncomfortable. "Er, not exactly, Sir. One of my men was...a bit rough with one of the crew trained for the operation, and that man died. The others are not very sure how to proceed. It is a very difficult device to prepare, they tell me."

The senator flushed with anger. "You idiot! They are stalling you! Do I have to send Psellos down there to persuade them? I am sure they will remember well enough if he is there to oversee the process."

Choumnos, standing behind Caravello, fidgeted. He did not like to hear Psellos being singled out for tasks that he could do well enough himself. The rivalry between the two had intensified since he had been wounded, and now he smarted every time the senator mentioned his rival's name. He suspected that Psellos was up to something.

Caravello shook his head. "No, Senator, I can deal with it."

"Good. Now we have other things to concern us. I think it would be a good thing if you returned to your ship and waited for orders. You have done well, and I shall make sure that you are rewarded."

Caravello, realizing that he was being dismissed, stood up and made his way out of the room.

Senator Spartenos resumed his seat opposite Basileios then beckoned Choumnos over.

"Now we know the fleet will be at Abydos very soon and a messenger will be here in less than a week. That will draw off a great part of the fleet, and our ally will make sure that those most sympathetic to our cause remain here, while those most loyal to the emperor are sent to deal with the threat. I want you to go around to all the locations where the Cilicians are hiding and warn them to be ready for the signal to move into place. Assess each group and make sure they are sharp and ready. I do not want a slipshod job done of securing the harbors."

Choumnos drew himself up and saluted. "I shall take care of this immediately, Sir."

The senator knew that he could trust Choumnos so he turned his attention back to his guest.

"Does the prince know where he must be once the fleet is on its way?"

Basileios took a sip of mulled wine. "Yes, all is in readiness. I still have grave reservations about using the Arabs, even for a diversion. We should have simply had a coup within the fleet."

The senator sighed at this display of nerves and said slowly as though to a simple person, "Basileios, my dear friend. The Prince is confident that his Cilicians can deal with any eventuality within the city, but he could not fully trust the navy. The High Admiral is a very loyal servant of the emperor and his men outnumber our supporters in the navy. They have to be neutralized, and it is highly likely that both fleets will destroy each other in the confines of the Hellespont in the engagement. The fire the Arabs now have will even the odds enough to keep our fleet very busy and out of the way.

"Our emissaries in the court of the Sultan were assured that all they want is a change of leadership and that their northern flank will be protected. Do not you see? With Manuel here we will be losing more battles with the Turks, and then we will not even have an empire. With his brother in charge and his nephew next in line there is a strong chance that we can crush the Turks between us and restore our lands in the east."

"What about the Varangians?" Basileios persisted. "They are dedicated to preserving the life of the emperor. Do you really think they will just roll over and accept a change in the palace?"

"They will be among the first to be taken care of. There are detachments of Cilicians waiting near the Grand Palace and the Blachernae palace. As soon as the signal goes up they will surround and disarm the Varangians and execute as many of the officers as time permits. The rest will go to the galleys, as their loyalty will be in question."

"Do we have enough men in the city to accomplish all of this?"

"I think so. We have been smuggling them into the city for months now. The ships provided by the Vice Admiral have more than done their job. Not only that, but the men of Antioch were very disillusioned with the emperor after the death of their leader Baldwin, and many are ready to change sides. They will come over, of that I am sure. Manuel does not even begin to understand how close to a mutiny his army is today because of the failure at Myriokephalon."

The senator paused to take a sip of wine and waved the servant in to stoke the brazier and place some more wood on the fire. The room warmed up noticeably.

"Prince Andronikos is ensconced close to the Purple Tower in readiness to seize the palace, so now all we have to do is to wait. He came into the city in an ox driven cart through the Charisius! Imagine that! No one suspected a thing. I am sure that Manuel would appreciate the irony of his nephew arriving in such style. But if he captures him then it will be the end of the prince. Manuel has pardoned him once too often for treachery and rebellion."

He smiled at his guest. "Fear not, Basileios, my friend. We will be avenged for the disgrace at the hands of the Turks, and I shall derive great satisfaction in putting Manuel...and his son...to death myself. It is time for a real emperor." He did not add that the death of his own son added to the driving force behind him. He kept that well under control.

*****

One of the first things that Talon did once they were sailing north was to go below and visit Aarif in the storeroom, taking Guy with him. Below decks the crewmen were settling down to rest for the night, the oars were stacked in neat lines in readiness to put out at a moment's notice, and food had been handed out. As they came below everyone acknowledged Talon as he went by with smiles and "God Bless, Sir." They were happy to have survived the ordeal and to be sailing north to the city and some well earned rest. But he was also aware of the respect they demonstrated as he went by. They would halt what they were doing and knuckle their foreheads in salute, only resuming their activities after he had passed by.

"You have a good, loyal crew here, Sir Talon," Guy remarked. "They know who you are now and their respect is high, especially after the incident with the Arab fleet and the ship we captured."

Talon nodded in the gloom. "God was on our side this time, Guy. It could very easily have gone the other way and we could all be pulling an oar on one of *their* galleys."

Guy barked a laugh. "Not me, Talon. Not again. Once was enough for me. I thank God he led you to us in Egypt, for we would all have died in less than three months."

Talon clumped down to the lower deck where the stores were kept, followed by Guy. They had to stoop almost double because of the low beams overhead, for the decks of the dromon were not spacious. It was dark down here and he heard rats scuttling out of their path as they made their way cautiously toward the dim light from an enclosed oil lamp near the storeroom. There they found Aarif. His turban had slipped and he looked disheveled, very angry, and not a little confused. When he saw Talon he almost shouted at him.

"Why have you done this to me?" He rattled his chains. "This is humiliating and not what you promised. I am a nobleman, not some common criminal!"

In the dim light of the lamp Talon could see there were tears of mortification in his dark eyes.

"Salaam, Aarif. I promised you one thing and one thing only. That I would not send you to join your crew in the not so warm dungeons of Abydos if you told me the truth."

"Are we at sea? It feels as though we are." Aarif said as though to change the subject.

"Yes, we are at sea, and you are coming with me to Constantinople. You are still my prisoner but that does not mean that I believed you. In fact I did not, but I decided that the Greeks would torture you and they would probably kill you in the process. You have told me all that I needed to know in any case. Now you will remain my prisoner until we can find a way to have your ransom paid."

Aarif stared at him. "I underestimated you, Sir Talon," he said slowly.

"Many do, and some live to regret it." He turned to Guy.

"Guy, you can release the prisoner from his chains and bring him on deck. When we come into port I want him to be held in the second smaller cabin under guard until I can decide what to do with him. He might come to Acre with us. Make sure that there is a double guard on his door all night long. I do not want him wandering about the ship while we are all sleeping."

Guy nodded, went to the hatchway and called upon one of the crew from up above to come below and release Aarif.

As this was going on Talon said to Aarif, "I must have your word that you will not try to escape, nor will you attack any of my crew, nor my person. Should you try to do so, I will have you put in irons again or even kill you."

"I understand and give my word. I swear to God on my honor," Aarif said. Talon decided that the fight had gone out of his prisoner, at least for the moment.

"Then I shall offer you the limited hospitality of my ship while we are en route to Constantinople. You must be hungry. When we get there you must come below and stay in the cabin with this man," he indicated Guy. You should compose those letters that we discussed. Your captain and the others of the crew who died will be accorded a decent burial. My sergeant is aware of the Moslem rites and will ensure this. I give my word. I shall in turn do my best to have a letter delivered to your family in Damascus asking for a reasonable ransom."

"Why are you doing this when you could have left me to my fate in Abydos?" Aarif asked him.

"Let us say that I have a debt to repay, and in a small way you are part of that repayment," Talon told him. His mind flew to the Fayoum in Egypt where his friends lived.

Guy then reminded Talon that their cargo of salt needed to be examined. The two of them went along the low wooden wall looking for places where water might have found its way in among the salt blocks. On being asked, several of the oarsmen volunteered that indeed water had come in through the oar ports and in several cases down the hatch despite it being shut, and they had gotten a good dousing, but not over much. Guy said that he would examine the cargo the next day with Giorgios and find out what they could.

They sailed for two days, clearing the mouth of the Hellespont that night as Orion, heralding winter, was clear to be seen amongst the stars. Henry had decided to sail through the night as the storm was well gone, leaving a clear sky by which to navigate. Evidently the captain of the naval galley decided that he could too, as it remained on their starboard side all through the night. In the morning they closed with another warship and their escort paused long enough to pass along the news. Evidently they became alarmed enough to turn about and join them for the final run to the city across the Marmara sea.

Guy, true to his word, went below with Giorgios, and with some of the crew examined what they could of the cargo. He came back with a mixed report. Some of the bottom ingots had been affected by water and were dissolving, so there was a loss to be expected, but a good percentage was left in reasonable shape. Giorgios estimated that perhaps a third of the cargo was damaged, but said that they would still come out of it with a respectable profit if they could unload the salt speedily once they made port.

Talon thought about the gold he had brought with him from Rodos, which had been paid for the silk and spices, and the chest of gold he had taken from the Arab ship. Giorgios had told him that after the fees of ten Solidari for the ship's entry to the city and the taxes for the cargo itself were paid, they would still come out ahead.

"If we had to pay thirty Solidari like the other Greeks, or even the seventeen, it would have been a little more tight, Sir Talon. Salt is always popular, as it is ever in short supply. I am sure that Makarios will get a good price for it." He appeared satisfied with the results, modest though they were.

"Do you think Makarios will be pleased?" Talon asked in a low tone.

Giorgios smiled at his obvious concern. "Do not be so worried, Sir Talon. You should remember that up until a few weeks ago the cargo we took to Rodos was rotting in a warehouse and going nowhere. Now it has been sold at a reasonable profit! Furthermore, we are bringing salt back to the city for more gold. Yes, I think Makarios will be very pleased, and so will master Alexios Kalothesos and the Senator. Even if we only made back the cost it would be considered a success, I am sure of it. And I shall be sure to inform them all of the risks you took to bring back their payment, Sir."

"And I shall inform them that I want you to come with me on the next venture as our agent, Giorgios. You are a very good negotiator."

Giorgios almost simpered. "I am honored, Sir, but...I pray to God that there will be much less excitement the next time. I am not the best sailor, and the fighting scared me."

"I too, Giorgios, I too. Storms terrify me. Alas, I do not think I shall ever be a good sailor." He laughed at the look of disbelief that Giorgios gave him.

Talon relaxed and was able to concentrate his thoughts on what he must do when they arrived in the city. He wondered where the Genoese ship might be. He badly wanted to have a talk with that captain.

Evening was glowing red in the west when they sighted the city of Constantinople and breathed a collective sigh of relief. There was no sign of the Arab fleet, and Henry suggested that they might have been scattered by the same storm that struck them and be regrouping south of the Hellespont.

"I hope they were wrecked all over the place, may God strike them all," he said with a savage look at Aarif. who was taking the air on the afterdeck. Talon looked across at the other two ships and noticed that the double eagle of the empire flew from the masts, so he asked Henry to run up their pendant. Giorgios agreed that it was a good idea. People would be keeping a lookout for them from the hills as they came into the harbor, and they would pass along the news of their arrival to Makarios and the family Kalothesos.

The three ships sped around the tip of the peninsula, past the Grand palace buildings and the Hagia Sophia, straight for the shipping anchored on the north side of the Golden Horn, and dropped anchor among the cruisers of the Grand Fleet. Talon cast a glance over at Aarif and smiled to himself. His prisoner wore the same expression Talon and the rest of his men had worn when they first saw the magnificent array of palaces, churches and villas on the hills before them.

Telling Henry that he should wait for him, Talon had himself and Giorgios rowed across the short distance to climb aboard the ship that had accompanied the *Falcon* from Abydos and was greeted cordially by Captain Petrous.

"I have a letter from the *Phalangarches* Meletios," he told Talon without preamble. "But it is important that we have your testimony to back it up."

Talon nodded his agreement and asked Giorgios to be permitted to accompany him. The captain nodded, and then they were rowed across the small military harbor to the jetty, where they had to explain themselves before being allowed to continue. Talon allowed the captain to do all the talking and just looked about him with interest. This area was off limits to the ordinary man on the street and there were many guards about. He was disconcerted to note that the ships they passed along the way were not heavily manned and wondered how long it would take to prepare them for an emergency.

They were finally provided with an escort that marched them through the gates of the harbor and up a short street along the inside of the walls to what was a small palace. Again guards wanted to know why they were there. Captain Petrous presented the missive from Meletios for proof to at least four officers along the way, each of whom checked the seal carefully before allowing them to proceed. Eventually they arrived before some large, carved wooden doors and were allowed entry. By this time Talon was becoming impatient. He badly needed a bath and a bed, and this endless officialdom was wearing on him.

The room they entered proved to be but an anteroom to an even larger chamber, where Talon could hear the murmur of voices. This was the inner office of someone of high rank. There was much activity, with eunuchs scribbling at desks in corners and others hurrying to and fro with papers tucked under their arms. He asked Petrous where they might be.

"We are in the offices of the *Topoteretes*, the Vice-Admiral of the Grand Fleet. It is he whom we must convince before he will inform the *Megas Drungarios tou Ploimou*, who is the Admiral of the Grand Fleet. Ultimately, it is he who will decide what we have to do next," Petrous explained in a whisper. He handed the sealed letter to a eunuch who asked them their business.

"We come on urgent business from Abydos, and it is vital that we meet with the Admiral. We bear grave news," Captain Petrous told the eunuch, who barely blinked as he took the letter and told them to wait while he delivered the message.

*****

They waited for nearly an hour before a young aide in a smart uniform, gold hemmed tunic and silver sandals with ornate breast plate and polished buckles, came to he door. He beckoned the three men forward. He sniffed and pursed his lips as they drew level with him. Their unwashed condition clearly offended his sensitive nostrils. Captain Petrous glared at him and the man hastened to lead them into the office.

They soon found themselves in a large, grandly appointed room with a good view of the harbor. A small group of officers stood in attendance around a grey-bearded man of very senior rank who was seated at a table covered in rolls of vellum and piles of papers.

Captain Petrous marched forward and saluted smartly, then stood silently, awaiting the portly senior officer to look up from the letter he was reading. It looked to Talon to be the same letter that Petrous had delivered. After some time the Admiral looked up and nodded to Petrous.

"Please explain in more detail what *Phalangarches* Meletios is saying in this letter. Also, who is the Templar he is talking about?" His tone was haughty.

Talon felt his heart sink. This was not the reaction he had looked for. The Admiral did not display any real interest in a situation that had the potential to be deadly. The man looked overweight and his features betrayed a liking for wine. His nose and upper cheekbones were riddled with blue and red veins. His puffy eyes regarded Talon's disheveled appearance with evident distaste.

"My lord, the Templar Knight is standing here with me at this moment. I wish to present Sir Talon of the Knights Templar. It was he who brought us news of the Arab fleet. He arrived in our port and delivered the news three days ago," Captain Petrous said formally.

The Vice Admiral barely glanced at Talon. "Did you see the fleet with your own eyes, Captain?" he demanded.

Petrous glanced uneasily at Talon. "Well no, Sir, not with my own eyes. But Sir Talon was pursued, and he captured one of their ships right in front of Abydos under very difficult circumstances."

"I repeat, did anyone other than this man who claims to have, actually *see* the Arab fleet, Captain?" the Vice Admiral demanded in a louder voice.

Captain Petrous shifted his feet. "No, Sir. We...we only have the word of Sir Talon here, but..."

"That will be all, Captain. You are free to go about your duties. Dismissed."

Captain Petrous almost gaped but drew himself up stiffly and saluted. Then he turned and marched out of the room.

All eyes swiveled to Talon. They regarded him with curiosity and he became acutely conscious of his bedraggled state. He did not think he looked very presentable, as he had not done more than change into his Templar uniform before coming ashore.

"Meletios says here that you captured one of the Arab ships right outside Abydos and towed him in with the storm raging all around. That sounds like quite a feat," the Admiral remarked. His tone was dry but interested nonetheless.

"It was more the work of my captain, who is a first rate navigator and sailor, Sir," Talon said.

"Ah, you speak Greek. Not many of you Franks do. That makes it easier. I have here the report made by Meletios which confirms the capture of the Arab ship, Sir Talon, which we will hold in Abydos until it can be decided as to what the Byzantine Navy wishes to do with it."

Talon tried to speak, but the Vice Admiral raised his hand.

"There have been many rumors of late of an Arab fleet out there somewhere, but we need better confirmation than just the word of one man, who is not even Greek."

Talon made to protest. "Sir, I sailed right through the fleet in question and I know its whereabouts. It is coming to this city."

He was about to explain that he had an Arab prisoner who could confirm his report when the Vice Admiral smiled with disbelief and waved a languid hand. "We thank you for your concerns, Sir Talon. But please do not waste our time anymore. I am sure you have other things to do."

Talon stood rooted to the floor, staring at the man in disbelief. Then with a shrug he whirled and stalked out of the room to find Petrous, followed closely by a bewildered Giorgios.

When he stopped to talk they were out in the middle of the courtyard. Talon put a hand on Petrous' sleeve. "This is wrong. I do not know what the letter said, but this is not only wrong it is stupid." Petrous was still looking stunned and Talon was still talking when Giorgios noticed a squad of soldiers emerge from the building and start to march their way.

"Look, Sir Talon, they are coming for us. I think they mean business," Giorgios said nervously.

"Both of you, walk away and get out of here as fast as you can; those men are coming for me! Giorgios, get the ship over to Neorion and alert Alexios. Petrous, find Nikoporus; he will know what to do." His two companions moved swiftly away and headed off into the rain without looking back.

To distract the soldiers' attention from his companions, Talon began to walk toward them. They met in the middle of the courtyard. The soldiers crashed to a halt and a young officer marched up to Talon and saluted.

"You are to come with us, Sir."

"What is this about?" Talon asked.

"I will need to have your sword, Sir. It is procedure."

Talon looked at the man hard. "Are you arresting me?" he demanded.

"You will come with us, those are my orders. Please do not make any trouble." He was tense and ready for a struggle.

Talon sighed. It would not help his case to resist. Even were he to escape, he would be a hunted man, and then his explanations would be even less likely to be believed. He unbuckled his sword and handed it off to the officer, who then motioned to his men. They broke ranks and surrounded Talon. At a low command they moved off, not to the offices of the Vice Admiral but in the direction of a heavyset door placed in the wall of a low, solid looking building at the other end of the compound.

*****

Giorgios and Petrous hastened away from the buildings and out of the main gates, then almost ran down to the harbor.

"You must take your ship and flee this place. There is something going on that I do not understand," Petrous said breathlessly. "I shall see if I can find Nikoporus and tell him what has happened."

He strode away, his cloak flapping in the wind, leaving a confused and frightened Giorgios standing on the quayside looking after him.

Finally Giorgios pulled himself together and ran all the way along the stone quayside to where the *Falcon*'s rowing boat was tied. Once he arrived on the ship he ran past the sentry, who shouted after him, and almost slipped onto his back as he dove down the wet steps toward the main cabin.

Giorgios banged on the door and let himself in without being invited. He found Henry and Guy eating at the table in the stuffy cabin. The table was strewn with chunks of stale bread and dried meat. They looked up at him with their mouths full and stared at his scared face. He was gasping for breath as he stood shaking in front of them.

"What is the matter, Giorgios? You look as though you have seen a ghost," asked Henry.

"They...they have arrested Talon! He told me that you must get this ship out of here without delay and across to the other side. So...so did Captain Petrous!" Giorgios babbled.

Both men registered shock. "Arrested? For what, in God's name?"

"I do not know, Henry, but you must get the ship out of here very quickly or they will arrest us too!"

Henry wasted no time. "You can explain later, but now, Guy, get forward with the men. We need to hurry."

Guy needed no persuasion. He dived out of the room and ran up the stairs, shouting for the men to get on deck. Within a matter of minutes the crew on watch had cast off and they were drifting away from the nearby ships.

The men who did the rowing were woken up and chased to their benches. With one of the senior crew members bellowing orders at them they pushed the oars out and began to pull while Guy prepared his men on deck to lower the sail when Henry gave the command.

They were none too soon. Giorgios, who had been watching the quay with great anxiety for any signs of activity, suddenly pointed.

"I told you, Henry! Look! They are coming for the ship!"

"Where are they?" Henry demanded. He peered at the quay.

"There...just coming out of the gates. They are coming here, I am sure of it."

The *Falcon* was well out into the bay and almost out of sight among other shipping. Henry watched the squad of men come to a halt on the quayside. The officer was peering out into the gloom at the ships in the harbor, but evidently he could not see the *Falcon*, which was now drifting behind two larger naval vessels.

"By God, but you were right, Giorgios. We must hasten before they can send anyone after us. He is marching his men away, but I am sure that you were right. They were coming for us."

"Guy, we must get over to the other side even if it is dark. Drop the sails and post men on the mast and in the bows to ensure that we do not run into anything."

As the *Falcon* surged out of the harbor past the lighted towers they drove into a choppy sea, but the ship pushed the waves aside and raced under full sail to arrive shortly thereafter and without incident at the Neorion bay.

While they sailed past the Golden Horn, Henry and Guy quizzed Giorgios. He explained what he knew and had heard and the response of the Vice Admiral to Talon's report. His puzzlement was matched by theirs. Henry, scratched his beard furiously and said, "There is something that smells bad here, Giorgios. What about the other captain? Did they not listen to him?"

"The Admiral dismissed the captain after asking if he himself had actually seen the fleet and he said no. They sent him away! He was with me when they came for Talon. He told Petrous to find a person called Nikoporus. Who is he?"

"I do not know, but one thing is clear, Giorgios: you and I will have to go to the Kalothesos house and tell them what has happened. Guy, you take the ship in and we will find our way from there."

"We will have to watch out for patrols," Giorgios said. "It is well past the curfew."

"Do you know how to get there without running into them?" Guy asked.

Giorgios nodded his head uncertainly.

*****

Alexios was playing chess by lamplight with Theodora when Joseph came into the room and announced that Henry and Giorgios had arrived. He looked his surprise at Theodora, who got up with an expectant glow in her eyes.

"They have returned!" she exclaimed, and clapped her hands.

Both of them went as fast as Alexios could limp to find Henry and Giorgios standing in the anteroom looking wet and very agitated.

Alexios took in the condition of the two men and the notable absence of his friend Talon.

"Gods Blessings, Henry and Giorgios." he said in Greek, then French.

Henry replied in broken Greek. "God's blessings. Sir, we have a problem."

He turned to Giorgios and said, "You must explain what has happened to the young master here."

Giorgios nodded and then fell into rapid Greek. "Greetings, Master and Mistress, but we have bad news."

Theodora uttered a little cry and put her hand over her mouth, her face anguished. "Talon?" she asked.

"Er...yes, but...Mistress, be assured he is not injured or dead but...Sir, he has been arrested!"

"Arrested? What in God's name for?" Alexios almost shouted. "Where is he? Tell me, man."

He put his arm around Theodora's shoulders as she slumped against him.

"Who has been arrested?" Joannina asked as she swept in. "Theodora, why are you crying?" she demanded.

"Mother, Henry and Giorgios have just arrived and they tell us that Talon has been arrested, and we do not know why," Theodora said, dashing her tears away and trying to look less concerned.

Henry ducked his head, holding onto his sea cap, while Giorgios tried to make a fashionable bow but only succeeded in dripping more water onto the tiles. Both men looked very uncomfortable.

Joannina took charge immediately. "Theodora, go and wake up your father and bring him to the dining room. Joseph, please call upon Eugenia and alert John that we will need refreshments and mulled wine. Come with me." She led the way into the dining room where it was considerably warmer than in the anteroom.

"Be seated and tell us all about it," she commanded as she sat at the head of the table.

Alexios limped over to join her while Henry and Giorgios sat on the edge of their chairs, looking bedraggled in that fine setting. Mulled wine appeared like magic and baklava arrived on small brass trays.

"You must be weary and cold from your journey, "Joannina said kindly as she waved at the food and drink. Neither man needed further persuasion. Eugenia arrived close behind a breathless Theodora and asked what had happened.

"The authorities have arrested Talon," Theodora told her before she sat down. "You must go to the Empress and tell her that there has been some mistake. He is guilty of nothing!"

"I shall need to know a bit more than just that before I do so, Theo. As usual you are overreacting. I want to hear more. I assume that is why we are here, Mother?" she asked, ignoring her sister's wrinkled nose.

"It is, my dear. I am glad that you are here as we might need some help."

Henry and Giorgios were still eating when John assisted the senator into the room.

"What is all this about, Joannina?" he grumped.

"They have returned, Papa, but somehow Talon has been arrested, and Henry and Giorgios came to tell us about it," Alexios said.

"Well? What happened?" He glared at Henry and Giorgios, who had jumped to their feet. "Sit down, sit down. You arrived safely enough, but Talon is now in jail? What is going on?" he demanded as he was assisted to a chair next to his wife.

Giorgios explained in detail all that had occurred from the day they had sailed from Rhodes. It took him well over an hour to recount all their adventures and his audience listened with rapt attention.

When he described the way they had slipped through the Arab fleet, and the subsequent chase and fight outside the harbor of Abydos, the senator slapped his thighs with glee and beamed at

Henry, as Giorgios had not been stinting in his praise for the Frank's seamanship.

"These Franks are fighters, by God. Most other men would have run for cover! Ha Ha!" he crowed happily to no one in particular.

"Let him finish, Papa, there is more to come," Alexios admonished his father gently, but he too was flushed with excitement.

The old man subsided with a grunt and took a sip of mulled wine, then waved for Giorgios to continue.

Eventually Giorgios arrived at the point where Talon had told him to come and inform them of the situation, at which point he stopped and waited.

There was a long silence as everyone digested the news.

"What do we do now, Papa?" Theodora urged. "Will the Empress help?" she demanded of her sister, who shrugged uncertainly in response.

"I think I want to find Nikoporus," Alexios said.

"I can always ask in the senate if anyone has heard anything. This is very serious. Why did the Vice Admiral not pay attention to either Talon or to Captain Petrous? I could understand if he did not like the young Frank, but Petrous is a Naval Captain and his testimony should carry some weight, even with a Vice Admiral."

Giorgios raised his hand timidly. "Sir the...the Admiral asked the captain directly if he had seen the fleet, and when he said no, the Admiral sent him away."

Alexios shook his head. "This threat is too serious for anyone to simply dismiss, and if I know Talon it is no fanciful mistake. Besides, you two are here to bear witness. You saw the fleet, did you not? You were there!"

Giorgios looked at Henry and spoke for both of them. "Yes, we were there, Master, and if Talon had not spoken Arabic we would not be here today."

They talked long into the night as to what should be done. It was late when Theodora went to her bed yawning and Joannina finally persuaded her two menfolk that it was time to leave for bed.

"There is little we can do for Sir Talon tonight, but in the morning we should do all we can," she stated. "John will see to your accommodation, Giorgios," she told him.

But after a short conversation with Henry he replied, "My Lady, the rain has stopped for the moment and Henry is concerned about the ship. If you do not mind, we will go back there tonight. There is still much to do."

Alexios had not yet left so he added, "You have done well, both of you. I shall send a messenger to Makarios in the morning to come and see you at the harbor.

*****

A dark figure slipped over the wall into the compound of the family Kalothesos. It made its way very cautiously up the walls of the house and then moved like a shadow along the loggia until it came to a lamp-lit room. Psellos had done so several times in the recent weeks. Following Theodora through the streets of Constantinople and to the study halls of the Great Palace had not lead to the discovery of anyone who seemed like the mysterious intruder, although there had been wounded men enough at the hospital she visited occasionally.

This was the time he liked best. On several of his visits he had been able to come and observe the girl. She was getting ready for bed and he could see clearly into the room. She was at her toilette and sat half undressed on a stool, brushing her unruly mane of hair.

Psellos experienced his usual rush of desire as he watched the adolescent girl and almost forgot that he was exposed should someone come along. He slipped out of the dim light coming from the window shutters and into the darker shadows. Just as he went into hiding, a guard walked by down along the garden path below the loggia. Psellos remained in the shadows while the guard, unaware of the danger, walked on.

The lamp had been turned out and the rest of the house was very quiet. Psellos was not ready to leave yet. He wanted to be a little closer to the girl and he smiled to himself as he considered his abilities and the risk of detection. He chose to see this as a kind of test that he could throw in the face of Choumnos one day.

It was easy to slip his knife under the latch of the shutters and very slowly ease one of them open sufficiently for him to glide over the window ledge and into the darkened room. He crouched in the darkness out of the dim light of the open window and listened. His orders had been to neither hurt nor trouble the girl or the family. His orders did not say that he could not come close to her, however.

He heard the deep breathing of the girl on the bed off to his left and moved as silently as a specter to stand over her. He inhaled the scent of the young girl and lingered near, close enough to reach out and touch her. The urge to simply take and ravish her was almost overpowering, but he knew he would not survive Choumnos' retaliation, so he contented himself with her scent and listening to her breathing, his heart pounding with desire. One day the senator would give her to him, he thought, and then his imaginations would become reality.

He got up to leave, but something might have warned the sleeping girl that there was a presence in the room, for she stirred and moved to turn over and then began to wake up. She sat up in the bed so abruptly that Psellos was almost caught as he slipped out of the window. He hurried out of the garden as fast as he could go.

*****

Back in her room Theodora woke up wondering sleepily what might have disturbed her, but then noticed that the thick drapes at the window were moving. She lay frozen in the bed, wondering. She could have sworn her maid had closed the shutters before she went to bed. Now, however, she could hear rain beginning to spatter on the tiles above the loggia and a chill wind was blowing into the room. She forced herself to climb out of bed, walked with great trepidation toward the window, then peered outside. Although she was half asleep she caught a slight movement in the garden. She stared hard out at the night and noticed a dark shadow at the edge of the garden moving away to quickly disappear into the night. Her hand went to her mouth and she stifled a scream.

She shuddered violently and made haste to close the shutter and make it fast before climbing back into bed, where she spent the next hour feeling cold and fearful of what she had seen. She was very afraid. Talon was in jail for no apparent reason, and someone might have just paid her a night visit. There were invisible enemies who wanted to do harm to them, but who? She could not sleep so finally she got up and went to join her sister in her bedroom for the rest of the night. Eugenia did not mind, although she was tired and mildly irritated that Theo would not tell her why she was shivering so much. Instead she took her little sister in her arms and comforted her.

Euripides

Chapter 24

Treason

Senator Spartenos was working late that same evening. He was seated in his library writing notes by the clear light of some expensive oil lamps when Markos tapped gently on the door jam.

"What is it?" the senator asked.

"A messenger has arrived, Master."

A man dressed for the outside walked in. A hood hid most of his head and face, the cloak he wore was soaked, and his boots muddy. He simply handed the senator an oilpaper-wrapped package.

"I shall wait outside for a reply—should there be one," he murmured and left the room.

Senator Spartenos opened the letter and swiftly read the contents. He shook his head as he read.

I understand that the fleet is closing with Abydos as planned. I have intercepted an unusual messenger. He is a Frank, who speaks Greek moderately well, but claims to be a Knight of the Temple. He informed me that the Arab fleet was sailing into the Marmara Sea with the intent to come to this city. Our agreement was otherwise; I do not yet suspect treachery. However you must investigate. I do not think the messenger has spoken to anyone else, and I now have him in a safe place. Another man, one Captain

Petrous, accompanied his ship but he has not seen the fleet, although he believes the Frank. He is at large and my people are looking for him.

There was no name to the missive, but Spartenos knew full well from whom it had come. The Vice Admiral Tarchaneiotes had done well. The news of the Arab attack on Abydos must be suppressed for a few more days. He needed that time to finalize his preparations.

The Frank again! This was the same man who had tried to get into his house, he was now sure of it. Who would have thought a Templar would be a capable night fighter. But now he had been thrown into a dungeon by no less a man than his ally the Vice Admiral. He was very glad of this, but the uncertainty of the Arab intentions worried him. Had they betrayed him? Were they now going to make a bid for the larger prize? They had promised a diversion, nothing more. If they came to Constantinople his men would be unable to move, for the city would come alive with military personnel.

He drew out a quill from the cluster stuck into a silver holder and dipped it into the ink.

Please inform me when the Captain is apprehended. It would be wise to dispose of him, and the impostor in the dungeon should be dealt with in the same manner. I want no possibility of anything being heard by the wrong ears at the wrong time.

He called for Markos and sent for the messenger, who took the note and disappeared into the night.

*****

As the first rays of light lit the eastern sky Eugenia ordered her litter and left the villa. The rain had stopped, the morning was fresh with the smell of wet roads, and the drops of water hanging off the already golden leaves presented a lovely picture. But Eugenia had no mind for the beauty of the morning. She had barely slept the previous night, and now she was desperate to reach the hiding place of the prince. She had to warn him that disaster was pending and he must flee.

If Talon was telling the truth, if the Arab fleet was about to attack Constantinople and people learned of it, the alarms would be going off all over the city. The gates would be locked and the ports sealed, and he would be trapped. She did not know if all was in readiness for his attempt on the palace.

Her thoughts turned to the events which had brought her this far. Prince Andronikos had made it clear that while he liked his women she was special, and he had promised her much. She believed him to be sincere. He had even hinted at the possibility of a throne, should he achieve the downfall of his detested uncle. His ambition ran high, and she was determined to try for the same heights with him.

Her lips tightened as Eugenia thought about her present position. She would not be relegated to the role of Lady in Waiting to an empress forever. While the Empress Maria was kind, she was not going to help her marry a person of any great substance. She had not been born to the purple and hence would receive no help in that direction. It irked her that her mother thought her position sufficient and had counseled patience. The right man would come to court one day and then she would be set for life, her mother had assured her with a condescending pat on the hand.

Instead she had to fend off pawing and lecherous whispers from men in the shadows of lower standing, who thought she should give her body to them for nothing. Other than the prince, there was only one person she had bedded. That man had been the Frank, and that was only out of curiosity. She had liked him and had enjoyed their brief liaison, but he was now a serious threat to her future and to that of the prince. She calmly thought of his death in a prison somewhere. The senator, once he knew of the situation, would see to that, and she was sure he did know. His intelligence system was wide-spread.

No one in the house would find it unusual that she had left so early. Ladies in Waiting were often called upon to rise early and carry out many preparations in the way of costumes and other toiletries long before the empress rose. But now, as she sat in the swaying litter carried by the brawny bearers up the Second Hill and then along the Mese, which was just waking up, she considered for the first time the ramifications of failure, and wondered if she had not made a mistake.

The bearers hurried along the slightly northern route toward the Palace of Blachernae, but just before the Palace of Porphyrogennitos she called out to them to stop and let her out. She paid them handsomely and watched them head back up the road. Once they were out of sight and she was alone, she made for a small church called the Savior de Chora that was located on another road well off the royal avenue.

Eugenia walked along a path behind the church and was admitted to a small walled compound that was heavily guarded by men who she knew to be Cilicians, men loyal to the prince. They recognized her and quickly led her to the house and then to the upstairs rooms, where she was admitted by another set of guards who were even more heavily armed. The eunuch in the suite of rooms was surprised by her appearance.

"My Lady Eugenia. Is everything all right?"

"I must see the Prince at once," she said in a low voice. He looked at her and could see that she was agitated.

"I shall notify the Him at once," he said. "Please wait here, My Lady."

Eugenia sat on a bench in the room and looked around at the very modest surroundings. The Prince was not living in the manner that he was used to, she reflected, but within a short week he would be in the palace—and she would be by his side.

The eunuch came out of the bedroom and signaled silently that she could go in.

The Prince was still in bed, sitting propped up on cushions, eating some figs. Nearby lay a metal tray with some bread, olives, and grapes, which he had not yet touched.

"Eugenia, my beautiful dove!" he beamed. "I am so glad that you have come. Have you eaten breakfast?"

She shook her head and smiled at him. It was all she could do to keep herself under control and not rush into his arms. Instead, she moved deliberately to the edge of the bed and leaned over him to be kissed.

"I missed you badly last night," he told her with a look in his eyes as he kissed her directly on the lips. The kiss lasted much longer than a simple greeting might and she could already feel her resolve slipping, but with a great effort of will she drew back and sat on the edge of the bed.

He looked a little surprised at this seeming lack of passion and lowered his eyes to look hungrily at her firm breasts instead.

"Your Highness," she began.

He took her hand. "Eugenia, my love. You do not have to call me that while we are alone. It is Andre."

"Andre, there is danger," she stated simply.

He started and gave her a sharp look. "Danger? Where?"

"Yes, there is danger...for you, perhaps for all of us. Last night a messenger arrived at my house telling that a man, you might remember him, a Templar knight who played *tzykanion* in front of the emperor, had come back to the city and told the Vice Admiral that an Arab fleet was approaching the city. I do not think this was supposed to happen. He appears to have been arrested, but you must see, Andre, that if any of this gets out there will be panic and the city will shut down, and then you will be in grave danger."

He was quiet for a long moment, staring at her, and then he got out of the bed and strode naked to the window. The shutters were closed but he opened them and looked down into the garden below.

"How sure of this information are you?" He turned to gaze at her. His eyes were very sharp and he looked at her in a manner that sent off a tiny alarm bell.

"The...the senator sent a messenger to tell me about it. I came immediately to tell you," she lied. She realized with a cold shock that she had nearly incriminated her own family. The realization that she might be close to putting her family in jeopardy struck her like a blow and left her with a cold feeling in the pit of her stomach. She would have given her life for the prince, but that did not include the lives of her own family. He was an ambitious man, and if he suspected that her family knew his plans he might take action against them. She knew, even as she loved him, that his moods were unpredictable and that for some strange reason he disliked the aristocracy intensely. Surely, if he could escape then all might yet be well.

"Andre, I am not aware of who knows this, but it will not be long before others do, even if the Templar is in a jail. People talk." She said this while admiring his strong body and wanting him just to take her in his arms.

"No one has talked as yet, and I have been in this city for over six weeks now," he retorted.

"I fear this is different, Andre."

He turned and walked toward her with a slow smile on his face. Observing his body as he approached she could not help but make the comparison between his almost unblemished muscular frame and that of the Templar with its scars and mute evidence of wars past.

"I do not think we need to fret, my darling. Our friends have it all under control. The Arabs will do as they are told. No one will believe the crewmen; they are foreigners after all, and their leader is in jail."

He took her cold hands in both of his and then slipped her into his arms. She laid her head into the crook of his shoulder, too weak from tension and lack of sleep to argue. Perhaps he knew best, she thought, as he fumbled with the strings on the back of her tunic. She felt a rush of warmth as he kissed her just below her ear, and then his lips proceeded to move down her neck and breast. She let out a small moan and gave herself up to the pleasure at which he was so skilled.

*****

Talon spent an uncomfortable night in prison. The soldiers had marched him through the large thick door at one end of the courtyard and down some narrow stone steps to a long corridor. The soldier in front had taken a torch out of one of the alcoves and walked ahead to another small door set in the side of the damp wall. He pushed the door open and Talon was thrust into a dark hole by rough hands. He stumbled in the darkness, and before he could turn and demand an explanation the door slammed. He realized there was no use shouting. He felt his way about in the dark and discovered that the cell was very small, barely three paces long and two wide. He reached upward but could not find the ceiling. There was some kind of straw on the floor that stank of urine and other foul smells; otherwise there was nothing.

He squatted on the floor and contemplated his situation. What could have happened? He had simply warned the Byzantine Navy of a threat and had found himself in prison. The unpleasant thought of treachery flashed into his mind. Could it be that he had gone to the wrong person? Was the Byzantine navy involved in this? If so, there was a very grave danger to the city. Who could he trust, if not one of the most senior men in the navy? In the light of that, could he even trust Niko? He had hoped fervently that Captain Petrous would find Niko, but now he wondered if that might be a mistake. More than once Alexios had commented on the depth of feeling against Manuel for the lost battle of Myriokephalon, so Talon could not be sure if even Niko was on the side of the emperor. He had a deep sinking feeling in his stomach as he thought about what might happen. He took his knife out of the inside of his tunic and fingered its razor sharp blade. The soldiers had not thought to check him for other weapons in their haste to put him inside this hole.

*****

Nikoporus strode down the hill to stop at the gates that led to the house of the family Kalothesos; he was concerned about a message he had received that morning from Alexios. A few minutes later he presented himself at the house. He was met at the door by Joseph the eunuch, who smiled and said, "Thank you for coming, Sir. Master Alexios is in the library with his father."

Joseph announced his presence to the two men, who were studying some papers. They looked up when he entered with obvious relief showing on their faces.

Alexios limped over and embraced his friend. "Gods Blessings to you, my friend. I am very glad you've come." He sounded strained and worried. Nikoporus noted that the creases between his dark eyes that had formed after the disastrous campaign were deepening.

The senator waved to Nikoporus from his chair. "I won't get up, young man. The weather is playing havoc with my rheumatism and I ache from neck to toe! But thank you for coming and please, have a seat. You are very welcome in my house. Will you have some refreshment?"

Nikoporus nodded with a smile. "I received your message this morning, but it said almost nothing other than it was very urgent, so I am very curious as to what it is all about, Sir."

"We dared not say more in the letter, Niko. We are very worried."

"Then perhaps you should explain, now I am here," he said, as John walked in and placed some wine on the table.

When Alex, with help from his father, had finished the account of Talon's arrest Nikoporus sat back, his face grim.

"Now perhaps I have an explanation for something that you do not know about," he told them.

"What are you talking about, young man?" Damianus said. His expression was tight.

"Captain Petrous was found murdered in a ditch on the other side of the Golden Horn this morning. I was told they thought it might have been robbers, but now..."

"Dear God!" Both men in front of him burst out, almost in unison. Their faces registered shock and alarm.

"Had you talked with him? Had he told you anything of what we have told you?" Alexios whispered, his face ashen.

"We were going to meet on my ship this morning, but then I heard about his death, and you sent me such an urgent message I thought I should come here before I crossed the water."

"I am very glad that you did, Niko. Do you know what this means?" Alexios demanded.

"I think I do. Either Talon is next in line or I might be, by reason of association with him and Petrous," Nikoporus said slowly, his eyes widening. "There is treachery here, and it would seem the Vice Admiral is involved. How they will justify the murder of a Templar I do not know but I must get to the right people or our own lives will be in jeopardy."

"You can't leave this house without a substantial escort, Niko," Alexios said flatly.

"I agree with my son, Nikoporus. You cannot just go wandering about on your own any more. Anyone in these crowded streets could slip a knife into you and no one the wiser."

"But I have to find a way to get to the Admiral of the Fleet! How am I to do that if I am cowering in this house?" Nikoporus said with frustration in his voice.

"My men will accompany you, and furthermore our...Talon's ship can take you across the sea to the military harbor, although his men are concerned that they will be arrested too. They got out just in time last night."

"I can use my influence as a *Mandatores* to see that they are protected until I can get to the main offices of the Admiral. It will be chancy though," Nikoporus said slowly. "I must leave immediately, as we do not know where Talon might be and what they plan for him next."

Alexios nodded and called for Joseph. "Get all the men from the stables here with their spears and whatever else they need for weapons, Joseph. I want you to take my friend down to the ship and ask Henry from me to take him across the Hellespont to the naval harbor. He won't like it but tell him that Nikoporus knows what he is doing and it is for Talon."

*****

Nikoporus jumped from the side of The *Falcon* onto the quayside and began walking casually toward the naval buildings. He was alone now and felt very vulnerable. He glanced behind him once to see that Henry, the grizzled Frank seaman who ran the ship, had already pushed off and the ship was being rowed out some distance to where it could not be surprised by anyone. Henry had been wary when he had first met Nikoporus, whom he did not know. It was only when Giorgios had shown up and had explained what was going on that Henry had reluctantly agreed to transport him. With the help of Giorgios, Nikoporus had told him of the most recent events and the death of Petrous. Giorgios was shocked and not a little frightened by what he heard, but he told Henry that this sounded like the only option they had and they must hurry. It had not taken Henry and his large and imposing looking assistant long to get the ship to the naval port.

Nikoporus braced himself for what might come. For all he knew he might be walking into a trap, but he did not know where else to go to for help. The thought had occurred to him to bring with him a contingent of Varangians, but he realized that he only had a flimsy explanation and time was running out. By the time he had convinced some of the army people Talon might well be dead.

He arrived at the gates to the large buildings and in his capacity of *Mandatores* he obtained speedy entrance to the outer offices of the Fleet Admiral. He was asked to wait by an unctuous eunuch as there was a conference taking place, but the Admiral would most likely be able to see him after that. He slipped a coin into the official's hand.

He was waiting impatiently at the back of the room when the first of the people who had been with the Admiral exited the room. Nikoporus gave a start, as he was looking directly at the Vice Admiral Tarchaneiotes, who came out of the room looking pleased with himself, followed by three other less senior officers. Nikoporus made haste to make himself look inconspicuous as the men sauntered out of the room. He glanced at the eunuch, and that worthy nodded. Nikoporus slipped into the main office where the Admiral Nestongos was busy writing.

He walked up to the desk and saluted smartly, then stood to attention while the man finished his writing and glanced up. "Ah, Nikoporus, what brings you here? I am quite busy you know."

Nikoporus took a deep breath. "Sir, I come because there is treason most foul in this building and you need to know about it before it is too late."

The Admiral put his quill down and stood up. He walked past Nikoporus and shut the door and then came back to his desk. "What in God's Name are you talking about?" he demanded in a low voice.

*****

Talon heard the bolts to the door being drawn and braced himself against the wall next to it. He had the knife down alongside his thigh ready to take the first man to come in the door and then strike for the others, hopefully taking them down with one of their own weapons.

A man began to step into the cell peering into the dark; he was holding a torch in his right hand. Talon seized his wrist and pulled hard and was on the edge of stabbing up when he recognized the officer who had placed him under arrest the night before. The man gave a startled yelp and fell forward to land on his hands and knees. The torch fell out of his hands and sputtered on the filthy floor.

Talon had pulled his knife back just in time, but now he waved it at the men in the doorway threateningly and placed it firmly alongside the man's neck who was still on hands and knees gasping with surprise.

"Stay where you are or this man dies!" Talon called up at the men who had started forward to help.

"We could rush him."One of the men on the outside of the cell who was peering in muttered.

"Then your officer dies with me and several of you with him. Who will be first?" Talon called upas he seized the collar of the officer and slipped his blade around the man's throat where it pressed. The man gurgled with fear and did not move from his position. It was a stand off that Talon did not know how to change. His mind was racing with options when there came another shout from along the corridor. He thought he recognized the voice.

"Stand where you are and do not move!" someone shouted and there was the sound of running iron shod sandals and the rattle of arms and armor.

"What are you doing here?" the same man with the authoritative voice demanded as he came to the doorway. Abruptly the narrow corridor was full of armed men and the former group of soldiers protesting loudly, were being hustled away from the doorway at spear point.

"Arrest these men at once and have them locked up." Nikoporus said loudly as he peered into the dimly lit cell.

"Ah Talon, I see you have everything under control?" he grinned but it was a tight grin. "You can let him go now, we have to hurry."

"How can I trust you, Niko, or anyone for that matter? Why am I here in this foul place?" Talon grated; the knife never wavered.

"Alex told me everything he knew. He told me you might not believe me, but I am here to take you to the Admiral of the Fleet. I told him everything that Alex had said, but you know more. You must come with me to tell him what you know!"

"Phew! It stinks in here! Talon, listen, there is not much time if your report is correct. The Admiral needs to see you and quickly. Will you come with me?"

Talon pointed at the men above. "Can they be trusted?"

"These are now my men, Talon. You can trust them. Come, my friend, we must hurry!"

After locking the officer in the cell with a couple of his men and placing the rest in another cell Nikoporus led the way out of the building. His men formed a protective screen around him and Talon as they jogged across the large square into another imposing building. It began to rain, the gusts of wind pulling at their cloaks as they hurried across the paved square. They ducked their heads and hurried past guards who saluted as they passed, along echoing corridors until they came finally to a grand pair of doors and Nikoporus was saluted by a junior officer and two guards.

As they walked Talon told Nikoporus about the Greek Fire. His friend stopped and stared at him aghast, then turned and almost ran into the offices.

"Is he in?" Nikoporus demanded.

"Yes, he is in, Sir," the officer said.

"I must see him immediately," Nikoporus said. "I am expected."

They were admitted to another anteroom that was almost deserted. "This will be my head if you are wrong, but I do not think we should be wasting time," Nikoporus said. "Follow me, Talon."

The man seated at the table was a marked contrast to the Vice Admiral. This man was burly but looked as though he was fit and used to being outdoors. He glanced up when Nikoporus marched up and saluted him.

"Sir, you need to hear this man. He is the one who I told you about," Nikoporus said. "I believe him. There is a lot more behind this than just an attack on Abydos. The Arabs have captured several fire machines and their crews."

The Admiral snapped his head around at this. "What did you say? They have captured some of our fire machines?"

"With me is Sir Talon of the Knights Templar, to substantiate the news. I feel that you should hear it for yourself," Nikoporus said.

The officer stood up and walked around the table. "I am Nestongos," he said. "I welcome you to Constantinople—although from what I hear you have not exactly had a fine welcome." He clasped hands with Talon, who bowed.

"I am honored to be in your presence, my lord. I come with news of the utmost import, and I do not understand why when I and the other captain had completed our report we were dismissed and then I was arrested."

The Admiral gave him a grim look, then went back to his desk and picked up a piece of paper. As he scanned the paper, he glanced from time to time at Talon.

"Nikoporus has told me something of you, Sir Talon, and it is all good. But there is another thing. Captain Petrous came with you to see the Vice Admiral, and he is now dead."

Talon stared at him and then turned to look at Nikoporus. "Is this so, Niko? Why would they kill him?"

"For the same reason they threw you in prison, Talon. To keep him quiet."

The Admiral waved the piece of paper in the air. "This is a very flattering letter of your courage, Sir Talon. However, Admiral Tarchaneiotes does not think that the Arabs will come this far north. It is his contention that they will lay siege to Abydos and do as much damage as they are able, then disappear as soon as we come and chase them away. What do you wish to add?" He looked hard at Talon. "Ah, yes, now I remember the name. You are the man who played alongside Nikoporus in that interesting game of *tzykanion*, are you not?"

Talon nodded. " I am, Sir, but..." He wished he did not have this reputation which everyone appeared to know about.

"Sir, if Sir Talon has anything to say, I for one will vouch for it on my honor," Nikoporus said.

"Why do not we let Sir Talon tell it in his own words," Nestongos said.

Talon wondered if he was committing another wrong move for an instant but there was little he could do. He trusted Niko, so he told Nestongos everything that had transpired. The Admiral listened intently, and when Talon got to the capture of the two warships by the Arab fleet, his eyes grew hard. He questioned Talon with great intensity, looking more and more grim as the story unfolded. He started when he heard about the use of the Greek Fire weapon and shared a knowing look with Nikoporus. Clearly Talon had struck a chord. By the time Talon had finished there was absolute silence in the room other than the crackle of the logs burning in the brazier at the other end of the room.

Admiral Nestongos sat back in his chair with the letters in his hands.

"These are dismissive of everything you have said, saying it is mere speculation. There is very little in either report to confirm what you have said to me, other than they accept there might be a fleet of corsairs out there and it might be heading for Abydos, nothing to warn me of any other intent, least of all that they are coming here to this city. But the officers flatter you for your courage in capturing the Arab ship. What do you say to that?"

Talon went on to recount how he had interrogated the prisoner Aarif and what Aarif had omitted rather than what he had confirmed.

"So, you speak their language? How can we be sure that he was providing misinformation? Why do I not order him to be arrested and brought in for questioning and torture to confirm what you think?"

"Because it would be a waste of time, Sir. I gave my word not to do so, and I believe I managed to gain more from that. If you torture him he will die first. He will think I betrayed him, and besides, it will be a while before you gain anything of value. By which time it might be too late to act upon it. The Arab fleet was heading into the straits when we left, of that I am sure, and not to tarry at Abydos."

"Sir, he might be right," Nikoporus interjected. "Is it possible that they have another strategy in mind? Perhaps they intend to sail here and surprise the fleet in harbor where it cannot maneuver. With the stolen fire weapon on board they would not only have the advantage of surprise but also flame to immobilize the foremost ships and prevent the others from being able to get out of the harbor to the open sea. It could be a disaster for our fleet."

The Admiral frowned. "Perhaps..." he said slowly. "But why would they want the Arabs to destroy our fleet if they're contemplating treason? They would be better off taking it over."

"Perhaps they do not...perhaps the Arabs have a different agenda? Would it be possible that the traitors do not realize this?" Talon asked.

His words were greeted with a long silence.

"Do you think the storm might have disrupted their passage?" Nikoporus asked Talon with a glance at the Admiral.

"Possibly. It was a fierce storm. But I am sure of one thing, and that is that no shipping will escape from Abydos to tell us what they are doing. But I am very sure that so many ships will not tarry long at that city other than to leave behind some to blockade the port and then continue north."

"Admiral Tarchaneiotes has totally ignored your report about the theft of our fire weapons. I wonder why," the Admiral mused. But his eyes were hard and his face tight.

"It should have been in the report you were given, Sir," Nikoporus said. "I do not know why it is not, but my guess is that Meletios did not want to mention it because the ships that were lost were under his command. I mourn their loss, but he should have mentioned it in the report, Sir. Talon here picked up a sailor who had been on those ships and he told a sorry tale. I am bewildered as to why the Vice Admiral ignored everything that Sir Talon has told you," Nikoporus finished.

The Admiral muttered something under his breath.

There was another long pause before the Admiral came to a decision. "Sir Talon, you may leave with your ship to go to the city harbor now. Be aware that I shall inform the emperor and the generals of what you have told me. Nikoporus, in your capacity as *Mandatores* you will stay here with me. I want to talk to the Vice Admiral."

As Talon was leaving the room he heard the Fleet Admiral say to Nikoporus, "I want the Vice Admiral here as soon as possible and you are to bring an escort of soldiers back with you.... Alert the harbor...Make sure you alert the men you most trust." He did not hear anything else, but it was enough to tell him that the Fleet Admiral was taking him seriously. He also sensed that there was more going on than he was aware of and the Admiral was alarmed for more than one reason.

*****

Talon made his way back to the ship in a thoughtful mood. He stood on the quayside looking for his ship and was alerted by a shout as it appeared around the side of one of the larger dromons. Henry and Guy were waving at him excitedly. They paused long enough to allow him to climb aboard and then pulled away from the stone quay with alacrity. As soon as he was aboard he told Henry to cross over the Golden Horn back to the harbor, and while they were moving across the water they talked.

"We could not believe it when Giorgios came running down the hill and told us that you had been arrested, Talon."

"Why would they do such a thing?" Guy asked.

"There's treachery of some sort going on, my friends. Giorgios, you did well. I thank you from my heart for reaching the boat."

Giorgios looked embarrassed at the praise, then said, "We went to the house and told them all about it, Sir Talon. They are very alarmed and I think it would be a good idea if you were to go there today."

Talon agreed.

A short while later they were guided into the walled interior of the harbor and the anchor stone was dropped. Leaving the ship in Henry's charge Talon decided to take Guy and a couple of seamen with him to call upon the family Kalothesos. Before he left he told Giorgios to find Makarios and arrange to have the salt taken off the ship as soon as possible. He glanced up at the sky. The clouds were dark and low, the wind from the north had picked up and was ruffling the sea; it was going to rain again before long.

As they made their way up the hill he glanced over the stretch of water they had just crossed and had the impression even at that distance that there was a lot of activity going on with the fleet. Small sail boats were driving across the waters toward a cluster of the galleys anchored in the middle of the channel and others were putting out from the harbor and racing eastwards in the direction of the Blachernae palace. He felt better for having been able to talk to the Admiral and blessed Nikoporus for having made it possible.

It was beginning to rain again when they arrived at the gates of the villa. Talon he was greeted respectfully by the guards, who knew him well by now, and even the dog merely growled at him instead of showing its teeth. At the house John looked relieved and pleased to see him and asked him to wait in the anteroom while he found the lady of the house. Talon handed Guy and the two sailors off to another servant who promised to make sure they were well fed in the kitchens.

Long before he saw her, he heard the slap of sandals on the tiled floors, and Theodora came running into the room.

"You are back!" Theodora rushed into his arms and kissed him. "Thank God for keeping you safe! We have been so worried, Talon. What were they doing to you? You look awful!" she cried, hugging him hard. He laughed and gave her a hug back and a peck on the cheek in return.

"I am back from our adventures with much to tell. How are you?" he asked, holding her at arms' length, enjoying her obvious excitement at seeing him back.

Joannina glided into the room right behind her daughter and admonished her.

"Theodora, you really must show better manners. What will Sir Talon think of us if you behave like this?" But she was smiling with delight, and with far more decorum she gave him both hands and allowed him to kiss her on the cheeks.

"God's Blessings. We have missed you, Talon." She stood back from him and sniffed, then said, "You must have a bath, and then you must tell us all about your trip."

"That would give me much pleasure, my Lady Joannina," he responded with feeling.

At that moment Eugenia made her appearance, almost as though waiting to make her entrance alone and with effect.

Talon looked at her as she too glided into the room, dressed in a simple tunic of shimmering colors that, while ankle length, did very little to hide her figure. He found himself staring for a brief moment but then he greeted her with a smile.

"I have returned to pay my respects and to inform the family Kalothesos that we were successful, Eugenia." He did not notice how pale she had become or the slight tremble of her hand as she gave it to him.

He bent over and kissed the back of it, then she asked him, "Did you achieve all your goals and sell all your cargo, Sir Talon?"

"I have more than a mere journey to report to you, my Lady," he responded with a smile. "We have been having adventures and there is much to tell."

At this point Damianus and Alexios made their more careful entry. Talon remarked to himself that they were both limping, but that the old man was staying close to his son. They were not at odds any more, he surmised.

They greeted him warmly and looked very relieved to see him.

"Your men came and told us what had happened, and we told Niko, then sent him to find you. Clearly he was successful, as you are here and unharmed. We were very worried."

"There is much to discuss, but I think the Admiral of the Fleet is going to take some action at last, and mostly because of Niko," Talon told them.

He allowed himself to be sent off to the baths and spent a comfortable hour in the warm water of the pool; then, feeling refreshed and clean, and dressed in new clothes, he returned to the family, which was now grouped together in the dining room eager to hear about his adventures.

He recounted to them all that had occurred since his arrival. Before long it was time for a meal. Lamps were being lit as they seated themselves. While they waited for the servants to produce the food Talon changed the subject and explained that his men and Guy were with him, as he had brought the first payment with him for the cargo sold in Rhodes. He casually laid a medium sized bag of gold on the table. It chinked as it landed and everyone stared.

He watched the faces of Alexios and his father intently as he waited for a reaction. Alexios was about to say something when Talon produced another medium sized bag of gold and dropped it onto the table; it too chinked as it fell.

Before anyone could say a word the third bag landed and fell open to spill coins onto the table; one coin rolled for a small distance before falling over and settling on the surface near to Damianus.

Theodora gave a cry of delight and Alexios let out a whoop of joy then turned to Talon. "You rogue, Talon! You had me so worried for a moment. I knew the cargo was worth more than the one bag. Father, he teases us!"

The old man chuckled. "I, for one, am very happy that you came back safe and sound and that the enterprise seems to have been a success, Sir Talon. Welcome back, my boy." He laughed. "My goodness, my son's face was a picture wasn't it? Ha, Ha!"

He banged his stick on the floor. "John, bring the wine. We are to have a celebration."

John appeared like a genie at the door holding a bottle of the prescribed wine. He poured a glass for all the adults. He paused at Theodora but the senator waved his hand. "Give her some," he said.

"Make sure it has some water in it John," Joannina said sternly.

Theodora looked up at John as though to say *not too much water* and smiled beguilingly. He made as though he was pouring water into her glass with a twitch of his lips. He was rewarded with a thankful grin from Theodora, then he stood back to wait for the senator to sip his first. There was a brief silence, before he nodded with satisfaction and said, "It will do, it will do, thank you John. Now, Talon, tell us all about it."

There was happy laughter as everyone joined in a toast to Talon while John supervised the distribution of food brought in by the servants.

In between the courses Talon told them all about his adventures up to and including the capture of the Arab ship and finally his discussion with the Admiral.

There were somber faces and Damianus grunted with alarm when Talon told them of his fears. He had not wanted to alarm anyone, but he also realized that he owed them the facts. But it was Alexios who saw the greater danger. He interrogated Talon about the nature of the fleet in detail and finally he said, "Despite what you have told us I still do not think the Admiral has fully understood the peril of what you have uncovered. This is more than just a casual visit by a fleet of Arabs bent upon mischief, Talon. There is more to this, though I cannot fathom it yet. One thing I can do, however, it to alert my regiment and have them put on standby. I shall have Joseph send a runner down to the barracks by the Tower of Belisarius with a message."

He called Joseph into the room and in rapid Greek instructed him to alert the regiment. "Ask the *Merarch* Philippos to send one of my colleagues to the house so that we can explain our concerns to him," he told Joseph, and dismissed him with a short note for the runner.

"We do not live very far from the Great Palace where the Varangian guard are bivouacked. Should we not alert them too?" Alexios asked the room at large.

"It would be a good thing, but I do not think the Admiral ignored what I said," Talon told them. "I saw a lot of activity as I was walking up the hill on my way here."

Then he remembered something. "Is not the house of Pantoleon Spartenos close by?"

Eugenia paled but it was her sister who spoke up. "Yes, it belongs to Senator Spartenos..." She was about to say more when she shut her mouth and stared at Talon. Her face went white as some of the implications dawned on her.

Eugenia abruptly got up and excused herself. "I am not feeling quite as well as I should, Mamma. Will you please excuse me, Sir

Talon? I am sure I will recover momentarily." She hurried out of the room.

"She is probably having her moon," Theodora said dismissively with a shake of her head.

"Theodora! What a thing to say in front of a guest!" Her mother was shocked. "You will be sent to your room if you continue in this vein, young woman."

Theodora was instantly contrite, but Talon sensed that she was not sorry her sister had chosen this moment to leave. He wondered what had occurred to disturb Eugenia so much. His mind went back to what had just been said. It had been the mention of the senator's house that had set this off, but he could not see any connection that could concern her. He dismissed it and concentrated on what Alexios was saying.

"You were right about unloading the cargo of salt at the earliest opportunity, Talon. From what you and Henry have told me it is still mostly in good condition, so first thing in the morning I shall instruct Makarios and Giorgios to complete the process. How did Giorgios behave on the journey?" He asked.

"He is a first rate negotiator. I would willingly take him on my next voyage, Alex. But he does not like conflict, so I hope that the next time is less exciting."

"What will you do with the other ship, Talon?" Damianus asked him. The old man had been gleeful at the story of its capture.

"Why, once it is repaired, I have a captain for it already and I thought that we might put it to good use, Senator," Talon responded with a grin.

The senator nodded and said, "You did an impressive thing there. Most men would have allowed them to sink, but you thought ahead. Well done, my boy. You shall have a fleet if you keep this up. I can promise you one thing, with your mandate from the emperor, there will be many calling upon you for help with their cargoes." He laughed and called for more wine.

"There is one thing you can be sure of, Sir. My ships will be carrying your cargos before all others."

*****

It was only later, after the senator had gone to bed accompanied by Joannina, and Alexios had limped off pleading tiredness, that Talon found himself alone with Theodora.

449

Talon rose to leave but Theodora said quickly, "Talon, do not leave. There is something...I need to tell you."

He returned to his chair. Theodora motioned the silent servants to leave and watched them go. Then she turned to him and said, "I am afraid, Talon. Something happened while you were in prison."

He straightened. "Can you explain, Theo?"

She told him of the visit that she thought had occurred, and when she had finished there were tears trickling down her face. She trembled and edged closer but evidently did not think it a good idea to crawl into his arms, where she clearly wanted to be.

She could see how upset he had become at the news, but for a long time he said nothing.

Eventually, when she thought he would never say anything, he turned to her and she saw his eyes. He terrified her with that look.

"Have you told anyone else about this?"

"No, because I did not want to worry them. It might have been just my imagination but...I am *sure* I saw someone, although I cannot be certain it was the same person who was in my room. It was just that, I felt so strongly that someone had been there. It frightened me so much! I do not know how long they were there nor why—she was crying now."

"Perhaps you should have told you brother, Theo. He could have at least taken precautions."

"He has enough troubles with getting better and I did not want to add to his problems, Talon," she said between sobs.

He reached over and grasped her hand. "You have nothing further to fear, Theo. I am here now and whoever contemplates harm to you will answer to me." He waited, still holding her hand, as the sobs subsided.

In the darkness of the corridor just outside Eugenia held her hand over her mouth and nearly choked. Then she hurried away, making as little noise as possible.

All we have of freedom, all we use or know—
This our fathers bought for us long and long ago.
Ancient Right unnoticed as the breath we draw—
Leave to live by no man's leave, underneath the Law.
Lance and torch and tumult, steel and grey-goose wing
Wrenched it, inch and ell and all, slowly from the King.

Rudyard Kipling

Chapter 25
War in the City

It had been three days since Caravello had sailed into port and delivered his report, then returned to his ship to await further orders. Now it was late evening at the villa. Senator Spartenos leaned back in his chair, and while he half-listened to the rain on the closed shutters he contemplated the situation as it had developed so far. He felt satisfied that all the pieces of his chess game were now in place and it was almost time to make his move. There was a low cough, and his eunuch Markos indicated that he had a visitor.

The senator motioned the eunuch to allow entry and there was a light footstep at the door and then his wife appeared with Eugenia at her side.

"You have a visitor, John," she said.

The senator stood up and said to his wife. "Thank you, Constance, leave her here with us and you may go."

His wife touched the girl on the shoulder and said in a low voice, "God protect you my dear, I shall leave you now." She disappeared back into her own rooms.

The senator looked after his wife and the movement of the leather curtain for a brief moment as she departed. Since the news of their son's demise she had become almost a wraith, eating very little and praying till the early hours of the mornings. Almost nothing could enliven her now, and he suspected that she was going to the church nearby to pray for the soul of their lost son once again. He gave a mental shrug. His anger with the emperor was sustenance enough and the thought of bringing that august figure down would compensate in part for the loss of Pantoleon. He beckoned to Eugenia to come into the room and waved the servant off who was standing near the door. He wanted privacy.

"What brings you to us at this time, my dear?" he asked in his most kindly manner.

Eugenia stepped warily inside and stood before him, dipping her head with respect. Her hair was wet and her outer clothing was damp from the rain.

"I have come as you ordered to inform you that the Templar has returned, Sir."

"That is not much in the way of news," Spartenos snapped.

Eugenia stared at him, and there was fear in her eyes when she next spoke.

"He has been release from prison Senator!" His eyes flew wide with surprise.

"Furthermore Sir Talon has spoken to the authorities, the Admiral of the Fleet no less, about an Arab fleet that is on its way to attack this city."

The reaction she got was unexpected. There was a stunned silence for a few moments, then the senator recovered himself enough to almost physically bring himself under control; he turned a death-like smile to the girl and said, "Tell me again what you just said, and you had better explain what has happened."

The last words were delivered in almost a whisper and the girl shrank from the now blazing eyes that glared at her.

"Sir Talon arrived the other evening with his ship. He has been south on a voyage for my father and brother, as I told you before. However, on his way back he encountered an Arab fleet and managed to evade them and sail on to Constantinople. Did you know he had been placed in prison but then released on the orders of the Admiral of the Fleet? He reported to the Admiral of the Fleet what he saw, including that the Arabs now have the use of Greek Fire. He thinks that the Vice Admiral has been placed under arrest."

The Senator took her by the shoulders and sat her down, telling Markos to bring some mulled wine. Then for the next half an hour he asked her many questions, most of which she could not answer, but after a while he drew back from leaning over her and sat back in his own chair, his mind in turmoil. The news of a plot would have reached the ears of the emperor by now. But far worse was the news that the Arabs were going to attack this city? This had never been the plan.

"What does this mean senator? Is my...the prince in danger?" She asked the last with apprehension in her voice, her eyes wide with concern.

"There is nothing for you to worry about, my dear. Have you told me everything that you know?" his eyes were hooded as he looked at her.

"Yes, it is all I know. What should I do now?" she asked, her hands plucking at the edge of her cloak in her agitation.

"You shall go home and wait there until I call for you. It is better that you do not go out anywhere, least of all to the palace tonight." His tone was cold.

Of a sudden all her dislike and revulsion for him surfaced and Eugenia blurted out, "I know that you have been having my sister watched! Why?"

"What in God's name are you talking about?" he demanded.

"I find it terrible that whoever it is that is doing so is coming inside our house to spy on her in her own room! How could you?" she cried, anger replacing fear at that moment. Instantly, she regretted her impulsiveness.

He looked at her in complete puzzlement. "I have not given orders for anyone to go to your house, other than in the street to watch over your sister, for her protection you understand," he said.

"Someone is disobeying your orders, Senator," she told him icily. "If it happens again I will tell my brother and father. I am tempted to do so even now. I am disgusted that one of your...your assassins has been doing this!"

"You need not fear for that, young lady. I shall be dealing with it sooner than you think," the senator said in a low tone. His face and neck were red with anger.

She got up to go and he patted her on the shoulder as she went past him. "Fear not, my dear, all will be well."

She nodded in mute acceptance of his words, almost cringing at his touch, but she was still seething with anger and her breath came in short bursts. She stumbled out of the library following Markos.

When Markos came back, Senator Spartenos sent for Choumnos. He arrived with an attentive expression on his face, the only indication that he had suffered an accident those several weeks ago was a small scab on his cheek. The expression on the senator's face was difficult to read but it made Choumnos nervous to look at him.

"Follow her quickly and dispose of her. Make it look like vagabonds or footpads robbed her and killed her. She has become a danger." The senator paused then said, "On second thought, send Psellos with her. Tell him to do it quickly and to make no noise. When he gets back I wish to see him. Did you know he has been going into that house over there?"

Choumnos eyes went wide. "No, senator, not at all. But...he did come back very late the other night and I wondered about where he had been."

"I cannot have a man like that jeopardizing our ventures with his rampant desires. You will deal with him when he gets back. I will not have it!" the senator said between clenched teeth.

Choumnos hurried off to find Psellos, whose eyes lit up at the prospect of doing his master's business. He leered at Choumnos, his pock-marked face distorted, and licked his lips. "She is a tasty bit, that one. Not your day, my friend, I suppose he wanted someone who could do it properly."

Choumnos stepped in closer, his eyes inches from those of Psellos. He said in a very low, menacing voice, "Hear me well, you scum. You will kill her and then get your sorry carcass back here. Do you hear me? This is not a real assassin's work. This is a job for a boy! I know more than you think. It is to be done quickly—*quickly*, do you understand? And no one, no one at all must see this; if they do I shall do to you what you intend to do to the girl. Do you hear me?"

Psellos grunted and glared at him. "All right, all right. But you hear me, Choumnos! You might be cock of the hoop for now, but just wait," he snarled. Choumnos turned away with an obscene gesture. Psellos did not dare to give one back. Choumnos did not have his reputation for nothing. Psellos hurried out of the building into the rain.

*****

When Choumnos had departed to pass the message to Psellos, the senator tried to bring the turmoil of his thoughts under control.

If the information was true then they must either move very fast and get the Cilicians into place or call it off, as the whole plan was on the edge of ruin. Had those cursed Arabs betrayed them? He had known that Saieed Fakhouri was a devious man to deal with. He was, after all, almost a pirate, but the present of the fire had surely been enough to make the man keep his word? What would the prince want him to do?

They were so close! But it could all fall in on itself unless he could move very fast. It was late night and raining. How was he to get his messengers to the vital points in time? His features hardened into a bitter mask. He remembered his son and the huge potential the boy had had until his life was wasted. He decided that he would deal with the girl first, then send some of his men into the Kalothesos villa to deal with all of them—including the meddling Templar—while he concentrated on the larger issues now confronting him.

Then without warning a wave of white-hot rage and grief washed over him. He snatched up a small porcelain vase and hurled it with great force at the wall, where it shattered into many small pieces that flew in all directions to scatter on the tiled floor. Markos, standing just outside the door, shrank from this rare display of anger and tried to become invisible.

*****

Talon was looking for Guy when he came out of the stables and walked over to him while chewing on a chicken bone.

"Hello Sir Talon. I was just walking about admiring this palace where your friends live. It is beautiful! I could live handsomely in the stables alone!" he exclaimed. There was awe in his tone. Then he said, "When can we leave? I want to go to the inn as soon as possible and take a bath."

Talon laughed out loud. "My goodness, Guy, You have changed since you came here! What have those women in the whorehouses done to you?"

"Well...you know. They just...prefer." He did not finish. Talon clapped him on the shoulder and laughed again. "I do not want to know, my friend. Just wait here for a while longer. I have a task for you to perform along the way back to the inn. I want you to go at once to the gates of the Great Palace and pass this letter to the Varangian guards at the doors. Can you do this for me?'

Guy nodded. "Of course, right away. Will I see you at the quayside tomorrow, Talon?"

"You will indeed, Guy."

Guy hesitated and then said, "You know, Talon, even the maids in this palace are beautiful beyond words. One went by earlier and left by the gate. She was in a hurry but I did get a glimpse of her face." He brought two fingers and his thumb to his lips and made a kissing sound.

Talon was barely interested. "How long ago was that?" he asked, puzzled that anyone, least of all a maid, would want to be out in this foul weather.

"About half an hour or so. Strange to send a girl unattended on an errand, and in this rain, too."

A tiny alarm bell rang in Talon's head. "Wait here for a moment, Guy. Where are the other two men?"

"Still eating, I suppose."

"Find them now and send one of them off with the message at once, and then come to the main entrance, Guy."

He strode off back into the main building where he encountered Theodora, whose eyes lit up at the sight of him. "Talon! I have been looking all over for you!" she said accusingly. "You are not contemplating leaving, not at this time of the evening or in this weather, are you?" she demanded.

"No, Theodora, I am not. But you will remember the...odd event that happened some weeks ago?"

"Of course I do. I am thinking that perhaps it might have something to do with what you have been telling us. Do you really believe that...the senator might be involved, Talon?" she asked breathlessly her eyes wide.

Talon looked at her. "Do you know where Eugenia might be, Theodora?"

"In her room, I suppose. What has she got to do with anything?" her tone had changed to become just a little petulant.

"Theodora, it might be important. Just find her for me?"

He waited in the anteroom while Theodora left to find her sister, but soon she came back with news from the maid who had told her that Eugenia had gone out.

"In this weather?" Talon asked.

"I think that is very odd. She hates getting wet and I find it very strange that she would go out into this mucky stuff," Theodora said, sounding puzzled. "Why do you want to talk to her, Talon?"

"I will tell you later," he told her. "For the moment, please stay here in the house. I should be back within a few minutes."

He left the house in a hurry and made his way down the short road to the gates, where his suspicions were confirmed. The guards reported that Eugenia had left over half an hour ago and turned right at the roadway.

It was getting darker by the minute as he hastened down the road, retracing his path from the previous time he had come from the other villa. The various houses along the way had torches in sconces set into the walls near to their gates, which illuminated the road after a fashion, causing the dark shadows of the swaying trees to dance and move in their flickering light. The wind had picked up and its loud soughing through the remaining leaves on the plane trees muffled the sound of his boots on the flagstones of the street. The rain pelted down, causing the torches to hiss and splutter, but he could still see about a hundred paces ahead of him, and this was when he noticed someone coming in his direction.

The figure was that of a woman who was about seventy paces away. He could make out that she was dressed in a large voluminous cloak and a hood that partially covered her head. The wind was blowing her skirts about her legs and her hair had broken loose of the hood and was streaming about her pale face making her look like a phantom.

But then without warning the figure staggered and fell forward. With a short grunt of surprise Talon started, thinking she might have tripped over her cloak. But the figure did not get up. Instead she emitted a cry of agony and rolled onto her side, her arm behind her trying to reach something in her back. As he raced toward the figure on the ground, his heart in his mouth, Talon now recognized the contorted features as the woman moaned and struggled with the shaft that protruded from her back; there was a dark stain forming around the shaft. He realized with a cold certainty that it was Eugenia and someone had just shot her with a crossbow bolt.

Talon went to one knee beside her on the wet street.

"Ah, Talon...I am...sorry," she gasped. She tried to rise, but then slumped face down onto the pavement, the arrow protruding from her back.

He was very lucky, for just as he bent to touch Eugenia, who lay limp on the road, he heard the hum of a bolt go overhead. Had he remained upright he would have joined Eugenia on the ground. She was mortally wounded.

His instincts took over and he whipped out his sword, staring hard at the shadows from where she had come, every nerve screaming, crouched and alert for more danger. He knew he had only a few moments before another bolt came his way. His eyes pierced the rain ahead, desperate to find where the assassin was located, and then he noticed a movement. He had no choice but to abandon Eugenia and charge at the flicker of movement praying that he was not mistaken.

Someone in the darkness gave a short harsh laugh and a cross bow flew out of the shadow, rotating as it flew at Talon's head. He dodged to the side, but the cumbersome weapon still struck him a glancing blow on the right shoulder before it clattered to the stones behind him, and as it did a tall, bare headed man carrying a long sword stepped out of the darkness. He carried himself in a half crouch and he seemed very confident as he came towards Talon. By the light of the nearby torches Talon could see he was grinning.

"What have we here then?" he grated, as though talking to himself. "A boy with a sword, indeed? Pity you were there to see this...pedestrian casualty, but that is just too bad."

He finished with a large step forward and a mighty swing with the sword. Talon evaded the blow easily and slipped back a pace to gain some room away from the walls nearby. They both heard a piercing scream behind them. Talon danced back from a savage thrust and then threw a rapid glance behind him. Even his opponent paused for a moment to look to where the sound had come from. Talon recognized the voice. It was that of Theodora; she must have followed him out of the gate, and now she was crouched over her sister wailing with fear and grief.

Theodora lifted her head and screamed again, but Talon had no time to console her. His shadowed opponent was coming at him again and this time seemed determined to finish it quickly. The sword no longer came at him with wild swings but with the controlled hand of someone who knew how to use it. Talon was using the sword he had received from Aarif. He hoped that the Damascus steel would withstand the clash and rasp of their crossing blades. He parried and struck, as did his opponent, who seemed to have developed a little more respect for Talon as he did not speak and was more cautious about attacking. However it was clear that he was in a hurry to finish it as he drove in towards Talon's guard again and again, forcing Talon to give ground.

The figure in front of him muttered something as though incredulous, then said out loud, "It is she! Take your last look at an assassin, boy. I shall finish you, and I shall have her when I am done with you." He attacked even more ferociously.

But Talon was watching his opponent carefully, watching for an opening. The sparks still flew as they struck blades and parried one another, but Talon now had his knife pulled out and waited for his opportunity. Psellos made his mistake at the same moment they both heard shouts from up the road from the Kalothesos house. Out of the corner of his eyes Talon could see men running down the road towards Theodora; they carried torches, and he knew Guy had arrived.

He flicked his eyes forward to see Psellos shift one foot forward like a dancer and then lunge at what he thought was Talon's exposed midriff. Instead of parrying and moving back Talon danced sideways and in; his sword hammered down onto the incoming blade, driving it away, but then his knife thrust straight into the oncoming man's throat. It was not an instantly killing blow but it was mortal. Psellos fell forward onto his hands and knees on the flags of the wet road and coughed. Then it seemed as though he could not get up again. He looked up at Talon, surprise written on his face, and croaked, "How did...?"

"I am one of you, but...better," Talon whispered. Psellos stared at him, his eyes full of terror, and then fell forward onto his face. Talon kicked the man's sword out of the way and turned him over onto his back with his foot. Psellos was still alive but was bleeding furiously from the gaping wound in his neck that he tried feebly to stem.

Talon cut a piece of cloth from the man's tunic, wadded it, then placed it against the wound, knowing full well that the assassin only had little time left. Psellos grimaced in pain.

"Who sent you?" Talon demanded as he knelt near to the man.

It was clear that Psellos knew he only had a few moments of life left. He groaned and then gasped. "You are good. The senator... he...wanted her dead. Wants you all dead. Pretty..."

Talon was about to check the dying man for a knife when Psellos in one last huge effort drew one and with his teeth bared in a snarl tried to reach up and stab him in the side. Talon easily caught the arm and twisted the wrist to force the blade point into Psellos' chest then pushed downwards. They stared into one another's eyes as the point of the blade came down slowly. Psellos grunted with the effort, but in his eyes there was now only stark terror. Talon thrust the last few inches hard and the blade went deep into Psellos' heart. Psellos gave an agonized gasp, his eyes rolled up and his head lolled over to the side while the other hand holding the wad fell away, leaving the gash exposed with a trickle of blood staining the ground. His feet drummed on the road with his death throes, then he was still. The rain began to wash away the blood on his neck.

Talon stood up to find himself surrounded by the servants from the Kalothesos house and many others from nearby houses who had heard the screams and had come to investigate. They regarded him fearfully, having seen the final moments of the fight. Talon was relieved to find Guy was there too.

"What happened, Talon? Dear God preserve us, but it is the woman I saw leave earlier from the house!" he said in a low tone to Talon. "Is she alive?"

Talon shook his head.

"No...she died from a cross bow shaft."

"Who is this?" Guy nudged the body of the dead man at their feet.

"Her assassin," Talon told him.

He went over to where the crowd was gathered around the body of Eugenia with Theodora still holding her and sobbing quietly now. The onlookers were babbling freely to one another but otherwise doing little to help Theodora, who was moaning and rocking herself over the still body of her sister. Talon put his hand on her shoulder and said gently.

"Theodora, you must come with me now."

She looked up at him vacantly and then seemed to recognize him.

"Talon, I...I never meant all those mean things I said about her. I didn't! Oh God, why did this happen? Why?" She began to weep and deep, racking sobs shook her body. Talon decided that they needed to get her out of the rain as quickly as possible.

"I intend to find out, Theodora, but you must help me by going with Guy and my men here. Guy, take Eugenia with you as well, back to the villa and lock it up tight. No one is to be allowed in unless you can verify who they might be. Make sure the guards are on high alert! Be ready for anything, Guy."

Guy nodded in the torchlight and was just about to help the sobbing Theodora to her feet when they all heard the tramp of marching boots and heads turned to stare up the street at the row of torches that were coming down the hillside.

"Quickly, Guy, get her into the house!" Talon whispered. "I do not know who this is, so let us be safe."

Guy wasted no time. He simply picked Theodora up in his arms and told his men to bring the body of Eugenia, while they hurried up the short distance to the torch-lit gates of the villa where the guards admitted them. Talon followed at a slower pace, drifting in with the curious crowd, careful not to be too prominent among them. The marching men came closer and soon they could see the gleam of metal as the light from the torches they carried reflected off armor, chain mail and steel helmets.

Talon did not at first recognize the armor and accouterments of the approaching men, but then realized these might be the men that Alexios had called for and gave a small sigh of relief. As the small detachment came closer he recognized the man in the lead as one of the officers he had met while playing *tzykanion*. He stepped forward to be seen.

A quick command and the squad of men crashed to a halt and the officer walked over to Talon. He recognized him with a smile.

"*Gregaros aggalon*, Sir Talon. We are here because Alexios Kalothesos sent a messenger calling upon us to come to this house. This is very unusual. Can you explain what is going on?"

"No, I cannot at this moment, but I do know that there is danger and it is a good thing that you have come. We might need you before long. Come with your men to the house as it is there that we will have to defend ourselves if anything happens."

The young man nodded, clearly curious, and ordered his men to enter the compound.

"What was going on out there when we arrived?" he asked.

"One of the women of the family was killed out there by an assassin. The reason is unclear, but I killed him. Before he died he told me that Senator Spartenos had sent him."

"Dear God. You cannot be serious? Senator Spartenos, the father of Pantoleon? Are you sure?"

"I am sure of very little right now, but I am certain of one thing and that is that this family is in danger and I am glad that you came."

Over the Golden Horn the lightning flashed, lighting up the roiling sea, followed by a crack of thunder.

Damianus and Joannina had been alerted to the commotion in the street and had come out onto the steps, despite the rain, to investigate. But now they were standing, looking stunned, in the anteroom. Alexios stood next to them just as numb, leaning on his cane. Their shocked expressions told Talon that they knew of Eugenia.

"What has happened, Sir Talon? Tell us what is going on?" Damianus demanded. His voice quavered, near to breaking. Joannina was weeping. She excused herself to attend to her daughter and hurried out, her face buried in her hands.

The senator eyed the newcomer warily.

"Who is this man, and what are those soldiers doing here?" Damianus demanded, as he realized that the man standing in front of him was in uniform.

But Alexios embraced the officer, exclaiming, "You made good speed to get here when you did, Gregaros. I thank you with all my heart. You find us grief stricken at the death of my sister, dead for what reason we do not know. God protect her soul. Talon, can you help us to understand what happened?"

"I do not know what you told the commander, Alex, but it is as though someone kicked over a hornet's nest at the barracks and I heard what sounded like fighting at the Great Palace as we hurried over here. A large troop of Varangians went galloping by heading for the Blachernae palace as we came to the Mese. By the saints, they were in a hurry! My orders were explicit, however. Not to turn aside for anything but to come here immediately," Gregaros said.

"Fighting at the palace? Dear God, what is going on in this city?" Damianus exclaimed.

"I do not know, Senator, but it is something very serious. Soon after the messenger came from your son, another arrived from the Palace telling us that an Arab fleet had been sighted only a day's sail from the city and to prepare for a siege."

Everyone blinked in surprise. They moved indoors to the warmth of the dining room where there was a brazier burning. Talon was comforted with the knowledge that the alarm had been truly sounded, so he relaxed somewhat. Although, there was unfinished business to deal with.

He told them in a few terse sentences what he thought he knew and what had transpired on the street. But their shaking heads and shocked expressions told him they could not believe him.

"Dear Lord help me, but I cannot believe it, I will not believe it! You must be mistaken, Sir Talon. John is my friend and fellow senator. I know him well and we all knew and loved his son Pantoleon. There must be some mistake!" Damianus groaned as he put his head in his hands. "What possible reason could he have to kill my daughter?" Alexios hobbled over and helped him sit, where he stayed with his head in his hands.

"I do not know, Sir, but I intend to find out." Talon turned to Alexios and said, "You must put aside your grief for a little while and prepare to defend this house. Call all the servants into the main building. Gregaros will assist you, but lock all doors and be ready."

There was a flash of lightning over the harbor and another rumble of thunder, then the rain came down harder than ever, thrashing at the shutters and creating a light mist on the ground outside.

Alexios stared at him as though he had just lost his mind. "What are you talking about, Talon?" he demanded.

"Please, Alex, do this. It may be for nothing, but you must prepare. I shall be back. There is something I have to do." Alex nodded reluctantly, but he clearly trusted Talon as he immediately began issuing urgent orders to the servants, who in turn began to run off and gather up the others. Servants were told to close the shutters on every window and the soldiers were placed at every entrance to the house.

Before he left, Talon sought out Guy and found him and his two sailors standing guard at the doorway of a room from which could be heard the wails of grief from Eugenia's mother and sister. The men were clearly uncomfortable with their role but he told them to stay where they were.

"Be on your guard, Guy. Make sure the windows are locked and one of you stays inside next to them just in case; there are assassins abroad tonight. We have the soldiers here to help, but you must protect these women. Tell Alex and his father not to leave the house under any circumstance until I come back."

Guy gave Talon a ferocious grin and said, "We will be here, Talon." They clasped hands and he disappeared.

*****

Alexios and Gregaros rapidly organized the servants and the soldiers into well armed groups and placed them strategically around the interior of the main villa. Alexios made sure that his parents and his sister were well protected by asking Gregaros to provide a couple of extra men to support Guy. He was impressed and not a little startled when Guy gave him a grin like a troll and told him respectfully that Talon had ordered him to protect the women. After that Alex was able to concentrate his attention on the pressing matter of what he might be defending against and trying to guess how to counter whatever it might be. He and Gregaros were seated in the main dining room with a couple of oil lamps for light when Theodora walked in. Guy was with her acting as her bodyguard. He shrugged when he saw them.

"I could not stop her so I am with her," he said in broken Greek.

Theodora was still in her damp tunic, her face was streaked with dried tears and her eyes red from crying; her hair was tousled and she looked very fragile. She almost threw herself into Alexios' arms and began to weep again, her head buried in against his tunic.

"Oh, Alex, what has happened? Why did someone want to kill her?" she sobbed some more while he patted her on her shaking shoulders, unmindful of the tears that were wetting his tunic. He held her close and whispered to her. "We will find out, my little sister. We shall be avenged for this. Before God I swear it."

She said something that was muffled and shivered. He reached for his cloak, which was lying near to hand and pulled it around her shoulders.

"What did you say, my Theo?" he asked.

"I asked, where was Talon? I have not seen him since he was fighting with that...that...assassin on the street."

Alexios looked up at Guy, who shrugged and opened his hands. "He is gone, Sir. That is his way. He does not say anything. But he will be back, of that I am sure. I saw how he dealt with the man who killed...er... your sister, God preserve her soul. He took his bow, I know that much. None of us know him well, but we all trust him."

Not for the first time Alexios contemplated this man who, along with the other rough companions Talon had accumulated, had a frightening aspect to him; but the most terrifying thing, he realized, was that Talon, who did not seem to be, was indeed the most dangerous of them all. He was glad that these people were on his side this night.

Theodora sat up sharply. "I know where he is gone to! Oh God, but they will kill him this time! They will be waiting for him!" she cried.

"Calm yourself, little sister," Alexios said gently, holding onto her. "Where has Talon gone?"

"I shall tell you, brother. When he was here the last time those weeks ago he...he was bleeding. It was late and I was um...reading in the library room, as I could not sleep. He came into the room and pretended that he was all right but he wasn't, as I noticed that someone had cut him on the side. There was blood all over his side."

"How come we know nothing of this?" Alex demanded.

"Because he made me swear that I would tell no one," she hiccuped.

"You had better tell me all you know," Alexios said, and his tone was ominous.

"I noticed the blood and asked him what had happened, but he told me that he had been attacked by footpads. I helped him dress the wound and then he went to bed, as did I later."

"Perhaps he was attacked. I know he can look after himself," Alexios said, but he sounded uncertain.

"I almost believed him, but the very next morning Senator Spartenos came to visit."

Alexios gave a start and exchanged glances with Gregaros. They both looked grim. "Go on, little sister. We are listening," he said.

"Well, it wasn't just a social visit, and in any case the senator does not really like Papa, as you well know; I cannot remember the last time he came over to visit, although his wife Constance does sometimes." She wiped her eyes with the back of her hand. "He was oily nice. I never did like him much nor that prig of his son." She sniffed, and Gregaros had to put a hand over his mouth and look away to hide a grin.

"Theodora, please stick to the point," her brother admonished her.

Thunder rumbled overhead and lightning lit up the gardens. The hiss of rain muted other sounds and the brazier that had been burning brightly earlier had almost gone out. Guy sensed what Alexios was thinking and went over to throw a log on the embers. The fire brightened and drove back the shadows that had darkened the room.

Theodora continued. "Yes, well, he kept asking questions, about whether we or the house guards had seen an intruder coming over the wall into our compound. Of course, Mamma and I did not know anything, nor did the guards, who denied ever seeing or hearing anything. But he insisted that his dogs had found blood at the base of our walls. He told us that there had been a disturbance in his compound and that his men had wounded an intruder who had tried to get into his house."

"You think it might have been Talon?" Alexios asked aghast.

"Do not you see? That very night Talon came in with a cut to his side. I am sure it was he, although I have little understanding as to why. He did mention the words Greek Fire and asked me about it, but nothing more. I didn't know what he was talking about in any case."

She stopped and wiped her nose with a cloth that lay on the table, but the tears came again.

"He killed that…that monster who killed Eugenia, and before the assassin died he told Talon something, and now Talon is back there. I am sure of it! We have to help him!" she wailed.

"There, there! Stop crying, my dearest!" Joannina swept into the room followed by the two sailors, who hurried after her then joined Guy near the brazier. Her face was puffed with weeping and her lovely eyes were red, but she looked determined to be brave and took the girl onto her lap and held her like a child, rocking her in a chair next to Alexios.

"What have you been talking about, Alex?" she asked, looking at him reproachfully over her daughter's head.

"She is telling us of the visit by the senator, Mamma," Alexios said, "but there is something you do not know. It is about Talon."

At that moment they heard a commotion outside. There were shouts and the clash of weapons. Alexios and Gregaros started up.

"You must go and deal with this, my friend. Sir Talon must have been right. I shall stay with my family. God go with you." Alexios' sword rasped as he drew it. He turned to Guy. "Do you know where my father is? Please have John bring him here as fast as you can."

Guy hurried off, while the men who had been with him moved closer to stand next to Joannina and Theodora. Gregaros drew his sword and ran out to join his men.

*****

Talon was glad of the rain and darkness as he slipped over the by now familiar wall near to the postern gate. No one stirred in the garden as he dropped onto the soft earth behind the bushes. He listened carefully for any indication that the dogs might be abroad, but so far nothing. He assumed that the guards might well be taking shelter from this unpleasant weather.

He watched the house, looking for any indication that there might be more activity than normal, but it was dark and very quiet. He began to head for the house when he sensed a movement off to his right. In an instant he had vanished into a dark group of bushes. He peered out in the direction of the noise. A flash of lightning over the Golden Horn briefly illuminated the garden, and he saw a man huddled in the shelter of the arch into which was set the postern gate. The man was peering in his direction as though he sensed something. Very slowly Talon stood up and notched an arrow. It sped true, hitting the man, who died with only a low grunt, falling out of sight at the base of the door.

Talon turned to leave, but then he knew with absolute certainty that a dog was rushing at him from the house. He caught a glimpse of the large shadow as it ran into the bushes about fifty paces away, silently speeding directly towards him. He dropped his bow and settled his sword in his two hands, its point facing the area where the animal might attack from. He did not have long to wait. Within moments the huge animal burst out of the bushes in a spray of water to leap at him, going for his throat.

Talon knew that he had a split second and thrust sharply forward at the huge black form diving at him. His sword met flesh and penetrated; he rammed it forward even as the huge jaws of the animal snapped within inches of his own throat. His sword went deep, almost to the hilt as it penetrated the chest cavity of the dog, which now dragged him down as it fell. Fearful of the noise it might make Talon drew his dagger and finished the twitching creature off before it could do much more than make some broken grunts and a low choking sound of agony.

He rose to his feet, panting, to again watch and listen for any more danger. Picking up his bow and slipping it over his shoulder and holding his sword in front of him he moved very cautiously away from the area of the gate and slipped though the bushes and under the low trees to arrive just in front of the loggia of the huge building. In the darkness he could only see the dim light of oil lamps in one or two of the rooms on the ground floor and one on the second floor. There did not seem to be much activity going on and he wondered if he might have been wrong all along.

But then he saw the movement of another dark figure standing in the deeper shadows of the loggia. The man came to the balustrade and gazed over to the place where the dog had encountered Talon. The figure was obviously concerned and Talon reasoned he had loosed the dog to go and investigate something the animal had sensed. The sentry gave a low call and then whistled.

The man never knew what hit him. The arrow went into his neck, quickly followed by another that struck his chest with an audible thump. The man doubled forward and toppled over the low railing into the bushes, where his body lay there inert. Talon heard an urgent call from along the loggia and another guard ran down its length, no longer trying to remain silent. He called out a name. When there was no response the figure leaned over the railings nearer to where Talon hid and stared out across the garden. A flash of lightning lit up the trees, followed by a loud crack of thunder, and the rain hissed, obscuring the far end of the compound.

Talon slipped behind him and thrust his dagger deep into the man's middle back, just to the left of center. He held the body as it slumped and then allowed it to fall over the rails to join his companion in the bushes. Talon looked around and wondered how many more sentries there might be. He decided to get onto the second floor. He heaved himself up to the supporting beams and then eased himself onto the tiles of the roof. To his consternation he found that the tiles were loose in places so it took a great deal of care to move up the sloping roof without slipping on the wet tiles, to arrive at the closed shutters of the nearest window.

Then he heard a commotion below him on the loggia. Someone shouted and there was the sound of running feet as the alarm was raised. He guessed that another alert guard had discovered the bodies of his companions. Using his dagger to prize open the shutters, he hurriedly entered the room on the second floor. He made sure that the shutters were closed again and then crouched, listening to the sudden increase of activity taking place below. He could hear shouts and running feet, then doors were opened and slammed and more running feet, now with female voices crying out in fearful tones adding to the commotion.

Talon guessed that it would be only a matter of time before someone came up the stairs to investigate. He slipped out of the room and went to the stairwell to listen and see what he could. The ground floor was a blaze of light and hurried footsteps told him that the staff was now wide awake. His work was going to become much harder. He made his way cautiously down the stairs and then hid behind a thick drape that covered the opening to a small archway. No one came by so he listened carefully and made out the sound of voices raised down a corridor he could see to his left. There was a guard standing in front of one of the doors further down the hallway. The guard was facing forward and alert. Talon drew his bow and stepped into the middle of the corridor. The guard must have sensed something at the last moment, for he turned to see the dark apparition lit from behind and the arrow already speeding toward him. He had no more time than to give a cry of terror before the arrow embedded itself in his breast. He fell without another sound, but his shield and spear fell with a clatter. Talon was already racing down to reach the body as the door opened. Without stopping Talon hammered against the door with his shoulder, knocking someone backwards.

As he crashed through the entrance Talon noticed the shocked face of a servant who had fallen to the floor and was now holding his nose and staring at him with stark fear in his eyes. Leaning over the man Talon seized his shoulder to stop him moving then hammered the pommel of his sword down onto the top of his head, sending the servant sprawling unconscious.

There was no time to pause and Talon was rapidly taking in the occupants of the room and its contents. There were two other men in the room besides the servant. One of them was Senator Spartenos in the process of rising from a divan, but his companion caught Talon's full attention, for he was already moving very fast in Talon's direction, a long sword held in front of him.

The man was dressed in a thick plain tunic of brown wool resembling a monk's habit, including a cowl, but Talon doubted he was a monk. The manner in which he held the sword denoted someone who knew very well how to wield it, and the half smile on the plain face told Talon that here was a man who was confident in his ability.

"You finally arrived. I hoped you might come back again," he said.

Talon said nothing but flicked his eyes around the room to familiarize himself with the furniture and other statues placed against the walls. The room was ablaze with light from a dozen oil lamps placed in niches and on the table near the senator, who was now standing watching him with narrowed eyes.

"Ah Sir Talon, this is a surprise! Were you the intruder who came here several weeks ago?" senator Spartenos said

Talon nodded and tapped the tip of his opponent's blade away with a clink. They were feeling one another out, but he knew within that split second that he was up against a master swordsman.

"I though you would be dead by now. Instead, here you are again! What are you doing here?" the senator demanded loudly, as though trying to distract him.

Without looking at him Talon said, "You ordered the killing of Eugenia?"

"Why yes, I suppose I did. I expect Psellos has failed to do what I asked of him?"

"He succeeded—but then he died," Talon replied, as he danced back out of the way of a vicious knee high swipe from his opponent. He saw the gleam in the eyes of his opponent at his words.

"Well, that was to be expected, I suppose. Psellos always did have an inflated opinion of his abilities. Now Choumnos here, he is much more modest, but you have made a bad mistake coming here. He is still peeved at you for wounding him. I doubt if you will be leaving on your own two feet this time."

Talon's eyes were fixed on Choumnos, who was watching him with a wide, unblinking, cold stare. They gave very little away, barely even flickering as he made his lunges and short sharp blows aimed at Talon's head and neck, which were now increasing in rapidity. His teeth were bared in a chilling smile as he attacked, swinging and stabbing at Talon in quick succession. Talon was forced to give ground.

He blundered backwards into a low stand shaped like a pillar with a plaster head on it, knocking both over with a crash. As he stumbled back Choumnos darted in and cut downwards. Talon only had a split second to raise his sword and deflect the blow with a shower of sparks. Choumnos snapped his blade high again in one smooth motion and brought it down once more. But Talon had scrambled out of the way and Choumnos' blade struck the corner of a small wooden table. The wood splintered and the table leaned over to allow the small items on its polished surface to slide down onto the floor and shatter in a noisy stream.

Talon barely heard the words, "Oh dear, my wife will not be pleased to see that. Have a care, Choumnos. This isn't your house to destroy."

But the two opponents paid the senator no attention at all. Talon, having regained his balance, was attacking with everything he had from blade to hilt to pommel. He discovered that the training he had received a long time ago from his uncle Phillip was paying off. He managed to bring them very close together at one time where he twisted his sword so that he could punch Choumnos in the face with the hilt. Choumnos blinked with the pain and blood seeped out of a gash on his upper lip He took a step back and made room but never dropped his guard. He glared at Talon as he wiped his mouth.

"You will regret that, Templar," he said softly, and then danced forward with another ferocious series of lunges and strikes that made Talon work hard to avoid being struck in multiple places. He drew his dagger now and used it to parry some of the lighter strikes.

Choumnos was grimly determined to wear him down, his sword was held in both hands and he used it more as a striking weapon than for lunging but Talon was quickly dissuaded from assuming he could get inside his opponent's guard very easily. They demolished another table, which Choumnos shoved aside as he backed off from a determined assault from Talon. It fell over with a crash and a pottery bowl shattered, its pieces getting under foot.

Talon realized then that Choumnos was edging him backwards toward the senator behind him. He slipped sideways very quickly and a metal object flew past his head to thump against the wall. He slashed at the senator, who dived out of the way of the flashing blade, tripped and almost fell over the back of the divan in his haste to get out of the way of the two combatants. The senator yelled in outrage as they blundered yet again into some priceless art object, which fell over with a crash, adding to the litter already on the decorated tiles of the floor. Talon could sense that Choumnos was tiring as the savage speed of the initial attacks had slowed, but he too was feeling the toll. They were both sweating with exertion now and he wondered how he was going to finish the fight. Choumnos gave so little away.

Talon had to get in close again, unappealing as that might be. He allowed Choumnos to come in and parried a couple of snake-swift blows. Just at that moment there was a huge flash of lightning that lit up the room with an eerie glow, followed by an immense crash of thunder directly overhead. For a split second Choumnos hesitated, and it was to prove fatal. Talon crossed blades then using all his strength forced his opponent's blade aside and drove for the opening to stab his dagger into the man's midriff. He had meant to strike at the heart but at the last moment Choumnos shifted his weight. Talon drove the blade in deep and at the same time used his own sword to make sure that Choumnos could not use his own blade. The agony showed on Choumnos's face and he dropped his sword with a metallic clatter on the marble floor, then leaned forward and dropped to his knees. He stayed there holding onto his belly, his head down, gasping.

Talon stepped back and watched for a few moments as Choumnos clutched at his midriff. Then the man groaned and looked up to whisper, "Finish it! Finish it, God damn you!" His eyes pleaded with Talon, who stared at him then gave a brief nod. He slipped behind Choumnos and with one huge blow struck his head from his shoulders.

The head bounced to the floor to lie face up while the body slowly fell forward to sprawl in a bloody puddle almost at the feet of the senator, who had been about to come at Talon from behind. Talon stood there looking at the body and the senator; his bloody sword shot up to point now at the senator's chest while he took great gulps of air. The senator backed off, fear in his eyes.

"I am not a fighter, do not..." he said with a tremor in his voice.

"Sit down," Talon's voice was low and curt.

The senator complied and Talon watched him while he recovered his breath.

"Why did you have Eugenia killed?" he demanded.

"Because she knew too much. She was not the innocent that a naïve fellow like you might have thought. She was a whore."

Talon flicked the bloody point of his blade up to the senator's face. A drop of blood splattered the senator's cheek.

"Do not call her that."

The senator stared into Talon's hard eyes and realized that he was a hair's breadth away from death. he wiped the blood off his face with the edge of his toga and looked at it.

"She knew where everyone was...is," he said coldly. "She was the messenger between me and the prince, who was bedding her... the fool! He just can't keep his hands off a pretty girl even when his future empire is at stake. Sad to say, she meant nothing to him."

"Who is this prince?"

"Prince Andronikos Komnenos, the emperor's nephew! You do not know of him, do you?"

He must have noted the surprise on Talon's face.

"Oh yes, Eugenia was being bedded by him, and when I found out I used her. She was terrified that her family would find out and that the empress would discover her indiscretion. That can get you blinded—or worse. The family would have been utterly dishonored."

"What have you to do with the Arab fleet? You have mentioned Greek Fire. I overheard you the last time."

"So you did hear something. That useless fellow over there let you get the better of him then, and told me that you could not have heard anything. Well, he has paid his price...and so shall I, but you are too late to stop what is in motion now."

"I warned the Admiral when I arrived, and I am sure he listened because the fleet is preparing for sea." Talon watched the senator as he spoke and saw a flicker of alarm.

"I heard that, damn you to Hell. We could have had an emperor who knew what he was doing but for interference from ignorant bastards like you, Frank."

"Who is it that you have been working for? Just the Prince?"

"You will just have to find out, because I shall not tell you. We might still be successful, and even though I know I shall not see it, my shade will have the satisfaction of seeing Manuel destroyed."

"I know the Genoese worked for you, so it was you who arranged for the Fire to be captured, using him as go-between with the Arabs?"

"Caravello? Yes, he had his uses. I imagine he is long gone now, unless he got bottled up in the harbor. You had better be careful if you chase him on the high seas, as he has the Fire. He will have no hesitation in burning you to the water if you confront him. He knows full well the value of that stuff—and how to use it. Pity...with his ship and the fire I could have carved out a place of my own on one of the islands, as I had intended to one day.

"As for the cursed Arabs, they were only supposed to sail to Abydos and create a diversion. Their commander must have become ambitious, greedy or both, the fool, but what do I care? If our own navy cannot protect us, who can?" Spartenos' voice was full of scorn.

"You are a senator with wealth and power aplenty. Why do you hate the emperor so much and risk all this on a gamble?"

"Even before the disaster at Myriokephalon he was useless. His waste of money and his exorbitant taxes were ruining what is left of the nobility. Then to cap it all led my only boy to his death at Myriokephalon. My son Pantoleon was a rising star in this city!" he was speaking in a lauder tone now. "My...my boy would have been a great general and even more perhaps, but that...fool Manuel let his army to destruction and I lost my only son." The senator put his face in his hands and sobbed. It was so unexpected that Talon stared at him in astonishment.

"It was your son and others like him who persuaded the emperor to go into that deathtrap against the advice of his own generals, senator," Talon said, his tone was sharp.

Senator Spartenos looked up, his lined face streaked with tears. "You are a liar, Frank. You do not know what happened."

"I was there, Senator, and I heard and saw. Later I and Alexios Kalothesos tried to find your son's body after the battle. I regret that we failed. But it was he, as much as anyone, who talked the emperor into the gorge."

There was a timid tap on the wall and they both whirled to see who was there. Standing in the opening was Constance holding a jug and some large silver cups on a tray. She looked like a ghost but appeared to be icily calm, and ignoring the chaos of the room and the headless corpse she walked slowly up to the two men.

She barely glanced at Talon but placed the cups on the debris littered table in front of the senator and said, "I have told the servants to leave the compound and to go to their homes. It is time we had a drink of wine, my dearest. You will need it after all this."

He looked down at the wine in the cups but did not touch it. "I need no wine, woman. Leave us."

"I could leave you, my husband, but I do not think that you will like having your eyes gouged out with red hot irons and your limbs torn from your body while you are still alive." She glanced at Talon, then continued.

"John, that is what is going to happen to both of us if they come and take us, and they will do so. Do you want this humiliation for me? Are you so selfish? All your little plots are finished and with them our lives. I wish to die with you, but with dignity," Constance said with icy calm.

"You will allow us that much, will you not, Frank?" She looked up at Talon. Her hazel eyes were those of a ghost, but there was a desperate plea in them that made him hesitate.

Talon stared into her eyes for a long moment and then finally nodded. "I shall stay with you to the end," he said softly.

The fight had gone out of the senator. His shoulders slumped and his features seemed to have aged ten years within a few minutes. For some long moments he said nothing and just stared off into space, but then he moved slowly. Without looking at Talon he picked up one of the cups and gave it to his wife. In a moment of tenderness he kissed her on the cheek and said gruffly, "You are right...dignity. Goodbye, Constance. You have been good to me. God be merciful to our souls." He then picked up the other cup, held it for a moment in front of him, then abruptly tossed the contents down in two gulps.

Constance followed at a slower pace and then placed her cup down next to his; her hand shook just a little. Then she moved so that she could be next to him. He placed his arm over her thin shoulders and said, "Make this house our funeral pyre, Frank. Will you do this for us?" He leaned his head back as though very tired and shut his eyes. His wife appeared already to be asleep.

Talon waited while the agonies of the poison finished their work and they were both finally still. He then went over to an array of candles and bundled some material into a pile. Pouring oil onto the bundle he set it ablaze. The flames spread quickly. The room was rich in material for a flame to catch. When it had taken hold and had flared, about to consume the entire room, he left.

Talon returned to the wall the way he had come; as he went over it he saw that the fire had taken hold and the entire downstairs section was ablaze.

The Grecian vessels not unskillfully
Were smiting round about; the hulls of ships
Were overset; the sea was hid from sight,
Covered with wreckage and the death of men;
The reefs and headlands were with corpses filled,
And in disordered flight each ship was rowed,
As many as were of the Persian host.

Aeschylus

Chapter 26
A Battle at Sea

Talon appeared as he had left, without warning. Neither the guards at the gates, the soldiers, nor the servants noticed his arrival until he was there in the house. The family Kalothesos was standing under the loggia, facing northeast, watching the huge fire that glowed in the night a few streets away. The sparks from the burning house flew high into the night sky and the people on the loggia could hear distant shouts as the alarm was sounded all about. Talon noticed that there had been a fight while he was away and resolved to ask Guy what had transpired, but for now it sufficed that he was back and the family was unharmed.

It was Alexios who noticed him first, and he exclaimed, "Where did you appear from Talon?" He registered genuine surprise at seeing him so suddenly back with them.

The others turned and stared equally surprised, but then Theodora rushed up to him and embraced him.

"We were so worried about you, Talon. Where have you been?" she demanded, although she was sure she knew.

He gently pulled away from her and smiled at the others.

"Let us say that much has been resolved. I see that you are all unharmed, Alex. Thank God for that."

"Everything is fine now, thanks be to God. Are you not going to tell us where you've been, Talon?" Joannina asked him. Her glance went to the fire.

"I cannot, my Lady, but you should know that a danger is past and we can take up our lives again. I am truly grieved at the loss of your daughter," he added.

Theodora gave him a look that said, *I know very well where you have been.*

Joannina looked back at him, the tears in her eyes gleaming in the light of the fire. "We will miss our daughter, Talon. She was precious to us."

Alexios gripped his hand and said, "Wherever you went, Talon, I am sure it was for a good reason. We had a small fight here. How did you know they would come? But they were not anticipating the men under Gregaros' command and were well and truly surprised. His men drove the intruders off, but we have still no idea as to where they came from or whose men they were. You would not know?" he asked staring hard at Talon.

Talon shook his head, but Alexios nodded as though he understood. "Very well. I am glad that you are safe anyway."

Damianus took his hand and said, "It has been a night of tragedy, as we have lost a daughter we loved. Yet you have been strong for us, and I am grateful, Sir Talon. Now it it is time for our beds. We can talk more in the morning."

That night Talon slept only a little. His mind kept going to the burning house where he had left the bodies of senator and his extraordinary wife. But later he had a dream. He was on a bridge where there were many people. From there he could see Rav'an with Fariba and Far'jan, and he knew, even though he could not see him, that Reza his brother was there, and to his joy, so was Jean. They were laughing and watching the sailboats on the river below. He heard the voice of a child, and looking up he saw that Rav'an was holding a young boy in her arms and smiling at him. She seemed to be offering the child to him, but as he reached for the child the dream faded and he could not recapture it. He called out her name as he woke up, his heart aching, as it had not done for some time. He knew then that he must find a way to return to Persia, even though he knew his uncle Far'jan was dead as was Jean. A cold dread swept over him as he considered this. Perhaps they were all dead and with his uncle, and they were calling to him from the other side. He sat up sweating and then wept, for he did not know if they were now alive or dead.

*****

The next day Talon rose early, but not so early that Joannina did not intercept him. She greeted him with a wan smile and kissed him on both cheeks.

"I trust you slept well, Talon, despite the events of last night?"

He looked into her red-rimmed eyes and drawn features and saw the pain. Rather than rushing off, which was his inclination, he decided to stay for a while.

"I slept, but I fear that perhaps you did not, my Lady?"

"It was difficult, Talon. I am so grateful..."

He put up a restraining hand. "Come, my Lady. I have found that gardens are the most precious of remedies for calming the spirit. Why do not we walk outside? It is a beautiful day and you have a lovely garden."

She nodded and placed her hand on his arm then they walked out onto the loggia pausing, for a brief moment, to look over the Golden Horn and the glittering sea now full of sails of all manner of ships, which had taken shelter from the storm the night before but were now free to sail again.

"How is it that you, a warrior, and my son tells me a formidable warrior, love gardens so much, Talon?" she asked him as they descended the steps of the loggia and walked along a pathway that led among the shrubs and olive trees that glistened with rain drops not yet burned off by the early sun.

"It seems like a long time ago, my Lady Joannina, that I was introduced to a garden in a land where they are especially prized because water is not so freely available. They are known as *paradise* and men and women value them highly as places to reflect and find peace."

"I come often to this garden, but alas, my two daughters do not...did not always often join me. I fear the young are always impatient to do other things that preoccupy them. Do you find peace here in my garden, Sir Talon?"

Talon smiled. "Your garden is one of those *paradises* and I love to walk in it. I know full well why your husband likes the vines too. He explained it to me and it made good sense."

"My husband is a good man, although he can be very prickly at times. You are aware that he has become very fond of you?"

Talon smiled at her. "I am one of those terrible Franks. How could this be?"

Joannina laughed and he was pleased that she could. There was much grief, but this one time she could.

Then she became serious and said, "My little daughter spent the night with me."

Talon said nothing.

"If you are not aware of this, then you should be. She is head over heels in love with you, Talon. She cried a lot, as I think she knows that you are not interested."

He stopped in surprise and stared at her. Joannina smiled. "Oh yes, I have noted it, and since the first day too."

"As I recall, she spent some time treating me like something the dog had dropped at the door," he said with a grin.

She laughed again. "Ah, but I am a woman, and last night it was confirmed. Talon, you do know that this is a family that would welcome you as a son. You have proved a staunch friend and comrade to our Alex and all of us. We are forever in your debt for that. But..."

"My Lady?"

"You carry many deep secrets and my instincts tell me that Theo will not be lucky where you are concerned. Am I right? Is there another woman in your life?"

"Yes, my Lady, there is. But you must know that I am very fond of Theo and would not hurt her for the world. She is amusing, resourceful and very intelligent, and will I hope one day be a formidable physician, but...there is someone...I left behind a long time ago."

"Where is this woman? Is she in Acre?"

"No, my Lady. She is in Persia, although I do not know if she is indeed still alive. I dreamt of her only last night and it left me very confused."

Joannina touched him gently on the arm. "Ah, Talon, it is as I feared. I imagine she is very beautiful. They say some Persian women are exquisite. I shall have to tell Theo before too long. Gregaros was making sheep's eyes at her last night. He is from a very good family and might be able to deal with that complicated girl of mine."

It was Talon's turn to laugh. "Complicated she is, but she is a truly wonderful girl, Joannina. I wish to be her friend. If Gregaros can woo her and hold her, then he is a lucky man indeed. But I am not leaving you for good when I depart for Acre, which I must do very soon. Sir Guy will be wondering what has delayed my arrival and I have urgent dispatches to deliver. But now that we have a trading license from his Majesty, I hope to be a frequent visitor to your house in the future."

"None of us would forgive you were you not to visit us, Talon. You will always have a family here with us." She had tears in her eyes as she kissed him on the cheek. "Look, my husband is bullying the gardeners in the vineyard again. We must go and defend them." She took his arm and they made their way down to the rows of vines where the senator stood holding up a small bunch of grapes while he harangued the long-suffering gardeners.

*****

Having spent the better part of the early morning with the Senator and Joannina, Talon quickly paid his respects to Alexios. He was evasive when Alexios asked him if he knew why his sister had been attacked, pleading ignorance, but it was clear from his face that Alexios was dissatisfied with his answer.

"I understand that Eugenia was attacked by a footpad, and I came too late to save her, Alex."

"But Theo said he spoke to you before he died. She also told us about a visit you paid to the Senator Spartenos' house some time ago, and she was certain that you went there again last night," Alexios said, indicating that he wanted to hear more.

"Yes, I did go there the first time, because I noticed someone I knew from a long time back go there in the night."

"Since when does a Templar go around visiting houses at night and uninvited?"

Talon spent some time explaining who Caravello was and what had transpired in Alexandria.

"Now I can understand something of what this is about," Alexios stated, "but what does he have to do with the senator?

Talon went on to explain what had occurred with the Greek Fire, which Alexios knew about, but not the source. When he had finished Alexios was silent for a long moment. Finally he looked at Talon.

"I do not want my father to know what you have told me, Talon. He might not have liked Spartenos, but he would be very disturbed to find out that he was a traitor."

"I agree, Alex. It will do no one any good to look further now. It is difficult enough for all of you to lose Eugenia."

"What did my sister have to do with him, Talon?" Alexios asked, his tone insistent.

"Before she died she told me she had delivered a message from the palace; that is all I know, Alex."

Alexios looked at him hard. "You are not telling me everything, but I think that you are protecting my sister, Talon. If her honor was at stake, then so be it. As far as I am concerned she died without dishonor and I shall mourn her."

Talon placed a hand on his friend's shoulder. "I knew her for but a very short while, but I too mourn her with your family. Alex, the danger is past and you can look forward to the future without looking over your shoulder. May her soul rest in peace."

*****

He made his excuses then left the villa with Guy and his men to go back to the harbor. The storms had moved away. The sun was well over the low hills of Galata on the other side of the Golden Horn and the day promised to be warm and sunny. There was even steam rising from the hillside as it began to burn off the moisture on the trees and grass along the avenue. As they walked down the hill to the harbor of Prosphorion Talon could smell lingering smoke from the burnt wreckage of the villa. They had seen a small crowd of curious onlookers gathered about the back wall, but they could not see much as the door was firmly shut and surly guards were posted outside to stop people climbing the wall to take a peek.

"Were you part of that, Talon?" Guy asked him with a nod in the direction of he smoldering ruin.

"Yes. That man had Eugenia killed, but it was much larger than that, Guy. In the end the fire was for the best. God rest their souls."

Guy gave him an intense look but said nothing, and then led the way down the hill without further comment. As they continued Talon stared across the Golden Horn. There were almost no ships in the harbor. The fleet had gone to sea. He wondered where it would meet the Arabs and what the outcome would be.

Makarios and Giorgios met them at the gates. They were there for the purpose of negotiating for a berth alongside the quay. Makarios greeted Talon warmly, which was a change from the last time they had met, when he had displayed distinct concerns as to Talon's capabilities. That attitude was gone, replaced by a pleasant smile and discussion as to what came next.

The soldiers at the gates, however, were on high alert and not about to let them in on just their word, so they had to wait while an officer was found. These were not the same men who had been there before. While one of them marched off to find his officer Talon had a moment of apprehension, as he thought this too might have been something the senator had arranged. Had the ports been taken over, he wondered? He was relieved a moment later to see a familiar figure in full chain armor stomping along the flagstones toward them. He had a slight limp to his gait.

It was Cuthberht, and accompanying him were other Varangian soldiers. He grinned when he recognized Talon.

"The Frank Templar, by God! I hope you are well?" They clasped hands.

"I am well, Cuthberht. I was not expecting to see you here guarding the port. What is happening?"

"Ah, Talon! Much happened last night while you were abed. We discovered a plot to depose the emperor, and scotched it in the making. We, the mighty Varangians, had a big fight on our hands rounding up a bunch of Cilicians and either chasing them out of town or throwing them into the dungeons!"

Talon looked shocked. "A coup against the emperor, you say? Dear God, I trust you crushed it completely? How are we to sleep in our beds peacefully otherwise?"

Cuthberht roared with laughter. "Oh yes, you missed a good fight. Well I know how you and Max like a scrap. It went back and forth for a while, I can tell you, for those Cilicians were determined fighters, but it is all under control right now. What can I do for you?"

Talon smiled. "I have my ship here, Cuthberht. Do I have your permission to bring it alongside the quay to unload its cargo?"

"Of course, Talon! By all means, and may your profits far exceed your costs!"

"Thank you, Cuthberht. Please give my sincere best wishes and deepest thanks for our deliverance to all your comrades."

A small bribe to the harbormaster and they were able to signal to the ship that it could come in to tie up. An alert seaman called to Henry, and soon they could see the anchor stone being pulled up, and then the oars went out and the ship began to maneuver through the crowded shipping toward the quay.

Talon stood and watched it coming in with an unexpected sense of pleasure. He found that to his surprise he was beginning to like the smells of the harbor and the noises that came with it, the wheeling seagulls and their shrill cries and the almost constant sound of water slapping against the stone walls, the bustle and activity. There was some kind of promise here, as though this was where adventures began. As soon as the ship was tied up Henry came ashore and greeted them. "What has been going on in the city, Talon? Guy, do you know anything?"

"There was a small group of people who wanted to burn a palace down, that is all we know, Henry," Talon said with a look at Guy.

"Then that must have been the fire we could see on the hillside up there." Henry pointed to where the villa had once stood high on the hill above the harbor.

"Henry, you and Guy should work with Makarios and Giorgios to unload the ship and prepare her for sea again."

"Where are we going, Talon?"

"There is a ship that I want to follow, Henry. Neither of you are to say anything to the others, but I want you to be ready at a moment's notice to sail out of here. Do you see that ship over there?" Talon pointed.

Henry and Guy shielded their eyes from the sun as they faced east.

"The Genoese galley?" Guy asked. Then he gave a start. "Is that not the one that you and Max have such an interest in, Talon?"

"It is, Guy, and I need you and Henry to keep a sharp eye on her, as I believe she is about to fly. If Makarios has a cargo for Acre, then we will take what he has, but it is secondary to keeping that ship under observation. We might even leave beforehand so that the captain does not get suspicious."

"Do we not need some cargo to pay for ourselves, Talon?" Henry asked, ever the practical seaman.

"Do not worry about that, Henry. It is all taken care of; we are no longer poor men."

Henry beamed. "I like the sound of that, Sir Talon," he said.

"Hurry with the unloading, or Makarios will get impatient," Talon laughed. "They are very pleased with us. We can come back to this city any time now."

Henry rubbed his beard with a pleased look on his weathered face and Guy grinned frighteningly.

"What about the prisoner?" Guy asked.

"He stays below if he knows what is good for him. This is not the time for him to show up on the deck."

"Very good, Sir."

As Talon walked away to talk to Makarios the two men looked after him.

"You once told me that Talon was a strange and dangerous man, Henry, but now I know that he is not at all a man to cross."

"Why? Were you thinking of it, Guy?" Henry asked with a chuckle.

Guy gave him a reproachful look and said, "You know better than that, Henry. I am loyal to the death for Sir Talon. He saved us from a fate worse than death in Egypt. You cannot repay that with anything less than complete loyalty."

"You are right, Guy. I was joking, but you are right. I do not ever want that look he sometimes gets to ever be directed my way. That is truly a look that can kill. Now tell me what happened last night. Do you know anything about that great fire on the hill?"

"Oh yes, I think so," Guy said, his tone that of a conspirator.

*****

It was already quite late in the afternoon when Talon arrived back at the villa with the aim of packing his belongings. He had intentionally stayed away because he felt that the family needed time to grieve and his presence might be an uncomfortable reminder of the night before.

He was engaged in packing his meager belongings when there was a knock on the door and Theodora walked in without waiting. Talon smiled to himself; the girl was not one for convention.

Her greeting to Talon was subdued. The first thing she did was to go up to him and put her arms around him and stay there for a few long moments. He put his arms around her and waited, smelling the clean scent of her tousled hair.

"I am so glad that you are safe, Talon. My brother says that you have avenged the death of Eugenia and that we must grieve, but not with vengeance on our minds." Her voice was muffled.

"He is right, Theo; it is time to grieve, but not to allow old wounds to fester. It will be difficult, but it is time to begin the healing."

"Will you be staying now, Talon? It is almost winter and not good for sailing." She sounded hopeful.

"There is another ship in Abydos that I need to attend to, and then I am going to have to go back to Acre before winter, Theo. I have documents to deliver to Sir Guy for the King of Jerusalem and cannot delay any longer. But I promise I shall be back in the late spring."

There was a discreet cough from outside. "I did not mean to disturb you, Sir Talon, my Lady," Joseph said from outside. "But my Lord Alexios told me to inform you about something going on that you should know about."

Talon immediately thought of what Cuthberht had told him, but Joseph sounded excited.

"A messenger came to tell us that there is a wondrous sight to see from the top of the hills facing west. The fleet is there! Lord Alexios said we must hurry, as the light is going."

Talon and Theodora looked at one another in alarm. "Come," he said. "I think we are about to see something momentous. I fear it is the attack of the Arab fleet."

They left the room immediately to find Damianus and Joannina with Alexios in the dining room waiting for them.

"Ah! There you are, Talon. Alexios says there is something up and we have to leave immediately to see it. Come with us, Theo, my girl. I have ordered John and Joseph to call for litters to take us there. You will go with Joannina. Hurry!"

Talon hastened to get his sword and join them outside the house. The small procession left within a few minutes, only to discover that the street outside was already filling up with people, all of whom were making their way toward the top of the hill. Word had gotten out that there was a spectacle and people were murmuring to one another with excited anticipation.

Talon walked with the bodyguards that Gregaros had left behind. Gregaros was no longer with them, having been recalled to the barracks that morning.

"If we want a good view we must move to higher ground," Alexios called out to the bearers and the eunuchs. "John, tell them to make for the Nymphaeum; we can see for a great distance from up there."

The procession hurried along, and the crowd made way for the litters as the bearers trotted by. By the time they were halfway up the slope to the Nymphaeum the bearers were panting and sweating in the evening air, but finally the western side of the city was laid out below them. An already sizable crowd was gathered on the crest of the hill. People of all walks of life were standing in small groups or families, talking excitedly and pointing out to sea. Talon sensed the tension in the air. All of a sudden they heard distant cheering and the people nearby exclaimed and pointed to the walls of the Nymphaeum. "The Emperor is here!" they whispered. "He is here to see the fleet."

Talon made sure that the senator and the ladies were able to see without difficulty and were attended to by their servants, then stood off to the side with Alexios, who was seated on a light wicker chair. The sun had already set but the western sky was streaked with red and gold clouds, making for a spectacular sunset.

Talon stared back out to sea and was astonished at what he saw. The water about five miles off shore was full of naval ships.

There were three large groups of galleys well spaced apart. He counted roughly thirty ships in each group. These were the war galleys of the Byzantine fleet and they were facing west. So the Admiral of the Fleet had taken him seriously after all. He said a small prayer of thanks.

But then the crowd noticed something else, and the murmurs became apprehensive. Moving toward the Byzantine fleet was another large group of ships, and Talon felt a prickle of excitement. The Arab fleet had arrived! He wondered what the commander was thinking as he took his fleet forward.

"I am sure that the commander did not expect to be met at sea by the Byzantine fleet," Alexios remarked with satisfaction.

"They probably hoped to attack the fleet in port where its superior numbers and fire ships could not maneuver and would thus have been easily destroyed," Talon replied.

"You were not with us today at the villa, but a messenger came from Niko, telling me that the Admiral of the Fleet had arrested the Vice Admiral and a group of other disloyal officers last night, Talon."

Talon looked at him in surprise.

Alexios nodded. "Yes, there has been a lot of discontent since the disaster that we were part of, but that is no reason for treason. Niko said to thank you for what you did. He says they are ready for anything and this is as close to an ambush the fleet could get. He will be in a ship down there this evening."

"Then this should be interesting. God protect Niko and all the fleet," Talon said.

Darkness was falling as the final glow of the sunset faded and dusk began to settle over the city. Smoke from ten thousand home fires began to settle as a light fog in the lower reaches of the city along streets and avenues.

They all heard it begin. Then the sound grew, and the crowd was still and absolutely silent as the bells began to ring. The sound was made by hundreds, even thousands of small bells of bronze being rung by hand or beaten with small hammers as each church took up the ringing until every bell in every church in the city was chiming. The tone and volume were at a pitch that indicated danger and alarm. The city of Constantinople was standing to as yet another enemy approached its walls.

The fleets were about to close with one another. Talon remembered Nikoporus' description of the Greek Fire, and his own encounter with it, and hoped that his friend was safe. As if to emphasize Talon's concerns a plume of fire arched out of a ship and a gasp went up from the crowd. The battle had begun.

He could not really tell but he thought it might have been an Arab ship that opened fire first, but instantly several arcs of flame shot out of ships nearby and soon the sea was a confused mass of shipping with long tendrils of flame leaving one ship and landing on another. The fleets were completely intermingled by now. Many vessels were soon on fire, and Talon thought of the crazed crews who would be trying to find safety in the water and finding none. An awed buzz came from the crowd on the hill with the occasional shout from someone calling encouragement to the distant fleet.

Talon wondered at the horror taking place on the ships they were watching. The crews manning the Greek Fire apparatus on the Arab ships were sure to have been Greek; they had more than probably been terrorized into using the equipment, lashed and beaten until they had fired on their own ships at close range, knowing full well what form the retribution would take. He doubted that any of them lived to fire their equipment more than once, as the Byzantine navy singled out those ships first and destroyed them with their own fire. He muttered a small prayer for their souls.

For the spectators on the shore and watching from the hills it was truly a scene from Hell, but eerily it was carried out in total silence. They could hear nothing at this distance of the battle shouts, the clash of arms or the shrieks of agony from the men who were dying from the awful flames that criss-crossed the center of the two groups. The two wings of the Byzantine group now joined the battle. Their lead ships struck the Arab fleet from both sides and poured flame into the flanks of the enemy vessels.

"They do not have the numbers of flame throwers that we do, Talon," Alexios said. "They were relying upon the element of total surprise and treachery."

Talon agreed, mesmerized by the sight of his first naval battle. As darkness enveloped the land and then the sea to the west, the scene became if anything even more hellish. There was a great pyre of flame in the center of the two fleets, while on the outskirts he could just make out the dark shapes of galleys breaking away and trying to escape, but the squadrons on the wings were waiting for them and gave chase, sending plumes of flame after them, setting them on fire. The ships stopped where they were and became isolated torches, while other vessels gave them a wide berth.

"The burning ships must be a hazard for both fleets by now. They will have to get some distance from the hell in the middle," Alexios remarked.

Indeed, although hard to tell in the dark, it was as though the whole battle was drifting away to the west. The sea was dotted with burning hulks and other small groups moving westward. Flames still poured from some ships, but it was all now far away from the city and there was a great pall of black smoke hanging over the area that further reduced visibility.

It felt like an eternity during the battle, but in fact it could only have been an hour before the ships scattered out of sight of the city and the subdued crowd began to disperse.

Talon and Alexios turned away from the distant spectacle and began to help Damianus and Joannina in to their litters. Alexios would have preferred to walk but the distance was still too great, so he elected to return with his litter. Theodora decided to walk with Talon.

As they walked, and possibly because it was dark and no one could see, she put a hand in the crook of his arm and held onto him.

"I think war is horrible," she stated in her matter of fact manner.

"I agree with you, Theo, but men will fight them for whatever reasons they can find."

"That is why I wish to become a doctor. I think I can do much good as a physician."

"You have chosen well, Theo. I know you will be a good physician, and I wish you good luck with your future plans."

"What of you, Talon? Are you to go back to that primitive place Acre and stay a knight of the Templars, or will you stay here...with us?" this last was said almost wistfully and its meaning was not lost on Talon.

"Theo, I cannot stay, even should I want to, for the Order has my fealty and I may not gainsay that. Besides I have packages to deliver to Sir Guy for the King. However, I shall be back in the springtime to help your brother transport cargo with my two ships."

"When do you leave?" she asked in a low voice, and her hold on his arm tightened.

"I think it will be tomorrow now that the battle is decided."

*****

The next day, once he was sure that Henry and Makarios had the cargo situation under control, Talon made his way back up the hill to the house of Kalothesos. Henry and Guy had told him that they suspected the Genoese ship was preparing for sea. It was time to say goodbye and he was very reluctant to do so.

John the eunuch met him at the door and smiled with evident pleasure at seeing him. He invited Talon to follow him to the garden. "The Senator will be there, Sir Talon, and he is sure to want to talk to you."

"Very well, John, I shall come with you. How is my Lady Joannina today?"

"As well as can be expected, Sir. She grieves, as does the young Lady Theodora. The funeral is to be in a couple of days at the church of St. Mary Diakonissa."

The senator was standing with his gardener in among the vines when John announced Talon. He looked up and smiled, then waved him over.

"The news is all over the city, Sir Talon. We won a great naval battle last night. From what John has discovered from the street our enemies were almost completely destroyed!"

Talon nodded and waved. He had heard the buzz of excited groups of people on the street corners and in the harbor itself. He noted that the fleet was still not back, so he assumed that they were scouring the Marmara seas for stragglers and hunting them down, even to chasing them out of the mouth of the Hellespont and stopping the siege at Abydos along the way.

"Come with me, Sir Talon, we are going to sit among the olive trees down there. I want to discuss something with you."

They were soon seated comfortably under an olive tree on a wide wooden bench. John was sent off for some wine. Just as John came back Alexios hobbled into the garden and came to join them.

"I suspect that you are coming to say goodbye, Talon," he said.

"I am, Alex."

The senator looked surprised. "I thought you might be staying for the winter, my boy?" he queried, looking disappointed.

"I regret that I must sail to Acre, as Sir Guy is expecting me with dispatches that cannot be delayed any longer, Sir. And there is a small matter of another ship to pick up along the way."

"We will miss you, Talon. God protect you until we meet again," the old man said.

"We shall indeed, Talon," Alexios added his own words. "With whom shall I play chess now?" he complained.

"You just do not want to be beaten by that little scamp of a sister," Damianus said, and cackled with laughter at the discomfort on his son's face.

Alexios put his hand on his father's arm in an affectionate gesture and grinned ruefully at Talon. "I have no friends here, Talon. I am quite alone! Come back soon to see us."

His father snorted and tapped his stick on the ground. "Where is that wine? We will have cargo for two ships waiting for you when you do come back, Talon. Make it soon, my boy."

*****

Henry and Guy appeared to have judged correctly. The activity on the galley denoted that the Genoese was preparing to leave. Talon asked his men if any unusual passengers might have boarded the ship, but the men informed him that unless it was done under the cover of darkness they had not seen anything.

Meanwhile all was bustle on the *Falcon*. Makarios, not being a man to waste an opportunity, brought wagonloads of iron and bales of hides to their ship and told Talon to try and get the best price he could in Acre. Henry nodded at Giorgios and Makarios, who were standing on the quayside as the last stinking bales of hides were loaded. "He has a good nose for business, that man. The hides are for sure wanted in the Holy Land, and iron is much needed in the forges. We will get a good price for them."

"Do they not need salt also?"

Henry laughed and placed a finger alongside his nose. "He thought of that too. We did not entirely unload all the salt. There are a good few ingots still in the hold, and Guy will be like a mother hen with them, have no fear." He was still chuckling as he went to the rail and called out to Guy to close down the hatches and make the ship ready for sea. It was mid morning and a good time to leave.

As they left with a wave to Makarios and Giorgios, who were standing on the quayside, Talon cast a look up the hill toward the villa Kalothesos and wondered if they could see his ship. They were leaving without enough notice for the family to come down to see them off. He sent a prayer of thanks to them and turned his attention to the activity going on across the water where the Genoese ship was hauling up its anchor.

Henry, Guy and Talon watched the other ship row out through the port gates, and then Guy went to the lower deck and supervised the rowers while Henry took up his usual station alongside the steersmen. A pilot who had come aboard a few minutes ago gave directions, which Talon translated to Henry, who guided their ship across the still waters of the harbor negotiating a course between the other shipping, then they rowed out between the huge towers of the entrance to the port of Prosphorion.

They paused long enough to drop the pilot off in a small sailing boat that had kept pace with them, and then Henry and Talon looked for the Genoese galley. It was making full sail for the chain, which was lowered to allow a squadron of naval vessels speeding in from the Bosporus to cross over. Talon stared at them, wondering.

Word had come that morning that Nikoporus had died in the battle. Talon and Alexios had both been struck numb at the news. Alexios had put his head in his hands and wept for his friend while sitting next to his father and Talon on the bench under the olive trees. Damianus, himself fighting back tears, had put his arm over his son's bent shoulders to console him, a gesture that Talon was sure he would never have considered a few months ago. Talon had finally left with a heavy heart, feeling that he was deserting the family. As he looked up at the distant roofs of the villa he prayed that they would know peace of a sort again before too long.

Now he looked at the ships speeding past and wondered if the Fleet Admiral might be aboard, but the distance was too great and it was impossible to identify him from among the splendidly uniformed men clustered on the decks of the warships as they swept by. He turned to stare at the Genoese ship, and despite himself there were dark thoughts in his heart. Caravello had to be made accountable.

Henry bawled some orders and Guy stood the rowers down and hurried the deck hands to get the sails dropped. The sails caught the wind, bellied, and then the *Falcon* came to life, surging forwards. Talon experienced an unaccustomed sense of pleasure as the ship pushed into the choppy seas. His attention was focused on the Genoese ship for the time it took to clear the cape and round the peninsula and start heading south; it too was under full sail and making good speed. They were accompanied by several other ships sailing in the same direction, so he did not think they would draw much attention from the Genoese captain.

Talon could not resist a final look back over the wake of their ship to stare at the receding city, which was glowing in the warm sun of late autumn. He observed the Hagia Sophia and the huge complex of the Great Palace, their copper roofs and white walls glowing in the sun, and remembered again the chariot races and the games of tzykanion, but also the incredible variety of this magnificent city and its multitude of people.

"You seem to get your sea legs much faster these days, Sir Talon," Henry said. He was braced against the side of the afterdeck whereas Talon was standing free. "Have you decided that you like the sea better now?"

"Truth be said, Henry, I fear the sea, but when I am on a good ship with a good navigator like you I feel safer."

Henry grinned. "You will make a navigator one day, that is for sure. All of us three sailors talked about it. The sea is for adventurers, Talon, and you are one for sure."

"Perhaps you are right, Henry. But I love most of all the mountains. They call to me, Henry, and I do not know how to explain it. There is always a mystery in mountains. What is at the top? What is on the other side that you cannot see?"

"The sea has its mysteries too, Talon." Henry said.

"I still have some things to settle, and then perhaps, who knows where the sea will take us, my friend? However, I will miss this city."

"We shall be back, Sir Talon. God willing."

"Yes, God willing, we will be back, and I hope it is not too long before we are."

"Guy tells me that you have had an interesting time of it, what with the campaign and the troubles in the city."

"Guy talks too much, Henry. But I will miss the family Kalothesos. The senator is a good man, and his wife and children are good people. The city is a gemstone in a world that is confused and uncertain."

Henry nodded. "I agree, Talon. We can winter in Acre, as you wish, and then we can come back and trade?"

"That is everyone's intention. There is trade for us, that is for sure, and once Nigel joins us at Abydos with the second ship we will be able to transport that much more."

Guy came onto the after deck and joined them.

"What of the prisoner below, Sir Talon? Can I let him up?" he asked.

"He can stay below for the time being."

"Are you going to ransom him?"

"Indeed I will, and we will share in the ransom, Guy."

Guy laughed. "You are a dark one, Talon. We must ask before you will tell us anything!"

"I shall tell you something about that ship over there before you ask."

They gave him their full attention.

"I wish to take that ship for myself. I think three is a good number."

They were still gaping at him as he descended the steps to go and talk to Aarif.

*****

They sailed south all day, and were witness to all the detritus of a naval battle. At one point they sailed into a sea of charred wood fragments and lost equipment formerly belonging to ships. Oars, spars, whole sides, and even the bows of ships floated everywhere the eye could see. Anything that could float to the surface of a ship that had been destroyed was bobbing up and down in the waves. Henry became so concerned that he ordered the sails to be reefed, afraid that they might ram into some large obstruction just under the water. There was worse to come as they approached the epicenter of the battle. Lifting and falling in the choppy seas in among the other wreckage were innumerable corpses of the men who had died one way or the other in the great battle fought the night before. Looking out in every direction Talon could see many of the Byzantine navy ships moving about searching the waters for survivors. One approached them and demanded identification.

Having shouted the right answers they were allowed to continue. The Genoese received the same treatment and had to stop, and this was the opportunity for Henry to fill the sails and get ahead of their quarry. They sailed past the Genoese, whose captain was being interrogated by a snappy looking naval officer. No one showed any interest in another galley going by. They were almost a mile ahead when their lookout told Henry that the Genoese was lifting sail and following them.

Chapter 27
A Debt Paid

Talon lifted his head and peered over the edge of the low cliff down at the inlet below. Anchored in the clear waters was the galley belonging to Caravello. It seemed from his perspective as though the ship was suspended in air, the water it rode upon was so clear and calm. He could see the plantation of seaweed nearer the rocks to the vessel's starboard side, and suspended above the sandy bottom of the small cove there was a small shoal of what he thought might be sardines moving left and right as one flashing mass, while several larger fish moved about in a more leisurely manner. The area he was watching could hardly have been more peaceful. Talon could make out every detail from his position in the tall grass, with shrubs and trees further back to ensure that his silhouette was not seen, neither from the ship nor the beach immediately below his position.

Talon glanced cautiously about. He saw nothing to concern him. Max had taken great care to place their men well out of sight. It was now late afternoon and they had been in position for most of the day, having moved into the area with the dawn to avoid being detected by some sharp-eyed sentry on the ship or from the beach. His stomach rumbled and he wondered if the others were hungry too. They had had nothing to sustain them all day other than some water in skins, which were now looking depleted. He looked up at the sky, impatient for the sun to set and to commence the business at hand.

His thoughts drifted back to the day Caravello had brazenly sailed into the port of Abydos a few hours after the *Falcon* and anchored not far from Nigel's ship. At Talon's request, Dmitri had followed Caravello onto the docks and had been close at hand to hear Caravello telling the port officials that he was on normal trading venture and asking if the way out of the straights was clear of the accursed Arab fleets.

The arrival of the Genoese had energized the officers and crews of both his ships. Talon had sent out the order that they were not to tell the port officials of Abydos that Caravello had been the cause of the loss of the two naval patrol ships. Talon had then brought his four companions together with Dmitri into his cabin and told them his plan.

His first question was to Dmitri. "Do you wish to stay with us, Dmitri? If you wish to stay here in Abydos I will understand and pay you off handsomely."

Dmitri looked around at the others. Nigel grinned at him.

"If it is all right with you, Sir Talon, I would rather stay with you," Dmitri said.

"May I ask why?" Talon asked.

Nigel roared with laughter and Max smiled.

"I will answer for him if you do not mind, Sir Talon," Nigel said when he had stopped laughing.

"Well?"

"He had gotten a pretty girl at a tavern with child and wants to leave in a hurry."

Talon looked sharply at Dmitri, who gave a sheepish grin and opened the palms of his hands and shrugged. "What can I say, Sir. Things happen."

This elicited more laughter, particularly from Guy, who felt that some of the heat was off him.

"You will work as Nigel's first mate. He tells me that you are a very good sailor, Dmitri. But stay out of trouble in future."

Dmitri glowed with pleasure and pride. "God bless you, Sir. I will not disappoint you."

"I dare say Nigel will see to that, Dmitri," Talon said dryly.

Then he addressed them all.

"We are going to intercept that ship and take it away from Caravello," he said, and watched their reactions.

Henry and Guy, having already been informed, enjoyed watching the reaction of the others. Nigel went through his usual performance of staring at Talon as though he had lost his mind, but Max slapped his thigh and said, "I knew you would not let it go at that. God bless you, Talon!"

Henry sat back on his stool and asked, "How do you propose to do that, Talon? He has the Greek Fire and will not be afraid to use it." His tone bordered on the skeptical but he was not about to underestimate Talon's propensity for daring. He scratched his beard furiously.

"I do not propose to take his ship on the high seas, Henry. Not where he could burn us down. But was it not you or Nigel, one of you, who told me we could watch another ship from afar and keep pace with him?"

Guy grinned. His teeth shone in the dim light making him look ferocious. "And he has to pull in for water some time, is that not what you are thinking, Talon?"

Talon smiled. "Yes, but it is a gamble, as we cannot do this in a populated port or they will only see it as outright piracy, and there is no guarantee that he will stop anywhere else."

"Oh, I think he might, Talon." Henry said. "He carries something that he does not want discovered, and not all inspectors can be bribed, so he will want to avoid the cities as much as possible and we should be able to follow him to a quieter place. We can certainly keep an eye on him. The seas around these islands are full of ships now that the Arabs have gone, and if we follow with first one ship and then the other we might fool them into thinking that we are just merchant vessels going more or less the same way."

"Then, Nigel, you must make ready for sea. Max, you go with him and the two of you make the ship ready to sail at a moment's notice. You've done a fine job of repairs. Now you must sail her well. Henry, we sail immediately."

Before he went over the side Max paused and said to Talon, "I was very sure that you would follow up with the Genoese scum, Talon. What happened in Constantinople?"

"It is a long story, Max, but our fears were well founded. The Arabs came with their fleet, but they were anticipated and the Byzantine fleet burned them to the water."

"By God, I am glad of it. That is too beautiful a city for them."

"It is a magnificent city, but it is also riddled with intrigue and much treachery at the top. That might be its curse and yet prove its downfall."

"The Arabs came here on their way through and left about ten ships to blockade us before sailing on but did nothing other than that. I imagine that the commander here was somewhat surprised at that, as he thought they would besiege the city. He told me so when I took the gold to him. He really did not believe us."

"I know, as he said as much in his letter to the Admiral," Talon agreed.

"We did bury the Arab commander of this ship, but where they have taken the crew, God alone knows. I imagine that Greek dungeons are no more comfortable than those of the Arabs. Do you still have your Arab with you?"

"Yes I do, and a hansom ransom his family will pay too."

"How is the family Kalothesos?"

"I left them mourning their dead daughter. You remember her? The very beautiful one, Eugenia?"

Max looked shocked. "Dear God. How did that happen?"

"The neighbor, the one I visited that one time where I was cut, had enmeshed her in an ugly plot. He is now dead by his own hand, and his assassins are as well."

Max gave Talon a long hard look. "May God be kind to the soul of poor Eugenia and send the rest of them straight to Hell. Are you ever going back?"

"God willing, yes, Max. You remember Nikoporus? He was killed in the sea battle. I liked him. It devastated Alexios."

Max nodded. "They were very good friends. God be merciful to his soul."

"We can say prayers for those lost when we get to the chapel at Acre. Meanwhile we have some ships to keep employed, you and I. These ruffians we call our friends are too good at navigation to leave on the beach; we have already done very well, as the crews will all find out when we get to Acre. And the family Kalothesos wants us back, they want our ships to sail for them."

Max nodded with satisfaction. "Yes. But first we have some business to attend to?"

"That we do, my friend."

They embraced, and Max went down to the boat where Dmitri and Nigel were waiting for him. He seated himself and looked up at Talon. "God protect."

Talon nodded. "God protect, my friends."

*****

The Genoese had sailed the next day. Nigel followed the vessel out through the water breaker and took up station just on the horizon where he could see the ship hull down. The *Falcon* had taken up station with Nigel and followed him a few miles astern and well out of sight of the Genoese. Talon had trouble containing his worry that the man might slip away from them, and disappear forever.

They tracked the Genoese vessel for four days and three nights, and oft times they thought they had lost their prey until one day they had a stroke of luck. The *Falcon* had been in the lead and they had sighted an island ahead of them, and the Genoese had not changed course. Instead it had sailed directly toward land and then vanished.

Henry had hauled in the sails and had the rowers prepare to hold station, then they waved Nigel up alongside. There had been a shouted conversation between Henry and Nigel as to the nature of the place, but it was Dmitri who told them that it was a very small island which had probably only a couple of small villages on it and those were to the south. The Genoese could well have gone into a cove that Caravello was familiar with to obtain water.

Knowing they had little time to take advantage of the situation, Talon had ordered them to make landfall but to be very wary of being seen. Fortunately they had seen the masts of the galley and had then steered clear to find another cove a few miles further down the coast. Hastily pulling the two ships into the protection of a tiny bay well protected from the surf, they had anchored and then landed on the shore. Having made sure of their own security, Talon led a small party overland accompanied by Max and Guy to investigate the location of the Genoese ship.

Now he was staring down through the long grass at the vessel, watching for activity that might indicate that they were making preparations for departure. He was taking a terrible risk; if the Genoese ship departed suddenly, they might lose it altogether. However, as the afternoon deepened to twilight Talon decided that the Genoese ship would be likely to stay where it was through the night.

He could see a lot of movement on the deck; all at once he was shocked to see a long gout of flame pour out of the side of the ship to land with a flaming splash on the rocks nearest to the ship. He gasped. They were practicing with their Greek Fire! The men near him stared wide-eyed and fearful and crossed themselves. The sight of the bright unearthly glow of the flames that still burned on the sea and the targeted rocks clearly unnerved them.

Talon and Max looked at one another in the gloom. "They have learned how to use it, Max. We have no time left, we must move tonight. Talk to the men; we do not want panic to set in just now."

Max nodded and moved off to reassure the other men and to tell them to prepare for the work to be done. There would be two parties, one of which would attack the crew on the beach, while the other group would capture the ship. These men all professed to be able to swim, although Talon had not had time to verify this. Those who could not would presumably sink. They were to take only their swords and knives. As soon as Max had overcome the sentries on the beach he was to come to the ship with as many men as he could put into the boat and assist Talon to secure the ship. Talon left his bow with Max and asked him to bring it with him.

"We do not know how many are on their cruiser, so we have to depend upon surprise," he had advised.

"I will lock down the hatches with my men as early as we can to keep the larger part of the crew down below decks." Guy had said. "There are two main hatches and then the after cabins," he had added.

"I can go to the after cabins and attempt to capture Caravello. I hope that once he is taken prisoner the resistance will fall away," Talon had said.

"We are only forty men against what looks to be a full crew of about eighty men. We must succeed at the first try. There will be no second chance, and I for one would hate to lose this man. He must be made to pay for what he allowed to happen to Montague" Max had spoken grimly.

Talon had nodded his agreement.

Now Talon hoped fervently that no one would be on duty at the fire device when they were swimming toward the ship. They stood no chance at all against that terrible weapon should it be used upon them. The nagging doubts worried him as night settled in and darkness shrouded the bay. Lamps were lit on the ship's bow and stern, which gave away its location, while a fire burned on the beach, its glow illuminating the forms of ten men who were sitting and drinking around it while a few others, presumably sentries, were seen walking around on the periphery with pikes.

They continued to wait. The plan was not to attack until the early hours when both the sentries on the beach and the men would be likely to be asleep, and the men on the ship hopefully in a similar condition. Talon yawned. It had been a long day. He took a sip of water from a skin lying nearby and looked up at the sky. It was going to be a clear night, which would not help if anyone on the ship was alert and watching the waters of the bay. They would be fully exposed and then...his mind did not want to dwell upon the consequences of that scenario. He put his head in his arms and tried to get some sleep.

*****

Orion was low on the western sky when Talon nudged Max, who was dozing nearby, and whispered the order for the men to move. Making as little noise as possible the men from both parties made their way down a narrow path to the sandy beach. Apart from the very occasional scrape of a foot on the sandy track or small stumble and grunt of annoyance from someone, the short journey was accomplished in almost total silence. They stood in the darker shadows of the cliff, listening and looking around for the sentries. None were to be seen. Max whispered into Talon's ear.

"It looks as though they are all asleep! Shall we deal with them silently?"

Talon nodded and left him to it, while he led the way across the sand to the water. He was quite naked, as were the twenty men with him, except for the belts around their waists holding their swords and knives. They had left their clothes in the dark shadows at the base of the track. Some put their knives between their teeth, and then they all sank into the calm, chill waters of the bay and began to swim. Pushing off into water Talon did not look back. The water was cold and his breath caught as he worked his arms and legs trying not to make a wave or to splash in the water. The weight of his sword threatened to drag him down if he did not keep in motion. He knew that the other men were working just as hard and thought he even heard some labored breathing behind him.

Max and his men were surely doing their deadly work as they swam. Indeed, he heard almost nothing until there was a small choking sound from the beach, but by this time they were almost at the ship. It rested on the water in total darkness. The lamps that he had seen before appeared to have gone out and he could hear nothing above him as he approached the dark hull other than the creak of wood and the light rattle of rigging from the masts towering over them.

In total silence the men withTalon, including Guy, reached the side of the ship and caught hold of ropes that dangled from above. Talon tested the air with his nose. There was a peculiar and unpleasant smell to this ship that he could not identify. The ropes had presumably been dropped to haul up the boat that now lifted and bumped gently against the side of the silent vessel. Still no alarm as he tested the one rope, and then when it held he slowly pulled himself up, dripping water as he went, pausing to listen every other pace. He finally reached the deck and peered cautiously over the edge. He was greeted with a snore from very close by. A member of the crew was lying in the scuppers almost under his nose, and he caught the rank smell of sour wine and unwashed body.

Talon pulled himself over the side and crouched in the darkness right next to the sleeping man. He stared around the deck for any sign of activity. Then he heard a snort as someone blew his nose. He flicked his gaze upwards and saw the figure on the afterdeck above him wiping his fingers on his pants. But the man was also staring intently towards the beach. He seemed to be quite alone, which was a huge relief to Talon, but it was becoming clear that the figure was listening very hard and what ever it was he had heard was taking up his full attention.

Talon could hear the very faint sounds of the men behind him preparing to climb the ropes so he moved like a shadow along the deck and slipped up the ladder leading to the afterdeck. He was one pace away from the man before his victim became aware of any danger, but then it was not from him. The man had heard something in the water alongside the ship and his head turned sharply in the direction of the sound.

He tensed and peered intently down to where the men were climbing the ropes and the steps up the sides. He had seen them and his mouth opened to shout the alarm. He got no further. His head was jerked back violently as Talon's knife blade slit his throat. All that he uttered was a gurgle of agony as he died, and his foot twitched once on the deck making a dull thump. Talon eased the body down onto the floor then hastened to the waist of the ship to give a hand up to the first arrivals.

It took only a few minutes before most of them were on the deck, dripping and naked. Guy led them over the side and then directly to the far hatchway, running as silently as possible with their swords out ready to attack anyone they confronted. They were almost at the hatch when it opened and a man put his head out as though preparing to exit. He spied the dark forms of the figures rushing toward him and let out a squawk of alarm. He threw open the hatch, then dived back below yelling the alarm to those on the lower decks.

Guy reached the hatchway just as more men popped their heads out, and they too shouted to the men below. Guy and his men mounted a ferocious attack on the crew trying to get out from below, while some of the other men with Talon rushed to the after hatchway and began to close the doors. But they too became engaged by men from below who, realizing that their fate was sealed once the hatches were shut, fought with everything they had to keep them open. Pikes and spears were thrust upwards at the men on deck, who only had their swords to counter them. Talon assessed the situation as best he could but he knew that he needed to get to the main cabin before all else.

Talon dived through the main doorway that led to the cabins below and hastened down the steps. He was met in the darkness by a large figure that shouted at him in some language he did not understand. Talon reached forward and thrust hard at the soft form with his blade. The blade sank deep into flesh, eliciting a gasp of agony, and the man fell backwards with a crash to the deck where he lay groaning.

Not waiting to see how much damage he had done and now desperate to find Caravello, Talon stepped hastily over the writhing man and made for the first door he could find. He rammed his shoulder into the door and almost fell into the cabin beyond.

There was a small oil lantern burning low in a metal frame that illuminated a room full of accouterments, armor and clothing, but no Caravello. The stink of unwashed bodies was heavy. Thinking he might have heard movement in the cabin behind the wall Talon dived outside and down the short corridor and was nearly knocked off his feet by another much larger body coming in haste the other way. Talon sidestepped a nasty swipe with an axe that would have killed him had it connected, and then tripped up the man whom he thought might be the bodyguard who had accompanied Caravello on his way up the hill during their visit to the senator's house.

The fellow crashed to the deck and his axe fell away. Leaning over him Talon struck very hard at the base of the prone figure's head. The dull thump of his sword pommel meeting bone and the second thump as the man's head hit the deck was enough. It went limp. Talon could hear the fighting on the deck intensify and still he had not found Caravello.

But then Talon heard some war cries above and knew that Max had arrived, so he decided to worry less about what was happening on deck and concentrate upon finding his quarry. Indeed Caravello was not lacking in courage, because the door of another, larger cabin was flung open and he appeared very suddenly in front of Talon, the light of an oil lamp illuminating his silhouette and the interior of his cabin.

Talon did not have any time to examine the cabin, however. Caravello came at him with sword and knife and appeared to know how to use them. The blades flashed in the lamplight as he swirled them about in an attempt to confuse his opponent. In the confined space of the corridor and the entrance of the cabin the two men confronted one another.

"You cursed pirates will not take my ship!" Caravello shouted almost into Talon's face in Greek, clearly thinking he was dealing with some local pirates. "What?" He jeered. "No clothes? You must be in a poor way. But not at my expense you do not, you bastards." He lunged at Talon's midriff, but Talon danced out of the way, blocking the thrust, and flicked the blade of his knife across Caravello's forearm, drawing a long red line. Caravello cursed and backed off very as though reevaluating his opponent, but he soon recovered and attacked fiercely again and again.

Their blades rang and rasped along their lengths, drawing long arcs of sparks. Each time Talon blocked or retreated enough to avoid being hurt, but he was concerned about what was happening above him. Caravello was slowing down, although he continued to swear in an almost endless stream of both Greek and his own language as they fought. He appeared to find Talon's silence somewhat unnerving.

Very quickly Talon flicked his blade onto Caravello's sword hand, cutting the wrist to the bone. The Genoese gasped and then yelled bloody murder as he dropped his sword and clutched his damaged wrist. He fell back with first a startled and then frightened look on his wide face as he contemplated the silent, naked and seemingly implacable figure before him with the blade of his sword settling on his throat.

"What do you want?" Caravello gasped. He winced at the pain in his wrist that was now bleeding copiously.

"You come with me. Now!" Talon said sharply in Greek.

He drove the large man out of the cabin and along the corridor past the unconscious figure on the floor, and then they walked up the stairs with Caravello looking back and down on his fallen companion.

"You killed Davide, you bastards. God curse all of you to Hell," he said as he climbed into the open.

The sight that greeted them was one of men still fighting, but it was instantly clear to Talon that Max and Guy had the upper hand. It was almost comical to see the men who had swum out to the ship prancing about their opponents, brandishing their swords while screaming and yelling like mad stark naked devils. This tactic clearly had the effect of unnerving their opponents.

"Tell your men to stop fighting and they will live!" Talon shouted to Caravello. He hauled him up the stairs onto the afterdeck and shouted again. "Do it, or you will die in front of them all."

The Genoese did not need further prompting. He took a deep breath and bellowed an order. His men hesitated and stared up at him. For some this was the last thing they ever did, as the naked savages capering about them, not understanding their captain's words, took quick advantage of their inattention and struck to kill. Max realized this and bellowed at his men.

"Stop! Stand back! Their Captain is a prisoner, look up there! Stop, I tell you!" Max's voice was as good as Caravello's and the two of them then shouted again to get the full attention of the remaining fighters.

Men stopped what they were doing and stared up at the former captain of the ship who had a naked man standing next to him with his sword at his throat.

"I did not realize it was 'im!" One of their own crew joked, referring to Talon. "Never seen 'im without 'is clothes before!"

The men around him laughed like madmen and began capering about like fools, further terrifying the Genoese crew.

"Who said that?" Max bellowed. "Get on with checking the prisoners, you idiots, or you will feel the flat of my sword on your bare arses." He was still a sergeant of Templars after all. The cackling and capering men settled down.

"Tell them to throw down their arms. Their lives will be preserved if they do. If not, they all die—and you first," Talon threatened.

Caravello shouted at his men in his own language again and slowly the men under his command began to obey. Their weapons dropped to the deck with a clatter and they stared with wide-eyed apprehension at their captors.

"You will tell all the remaining crew to come out onto the deck without weapons. If anyone has a single knife in his possession we will have you all butchered," Talon told Caravello in Greek. "Anyone who remains below will be killed when we find him."

The man nodded and with apparent reluctance shouted some more orders. His men passed the orders down below and other men began to emerge. Frightened men and boys came onto the deck, where they were searched and then their hands tied behind them. Guy came bounding up onto the afterdeck with some of his naked cohorts and some rope with which they tied Caravello's arms behind him. Talon noted with some distress that there were naked men among the dead and wounded. Not as many as he had feared, but still these were his men.

Talon's reflections were interrupted by Caravello who was now standing by the steering oar looking more and more angry and fearful.

"Who are you people?" he demanded. "By God, I wish to know who is pirating my vessel! You cannot get away with this!" he shouted, his eyes bulging with rage.

Talon was beginning to feel the cold as the excitement of the fight ebbed away. He shivered and said to Guy in a low whisper, "Send a man down to the boat and get our clothes, you did bring the clothes Max?"

Max nodded and grinned.

"There is a man below whom I wounded, some men need to go below and tie him, he is lying in the corridor. Tie him up, but hurry. Guy, we have to sail this ship away before the dawn. You will be the captain."

Guy stared at Talon with surprise, followed by joy written all over his face. Then he gave Talon the benefit of his fearsome grin, nodded, and hurried below just as Max came up the stairs to the afterdeck.

Max stared hard at Caravello, and Talon watched his friend closely as he strode up to the captured captain, who backed away from the baleful stare. Max stopped and examined him in the dim light of the growing dawn. Talon was afraid that Max might take his revenge there and then, his emotions appeared to be so great. But they had agreed beforehand that they would not kill unnecessarily. Finally, Max turned to Talon.

"It is he all right! I would know him anywhere. God damn him," he muttered to Talon.

"You know we must leave, as it will soon be dawn," Talon spoke in a low voice to Max, who nodded and went back down the steps without a further look at the Genoese.

Max took control of the waist of the ship where the despondent former crew was gathered.

"Who are the men who know how to use the Greek Fire?" he demanded.

There was silence, but then Talon added his voice. "We have to know who it is who can use the Fire apparatus? Are any of you from the city of Constantinople?"

Several raised their hands. "Are you the men who made the fire last night?"

Only one man raised his hand.

"Step forward and be seen," Max ordered, and when the man complied Max reached for his arm. The man flinched and tried to pull away, his face a mask of fear. "No! I will tell you! Do not torture me any more!" he wailed.

Max glanced at Talon and said to the frightened man. "We are not here to hurt you, but you have to tell us what you know. See that man there?" he pointed to Talon. "He is our leader and he would talk to you about how this all came about."

The man nodded and spoke rapidly in Greek. "I will tell you, but I am afraid. They killed all my companions to make us talk...in the end I told them, and then they made me work it."

"Do not be afraid. Sir Talon here will just talk to you. Are there any more of you who know this device?"

The man shook his head in mute denial then spoke. "They, he killed them, all three of them, right in front of me. God curse him to Hell for that." The thin-looking man pointed to Caravello, who stared back defiantly.

As soon as Guy had returned with some clothes, Talon indicated that Caravello was to be taken below. As they passed by Talon glared at Caravello.

"I was going to leave you on this island with your men, but now, after hearing what that man said about your murder of his companions, you are going to come with us to Acre."

Guy ordered his men to hustle the prisoner below, lock him in the storeroom, and stand guard at the door.

Max then told the crew of the Genoese ship in his broken Greek that they were free to go. He pointed to the beach where their dead companions lay by the now smoldering remains of the fire.

"Go!" he said loudly. "Go!" There was no mistaking his words, which were followed by the unkind prodding of the *Falcon*'s men with the points of their swords. The first of the crew who now had their hands untied began to jump into the water and swim for the beach. Some protested but were still told to jump, and those that hung back fearfully, begging not to have to go into the water, were picked up and tossed wailing with fear as they fell to plunge into the water with loud splashes. These men were helped by their companions to splash their clumsy way to the beach where they stumbled to the sand and sat down, soaked to the bone and shivering there to contemplate their fate. Others discovered their dead companions and shouted their anger and their fear to the new owners of the ship. By this time, however, their voices were faint, as Guy gave the order to lift the anchor stone and haul down the sails. The vessel began to head out to sea, just as the first real streaks of dawn turned the eastern sky a light blue.

They sailed around the point of the island to see the other two ships still at anchor and drew near to the cheers of the crew who had waited for news all night long. By this time the rest of the men were dressed in some semblance of clothing pilfered from the recent crew and what Max and his men had salvaged from the bundles they had left on the beach. They stood proudly on the sides and climbed the rigging to gleefully yell and wave at their companions before Guy shouted at them to get to work hauling up the sails and making sure that they anchored safely.

Henry and Nigel came aboard with huge grins of delight written all over their faces to embrace the three men on the afterdeck. They were both enormously pleased for Guy when they heard what Talon had made him captain of the ship. They thumped him on the back and shouting their congratulations as he wore an ecstatic smile that would have terrified anyone who did not know him. Henry took Talon aside.

"I do not know how you took this ship, Sir Talon, but you will not regret having Nigel or Guy as your navigators, of that I am sure." He rubbed his beard furiously for the next few minutes while Nigel ribbed Guy mercilessly about his navigational skills. Looking at the two of them Talon smiled and thought that together they made for the perfect nightmare for anyone who met them in the dark after a few skins of wine.

Eventually, impatient to leave this island, he called his companions to order and told them to come below for a conference. When they were all seated in the well-furnished cabin formerly belonging to Caravello he told them that they were to set sail together for Acre.

"Not for the great city, Sir Talon?" Guy asked, clearly disappointed.

Nigel laughed and Henry and Max looked at one another and chuckled.

"We all know that you would like to winter there, Guy, but no. You have a ship that we have pirated and I want it changed beyond recognition in a place where we will be secure. The prow must be changed to a bird of prey, just like a falcon, as will the ship you have, Nigel."

"What about trade and so forth? Is the city not the best place to do this?" Nigel asked slyly.

Talon grinned.

"We have booty aplenty to see us through the winter, my friends. I shall share it with you when we get there. Some must go to the Templars, as is only right, as we do sail with the charter that Sir Guy allowed me, but I do not think he anticipates that we might now have three ships to run instead of one. Thus I must keep my newfound fleet paid for. Fear not, my friends, we will have many a chance to trade with the Golden City in the spring and summer of next year. My friends want us back."

"What do we do with the Genoese?" Max asked.

"We have to take him with us, Max. He has betrayed the Greeks and he murdered innocent men in order to obtain the knowledge of this fearsome device we have on board."

"I realize that, Talon, but I would sooner drop him overboard with a stone tied to his ankles than take him back to the Byzantines."

"I wanted his ship, Max, and now we have it. He can wait out the winter as a prisoner in Acre, and with the warmer weather he will go with us back to the city to face his fate. He deserves to be handed off to them. They will not be kind to him."

Talon decided to remain on the ship with Guy because, as he told them, he wanted to find out how the Fire apparatus worked, or at least have it demonstrated to him by the timid little man.

They set sail within the hour and before noon their ships were well out of sight of the island. Henry as the lead navigator led the way with the *Falcon* toward the south and Acre, the other two ships following in his wake.

****

Caravello was kept under tight security for a couple of days while they sailed. Talon had other things to worry about, and one of them was the apparatus that squatted on the starboard side of the ship. He had the crew take off its coverings and then examined it with great care, with the skinny Greek named Ioannes in attendance. Ioannes spent some time trying to explain the system to Talon, who, not being of a very technical bent, found it difficult to understand.

Ioannes pointed out its main features. There was a bronze riveted tank suspended over a fire box that was enclosed inside metal and which could be resupplied with either charcoal or wood, but this fire had to be going very well before anything could be done. Ioannes indicated the large bellows, the snout of which went into the base of the fire tank.

"The bellows make the fire very hot, Sir. Then the upper tank that contains the thick infernal liquid will become heated to a very high temperature and much thinner than when cold so that it flows better."

Talon looked at an attachment that led into the tank from the deck side. "What does that do?"

"It is the pump that is manned when the temperature is getting close to the right heat. Several men must pump air into the tank. It is very hard work."

"What does it do?" Talon asked, puzzled.

"It makes the air inside become thick and the liquid is now put under pressure like a fountain. Do you understand, Sir? This is when the whole thing becomes very dangerous, as a mistake can lead to the liquid not coming out in the right stream which could pour onto the side of your own ship, or the tank can sometimes explode and burn the whole ship and the crew to the water."

Talon stared at the thin man in front of him trying to judge whether he was just trying to scare him or not, but then he nodded. He believed that now he understood. He suppressed a shudder. He looked again at the stinking object squatting on the deck of his ship and observed a large pipe that led out of the heating tank to a long bronze tube mounted on a wood platform that pointed over the side of the ship.

"When everything is ready we light that small flame on that oil torch over there." Ioannes pointed out a thick wick that was placed just before the opening of the bronze tube that had an opening about the size of a man's fist. He touched it and found it to be sooty and burned black at the muzzle.

"It takes a great amount of skill and training to know exactly when the upper tank is ready to use. I am only just trained enough to make it work," Ioannes explained to Talon.

He showed Talon the device in the middle of the large copper pipe. "This is a vent that allows the fire liquid to escape when the pressure is high enough." He began to turn the tap but Talon stopped him, fearful that he was about to make the fire operate.

Ioannes gave him a sardonic smile. "It is not going to do anything, Sir. The tank is not full and it is cold so the liquid will not flow."

Talon stood back relieved. The image of the flame reaching out from the ship was still vivid in his memory.

It all sounded very complicated to him. "Where does the liquid come from?" he asked.

"I am not sure, but I think it comes from the north of the Black Sea where it is collected. Do not ask me what it is, because I do not know. There are men in Constantinople who process it when it comes to the city in ships."

"Is that what makes this stink?" Talon asked him, wrinkling his nose because up close to the apparatus the smell that pervaded the ship was very pronounced. It burned his nostrils. "It stinks like a whiff of Hell," he added.

Ioannes nodded with a wry smile on his scantily bearded face. "It is kept in copper tanks, and we have only one more on this ship which was brought on board when the Arabs captured the men-of-war. Yes, this stuff stinks."

Talon let him go while he continued to stare at the device, trying to fully understand the mechanism.

*****

Several days later Talon brought Caravello up from below. The man looked very much the worse for wear. His clothes were still bloodied from his wound and the bandage on his wrist was encrusted in his own blood. He looked haggard and frightened, which was what Talon intended. He looked about him, blinking and squinting in the daylight, and then, seeing Talon on the afterdeck beckoning, he walked stiffly up the stairs and came to face him.

"You have stolen my ship. Who are you, and why? You know that you are pirates, and I shall inform the authorities as to what you have done." He sounded unsure of himself, however.

Talon gazed at him from where he stood next to Guy and the steering men.

"You do not remember me?" he asked Caravello.

The Genoese stared at him. "How should I know you?" he said, anger beginning to flush his jowls.

"Hark back to a time in Alexandria, captain, when you and a friend of yours took silver from three men who just wanted to go with you to Cyprus. You have been to Alexandria, have you not?"

The captain nodded slowly. "I have been there, but what has this to do with me?"

"You and your friend took our silver and agreed to take us to Cyprus, almost three years ago, captain. You do not remember the fight on the quayside, where your friend betrayed us and one of my companions was killed?"

Recognition slowly dawned in Caravello's eyes. "It was you?" he asked with a puzzled frown.

"Yes, it was I and my companions. One died on the docks right in front of you, and the other two were taken away to become slaves," Talon said this last with enough venom to cause Caravello to take a nervous step back.

"I could not prevent it!" he said. "He was the one who betrayed you, not I."

"I realized that at the time," Talon said with less force. "But you have been involved in another piece of treachery, and this time it involved Greek Fire and the stealing of it for the Arab fleet."

Caravello was by now looking nervous and trapped. "How do you know this? Who are you?" he demanded again.

"My name is Sir Talon of the Knights Templar, and you will be my prisoner as we sail to Acre, where you can kick your heels in a cold Templar dungeon before the spring comes when I shall take you back to Constantinople to account for your crimes."

Caravello gasped and then stammered, "I am not guilty of any crimes, I swear it."

"You do not know the Senator Spartenos? You do not know of the betrayal of the two naval vessels to the Arab fleet and the theft of the apparatus on the deck below?" Talon looked at him with contempt. "It was pure chance that we came upon some debris in the sea and found survivors who told us all about it. Not only that, we now have another witness who is on this ship with us who will,

I am sure, testify against you for the murder of his companions whom you tortured for the knowledge of the apparatus down below."

The Genoese twisted his mouth downwards and shook his head. "No! No. Before God I swear I was given this apparatus to take to Cyprus," he almost whispered. He was clearly very frightened now.

"How do you know all this?" he finally asked the silent Talon. He could not look him in the eye.

"For your information, the senator is dead, as are his henchmen. And you know that the Arab fleet was destroyed. I heard that there was a prince involved, but he too must be running for his life as the attempts upon the palaces also failed."

"God will surely judge you and I fear find you wanting, but the Byzantine people will be less kind. You betrayed those ships to the Arabs and allowed them to obtain the Fire. They who wished to destroy the city! But thank God those devices are now at the bottom of the sea."

"I...I have riches, I can pay! I have much that I could give you for my release," Caravello whispered his entreaty to Talon, all pretense was now gone. There were beads of sweat on his forehead even though it was not hot.

"I have enough and do not want your pieces of silver, Caravello. Were it not for the fact that innocent people have died because of your greed and treachery I might consider your release, but that cannot be so now," Talon said. He turned to Guy. "Have your men take him below. He may have the smaller cabin until we get to Acre where his accommodation will not be so good. Make sure he is guarded well."

Guy nodded to the two men who had escorted Caravello to the afterdeck. They took his arms and walked him down the steps to the main deck. They were about to lead him down the short steps when Ioannes calmly walked up to them and threw a large pot of some stinking liquid at Caravello. Caravello staggered back with a scream, his hands flying to his eyes. It covered his face and hair and the entire front of his clothing. Ioannes had made sure that none of it landed on the escort, but then he shouted in Greek.

"You will take the short road to Hell, Genoese! This is for my friends, and for me." Then while Caravello staggered back to the side of the ship roaring with pain as the liquid burned his eyes, shaking his head and trying desperately to wipe it from his face, Ioannes threw a lighted oil lamp at him. The flames instantly took hold and within a very short moment Caravello was transformed from a man into a flaming torch that shrieked with agony as he battered at the flames that now engulfed him.

The men who had been nearby shrank away with horror. Talon leapt down from the afterdeck in two bounds to try and help but there was nothing he could do, the heat of the fiercely burning flames drove him back. Caravello staggered about the deck jerking his arms up and down beating uselessly at the flames that were consuming him, shrieking in a high pitched tone that penetrated the head of every man standing on the deck nearby.

Caravello gave one last choking scream that died into a whimper and then turned and toppled over the side of the vessel. The ball of flame that had once been a man tumbled into the sea with a loud hiss to sink rapidly beneath the waves, leaving steam hissing on the surface and the stink of burning flesh. Talon rushed to the side with other men and peered down, and to his horror saw the figure still burning as it sank deep into the water, where it finally disappeared in a plume that obscured their view. He stood back stunned with the shock at what he had just witnessed. Other men nearby were crossing themselves and praying, shock written all over their faces. Some were even on their knees praying and weeping. One was even retching over the side.

Talon cast a frantic look about the deck to see if there was any risk to the ship and found that Guy with great presence of mind had strewn sand over the stained deck and thus effectively prevented further fire. But lying on the deck on his face in a puddle of blood lay Ioannes whose thin features wore a frozen expression of triumph.

"He stabbed himself, Sir! I could not stop him. He...he said..." The man stopped, his eyes wide with the horror of the awful event he had just witnessed.

"He said what?" Talon almost shouted.

"He said he would see that man in Hell and we could all go to Hell as well. Then he stabbed himself, right in front of me. But we were all looking at the other...man. I noticed something but I was too late to stop him. God save us!"

Talon looked down at the inert body of Ioannes. The man had a small slim knife protruding from his chest where he had thrust it up under his ribs into the heart. One hand was still gripping the handle. Ioannes had planned the killing of Caravello carefully, awaiting his opportunity and then executing it with mad determination.

Talon looked hard at the crewman, but there was no question that the man was telling the truth. He was clearly very distressed at what he had witnessed. It had been a self-inflicted killing and there was now nothing to be done about it. He looked up at Guy who was standing at the rail looking down. Guy shook his head sadly. "He was crazed, Sir Talon. He wanted to have his revenge for his companions and he wanted to die. No one could have suspected he had it in him."

*****

Talon sat in alone the main cabin for the rest of that day and thought about what had happened. The creaking of the ship's timbers and the muted talk of the crew on the upper deck did little to intrude upon his thoughts.

He could never have wished upon any man the death he had witnessed that day, and he knew the awful image of what he had seen would stay with him for the rest of his life. He had heard that Nikoporus had died in the early stages of the battle in the center of the fire that had consumed half a fleet. In some cruel way, Niko's death had been paid for. But now he was faced with a decision.

The one man who could have operated the Greek Fire apparatus was dead. Perhaps it was for the best. The infernal device was better off in the hands of those Byzantine Greeks who knew how to use it to protect their empire. It was not for the likes of Caravello, who had paid a dreadful price for it, nor was it for the likes of him, Talon. He gave a mental shrug. Let them keep their secret. He did not want any part of it.

He thought back over the last months and the cruel intrigues that had led up to the events he had seen in Constantinople. That great city would see more of him, now that he had ships and good men to sail them, and—just as importantly—the right to trade with the city. But in the silence of the sumptuous cabin he knew too that although the trade and spoils of war had made him and his companions very rich and would continue to do so it would have only half of his attention. The quest to find his friends was not over, simply interrupted. He calmed himself with thoughts of a garden in Isfahan.

When Talon finally came on deck the sun was setting on the western horizon of a sea empty of land and vessels other than the three ships, one behind the other under full sail. The crew members who noticed his arrival stopped what they were doing and saluted him respectfully. He went and took a long hard look at the apparatus that squatted on the deck under its coverings of protective cloth. It sat there like a crouching monster, and it stank like one.

"Guy," he called up to the afterdeck, "I want that...thing to be thrown overboard and all the trappings that go with it. Everything."

Guy, after a look of total surprise, opened his mouth to say something, but then nodded reluctantly and held his tongue. He bade the men to do as Talon had ordered.

The rumble of the heavy equipment being hauled across the deck and pushed overboard, then the sound of the splashes as it fell into the sea and sank, bore a strange note of finality.

"God willing, if this good weather holds we will be in Acre within two weeks," Guy said, as Talon joined him on the after deck.

—*End of Part IV*—

About The Author

James Boschert

James Boschert grew up in the then colony of Malaya in the early fifties. He learned first hand about terrorism while there as the Communist insurgency was in full swing. His school was burnt down and the family, while traveling, narrowly survived an ambush, saved by a Gurkha patrol, which drove off the insurgents.

He went on to join the British army serving in remote places like Borneo and Oman. Later he spent five years in Iran before the revolution, where he played polo with the Iranian Army, developed a passion for the remote Assassin castles found in the high mountains to the north, and learned to understand and speak the Farsi language.

Escaping Iran during the revolution, he went on to become an engineer and now lives in Arizona on a small ranch with his family and animals.

James Boschert

Excerpt from

Hawk of The Desert
Book V of Talon

...There was new respect in the eyes of the Captain when he asked the next question. "How do you know so much of these people?"

"I suggest that we ask questions of Talon later when we have dealt with the enemy, Captain. I for one want to sleep in my bed with both eyes shut. Not waiting for a dagger in the night."

"You are right, Sir Guy," said the Captain. He turned to his men and began to issue orders. The fighting in the yard had died out and the men were going round killing the remaining wounded. He called over to them and told them to bring two captives to Talon before continuing the search for the hidden Assassins.

Two of the wounded 'Assassins were carried to where Talon stood in the middle of the yard with Sir Guy. Having dumped their prisoners unceremoniously and none too gently on the bloody ground, the knights went off to help their own wounded.

The two young men on the ground were weak from their injuries but still defiant. Talon went up to one of them and without warning slapped him very hard on the face, knocking him flat on his back. The wounded youth gave a startled cry of pain. Talon stooped and very quickly searched the groaning youth. He turned up a knife, just as he expected, and stood back, allowing the angry young man to lie back and glare up at him.

"Why did you attack this castle?" Talon asked quietly.

There was only the glare in response while the youth clutched at his wounded chest.

"I know it was Simon Rashid Ed Din who sent you, and I respect your courage, but you will tell me why you were sent," said Talon ominously. There was silence.

"Are you *Fida'i* or *Rafiqi*?" he asked in Arabic.

There was a startled look from the pair of youths on the ground. Then one spoke to the other in Farsi. "How does this Ferengi know of the *Fida'i*, or the *Rafiqi* for that matter?"

"I do not know, but he speaks Arabic very well for a *Ferengi*."

"I also speak Farsi; I am a *Fida'i* from Alamut," said Talon, very quietly this time.

They stared up at him speechless.

"You should not have attacked this castle, but I will let you and your companions live if you tell me why you attacked us. You must tell me quickly, as the Knights Templar are thirsty for blood and want to kill you all."

"I am dead anyway," said one of the youths. "We were told to take this castle in revenge for the attack on one of the caravans by your Duke Raymond, may his soul burn in hell." He gasped with the pain in his chest and lay back. There was blood on his lips and he was very pale.

Talon knelt by his side. "Have you come from Persia? Did you come from Samiran?" he was referring to the great castle of the 'Assassins situated at the entrance to the Alborz Mountains, in far away Persia.

The youth nodded, as did his companion, who had a bad gash in his leg and on his right arm.

"Is Timsar Esphandiary here in Syria?"

Again the surprised looks. But the youth with the chest wound was going fast. Talon lifted his head and asked Sir Guy for some water. One of the nearby retainers brought over a skin and Talon allowed some drops to wet the parched lips of the dying youth.

"Your bravery will be remembered. What is your name?" he said.

"Kemal. Tell me, what is your name, Templar?" the youth whispered.

"Talon, I am Talon," he told them.

"Are you the one that killed the lion when only a boy at Samiran?" There was genuine surprise in his weak voice.

"I am that one."

"They still speak of the Ferengi Tal'on who killed the lion," whispered the youth, then his body racked in Talon's arms and he died. Talon closed his eyes and laid him back on the bloody ground, covering his face with his head cloth in respect.

He stood up and went to the other youth.

"Let me bind up your wounds without fear," he said.

"It is Allah's will that my companion should die. We are *Fida'i*, Tal'on - Kemal, you and I. What are you doing fighting for the *Ferengi* as a Templar? I will not fight you now."

"First let me bind your wounds, and then we must call your companions and ask them to surrender. I shall ask for quarter and try to send you back to Simon Rashid Ed Din or...is it to the General?"

"It is to the General, he is near Allepo with the Master of the Syrian Ismaili."

Talon's heart began to pump violently but there was no time to dwell upon the one thing that he wanted to ask most. There was the clash of steel and more shouts as the Templars, their Sergeants and retainers hunted down the remaining 'Assassins.

Talon quickly gave Sir Guy the gist of what had been said and told him, "Sir Guy, I think we can do ourselves some good if we do not massacre these people. You should know that we and they both hate the Seljuks and the son of Nur Ed Din."

Sir Guy nodded agreement. He shouted for the Captain of the Templars, telling some of the men to run and fetch the Captain and to ask him to pause in his searching while Talon tried to get the 'Assassins' out with words rather than by force.

"I have to have real assurance that they will not be killed if they do come out," Talon told Sir Guy.

"I shall be the guarantor of this, Talon, if you really believe this to be the answer."

"If we miss even one of them he will wreak havoc with the survivors during the night, Sir. That I can promise. It will be easier for all of us to get them to leave of their own free will."

Sir Guy saw the sense of that, and then they waited impatiently for the Captain to arrive. He eventually came striding out of one of the towers.

"Well, it is going to be very hot work prying these people out of the nooks and crannies of the castle," he agreed. "They certainly know how to fight, and to die," he added as an afterthought. "What do you want of me, Sir Guy?" He glanced down at the living prisoner and the dead youth.

"Talon thinks he can talk them out of there, Captain. He spoke to these two and they are from Persia. The rest come from both Persia and from Syria. It would do us no harm at all to let these people go as a sign of respect and to gain their allegiance if not their friendship."

"Do you really believe this?" the Captain asked him forcefully, glancing at Talon as he did so.

"Captain, I have come to trust Talon in these things and one day I shall explain why," said Sir Guy, standing his ground.

"Very well then. I shall command the men to assemble out here where we can take a roll call, and then Sir Talon can try to get them all out."

"Thank you Captain," said Sir Guy.

The Captain bellowed orders that were quickly relayed to the houses and buildings where the hunt continued. Slowly men in small groups filed out and assembled in the yard. The men on the battlements remained where they were.

It was a disheveled and very bloody group of men who assembled in front of the Captain and Talon. They murmured angrily when told what was wanted and were not a little skeptical. They had felt the hard edge of these phantoms from outside and didn't really believe that it would be possible to achieve what Talon wanted.

Talon, who had been binding up the wounds of the youth on the ground next to him, spoke to him.

"I shall help you to stand and then we must go to the buildings one by one and call them out. Can you do this? Will you do this? Also, what is your name?" He spoke in Farsi so that none of the assembly could understand. The Templars had a few men who spoke some Arabic, but no one who spoke Farsi.

"Do as you will, Ta'lon. My name is Mehmed. Yes, I shall speak to them," the youth said.

Talon asked the Captain to provide two men who would support the wounded youth and then they headed for the nearest building.

At the entrance they stopped and Mehmed called out loudly in spite of his pain. Although his wounds were now bound up they were not insignificant and he had lost a lot of blood.

He called to his companions, telling them that he had been spared by another one such as themselves.

"This man with me is called Tal'on. He is a *Fida'i* and is one of us although he is a Frans and now a Templar. He will protect you and make sure we can all leave the castle safely if you come out now. We have his word and that of his chieftain."

The whole castle was eerily silent after he had spoken. Even the men in the yard grouped with the Templars were quiet, waiting tensely for whatever might happen.

There was a slight sound within the building. Talon tightened his grip on his sword and the two men holding Mehmed upright looked fearful. But they all relaxed a little as a youth much the same age as Mehmed, dressed in the remnants of a monk's habit, came cautiously to the door. He was armed with a sword and looked very wary. He called out to Mehmed.

"What have they done to you that you are now calling for us to come out and die in the sun, Mehmed?"

"This is Ta'lon, killer of the Lion in Samiran, who has spared me. He is a *Fida'i* just like you or I, Mahmud. Remember the tales of the Frank who slew the lion when only a boy? This is he. I trust him as no other."

Mehmed had called this out loudly to ensure that any other listening would hear and think about it.

Slowly, very slowly, the 'Assassins came out of the buildings; one by one they came towards the small group standing by the entrance to the main hall. They did not give up their weapons nor did they say very much. They looked warily over towards the glowering Knights clustered in the middle of the yard, but on the whole they concentrated their attention upon Talon.

Many were the questions thrown at him in Farsi by the Persian survivors, who then explained to their Syrian counterparts the story of his time with the 'Assassins in Alamut.

Talon heard it all but said nothing and finally Mehmed asked him, "You have said nothing, Ta'lon, I have kept my word. Are you going to have us all killed now?"

Talon looked him in the eye. "My word is my life, 'Assassin. I shall personally escort you away from the castle. Are they all here?"

"I think so," Mehmed said. He talked rapidly and forcefully with the others, demanding to know whether there might be someone still hidden; most looked around and told him that they were sure that they were all there were left. There were fifteen in all.

Talon beckoned to the men gathered in front of him. In Farsi he tersely told the startled men to lift Mehmed and carry him, as he was sorely wounded. The two retainers who had been supporting him thankfully walked quickly off to join their fellows among the Templar contingent. Talon then asked the youths to follow him.

Walking in front of the 'Assassins, he led the way to stand in front of the equally surprised Templars.

"I shall lead them out of the castle, Sir Guy, with your permission," he said to a bemused knight and his Captain.

"Can we trust them not to kill you when you go out with them, Talon?"

"No, but I gave my word that we would not kill them, and now I must keep it."

Sir Guy looked hard at the 'Assassins. "Very well, may God protect you."

The knights stood aside and watched while Talon led the hesitant group of ragged youths towards the gate.

There he told them to wait while the portcullis was reattached to its rope and then winched up out of the way. This was going to take time, so he told them they could take their dead with them or they would be interred outside the castle walls within one day as per the proscribed rules of Islam. They nodded acceptance.

The while they squatted in the bloodstained dust Talon was subjected to a barrage of questions. The Persians all knew of the legend of his fight with the lion. Few knew of his involvement with the killing of Ahmand or his uncle those long years ago, for which Talon was grateful. He started asking questions of his own.

"How was the General Esphandiary?"

Still the mightiest warrior that ever lived, they bragged.

"What of Reza...does he still live?" Talon held his breath at this point.

"The Reza of fame, who had saved the life of the Master?"

Talon nodded.

"He has not been seen for many years," one of them said.

"He is somewhere in the south with the Master's sister."

Talon's heart began to thump very loudly in his chest. He spoke very carefully. "The Agha Khan had only one sister, as far as I know."

"He *has* only one sister and she is living somewhere in the south," the leader of the group of young men told him.

"What is her name?"

"Why, it is Rav'an. If you had been in Samiran you should know this, as she grew up there they say, around about the time you were there."

Talon had to stare at the ground. "Yes, I know," he whispered almost to himself.

Work on the portcullis was finally finished and the winch turned by two burly men in the tower. Talon watchfully herded his new acquaintances out of the castle.

"Please convey my deepest respect to the Timsar Esphandiary and tell him that this was the wrong castle. He should punish Lord Raymond in the manner that he would normally use, if indeed Lord Raymond deserved it," he told the man who led them out. "Tell me, where is the General?"

"He is in Aleppo," was the reply.

Taking care not to seem too interested Talon managed to obtain a fairly detailed understanding as to where the youths would be going, and ascertained that would also be the place where the general would be staying.

The youths came up to him one by one. "*Khoda Haffez, Genab Agha,*"—God Protect, honored Sir—they said in unison, clasping his hand between their two. His onetime enemies were almost ready to embrace him. But he would not permit it. His own mind was racked with a different kind of emotion; he barely noticed them anymore. But he mustered himself and bade "*Khoda Haffez*" to each as they came to him and clasped their hands in his. They had been trying to kill each other only half an hour ago but fate had changed things for all of them.

The youths were barely gone when the fearful retainers hurriedly closed the main gates with a loud crash of wood and iron on stone.

Talon was left alone in the archway of the gate to ponder what he had heard.

Rav'an was alive? How could this be? His mind was ready to explode and his heart was thumping so hard he could hardly breathe. He sat down abruptly on one of the steps leading to the tower nearby and put his head in his hands. How could this be? He had lived for nearly six years with nothing inside him to be called hope and now fate had come and laughed in his face.

******